INDIGO LOST

Dear Phoebe,

Enjoy the adventure!

Published by Somerset Press

Second Edition published in 2019

Somerset Press Limited
3 Church End
Radford Semele
Leamington Spa
CV31 1TA

Printed in the United Kingdom by
TJ International Ltd, Padstow, Cornwall

This book is a work of fiction. Names, places, characters and incidents are the product of the author's imagination or are used fictitiously. Any resemblance to events, locales, persons living or dead is coincidental or they are used fictitiously.

Paperback 978-1-9161480-4-8
Hardback 978-1-9161480-5-5

Cover design and layout by www.spiffingcovers.com

INDIGO LOST

BOOK ONE OF THE INFINITY SQUARED SERIES

∞

S R SUMMERS

Also available in the **Infinity Squared** series

Available on Amazon

and somersetpress.co.uk

PART I

STOP IT! PLEASE STOP!

The words were a silent scream inside her head, echoing the plaintive cries in the room behind.

She backed up against the wall; not that there was anyone in front of her, but because she needed to hold on to something. Her small fingers clung to the edge of the doorframe and she pressed hard; it hurt the back of her head she pressed so hard, but nothing, *nothing*, blocked out the sounds she heard from the kitchen that had witnessed more violence than it had cooking in her short life of seven summers.

How much longer until he stops?

Knowing how often she had endured this filled her with hopelessness, and as much as she felt like a coward she couldn't look, couldn't go in there. She was afraid that if she showed any part of herself around the doorframe she would end up with the same fate. Besides, she did not need to see to know what was happening. Her mother's crying told her everything. Gabbled sentences in between the screams, in that soft sweet voice she knew as well as her own, were trying to appease the monster of rage that was currently tearing their kitchen apart. The same monster that tore apart any sense of security, of peace, for everyone in the house, daily.

Taking in a lungful of air as quietly as she could, the child forced her eyes open, and pressed her lips into a determined yet tremulous line. *I wish I was older. I would go in there and get him off her. I would tie him up and–*

A higher pitched shriek of agony interrupted her grand plans for heroism, bringing her back to the present as effectively as a punch to her gut. (She knew what that felt like. It had happened plenty of times before.) Angry silent tears then streamed down her face; she had long ago learnt to cry silently as well as breathe silently.

Some days she thought she might go mad from wanting so badly, in her heart, to save her mum, but there was nothing she could do. She'd learnt that lesson a long time ago, aged five. She hadn't stood a chance. She had tried to stop him . . . and had been off school for a week she had been so bruised; too bruised for her to have gone without questions being asked. And her mum would have been blamed, not the one who had put so many colours on her – he who lived a life of alcoholism and violence. She was young, but she'd already lost innocence to the brutal propensities of human nature.

The terrified shrieking from behind her built into a climax. *Please stop.*

Proximity was never advisable. The monster was wont to look for a second victim when the fury was in him. Flight was the other viable option . . .

Through tear-soaked lashes she saw the door to the hall was open; her brain knew she could make it if she was quick. For her own sake, she needed to be just a little further away. The adrenaline-fuelled tension that poised her to run felt like it might break her into a thousand shards, but pushing away she ran towards the door, fearing any second a hand upon her shoulder – a hand she knew might hurl her against a wall or crush the life out of her.

Out in the hall it was gloomy because it had so little light, and in the grim late-afternoon of the winter's day, it was as cold and as depressing as a crypt. The wallpaper had long ago lost any attractiveness or vibrancy and had peeled off at the edges. The light fitting was so old it was almost antique, and the bulbs were no longer working. The child knew every single detail and despised them all equally. No amount of cleaning would ever improve their home. God knew her mother tried hard to keep the house spotless, but it was an impossible task. Sitting motionless on the stairs now, captive, and refusing to move any further from her mother, it was the most she could do to just keep breathing. She knew this was how he wanted it. Wanted reason to find fault. Nothing her mother did ever made a difference. He just wanted a reason, *any* reason, to beat her down. Voice or fists, it didn't matter.

She knew he was the one who had control over the money as it was he who worked; and he who drank or gambled it away, leaving her mother with barely anything to feed them, let alone money for some paint to brighten the house. But what did any of them care for a bright house when there was never any sunshine in their lives no matter how much the sun shone in the sky? All three of them – her mother, her sister and her – lived in perpetual fear of the moment he came through the front door. Some days he was so drunk he just fell on the sofa and slept. Those days weren't so bad. Some days he won something – never anything compared to his losses, but at least there would be no screaming that night. No fresh bruises. No taxi rides to the hospital. And those days weren't so bad. But the other days. These sorts of days . . . Her mother had to be the clumsiest person in the whole of the state; she had walked into cupboards and fallen down stairs so many times . . .

As if the ER staff believed it.

THREE THOUSAND MILES away, Daryl Augustus Bartholomew Blackmoor allowed himself a small smile of satisfaction as he lazed on his personal sun lounger. The raised dais and the tilt of his upper body on the cushions gave him the perfect vantage point from which to survey his birthday party. The party would go on until early dawn. Night would become day, the exotic made plentiful, and a new definition given to the meaning of 'excess'. He was not a man to obey the rules of convention nor nature, and if there was anyone who thought himself above mortal limitations, it was he. At the relatively tender age of eighteen, there was nothing tender about him at all. Not even if one tried to look for it.

He surveyed the scene of his own creation from the elevated position he held above his guests, a luxuriously-decked out gazebo behind him, bodyguards and waiters standing in their positions, silent and waiting. A table to his right had his favourite cocktail of the moment on it: a Belvedere, which was a combination of apricot juice, a rare Charles Heidsieck Champagne from 1981, and an even rarer Louis XIII Black Pearl Cognac – all decades older in vintage than the young man drinking them. The ingredients alone cost over $200,000. The drink had never tasted so satisfying, and he didn't have to care about the cost. Didn't have to care about much at all really. And as he watched the beautiful people, mostly the same age as himself, enjoying themselves on the top of the skyscraper he owned, he had every reason to feel happy. His rooftop had been transformed into a tropical-themed pool party that would set a new personal best, even for his high standards of extravagance and debauchery. The night sky was dark and distant beyond the lights, making the expanse of space around their bright island of frivolity and naked flesh somehow even more decadent, the laughter, music and singing contrasting with the muted tones of a city at night. Before him was a new generation of glitterati; the jewels of America's wealthiest families and most of the world. Millions wished they were part of it; millions would never come close to imagining the reality of their experience.

He detected a certain thrill of smug satisfaction, knowing everyone was enjoying themselves at his expense, and it was savoured in the same cynical way he had tested the fine champagne, the bubbles now playing on his tongue. He was the only son and heir of the richest man on the planet – Richard Blackmoor – yet he was also a billionaire of his own making. What was a little party with wealth like that?

But to think it was his eighteenth birthday party. He felt older. Much older. His body was young and fit, his lean but muscular six-foot-four frame enough to make any female stop and look again – and it made him perfect for his position in the Harvard football team. His body was yet to become its full adult shape; his mind, though, was already honed to adulthood. He had already done so much, had experienced and tasted plenty of what life could offer and, well . . . things tended to bore him. Even here, at this spectacular party with so many amusements and so many people, he felt alone. Had always felt alone. It was like a shadow that accompanied him no matter how many people he surrounded himself with.

Daryl turned his head slightly and saw one of his best friends, Luke, easing the bikini top off one of the gorgeous brunettes he recognised from their Harvard business group, head dipping to taste her breasts. It was happening all over the place, girls and guys losing their few clothes – and it was happening all over the country. It was Spring Break, and he was throwing the party early to set the benchmark, well aware no party would top this one. No one had turned down the invite; people had rather been begging him for one. Inviting most of his fellow students had clearly been a good idea as his popularity rating would skyrocket – even though he knew it was an empty achievement. His true friends he counted on one hand; the rest were in awe of him, hoping to keep him in their sphere in case they needed his influence.

So many people that need or want something from me. But what do I want?

Despite being a year younger than many at Harvard, his acumen and who his father was had got him a place a year early, and he had done nothing if not proved why he should be there. He partied hard, but he worked even harder, settling for nothing less than top grades even whilst launching a new company almost every month. Entrepreneurial profiteering online was easy money when he had fingertip access to web developers and products *and* the means to make happen. He'd had no intention of living in his father's shadow or living off his father's wealth. One day, Daryl had promised himself, many times over, the world would remember him for far more than his father. He had already made a good start.

A slow smile of intent curved his perfect lips at the thought of how much success lay in his future. He was unstoppable; he had the world as his proverbial oyster . . . and he was intending to swallow it whole with some more ludicrously fine champagne.

He caught the eye of the girl he had noticed earlier on his way from the hot tub to his dais. He had spotted her in the crowd and liked what he had seen sufficiently to have trailed a finger up her arm as he passed, confident – even if she did not know it yet – that she had been told. Such a gesture indicated his interest, and it would be prudent of her if she did not ignore it. He now tilted his head a tiny fraction in her direction, her gaze completely held. Within seconds she moved away from the friends she was with without a word, and came towards him through the crowd of gyrating bodies moving to music and raising hands to the sky like pagans of a new age, alcohol and confidence an addictive combination.

Daryl leaned his head back again, slipped his bespoke shades over his green eyes and sighed. It was almost criminal how easy life was sometimes.

INSIDE THE HEAD of blonde curls, hope wrestled with despair in an unending war; moments like this one, it felt like a fight to the death. The child clutched her knees against her chest as she hunched over, praying so hard she could change this. It was a childish dream, yet it was the thing she clung to: I pray tomorrow will be different; I pray he dies in a car accident when he's drunk; I pray that when I'm old enough I will earn enough money to get us away from here. *Because it's like prison here.*

But had she been older, she would have known that it wasn't really like prison at all, for even in prison there were rules against bullying, against fighting. And there were three meals a day.

She jumped out of her skin as she heard something smash and then a slam. And then footsteps.

He's coming.

She scrambled up the stairs, out of his line of vision, and watched as he strode through the lounge door into the hall, hating his face, hating him. She watched, still and silent, as he yanked on his coat, angry that his leaving for the pub had been delayed by the need to discipline his wife – a burdensome chore that he must undertake to keep her in line.

He slammed the front door behind him and disappeared down the path to the heap of a car that only served to facilitate his consumption of alcohol – and ate up more of the precious money that was needed for food. She held her breath until she heard the car wheeze and start up, and then he drove off. A second later, she scampered down the stairs and threw herself through the lounge door into the kitchen, hearing the quiet weeping that made her want to weep herself. Any fleeting relief she had felt that the perpetrator of the storm was gone disappeared; didn't she already know the aftermath was a different kind of ordeal altogether?

She paused in horror, went on hands and knees across the horrid linoleum floor to her mother, tears already sliding down her cheeks. What she saw, no matter how often she saw it, always shook her to her core. *Why can't I stop this? I think I'm going to break. Just like that pretty blue vase mum loved so much.*

The vase had been smashed on the same floor where her mother was now lying, both victims of the same violent temper.

"Mum?"

She gently touched the arm cradled over her head; the other was holding her ribs where she had been thrown into the kitchen unit. She prayed nothing was broken this time. There was no money left for any treatment at the hospital. This was the reality of the overly populated, economically struggling, small US town they lived in with no free medical services.

"Mum . . ."

Her tears dropped onto the bare arm already smeared with blood and the arm moved, a little, letting her see her mother's face. She froze as she saw the 'W' carved into her cheek. She didn't have to ask. She had heard the word 'whore' hurled at her mother enough times. In his worst rages, she had been called the same, despite being just a child.

Thin arms reached out and she covered her mother with her thin body, doing her best to protect, to absorb some of the pain, to try and console the inconsolable.

Her mother put one arm around her youngest daughter and held her as tight as she could, unable at that moment to move off the floor. She clung to the fact her daughter was there with her, felt the gentle hand that smoothed over her hair; but it was a caress a mother typically shared with a daughter, not daughter to mother, and she felt ashamed.

"I love you so much." It was the whisper of a child not sure what to do to make it all better, and the woman silently thanked God for her.

She slowly rose, once more, above her own traumatised state, knowing she had to be there for her child, that she had to ease some of the distress for her.

"I love you, my beautiful girl."

Her words caused fresh tears to tumble down pale yet baby-soft cheeks, and they held each other, matching blonde curls in disarray as their heads pressed close together. She felt a small hand, with surprising strength in it, squeeze her a bit closer. The child could not get close enough. Her mother's arms were her favourite place to be.

"Come on. Help me up and I'll get you some dinner. We can sort me out at the same time." The hand that cupped her cheek created a dark smear of blood, but that could not be helped. In truth, she didn't care. She wanted her mother's touch more than anything else. "Where's your sister?"

"In the wardrobe."

She didn't have to think about the answer; she knew her elder sister would be there, had seen her run for the stairs the moment the first shrill cry of protest had rent the air. How many times had she wished her sister would give her some comfort, would help? But she always hid. Had never come to the hospital once. Her sister did everything she could to ignore what was happening, having given up hope that things would change. But she knew really it was her way of protecting herself.

Slowly, her movements so pained she might as well have been hit by a truck, the woman sat up, helped by willing hands that were more encouraging than they were truly helpful. The child hooked her mother's arm over her shoulders and, with the help of the table, managed to get her onto a chair. It was a hard, uncomfortable chair, and both knew it was little better than the floor.

Immediately after, she reached for the kettle, stretching and filling it with water. With practiced ease, she jumped up onto the counter to get to the top of the cupboard to bring down the first aid kit, her litheness in heart-breaking contrast to the weariness of her mother sat mutely watching her daughter. Her daughter of just eight years; her own thirty-three-year-old body feeling like eighty.

She wondered for the thousandth time how much more she could take. The man she loved, had loved, probably foolishly still did love in some unexplainable way, had ruined her life and hurt her more times than it paid to remember. She observed her daughter with sad loving eyes, knowing every detail of her so well. She was so proud of her . . . and yet hated that every day they shared was marred by the brutality of the drunken, spineless man that she had been so foolish to marry. And not found the courage to leave. She'd had such hopes. And had lost them all. Never to be regained. Just like her freedom, and peace of mind. And to have to watch her husband's brutal selfishness disfiguring the lives of her daughters? It was the same insoluble nightmare she had faced for the last five years. Or was it six? Did it matter anymore?

Her daughter started to clean the cut, making her wince with pain at the sting of anaesthetic, using it sparingly, knowing it would cost precious dollars to replace.

Then the fridge was opened and a box of eggs taken out. The frying pan was put on the stove, and the familiar sounds of cooking began: the toast going in the toaster, the sizzle of the oil, plates being fetched.

She then eased her mother's hand from where she was clutching the faded summer dress she was wearing to undo the buttons, to inspect the bruised skin.

The woman gathered herself, feeling ashamed at the valiant attempt of her daughter to step in, to make up for her weakness. She felt guilty watching her fetching the food, making a simple dinner – not that she could have cooked anything different. Food was a rare and precious commodity. *Dear God, I can't even manage to feed my children well enough to put meat on their bones.* She would happily have got a job to earn more money, but she wasn't permitted. Knew she would face another beating for just suggesting it.

"Go fetch your sister. I will finish this."

She took her daughter's hands and set them aside firmly but gently, not wanting it to be a rejection, but wanting to stand up and take the lead again. It was not for a daughter to do, to have to take control. The woman stood, carefully, keeping hold of the chair as she was watched with wide, worried eyes, eyes that were so beautiful, so unusual, soft indigo etched with concern.

"Wash your face and then come down and set the table. Your sister can pour everyone a glass of milk."

The girl did as she was asked, but with a reluctance that made her mother's heart swell with love.

Such a strong child. Oh God, what will happen to us?

The woman took a breath, trying to hold the emotion in. She washed her hands in cold water – they rarely had hot water – trying to get rid of the blood with a flare of angry determination. She went to the stove to check the eggs, exchanged the toast in the toaster for another two slices of bread. She looked at the loaf. It was meant to last another two days, but she was sick of knowing she and her children were going to bed hungry. She got out another two slices, deciding she would find a way to make it last; maybe dip into the secret pot of change she had hidden for emergencies. Usually it paid for taxis to the hospital. And then the treatment. Or, if she could, a present at Christmas or on a birthday.

A sob of despair escaped as she realised there was nothing to go on the bread. No cheese. Not even a scraping of butter. And there was no one she could turn to for help in this town. Even if anyone was willing to listen, her husband would half kill her if he thought she had sought advice from anyone else. She was so utterly alone.

Somehow, she forced a smile onto her face as she heard feet on the worn thirty-year-old linoleum flooring. Her daughters arrived, the taller, darker haired girl just as thin, her face haunted with fear, eyes apprehensive at seeing her mother, or rather, the state she had been left in.

The atmosphere was unbearable.

"Cassy, can you get the drinks? This will be ready soon."

For her children, she would pretend everything was normal. That there wasn't still a dribble of blood seeping from the 'W' carved into her cheek.

She prayed to God her daughters would never have to live with this terror.

But she knew they already did.

DARYL PONDERED THE work waiting for him, his eyes closed, and absently totted up figures for a business investment he was eyeing up even as he felt a hand trail up his leg, followed by another . . . but he refused to react, curious as to what might follow. A body joined him, and he knew she had a knee either side of his legs, felt the wetness of damp hair against his thighs and fingers on his swimming trunks. Her body shielded him from anyone else, and he let himself enjoy the touch of her fingers as they loosened the tie on his shorts, eased them down, and then played with him until his body responded, filling and swelling in her hands, sensing admiration in her touch. Suddenly, her mouth took him, almost all of him, and it was enough to make him open his eyes as a wave of pleasure soared though him. Her head bent to take every inch of his ample erection as far down her throat as she could, lips closing around him and sucking, tongue caressing, and he put one hand in her hair and grasped a handful of the wet dark tresses, liking this birthday present very much.

He was impressed. It was good. And he'd had plenty of experience to judge. He watched with amused detachment as her head bobbed up and down over his crotch, letting the pleasure build, knowing well enough his release was near. His hand tightened on her hair, perhaps a little too tightly, and he held her head down, forced her to keep him in her mouth as he climaxed, the force making him thrust into her as the ripples shook him.

"Swallow."

He felt her obey him as he was still deep inside her throat, and then released her head, letting her come up for air, her eyes going nowhere near meeting his. She licked her lips uncertainly, unsure, the catlike confidence gone in the aftermath of her pleasurable offering.

"I trust you can put back what you took out to play with?" he asked arrogantly.

He then watched her tidy him away and retie his trunks in silence, satisfied she was beginning to understand that he was to be obeyed, at all times, by everyone. Daryl took hold of her arm and pulled her to lie next to him, surprising her, because his authoritarian attitude had been unfriendly to the point where she had thought he would send her away having served her purpose.

The girl didn't argue though. She was smart enough to know this man was worth pleasing. Every girl was aware that he was the prize; every girl wanted to be the one he married. It was true he was arrogant, but did he not have reason to be? Even being his girlfriend for a few weeks would be an achievement – something every woman secretly competed to be. She settled herself obediently where he seemed to want her, aware she was the first girl to have been invited to his lone seating arrangement that evening, wondering how she had managed to catch his interest. She could still taste him on her tongue.

A hand lazed up from her hip to her ribs, then her bikini top, warm against her skin, the fingers pushing up under the fabric and playing with her nipple. The languid touch made her want him, made her curve her body against his, for although he paid her little sincere attention, it was impossible not to be seduced when his hard, toned body was pressed against her, and her mind was buzzing with the knowledge of his reputation. It made her wet just to think of the things she had heard about him, combined with the quiet power exuding from him, and her heart started pulsing faster with the wild hope he would take her into the veiled interior of the gazebo and take her bikini off completely for a more thorough inspection. How her friends would envy her. Even her mother would be proud of her. All the years of seeing him from a distance, and here she was lying beside him having so intimately pleasured him less than two minutes ago. The evening took on a dreamlike quality.

Daryl, however, was not after an evening so singularly tame, although it would be intimate. The platinum-blonde he had seen in the bejewelled turquoise bikini earlier caught his attention, and he recalled the inviting look in her eyes. He had also noticed the obviously enhanced breasts that strained against the wisps of material that barely covered them, and decided to appreciate her investment, or, more likely her parent's investment. It was the tendency of the rich to do everything they could to beautify their children, no expense spared – especially if they thought that child might snare *him* into marriage; indeed, every parent with a daughter at Harvard hoped for one particular set of nuptials.

The second girl responded to his look much like the first, moving away from the group of people she was with, and he admired her again as her long legs carried her towards him, his appreciation of her figure ruined by cynicism he did not try to control. He was arrogant enough to know he had the choice of all women, and could take his pick from those without surgical improvements, but still . . . He was reminded as he observed her of the one thing that still eluded the wealthy of the world he lived in: genuine beauty. So few had it in the truest sense; so many paid to try and achieve it. Even in this world where those who could chose the genes for their children to get 'perfect' designer babies. He, however, was blessed with a natural masculine beauty that he could thank both of his parents for, yet knew he was desirable not only for his face and body, but also his bank balance. Hence the reason he was a model. Hence the reason he had been nominated for The World's Most Handsome Man – one of those media inventions that he didn't really care about, yet still allowed to pander to his youthful male pride. His eighteen-year-old psyche, however, did not spare a second to think of the invisible kind of beauty; the kind that existed inside the physical shell he judged so arrogantly.

On impulse, he chose another: a red head, slightly more curvaceous, and wearing a daring yellow bikini, all pale skin and freckles. She was also minus any silicon enhancements, as he preferred. The two reached him at the same time and he stood up, dislodging and encouraging the brunette to her feet, stroking the backs of the two new women, guiding them towards the doorway of his gazebo, picking up his cocktail as he went, knowing one of the waiting servants would let the silken curtain fall closed.

Inside, under the glow of more gentle lights that showed off the exquisite shimmer of the cushions and rugs that covered the floor, he sat down on the wide chair and watched them for a moment, taking his shades off and tossing them on the low table to the side. Daryl knew they were waiting for him to tell them what to do. *God forbid they should take the initiative.*

Teeth ground and a muscle jumped in his jaw as he fought to control the burst of rage, not sure if he was more frustrated that they stood there waiting for instruction, or angry they were so overawed by him. Normally he enjoyed intimidating people into submission, into fulfilling his wishes, but sometimes it would be nice not to have to orchestrate everything.

"Why don't you put on a little show of your own while I have my drink, then we'll see what happens."

It was not a suggestion. At least he had chosen well and the women did not seem to find the command at all shocking. No one would accept an invitation to one of his parties if they weren't prepared to fuck or be fucked. There had only ever been one uncomfortable moment of such kind, a while back, and since then he was always very careful to make sure it wasn't repeated. He had no time for it. Not so much as a second. There was no room in his life for weakness, innocence or sentimentality. They were alien concepts to him and he was happy with that state of affairs. Emotions were complicated. He engaged with as few as possible. It kept life simple.

The platinum-blonde took the lead and turned on the redhead, the clash of hair colours interesting – he knew they were both fake, however, as although they looked good, the colours were too bright, too perfect to be natural. Perhaps the brunette was natural though, he mused, but had had some highlights put in . . . Daryl sipped his drink in silent contemplation as he watched them kneel on the soft rug on the floor. There was a good collection of pillows piled around them and the redhead lay back, sharing a relatively believable kiss with the blonde, the brunette getting on her knees and trailing kisses up the blonde's back. The tangle of limbs and seeking lips ended with the redhead lapping at the brunette's cleft, hands clutched around her bottom, the brunette using her mouth on the blonde, and the blonde satisfying the redhead with her own teasing fingers, her bottom raised up in front of the brunette.

The writhing collection of limbs and whimpers was having an effect and Daryl felt himself responding, took one final swig and set the beautiful glass down, even as he saw the brunette's lips part with a cry of ecstasy, the tilt of hips and arch of spine so familiar. Stepping forward, he covered those lips with his own and felt her respond, kissing him back as he finished the work of the fingers on the redhead, watching both the blonde and the redhead climax with the ache of not being joined fully with flesh. A state of affairs he would rectify shortly.

The touch of his hand and bodies moved. This time he was stripped of his one item of clothing, and the females joined again, only this time they were centred on him, and he closed his eyes to enjoy the power of the blonde riding him as hands and lips busied themselves above and below his waist, the blonde leaning down to kiss his neck when he pulled her head towards him, feeling her hair brush against his chest.

Midnight and a whole night ahead of him. And at least another fifty beautiful women to choose from.

Dear God, it's good to be me.

THE FRONT DOOR slammed and the child crept out of hiding once more onto the landing, watching him leave.

The deafening silence was like a vacuum and she paused for a few seconds before descending, bracing herself for what she might find. She'd come home from school only an hour ago; ten minutes later the world had turned into a warzone. The broken picture frame lay in the hall where he had thrown it, after ripping it from the wall and hurling it at her mother's feet. It was one of the very few ornaments in the house, and it was of his daughters when they were much younger, both with rather fixed smiles on their faces. No one had bothered to take any more recent ones, and there wouldn't be any smiles; it was far more likely they would run out of tears before they smiled again.

She stepped over the mess and went through to the lounge, reaching for the phone on the table before she went to her mother in the kitchen. It was nearly always the kitchen that the bad stuff happened. *Please be OK.*

The quiet boded ill. And the child's prayer went unheard, as she found her mother prone on the linoleum. Blood seeped from a cut on her head, and with her arm twisted the wrong way the damage was conclusive enough. It was a shaky but calm voice that asked for a taxi, knowing that was cheaper than paying for an ambulance. She'd made the mistake of dialling 911 before, and it had not been pretty when the bill had arrived. She'd learnt not to make those mistakes twice.

Putting the receiver back down she knelt on the floor, not sure where to touch. She just wanted her mother to do something to indicate she was . . . *How could anyone be alright after this?*

"Mum?" The voice quavered and she tried again, "Mum, I've called a taxi, we have to go outside now."

She got up, ignoring the smear of blood across the kitchen cupboard, and the bloody handprints on the fridge. She blocked it out. She'd seen so much. Too much. She took the towel and a damp cloth, waiting. Her mother stirred, her eyelids fluttered, and then her face creased up as the pain hit her consciousness.

"Mum, the taxi will be here soon."

"We don't have money for a taxi, baby."

She said the words automatically, knowing there was never any money. Knowing that spending money they didn't have led to more pain and more blood. There was no escaping the downward spiral from which they were powerless to save themselves.

The child ignored the protest and finished clearing the worst of the blood from the bruised skin, then wrapped the towel as gently as she could around her mother's arm and wrist. Her mother watched her do it as if the arm was not part of herself, unflinching despite the pain of moving it.

Not taking no for an answer, the child chivvied and pulled and eventually got her mother to her feet, her small body buckling to steady her as she swayed. Together they shuffled to the door, making excruciatingly slow progress compared to the man who had left in his usual storm of fury. The door was opened with one hand as she kept the other on her mother. The cold April wind hit them both, and she began to wonder how she would get her to where the taxi would be parked on the road. A car door slammed and she looked up: the taxi driver they'd had before was running towards the house. She could see the concern on his weathered face even in the dim light of the cold evening.

"Jesus Christ! What is it this time? Come on, give her to me."

The child relinquished her hold on her mother, warning him about the broken arm. She then ran ahead to open the rear door ready for him to slide her in, before running back into the house and up the stairs, diving into the bedroom she shared with her sister and pulling the box out from under her bed, gathering all the money she had saved from washing neighbours' cars, her prize money from a competition at school . . . literally, everything she had. She ignored her sister who was sitting huddled under the thin duvet they had to share, and belted back out to the waiting cab, a pall-mall dash of legs and arms, one arm pulling the door closed behind her as she went.

She jumped into the back seat next to her mother, and no sooner had she shut the door than they pulled away, the driver using all the urgency she would have employed had she been old enough to drive.

"Next time I'll bring my own flashing bloody light to put on the roof!"

He spat the words out angrily, knowing the family. It wasn't such a big town. They had all seen the beautiful young mother turn into this wreck of a person, or had heard about it. He knew the girls too. Went to the same school as his own children.

"The hospital, right?" he demanded of the child, looking at her in the rear-view mirror, his face taut, eyes glancing at the barely-conscious woman he had strapped into his cab.

"Yes. Please."

He watched her reach over and take the hand of her mother's uninjured arm and hold it tight. Tears began to slide down her young face, and he dragged a hand over his mouth to hold in further angry words, knowing they were not for him to say, nor for her to hear. *This isn't right.*

"Please take us as far as $25 will go. We will walk from there." Her voice assertive.

He looked again at the girl, and met the eyes waiting for him in the mirror.

"*Walk?* Are you crazy? She can't even stand up!" The child blinked at the rebuke but stubbornly refused to look away. "I'll take you to the hospital all the way and it'll cost you $10. Save the rest for having your mother looked after. When you win the lottery come back and buy me a new cab."

The child bit her lip, tasting the tears that couldn't be controlled. She wasn't good with kindness, not from a man, and certainly not from an almost total stranger; but she didn't have any choice. She didn't know what to say. She'd never let herself be in anyone's debt before, and she didn't want to be now, but he was offering her a lifeline.

"Thank you. I promise, when I can, I'll pay you back everything."

"Sure, kid, now try and keep your mother upright, I'm going hit the gas."

Without her own seatbelt on, the child slid closer to her mother with the momentum of the car, and a loud growl was heard from the engine as he pressed the accelerator down hard.

The rest of the journey – the rush to get her mother into the hospital, and the reaction of the nurses upon arrival – was a blur. Being around so many people who were all trying to help rather than hinder was always a disorienting experience. So different from being at home, or school, where she was largely left alone. Her family was tainted. No one wanted to get involved. No one wanted to be her friend. Not even her own sister.

She had felt so useless as the taxi driver had screeched to a halt, dived out and come around to carry her mother into the hospital, and she'd had plenty of time to see the looks of disapproval, and sadness, on the nurses' faces, combined with not a little frustration at just who was coming, once again, through their automatic doors. Somehow, she had answered all the quick-fire questions thrown at her by the medics, and managed to send a grateful glance at the taxi driver, before following her mother, who was then wheeled away to one of the cubicles further inside the building. He had seemed somehow relieved to hand his burden over to medical care, but unwilling to leave all the same, wanting to know if she would be alright. And when it came to the part where she was sat waiting outside the room on a plastic chair, her feet dangling, she dearly wished she asked his name. Why was he so kind? He didn't have to be?

Time slowly ticked by. The fear that she wouldn't have enough money to pay for the treatment began to gnaw at her. Fingers stayed clutched around it in her pocket, fearful it would somehow fall out and get lost.

"Hey there."

Her head snapped up. She had been concentrating on the low voices in the room behind her, trying to hear what they were saying about her mother, but happy not to be in there. She didn't want to see any more blood, or her arm all twisted and bent. *How would she ever fight him back now, with a broken arm?*

She blinked, trying to focus on the person before her whose head seemed right up on the ceiling. The man looked back, calmly and unmoving, seeing a frightened child. He didn't want to add to that; not any more than he had to.

"Can I sit down?" he asked politely, wanting her to feel unthreatened, and that he was one person who wasn't going to force her into anything. To talk. Or to trust him. Except that he did need her to talk, and to trust him.

"Sure."

It was a small word, spoken grudgingly. She suspected him, and he sensed she knew what he needed. Slowly he sat, aware they would make an odd picture. His size was not to his advantage with this witness; his giant bulk next to such a little kid. Sheriff Joshua Mackenzie made a mental note to keep his body language as gentle as possible to avoid spooking her.

"So . . ." *How do I have this conversation?*

He looked down at his hands, leaning forward as she did, elbows on knees, hands knotted together, head hanging low. How to even broach the subject was eluding him. He knew about her and her sister from his own kids; knew from the previous summons to the hospital about their mother. Had even ordered some of his men to resist from finding her husband DUI (driving under the influence) because he knew it would mean their mother would have the living daylights beaten out of her when he returned home in a foul mood. He knew the type. Had met the man. At least thieves and drug dealers knew they were wrong; didn't think they actually had a right to anything. Men like him, they were so convinced of their absolute right to do what they did, it was pointless arguing, and knew it was a waste of breath going to see him for a 'quiet chat'.

"Quite a night."

"Yes."

DARYL BLACKMOOR STRODE through the apartment, as if, quite rightly, he owned it. But only just. For the one reason he did not want to own anything.

He didn't see any of the priceless antiques, the art collection that put galleries to shame, the furnishings and décor that was kept so impeccably; everything was just so, no expense spared – indeed, why would it be? Entering the largest lounge, he watched everyone stand with hard cynical green eyes. He reacted to nothing. If it were not for the healthy glow of his skin, he might well have been carved from stone.

"Mr Blackmoor."

Mr Tyler stood forward slightly from the line of fellow lawyers arrayed in the room, all looking at him solemnly, and extended a hand.

"Mr Tyler."

Daryl stood on the other side of the coffee table and did not move his hands from where they were clasped behind his back, refusing to acknowledge the gesture of greeting or well-meant comfort. Nothing in his body language invited any further comment or solicitation.

Mr Tyler was not surprised at the rejection of the hand; indeed, it seemed quite typical for one who seemed so much older than his eighteen years, and who possessed the authority and reserve of a much older man – something few could even hope to achieve during their entire lifetime. The young Blackmoor heir had a commanding presence that was wholly his own, as much as there was a physical resemblance between the son and the late father Tyler had known so well. Somehow, he knew that the son was going to excel even the monumental legacy his father had created. Born to it. Prepared for it. Bred and reared to endure the weight about to descend on him.

Clearing his throat, Mr Tyler began the official proceedings. "We are all very sorry to be here, Mr Blackmoor."

Silence.

Daryl was so sick of these platitudes, these well-intended comments. They didn't mean anything, not really. Even if they were sincere, they didn't affect him in the least.

"I confess I always thought your father would outlive me. I never thought I would need to read his will," he continued.

Mr Tyler slowly read the hint in Mr Blackmoor's stone-still face that it was best to move on to the business at hand, and leave the flowery sentiments of condolence behind.

"Well, I'll make a start, then . . ."

Daryl made no move to sit, so no one else did, and men used to sitting in plush chairs in their smart suits stood a little uncomfortably.

"Your father, as you might have anticipated, named you, and you alone, as his sole benefactor. As did your mother."

Daryl's face didn't reveal any pleasure at hearing the news. He breathed in, but outwardly he showed nothing else as words just kept coming – words he had already anticipated would leave him feeling cold and empty.

"Every property, every investment, every company, every position in said companies is now left to you. Your father made very explicit instructions and full provision in his will to avoid any complications handing everything over to you. A complete portfolio has been sent for your personal attention to your email, and we have brought an additional copy here today, on a datacard, along with hard copies of everything. It will give you a full breakdown of every aspect of your father's business empire. It will take a good long while to go through, but if anyone can make sense of it all, you can. You are your father's son, after all."

Mr Tyler hoped he might see some reaction to this, but he was disappointed. He gestured at the smartly dressed individuals on either side of him.

"These men all helped your father with the legalistic side of the businesses and the investments enclosed in those documents. Any questions you have they will be able to answer for you. In due course, you will undoubtedly want to visit or speak to the individuals involved, at least in the most important cases which are earmarked as such."

Mr Tyler suddenly realised he was talking far too much, as there was now a hint of anger and impatience in the intense green eyes.

The tight-closed lips moved purely to say two words: "I understand."

"Of course, of course . . . Would you like to ask any questions at this time?"

"No. I think everything I need to know will, as you say, be in those documents."

Mr Tyler nodded, and everyone else – busy staring at the floor or the coffee table to avoid the chill of Daryl's eyes – relaxed slightly, seeing an end in sight to the strained meeting.

"I take it nothing has changed? They are confirmed dead?" Daryl then asked. Two questions that hinted not only at the amount of pain the young man was holding inside, but also a hope, so distant yet still there, that perhaps a mistake had been made.

"I'm afraid so, Mr Blackmoor. Police reports, the divers . . . you know the Marines were called in again to help search for them when they thought they found something? But there was nothing. It's been six months now. . ." He went quiet, afraid once more that he had said too much.

"Well, then. I should say that concludes this meeting."

Mr Tyler allowed himself to breathe out properly, hearing that unmistakable dismissal.

"Anything you need, Mr Blackmoor, please just say. I greatly liked and admired your father. I will do whatever I can to help during this most difficult time."

Mr Tyler hoped his words might allow the man standing before him, who had just inherited an empire, but who had lost his parents, relax just a fraction, maybe even acknowledge the kind words. But no. The successor to the claim of being the richest man on the planet was ramrod-straight and as tense as he had been the moment he had arrived in the room. Mr Tyler was aware he had no idea how it felt to be the second Mr Blackmoor; the weight of responsibility; the mantle of greatness of merely being who he was. It had been incredible enough knowing his father, but his son . . . He opened his mouth to say so. Then closed it again.

"Thank you, Mr Tyler."

The lawyer ducked his head wordlessly as he took his leave. He naturally went to offer his hand again, but changed his mind and clasped them together instead. As the most senior lawyer there, he led the way from the room, the small herd of fellow lawyers moving after him.

The door was shut. Finally.

Daryl allowed himself to move.

He did not go to the table where the huge books sat, twenty-two volumes in all, each at least five inches thick, and God knows how many pages. He didn't care for the wealth he knew would be written on those pages.

He felt no satisfaction.

He felt no enjoyment knowing he was now the richest man on Earth.

Felt no sense of power.

He just felt . . . alone.

He hadn't believed it when the news had come; had never stopped believing they would be found. *My father mustn't die. It is unthinkable. He holds entire national economies in his hand.*

His father had been the only person who might have understood how he felt in these moments of silence. He knew what it was to be so revered, so awed, so . . . apart. How he was looked to for instructions and orders every minute of every day. Expected to have answers that no one else could give. Who would ever know how he felt now?

He had never been particularly close to his father. His father's businesses, since Daryl was a small child, were the driving force of his life, and left him little time to indulge in being a parent beyond making sure his son was well provided for with a fine education, material possessions, and a life that befitted one whose father had achieved so much. And Daryl, subsequently, had led a largely singular life, always aware of how different he was. And his superiority, and having limitless wealth, had meant he had selfishly enjoyed his life any way he wanted. He'd had his self-worth and status imprinted on his mind every step of the way through growing up, but with a firmness borne of what felt like necessity, not love. He had therefore developed a relationship with his father that was little more than passing conversations involving business advice, and commenting lewdly on women – whom they both considered themselves connoisseurs of – and he now realised just how much time had been wasted. He wanted to go back and find something more meaningful to share with those who should have been the closest people on Earth to him. He wanted to go back and say all the things he never had. And how he wished there had been something more, something warmer, between them.

He also wished he had paid more attention to his mother; but he had always found her largely irrelevant as she'd had so little to do with anything he did as a child, as a growing boy, as a young businessman. She had her haircuts and manicures, dress shopping trips and magazine interviews to occupy her. He had taken her existence for granted, always trusted she would be there, somewhere in the background, floating around in one of her gorgeous ensembles and clouds of perfume, nagging him to find a steady girlfriend.

And now they were both gone. Without even a proper goodbye. He had rung them briefly before they'd left to wish them a happy anniversary, but he hadn't thought much of it. They had done so much travelling whenever the fancy had taken them, since he was a baby left in the hands of nurses and nannies, and the conversation had been so ordinary, never thinking it would be the last they ever had.

Hadn't he always hoped for more? One proper hug from his dad, like on the day he drove a car for the first time? Getting accepted into

Harvard, despite being over a year younger than most? His first million from his own investments? He'd always hoped at some point his father would say something to show his approval. Yet the money – all the money a mortal man could ever dream of possessing – had not bought moment's natural affection between father and son, had not bought immortality.

Daryl looked out at the rain now hitting the windows of the penthouse apartment that had belonged to his parents. He did not see the incredible view of the city, the urban splendour of Manhattan real estate that he probably now owned a good chunk of. The silence was huge in his ears. The longer he stood utterly still, the deeper the sense of loneliness became. No one else was there. He was alone. Always alone.

He had no choice but to continue. Could not give up what was now his, what was his father's legacy. But why, when he had so much, did he feel like he had so little?

HE NOTICED HER shivering, her eyes fixed on the floor in front of her, the lights reflecting with painful brightness off the clean surface. She was staring so hard, but he knew it wasn't the shiny tiles she was seeing. And no wonder she was cold. All she had on was a thin t-shirt, a pair of leggings that were at least two sizes too small and full of holes, and battered old trainers. *She's all elbows and knees. Healthy but underweight. Kids her age need so much feeding*. He felt a surge of anger that she should suffer, knowing her father drank most of their money away in the town's worst bar, only caring about quantity; that blurred trip to oblivion he took as often as he could, as if he had no responsibilities to the living.

"Can I . . . may I ask what happened?"

He held his breath, waiting, hoping she would say what he needed her to so he could actually do something.

She blinked. "My mum fell over. Down the stairs."

He closed his eyes and tried to reign in the disappointment, wanting to bellow with frustration. It was so wrong that this small child was so petrified, so trained by circumstances to lie to protect the man who did not deserve anything except a bullet in the head. The lie hovered in front of them like a grotesque spectre, mocking her. Yet he could feel the truth trying to burst out of her, so desperately did this child want to be free from the fear and the deceit. Small hands clutched each other in her lap.

Taking a calming breath, anxious to not let the silence go on too long, the sheriff spoke again: "That's strange. Your mother said she fell over a kitchen chair and fell on the floor, hitting her head on the kitchen unit and landing on her arm."

"That's what I meant."

He rubbed his eyes with his large hands. Years of working within the law could never really prepare a man for this. This was the kind of interrogation he did not feel he could win. He'd known the occasional domestic abuse case, but nothing like this. The worst part about it? It was escalating.

"Kid, you know this will happen again unless you or your mother tell me the truth."

"We don't have any money for a lawyer. Unless you can send him away for life, he'll kill her for saying one word. *You know that.*"

Her fierce answer took him by surprise. He never thought she was stupid, but that was something far beyond her years to know. She was what? Seven? Eight years old? It didn't sound like it was something she was repeating either. Where had she learned that?

They sat in silence for a few minutes.

"Where's your sister?"

"Hiding upstairs. She'll probably still be there."

"You did a brave thing tonight. You're always such a good girl, looking after your mum."

"I don't care about being brave. Or good. I just do what she needs me to do." Whispered words, yet just as fierce as before. "I wish I could . . ."

Her hand went to her mouth, holding the sob inside. His words had sounded patronising, even to him, and he hadn't wanted them to. He wanted to put an arm around her and give her a hug. He could feel the acute distress in the trembling body beside him that quivered with shock, fear and cold; but like an abandoned puppy, he did not think physical touch would give her much comfort, just scare her more: she had so many reasons to distrust it.

But he dared put a hand on her shoulder; no pressure, just a touch. She did not react. Just kept her eyes squeezed shut, keeping herself silent, her hand still muffling her sobs. He wished he had his wife with him. Angie would know how to give her the comfort she needed so desperately. He felt like he was failing her as well as her mother.

There's so little I can do unless her father is actually accused of something. Anything to give me half a chance to slap some handcuffs on him and throw him as hard as I can in to a cell.

He could feel bones beneath his hand. He thought of his own sons. Healthy, athletic and properly fed. It gnawed at his gut to know he would have to leave her at some point to go home to the warmth and love of his family. Knew when he saw his own children the sadness would hit him afresh. Worse, he knew there would be more nights like this.

"I need some coffee. You fancy something? We could get some cake? Crisps?"

He hoped the lure of food might tempt her.

"I don't want to leave my mum. She might need me."

He sighed, yet knew it was foolish to have expected any other answer.

"I'll tell you what, I'll ask the nurses how long they're going to be, and tell your mother where we're going, then they can always get us if they need to. Is that alright?"

She nodded, hesitantly, and he knew she wanted to agree; but kindness was probably not something she was used to, nor would trusting kindness be something she would be good at.

Mackenzie stood up and slipped into the room behind them, almost surprised she did not try to rush in with him; but he concluded she had probably seen enough, and was happy to trust the nurses to look after her mother for a short time so she could be free of that responsibility, even for a few minutes. *I wouldn't trust my kids with a goldfish.*

"At least another half an hour they said, so we're all good to go raid the canteen. You in?"

He held out a hand, looking down at the top of her head, willing her to look up and take it. *Come on, let's go and get a cake . . .*

His patience was rewarded when she moved, not looking up, but slipping forward off the chair so her feet found the floor. She then took his hand, and together they walked down the corridor, three steps from her for every one of his, but still a moment of normality in a very turbulent world.

Neither of them could possibly have imagined the circumstances the next time they would meet.

PART II

TWO YEARS' LATER

"*THIS IS ALL YOUR FAULT*!"

Her sister's words cut like a knife, shouted from her refuge in the wardrobe. She clutched hold of the banisters more tightly, as if she could channel her strength through to her mother by doing so.

It was her ninth birthday, and her mother had tried to do something for her, had made a cake, bought some balloons, invited some other children from school round to share a birthday tea. The mums had come after an hour or two of games in the garden to collect their children, and all might have been fine if it hadn't been for the fact that one child was picked up by her father.

"Whore!"

The birthday girl jumped in fright as the word shattered the momentary quiet of the night, the argument having raged for a good long while now; much longer than usual. It had started the moment the last of the children and parents had gone, all of them made to feel unwelcome by the brooding presence that had come home to find his family celebrating, even in such a low-key and inexpensive fashion. They should not smile, should not laugh without him.

"You would find any reason to invite a man to the house. And such a reason! Your own daughter's birthday! You disgust me!"

"No! He came to pick Eliza up. I only know her mother, Clara. I've never seen him before!"

"Don't lie to me! Did you think I wouldn't find out? To think I've tried so hard to be patient with you, to forgive you, and yet, even having neglected yourself, you still draw men to you like a hooker on a sidewalk!"

There was a screech of chairs over the floor. The girl's legs braced ready to spring, the burden of guilt on her mind that this really was her fault. If she hadn't had a birthday this would never have happened; if her mother hadn't tried to make it special, hadn't invited anyone, then her sister and she wouldn't be cowering upstairs again.

"*No!*"

A scream followed the shout and a slap resounded. Then another.

"Traitorous *bitch!* I should have ended this a long time ago! Not had you and your stupid daughters driving me to madness and drink! I could have been someone! I could have been a success but for you!"

Something got broken – a chair? – and then the thumping began. The girl let her forehead sink to the thin worn carpet. She couldn't take any more. Both children listened in fascinated horror. Both too scared to move. Trained by years of terror not to interfere.

They then heard noises from the garage, things being moved impatiently, someone in search of something. Their mother would be shaking, terrified. They could imagine the scene. But they did not want to.

She lay on her back on the table, blood seeping from her mouth, another cut near her hairline. The dress she kept as best – the least old – was now ruined. Bloodstained and ripped. It had been shoved up to her waist as her husband had raped her, once over the table, then on the table. Her mind was swimming. How on earth was she was going to clear up the mess in time for the girls' breakfast in the morning? The real danger she was in was not yet apparent, so used was she to such abuse, so she had already jumped ahead to the clean-up. But this was one time she wasn't going to have to clean up . . .

Her arm, the one that he had broken before, lay weak and useless against her side. And she could not move her legs. Had he tied them or had she literally become paralyzed by fear? She felt blood trickling over her thigh, wanted to wipe it away but could not reach. Did it matter? There would probably be more. *Where is he?*

He reappeared, his face contorted. The days when she had thought him so handsome, his face that of an angel, had long gone. Just like her sense of hope.

"You have gone too far this time. You're teaching your sluttish ways to children, and I won't have it. You are not a fit mother for them. *Never have been.*" Spittle flew from his lips to hit her face his vehemence was so acute.

She shook her head in denial, but was given no chance to reply as a rag was stuffed into her mouth. *Oh no . . . no.* Her heart fluttered as the panic rose, and her good hand went up to take it out, but he grabbed her wrist and looped the garden twine around it that he had found in the garage. He tied her hand to the table leg, did the same with the other, and then her ankles. He looked down at her when he had finished, his eyes dark, shadowed. She could only look back, her whimper muffled by the cloth. What was he doing? Terror the like of which she had never felt before caused bile to reach her throat. She closed her eyes. Perhaps in defeat. A surrender of sorts. Or perhaps to seek a rare moment of quiet. *Why didn't I find the courage to leave this man?*

She heard the rustling of plastic, heard a drawer being opened and shut, then a cupboard. Something was plugged into a power socket and he pressed a button. The noise was loud in the quiet room, the silent fear of the woman palpable in the air, mingling with the fury of the man whose clothes were already stained with blood. His shirt was half undone, his tie lost somewhere.

He came back into view. Vincent Sinclair Earl.

How she had loved him. Had been so happy. Could remember the wedding dress – so pure and white. How easily, she learnt, white showed up the red stain of blood. In the beginning, he had been apologetic; but time had made him more embittered, more paranoid and more violent.

She recognised the whir of the electric carving knife – a present from his family for their wedding – unused as they had never had enough money for proper roasting meat for dinners. Why had she given up her life and family in England for this monster? How had she been so stupid?

Tears slipped down from her eyes into her hair as she gave herself up. Knew with heart-stopping certainty that this time she was going to die. Knew she would never see her beautiful daughters again, never have another chance to kiss their hair, hold their hands, tell them she loved them. She would never see them grow. See them marry or have children. See the women they would become. So much she would never know.

Some of the scream that then erupted from her chest made it into the rag as the blade cut into the smooth skin of her thigh.

She had hoped for so much. Given so much. Had all of her life been a waste? Why had the simplest pleasures and hopes been denied her?

She felt sensations through her flesh she had never felt before, the grinding of the blade against bone, then light-headedness.

She knew was going to die. And there was nothing to save her.

Why didn't I fight harder? Why didn't I leave?

But these seconds were too few and too precious to waste on regret.

Images from her life fluttered through her mind in a desperate carousel: days of sunshine and laughter, England in the autumn, leaves in the wind, the smell of cut grass in the garden in the summer, her mother's smile, her days as a student, the joy of learning and discovery, the birth of her children, seeing them run in the garden, their first steps, their first teeth . . .

She wanted to scream to her children, say a last goodbye, but it was not to be. She would be denied as much in death as she had been in life. And her heart ached knowing that.

"WHAT IS HE doing to her?" the younger sister demanded from her sibling, looking for some guidance – anything but the muffled accusations from her hiding place.

"I don't *know!* Just don't make any noise. We don't want him up here!"

They fell silent again as the awful noises continued.

The girl felt sick. Could feel the small piece of birthday cake in her mostly empty stomach, the unfamiliar taste and sensation of sugar. Such a brief moment of happiness. Look at how it was being paid for . . . *What is he doing?*

After about half an hour, it stopped. They then heard the patio door being pushed open. Easily recognised. They hadn't heard a sound from their mother since the last muffled scream.

The girl unravelled herself from the banisters and went to the bedroom window, climbed up on the bed and looked down into the garden, keeping to the side so she wouldn't be seen. She hoped for a glimpse of her mother, but there was only her father. It was dark, and the light from the moon and the kitchen light made strange patterns on the grass. Why was her father digging a hole in the garden so late at night? He was moving with a focussed energy, his eyes on his task, the spade thrusts angry; and he just kept digging, deeper and deeper, stepping down into the hole to keep going. Finally, he stopped, seemed satisfied, and thrust the spade into the grass leaving it upright, turning to go back into the house. *Why is he wet?*

She could see his shirt sticking to him and his skin looked shiny, it didn't make any . . . She looked closer. He was covered in something red. Red water from the ground, from the hole? The pieces fell into place with horrifying clarity, slowly, leaving a stark picture of ugly truth: it was blood. Blood belonging to her mother.

She stood open-mouthed in front of the window, her concealment forgotten as she watched for confirmation of her conclusions. Her heart pounded, yet she felt nothing. She didn't know who she was, what this was, only that her whole world was changing.

Her father came back into view, carrying black rubbish sacks. But they weren't full. Not like the ones they put in the dustbin. These were small, bundled up parcels, carried in his hands or under his arms. He stopped at the hole, paused for a moment, then dropped the first ones in. The weight of them carried them down quickly, and it was strange not to be able to hear the thump as they hit the ground.

He disappeared, reappeared with more bags. And again. But as he dropped the last of the bags, a startled shriek left her lips without her meaning it to. From the top of one sack trailed hair, and the colour was clear, even in the moonlight. The length and the colour and the curl told her it was her mother's hair.

Her father turned at the sound and their eyes met. He stood alone and demonic in the garden, the whites of his eyes bright in the shadowed, reddened face. It was a moment that turned her whole body to ice. Such accusation, madness, and rage. Such hatred. And then she saw the intention in his expression: you next.

Then he moved, striding forward with new energy, snatching up the spade as he went, straight towards the house.

He was coming for her.

"We have to go!" she cried, turning to see, in horror, that her sister was now standing behind her. Had she seen? She grabbed her arm.

"I'm not going anywhere! Get down or he might see you!"

"He already has! She's dead! He's killed her! He's burying her in the garden!"

"Get off my arm!"

The girls paused their panicked bickering as they heard the patio door slide shut and movement in the hall. A split second later the girl turned, saw the stubborn pout and hard-set eyes of her sister, full of fear, full of denial. She didn't have the time to convince her, not if she wanted to live. Primitive human survival kicked in, and she knew she had to leave.

She ran, darting out of the dark bedroom and across the landing as lightly as a fawn into the bathroom, flipping the lock on the door and going to the window, even as she heard footsteps on the stairs. Heard the door of the bedroom creak. She opened the window and climbed up onto the ledge. She didn't want to think about the drop down onto the drive two storeys below.

It's not that far. It's not that far.

Her heart beat wildly in her chest as she heard his footsteps outside the bathroom. Then felt the same rush of adrenaline as she did when she was at school doing gymnastics or her dancing – she'd joined as many clubs as possible; they kept her away from home – as she looked down.

She was too terrified to think about being afraid.

It was now or never.

And she wasn't ready for never.

His fist pounded into the door.

And she jumped.

She landed, then rolled, as agile as a cat. And paused, stunned for a moment. How had she done that? A crash from above confirmed the bathroom door was now smashed from its hinges, and she crouched down behind the car, hiding, wanting to run . . . but she did not want him to see her.

An angry growl of frustration was heard and the window was slammed shut. She peeked over the edge of the car.

Now!

Thin, strong legs carried her away, heading instinctively for the police station, wanting to find the man who had taken her to the canteen in the hospital. He would make everything better; he wouldn't let her father hurt her as well. She couldn't think of anything or anyone else. Not her mother. Not her sister. Just him. *Please be there!*

She pelted through the small town that seemed alien in the darkness, petrified of her father's hand appearing from every corner or shadow to grab her, or seeing him in his car.

She saw the police building and ran up the steps, throwing herself into and through the doors, not caring that it hurt. Heads looked around as she came to a halt, suddenly unsure.

"Kid?"

The night duty cop on the front desk stood up and looked over at the wild-eyed girl who was breathing like a racehorse, her legs quivering.

"What are you doing here this late? Where are your parents?"

"My mum. My mum is dead. He killed her."

The words came out as a whisper as she stared at him, seeing his face but not seeing anything at all. They had to believe her, right?

"Who killed her?"

Everyone was standing up now, cups of coffee or paperwork forgotten on desks, the clear distress of the girl and her words going off like a fire alarm in their heads. This was a quiet town. Murder was an event that happened once in a decade . . .

"My dad. He's . . . he's cut her up and he's trying to bury her in the garden." A sob burst out of her chest, and she glanced back. "And he might be after me now!"

She lurched away from the doors as if afraid something might follow her through, at the same time as people came around from behind their desks, their orderly uniforms and tied-back hair a strange contrast to her mother's shabby dresses and her father's dishevelled appearance.

"Kid, have you been drinking?" one of them asked, trying to get her to sit down on one of the chairs in the waiting area; but she jerked her shoulder and shook him off, not wanting to sit.

"I'm nine! Today! Are you listening to me? She's *dead*!"

The vehemence of the declaration got their attention.

"Get the sheriff down here; we'd better check this out."

She was hustled past the lines of desks and into a room with comfortable chairs, a small water fountain, a big green fern plant. Sat down in the silence. The blessed silence.

Except all she could hear was that muffled scream.

Someone brought her a glass of water, but she held it in her hands unacknowledged. Putting the glass to her lips felt like a physical impossibility.

She couldn't move. Didn't want to even blink. Just sat, waiting for some of the pain or the confusion or the fear to . . . to do what?

She was vaguely aware of the bustle beyond the glass walls of the room. Aware of phones ringing and being answered, and phone calls being made. Of the female officer by her side. Did she bring the water? She smelt of soap, and something else: perfume? Unfamiliar smells. Comforting smells.

"Hey, kid."

She looked up at a face and a voice she recognised: the big bear-sized sheriff was standing in the doorway, and from the look of him, his clothes had been hastily thrown on and his hair was awry – had they woken him up? At that moment, he could have been dressed in a tutu or a tux, it didn't matter. His was the only voice she wanted to hear. But now it felt strange. She had shrunk so far into herself, that even the relief of seeing him felt alien.

"Can I sit down?"

He gestured at a chair opposite her and she nodded, a tiny movement, watching him with the soulful eyes he saw sometimes in his mind when his own children were playing in the back garden, happy and secure.

The sheriff moved his large frame towards the wide leather chair, his body well-padded from lots of lovingly prepared home-cooked food and a few too many snacks at work. He looked up at the officer who'd followed him into the room.

"Tony, see if you can get the little lady a hot drink. Tina, if you could stay with us that would be great."

She wasn't there as a witness – they didn't need one as the voice recorder and video camera were already turned on in the room – but he could see the child was traumatised and scared, and thought a female presence might be helpful.

"Now . . ." The door shut as Tony left the room. "Can you tell me what happened?" Kind, soft.

A shiver ran all the way through the child's body, he saw it. She was still just as skinny as he remembered.

"I don't want to."

He wasn't surprised she didn't want to, but he had to know. Eyes begged him to leave her alone. But also to tell her everything was going to be alright.

"Unless you tell me, I . . . I can't help." He answered her as gently as he could.

Her eyes lowered from his and stared at the carpet.

"It's all my fault." Such tortured words.

"How is it your fault?"

His heart squeezed inside his chest and he knew Tina shifted in her seat; she had a child of her own, just a little older than this one.

"It's my birthday."

Still looking at the carpet.

They waited.

And then a torrent: "My mother made a cake, and we had some friends from school come around, and we played in the garden with the balloons. Everyone was being collected to go home, then my dad came home. Sally Travis' mum was ill and her dad came to pick her up instead. My dad . . . my dad said my mum arranged everything so she would see him. He called her a . . . slut and a whore and everything went horrible like it always does." She gasped. "We – my sister and me – went upstairs where we usually go. She was in the wardrobe. That's where she always goes. There was shouting and crashing. Something got smashed, then there was thumping. I wanted to go down but I . . ."

She froze. Eyes back on the carpet.

Neither spoke.

"Then he went in the garage. I could hear the door and the noises, I was listening, hoping to hear him go out, waiting for it to be over so I could go and help my mum."

She looked up once. Quickly. To his face, wanting him to understand, and he nodded, his eyes on hers, kind eyes.

"Then I heard him open the cupboards in the kitchen, banging all the doors. Then this whirring sound, like a lawnmower but not as loud, and he said something to her, and then . . . and then she screamed."

She swallowed. And again.

"She screamed but it was muffled like there was a pillow over her face. Then she stopped, and the other noise kept going."

She paused.

Apart from the indistinct sounds of the building, there was silence in the room.

"When it stopped, I heard the patio door open, so I went to the window to look out. My dad went to the back of the grass and started digging with the spade from the garage. Dug and dug and just kept digging. He never goes in the garden. He climbed out the hole and came back to the house. He then came out with the black rubbish bags and . . . and . . . he threw them in the hole."

She choked on the next attempt to speak. At the words she knew she had to say next.

The sheriff held back from reaching out a hand to her, not wanting to do anything that might mean she didn't finish.

A huge breath of air. Somehow, she had to say it. *Say it!*

"I saw . . . my mum's hair coming out the top of one of the bags. I made a noise by accident, I screamed – *I didn't mean to*! *I didn't mean to*!"

"I know."

Two words. Should he have said them? Had he spooked her?

He could see her wresting with the horror. Prayed she would continue.

"I saw in the light from the kitchen he was covered in blood. All of him and his clothes. And his face. His eyes stared at me. Then he came into the house. I told my sister. I said *we had to go*. But she wouldn't move. I ran into the bathroom and locked the door and I jumped out the window and hid behind the car. When he slammed the window shut I ran. I ran straight here. I didn't want him to come after me. *What if he comes after me*?"

Her eyes came up again, searching for his. She saw the tension in his face; saw the sadness that she recognised as an echo of her own.

"I can still hear my mum's scream. The one that was muffled."

The whisper was so awful, so soft, and spoke of such pain that he could not bear to sit apart any longer. He moved onto the sofa she was perched on and put his arms around her. She was so cold. It had been a warm day and she was wearing faded denim shorts, another ragged t-shirt and the battered trainers; but the evening was cool, and she was traumatised.

And it was then she let herself cry. Finally. As she had never let herself before. Even when they'd been in the hospital. Control shattered, the dam burst.

Little wonder.

He glanced at Tina. Tears in her eyes. Where was Tony with a hot drink for the girl?

Finally, the tears ebbed and he felt it safe enough to speak.

"Tina, get a patrol car to the house to keep watch, see if anyone leaves. He might try running. Send out a warning to all units and get a team ready to go and investigate, full body kit."

His words helped steady the young woman, and she nodded and got up, glad to throw herself into her job, not just sit helplessly as a small child grieved.

Then there was a knock at the door, and Tony was there with a rather worried expression and . . . a cup of coffee . . . the sheriff could smell it. *Geez, easy to tell this guy doesn't have kids. What nine-year-old drinks coffee? What about hot chocolate? Or warm milk?*

"Tony, can you take the little lady upstairs and get her settled in one of the rooms along from my office. See if there's some food in the kitchen, and if there's a blanket or some extra clothes in Lost Property that'll fit. She's freezing cold. And, erm, get her a cup of hot chocolate, yeah?"

"Yes, sir."

Tony nodded, relinquishing the coffee cup to his boss. He waited, rather daunted by the new job assigned to him. He was used to loud-mouthed speeders or brawling bikers, not fragile girls who'd obviously been sobbing. It made him uneasy. He felt a little out of his depth.

"Tony is going to take you upstairs and look after you, alright? I'll be back to see you soon. You've done so well, you let us do something now? OK?"

He said the words at the same time as guilt gripped him, and he knew he had failed her – failed her and her mother. The law had, and society had. Nothing was going to undo the damage. But the other part of the tragedy? She would pay for that for the rest of her life: a life in care; a life in social facilities for orphans. Probably not even getting the counselling she needed. There just wasn't the funding for it anymore.

What have we done?

She nodded and took a deep breath, not wanting to weep anymore, instinctively used to staying quiet. As she was helped to her feet, Tony and the sheriff exchanged a look over the top of her head, their expressions grim.

Sheriff Mackenzie stopped off on the second floor, while Tony and the kid continued their slow progress up to the third. At least she'd talked. He'd known kids clam up completely after something much less horrific. He pushed open the door to AIC – Action and Information Centre – and putting his emotions aside, became business-like and formal again.

"Trudy, what have we got?"

"Patrol 152 is just approaching the residence."

He'd not needed to tell them any names. They all knew the kid. And where she lived with her unfortunate family – thanks to her father.

"Let's get it up on screen."

Everyone in the room turned to look at the large screen which covered most of one wall.

"Base, this is Patrol 152, at the Earl residence now. Going to take a look."

The familiar voice of Officer Jonathan Tweed came over the speaker system and Mackenzie put on the earpiece that hooked him in with the rest of them. Tweed was a local boy turned cop, a good lad, full of enthusiasm after college. Not who Mackenzie would have chosen for this job, but the rookie could handle himself.

The car's on-board camera followed the officer in his blue uniform, his trim young body not yet ruined by hours sat doing paperwork (and late-night snacks), his mind not ground down to lethargy by hours of overtime. The sheriff could see the house now that it had come into view: the bare front garden, a sorry-looking patch of grass, one balloon still tied to the tree. It was clearly in need of repair, but a lick of paint would not help it. The house reflected the abuse that had gone on inside it; a symbol of the neglect within.

It was eerily quiet. The only sounds were coming from the rustle of the officer's movements, the swish of his trouser legs, the clink of keys against items on his utility belt, the crackle of his radio.

"No movement detected. All seems very quiet," Tweed said calmly; though in truth he was a bit freaked out by the silence, by the unlit house. He'd been told only that there was a possible suspect inside, considered violent and dangerous. His hand stayed on his gun, the other on his Taser.

Mackenzie and the rest of his watching team held their breath, not liking the look of the house. They knew now what may have happened in there: knowledge made all the difference.

Shall I pull him out? Where's back up?

"Alright, Tweed, go back to your vehicle and move away a little. The other unit will be with you soon."

"Yes, sir, sheriff."

Mackenzie smiled at the familiar address. Tweed always called him sir *and* sheriff, rather than one or the other. He'd told the rookie often that he could just use one, but it hadn't made any difference.

The camera feed was filled with the body of the officer as he walked back to the car, blocking the view of the house. Most people turned away now, getting ready for the arrival of the unit, ready to get the forensic guys alerted and sent over depending on what they found.

Mackenzie's shout of alarm came too late. Having seen a glint of something metallic he had first thought it was a gun, he'd not even had time to turn, draw his gun, before the spade crunched down on his head.

The camera showed in horrible clarity the moment of agony on Tweed's face as Mackenzie's shout registered . . . then nothing as the body crumpled forward, the skull smashed like the shell of a boiled egg.

Everyone's attention was once again fixed on the screen, all watching open-mouthed as, still holding the bloodied spade in his hands, a face that none of them would ever forget was picked up on the camera and streamed back to the office. Even in the streetlight, the shimmer of red on his skin was clear, and as mad eyes looked into the camera, as if he knew they were watching him, they all shuddered involuntarily. It was a face of outright evil.

He stepped out of view, and in the doorway of the dark house, the camera now picked out the shape of a girl similar in age, perhaps slightly older, to that of the one upstairs, her face not quite in focus, her darker hair long against her pale skin.

And then a bloodied hand grabbed hold of the camera and wrenched it off the car.

The feed went dead.

Then: "Get medics over there! Chase the unit – *where the hell are they*? Get another unit over there now! Trevor, you're with me! We go too! Make sure everyone has a weapon!"

The room burst into activity, shaking off the momentary shock in a frenzy of action, everyone wanting to do anything they could to get the man who had just attacked one of their own, do anything to get to the other child in time.

Mackenzie cursed as he raced down the stairs, pulling on his Kevlar jacket and belting his gun around his hips. Why had he let Tweed get so close? And alone? Why? Was it that he hadn't quite believed the kid? If he had he wouldn't have underestimated the threat of the man in that house. Damn it! Worse, Earl now knew the police were aware of what had happened and would be on the run! God knew where he might go or who might get hurt as he tried to escape. Was he going to hurt his other daughter or use her as hostage? Too many questions; all impossible to answer.

Feet thundered down the stairs around him, following his lead as they threw themselves into the set of SUVs, glad to see shotguns and automatic weapons in the hands of some of his team. He wouldn't hesitate the give the order to shoot on sight, to disable the man they desperately wanted in custody.

It was only when Mackenzie stood in the blood-splattered kitchen that he got a taste of the horror that had occurred there on this night. And it was only when he saw the hastily dug hole half filled with its gruesome contents in their black bags that what the child had said truly hit home. But even after seeing Tweed have his head pulverised by a spade, there was nothing to prepare him for the carnage in the kitchen. He wanted to throw up. It looked like some kid with a paint can had gone crazy . . . only this was no can of paint, and no kid. Incredibly, the electric carving knife was still plugged in and lay on the kitchen worktop, and still slick with dark red, testimony to the butchery that had been trodden through into the lounge and hallway, even up the stairs.

The two units had burst in, a frenzy of activity and bristling with weapons as was standard procedure when entering a property with a potential murderer inside; but as Mackenzie had known would be the case, Vincent Sinclair Earl was gone, and his other daughter was almost definitely with him. *Please God, don't let there be more innocent blood split tonight.*

"Sir?"

Mackenzie ignored the white-suited forensics officer, who then asked him to look up to the bedroom window he guessed belonged to the girls, as indicated by the Disney stickers on the window. Did he agree that was the girls' bedroom? It would not have been hard to see straight down into the garden from there, even for a child, did he agree?

"Sir?"

The officer tried again, seeing the distracted look on the sheriff's face as he eventually glanced up at the window and nodded. Once.

"Yes?"

"Yes. I believe that was the window from which the girl witnessed her father's activity in the garden."

"I need you to step away from the evidence, sir. We need to take pictures and moulds of the footprints, and the remove the . . . evidence . . ."

Parts. Body parts. Say the words.

They hadn't needed to look in the bags – though of course they had needed to open one to be completely sure, beyond doubt, that it was human body parts in the bags.

Mackenzie's mind returned to the electric carving knife. *Had he intended to use it on the children too? Where was he? Where would he go?*

"Trevor!"

He walked back towards the house, using the side gate to get to the front of the house to avoid the melee of white suits in the garden and kitchen, taking pictures, bagging items. It seemed to him that this was a building that wanted to give up its secrets, not keep them. It was a house already so desecrated it did not seem like the intrusion it sometimes did at other crime scenes.

"Yes, sir?"

His deputy started walking towards him, having finished talking to the officer and medical officer who'd attended Tweed's body where it still lay by the car.

Why did I send Tweed alone?

"Get a perimeter set up and maintained, just in case Earl is crazy enough to try and come back – though he must know we're here. I don't want any more deaths tonight. And those boys need to work the scene in peace. And if any reporters show up, make sure they stay behind the line, and only very basic information at the moment; in fact, as little as possible until we have Earl in custody. Any news?"

"Nothing, sir, though I have sent out the APB," – the All Points Bulletin system they used to relay information – "to all units and stations. The announcement is on the airwaves as well as the news channels that people must report any sightings but must not approach. Hopefully if he's still covered in blood that'll warn people off."

Mackenzie only nodded, approving the action taken so far.

"I'll head back to the station, see if the kid can give us any ideas where her dad might go. Let me know if anything develops."

"Yes, sir."

Mackenzie placed his hand on the shoulder of his trusted friend and colleague, knowing he was fully capable and understood the situation.

He climbed into his car and pulled away, zooming back through the silent streets to the station, impatient to see the girl, who now felt like the key to so much.

Tony was standing guard outside the third-floor room where he had been instructed to take the child, and was looking pale and anxious. The handheld screen he was looking at showed the data feed of the evidence being logged, including some of the pictures from the house; no wonder he looked the way he did.

"She alright?"

Tony looked up as the sheriff approached.

"As much as can be, sir. I got her to eat a slice of toast and drink some hot chocolate, and then she fell asleep, which is a mercy, sir."

Both men went to the door and looked through the window. A small, still shape lay under a blanket on the couch. And Mackenzie's heart broke for her yet again.

"I really don't want to have to wake her up, but we need to know anything that might help us get her father." The sheriff rubbed a hand over bleary eyes. He looked at his watch: 2.06am – no wonder he felt rough. "Wish me luck."

He pushed open the door and let it close quietly behind him. Sat down on the opposite sofa. Reaching across, he gently touched her shoulder.

"Hey, kid."

The child jerked up from under the blanket and leant away from him, eyes alarmed and wide; and then they relaxed a fraction.

"W-what happened?" she whispered.

"We've been to your house. My team are there at the scene, gathering evidence."

She clutched at the blanket. The luminous eyes gleamed bright with unshed tears, the tangle of blonde hair about her shoulders.

"Is it OK if I tell you what happened?"

A nod.

"Your father attacked the patrolman who went to wait outside. He also ripped the camera off our car, but just before he did, we saw your sister standing in the doorway of the house." He kept his voice calm and controlled. He did not feel it was necessary to tell her that her father had killed their patrolman in cold blood; he didn't want her feeling responsible for that. But the situation was dire. They had to find him. *Damn it, I don't have time to be as gentle as I want to be. She's my best witness . . . my only witness.* "But when we got to the house, your father wasn't there, and neither was your sister, which is why I woke you. You're a smart kid. You can understand how important it is we find them."

She seemed to close down at mention of her father. He needed a different angle. But there were questions he needed answers to. Urgently.

"How old is your sister?"

"Eleven."

"It must be good to have a big sister."

He cringed. *What a dumb thing to say. What can I do here*?

"I need you to tell me if you know . . . if you have any idea where he might go."

He saw her face register the request; the appeal for her help even though she was drowning in misery. Mackenzie felt like a bastard for pestering her with questions, but he had to know.

Slowly she shook her head. "I don't know. I . . . did he go in the car?"

Mackenzie looked at her for a second with stark astonishment etched on his face.

"Did he steal your police car or did he drive his car?" she asked when he didn't answer.

Her words only compounded his stupidity and he cursed himself angrily, leaving her rather surprised. Earl hadn't taken the squad car as it was still parked on the road . . . but he hadn't thought to check if he had a vehicle of his own!

"What colour is your father's car?" he asked gently.

"It's black."

"How many doors?"

"Four doors. And the trunk is big. It's very old."

"Good. You stay there. I'll be back. Tony's just outside the door if you need anything."

He strode from the room and down the stairs to AIC, buzzing Trevor on his radio: "Trevor! Is there a car on the drive? Dark. Black. Five-door."

"A car? Earl's car?"

"Yes. Is it on the drive or has it gone?"

"I'll check." There was a pause. "It's not here."

"OK, thanks." Mackenzie looked around at Trudy and her assistant Janice. "Get me the plates on Vincent Sinclair Earl's vehicle and send out to all units and neighbouring forces. I want this bastard found by dawn.

Rerun the footage from the town's street cameras and find which road it left on!"

There was a ripple of "Yes, sir" around the room; then: "Sir!"

Mackenzie looked over at the officer who had called him, trying to ignore the footage on the screen of the people in and around the Earl household. It brought back images he didn't want to think about.

"Got a call from Ellias Hospital. They've got an emergency over on route 986 by the West Valley: a truck driver found a guy on the side of the road badly beaten up. The guy, a Mr Steven Thompson, was taken to hospital, and when he came around he said some bloke had flagged him down. The bloke punched him when he'd let the window down, and then dragged him out of the car and beat him until he lost consciousness. When he regained consciousness, his car was gone. I have the registration of the vehicle. Shall I get Observation to put it into their data feeds?"

"Sounds like our guy. Yes, do that, and let me know if you get any firm sightings." Mackenzie felt a surge of hope. "Did Mr Thompson say anything about a girl? Eleven years old. Skinny. Pale skin. Long dark hair."

"No, sir, nothing."

This was bad. Yes, grab a different car to keep them guessing, but where was the girl?

I don't want to lose another person tonight.

He ducked into his office and started on the report notifying his superiors of the developments, and made a note of the next of kin for Officer Tweed. He knew his parents, knew he was engaged to be married. It was a duty he wished he did not have to undertake.

"Sir!" He looked up, knowing from the tone of voice it wasn't good.

"Yes, Trudy?"

She was in the doorway, headset on, wires dangling, a handheld screen held out to him. The drawn expression on her usually calm face did not bode well.

"Just had reports come in, sir. A car has gone off the bridge alongside the lake off the B36. Vehicle said to be dark, five-door, not new. That's the best description we had. A householder up on the hill saw it happen through the bathroom window. Thought they were seeing things but–"

"The description fits that of the Earl family car." Like he needed it confirmed. "What time was this?"

"He says about 1.25am."

"Enough time for Earl to get over to the highway and flag down a driver and steal another car," he mused out loud. "And the car?"

"It sank fully, sir."

His heart hurt; he felt like he'd been sucker-punched in the gut. The movements of their murderer were important to him at that moment, but the knowledge of where the other daughter more so . . . somehow, he knew where she was: at the bottom of the lake.

"Get Search and Rescue over there and ready to dive as soon as dawn breaks. Get an officer out to the witness and get a formal statement taken – the morning will do, as God knows we haven't got enough people to spare right now." He looked back at the team in AIC as he headed for the door. "And find me that stolen car!"

He leapt up the stairs and back to the girl with a speed and agility he had not employed for a good long while – nothing had happened to warrant it, and tonight was certainly payback for all those lazy afternoons of form-filling and working lunches. He looked at his watch: 2.47am.

Sweet Jesus, the longest night of my life - apart from the wife being in labour with the kids. I want the dawn to come; want to nail this bastard.

The girl was waiting for him, huddled up with her knees against her chest, wrapped in the blanket as if unwilling to give up its warmth now she had it. He didn't blame her.

"Hi. You OK, kid?

A nod.

"Is it OK if I tell you what's been happening?"

Another nod.

"Your father took his car, but now he's stolen another one," – he decided not to tell her about her sister – "Do you know where he might go? Does he have family around here?"

He tried to sound relaxed, but there was no mistaking the urgency in his voice. She did not seem put off, however, and when Tony entered the room as well, he sensed that she had overcome some of her initial shock and was perhaps keen to join them in their attempt to hunt her father down, to be useful. The short sleep seemed to have done her good.

She looked up.

"His parents died and his grandma died, so did his grandpa. They're buried in Charlesbury. My grandma has a house in Dewlan, up the hill. He went there once but not again because he hates my . . ." She fell quiet. "He hates my grandma coz she's my . . . my mum's mum." Her face darkened.

"Do you think he would go to the house? Do you know the address so we can go check on her? Make sure she's alright?"

Mackenzie realised the kid understood the implications of the questions, and the panic rose again, instantly, making tears brim in her eyes.

"I don't know it!" she cried. "I only know how to get there from going there in the car and we haven't been for the longest time as it always made my dad mad if my mum went to see her, so she stopped going!" She started rocking, and the tears fell.

"It's OK. We'll find it. But can you remember anything in the address?"

"I never saw it. My mum had it written in her address book by the phone in the kitchen . . ." Her words trailed off as the horror of the last few hours came back full force. She pulled the blanket up high, like it might protect her from the questions that made her remember too much.

He stepped out into the corridor and closed the door behind him.

"Trevor?"

"Boss?"

"Can you fight your way past Forensics for me? I need you to find Mrs Earl's diary and message me over the address for her mother, in Dewlan. I need it ASAP. In fact, that's not soon enough. *Hurry.*"

"The forsies aren't going to like it, but I'll try and get in through the lounge. They're mostly still in the garden and kitchen."

"Tell them I sent you; they can bitch at me when they next see me."

"Will do, boss."

They clicked out and Mackenzie realised how tired he was, yet wide awake at the same time.

Adrenaline?

Guilt?

Both.

He glanced through the window, saw the girl look up as Tony said something to her. Saw her respond, tentatively. Should he tell her about her sister now? No. There would be plenty yet for her to deal with. Let her have a few hours of relative peace.

'*WE BRING YOU this breaking story from a small town in the . . .*'

A loud female growl of frustration and annoyance drowned out the news report on the huge state-of-the-art screen on the wall in front of the large, soft sofa on which Daryl Blackmoor was trying to relax. He had his tuxedo on, hair slicked back, so he was ready, but he wasn't in the mood for rushing anywhere. As a rule, he didn't rush. He closed his eyes and winced, trying to keep his seething irritation at bay at the sound that reminded him he wasn't alone.

Why the hell did he put up with it? She had been annoying him for at least two weeks now. Sure, she was beautiful, but to be honest, there were lots of beautiful women out there, and it wasn't like he actually gave a damn about her. Why was he putting himself through this? This pointless charade of togetherness? To begin with she had been suitably grateful and appreciative; more recently, however, arrogant and increasingly assertive, which he didn't like at all. That was the one thing no one ever did: tell him what to do. He didn't want to waste time thinking about what had caused her annoyance. It was probably a broken fingernail or something else stupendously trivial.

Daryl was drawn back to the news bulletin and saw a familiar news reporter with a coat on, the world dark around her, and behind her lots of parked police SUVs. A swarm of forensic people were moving about in the shot.

'*Local forces were alerted to a crime here at this small house behind me . . .*' The camera panned away and showed the house: a sorry heap of a building that Daryl would have had no hesitation in pulling down. '*From what we can gather, the father of the household, who is suspected of domestic violence, killed his wife and planned to bury her in the garden. And it is thought from what our news cameras have picked up, and what we have seen being carried from the house, that the mother's body was not in one piece.'* The reporter's face showed a flicker of emotion as the gravity of the words registered somewhere deeper inside her. '*In what will surely be a case to shake this small town to its core, it is understood one of the children managed to escape the house and get to the police station. A second child was seen alive, picked up by a patrol car camera, just moments before the patrol guard was also killed. However, when response units got to the house, both the child and the father were gone. The latest update is that the family car has been driven off the bridge on the B36 into the lake, just outside the town.*'

The shot changed to footage from a helicopter over the choppy waters of the lake, police and their vehicles on the road, the focus on the broken fencing and the dark water that gave nothing, despite the strong lights shone down onto it.

'*Fears are that the father has killed himself and the second child to avoid being apprehended by the police, but Search and Rescue teams are having to wait until dawn to safely recover the vehicle. Naturally our thoughts go to the remaining child who, we believe, is in police care.*'

"Daryl!"

The picture cut abruptly from full-screen to blank screen. His date was standing in front of the TV, remote control in hand. Once he would have been tempted by the curves that filled the black and white dress – haute couture, the best money could buy, obviously – and the sleek limbs and coiffured hair. It would have impressed him sufficiently to have forgiven the interruption. Now? Nothing.

"Daryl, we have to *go*! We'll be *late*!"

Who does she think she is? My mother? My wife?

He stared at her for a moment, amazed at her stupidity. Despite everything he had done to impress upon her the rules of their relationship, it seemed she had a much shorter memory span than he had thought. The voice grated on his nerves: whining, vapid, weak. How he hated the way she said his name even. Why hadn't he dealt with this vexation sooner? How sick he was of these insipid creatures – this one in particular.

He stood, towering over her even in the six-inch heels she balanced on, his broad muscular shoulders tapering down to slim hips. He knew why he had been awarded the World's Sexiest Man and the World's Handsomest Man for three years on the trot. His physical perfection was a miracle of genes and healthy lifestyle, and his body obeyed him just like everyone and everything else. That was just how he liked it.

"Just what. . ." – his tone made her face falter and lose some of the demanding attitude, made her go perfectly still – "do you think you're doing?"

Her mouth opened and closed twice before she managed to get any words out, never having faced his anger before. All the brooding power and authority that he carried around inside was now being unleashed, albeit partially, and directed at her. It was frightening. Much worse than she had imagined. Why hadn't she kept her mouth shut?

"Daryl, we need to go. . . you . . . you can't just watch the news all night."

Daryl noticed the change in her voice: softer, persuasive, seeking forgiveness. He wasn't persuaded. And he didn't feel at all forgiving.

"*I* can do what *I* like. Do you really think they'll start without me? Have you forgotten just *who I am*?"

His correction was like a slap and she flinched at the last question, louder and angrier, and so dangerous in its tone she couldn't move. He stared at her with those beautiful, terrible green eyes, eyes that had seduced her so many times . . . but now they seemed to despise her. Made her feel shorter, despite the heels. He straightened up to his full height, and stood tall, unreachable.

"Take off the dress."

It was such a change of tack, and her face betrayed surprise. And relief.

"If that was what you wanted, you should have just said. We will be even later though . . ."

Her hand went to the zip, glad he appeared to be merely sexually frustrated and just needed a quick fuck to calm down. She was used to those kinds of needs.

But Daryl felt disgusted with himself indulging such base instincts with her, and barked, "Just take the dress off."

His impatience and the biting tone made her look at him quickly . . . this wasn't quite right. She complied though, his eyes warning her that if she didn't she would regret it. She hated the way his hands were clasped behind his back, as if he couldn't bear to touch her. Her mind tumbled in frustration. She would never understand this man. He was a mystery as far as emotion went, like a living storm cloud, always changing, always so potent, and she was never sure where the direction of his temper would blow or the lightning would strike next.

The dress slipped off and she bent down to pick it up. She held the expensive garment uncertainly, not sure where to put it, not feeling able to move from the spot where she stood.

He solved the dilemma by reaching forward, taking it in one hand and then tossing it behind him onto the sofa with a force that expressed some of his displeasure. She stood there in her hold-up stockings, her lacy bra and tiny panties, knowing she didn't look at all bad. She leaned her weight back on one heel and let a hip slip forward, trying to look a little provocative, hoping it might sway him. Disappointingly, his eyes didn't even drop to her breasts but stayed on her eyes, boring into her, making her confidence shrivel. She felt like a beetle at his feet. How could eyes convey such displeasure, such disgust?

"And the earrings."

She paused. Then did as she was told, putting them in the hand that he held out. He didn't look away from her or at them as he put them in the pocket of his jacket as if they weren't worth a few hundred thousand dollars alone.

"And the necklace."

Again, into his pocket.

She was then treated to another scathing look that made her feel a lot more naked than she was. His eyes tore at her soul and made her feel nothing more than the flirtatious whore of the man before her, as if she was a toy that had offended its owner and been found wanting – and about to be discarded in the trash.

"Keep the underwear. Or not. I don't really care. Find some of your own clothes and put them on. Someone will be here in five minutes to escort you from the building, and a car will take you wherever you wish to go. Do not try and stay; do not try and contact me; but do try to keep that mouth of yours from saying anything foolish. To anyone. Remember you signed an NDA. I would hate to have someone pay you a little visit, at my request."

Words so quiet, yet so full of menace. She couldn't have spoken a word in her defence if she'd tried. She knew it was pointless. She had fallen from grace. There was no redemption.

With that he turned and strode to the door, leaving her standing there. Tears slid down her cheeks as his expressionless face passed in front of a mirror for one last check of his appearance, then he was gone from the room. She knew that would be the last time she ever saw him except via the pages of a newspaper.

Daryl didn't look at his chief of security as he walked him to the elevator that would take them from the penthouse to the ground where the Bentley would be waiting. Not a word was said about Daryl being there on his own rather than accompanied by the girl, as had been planned. The fact she wasn't there said everything. And there was a strong possibility she would be replaced by the end of the night. It wasn't the first time; it wouldn't be the last.

"Have a car take her wherever she wants to go, and ensure she takes all of her possessions. I don't want a trace of her left. She is not permitted to take anything else whatsoever. I am not feeling generous this evening."

Usually he let them take whatever he had bought them while they had graced his bed, and usually they parted company because he was simply bored of them – not bored *and* annoyed. Mac didn't respond. Daryl didn't expect him to. Orders were given to be obeyed. There was nothing to question.

"And put these somewhere safe."

Daryl reached into his pocket and took out the earrings and necklace and handed them over. If Mac was surprised, he didn't show it. He knew his job description: keep Mr Blackmoor safe, alive, and see that whatever he instructs you or anyone else to do is done. In return, Mac was given a salary that would ensure he would never want for anything – if he lived long enough to see his eventual retirement.

The elevator doors opened and they both strode out, Mac handing the gems to another bodyguard positioned just outside the doors with a look that said all it needed to. He stayed at his boss's side, eyes everywhere, listening to his earpiece, as alert as a hunting cat.

"And Mac, have Clarice brought over for when I get back. I want a bath and champagne ready as well – I don't care which, just one of my usual selection."

He sighed. At least some of his women knew how to please him – a select group he had called his 'Cherries' – and they were deliberately kept out of the limelight, hired for their performance in the bedroom, not for appearing at his side in a public capacity. Each of them had a particular forte, and he got to pick and choose which he wanted whenever he wanted. And in return for being exclusively available, and keeping themselves as beautiful as nature, cosmetics and science could manage, they were kept in luxurious apartments and allowed to enjoy a relatively carefree existence, all bills paid for, a large allowance for any shopping they needed, and a car supplied and replaced every year. If they lasted that long.

Daryl had instigated the set-up not long after his eighteen birthday for several reasons: firstly, that he did not have the time for socialising as much as he had been used to; secondly, he had a care for his health, so all his Cherries were vetted and checked, as well as monitored by cameras that ensured they stuck to the 'agreement' – it was all very well being a womaniser, but he did not want it to be his undoing; thirdly, he was aware of his increased status as 'the prize'. He was the bachelor every society madam, call girl, bored housewife and young debutante on the social scene wanted to call their own; he was a fantasy, the man they all wanted to 'net'. But he only ever wanted a woman for her body, for the temporary diversion they offered him from the stresses of being who he was, and did not have the patience to field limitless expectations and naive hopes of marriage. He was not looking for anything meaningful. He was looking for physical satisfaction and pleasure. Emotion was an inconvenience he had no time for. Nor was he going to be tricked into marriage or alimony payments because of an accidental conception. He was wise to the games women played, and his Cherries meant he was protected from all inconveniences associated with them.

He did not expect the world to understand, and he did not care if it did or did not. Who was anyone to tell him no?

He got in the waiting car, and the door was closed.

"Good evening, Mr Blackmoor."

"Evening, Geoffrey," he replied automatically, staring out of the blacked-out security glass of the window as the car pulled away.

His mind slipped back to the story on the news. He generally didn't watch much else other than the business news, sometimes the sport, but even he, who had little room for such trivia and even less for sympathy, knew that the circumstances behind the story must be awful. A child drowned by their own father? Their mother dismembered in the family home? A child somehow brave enough to run away and get to a police station?

"Are you alright, Mr Blackmoor? You seem very quiet."

He looked around, realised he had been frowning rather ferociously at the world beyond the window. Geoffrey was being kind. Clearly his dark thoughts were loud inside the car.

"Just thinking, Geoffrey. Something on the news."

"I try not to listen to it any more, sir, nothing ever good on it."

The chauffeur realised after a few seconds of silence that nothing more would be forthcoming. For Mr Blackmoor, however, in his mind that was not a bad 'conversation'.

"Would you like some music, sir?"

"Something soothing. I'll have enough noise to put up with soon enough, I'm sure."

He grimaced at the prospect of the awards ceremony. All those smiling people wanting to shake his hand and toast his success and his health. Lots of people thought it must be exciting. It was not. It was monotonous, and he'd been promising himself a night in on the sofa to watch some football and relax for a very long time . . . but it never quite happened.

He made a mental note to make a donation to a victim support charity. He wondered how old the surviving kid was. What on earth would happen to her? No mother. No sister. Her father a murderer or dead – which might be a blessing. At least he knew one thing: for one young person, the night had turned into a terrible thing, and for far worse reasons than he could claim.

IT WAS 7.37am. The long nightmare unfolding seemed surreal; like it couldn't possibly have happened in such a short space of time; like it couldn't have happened at all in such a small town. But then Mackenzie looked through his office window into the next cubicle and saw the child. Looked at the evidence continually updating and uploading on the data feed. Looked again at the piece of paper with the phone number on of Officer Tweed's parents. He closed his eyes for several long moments and remembered every sickening minute spent in that gloomy, tragic house. He had already visited the lake. Watched as they hauled the car up, the sun just peeking over the horizon. Already seen the lifeless body of a girl whose hands were handcuffed to the steering wheel, her skin luminescent in the dawn light, her dark hair plastered to her white, bloated face.

They always say there's one case that gets you. One case you never forget.

Sadly, he wished it was one that he had made fewer mistakes conducting. Why had he let Officer Tweed get out of the car? Why hadn't he had Earl arrested before he slaughtered his wife and drowned his eldest daughter?

He looked at the kid again. She was watching, alert as a baby hawk, her astonishing blue eyes on the movement of his people and the screen. She had the same bright blonde curls of her mother. She would look almost exactly like her mum when she grew up, he'd put money on it. He checked himself, feeling emotion rising.

No point thinking along those lines.

He recalled the hatred in Earl's eyes as they had focussed on the patrol car's camera for that moment. Real hatred. No remorse, no trace of regret. It was unnerving. No, it was . . . inhuman. And he wondered, once again, how the girl would ever recover from this.

Jesus, he needed to sleep. But not until they at least had some idea where her father was. He had check points on all roads, all surrounding forces on high alert and offering any manpower he needed. But they still hadn't managed to find that damned address book the child mentioned. He was considering taking the kid for a drive and letting her direct him there, but he just didn't feel comfortable about that for two reasons: it would be downright cruel to make her retrace the route in her mind from her 'home'; and he did not want her leaving the building until her father was locked up in a cell with restraints pinning every limb down.

She looked around, as if sensing his gaze, and he would have tried to smile but for the tears that were travelling silently down her cheeks again. He'd had Tina find her some clothes from their lost property room – a pair of grey sweat pants, a white t-shirt and a navy hoodie – and she had reluctantly put them on over her own clothes, as if it felt like stealing. He had also been glad to see her eat some pizza that morning – an unhealthy breakfast that would have got him into lots of trouble with his wife! But it hadn't mattered, she was starving hungry and had eaten it all. She had then wrapped herself back up in the blanket.

He dropped his eyes down to his screens, longing to make inroads into the tasks waiting for him. He was going to have to send in another news update for the press, and another report to his superiors – and no doubt he'd get an earful for not having caught the guy yet. He looked at the number again for Tweed's parents and decided he should call them first. Invite them into the station maybe? He reached for the phone, dialled the extension for an outside line, and pressed in the first number, thinking how glad he would be to see his wife and kids, whenever that turned out to be.

Then he heard a gunshot.

And screaming.

He looked up and saw his own shock replicated in Trevor's face across the room.

"Everyone stay calm," he said quickly.

He clicked the icon for the video feed for downstairs, and immediately saw at least five officers without their bulletproof jackets on – his was still on only because he had forgotten to take it off.

The screen showed a scene of chaos: someone on the ground in front of the desk with blood pooling around them, and someone else behind the desk flopped unmoving over their chair. The rest he could see huddled at the back behind desks and chairs. There appeared to be no civilians in the room. Then he spotted a man hustling a female officer up the stairs. The image was blurred, but he saw a gun pointed at their head with one hand, the other hand removing the officer's weapon. Damn it! Now they had a madman on the loose with two guns! And he wondered, not for the last time, why he hadn't been given the go-ahead to get the ID-sensitive weapons upgrade.

"He's coming up and he has a hostage!" someone shouted.

Mackenzie took one last look at the screen and his blood ran cold: it was Earl.

All moved, finding somewhere to hide with their eyes on the double doors, everyone drawing a weapon. He pulled out his own heavy-duty pistol – his preferred choice as it sat well in his big hands – and slipped out of his office. He hunkered down behind a metal cabinet, the same side as the double doors. He could see the rest of the room, and kept half an eye on them and half on the door, waiting to see who sprang through them.

"If you get a clear shot take it!" Mackenzie instructed, "but do not shoot to kill. I repeat: *do not* shoot to kill! I need this man alive!" He realised he was furious. How dare this madman cause more bloodshed? "And can someone get an alert out to the hospital. Have crews sent here ASAP. Make sure they stay back before given the go ahead to come in."

"Yes, sir," called one of his men, sending a rapid comms through on his radio.

Mackenzie leaned back against the wall, closed his eyes for a single second, trying to reign in the emotion, control the adrenaline rush that was coursing through his sleep-deprived body. When he opened his eyes, he saw the one person who had no weapon: she looked back at him, horror on her face, all the fragile calm that eight hours in a safe place had managed to give her gone . . . it was the same petrified expression he had seen when he had arrived at the station just a few hours ago.

He was considering moving to her side to act as a shield, when the door burst open, kicked so hard that it swung back and slammed into the wall.

"Drop your weapons or I'll kill her!"

The shout was angry, and determined. He peeked over the top of the cabinet. The fear on Officer Jennifer Mattis' face was clear to see. She was only twenty-three, an absolute godsend on the front desk, and her body was held against his by an arm over her chest, the hand holding a gun.

"No one has to get hurt! I just came for my daughter! Hand her over and I'll go!" he then yelled.

Hand her over so you can torture and kill her as well?

"What do you want her for?" Mackenzie yelled back after a moment of silence, trying to buy time, trying to work out how to get all his people out of danger *and* keep the girl safe.

"That's my business! She's my daughter isn't she? I can do what I like with her!"

Mackenzie hadn't expected any other answer, and he could see the look on the kid's face, could see her breathing was rapid as she succumbed to panic.

She's still sitting on the sofa! Why isn't she hiding?

Mackenzie desperately gestured at her to get on the floor but she didn't move. Couldn't.

"I don't think I can do that," he replied, trying to think. He needed his response team there and they were out searching for the person who had just stormed in and surprised them all. This was AIC. They weren't combat specialists!

"Yes, you can! *I want my daughter*!"

Silence.

He heard a whimper from Jennifer. His arm was now around her neck, her body still protecting most of his – too close to risk a shot.

"I'll count to ten, then I'm shooting her in the head! And I'll shoot anyone who tries to stop me! Then I will find my daughter!" he shouted, eyes going over the room, identifying where people were.

No one moved. The computer screens that kept updating and changing were the most active things in the room.

"I just want my daughter!" He paused. And then counted: "One."

Mackenzie refused to give the man a chance to kill the girl, the courageous child who had done nothing wrong and deserved a chance at life.

"Two."

He looked around at Trevor, who he could just about see.

"Three."

He held up nine fingers and Trevor nodded back, passing the message on to the two next to him – who had bulletproof jackets and weapons, men who he knew were good enough shots.

"Four."

He hoped they were on form today, because lives were hanging in the balance.

"Five!"

Silence.

"Six!"

He ran through what he was going to do in his head. He prayed that the girl frozen with terror remained frozen. If she moved, she'd give herself away, and all would be lost.

"Seven!"

Silence.

"Eight! There are two of you already dead downstairs! I didn't think you cared so little about your own people . . . are you going to let more die now?"

Silence.

Mackenzie held up a hand to the child, a flat palm that said *hold still, don't move*, his lips saying the words silently.

"Nine!"

He gave Trevor a nod and the three moved as one, and Earl, caught by surprise, swung the gun that had been aimed at Jenny's head wildly, from left to right and back again, his eyes wild. Two other officers pushed the desk for all they were worth to provide another distraction – and to create a shield to get them closer. At the same time, Jenny grabbed the arm around her neck and twisted out of it, hitting him in the stomach with the full force of her elbow – a mixture of panic and intent – and lunged towards the door . . . but the bullet got her in the back and she fell. Earl, suddenly refocussed, then loosed bullets at those in front with the second gun, the first officer going down with one in the shoulder. Trevor and the other officer put bullets in the outstretched arm that held the gun and he dropped it; but like some indestructible fiend from a horror movie, Earl stepped forward and shoved his first gun into the officer's belly under the black Kevlar jacket and pulled the trigger twice, before ducking under a desk, avoiding Trevor's shot. Trevor threw himself to the floor.

It was all happening too quickly. Mackenzie had his gun ready in two hands to fire . . . and then the small figure in the room beside him stood up and turned to stare at her father. To face the monster she had run from. To face the fate she had feared would be hers.

Her movement distracted Mackenzie for a split second and his eyes flicked from Earl's to hers.

Earl saw the movement and followed his gaze, saw his daughter and then turned and fired at him. The bullet pummelled into his jacket, throwing him back and to the side, slamming his body against the cabinet with the combined force of his weight and the shot.

His stare had given the child away, and there was a momentary pause as Earl's focus changed from shooting down law officers, to the helpless figure of his daughter. Mackenzie watched then in horror as the gun was lifted to aim at the child . . . he would never be in time . . .

The gun reported, and again, and again, and as Mackenzie fired at Earl, he saw the blanket that had been around her shoulders fall to the floor, and his heart stopped. He then felt fury for this man, and raised his own gun again and fired once, twice, watching him crumple further under the desk, saw Trevor stand and point his gun at Earl's head, yelling for him hand over his weapon and be still. Although badly wounded, Earl still struggled to rise to finish what he'd started, wanting to see his daughter dead. It was the only thought in his crazed mind and a roar of rage erupted from his mouth. But he was cornered, unable to escape, like some wild animal, blood pouring from his wounds, and he went quiet.

For a moment, there was silence. Then there was noise everywhere: shouting as people emerged from hiding to call for back up, for ambulances; others rushing forward to help those bleeding on the floor. Mackenzie looked at the scene of carnage, the blood all over the floor, walls and doors.

In what felt like slow motion, he pushed himself upright and turned around to go to the girl. To pay his respects to her dead body, or hold her hand while they waited for the med crew to get there and try and keep her alive. Four, or was it five bullets . . . there was no way she could have escaped.

He found an empty room. The blanket still lying there where it fell. He saw the bullet holes in the wall, pock-marking the otherwise flawless surface. He stepped around the door, looked into the corner, preparing himself to find the small crumpled body, his heart in his mouth.

But there was nothing. He looked up the corridor, his gun still in his hand. Nothing. Until he saw the broken window at the end of the corridor. He started walking, even as fear arose at what he was going to see.

Oh, no. She jumped. She was so afraid she jumped.

The bottom pane of the window was smashed, but how? Had it been the small body of a child, travelling fast as it hurled itself through in desperation?

He placed his hands on the sill, felt the shards of brittle old glass under his palms, and braced himself to look down.

He saw the pavement and his stomach flipped.

Nothing.

What the hell? We're three storeys up!

It was a good thirty feet to the ground. How could she not be down there, broken, or perhaps worse? There was nowhere else for her to be. Nowhere else she could have fallen.

He ran back into AIC, saw the furious work of the medics on his people, glad to see Jenny sitting up. He then flew down the stairs, his pulse racing, his mind telling him it just wasn't possible. She had to be hurt at least?

He got outside the building, past the flurry of more medics, past the response units that had just pulled up outside and unloaded themselves. He ignored all of them and hurried to the patch of grass beneath the window where she would have landed, marked by the littering of glass that gleamed bright in the morning sunlight. But no child. Not even any blood.

Mackenzie heard footsteps behind him: it was Trevor, and Alfie Duncan, one of the response team's leaders.

"She's gone," he said, without waiting for them to ask.

"What do you mean, sir? Where?" Trevor asked, confused, his look mirrored by Alfie, in full combat gear, armed to the max.

"She jumped through the window." Mackenzie pointed upwards, and then down at the ground. "But she's gone."

All three stood silently, completely flummoxed by the conundrum before them.

"Can we get video footage for the front of the building? Surely we'll be able to see her?" Trevor asked.

"She can't just disappear, she has nothing, she'll . . . get the video footage. And get a search organised. She'll not survive out there on her own . . ."

He didn't need to say any more. They hadn't worked cumulatively over sixty years in law enforcement to not know what happened to runaway kids. And she was a pretty girl with no means of defending herself. She was about as vulnerable as it got.

"Get Forensics down here and get it all photographed. Is Earl secure?"

"Yes, very. The medics are tending him. All shots were clear of vitals. He'll survive, so he'll pay for his crimes, as he should."

"I'm glad I didn't put a bullet in this head; that would have been too quick," Mackenzie said, bitterly. "Put out a general alert to keep an eye out for the kid on the radio and the news, and use a description. We've only got the video feed to get a picture from, but it should be enough. Maybe ask the school if they have a photo we could use? Let's hope we can find her before something else happens to her."

They all turned, walked up the steps and back into the building. *The slaughter has ended*, Mackenzie thought as he wearily climbed the stairs to his office, *but this is not over* . . .

He did not realise that he was both wrong and right.

THE GIRL RAN. Ran like she had the night before, away from her house. Ran like she'd been wanting to the whole time she'd been at the police station. She ran from the hurt. From her father's final, hateful stare. And from his bullets.

But finally, she had to stop. Chest heaving, breaths coming in gasps, she knelt down, hands on the ground to keep her from falling forward. If she lay down, she feared she'd never get up, so she stayed in her crouch, her whole body trembling.

She closed her eyes, amazed that she was alive, amazed the bullets had missed her. Everything rushed back in such a tumble it was a struggle to piece it all together in the right order. All she remembered was the fear that drove her to run as fast as she could. To escape. She remembered the corridor, brightly lit with the sunshine coming in through the window at the end. Remembered the doors that opened onto the corridor. She'd just wanted to get out of the building. He was coming for her. So, she'd just pulled the hood up on her sweatshirt and ran, launched herself through the doors and down the corridor and into the window, hitting it with her shoulder and curling around to protect her head. She remembered that her breathing slowed as she uncurled in the air outside, responding to the feeling of space around her, the strange sense of peace. And she hadn't been afraid.

She'd seen the ground then, rising up beneath her, her mind working out the distance in the split seconds left, her body curling again and turning over a full rotation, remembered her hands reaching out at the point of contact in the long grass. She had rolled twice, and tumbled down the hill, allowing herself a brief pause before she took off again, not consciously thinking where to go, just away.

She looked at her hands as she ran. Looked over the rest of her. All there. Nothing missing. Nothing particularly hurting except for an ache in her shoulder. How had she jumped and landed? Perhaps her gymnastics training had helped, as she knew she could do flips and turns and not ever stumble.

She crouched lower as she heard a car go past, music blaring from the windows, and then ducked down behind bush on the side of the road, keeping out of sight instinctively. Somehow she knew if she was seen they'd take her back. Take her back and make her answer lots more questions. Perhaps even make her see her father again. Had they caught him? Was he dead? Where was her sister? She looked at the back of the car now turning into a distant blur on the road, the long straight line of asphalt cutting through the greenery around her.

She couldn't go home.

Don't think about home.

She stood up and pulled the hoodie off and tied it around her waist. And then she ran some more, looking for the sign that would tell her where to go. She then recognised the signposts for her grandma's house and a small part of her celebrated. She'd found it. She could go to her grandma, she would know what to do! She'd be so pleased to see her, give her some of the lemonade she always made.

She followed the road as quickly as she could, half-running, half-walking, her brow furrowing as she realised she'd have to tell her grandma about her mum.

Don't think.

IT WAS LATE afternoon when she finally stumbled her way through the front gates and up the stony, uneven driveway. It was a ramshackle house with a veranda, plants and flowers trailing everywhere. She loved this house. Loved the rare visits, playing in the garden and feeding the wild birds. And the thought of seeing her grandma made her forget the blisters on her feet, the scratches on her arms from hiding in hedgerows every time she heard a car, her thirst, her hunger, and . . .

She staggered up the steps onto the veranda, her hand brushing the old paint on the handrail. It was odd that the door was open – but it was a warm day. Maybe her grandma had been in and out of the garden, tending her plants.

Then a strange smell. Like going past the rubbish bins in summer when they needed collecting, but kind of worse.

"Grandma?" she called, as best she could, her throat raw from running.

She went through the hall and into the lounge. Everything was normal, as it should be. Tidy. Flowers in a vase in the window. Had an animal got into the house and died? The smell reminded her of the time they'd found a dead rat in the garage; it must have been there weeks.

She turned and went into the kitchen.

And there was her grandma.

She wanted to shut her eyes, or look away, but they were fixed on the kitchen table. Bile rose in her throat. She stood completely still. The only living thing in the room.

Every joint was cut. Knee, ankle, wrist. Her loose, milky-white skin splattered with blood. Blood splattered everywhere, deliberately spread across walls and cupboards and floor. The light had been left on, she noticed, and the bulb shone a strange light onto the scene, illuminating that which should never be seen.

While so much lay limp and lifeless, one lethal kitchen knife stood proud where it was stabbed down into the shrunken, bird-like chest.

But even as she stood, unable to look away, part of her said it wasn't possible. Could not be true. Yet she knew it was. Her father had hated the woman who had given birth to her mother, and this frail, mutilated body was his way of proving his point.

What she couldn't see was her grandma's face, and she did not want to. Wanted to keep the image of her untouched by this. Wanted to hug her. Wanted to run. Wanted to curl up on the floor and never move.

Her eyes were drawn to a slight movement. And she watched a single drop of blood fall from the edge of the table to the pool on the floor. She couldn't take her eyes off where it had landed. She realised she wasn't breathing.

She finally turned and left the room, fell to her knees on the veranda, and tears she didn't think she had the energy to shed came tumbling out, choking her. Minutes passed before she could do anything else but try and understand what she had seen, what this meant. She had no refuge of any kind, anywhere. And this felt worse than even what had happened to her mother. Or her grandma. Was that possible?

Where is my sister? Did he get her too?

She wobbled to her feet, knowing she was going to throw up, but she retched on nothing. She was so thirsty. She saw the garden hose and struggled with the tap, and when it spluttered and then burst into life, she turned it on herself, washing the blood from her trainers, drinking in the metallic water, not caring that she was getting soaked. She drank until she started choking.

And then she heard a siren.

I have to go.

She ran back into the house and went to the drawer in her grandma's bedroom where she knew she kept a zipped wallet of money, having seen her take some dollars out sometimes and insist her mother take them to buy food. She opened it; it was full of rolled notes. She emptied the handbag that sat on the chair, pulling stuff out that she did not want or even know how to use – hairpins and lipstick and hankies – and replaced it with the money. She then grabbed a blanket from the bottom of the bed, catching her grandma's soft lavender scent. She slipped the strap of the bag over her head, bundled the blanket under one arm and scurried into the lounge, heading for the cupboard where her grandma always kept a tin of biscuits and packets of crisps. Another blare of a sirens sounded. Closer this time. She took the tin, and then ran, back down the steps into the garden, out the gate at the far end and into the wilderness beyond; the beautiful beyond that she had always been forbidden to roam in because it was dangerous; a beyond that was now an escape she could not refuse to take, and a kind of dangerous that felt like the least terrible option.

She ran again, up the hill, stumbling over the uneven ground. After she'd cleared the brow of the hill and down the other side, she tucked herself under a hedge, breathing hard. What the police would find at the house would keep them busy for a long time, and she could hear their shouts, felt a flutter of fear because it seemed like there were so many of them.

They mustn't find me.

She pushed her way further into the hedge, ignoring the branches that snagged her skin, and pulling the blanket around her, she opened the tin and ate. But instinct told her to eat slowly, and not eat everything.

SHE MUST HAVE slept for a long time, as when she awoke, still hugging the tin, and with the handbag digging in her side, she could no longer hear voices or sirens and it was almost dark.

She knew there was no one left to trust but herself.

NOT SO FAR away, the man who had offered her such welcome, temporary comfort had seen the wreckage and turned on his heel, gone back outside into the gathering dusk, unable to bear the sight of it for another moment. It felt like a taunt for having failed. Again. Another life snuffed out with such violence as to make angels weep. He felt the threat of tears behind his eyes with the knowledge that three generations of a family were all but wiped out by the man now apprehended . . . but apprehended too late. Why in God's name had they not been able to locate this woman's address in time?

Mackenzie had dreaded having to break the news to the grandmother that her daughter and granddaughter were dead; but that conversation would have been infinitely preferable to what he had been left with here. Paperwork seemed like the least punishment he was owed.

The investigative officers and Forensics had not missed the signs of another person having recently been there, and though the sheriff would need evidence to back it up, he knew it was the child. That brave girl had somehow found her way to her grandmother's house in the hope of finding some shelter from the madness of her world. And to find what? Desecration. Even that word didn't feel adequate. No word would ever describe what he'd seen here today.

He felt the pulse of frustration and anger, because now she had disappeared again. Instinct told him she was alive. But where? *Only a miracle is going to save her now.*

DARYL BLACKMOOR SWAM to the edge of the pool, and with enviable ease and athleticism, pushed himself up and out of the water. With leonine fluidity, he strolled over to the table shaded by a large blue umbrella – a contrast to the impeccable whiteness of the pool area. There was no other person in sight, the roof of the skyscraper so high that nothing but the tallest buildings could be seen. He slicked the water out of his hair with one hand as he reached for the drink that was waiting for him on the table. He caught sight of himself in the mirrored reflection of the patio doors that led into the beautifully furnished apartment, and enjoyed watching the ripple of muscle through his arm as he lifted the glass. He admired his torso, the definition of his shoulders, chest and belly obvious and well-defined, his legs long and muscular.

Success had bred success and hunger in him, his expectations always so high that they only ever went higher, including those for himself. For although he could eat whatever he wanted any hour of any day of his life, had personal cooks and chefs employed at his offices and apartments or mansions throughout the world to make travelling simpler and safer, there was not an ounce of excess on him. And though he never said the words out loud, he was proud of it, knowing this fact alone made him different from most men, let alone men who were in any way in his sphere of business – though none came anywhere near in terms of wealth. When he had challenged himself on the matter during one of the many conversations he had with himself about such things because there was no one else around to talk to, he reasoned that he wanted to be as fit and healthy as he could be so he might live longer – or certainly long enough to enjoy the fruits of his labours, not just the labour.

This afternoon, however, he was taking a few hours off; he'd worked so hard the last couple of weeks that he figured he deserved it – and he was intending to enjoy himself very much.

He carried the cocktail into the lounge, having dried off in the roasting hot sun sufficiently that he wouldn't drip water onto the carpet, and saw the woman reclining on the sofa, wearing only a matching red satin corset and panties and a pair of very high red heels. It was a sight to gladden the heart of any hot-blooded young male, especially when combined with the mischievous smile, mahogany tresses and brown eyes, lashes heavy with mascara. She was looking stunning, as Daryl expected her to.

"Mr Blackmoor."

His girls knew never to call him Daryl. Almost no one did.

"Leanne."

He watched her eyes skim over his body, knew they all enjoyed what they did. Taking a trip up to his penthouse suite was quite different from servicing wrinkled old men who simply had too much money and boring wives. And now that Leanne was one of his Cherries, she'd never have to 'service' such men again . . . unless of course she somehow displeased him and was fired.

She stood up slowly and paused, letting him admire her, knowing her employer liked to know what his money had bought. She also knew that he didn't tolerate pointless pleasantries – which was why she repressed the urge to ask him how he was, or some such, as it would only make him scowl. She hated it when he scowled. It was fearsome, even without any accompanying words. It was her worst fear that one day he would tell her she was no longer required, and her pampered position as one of the Cherries would be over.

"Where would you like me?" she purred.

A rather coy smile curved her reddened lips, and she lifted her eyes to meet his for just a moment, taking two steps towards him, slowly, sensually. He finished his drink and put the glass down on the nearest table.

"Such a choice."

He moved to her and let a finger trail down from her lips to her throat, down her back to skim over the bodice and her buttock, before coming back up to rest between her breasts. He pushed her slightly and she stepped backwards, trusting him, confident that he always knew what he was doing. Her blood was tingling in a low simmer in anticipation of what was coming. It was very enjoyable for her also. Daryl's pride was such that he always gave his girls satisfaction as well – except when he was in a very, very bad mood.

"I aim to please."

She saw him smile slightly, and she felt something bump into her bottom. They stopped.

"Is that right?"

"Absolutely."

His fingers hooked around the side of her panties and pulled, and the flimsy fabric gave way to the pressure. Daryl let them fall, his eyes dipping to the swell of her breasts. He untied the bow at the back of the bodice, and with skilful hands undid the hooks, one by one, and her body responded, as did his. The bodice was dropped and moved aside with his foot, and he turned her naked body, his hands roaming over her skin, exploring all the dips and crevasses, possessive and hungry. The same sure hands pushed her forward, bent her at the waist and pressed her face down on the marble dining table, spreading her legs apart, making her body shudder at the contact with the cold stone – though she knew better than to say anything.

She moaned as he pushed into her, her response genuine and unrehearsed. Mr Blackmoor was an expert lover and she was happy to give him full tribute to his efforts. His hands slid to her hips, holding her to meet his thrusts, and she tried to push back as best she could, to give him as much pleasure as possible, but it was difficult when the table was so smooth: there was nothing to hold on to, and she was powerless beneath him. She closed her eyes, feeling bad that she wasn't doing enough, but loving the feel of him inside her, that his focus was purely with her. Of all the women, of all the places he could be, things he could be doing, he was there, with her. She knew for this man that this was just sex; but as a woman, as a female, and despite the fact she was a professional, she couldn't help but feel seduced into wanting more. He was like that. He was so untouchable, such a mystery. He had such magnetism that being summoned to him was never a chore. It was astonishing that a man with so much was also so unmatchable in bed.

She felt her own climax looming, tried to hold on as he was sometimes a little irritated if they came too soon, but she couldn't, and she cried out, her head pressing against the hard marble that was so cool to the feverish heat of her skin, ripples of pleasure shuddering through her even as he carried on. Hands slid up to her breasts and her nipples squeezed hard between finger and thumb, and she writhed as the pleasure kept coming in deeper waves that drowned her senses.

Leanne felt him shudder and pause, push down on her hips again and hold himself deep inside her, trying to draw it out . . . another thrust and she heard a small groan of satisfaction and she waited, contentedly, as he enjoyed his release, smiled at the knowledge of his finding ecstasy with her.

He stepped away, tucking himself back in his swimming trunks, letting her push herself up from the table. She followed him obediently to the bedroom. Knowing him like she did, that was just the opening number. She was there for three hours; there was plenty more to come.

"You're far too good at that, you know. Perhaps I should pay you?"

He raised an eyebrow at that as he slipped off his trunks and lay on the bed on his front, every magnificent inch of him an invitation to be touched and kissed. She couldn't wait.

"I'm thinking of it as practice."

His answer encouraged her to try a little more conversation, even though it felt like walking a tightrope. Having already made the mistake once before, she had been told sharply with one of those dreaded scowls that she was not paid to talk.

"Practice? But you don't need any."

Leanne slipped off her heels and crawled over to him, kneeling by his side and expertly massaging the beautiful back.

"Practice for keeping my wife happy," he answered shortly, his head towards her on the pillows but his eyes closed.

"Your *wife*?"

"Yes. I've decided to get married."

IT HAD BEEN three days and the girl hadn't stopped running, despite the hunger and thirst. She been too afraid to go into towns or even fuel stations in case she was recognised, but she was finally driven to stop, close to collapse.

Choosing a dimly lit truckers' café on the edge of a town she decided it must be a good place – everyone inside looked happy – so she rolled her precious blanket up and tied it with some string she had found, brushed herself down, and ran her fingers through her hair in an attempt to tidy it up. She hoped she didn't look so bad. Peering through the window again, she saw that everybody looked a bit dusty and tired, so perhaps she would fit in OK. But then she imagined they would look at her and know instinctively she was running away from the police, and every innocent glance her way felt like a threat.

Looking up at several of the lorries, she noticed the heads leaning on windows or on elbows as the drivers slept before setting off again. Even in the calm atmosphere of the place, it felt odd to be amongst people, and she again felt a quiver of apprehension in her body.

But she needed food, and knew she must go inside. Before, she'd rarely eaten a proper meal because there hadn't been enough money; now it was fear of discovery. And both were because of her father. Even far away from home he had power over her.

As soon as she got through the door she knew she'd made the right choice. The food smelled like heaven – bacon, eggs, hot toast – and it made her stomach ache with anticipation not just with hunger. She tried to ignore the curious looks from the one or two customers who sat alone while they ate, and had nothing else to distract them but the new customers that came in, and went to the counter. She saw the surprise on the woman's face as she saw not a tattooed, chunky truck driver, but a young, scruffy girl looking up at her.

"What I can getcha?"

Everything, her stomach said.

"Bacon, scrambled egg and toast please, with a glass of milk, if you have any?"

The woman nodded slowly, turning to pour the glass of milk from the jug in the fridge behind her while her brain did some thinking: *Don't normally get kids in. Loud-mouthed gum-chewers with fancy jeans and haircuts, or smelly truckers, but not a child . . .*

"Just for you? No one with you?"

The waitress asked this carefully, not looking at the kid so as not to intimidate her. She had two of her own, and she worried about them enough. But this skinny waif didn't fill the woman with any sort of confidence that she was being looked after by a responsible adult. Some motherly sixth sense . . . When had the girl last had a clean change of clothes?

"No, my pa's in the truck having a sleep. He wants to eat later. I'm starving so he let me come in on my own."

The girl had seen her glance at her worn clothes, and she felt ashamed for looking, and the explanation satisfied her: she knew both truckers and kids' appetites pretty well.

"No problem. That'll be $7 then. You grab yourself a seat. I'll bring it over."

It was the first $7 she'd spent, *ever* spent, on herself, and it was worth every cent.

The girl slid onto the bench at the edge of the room and waited, sipping the milk, holding on to one of the memories of home and forcing the bad stuff away. That was how she managed, by pretending it hadn't happened. She was just on a big adventure, that was all.

Everyone else around her seemed lost in their own thoughts, or conversations, or engrossed in a newspaper, so she let herself relax a few notches, and tried not to jump at the sound of an old man blowing his nose, or the scrape of a chair on the floor.

The food arrived, and the woman brought Ketchup and Daddies sauce too. It was the best meal of her life. The eggs soft and hot, the bacon crispy. And, for once, she was full, and even wrapped two pieces of the four slices of toast that she couldn't finish in a napkin and put them in her bag. And unaccustomed as she was to the effects of a whole meal, she dozed off, her head tipped back against the wall.

SHE WOKE UP to the blaring noise of the TV mounted up on the wall. It seemed to be the most entertaining thing in the room, as everyone was looking at it. She turned her head to see what they were watching. The picture was rubbish, but the sound was clear. Even the two guys at the counter who had been ordering now turned and listened, along with the woman serving at the counter.

'*And now an update on a local case that has caused a lot of concern and upset, so here's Annette Carlton to give us a report from outside the police station where the shooting took place just a few days ago. So, Annette, what can you tell us?*'

Under the table, her hands curled into fists, she considered bolting for the door to avoid the truth; but half of her wanted to stay and find out. . . if . . . they had him . . . her father. She would be able to breathe a little easier if she knew he wasn't hunting her like the animal he was. The evil in his eyes, even in the blurred shot on the screen, had penetrated the room. No one was talking.

'*Well, Mick, it's a bit of a mixture really – both good and bad news. As you know, Mr Earl, now formally charged with the murder of his wife and daughter, is recovering in a secure unit after gunshot wounds to his shoulder as officers tried to stop his killing spree in their AIC room. He had gone to the station to kill his second daughter, who he guessed was there under police protection. A third charge of murder has now been added after the remains of his mother-in-law were found at her house in Dewlan. Further charges have been brought as it has emerged that Mr Earl also brutally attacked and killed a police officer outside his residence. He has also been charged with assault following his attack on officers at the police station in Meriden, and the assault of a driver and theft of his vehicle . . .*'

The delicious food her stomach had so eagerly digested rose in her throat at hearing the words.

He killed Cassy.

Dizziness came on the back of a carousel of images as the words on the TV kept coming. She glanced about, her heart pounding; but no one else in the room had noticed her distress.

'*. . . although the grandmother was discovered several days ago, a police statement made clear that due to the horrific nature of the murder there has been a delay in making this public. The surviving daughter is still missing after she ran from the scene of the shooting at the station, and police are doing everything they can to find her as she has experienced events we cannot even contemplate and may be deeply traumatised. Police are urging anyone who sees a young girl, travelling alone, to call in and report it. The number is at the bottom of the screen. They underline the fact she has done nothing wrong, and it is for her protection and wellbeing that the police wish for her safe return. She is nine years old, has blonde curly hair, and is of slim build. She is . . .*"

She thought she would collapse when her picture came onto the screen, obviously taken from video footage at the police station. It was poor quality, but her hair and the blue hoodie were clear.

"The police prosecutor is confident of a conviction, and Mr Earl is looking at several life sentences. Some judicial commentators are using this case to argue in favour of the lethal injection being brought into force in this state. . ."

The commentator, Annette Carlton, continued, but she had stopped listening, stopped breathing. She had to get out. Why had she stayed? She hadn't noticed the couple who had appeared at her table.

"You say your pa was outside in a truck, little missy?" the man said slowly, clearly suspicious. It was the lady who'd served her, and someone else – maybe her husband or the boss? His ragged moustache and tired eyes made him look like he didn't have much excitement in his life, like he didn't like surprises, but the gentle lines of his face told the girl he was a kind man, not a man with a temper.

She knew the difference.

"He's in his truck – the red and white one." She'd noticed it on her way in, and she tried not to feel bad for lying to them. "You want me to take you to him? Though he'll be mad if I wake him up. . ."

She saw the guy nod, slowly, lethargically. She noticed the woman was a little overweight, and she shifted on her feet as if they were sore from standing. They glanced at each other. Even with a full stomach she was sure she could outrun them both.

She stood up from the bench, slipped her bag over her head and gathered her rolled up bundle, as relaxed as she could, actually angry at her beloved blanket in that moment for being such a giveaway. Next time she'd have to hide it somewhere.

The woman was called back to the counter, but the guy followed her to the door, and she was just about to run when she felt his hand on her shoulder, holding her in a grip she'd not break from easily. Stifling the cry of panic, the child kept walking, knowing if she fought it, he'd shout for help and then it would be over.

Gritting her teeth every second, she kept walking, out of the door to the far side of the car park, appearing to head towards the farthest truck – the red and white one. She heard a deep rumble as one of the trucks behind her started up, then began to pull away onto the road, the sides built of wood. It was an old-fashioned out-dated truck that was nothing like some of the modern lorries parked around her, but beggars couldn't be choosers.

"I-I'm really sorry about this…" she said as she stopped. And turning towards him she punched once, hard, him in the groin. She felt his hand leave her shoulder – and couldn't help but watch, mesmerised, at the real-life effect of the move she'd seen once on TV as he doubled over, clutching his manhood as he let out a long groan! – and then ran.

Her bag bounced on her back and she almost dropped her blanket as she made her dash across the car park, a desperate collection of legs and arms. She headed for the truck, now on the road and accelerating away – though because it was such an old engine, it was painfully slow, which gave her a chance to catch it up.

She launched herself, grabbing hold of the straps holding the tarpaulin in place, and pulled herself up. Hardly believing she'd done it, she hung there for a moment, looking back at the limping man attempting to chase her. He yelled something that she didn't hear, just as she heaved herself up and over, letting herself down gratefully into the dip she had made in the tarpaulin. She huddled in the corner with her blanket, breathing hard. But a slow smile of victory lit up her face, and once again, with a full belly of good food, she did the most natural thing in the world: she fell asleep.

"HEY, KID. HEY there."

She opened her eyes and looked up.

Oh, no, not again.

She'd fallen asleep and now she'd been seen. Again. The face above her was a few feet away and upside down, as well as obscured by the light behind him.

"Hey, sleepy. I need to unload now so you're going to have to move."

She stalled for a few moments, blinking in the sunshine, trying to catch up with the fact that this guy – whose truck she had stowed away on – didn't seem at all bothered, and quite possibly wasn't going to try and grab her like the last guy. And hopefully this one didn't listen to or watch the news either.

She struggled to her knees, her bag over her shoulder, chucked her blanket over the edge and jumped down, forestalling his offer of help with her agility. From his facial expression, she guessed he was surprised to find someone so small staring back at him. But she also saw in him something like the sheriff, something trustworthy. Despite this though, she still kept her distance.

Assessing each other in silence, their following conversation was relaxed, given they were complete strangers.

"Thanks for the ride." It felt like the right thing to say, even though speaking felt odd. And in situations she'd never encountered before. Independence was a strange, encouraging discovery for her young mind.

"No worries. You should have asked me and you could have ridden up front." He spoke gently. He was still getting the measure of her. For although this little mite with the messy hair was scrawny and in need of a wash, her face was pretty, and her eyes – her eyes were brilliant with colour.

"You want me to pay you? For the ride, I mean?"

She reached for her bag, but he held up a hand. "No, you keep it. Buy some food instead; you look like you could do with feeding up."

She blinked and looked away. His kind words stirred too many emotions for her to handle. She just wanted to be gone now. Kindness from a stranger was just too confusing. And for a moment she thought of the sheriff again. Properly. She knew he would be looking for her, be worried about her. But she'd had no choice. She had to run.

He saw the distress and realised he'd said something wrong.

"You running away? You look awful young to be out on your own?"

She kept her eyes away from his, not wanting to see the concern in his face, knowing it would not help her control her emotions. She didn't need anyone but herself. It was just her now.

"I'm . . . travelling. I like it." She edged away slightly.

It was a poor answer that didn't satisfy; but he knew better than to push it. He'd seen enough people trying to get somewhere or get away in his life on the road. He realised she didn't want to lie to him; but didn't want to tell him the truth either.

"I remember wanting to run away when I was fifteen. I'd managed to prang my dad's car messing around one Sunday afternoon and, boy, was I scared he'd lynch me!" he told her, in the hope it might sway her back, but she only edged away a little more. "Is it something like that? Coz I'm sure you can't have done anything so wrong that your folks won't–"

The rest of his words went unsaid.

"No, it's nothing like that and I've not done anything wrong."

Her denial was fierce but firm, and he didn't detect any deceit. There was something too desperate, too heartfelt about her to doubt her motivation for running. Who was he to judge?

"You know where you are?"

"Nope."

"You heading somewhere?"

"Not really."

The girl didn't dare look at his face to see what he thought of that answer.

The guy reached a hand up to rub his face. *Jesus Christ! Either she's crazy or she's the pluckiest little thing ever.*

"Well, we're in Tatesville, at the moment. Go that way," he said, and pointed east, "you're heading back the way we came; go that way, you're heading west, and if you keep going eventually you'll fall into the ocean. That help?"

She nodded, knowing exactly which way she'd be going.

"I really did appreciate the ride," she then said, still not looking at him.

"That's cool. I'm impressed you managed to find it comfortable enough to fall asleep up there," he added, indicating the tarp. His smile almost reached her, but not quite. She wasn't up to smiling yet. Probably wouldn't be for some time. "Well, goodbye, then, and good luck," he said, offering his hand.

She nodded, didn't see the hand, just started walking along the road, keeping to the far side of the pavement, far enough away to avoid the dust from the traffic.

The man stood and watched her for a moment, shading his eyes against the glare of the setting sun, cursing himself for not challenging her more. *It's madness, that little kid heading off just like that.*

He turned away and headed to the depot where he'd pulled over to make his delivery. If his wife knew he'd just let a kid walk away like that, she'd have his balls nailed to a plank. It was just that there was something . . . resolute about her, refusing to back down, holding her own. She was a fighter, certainly . . . he just hoped she didn't pick a fight she couldn't win.

"GET *MARRIED*?"

"Yes. Get married." *Because, apparently, I need to find a wife and have children to secure the future of my empire; because, apparently, it would add to my public image.*

"But what about us?"

He opened his eyes in alarm. *Dear lord, don't tell me she thinks she's special!*

"The girls? What about the Cherries?" she asked, genuinely concerned.

Daryl smiled and closed his eyes again. He was rather pleased to hear the distress in her voice; clearly she – they – valued their role as his chosen girls.

"Nothing will change . . . unless you wish to leave?"

It was the nearest he got to teasing; but his face was serious and without his eyes open she had no way of knowing whether he was teasing . . . or not. She began again, albeit more tentatively, on his shoulders, easing some of the tension out.

"No, how could you think I would want to leave? Only … with your wife? . . ."

"She will learn to be very understanding and keep her mouth shut. She will be beautiful, of course, whoever she ends up being, but do you *really* think one woman would satisfy me?"

He rolled over and his eyes invited her. Arrogant, condescending eyes that were so bright and yet so hard. He didn't need words when his eyes spoke so well for him.

Leanne moved forward obediently, straddling him, her eyes boldly staying connected with his as she slipped lower, trailing kisses over his muscled torso and down the belly that moved as he breathed.

"She would have to be *exceptional* to manage that. A goddess among women no less, if she were to even have a hope of satisfying you alone."

Her fingers found him, caressed him, making him hard, and she licked her full red lips, enticing him with the promise of the next few minutes.

"My, my . . . We are full of compliments and wisdom today."

His smile told her he was actually enjoying himself. He so rarely smiled.

"It's amazing what happens when you get bent over a table and fucked so very well . . ." she murmured, her words ending as her lips closed over him, her slow and gentle movements increasing as she took as much of him as she could, feeling him swell a little more and flex his hips up at her. She knew what she was doing.

Daryl smiled as he let his head drop back on the pillows, thinking about her words. *Where am I going to find a goddess to match the expert attentions of my Cherries? Why should I give up a banquet for a much smaller menu? No, my wife must be as suitable a woman as I can find in order to bear me children; but beyond that, that will have to do. I need not even see her much.*

He had long given up hope of feeling anything more for anyone, let alone a woman.

TWO WEEKS HAD passed and the money from her grandma that she thought seemed so much and would last so long was running out. After her first trip on a truck, she had got used to riding on their roofs, and was undaunted by the height or the speed or the danger. In fact, she had turned it into quite an art form, watching and waiting for a truck to leave, then jumping on if it was going in the direction she wanted. Sometimes she would hear where a trucker was going from their talking to each other in the café, or hanging around in the sunshine, or when they got out and rang home or the office. Patient observation was essential, and she had enjoyed the success of it, of travelling a lot faster than she would have done on foot. And the rest she had when lying on the roofs was giving her body and mind a chance to recover and strengthen after the battering and neglect it had suffered so long.

She knew she needed to earn some money – not wanting to try and steal some before her funds ran out completely – and fear of starving was enough of an incentive. She chose to leave off jumping on a new truck when she heard that three days of scorching sunshine was on the way. Being exposed on the roof was hell when it got that hot. She felt like an egg in a frying pan. It would be a good time to try and get some work.

She walked through the town that obviously passed as a stop-off for the truckers that flowed through. It was small, but with more houses being built, it had a bustle about it that she liked – and it meant everyone was too busy doing their own thing to worry about her. However, she quickly realised that 'small' didn't really provide much scope for finding a job.

She ignored the gnaw of hunger in her belly, refused to buy anything until she had tried harder to find some work, but what could she do? She was a school kid! She couldn't wash cars, as she didn't have any stuff – and she didn't have the money to buy what she needed. And from the look of the dusty cars in the streets and bumbling along down the road, no one seemed to care much anyway. They let the dust win.

"Goddamn it!"

She turned at the sound of the angry curse – the only human voice she'd heard for a while: the place was so quiet, as people were staying indoors out of the heat. She saw a grocery store at the corner of the street and walked a little closer, following a clattering noise to where she found an old man with a cane sitting leaning on a stack of boxes, another two pallets close to the road. There was a pull-down security door raised up high, the dim interior showing that it was the storeroom for the shop.

"Are you alright, sir?"

She inched closer so he could see her; close enough to see him and offer her hand to help. It was instinctive. Even though she was happier staying away from people, seeing someone in need, someone who could be hurt, brought out the reaction to help. Something she had learnt from taking care of her mother . . . within seconds, images flooded her brain. *No. No. Don't think. Don't think about that.*

The old man looked up at her sharply. He'd been far too busy cursing his old body, his frail arms, the children who hadn't stayed around to help, and the wife who had left him to go to God, to notice her.

Eyes narrowed suspiciously, too angry initially to appreciate the helping hand she offered; then he registered the offered hand, the fact she was a child, dirty and dusty, thin too, but not a threat. Even in his shrunken old age he thought she possibly looked more worn out than he did. He took the hand and she pulled, then moved in closer. She realised one of his legs was straight and couldn't bend, which was why he was struggling; the rest of him was sinewy, but still lacked the strength to get his body up . . . or to move boxes.

"You alright?" she asked quietly, standing back to let him brush himself off to regain some of his dignity, and transfer his weight back comfortably onto his good leg.

"I am now. Dang leg always lets me down. Might as well have chopped the damn thing off!" he huffed angrily, adjusting the grip on the walking stick. Seeing her face pale, he realised he shouldn't be so angry in front of her (not realising her reaction was for a whole other reason than merely his cursing and frustration). "Anyways, thanks. I'd have probably sat there for another half an hour swearing myself into the good lord's bad books if you hadn't come along."

"It's OK. Lucky you swore so loud, else I'd not have heard you."

He liked her answer, and the glimmer of intelligence that shone in her bright eyes. He smiled.

"You need help moving the boxes, sir?" she then asked simply, indicating them with a hand.

"You mind if I ask who you are, and what you're doing here? I know most folks in this town, and I don't know you," he replied, quick as a flash.

She could hear the edge of suspicion; realised he was afraid she might be trying to steal.

"My pa's a trucker. He's left me here for a few days. Said it was going to get too hot in the cab for me, so I'd best sit out the last bit of the journey. He'll pick me up in two days' time on his way back." She shrugged. "I'm just looking to be a help and earn a few dollars if I can. I don't have anything else to do."

This disappearing trucker-father figure was her best invention, and it had got her out of so many questions already, despite it making her feel sick to know the reality was so different from this hard-working, caring pa she'd created. She stared back at him, hoping her lie wasn't written in her eyes, trying to stay relaxed.

"Alright. That's fair enough. I'll pay you $50 if you move all the boxes inside, then I'll give you another $50 for restocking everything in the shop from the boxes. If there's any time left over, I've probably got another job or two for you. Lord knows I could do with some help around here." He paused and looked at her, saw the delight in her eyes; her face was a little expressionless for a kid, otherwise, but he guessed some kids grew up quicker than others. "That sound fair?"

"Yes, sir."

"OK, let's shake on it."

Switching his stick to his left, he offered his right hand to her, and the contact felt strange – how long was it since she'd touched anyone?

"Well, I'll leave you to it. I'll be in the shop, so just holler if you need anything."

He turned to go.

"Um, sir?"

"Yes?"

He turned a little, the motion not easy with his leg.

"How do you want the boxes stacked?"

"You stack 'em how you like, kid. You're the one who'll be emptying most of them. But if you can organise it so I can reach everything, that'd be a help."

His smile, and then the sight of his back as he limped into the dim storeroom and through to the shop, spurred her to action.

She looked at the pile of boxes, the sudden responsibility to get the job done exciting. She missed school so much – the happiness of learning stuff and doing stuff – that this first chance to really *do* something made her feel a rare happiness. And an extra $100? Fantastic! It never occurred to her that he might not hold up his end of the bargain. There was just something about him she trusted . . . and not for the first time did she wonder where this instinct came from.

She put her bag, her hoodie and the blanket on the floor inside the door. She found the stock list that had come with the delivery on a clipboard, and picking it up, she scanned it and looked back at the boxes. Grabbing the pen that was tied with string to the board, she got to work.

A few hours later, she heard footsteps and wheezy breathing. Turning around, she saw to her surprise that the old man was leaning on the doorway looking at the storeroom with smiling eyes.

"Quite a bit of progress you've made."

She looked up at him, suddenly worried she'd done something wrong and would be shouted at – that was quite usual when she had been at home.

"You don't mind that I moved the older boxes? It all makes sense, I promise."

He looked back at her, saw the sudden fear etched into the pretty features. How old was she?

"I don't mind. I can see it makes sense. You've done a better job than I ever did after hauling the darned things in here. You got the list there as well?" He nodded at the clipboard in her hand.

"I was just checking everything off, and I've counted whatever was in the old boxes and added it on so you know what's here. When I put the stuff in the shop, I'll write down the new numbers. Well, I will if that's OK?"

"Hell, yes. Then I might know what to order next time, rather than ending up with two hundred tins of sweetcorn like I did once . . ." – his attempt at humour worked and she lost the worried look! – ". . . now why don't you go into the shop and grab yourself a soda from the cooler or something? You must be thirsty. Least I can do is offer you a drink." He stood back and invited her in.

She was thirsty, but hadn't wanted to say anything in case he thought she was shirking.

"Are you sure? I'm very thirsty," she said.

"Course I'm sure," he chuckled. *What a polite kid!*

She went through, and he followed, and she instantly liked the shop. It was spacious and well-ordered. It was also neat and clean and she could smell something good. Her tummy rumbled and she realised how hungry she was too.

"Sounds like you could do with some lunch as well. You want a sandwich? I'm having one . . ."

She tentatively nodded her head and he pointed down the aisle to the fridge that towered over her, the shiny cans arrayed before her. She'd never drunk soda before, only squash, milk or water, and she must have looked a little confused as he asked, "You don't like soda?"

She looked around, still unsure. Her mum wouldn't have let them drink fizzy drinks anyway, as they were bad for them, and all the labels and writing and colours were a bit too much for her to fathom.

"I . . . my mum never liked me drinking soda drinks . . . she always gave us milk or water," she answered, clearly a little embarrassed by her ignorance of the vast display of cans.

"Well, she sure sounds like a sensible woman. Come on, I've got milk you can have. There are some big bottles of it in the other fridge, but I've got one already open."

And so, in a most unexpected fashion, the girl found herself sat down at a small table, in a sparse kitchen, eating a cheese sandwich and a packet of crisps and drinking a big glass of milk. It was heaven.

As a widower, he didn't feel the need for huge amounts of conversation. Her company was enough, and he felt at ease with her. She compounded her good behaviour by doing the washing up afterwards and stacking it up neatly on the draining board.

"You know, it's strange having someone else here after so long on my own. You're a good kid," he eventually said.

She didn't know what to say. She was not used to praise. She had a hundred things to confess: she wasn't good, her birthday had got her mother killed, she'd been so stupid not to know her grandma's address so that the police could have saved her. . . The confessions railed inside her head, but stayed silent, where they belonged.

"I'd better get back to work . . ."

There was something about her hesitation that made him, just for a second, doubt her assurance that her father was coming back for her, or even that he existed at all; but he dismissed his doubts. She was a good kid. And a damn fine worker for such a skinny thing.

"Sure."

He watched her leave the kitchen, stayed sitting at the table. A little mystery had come to visit. But she sure was a help.

IT WAS ALMOST time to go. The shop had been replenished, and after another great day of quietly working, being brought a glass of milk or water every now and again, or another sandwich, she was breaking down the cardboard boxes to put out by the bin, her movements slowed with the knowledge she'd be going. Part of her didn't really want to, and she moved with a heaviness as she carried the first boxes outside. But she didn't come back empty-handed from the recycling bin, and carrying a box containing a strange mechanical-looking item with a wire and tiny set of headphones attached to it, she called out, "Mr Matthews, sir." (He had eventually told her his name. Had waited to hear hers. Had walked away when she hadn't told him, without questioning her.)

She looked at it in wonder, at the other rectangle cases that were in the box with it. What was it? Why was it in the bin? Was it broken?

She went to the counter where he was perched on his stool with the newspaper. (She knew by now that he liked to be here, able to serve customers at the till and keep his leg comfortable.)

"What is it, kid?"

"Look. I found this in the bin outside. Do you know what it is? Do you think it got thrown in there by accident?"

She held out her trophy, and he looked at it; then his eyes met hers, rather amused.

"I put it in there this morning after clearing out some old boxes from upstairs. Don't you know what it is?"

He folded the newspaper and beckoned her around the desk. He took the box from her and set it down, picking up the cassette player as she shook her head, watching him closely.

"It's a cassette player. Very old; practically an antique. People started playing CDs and then MP3s, and then iPods and all that downloadable stuff. I used to be quite a music-lover in my day, you know. I found this at the back of the cupboard." He removed a cassette from one of the boxes marked 'Queen' in big red letters. "Run and get a pack of batteries for me, will ya, the regular size? I'm not sure if it works, but we'll give it a try."

He fiddled with it and put one of the earphones in his ear, waiting for her to come back. After a few more moments of anticipation, he opened up a slot at the back and inserted the four batteries she handed him and pressed Play. There was a burble of noise, and he smiled, and offered her the other earphone. She put it in like he had . . . and her eyes lit up! She'd never heard music like this! There had been no music and barely any TV at home for a the last few years – because of money, and the fact that if the radio played the wrong song, or the TV was on the wrong channel, it meant her father would go crazy – and she couldn't believe what she was hearing.

"You like it?"

"Yes!"

"This is Queen. 'Bohemian Rhapsody'. An amazing band in their time, in the late 1970s and early 1980s, when there was real talent in music." He watched her for a moment, enjoying the expression on her face, saw the little bob of her head. He then pressed the Stop button, took out his earphone. He handed the Sony Walkman to her, along with the extra batteries. "Here, you have it. I had thrown it out, but now I know it'll go to a good home. You enjoy it."

She looked at him with such disbelief that he had to smile.

"I won't take no for an answer. You should know I'm a grumpy old man, and you don't want to go upsetting me now, do you?"

He pretended he couldn't see the tears that had gathered in her eyes as she accepted the gift he held right in front of her. His doubts about this kid's story rose again, but he didn't want to ruin the moment by demanding answers she clearly didn't want to give him. She'd not done anything wrong. Not to him.

"Thank you, sir, Mr Matthews," she whispered.

"You almost done back there?" he asked gently.

"Yes, just a bit of tidying up, sir, and then it's all done."

She didn't seem glad. He wasn't either. She was a good little worker, and didn't mind his crotchety behaviour, or his leaving things to her to organise and tidy up.

"OK. Well, you go finish up and then come back in here and I'll settle up with you."

She nodded and backed away, hugging the box.

HE WAS AT the counter when she re-joined him, her hoodie back on, and her blanket and bag in her arms. She also carried her new, most precious cargo – the box with the cassette player and tapes.

"I believe this is yours." He picked up the twenties and tens and handed them to her, glad she didn't count it as there was an extra thirty bucks in there. (He knew she'd refuse if she found it.) "And this." He then reached down and pulled up a rucksack which clearly had stuff in it. "My son used to use this for taking his sports stuff to school; he's too lazy to even walk the dog now, so, I think you're the best person for it."

"I . . . no, Mr Matthews. I can't!" She shook her head, thrown by his generosity and thoughtfulness, again.

"Yes, you can." He unzipped the top and revealed the basic set of supplies he had packed: bread, crisps, bananas and a big bottle of milk. (He'd also written his name, address and phone number on a piece of paper and tucked it deep inside.) "You can put your blanket in there, too, and the side pockets – see – for the recorder." Years of being a parent came to the fore and, with patient hands, he stowed everything away for her, even the handbag that she had put the money into and tentatively handed him. "See, you're all set now."

He turned it round, held it out so he could put it on her shoulders, having shortened the straps for her already.

"You didn't have to give me this."

"You didn't have to help a grouchy, cursing man to his feet, or do such a good job with my stock."

"You gave me the tape machine, as well," she reminded him quietly, biting her lip.

"I was going to chuck it, remember?" His smile reached her. "Come on, kid, no debts between friends. OK?"

He lifted the rucksack towards her and, after a long moment, she nodded, and obediently turned around.

"Sure. No debts between friends," she repeated, feeling the weight on her back, finding it heavy but not impossible.

"You drop by any time you're passing through, you hear?" he told her sternly, seeing her gauging the weight and feel of the bag. It was a bit big, but she'd grow into it.

"I will. I promise."

It was a promise, but she knew the chances of her coming back were . . . well, she hadn't even thought about the future. The future was tomorrow. In those few seconds, she realised how much her life had changed. Once all she thought about was escaping with her mum and sister; now all she thought about was her own survival.

Mr Matthews offered his wrinkled old hand, as he had that first day, only two days ago. It felt like she'd been there a lot longer.

"Well, then, good luck. You take care now."

She didn't speak. Stayed silent as a mouse. As if saying anything would be the wrong thing. But she took the hand and shook it, meaning it, wishing she had the courage to say something else, that she could do something to show her appreciation. But what could she do? Somehow, though, he seemed to understand her silence, respect it even, and his warm smile comforted her, allowed her to walk away without feeling any guilt.

She stepped into the late afternoon sunshine, headed for the truck stop to find her next ride.

Half an hour later, she was zooming along on the top of another truck, earphones in, learning all the words to Queen's *Greatest Hits* . . . her love affair with music was born.

IT WAS DARK and she didn't like the feel of this new town one bit. She'd got off the truck and taken shelter because rain was absolutely hammering down, huge heavy drops that really didn't show any signs of stopping. She'd not had the chance to earn any more money since the grocery store, and she knew she should try, but . . . this was not a happy place. She'd passed through enough to know the difference.

None of the trucks were going anywhere while the weather was so bad – there were reports on the radios of flooding and accidents – and anyone sensible was waiting it out, waiting for the deluge to stop. She'd also resigned herself to spending another day or two here, was keeping low, but the looks she got were aggressive, unfriendly. She really wanted to leave.

She bought some apples, cheese and bread, and told herself the food would have to last. Then she walked along the main street, telling herself this was just another part of the adventure, not thinking how sad it was she was sheltering in a hedge like a wild animal. If she could have afforded a room, and been able to do so without the fear of being asked a hundred questions, she would have.

She had quickly learned that her age was a significant problem. Luckily, she was quite tall so she had managed to pass herself off as thirteen, even fourteen when pushed to it. And she wished, not for the first time in her young life, that she was older – the world seemed so different when you were older. She didn't know that her innocent femininity, the blonde curls that had escaped her hairband, and her beguiling eyes made her an absolute picture; for although she was thin, her face was enchanting, her demeanour mesmerising.

There was a group of men standing talking outside a bar, under the awning, one of the few in the town, and she thought of the few notes left in her bag and decided to brave it. She would have been happier if it had been lighter, if the mood had been lighter, but she needed money.

"Excuse me, sir," she addressed one of them; but obviously they all turned at the sound of her voice, so unexpected. "I just wondered, do you know if there is any work around here?"

The lead man turned fully to her, and she felt his eyes going over her, glad she had left her bag hidden in the same hedge she had slept in so she would be able to run if she needed to. The man's look was not friendly, it was aggressive, and the smile that played on his lips was not nice, both before and after he looked around at his mates, who were all smiling the same way.

"Sure, sweetheart, I got some work for you, and that pretty little mouth of yours." He must have seen the confusion on her face because he stepped closer, a slow, prowling step that made her want to move away, but she sensed two of them circle around her, out of her line of vision. "I'll give you $15 to suck me off."

"W-what?"

He mistook her reaction for disgust at the price, not genuine innocence.

"Oh, come on, that's the going rate – unless you know some special tricks that might induce me to give you a little more? Hmmm?"

He reached forward to touch her chin, to hold it between finger and thumb, and the touch of his fingers jerked her out of her confusion.

What is he talking about? Why is he touching my face?

She slapped his hand away angrily, indignant that he thought he could touch her. Fear stole through her body and started the adrenaline flowing, awareness of the threats of these big men palpable. She saw his face harden into a mask of anger at the slap. The same nasty anger she had seen on her father's face. *You're a whore! Her father's words . . . oh no . . . they think . . .*

"Bit of an attitude. Think I might need to teach you a little respect, girl!"

He grabbed her top, intending to prop her against the wall of the bar, and he wasn't counting on meeting any resistance; but a small balled-up fist smacked into his eye, making his grip loosen enough to let her go. Then another hit the other side of his face, a knee got him in the balls, and as he bent to grab his crotch, she kneed him in the face, causing him to stumble backwards against the wall. And it all happened way too fast for him to react.

They all glanced at each other, at the girl, who was coiled like a tight spring, ready. She was breathing hard, staring at them with a look they couldn't decipher. Their leader was still leaning on the wall, testing his jaw, tasting blood in his mouth, and massaging his crotch. What should they do?

"I suggest you let the kid go."

She spun around to locate the voice and saw a man with grey hair, old wise eyes crinkled round the edges and weathered skin. The checked shirt and jeans were similar to those of the men she'd just encountered; but his attitude was non-combative, calm . . . in fact there was something strangely peaceful about him.

"Stupid little bitch. She was the one come asking for 'work'!"

The leader shoved off the wall and came forward, his friends arranging themselves on either side, all ready to defend themselves.

"Not *that kind* of work!" she threw back, fists clenched by her side, angry they were trying to blame her.

"You didn't say that!"

"She's a *kid,* Charlie, you should know better."

The newcomer calmly planted himself in between the two factions, providing her a barrier of protection.

"How old is she, anyways?"

"I'm ten!" She wouldn't say nine, in case anyone was still looking for a nine-year-old; but ten was still young enough to make her defender look round in surprise and dismay.

"Jesus Christ." He looked back at Charlie. "She's the same age as your daughter, isn't she?"

The question struck home and the man bridled, his eyes going accusingly to the girl, as if she had purposefully deceived him.

"Piss off, old man. Take her with you."

"Come on, let's go." The older guy turned to her and shepherded her off down the road, leaving them to fume, and then, no doubt, return to the bar for more drinks to fuel their bad attitudes. "I'm Mr Gibson, by the way."

He did not ask for her name; she didn't offer it.

The girl hurried along by his side, his pace fast, his manner not inviting any words. Something told her that it would be best not to run away. Having come to her defence, for which she was grateful, she clearly owed him something. Maybe he wanted an explanation? Maybe he was going to lecture her on being on her own? Whatever it was, she was relieved he'd made no move to grab her, or force her into following him, had just assumed that she would, perhaps.

Eventually, after taking a left then a right, they got to a building that reminded her of her dancing hall back at . . . at home. Doors in her mind slammed shut on that thought, ignored in favour of concentrating on the present. He opened the door in the large blue-painted wall, and gestured through.

"Inside, and no, I'm not going to hurt you. I just want to check your hands. Have you noticed your knuckles are bleeding?"

He pointed down at her right fist and she looked, saw blood, and then her stomach flipped over. She was not good with the sight of blood.

His hand caught her arm before she could fall and he led her gently through the door. She found herself inside a boxing club, equipment hanging up, the ring empty, seating on two sides facing it . . . the smell of men and sweat. She looked up at him. And he looked at her with a question in his face, and she nodded: she had herself back under control.

He released her arm and she followed him into an office, where he indicated a chair. She sat on it, tentatively, watching him, not sure why she was trusting him; but no instincts warned her off, just as they hadn't with Mr Matthews. Sometimes it felt like some kind of faith in some kind of good was growing, and that she would not give up all together in the despair and struggle of life, like a lone ant faced with a mountain.

He got out a first aid box and came to her, knelt down and took one hand, not looking at her. The toes of her trainers just touched the floor where she sat. She could see his nose had been broken and had healed a little wonky. He also had a scar near his left eye, and another down the opposite cheek. This man had seen lots of fights. Surely he wasn't going to pick another one with her?

"You have some moves there, kid," he said eventually, his brow furrowed by his thoughts, still not quite sure he had seen what he had seen. "Where did you learn to fight?"

That was a question she was not expecting.

"I don't know. I mean . . . I've never hit anyone before. I just . . . reacted . . . I guess."

Her answer made him smile at her innocence.

"I guess you did."

He looked at her when he had cleaned all the blood off one hand and let her take it back.

"You have some of the best reflexes I've seen in my life. And I've seen a lot," he then said.

She didn't know what to say, so she just looked back at him, the big beautiful eyes that questioned constantly silently delving into his.

"You on your own?" he asked.

She instantly looked away. She wanted to be honest. It felt bad to lie to him when he was helping her. And something straightforward about his question, and the way he'd dealt with the men outside, told her he would rather have the truth – and that it wouldn't shock him.

"Yes."

He picked up her other hand and started on the blood, though there was much less on that hand: clearly her right was her leading arm.

"You're very young."

"Yep, but I'll get older, I guess."

Her shrug and her words made him smile again.

"Then how about I give you some tips, so next time you'll know how better to move, to fight, and you'll be safer."

"I don't really want to fight people."

"I don't think you'll have much choice. Not with your face. And not in the world you're in."

He glanced at her again, briefly, wondering if she knew what she looked like; she seemed so unaffected, so unassuming, so naive. Which wouldn't last long. She seemed smart enough, though, and life would do the rest. Fill the gaps in. He let her think about it, hoping from what he knew of her already she'd be wise enough to see the merit in his argument.

"OK, then. I think that would be a good idea."

"Right. Good. Well . . ." He reached behind him to get the antiseptic cream and spread it over her knuckles, impressed at the way she didn't complain about the pain.

"First, don't forget to use your left hand. If your right misses, or doesn't hit hard enough, then a follow up with your left will save it from being a wasted effort. But take into account their reaction. You can even use your right as a lure to make them dodge and make it easier to hit with your left."

He then demonstrated by holding her hands up and aiming them slowly at his face, making her smile.

"Second, keep your hands up, protect your face. If they hit your head it can do a hell of a lot more damage than if it hits some other part of you. A face hit can disorientate you, make you dizzy, or hit your eye, like you got Charlie, and stop you seeing well – and that'll make you more vulnerable, understand?"

"Yes." She nodded decisively, and he let her hands go to reach for some tape to wrap around her right hand.

"There are three main hits which you can do with either hand: cross, jab and uppercut. We could get more in-depth, but I think for now that'll do you well. So, we have a cross, jab and uppercut. Watch."

He demonstrated in slow motion, his own hands going towards her face, leaving them short by a couple of inches.

"The uppercut is quite hard as it's so dependent on timing and opportunity, but can be very effective."

She nodded solemnly, and he paused, taping up her left hand, knowing he was training her to protect herself, but also to fight. She seemed so innocent, and telling her how to wreak violence felt wrong somehow. He saw her waiting for more information, however, and got up, gesturing for her to follow, and they went out into the gym area where there was more space. He took a stance opposite her, so that she could mirror him.

"Other places to aim for…" he began.

BACK IN HIS office, they shared a bag of chips. Both ate with relish. He from a feeling of positivity from having done something worthwhile for the first time in a long time; and she because . . . because she was always hungry. But more than that: sharing a meal was a very pleasant exception to the solitude, for them both.

"Where is everyone?" she asked, indicating the gym, the ring.

"There used to be a lot going on here. I trained some fighters, even had one turn pro; but the mine was closed two years ago and laid off a load of men. The town depended on it for jobs. Those guys at the bar . . . they never used to be like that, but having no money, wanting a job and not being able to get one . . . it grinds a person down. And no one has money for coming here anymore. I do have some clients, but I'm so quiet now I close two full days a week."

His explanation seemed to satisfy her and she nodded, thinking; then she paused her eating and looked at him seriously.

"I do appreciate you helping me today. I know you didn't have to. And then all those tips . . . they could save my life one day, but I have nothing to give you in return."

Her sweet honesty was refreshing, and her young body so vulnerable, but he'd seen her speed and her strength today, and who knew what she might be when she was grown? She was fighting right now to stand up for herself with the basic bravery and gutsiness he admired in anyone. He thought again about her words. Was she worried he was going to ask of her what Charlie had demanded?

"You don't need to give me anything. It was good to pass on something worthwhile. God knows I do little enough coaching now," he said. "But I want one thing from you," he added.

Her face was still. Eyes intense.

"Promise me not to pick fights you can't win, and to make the most of those reflexes of yours. Hell, if I'd had that when I was your age, I'd have been world champion by the time I was eighteen."

His look of praise made her smile, but then look away. What had happened to this kid? Getting her to accept the bag of chips had been hard enough, but he could recognise a hungry child when he saw one, despite never having had any himself, and knew instinctively she needed to eat.

"Well, you promise?"

"Yes, I promise."

"Where are you going to?"

"I don't know really, just going west."

"Head to Vegas, there's always money there."

Her face did not show any acknowledgement of knowing where or what Vegas was.

"You know, Las Vegas? Gambling centre of the US? Possibly the world? Cirque de Soleil?"

"I've never heard of it."

The girl seemed embarrassed about her ignorance, and he wondered where on earth she had come from, how far she had travelled and for how long. *Where are your parents? Everybody knows about Vegas. Why are you alone?*

"Well, trust me, it's a good place to head for. You can pass yourself off as older, for sure, and try and get a job – there are lots of hotels and tourists. You should be fine. I remember going there years ago, and I don't imagine it's changed much. Bright lights, fountains and gambling tables."

She nodded, thinking about the new information; the idea of having a destination appealing to her.

"Your . . . are your parents looking for you?" he ventured.

She swallowed the emotion, knew he would ask at some point because everyone always did, and looked at him so he would know she was telling the truth.

"No. My parents are dead."

Her father might be. Could be. Either way, he was dead to her. She would never acknowledge him. *Ever.*

"Have you got somewhere to sleep tonight?"

"The same hedge I slept in last night." The answer came with a shrug that spoke of normality.

He thought he'd had it tough, watching his business sink into a slump from which it would never rise, and his bank balance slowly depleting, but she? She had it worse by far.

"You can sleep here if you like. I have a house opposite. You'll be alone but safe. And probably a little warmer."

She realised he was trying to help, again, even more than he had already, and she decided she loved chips.

"I . . . that would be great. If that's really alright?"

"Sure. Might as well have the place used, after all. There are showers through there as well, so, err, if you want to…"

"You're going to make me feel really bad," she said sadly, closing her eyes, uncomfortable as always with generosity.

"No, don't feel bad. Just one day, if you remember me, come back and say hi. You can buy me a bag of chips and tell me all about the excitement you found in Vegas."

This time she knew what to say: "I'll not forget you."

"Then shall I walk you back and you can grab your bag – you must have one somewhere?"

"Yes."

"How are you travelling?"

She stood up, following his lead. He took the empty chip paper, screwed it up and dropped it into the bin.

"Well, I kind of . . . ride on the trucks."

"You *ride* on the trucks!" he repeated in disbelief, going to the door, turning the lights off as they stepped out into the air.

"Yes. I just lie on top."

He looked at her for a second and shook his head. This was one resourceful kid. She didn't need to go to Vegas; her life was one big rollercoaster of excitement already.

"SO, DARYL, WHO'S it between?"

Daryl didn't look at Harvey, who he had seen approach through the crowd and progress unhurriedly up the steps to join him on his balcony, overlooking the splendid party he was holding. To everyone else's knowledge it was a frivolous midsummer party; but known only to his closest confidantes and himself, Harvey included, it was a chance for him to have a closer look at the five women he had decided were candidates for marriage. Honing it down from the fifty or so available as realistic possibilities with the right age, beauty and social connections had been a time-consuming process, and his criteria had changed or increased as the process had gone on.

Now, looking out at the sea of people – the women all manicured and beautiful; the men all dressed in their smart tuxedos; the older generation dignified and poised – he despised the whole issue, so was steeling himself to get it done. Everyone was enjoying themselves in the tastefully excessive luxury of one of his mansions in New York, and all the leading people were present – his social parties were ones people did not turn down – knowing it was the place to see and be seen, especially if one was young, gorgeous and single and hoped to catch the hugely eligible DB's eye.

"You assume I have already chosen?" Daryl asked calmly, trying to find the five women he had selected in the crowd, wanting to observe from a distance and later, up close and personal. Depending on what he found, possibly *very* up close and *very* personal.

"Come on, Daryl. I haven't been your pal for almost my whole life without getting to know you just a little," Harvey chided gently, coming to lean on the banister next to his friend. A glass of the finest champagne sparkled in the crystal flute in his hand, his tailored black-tie ensemble almost as fine as that of his wealthier friend who stood casually, shoulders a little relaxed for once, one hand in his pocket, one hand holding his glass. "You may have invited a great many here, but I know you will have already scouted out the ground, investigated and examined, and come up with a short list."

"I may change my mind."

"You told me yourself, spontaneity has no place in our world."

"Then I was right. It does not. I will undoubtedly choose one of the five I have so far selected, else I will reject all of them and start again," Daryl replied simply. Having located three of the five, he was looking for the other two.

"So, who are they? And of course, the information goes no further than myself." Harvey held up his hand to pre-empt the request he knew was coming.

Daryl allowed himself a small smile, actually admiring the fact that his friend knew him so well.

"Dawn Ferguson."

"Very beautiful. A little older than I thought you'd go for. Her mother would be an irritation."

"Michelle Carstairs."

"Oh. A very fine choice. Very rich father – not that that is a consideration – but hasn't she got the most annoying laugh?"

Daryl quirked one eyebrow; that was a concern of his as well.

"Nicola Troubert."

"Mmm, a little too frivolous I would have thought. Not got the brains for it. Though I grant she is still very lovely."

"Alexandra Harrison."

"Oh, definitely. I'd pick her without hesitation. Superb legs, and a pair of breasts I could eat."

Daryl looked round at his friend with a rather amused smile.

"And Rachel Huntley."

"Oh dear, now you've torn it. I was all set to pick Alexandra and now . . . couldn't you marry both? Surely for you they could make a dispensation? Maybe ask the Pope?"

Daryl laughed out loud. Trust Harvey to find some way to make light of the matter.

"Surprised you haven't got the president's daughter in that selection."

"Why would I ally myself with a presidency that is everchanging? I intend to always have good relations with the president – whoever he is, or she is – but I don't want to get into bed with a particular family . . . makes things very awkward next term."

"Quite true, very sensible," Harvey agreed. As usual, Daryl had infallible logic. "So, criteria?"

"It's quite a long list, but as long as she's beautiful, can keep herself faithful, and be a model wife – and, of course, provide me with children – then I'm not overly bothered about the rest."

"Quite like choosing a race horse, I suppose," Harvey remarked dryly, wondering how on earth he would find a wife. He was damn glad his friend was leading the way, as no doubt once Daryl was hitched, his own parents would be on at him to follow suit and start making grandchildren.

"Not quite. I know for a fact I've never fucked any of my race horses."

Harvey threw back his head and laughed.

It felt good to relax, to relieve the tension he felt at the daunting task he had set himself. He had started it, so he would finish. Daryl knew it wasn't marrying that made him nervous, it was deciding. Businesses, houses, investments – he could make those decisions with unstinting accuracy and success – but a woman? Completely different. So much less predictable.

"You get to put them through their paces though, right?"

"What do you mean?"

"Well, if I were you, I'd want to ride the filly before marrying her. What if she turns out to be a frigid little so-and-so?"

Again, Harvey's type of infallible logic. Never could resist an excuse to take a woman to bed.

"I think we both know, fairly certainly, that none of them are."

"Yes, but wouldn't it make the process more fun? Let them know they have competition. Turn it into a fuck-off fuck-a-thon."

His friend's winsome face was utterly cheeky; his grin too much for Daryl to be serious.

"Harvey, having you around makes me feel positively scrupulous compared to the things you come up with."

He finished his champagne and set it down on the balustrade; one of the waiters would find it.

"That's what you rely on me for: honest opinions, dirty jokes, and outrageous behaviour that makes you feel more noble," Harvey declared grandly, speaking with confidence because they both knew, to a point, he was right.

Daryl smiled and patted his friend on the shoulder.

"Wish me luck."

"I do. Very much. Let me know if you need any second opinions if there's a draw."

Daryl sent him a crushing glance of mock annoyance as he started down the stairs and aimed at his nearest target.

He got within five yards of Michelle Carstairs, heard her laugh and carried on. She had a fine pedigree, a good education, a lovely face that would complement his own in press photos, and no doubt would produce attractive children but . . . there was no way he could put up with that laugh. He could bear it for a month maybe, if he tried, but after that? It was too glaring a blemish to be allied with his own flawlessness. He would come to despise it and her.

Alexandra Harrison wrote herself out the running by declaring quite by chance, within Daryl's earshot, that she had no intention of losing her gorgeous body to motherhood anytime in the next six or seven years. Daryl wasn't sure if such swift elimination was a good thing or a bad thing, but concluded it was only natural given that the rest of his calculations had been based on pure fact, not the women themselves.

He managed a brief chat with Dawn, who was as reliable as usual: not a hair out of place, her dress not too loud or over the top, nothing wrong with her just . . . nothing particularly right either. She would bore him within a month or less he was sure. Though she would make a relatively good mother and a steady partner in life; would never be thrown by having cameras shoved in her face; and never expect too much from him after a long week working. So perhaps she wasn't such a bad choice . . . if one wanted practicality over everything else.

But could he not do better?

Nicola Troubert got an attack of nerves when she came face to face with her host, and gushed irritatingly, blushing and not quite knowing what to say – even to perfectly harmless questions. Daryl gave up in frustration, though did accept that her reaction was in a way flattering and wouldn't be so acute over time. He had been told he could be quite intimidating. Still, he did not want a mouse or an idiot for a wife. He had enough responsibilities and problems to deal with, and he didn't need extra from his spouse's inability to deal with everyday matters or when things went a little awry. Picking up the pieces after some disastrous press interview was one extra concern he could do without.

"Miss Huntley."

He had tracked down his last target and walked out onto the balcony looking out over the city. The night air was cool and her arms were wrapped around herself as she observed the view. She turned abruptly, surprised at seeing who it was who had spoken her name. Daryl looked her over, liking the combination of pale alabaster skin, red lips and dark hair, coiled up and intricately fastened. It was a chic affair, complimenting the dark red figure-hugging dress that matched her lipstick. *Very beautiful,* he decided, *and shapely with it. Slender but not weak.*

"I trust you are enjoying your evening?"

"Of course. How could I not? No one comes to your parties without enjoying themselves, Mr Blackmoor. You are a world-renowned host, are you not?"

He liked her answer; liked the fact she had spoken to him without boring him or making a fool of herself; liked the way her lips curved as she spoke, trying to restrain a smile.

"I would like to think so."

Daryl continued his slow approach and joined her at the rail, leaning one arm on it just as she did.

"It does feel wrong, though, to be hosting them alone. I sometimes think they would be improved by a woman's touch."

He had been looking out at the city, but he was wholly aware of her, knew she'd frozen for a second as the implication of his words hit home. She wasn't stupid; she would fathom the significance of his topic of conversation.

"I'm sure whomever you chose as your hostess would always try her best to make sure the parties were just as fabulous," she replied carefully, keeping her eyes on the dark world speckled with lights.

"Yes, I would hope she would . . ." He paused. "Quite a daunting task, though, don't you think? Not every woman would want to take on such a role."

The most testing question he had put to any woman so far.

"Daunting, but not without . . . advantages, such that they would far outweigh the challenge."

"Do you speak for yourself or for women generally?"

Daryl turned his eyes to her and caught hers, disarming her completely with his question. His powerful gaze pinned her to the spot, forcing her to answer, daring her to deny him the truth, even though she sensed he already knew the truth.

"I speak for myself."

She waited. And there was just silence. Then he blinked and looked away.

"You do not find the idea so terrible then?"

"Not at all. How could it be anything other than . . . an honour? Knowing the man you are?"

He didn't bother to point out that she didn't know the man he was, not at all. But she was respectful, suitably humble and appreciative. At least she seemed to think she knew how incredible his position of power was – that was more than some people managed. He could enlighten her to the reality in good time.

"I have very high expectations," he warned her seriously, looking out at the night again, careful not to appear too interested.

"Then I would aim to meet them," she countered, with as much feeling and confidence as she dared.

"I would expect you to."

A rather crushing answer, and he saw the flicker of hurt in her face, her answer meeting with the impenetrable wall of arrogance and indifference.

"Good night, Miss Huntley. Do enjoy your evening."

He sauntered away, his night's work done. He could relax now, having made the first set of inroads into his nuptials. He ordered Melanie be brought to his apartment for three in the morning, by which time he would be clear of the party, and then set about helping a few good friends to lose some of their plentiful funds to him over the gaming tables.

DARYL STOOD UP lazily with a modicum of respect as Miss Huntley walked towards him, led by the maître de of the exclusive and rather expensive restaurant that he owned. He was at his personal table, always reserved for him in case he dropped by, regardless of how busy they were.

He analysed her again as she approached – this was a fairly important decision after all. Her face was just as lovely as he remembered. Diamonds dangled from her ears, a matching necklace trailed down in between her breasts, and her hair once again was lifted from her neck, exposing the slenderness leading down to the shapely shoulders and delicate collarbones. Her black dress was a beautiful fit, from the bodice to skirt that had a slit all the way up her thigh. What a stunning vision she made. Mascara darkened her lashes, and he saw the lushness of colour on her lips from the glossy lipstick which contrasted with her pale skin, making her look a little gothic, yet fragile. He could have her worked on. There was room for improvement, though she had all the essentials: good cheekbones, good skin and well-shaped lips.

"Rachel."

He took her hand and indicated that she sit in the chair next to him, watching with approval as the waiter pushed in her chair for her. He then sat also, letting her hand go and seating himself comfortably again. He lounged back yet retained the commanding posture, his greater height meaning she was always going to be beneath him.

"Mr Blackmoor."

She has a good voice, tolerable at least. Not too high, not too low. Controlled. And without an irritating laugh. Always a plus.

"You look lovely."

Always compliment a woman; it smoothes the way.

"Thank you. I admit I was surprised to get your invitation. I . . . I had the distinct impression when we last spoke I had displeased you in some way."

He raised his eyebrows at her words, and realised he needed to lay down some ground rules, and make her perfectly aware of who she was dealing with and why. This was not a whirlwind romance; this was marriage, on his terms.

"Not at all. You must understand, I am very busy almost all of the time, so I keep my words to the point rather than waste my breath. Even now I am ignoring a number of business appointments to be here with you." He paused so that that fact was not lost on her. "To answer your original point, you did not displease me. I wanted answers and you gave them to me, and I merely needed time to think them over."

She was silent for a moment and held his gaze, then looked away, accepting the glass of wine being poured for her by another waiter.

"I trust you have not forgotten about that which we spoke?"

His raised eyebrows again, and the tilt of his head made her feel very small, as if he suddenly suspected she was rather stupid. He seemed more dangerous this evening, letting some of the raw authority show, not the charming if aloof and mysterious man who had come to speak to her unexpectedly on the balcony and intrigued her completely. The mere whisper of the possibility of what he had implied was enough to send her into distracted daydreams, excited moments of dizzy joy – and then moments of paralyzing fear at the reality of it, of being so close and then even more closely tied to this powerful man. It was daunting. But irresistible.

"No, not at all, Mr Blackmoor. Not one word."

"Good. For I do not like repeating myself. And I do not like to be disappointed."

She didn't answer. She realised what this was: the reality check to go with the amazing possibilities he had started her thinking on.

"We spoke last time of the challenging role of being the next Mrs Blackmoor. A wholly envied position, as you are no doubt aware. Yet the woman who takes on that role must be conscious of the many responsibilities she will have and the need for her to be, at all times, far more than just an average woman."

She did not offer any comment, but nodded, sensing he did not want to be interrupted.

"In public, in the media spotlight, as a wife, a hostess, and at some point a mother, your behaviour must be above reproach. And you will be expected to be fully capable of dealing with all domestic issues without my guidance or interference. I have enough to do. Does any of that sound at all unreasonable, taking into account the amazing opportunity that is being offered you?"

His question was patronising and she didn't like his imperious attitude all that much, but she bit down on her irritation. *Remember who he is, Rachel, what marrying him could mean! Imagine how proud your parents will be, and how envious all your friends will be! You, marrying the richest man in the world!*

There was only one answer she could give, unless she wanted the interview to come to an end right then and there: "No, Mr Blackmoor."

"Super. Now, other matters." He had already taken her answer for granted and moved on swiftly. "Are you aware, per chance, that your father has kept a string of mistresses since before you were born, in fact, all through his marriage to your mother?"

His words completely threw her, the focus suddenly switched so completely and so close to home, that she didn't know what to say for a moment. *Is this . . . true? Has my father really? . . . But my parents are so respectable. They are the centrepiece of Texan high society! My father is such a good husband . . .*

"No, I was not. Are you sure?"

His bored look told her he had already anticipated her question.

"Am I *sure*? Do you really think I would say something without being completely sure?" He smiled at her in a mocking fashion – and it brought her out of some of her shock. "Have you forgotten who I am? Have I not made a fortune out of the advances in security, surveillance and the gathering of information I designed myself? Government contracts? Billion-dollar contracts for some of the world's biggest corporations? Do you think I have not had *you* investigated, Miss Huntley?"

A blush stole over her cheeks and she looked down at the diamond bracelet on her wrist, one that her father had given her; apparently not quite the same admirable father she thought he was.

"No, of course you have," she replied quietly, feeling rather vulnerable, like rabbit lured into a large lush green field only to find a wolf there.

Her distress clearly didn't mean anything to him and he carried on. "Exactly. Anyway, my original point is this: while I will expect you to be wholly faithful, I want to be quite clear from the beginning, my private interests and habits are of no concern of yours. I am being perfectly honest with you, for I do not wish you to either agree to something that you do not fully understand, or feel responsible for later on. I do not expect you to be able to satisfy me – and I do not hold you responsible for that – but I will amuse myself as I wish. Is that completely clear?"

She could not believe his utter calm in discussing such things, as if she wasn't aware of his personal five-woman harem of specialist lovers. And she was meant to tolerate him keeping them?

"How can you know I won't be able to . . .?" But she faltered, blushing scarlet over her cheekbones at her attempt to contradict and protest. The fact her own sexual performance was being brought into question in such a matter-of-fact way, by him of all people, and at the dinner table, with his head of bodyguard only steps away . . .

"Because I don't think any woman could. Do you understand?" He brushed aside her words like the wind blowing over a feather.

"Yes, Mr Blackmoor, I understand."

She forced out the words, though it cost her her pride. Somewhere dreams were crushed and the golden fantasy in her mind warped into a different shape with this staggering statement of intent. Not even married, not even wedded and bedded, and he was so convinced of her inadequacy? He seemed so assured, as though this were so . . . reasonable.

"There are two simple rules that will make your life very easy, Rachel: please me, then please yourself in a manner I would approve of. As long as you keep me happy, there is little for you to worry about."

She nodded; but his attitude, the shocking revelation about her father, and the way he spoke of everything as though his was the only opinion in the matter was beginning to take effect, as was the magic of his magnetism, that handsome face that she could find no fault with. The way his body filled out his suit. He was a physical god. And she knew she wanted him to be hers. Knew it more than anything else before in her life. She would be more socially important and famous than even the president's wife. The world would be at her feet if she could stand by his side as his wife. She wanted to be his wife. She would have to make sure he knew she understood, and that she was willing to play by his rules. What else mattered, because she was going to win the prize every other woman wanted?

"And when am I allowed to start pleasing you, Mr Blackmoor? Am I to suppose we must wait until a wedding?"

His eyes rose back up to hers from where he had glanced down at his LifeTime, a brilliantly designed item that did so much. *So, she still wants to play the game.*

A small smile almost made it onto his lips.

"You can start tonight, unless you're too busy?"

Again, his inference implied she needed to prove herself to him, despite the offer in her words. It was a challenge couched so perfectly, giving her a chance to back out and be a coward if she chose; but Rachel knew full well if she did, she would lose his respect – or any hope of having it. Despite his charm, the smile, the discussion of marriage, she had yet to have any reason to think he actually respected her. It was a strange revelation to have in that moment.

"I can't think of anything more important."

She allowed herself a smile as she reached for her wine glass and took a sip. Part of her elated she had run the verbal gauntlet and survived; part of her afraid as to what the night would bring and then . . . what she had truly let herself in for. The image, the icon he was in her head, the media creation of his greatness, was nothing to the man himself in flesh and blood. He was far more than she had ever expected – or rather every bit as impressive as she had dreamed he would be, and that made him incredibly dangerous. This was a man who thought he was next on the ladder from God. He controlled so much, ordered so many people . . . was it any wonder?

Which was why three hours later, when she found herself being led to the exclusive Blackmoor penthouse apartment down an impeccable corridor with two expressionless security personnel behind her, she felt nervousness creep up her neck and send a shiver down her back. She looked at the broad powerful back of the man who was proposing to marry her – not that he had been so romantic as to say it nearly so nicely, but instead had offered it to her like business deal. Yet not even a deal. He had laid down terms, and she had to comply, and she sensed that would set the tone for their whole marriage. But could it be any other way, when he had such responsibility on his shoulders? Was it not that commanding nature that made him the great man he was? Was she really going to throw away the chance of a lifetime because he wasn't romantic enough? She prayed all the sexual dalliances she'd had before had prepared her sufficiently not to fluff her lines now. There was no way this bold, virile, demanding man wanted a shrinking violet in his bed.

At the front door – after the retina and fingerprint ID check and the door unlocking – they entered, and then they were alone.

Immediately he pulled off his bowtie and tossed it on the table by the door; arrogantly relaxed in his own home he paid no heed to the uncertainty that was obvious in her body language.

"The bedroom is that way, if you want to acquaint yourself with it."

He pointed down a corridor, not offering her a drink or inviting her to sit down on one of the luxurious sofas first. He was busy scanning various handhelds for information of business updates that had occurred since he had last looked, before he had left to go out to dinner. Clearly, this marriage would be another form of business to him from the efficient way he chose to spend his time with her: no romance, no subtleties.

Rachel walked down the corridor slowly, not wanting to rush or let him think her nervous, or overly keen, or surprised by him. To get any tiny measure of respect – for she feared, once more, that he didn't respect her at all – she would have to match him as best she was able, not let whatever he said or did put her off. Though she was excited all the same. He was a legend when it came to sex, for his stamina and technique. She'd heard the divulged secrets between women over the years, and no word was ever heard to dispute it. His ex-girlfriends were always upset at losing him, for all it heralded their fall from grace; but none of them ever had a bad word to say about him in bed . . . and there she was, not as a girlfriend, but as a potential wife.

She got to his room, and she was about to take a step inside when she felt a hand on her back. She could smell the aftershave she remembered so well from their encounter on the balcony, knew it was made exclusively for him. He guided her through the door and then closed it, pulling off his jacket and undoing another two buttons on his shirt. He looked so tempting. He would be the best-looking man she'd ever met, let alone slept with.

He watched her for a moment, putting his hands in his pockets, and then strolled towards her, two steps, leaving another eight between them.

"Were you waiting for something?"

His eyes half mocked her, half dared her, and she knew this was all still part of the test, part of his decision-making. That being the case, she was going to have to do whatever she could to keep his interest.

Her hands went to the zip at the side of her dress and with a wiggle was left in only her thong and black high heels. She stepped towards him, watching his eyes skim down, praying he liked what he saw. Hands reached up to cup her breasts and thumbs grazed over her nipples, already reacting to the cooler air in the room.

"You have very fine breasts, are they natural?"

She smiled, glad she had something he liked.

"Every inch," she replied.

Slowly, she reached out a hand and undid his shirt buttons, then his belt, then his trousers, amused that he didn't move, just let her do what she liked. She felt a flare of anger when she thought about his women doing this for him as well, and a hot bright jealousy that she had not anticipated flowed and gave her courage to continue despite his unwavering scrutiny.

She broke with his gaze and knelt down before him, easing his trousers down and unbuttoning his briefs, pushing his shirt aside and letting her hands stroke down from his belly to that part of him that had already begun to react.

Daryl closed his eyes for a moment to enjoy himself, imagining those rouged lips wrapped around his hardened cock, sucking him in deeper and deeper, and then opening them again to enjoy the reality. Hands then cupped his buttocks and nails dug in, pulling his erection nearer to her face as she buried his length in her mouth and down her throat, those very clever lips every bit as good as he had hoped. Her enthusiasm did her credit and he ran a finger up her neck as her head bobbed against him, tongue busy, using every little detail she knew to try and please him, and when she did, a hand cupped her head and held her there, forcing her to be still or choke, and he came inside her.

He let her go, and looking down at her as he withdrew she felt a horrible sense of worthlessness, the way he looked at her, judging her, that even going onto her knees for him wasn't enough. He hadn't even kissed her.

"A very good start, I'll give you that," he commented dryly, as he helped her stand up with one hand, then shedding himself of his clothes with practised efficiency and nodding to the bed.

She climbed on at the base, intending to go up and lie against the pillows and admire his beautiful body, but she'd got no farther than halfway when a hand caught her waist and held her still, his body moving up behind her and hands pulling her legs apart.

She froze. *What is he going to do? Is there going to be any foreplay? Hasn't he just spent himself?*

She was then laid down on her front, her arms by her sides bent at the elbow, and she could feel his knees against her thighs, so he must be kneeling on the bed. She looked around at him, caught sight of the amazing musculature of his torso and wanted him, wanted to feel the strength of him and touch him. His hands smoothed her back, up to her shoulders and then down again, sliding over her buttocks with delicious deliberation, and she felt herself go wet with anticipation. She heard her thong snap as he pulled it off, and hands lifted her thighs and her hips and pulled her back, raising her over his knees, the tip of his cock on the edge of her cleft, touching, teasing. She felt a twinge of pain at the position he was insisting she bend into, and she was about to say so when he took her hands and pulled them behind her back, leaving her helpless, at his mercy. Yet still he teased her, and she bit down on a whimper of pain as the bend on her back increased now she could not support herself on her arms.

"You wish to please me. What if I want this? Will you deny me?"

His voice spoke in her ear and she realised what this was: it was conquest and domination. He was the master, and she would never be allowed to forget it. Ever.

"No, no, I want you to have what you want. Whatever makes you happy."

She forced the words out, trying to ignore the pain stretching from her lower back into her ribcage, feeling the pleasure of his erection against her. There was a moment of perfect silence, and then he drew back and pushed into her, filling her, and her eyes widened in surprise, his thrusts exquisite. All pain was forgotten as he drove into her, again, and again. A hand pushed her head down on the bed, refusing to let her move. She gave herself up to it. Felt the thrusts get harder, and she climaxed sooner than she expected, after which his movements became even more urgent, pounding at her with a force she'd never felt, leaving her feeling helpless and used, totally at his mercy, before he finished himself.

Not moving for a moment, and looking down at her naked back, he wondered why he felt such a rush of dislike, why he suddenly despised being there. He didn't quite understand his own feelings, but let it go. He should be pleased, considering how his evening was going.

He released her, withdrew and shifted her off him. He then got off the bed and walked in shameless nakedness to the large dresser on one wall. He pulled on a silk robe and then poured himself a drink, not offering one to her. He took a swallow and then turned around to find her watching him, sitting on the bed.

"Take your heels off."

Willingly, Rachel complied with such a simple instruction, slipping them off and pushing them onto the floor, thinking the worst was over, that maybe because she'd already passed through one hard set of hoops he might be kinder to her now. She hadn't meant to keep the shoes on, it was just . . . everything had happened so fast.

Daryl sat down in the chair by the window, with a suave elegance more fitting to sitting down to a business meeting. She felt foolish, out of her depth.

"Make yourself come," he told her with breath-snatching simplicity, and took a sip of his brandy.

Rachel stared at him in shock. "What?"

"You heard me, and I'm sure you know how. I want to watch you."

He saw her confusion. She may have been a practiced bed mate, but she obviously wasn't quite up to his bold demands.

"Use your fingers; imagine it's me."

He sat back and took another sip, watching her. Saw her confusion turn to something else: determination?

"I hope I haven't worn you out already?"

His last piece of subtle mockery did the trick.

She lay back on the bed and ran both hands over the breasts he had so admired, down to between her thighs. She arched her back as she touched herself with one hand, the fingers of the other sliding inside, and Daryl watched with cynical interest as she worked magic on herself, her hips working with her hands. After a few minutes and a whimper or two she cried out and her head fell back on the pillows. He finished his drink and went to the bed again, surprising her by straddling her. He took hold of the wrist of the hand that still gleamed with her wetness and raised it up so she could see it, looking down at her with eyes that held her captive.

"I am pleased to see you are so well practiced in satisfying yourself. That is what you will do whenever I am away, or cannot be with you. Don't ever think about finding satisfaction with another except yourself, for you will not want to suffer the consequences if I should find you have."

The threat was clear and she barely dared breath, let alone speak. *Of course, the ego of a man like this would never even contemplate that his wife would sleep with another man.*

"Now." He got off her and leaned back against the pillows, the untied silk robe spread out around him so that he looked like some kind of Greek god. "There is a car coming for you in forty-five minutes. Do you think you can keep me amused until you have to go?"

Rachel sat up, still reeling from everything that had happened in the last hour, but couldn't stop herself from going to him again, refusing to back down from his challenges. She slid over him, letting her wet cleft rub over his hard, muscled thigh as she dropped kisses up his chest, then moved herself down onto him, unsurprised to find his eyes watching her.

She began to move, focussing all her energies on him. Already feeling spent herself, this was all about him, and for the moment she was happy for that to be so. Once she had his ring on her finger then she might see if she could improve his attitude somewhat. She saw his lips curve into a smile as his eyes closed, hands going to her hips to urge her on. She tried hard to bring him the release that would at least impress him a little more. His smile was a good start. She didn't know he was smiling because he was remembering Harvey's words about race horses. Or that he had already enjoyed two quite similar nights with the other prospective Mrs Blackmoors.

Choosing a wife, it turned out, wasn't all that bad at all.

GETTING TO VEGAS had been so hard; or perhaps it just felt like that because once she had a destination, she'd just wanted to get there rather than just get taken anywhere. But as long as it had been westward she had been heading, on her own personal *ad hoc* mode of transport, she had been OK. She had almost got caught once or twice when she'd fallen asleep, and once had made a mistake and ended up going in the wrong direction, but she had made it.

She couldn't quite believe it. Vegas was in a desert. And it was so hot. She'd quickly got used to the heat, the sand, the thirst, but as the truck drove through the extensive suburban sprawl that led to the centre, the main Strip, the casino and hotel area, she felt a little overwhelmed. This party-land of excess and bright lights had grown after massive urban renewal projects, and nothing prepared her for the giant-sized buildings, the fountains, the people, the cars or the noise. Despite this, she took it all in with the wide-eyed wonder of an ignorant tourist.

She slipped off the back of the truck, stood in the shadows for a long moment, before squaring her shoulders and heading out into the melee. But after she'd got bumped into for the tenth time in as many minutes by people rushing past her, and got another dirty look from a suit who looked down at her, she realised just how out of place she was. The fast-flowing streams of people all seemed to know where they were going, and had no time or room for a small dusty person with a rucksack who was doing a world-class impression of a stray dog. No, she did not fit in at all. In fact, she was an eyesore compared to the dapper men and women who were all so well-groomed – even if some were remarkably overweight.

She'd never seen people so fat! *How much food did you need to eat to grow so big?* she wondered as she looked at her thin arms and legs.

She didn't know how long she had been walking, but she forced herself to leave the lively streets behind, the colourful flashing lights and the music that drifted out of the hotels into the street. It was all so interesting, but she knew from experience she needed to find somewhere to sleep and some work. She headed back the way she'd come, trying to focus, knowing on the poorer outskirts there might be somewhere to take shelter, at least for the first night. She'd never arrived anywhere with the intention of staying there more than one or two nights before, so everything was going to be a little different this time. But ten months travelling had made such basic concerns second nature; she knew roughly what she was looking for.

She tried to swallow and her throat ached. She'd drunk the last of her water on top of the truck, which was at least an hour ago. Time had seemed to disappear so quickly when she'd been amongst the crowds, staring up in wonder at the creations man saw fit to build. Were all these people really here so they could gamble? Isn't that what the man in the boxing club had said? Didn't they have better things to do with their money? After a short lifetime of witnessing the results of her father's gambling, it was hard to compare the two worlds . . . and she didn't want to. *Don't think.*

Worn out by the spectacle, the journey, and the questions the big city had already thrown at her, the girl spied a small grocery store set in amongst a row of shops – a hairdressers, a laundrette and a take-away restaurant – all quite normal by comparison. She went into the shop, looked around for a moment, and then saw a woman by the till. She was reading a magazine, chewing gum, one hand resting on the page ready to turn it, the other resting on her very pregnant belly. The girl offered a smile and got one back, and went to the fridge, contemplating buying a bottle of milk as well as water, but she was horribly conscious of the three notes she had left in her wallet, so doing anything at all frivolous was not a good idea.

She took the two-litre bottle of water back to the counter, and the woman looked up and scanned the item. She handed over the money without the woman needing to say the amount, there was no need. They both knew it.

"There you go, doll. $7.85 change."

"Thanks."

She put the money back into her wallet and pushed it back, deep into the rucksack.

"I don't suppose you know anywhere with any jobs going, do you?"

The woman looked at her properly then, having been ready to go back to her magazine the moment the transaction was done with.

"I've just arrived in town and I'm trying to find some work you know, so . . ."

The woman blinked and popped a bubble, then picked up the phone next to her – one of the old-fashioned types – eyes not leaving the kid in front of her.

"Carl. Yeah, it's me. I've got a girl here says she's looking for work, and you know how you was saying about getting someone to help me now I can't lift stuff . . ." She paused, listening, and the girl tried to keep the hope from growing too fast. "Yeah, OK, I'll tell her, she's still here. OK, see you in a moment."

She put the phone down and looked back at her, a big smile on her face; even the chewing paused for a moment.

"That was the boss. He's coming down. He says he'll talk with you."

She looked the girl over in the spare moments, watching as she gratefully drank from the bottle of cool water, clearly tired, dusty; but her smile was friendly.

"Makes you thirsty this heat, don't it? I'm drinking so much my mother started threatening to put me in a bowl with some gravel in the bottom."

They shared a smile at the humour, and then a man appeared from behind one of the displays of cereal. He wasn't too tall, but he was quite a big guy, mid-thirties she guessed, and not one for too much exercise. There was sweat on his brow, and his hand when he offered it to the girl was clammy. Even natives felt the heat.

"You after work?"

"Yes, sir."

He looked like he could be Mexican, but he spoke in English with no accent – except the American drawl.

He hadn't been expecting such a polite reply, or for the words to be so well-spoken.

"Where you from?"

"Back east. I only arrived today."

"You staying?"

"That is the plan, sir."

She waited and he weighed her up, saw a pair of bright, intelligent eyes and an open, pretty face. She looked healthy, if a little on the skinny side, and there were no tell-tale signs of drug use or alcohol, or anything other than honest dirt that a good wash would sort out.

"Come with me."

She followed him to the back of the store, and through the door marked 'Private,' past a storeroom and then into an office that was so deep inside the building there were no windows. The harsh glare of artificial lights glowed down on them. His computer was on and there were papers over the desk.

"So, what's your name, kid?"

She looked down at some of the sheets.

"April." She grabbed the word she read on the nearest sheet as she sat down on the spare chair, while he sat down in the bigger office chair and pulled up a new page on the computer and typed in information.

"April what?"

"April Megson."

She thought he might take issue with her surname – after all, it was just a mash of letters she had desperately pulled out of her head; but he didn't seem to care or think it odd. Clearly Vegas was a jungle of everything, including names. Either that or he really didn't care.

"OK, so, how old are you?"

"Fourteen."

He looked up, eyes scanning her over.

She held her breath.

"You'll pass for fifteen," he told her. "I've got enough paperwork to do at the moment, and obviously I don't know if you'll work out permanently. There's always a trial period of three weeks, and I'll pay you in cash, alright?"

"Yes, sir."

"It's $7.00 an hour. Then after three weeks it goes up to $9.50, OK?"

"Yes, sir." *Wow! Real money!*

"Now, I only have fourteen hours for you a week at the moment – two hours a day. Janice, as you saw, is pregnant, and likely to go in in the next few weeks from what I can tell, so if she does then you can take on some more while she's with the baby. For the first three weeks, you can do the shelves, load the boxes – you know the kind of thing?" She nodded emphatically. "Then, if you're OK and I trust you, we'll train you on the till. Clear?"

Another nod. Not big on words, but he certainly didn't think she was stupid. More of a worker than a talker.

"Now, have you got any papers or references?"

She held her breath. Then, "No. I don't have anything." Her face confirmed her words.

"Why are you here?" He realised he should have asked this much earlier, annoyed at himself for not having done so, irritated that he might have just wasted his time. "You're a kid. Where are your folks?"

"My family are dead. They died in a car crash. I didn't want to stay so I . . . I left."

A gloss over the truth.

"How come you're not dead?"

A rather brutal question, but she could understand him asking, so she didn't take offence.

"I was at a friend's house when it happened. Else I would be."

He was quiet for a moment. It was plausible, and she looked utterly serious, solemn even at remembering. If it were him, he would have left too.

"OK. Do you have any experience in a job like this?" He wanted to give her a chance, but he did need something else really.

"Well, I worked in the stock room and shop of a grocery store back east. I have his number if you want to call him? His name is Mr Matthews. Here . . ."

She delved into the zipped pocket inside her rucksack. Along with the cassettes and another pack of batteries for the Walkman – that had been her constant companion – she had the postcard with his name, number and address on that she'd found. She had wanted to call him more than once, just to say hi and thank you, but had never quite worked up the courage . . . She handed the postcard over to the waiting hand and he read it then dialled.

"Hello? Hey there, my name's Carl Cambrero. Is that Mr Matthews?"

A short pause. He scowled. The child prayed Mr Matthews didn't put the phone down.

"Yes, well, I've got a girl here, name of April Megson, says she helped in your store a few months back?"

He looked at her and she nodded to confirm his guess.

"I run a store myself, so I'm ringing to get a reference. She hasn't got any papers, but she had your number . . . Yes, she's fine. . . I'm calling from Vegas . . . Yes, she's a little dusty but she's OK."

Mr Cambrero looked at her again and smiled, and relief flooded through her.

"I've got a vacancy for someone in the stockroom and refilling the shelves. Is she any good?"

The girl crossed her fingers and sat in pensive silence, wishing she could hear the other side of the conversation.

"Great. That's good. Very polite, yes. Yes. Definitely. Of course. I'll tell her. If you could that would be great. Yes, OK, bye now."

The phone went down.

"Seems you made yourself useful, young lady. He says he wants you back."

He handed the postcard back after making a note of the details written on it.

"It's a bit of a way to go," she said quietly, pleased and relieved. Thank goodness he'd had the sense to put his details in her bag, else she would have been sunk.

"He's going to send me a written reference for you, so I can put that in your file, and he asked me to tell you to give him a call and tell him how you're doing. So, if you can just fill in your details on the computer – name, date of birth, etc. – that would be great. Saves me asking you for the spellings. I'll just go get you a shirt."

She sat down in his chair and tentatively typed in the letters, never having used a computer like this one, or any type of computer for so long. Days at school were part of another life.

She had just finished making up a whole load of information about who she wasn't when he came back. She had been glad he'd left the room, as she would probably have fluffed it if he'd been there watching, and she'd have felt so guilty. Being on the road had a certain freedom, but she hated having to lie to maintain it. One day she wouldn't have to lie. She hoped. But caution won over conscience.

"We don't have any shirts in your size. You're smaller than most around here. You can wear anything smart but practical, for now. I guess you're probably quite low on funds right now, but just do your best. You can get a blue shirt similar to these at the clothing store two streets over, and that'll be fine. OK?" He held up a navy polo shirt that would have probably fitted her to her knees.

"Yes, sir, Mr Cambrero." She stood up, vacating his chair.

"You can call me Carl." He tossed the shirt on the desk and held out a hand. "Welcome to the company." She shook hands and let herself smile. "Your first shift is tomorrow. Nine till eleven. I'll be here, so just get Janice at the front to let me know when you've arrived and we'll go over everything. You erm . . . you have someplace to go tonight?"

"I'll find somewhere."

He nodded, not sure what to say, so didn't. She wasn't asking for help, despite looking like she needed some just then. He led her back through the storeroom and to the door to the shop, opening it and standing so she could go through.

"You could do with a wash, too, you know. I think you have half the desert on you."

The words were said gently, jokingly, and her smile slightly lessened at the obvious embarrassment she felt when and she looked down at herself.

"I'll be clean, sir, I promise."

"OK, then. Well, till tomorrow."

He nodded goodbye and she walked back towards the counter. Janice looked up as she appeared from behind the stack of potato chips and a bubble popped.

"How'd it go?"

"I start tomorrow. Nine until eleven." Her smile said everything; Janice smiled back. "I'm April, by the way."

She held out a hand and Janice took it, bracelets jangling down her bare arms. She was wearing a dress that covered her bump, but left much of her body free to the air.

"Janice, nice to meet you. He says hi as well." She rubbed the bump and sighed, stretching her back. "I'm ready to have him now. He's awful heavy to carry around."

"Will I see you tomorrow?"

"Sure thing, doll, I'll be here."

A couple of customers came up bearing their handfuls of stuff, taking Janice's attention, and the girl slipped out the door. She had a job! She looked at the laundromat across the street and decided to get everything washed. She'd picked up a few spare clothes from thrift shops along the way, and she knew they needed cleaning, just like she did, and now she could afford it. She'd see if they had a bathroom she could use. Then she was going to need some food, then somewhere to sleep.

SHE TURNED UP for work at 8.50am, feeling cleaner than she had for a long, long time. Getting back down to earth from the rooftop where she'd slept without doing anything to dirty her clothes had been a bit of a struggle, but somehow she'd managed it. After spending so much time on the tops of trucks, and having twice redefined the rules of gravity and survived falls that should have killed her, or at least hurt her, she had no great fear of heights. Hence, climbing up the pipework outside of a four-storey building seemed a good idea when there was nowhere else to sleep that would be relatively safe. But perhaps the effort to get down meant she'd have to reconsider where she slept tonight.

Janice waved at her as she came in, and Carl showed her a room where she could leave her rucksack. He had no reason to complain, as she looked clean and respectable, her long, curly hair pulled back in a ponytail at the nape of her neck. And she was clearly ready for work as she settled into it quite happily once his tour and explanations of procedure were complete.

While she worked, she pondered the problem of where to live, knowing it would be a long time before she could possibly afford to rent a small room somewhere. She had already looked at the prices pinned up in shop windows, and they started around $450 for a month for a single room with shared bathroom and kitchen. She had a long way to go. It felt strange to be in the same place, rather than just moving on, but she knew if it didn't work out, she'd move on again. She wasn't tied here. *Vegas is just one place. There must be other cities.*

IT WAS THE pure chance of her getting her bearings wrong that took her past a fenced off old building after work, sad to leave but no excuse to stay. She looked at the husk of the building, so big it looked like it could have once been a hotel, but it had deteriorated greatly. One side, where the black stains of flames still marked the walls, looked beyond repair; but the other side looked OK. Could she? No one would know if . . . if she was careful. And certainly no one would care.

"Shame isn't it, dear?" a voice said behind her, and she startled, turned to see an elderly lady trundling down the road with her wheeled frame, heading towards the shops at the end of the road.

"I'm sorry, I didn't hear you?"

"Shame they've just left it. Not done anything with it for five years since the fire. It was beautiful in its day, dear. Now look at it. No one wants to touch it because of the money needed to restore it. Bit of an eyesore now. They should tear it down, but everyone's too busy building new things. They don't have time to worry about the old." She kept walking with her little staccato steps as she spoke, not pausing as she went past the girl. "It'll probably be there after I'm dead!" she added, and she gave a little bit of a cackle, seemingly happy just to have had an audience, not worried about the fact she hadn't had any further response.

The girl watched her walk down the path, never changing pace. The old lady would probably have said all that to whoever had been on the pavement, possibly even without hoping for a response, and she wondered if she should have replied. But what would she have said? And besides, she didn't want to draw attention to herself.

She looked around, seeing no one else. She was on a back street, half of which was taken up with this monolith of a neglected building. She judged how long it would take to get over the fence and into the shadow of the building and then inside. She would find a way somehow.

She took her rucksack off and swung it, heaved for all she was worth and let go, watched it fly up and over the wire fencing. Then she backed up, ran and jumped, grabbing onto the top with her hands, swinging her legs around and over. She was stronger now, and good at moves like this after her truck climbing.

She then burrowed her way in through a broken doorway and made her way upstairs, the massive hall and grand staircase feeling lonesome with all its splendour now gone. It was all grey, black or brown, and she imagined the rich colours it might have been before. It felt doubly lonesome to be there on her own, when it was designed for so many others. Going up cautiously, not sure how much decay might have taken place during the five years since the fire, she found herself on the next floor. The size of the building was astonishing as she stood in its heart and looked around. Putting her rucksack down, listening out for signs of life at every second, she proceeded to explore every room. She had never had such an adventure, and knew she was going to have to buy a torch, more batteries, some more bedding . . .

After exploring some more, she chose her room. It was large, with little furniture, as with the rest of the place, and most of it was too broken or smoke-damaged to use, but she didn't care. Below her room was a ballroom, and she wanted to be close to that, as finally she had found somewhere to dance to the music on the cassette player! She mentally made a list. And unexpectedly, a frisson of excitement blossomed through the scar tissue in her mind, like a new sprig of growth on an amputated tree branch.

RACHEL TURNED OFF the television, irritated by the ridiculous size of it – just like everything else Daryl owned. She had moved into his New York penthouse, though she hadn't really brought anything of her own to it yet, and didn't see any more of him as he was so often at the office, or travelling, or out for dinner meetings . . . Still, she was proud of the media coverage. There had been so many pictures posted of them together, and it was all progressing well, which, she discovered, was the same with everything Daryl did.

They made a stunning couple, and when the news had hit the world that she was a permanent fixture in his life it had created tidal waves of speculation and intrigue that Daryl Blackmoor was finally marrying. . . but not really so much about who he was marrying, however. But, she reasoned, that was as it would be – for now. She was intending to make a reasonable splash when she got her chance, else what was the point in marrying the world's richest man? A glance down at the sparkling diamond on her finger reminded her of one significant reason.

She tossed the remote control onto the sofa and looked towards his study where she knew he would be. It was 10.15pm, but she knew he was working, could hear the occasional conversations with others who were still working away, hear the commands to the computer, the tap-tap of fingers on buttons. Should she dare go in there? Why was Daryl marrying if not to enjoy being a couple, if not to have someone there in the evenings to tempt him away from such things?

He had already 'made love' to her shortly after he had got in from the office at eight thirty. Having announced he was going to take a shower, she had gone to see what he wanted for dinner and found herself tossed on the bed. It made her smile. He was devilishly good in bed. In a different league to anyone else she had ever known. And he was teaching her things about herself and her body even she hadn't been aware of, and although sometimes it irked that he took such a high-handed approach, she ended up loving every second.

But what annoyed her – and it was a niggle that hadn't gone away since the beginning – was that he hadn't actually kissed her. Not a proper deep kiss of passion. They had done so much else, enough to make her blush he was so virile, and nothing seemed to wear him out, but she couldn't work out why he wouldn't kiss her. Was it just her?

A fresh bout of determination and frustration brought her to her feet, taking her to the study door. Rachel looked through, could see him sitting in his towelling bathrobe still, a luxurious affair that made him look so handsome, and she felt her insides quiver knowing what was underneath. His feet were resting on a perfectly placed footstool, seemingly relaxed – except for the scowl of concentration on his face.

"Daryl."

She walked into the room, deciding she was only going to get more strung up on the kissing issue if she didn't do something about it.

"Rachel."

He said her name automatically in response, not looking away from the screens on his handhelds as he reclined in his luxurious chair: a godlike throne of control, everything at his fingertips.

"Are you going to stop work soon?"

She wanted to add an endearment but didn't really feel it was appropriate. If there was one thing she knew very well, it was that there was no love in this match; it was practical and satisfactory but not sentimental. 'My dear' or 'my love', even 'sweetheart' felt . . . well, it just felt wrong. And even *thinking* the words 'make love' felt like a little bit of a lie. They didn't. They had sex.

"Not as far as I can see right now," he answered in a monotone voice, reaching around for a different handheld from the table by his side to compare the two. She didn't even try to see what was so damned enthralling. And if she asked she knew she'd get a withering look, as if she was being ridiculously stupid to think she could possibly understand what he was doing.

"I was just wondering if I could ask you a question? . . ." she tried.

Out of his line of sight, she pulled the tie of her lacy robe undone – which she knew she looked fabulous in as she'd checked in the mirror a hundred times – and let it slip open to allow him a view of the curves of her breasts, her nipples just visible through the lace. But he didn't look up. And even when she walked in front of him, his eyes stayed on the screen in his hand into which he was typing.

"Will it take long to answer?" He typed something else.

"I hope not."

"Ask then."

She controlled her frustration. Was she a child or his fiancée?

"I just wondered why you've never kissed me."

Daryl went completely still, yet his eyes rose to meet hers, noting on their journey her state of dishabille and the temptation she was trying to put in front of him. Did she really think him so easily swayed?

The resounding silence following the question made Rachel wish she'd stayed in the lounge with the TV.

"I believe I have," he replied steadily, wondering what on earth this was about. Had he not given her everything she had wanted? Spared no expense in dressing her and pampering her so she looked absolutely gorgeous for the cameras, and let her preen as much as she liked? Taken her out to dinner and had her feted amongst their social circles as his fiancée?

"I mean on the lips, not everywhere else," she replied impatiently, partly due to her embarrassment at having to speak of it, partly at his dismissive reception of her attempt at discussing the subject.

"Is that a complaint?" he asked dangerously, his head going back, those eyes on her so that even from his reclining position she felt about ten inches tall.

"No, Daryl, it's just . . . I just wondered why."

"No particular reason. I haven't felt the need to."

It was exactly that kind of answer she had feared. She so desperately wanted to reach him, to not allow this reserved man to continue keeping her at arm's length. Even just a little sign of affection that she was more than just a piece of furniture would do. She walked to his side and knelt down on the thick carpet by the side of his chair, knowing he liked her on her knees, knowing he liked to feel in control. She thought it might sway him.

"Won't you kiss me now?" She pouted a little, knowing he liked her lips, he had told her so.

"Are you demanding, asking, or begging?"

She realised she was going to get what she wanted, but at a price. And, as usual, it would be her self-worth.

"I'm begging you, Daryl, please, just kiss me. Like you want to."

She refused to look away, his features so chiselled, his face so expressionless . . . but then she saw a little slant to his lips. She thought for a moment it was a smile of invitation. She was wrong.

"Come, you can do better than that," he chided her mockingly, not moving, not putting his handhelds down, even though she was there right next to him, her naked breasts pushed against the arm of his chair.

She blinked and shrank back a little, looked away to his naked feet on the footstool. Strong, shapely feet. Just as perfectly formed as the rest of him. Then she looked back at him and his eyes only confirmed what she already knew: he would never stop asking so much of her.

She crept down to his feet across the carpet, swallowed, and kissed his feet. Both of them.

"Much better. Come here."

She went back to him while heat suffused her cheeks, and he put the handhelds on top of each other and held them in one hand. She felt his other hand slip to her breast, cup it and then slide up, fingers circling her neck and her head . . . and he pulled her lips up to his. She shut her eyes and let herself enjoy the moment, her expectation not disappointed: as usual, he excelled at everything, and his firm sensual lips were demanding with restrained but enticing passion, teasing her tongue, the kiss confident, just like his performance in bed. He was nothing if not confident, totally assured of his own brilliance.

The kiss ended when he pulled away, and he held her close for a few seconds, his eyes waiting for her response, analysing what he saw in her face.

"Thank you," she said softly, wishing she could ask him to do it again, do it and then lay her down on one of the soft sofas and take her slowly, make her whimper like she knew he could. The closest she ever got to him was skin to skin . . . but if that was how it would be, then so be it.

Daryl let her go and she leaned back, preparing to stand, but his hand pressed down on her forearm and stilled her. It was unexpected, and there was force enough that she couldn't move away. Her eyes went back to his and she saw they were angry.

"I do not like being interrupted when I am working. Especially for something so trivial. Remember that and do not do it again."

She felt the small nugget of happiness at her success at finally sharing a kiss with him melt into a puddle in her chest. Failure again.

"Can you think of something you can do to lessen my annoyance with you?"

His eyes were hard and demanding. And she knew what he wanted. That was the usual penance for having stepped over the line of familiarity, of misjudging her importance to him. A length of hair fell over her eye as she turned her head – shorter hair than before after stylists had worked their magic on her, changing her appearance slightly, making her more sophisticated to suit his own debonair image.

She crawled to his feet and then ducked under one of his raised knees, pushing the robe away, reaching for the tie and letting it fall open. He was naked underneath. Her eyes didn't dare go up to his. Didn't want to see the expression in them. She lay her hands on his toned thighs, instead, and stroked upwards, teasing him to life.

"No hands. I want it to last. And seeing as you were so keen to use your lips, you can do so now. If I am sufficiently mollified, I'll take you shopping at the weekend and we can find you something sensational for the engagement party."

She felt like a whore, performing at her master's whim; in fact, was she really anything else? She had expected him to be demanding, but this? She dropped her hands down and closed her eyes as she lowered her mouth to him, using her lips as he had ordered. And she felt another piece of her self-respect crumble as she heard him pick up the handhelds and go back to his work . . .

But still, it was she – she out of the whole world – he had chosen! Could *she* not have the world at her feet too? After the wedding, they would settle into their separate lives – lord knew their lives were already separate enough – but if she were pregnant that would surely please him no end? It was all still to play for. This was just his way of testing her. It wouldn't always be like this. One day he would feel something more for her. He would.

IT WAS SUNDAY afternoon and she was bored. They had barely seen each other all week and she was annoyed that now, finally with some time to themselves in the penthouse, that all he was doing was lazing back on the sofa reading a book! So what that he had taken her shopping the day before and blown a fortune on her dress and some new jewels for their engagement party next weekend . . . could he not pay her any real attention? Even then he had been taking phone calls and ignoring her in favour of his handheld. She ended up feeling like she might as well have been on her own, sensed he knew what he was doing, playing the role of fiancé to a sufficient level for those romance-related headlines to hit the press. The reality was somewhat different. Not that anyone would ever know it. And she could never say anything against him, not to him or the press. It would be a suicide of sorts. It would certainly end the engagement.

She tapped her nails on the coffee mug she was holding, trying to think of some way to entice him to do something with her, or just to *talk* for goodness sake! Trouble was, he never seemed to want to hear anything she had to say.

"Can you not think of anything else to do rather than sit there making noise?" His voice cut into her thoughts and she looked at him across the large room. He hadn't bothered to look up, but his voice betrayed his irritation. "Why not go and paint them. It'll give you something to occupy yourself with," he remarked impatiently, turning the page of the book.

She had noticed he liked books – the old-fashioned kind, not the digital versions that could be viewed on any handheld. She didn't comment, just moved the mug so it sat on the table, away from idle temptation.

"I wonder at how little you seem to have to do considering there is the engagement party to organise, not to mention the wedding," he then said, his words airy but laced with a dangerous hint of menace.

"It's all under control. I found the most brilliant company who organises everything. I just have to make the main choices, and they source everything. It's so much easier."

She looked up from examining her already painted nails, a deep red, and then froze. His book had been lowered and his face looked thunderous.

"Are you utterly stupid, or did you really mean to insult me?"

His voice a dangerous purr. She had only ever heard it like that once before when he had used the same tone on a driver who had made him fifteen minutes late by taking a wrong turning. The man had been fired without hesitation.

"What do you mean?" she retorted desperately, alarmed when he stood up and threw the book down on the sofa he had been so relaxed on only moments before.

"It is the *one thing* I asked you to do. *You*. Not anyone else. Not a company. The one thing I asked *you* to see to personally, and you fail me. Are you a total idiot, or do you not understand simple instructions beyond how to suck someone's cock?"

Rachel recoiled at the anger in his words, at the crudity, and she stood up, backing away, his fury so quick it shocked her. Like a cornered lion in the room, his rage was unleashed, and from the calm of the afternoon came the ominous threat of great danger.

"I've no experience with engagement parties or weddings. I thought it would be better left to those who know how!" she threw back quickly, desperate to explain.

"You have all the helpers you could wish for; you have no budget; you can ask advice from anyone you choose, and yet, *and yet* you still chose to pass it off to someone else rather than attempt to fulfil my request *yourself*? I'm beginning to wonder what kind of wife you will be!"

It was the worst thing he could have said, and it made her feel foolish and inadequate, and ache with despair. She couldn't lose him!

"Daryl, please! I just didn't want to make a mistake!"

"You agreed to be my wife *and* my hostess! Is every party going to be someone else's creation rather than your own? Is it too much to ask that you could spend some of your time being *useful* rather than just shopping, painting your nails, or taking your girlfriends out to lunch? Why am I paying a company to do what my *bride* should be doing?" He paused, but she didn't dare reply. There were too many words in her head, but certainly none that would help her. "Dear God!" he roared.

He turned away from her in disgust and strode a few paces, so angry, so disgusted. The one thing he had entrusted to her and she hadn't even *tried*. It had been the perfect opportunity to show what she was made of. Theirs would be the wedding of the century . . . and yet she was happy to pass it off to a *company* to do everything?

"You will cancel any agreement you have with this company right now. I don't care how, just do it without making a bigger mess of this than you already have. You will tell them you have decided to take a more central role in the organisation and no longer need them. Then you will use the people I put at your disposal for the intended purpose and arrange everything *yourself*! From the menu to the colour of the waiters' jackets. *Have I made myself clear*?"

His rage was wondrous and wholly terrifying, and she jumped at his voice, genuinely afraid of it and his temper, all the poise he credited her with gone as she trembled before him.

"*Answer me*!"

She jumped again, glad there was a coffee table and a sofa between them. He looked like he might wring her neck!

"Yes, Daryl, I understand."

He fumed as he regarded her, noting the trembling in her body and her voice, hating her for having failed him, for her weakness of character. He had thought she was better than that, and he detested being proved wrong. He had made a decision about her too quickly, obviously, and now he was paying the price.

"I hope to God you do."

He strode from the room without looking back.

She wandered trembling in the opposite direction, going to the room she had taken as her own private lounge space where she could be without disturbing him, realising that was often a better place to be than irritating him with her presence. She felt a sob rise in her throat, a sob she had held in for so long. She wanted to please him, however he wanted, if that was the price to pay for the prize he represented, but it was so hard! She didn't want to give up or admit defeat, but sometimes he . . . he was impossible.

Tears fell now, and she knew her make-up was going to suffer unless she stopped, which would make her feel even worse if he came in and saw her, knowing that her own beauty was not as flawless as his. He so naturally beautiful. And so much smarter. He had so many more achievements, and was wiser in ways she would never be, and combined with everything else . . . well, she would never win, because she knew he had the measure of her, knew he found her wanting.

And it felt so futile.

Rachel sat down on the sofa wearily and ordered the call to the company, and someone picked up on the second ring, even though it was a Sunday. Reining in the emotion, she explained the situation, the change of plan, and was glad when she could disconnect the call, not happy that she was taking the opportunity away from them to organise such a momentous event.

"Rachel?"

She looked around in wild hope that it was Daryl coming to apologise; it died as swiftly as it had arisen when she saw Harvey's head poke around the door. He saw her tears and took a few steps into the room.

"Rachel, you're crying." It was so matter-of-factly said, and he swayed slightly. Then she smelt the alcohol. But at least he was sympathetic. At least he wasn't spitting fire at her. "What is the matter?"

"Oh, I just . . . I upset Daryl. I did something and it made him so angry, and I didn't mean to . . . of course I didn't mean to."

"Of course not."

He came a little closer and leaned on the edge of the sofa arm, his handsome face kindly and such a contrast to the impersonal treatment she had just received from her apparent nearest and dearest. It made her want to weep more. He was high on the euphoria of good news and drink, and a soft touch with lovely females – especially tearful, lovely females – and he placed a hand on her shoulder, giving it a squeeze.

"Nothing I do seems to please him, and I try so hard but . . ." She waved a hand in mute frustration, uncaring of the tears that fell. "He doesn't even kiss me for Christ's sake, and we're meant to be getting married!"

She let some of her deep-seated anger out, and her voice sounded harsh even to her own ears, but the release of saying it feeling good nonetheless. She was surprised to feel his gentle hand move to her cheek.

"Who wouldn't want to kiss you?" he said softly.

She looked up at Harvey's kind eyes, and then he moved, sat next to her, dropping himself heavily on the sofa as an almost-drunk person would do.

"Daryl is just Daryl, Rachel. There's no one like him in the whole world. He's brilliant in so many ways, but he's not emotional. You just have to accept it."

It was brotherly advice, but she wasn't in the mood for brotherly consolation. Her eyes lowered from his and looked at his lips, her whole body and mind rebelling against the strictures and shame loaded onto her over the past few weeks, and she closed her eyes as she leaned forward, closing the gap between them. She wanted more. She wanted comfort, solace. She wanted this man to want her, to make her feel less than worthless as Daryl did. She kissed him, and he responded, but then cried, "Rachel! We can't!"

Harvey leaned away from her, tried to stand up, but she wasn't going to take no for an answer. She moved quickly to straddle him, flexing her hips, pressing into him as she kissed him again.

"Rachel, we *can't*! You know Daryl is here! He might *hear us*!" Harvey groaned, horribly aroused, the alcohol blurring the moral issue from the practical.

They heard a door open and shut and then silence. Both were still, her hand on his face, another arm around his neck, her body pushed up against his. Their eyes met. She didn't care if he was a bit drunk; she just wanted him to want her. Wanted this man to treat her like a woman, not just a toy. She unbuttoned and pulled off her tailored shirt and unclipped her bra, a hand going to delve in between his legs, where she discovered that even if he wasn't moving, he was certainly reacting.

"He'll never know," she whispered in his ear, like the snake to Eve in the Garden of Eden.

He felt his vague resistance falter. Male instinct was over-riding all the thoughts he had had about walking away and . . . my God she had beautiful breasts. His lips found her right nipple and she sighed as she cradled his head to her chest, her fingers running through his hair. Hands ran up her back and down again over her buttocks – kinder hands, hands that praised her curves rather than tested them for faults – and hers went to his shirt and jacket, and in a frenzy of fumbling hands and desperate kisses, Harvey surrendered as she removed his clothes. But Harvey wasn't satisfied with letting a woman take such control. He pushed her off and sat her down. Pulling her forward, he knelt between her legs, momentarily lost in the hot wetness of her arousal as his mouth teased her, before moving to kiss her neck, her lips, and then unable to wait a moment longer, he pushed into her and she emitted a low groan. But then she took control again, and this time he let her as she pushed him away and onto his back on the sofa, mounting and lowering herself onto him, riding him until she collapsed onto to his chest, both of them gasping.

When he wobbled up off the sofa sometime later – had they fallen asleep? – to try and put his clothes back on, his brain horribly fuzzed and his body telling him all sorts of things he only half-believed, he found hands wrapping themselves around him again and he turned and looked at her. Saw her lips parted in wantonness, beckoning him once more, her dark eyes enticing him closer, and he picked her up as he kissed her and her legs wrapped around his hips. He walked them back until they hit the wall and the force stole her breath and a small shriek of delight filled the room. She clung to him as she bit his neck, encouraging him as he entered her, urgently, harder this time as he sobered up. She loved the way he wanted her with a desire and passion she had not felt from Daryl, loved the freedom of pure emotion it released in her. Daryl was good, of that there was no doubt, but it was all calculated, and he did not give to her or enjoy her with sheer abandon. She had discovered that despite hoping otherwise, there was always distance between them, even skin to skin.

Finally, her desperate cry of ecstasy still in his ears, Harvey set her down, the intensity of the emotion having cleared his head somewhat. He looked at her, at her beautiful body, from the fine mahogany tresses and those lips down to her full breasts and slender waist. His best friend's fiancée and he had just fucked her twice in less than an hour. And his best friend wasn't just anyone . . . he just happened to be one of the most influential men on the planet. He knew how much this marriage meant to Daryl, at least from a practical side of things and, in a sense, an emotional one too. Knew his friend craved a partner to stand beside him to lessen the loneliness that he didn't even dare fully acknowledge to himself. Oh God. His best friend. He'd never dreamt of betraying him like this. Dear God, he had been really drunk, and he was now in seriously deep shit.

Rachel noticed his look, the way he stood still and stared at her, as if seeing her for the first time despite what they'd done. Reality was catching up with the thundering inevitability of a runaway train. She didn't know what to say. She could see he regretted it. Could see him adding everything together . . . and the result wasn't good. His was not the satisfied look of a lover.

"You can't tell Daryl. It was an accident. You know how much it will upset him." Her voice was low and husky.

Harvey picked up his clothes, pulled them on hurriedly, and with enough abruptness to indicate that any attempt at stopping him or talking wouldn't do any good. And then he left without putting his jacket back on, and without looking at her again.

She sank back onto the sofa that bore the musky scent of lust, the invisible reminder of her ill-advised moment of madness. What had she just done? Surely Harvey wouldn't tell him? If he did, Daryl would kill them both.

DARYL WASN'T ALL that pleased. It was Monday, and he hadn't really enjoyed his weekend. He was having doubts about his intended bride, and to complicate things further, everything that he'd done for the past five weeks that had been directed at building her up, giving her excellent press coverage, making them a 'couple', spending enough money to raise eyebrows towards hairlines to ensure everyone knew how serious he was about marriage, seemed to have been . . . well, now . . . now he wasn't at all sure. He was sat in the limo that was taking him home from another exclusive restaurant where he had just toasted a rather exciting deal. The deal was for the broadcasting rights that would mean all revenues from downloads and viewings for most of the western world were his – and because he was rich enough to have the satellites, the technology and the infrastructure that made this a reality, there was no way it could fail. He was communications god of the world; even China and Russia were willing to do business. It would mean billions in revenue for as long as there was enough on air to tempt people to part with their money to view . . .

He knew he'd needed a meeting with his entertainment committee to start making that happen, however, because for a global audience of almost seven billion people, there really wasn't enough on offer. At least, not enough *good* material. There were soaps, sports events and some documentaries, but the music and film world had struggled somewhat, and almost didn't know where to go with all the new technology, plus no real talent had shone through in recent times. The pool of 'celebrities' was waning too, and nothing felt quite like the last three decades of the twentieth century, the heyday of entertainment.

And there were obviously the effects of recession in some countries, meaning people were fearful of a repeat and cautious about how they spent their money. Such things naturally re-ordered priorities in people's lives, as well as opportunities available. The contract signed only hours ago was almost as big as the contract he had renewed last Friday with the US Government, Canada, and some other territories for surveillance and security, both to be continued and upgraded. His was acknowledged as the best, and those who didn't want his involvement had to pay for the information to make their own versions. Despite being a business genius, his original strengths had been computer software, and it was because of this that computers were what they were now. And having made his talent clear with software from when he was just sixteen, let alone at Harvard, he had been helped along the way by the limitless money he could use on testing and research.

When this was combined with his lifelong love of photography, he had made a breakthrough in camera technology to create smart cameras – ones that could obey complex sets of in-program instructions and operate independently, and at the same time data-stream the information moment by moment in the picture, much like the fantastic ideas used in sci-fi films of the past. But the reality was even better.

Will anything ever be enough? he pondered, anticipating the revenue growth from the contracts. *Will I ever stop? Let myself relax? Do something I want to do?* But what was the point when he ended up doing most things alone anyway? Harvey and his bachelor group of roués and rich boys had made it big like he had, albeit more modestly, but they weren't really the social company he wanted all the time.

He had thought marrying would make a difference, but still no. Now he was not enamoured with the idea at all, and Rachel was proving more of an irritation than anything else. Was he going mad? Was he being too harsh on her? He had warned her repeatedly what he did and did not like; what he would expect and wouldn't tolerate. He'd kept it very simple – or tried to – but she just didn't seem to get it somehow.

In public, she was fine. She simpered and smiled and clung to his arm with suitable convincingness, and said the right things to the press – with a little coaching. And she was adequately beautiful for them to make a convincing couple, for her to be a good child-bearer. He had already had her checked and she was perfectly fertile: her children would be fine specimens to carry on his name. But in private? She did not excite him in any way, nor interest him – not even close. She satisfied at best and irritated at worst. He had thought her the type of woman who would, upon closer examination and encouragement, blossom rather than stagnate.

And as for her passing on the party and wedding organisation to a company . . . he could still feel the stir of anger in his mind just remembering it. But he wasn't sure if he was more annoyed that he had been told about the party arrangements she had delegated, or relieved he had found out before it was too late. He sighed, hoped that tonight she'd just leave him alone and not pester him. At least he had already eaten so had no reason to sit down for dinner with her and endure her frivolous chatter about nothing. All she seemed to talk about was herself, her girlfriend's latest falling out with her boyfriend, or what her mother was saying about them being a couple and how excited she was. He wasn't sure how much more he could take.

The car pulled up and he waited until the door opened before moving.

"Good night, Mr Blackmoor."

"Night, Geoffrey."

He was so tired of speaking. Using words to further his business, to charm, to smooth the way, to appear so courteous and professional. What would he give, he wondered, to have an evening with a beer, a steak and a football match? Why didn't he ever make it happen? Was he afraid even that would be a disappointment, and he'd be left feeling even more alone if he indulged his dream evening? *Or* that he'd enjoy it too much and wouldn't be able to get back to being Mr Serious?

He strode through the lobby, nodding to the desk clerks vaguely but without paying attention. Mac was walking by his side, his silent shadow, and they entered the lift, they were joined by two more security guards, one on either side, who remained still as the doors closed. Daryl knew there would be two more outside the lift when they exited on the 89th floor.

"I've just been told, Mr Blackmoor, that Harvey is in the apartment below waiting to see you. Shall I ask for him to be brought up?" Mac said.

No one went into Daryl's apartments or houses without Daryl himself being there. Except security and staff. And even then, there were grades of access. He kept the whole floor beneath as a mirror apartment so if anyone needed to stay they could do so.

"Yes. Did he say why he had come? I wasn't expecting him."

Daryl scowled, wondering why Harvey would come unannounced; he wasn't meant to be seeing him until next Saturday for a casino trip, but tonight? Monday?

"No, sir. Perhaps he forgot something when he visited yesterday afternoon. He was very drunk when he arrived, if I may say so. I let him in because you were there, and he was most insistent. But he left after you. Did you not see him, sir?"

"Yesterday? No. Not at all. How strange."

Daryl scowled a little more. Harvey visited yesterday, very drunk? He had left the apartment after the incident with Rachel, gone to one of his clubs for a quiet brandy and a bite to eat. He had then gone to the office to work, not wanting to see her nor, in fact, remember her at all for that short while when he could concentrate on something else entirely. When he'd returned home, she was in bed, and he was glad he'd had no reason to see or speak to her. And he had purposefully left that morning before she was awake, not trusting himself to keep his temper. He hadn't wished to start his day badly by being reminded of her failing him. But he had got to the office in a foul mood anyway, wondering why he should be the one avoiding being at home when it was his home!

"You will let me know if there is anything I need to do, sir?"

Daryl nodded, understanding the covert offer, knowing that Mac's loyalty was unquestionable, that he would do whatever asked of him – including dealing with Daryl's friends in whatever way necessary.

"Is she there?" *Please say no.*

"No, sir, she's on the way back from Lexington Avenue; she's been shopping."

"Again?"

"So it seems."

Daryl sighed. What on earth could she need now? Had he not bought her so much already? Was nothing ever enough for her? He wandered over to the sideboard behind one of the sofas and poured himself a brandy, rolling his shoulders alternately to try and ease the tension.

A door opened and closed, then footsteps – fairly swift and decisive – along the polished wood floor.

"Daryl?"

"Harvey. What an unexpected surprise! How did you know I was in dire need of a friend to brighten my Monday for me?"

Daryl forced a smile of welcome, despite his fatigue. He saw Harvey's face was tense and showed no friendliness in greeting; instead it was worried, anxious. What on earth could have happened to make it so? Harvey was one of the most laid back, carefree individuals he'd ever known. They had once been in a car accident, as teenagers, and Harvey's only comment was that he 'hadn't expected that'. And then he had brushed the glass off his lap got out of the car, and carried on chatting as if nothing had happened.

Harvey had stopped a few metres away, not coming forward to offer his hand in greeting.

"Harvey, are you alright? You look like you've had a worse start to the week than I have."

Daryl gestured with a hand to the sofa; but Harvey's distress only seemed to increase. His hand went through his hair and rubbed the top of his head, before slapping back down against his leg.

This was very odd. Had Harvey lost a load at the gaming tables and didn't want to tell his father?

"You won't want me to sit down once I've told you what I have to tell you."

Oh, God! He'd done all kinds of wicked things in his life – treated people far worse than they should have been, used and discarded women with reckless insensitive abandon, and ruthlessly approached his business interests – but never, *never* had he betrayed his friends. And certainly not Daryl, who he considered his closest friend. For despite him being so busy, and often reserved, they'd never not shared something important. Daryl trusted Harvey as much as he trusted anyone. And he knew that trust would at worst be lost, or at least severely damaged by his confession. Knew how utterly he had let his friend down. He felt sick. He hadn't meant to. What a terrible mistake he had made.

"Harvey, please tell me what is upsetting you so much. I count you as my best friend. What is it that is so bad it's making you so hesitant to speak?"

"Don't say that!" Harvey told him in forcefully, feeling guilt gnaw at his insides like acid. Daryl's words were making it all so much worse. "Oh, God, if only I hadn't been so drunk!"

He put a hand over his face for a few moments to compose himself, and Daryl immediately felt a horrible sinking sensation in his gut. He very rarely felt that, because so rarely did anything ever go wrong, because he organised and controlled everything so well.

Harvey's hand dropped away from his face and he held both out in appeal. Then said, "Daryl, I know you're going to hate me, so before I tell you what I have to tell you, I want you to know I'm more sorry than I can ever say. I haven't slept or felt a moment's peace since it happened and I-I never meant . . . God knows I never intended . . . I could barely stand up straight . . . but I'd never forgive myself if I didn't tell you. You have an absolute right to know because I know you'd want to, considering the circumstances."

"That is one hell of a riddle, Harvey. Please, just tell me."

Daryl's grip on his glass tightened and he felt his own emotions tense in anticipation, Harvey's desperate and acute unhappiness infectious.

"Yesterday, I was as drunk as a lord. I'd just found out I was an uncle – my sister, you might remember, was expecting and she had the baby, her first, and I was so overjoyed. I came over to see you, as I knew you'd said you'd be home on Sunday. I was going to suggest we go and wet the baby's head with a trip to a club or whatever, when I heard Rachel crying. I only poked my head around the door for a moment, and I asked her what was wrong. She was weeping and very upset and said she'd made you angry, even though she hadn't meant to, and I sat on the sofa and tried to tell her something sensible – something about you just being you and . . ."

Harvey looked up at the ceiling, trying to get his brain to remember all the details. Then said, "Well, I told her that you just had high expectations." He looked at the floor and then his eyes rose to meet Daryl's, refusing to cower away from the truth of his crimes any longer. "Then she leaned over and kissed me. I tried to push her away, but she got on top of me even though I said no. And I heard the door shut – that must have been you leaving – and then she took her top and bra off. I-I'm sorry, Daryl. Sweet Jesus, I'm a fool! I-I don't remember all that much, except she was hungry for it. Very hungry. She wouldn't take no for an answer, and she made sure she got what she wanted. I . . ."

Harvey's misery was all too plain. His commentary ground to a halt.

Daryl felt fury blossom. Cold, hard fury and disgust. But not with his friend. His brave friend who had been unfortunate enough to be drunk, but who had been honest with him – unlike his lovely bride-to-be. He then realised that part of Harvey's confession was because he had doubts about him marrying such a woman, who hadn't even got a ring on her finger before she'd managed to betray him, and in his own home. He was clearly worried, on Daryl's behalf, and despite the fact that it was he who had been part of that betrayal, that he was about to marry the wrong woman . . . and he couldn't agree more.

"How many times?" Daryl's voice was surprisingly calm.

Harvey's eyes snapped back to his. "Does it matter?"

"I want to know."

"Twice, as far as I remember. She'd probably have gone again, but I came to my senses and realised what the hell I was doing, so I pulled my clothes on and left."

"And she?"

"She told me not to tell you, that it was an 'accident', that you'd be angry – and I know you are. I know you have every reason to throw me off the roof, but I can't live with knowing what I did. I can't keep the truth from you, and stand there as your best man and let you marry her knowing–"

Daryl could not bear to see his best friend tearing himself apart any longer. He knew exactly what Harvey was like when he was drunk: he simply didn't have the self-control to resist a beautiful woman, especially one who had taken her clothes off and was sitting on top of him.

"Harvey, please just stop for a minute. You're going to go grey and we're still in our twenties."

Harvey stopped trying to find the words, glad that Daryl had interrupted. He stared at his friend in amazement. Where was the rage? Where was the blizzard of hate at his betrayal? Why hadn't he been punched yet?

Daryl pondered for a moment, analysing his feelings. He took a swig of his drink . . . and realised fate had kindly given him the answer he had been looking for, and a perfect reason to end everything. He turned back to the sideboard.

"I'm not angry with you, Harvey. I know you, and I know you would not intentionally seduce my fiancée, and certainly not in my own apartment. You couldn't have known she'd be here. I know from Mac how drunk you were. . ."

Daryl paused and turned around with another glass of brandy in his hand, his own topped up, and took a few steps towards his friend – whose face was drained of all colour. He offered the glass, leaving it for Harvey to come the last few metres and take it; the olive branch of friendship that he had to come halfway to receive. And he did, after a moment of stunned silence. He stepped forward into the proximity of the friend he thought he would lose forever.

"Here's a toast to the end of my engagement, and a long and happy life as a bachelor." Daryl raised his glass and Harvey matched him; then they both swallowed the measure down in one, as they had as boys and then young men. "Unless a miracle happens and I find a goddess – with both brains and looks – who just happens to be single," he added with a rueful smile.

Harvey let himself return the smile, and was so relieved he collapsed onto the arm of the chair.

"Christ, Daryl, you know how scared I was coming here to tell you?" He shook his head, still unable to believe his good fortune: he still had his best friend and he wasn't going to get thrown off the roof. "Oh, God, I never want to feel like that again in my whole life," he groaned.

"Don't go so far as to say you'll never get as drunk again, because you know you will."

Daryl saw the remaining distress in Harvey's face and reached out a hand to grasp his shoulder so he would know he meant what he said. But Daryl's easy banter and gesture was not doing the trick. Harvey's emotions had been far too turbulent to respond to such simple comfort, and he still looked distinctly uncomfortable.

"Harvey," Daryl then said, "the fault doesn't lie with you, and you have proved yourself by coming here and not lying, and not pretending –

as my fiancée has done – but to tell me the truth, despite anticipating my being very angry. I forgive you, truly."

"You don't know. . ." Harvey began to say, relief slumping his shoulders as he let the emotion go. He brought his hand up to cover Daryl's, his grip just as firm as his friend's. It was a perfect moment of peace enjoyed by both. And a very rare moment in a desert of meaningless physical contact for Mr Blackmoor. Not all was lost; in fact, amazingly, they had discovered something far more precious about themselves.

They heard a door open and the clip-clop of heels, as well as another set of feet, but quieter, and Daryl saw Rachel emerge from the corridor, followed by a maid carrying her purchases in their designer bags – who dropped the bags in Rachel's room and then scuttled off. She had been going at a brisk pace but came up short when she saw them, and the uniting gesture they had momentarily shared broke apart slowly, and both of them stiffened at the sight of her.

Daryl saw Rachel's eyes move from one to the other as she was confronted with her guilt, and he whom she had betrayed; it was something he wanted her to feel every second of.

"Sweetheart."

Daryl put his glass down and moved towards her slowly, watching her trying to work out why Harvey was there, what he might have said, clearly alarmed and confused. Why was he being nice? He never called her 'sweetheart' . . .

"You went shopping?"

"Yes." Her brain was too busy fumbling over facts and possibilities to think of anything else to say.

"Will you not say hello to Harvey?"

Her eyes fixed on Harvey, her partner in crime. Daryl stopped close to her, close enough to touch her; but he didn't. Didn't want to. Except perhaps to strangle her, which would be far too much bother to deal with afterwards.

"Hi, Harvey." It was a wooden reply, automatic, the horrible dread that was creeping over her whole body making her want to turn and run; but she knew she had to stay and face her fate.

"Harvey is my best friend, my sweet, could you not be a little nicer to him? For me? You know, maybe . . ." – he pretended to think – "a kiss? Or maybe you could just pull your clothes off and fuck him a few times. Like you did yesterday. What do you say? Maybe fit me in afterwards, perhaps? If you're not too tired, that is? . . ."

Red-hot shame scorched her face, and tears sprang into her eyes. She heard the scorn, the reined-in fury of his voice. She closed her eyes and felt the wetness of instant tears streak down her face, suddenly feeling utterly naked, as if she were not clothed in the cashmere dress and heels most women would give their right arm for, plus the tasteful amount of rather expensive jewellery.

"Is there anything you would like to tell me, Rachel?"

His voice was dangerously low next to her head, and she opened her eyes, looked at Harvey with eyes that begged him for help; but he just looked back, face as hard and unyielding as Daryl's.

"I'm sorry," she whispered. With no defence to hide behind, she might as well apologise, humble herself however he wanted her to . . . it might appease him . . .

"Sorry you fucked my best friend while he was too drunk to refuse you? Sorry you betrayed me in my own apartment? Sorry you thought you could get away with it? Or sorry that you are so gutless you could not tell me? Please, *be more specific*." Hard granite-carved words.

"I'm sorry for everything," she replied, her voice soft, tortured, in stark contrast to his.

"I'm pleased you had such a lovely afternoon and played hostess to my friend so very thoroughly. But I should have known you were untrustworthy considering you lied to me so easily in the beginning . . . very fine breasts, Rachel . . . how much did your father pay for them? Thirty thousand, wasn't it? An investment for your future to help net you a wealthy husband?"

He knew real flesh when he felt it. He'd re-checked his files, and discovering that she had lied had been a sad moment . . . but he had put it down to vanity. He'd never thought it indicated more.

"Daryl, please–"

"Do *not* say my name!"

The blast of rage hit her like a bucket of ice and she flinched.

"You thought you could take on my name as my wife? You are not remotely suited to such a position. You have proven that countless times already, regardless of yesterday! I blame myself for having been so poor a judge."

He did not unbend a fraction, even as she stepped back, unable to bear his anger so close to her. Everything about him was so forbidding that she could barely breathe she was so afraid. He reached out and took her left hand, took the ring from her.

"To think I was willing to give you so much, and this is how you repay me?"

He had taken the magnificent engagement ring from her finger! She looked at him as the shock dawned through the haze of fear and distress, and she realised with horrible clarity that the situation was utterly irredeemable. *This was it.*

"You were little more than nothing before I elevated your status, and just as quickly you will descend to where you belong. You will go back to your father's estate in Texas and stay there for a very long time. You will never try to contact me, never try to see me, and certainly never say anything negative about me to the press, because I will not hesitate to have you dragged through enough mud to keep a herd of pigs happy! Have I made myself clear?"

She nodded, her shame only increasing as she realised her fate. The power that made him so great also made him dangerous, and that which had tempted her now terrified her. She didn't know what to say. Her instincts told her it would be best not to say anything at all, as much as her mind screamed to try to appease him; but if she had learned anything, it was that Daryl did not change his mind.

"Mac!"

The bodyguard appeared within moments, with another.

"Have Miss Huntley escorted downstairs. Put her on a plane to Texas. Have anything of hers sent after her, and anything I have bought for her I will decide what to do with. See to it that someone observes her to make sure she keeps her mouth shut, and call my press secretary and have him meet me at my office at 7am tomorrow."

"Yes, Mr Blackmoor, sir."

Mac took Rachel's arm and drew her away; she went without resisting.

The front door closed.

The two men stood in silence. One trying to let go of his anger; the other knowing to keep quiet while he did so. Harvey hadn't spoken a single word during Daryl's confrontation with Rachel, and he didn't intend to now.

Then Daryl broke the silence. "It's a small comfort."

He looked around at Harvey, who said, "You'd never have had that kind of problem with a race horse." He could not believe he was attempting a joke, but saw Daryl smiling, willingly, at the reminder of their previous conversation.

"Might I suggest *you* never try and marry any of them either? Frankly, I don't want to think about marriage for a while," Daryl replied. "Although it'll be a real headache for my lawyers if I never have an heir, but it's about time they earned their fees."

Daryl suddenly felt so much better. It was over! No more dreading coming home, or inane conversations, or crushing disappointments.

"Don't give up, old chap, there's plenty of time yet."

"Hmmm, well, I shall wait to be convinced." Daryl slapped his friend on the shoulder. "Do you want a beer? Another brandy? Cigar? Come on, it's a nice night, let's go on the roof and talk like we used to before we grew up and life took over."

Harvey didn't argue; it was good plan. Generally, all of Daryl's plans were good, or exceptional. His only failure had been his plan on how to acquire a wife. Perhaps next time . . .

THE GIRL COULD NOT believe how much had happened in four weeks; four weeks of working and then going back to work on her 'home', having accumulated a supply of blankets and pillows from thrift shops on the edge of the city, carefully getting all her purchases back to her nest without anyone seeing and setting up camp. She had torches and a supply of batteries; but didn't have quite enough money to get one of the glow-lights that would give her a powered light source yet. Food storage was basic because she had no fridge, but at least there was food. And she bought a bottle of milk a day when at work, knowing from having tried to keep it overnight that nothing survived the heat of the daytime, even in the shade.

One of the things she had been worried about was water for the toilet and bathing, but she discovered – when she eventually managed to turn the seized-up tap on – that no one had turned the mains supply off, and after a loud spout of discoloured water, she saw that it was clear and clean, although freezing.

She'd had to get used to the dark sleeping outside, or wherever she could, and to conquer her fear of the shadows and shapes in the blackness, but she still didn't like it. Afraid something – someone – would find her, she barricaded the door every night, still telling herself she was on an adventure . . . but all the imaginary circumstances she concocted didn't take away the fear, nor did it stop the nightmares that haunted her sleep.

Which was how she ended up dancing to the music on the cassette tape. Not only was it a distraction, but she loved to dance, and had since she was tiny. She'd gone to every class she could at school, but this. . . this was different! And not just because of the music she was now exploring, but because she could do whatever she liked! She found she could bend, stretch, turn . . . and have endless hours of fun repeating the moves until she knew them by heart, pretending her mother was there watching her, encouraging her as she always had, remembering the stories she had told her of her own love of dancing as a child.

To her delight she had found a thrift shop not far from the grocery store – with the help of Janice's directions – and found a portable CD player for $2, which she had worked out played thin flat discs of music. She bought some of these CDs as well, for 50 cents each, as apparently cassettes were very out of date! She discovered music from twenty years ago. Christina Aguilera's *Stripped* album made her lie on the floor and cry long and hard, especially when she listened to 'I'm OK' and 'Voice

Within'; had this girl known despair and climbed out of the hole too? For the first time since the day she had started running, she finally let out some of the emotions she had ignored. And in the dark shadowy walls of the abandoned hotel, the girl discovered a new passion she had never anticipated: not just dancing, but singing, learning every line and nuance of the songs, breathing every second of the music that lifted her soul and helped her carry on. Hours spent away from work saw her time divided between setting up home and her music, wanting to do nothing else as it made her feel so much less lonely. And out of the ragged remains of a small broken child who had refused to give up, began to emerge something wonderful: an energy, a force that she had never felt before.

So it was that, humming to the tunes in her head, she went to work one sunny morning – every morning had been sunny so far – and greeted Janice in the same way she always did: a smile as she got called 'doll face', got told she looked far too happy for someone coming to work at 7am every day (her hours had doubled to four hours a day), and set about her stocking up the shelves.

Carl had trained her on the till, but it was tacitly agreed Janice would stay on the till until she left to have the baby, and April would look after stock. April didn't mind in the least as it gave her time to hum and choreograph more songs, to anticipate going home to sing, and perhaps start cleaning the large ballroom with mirrors and dusty chandeliers she had discovered where she could dance to her heart's content in lots of space. She was so busy in her happy thoughts, that she was unaware of the threat in their midst.

After the pre-9am rush, things had quietened down, and Janice had grabbed a coffee and started reading her magazine, as she usually did, relaxed and contented, with one hand resting on her bump that so far hadn't decided to make its entrance into the world. Which was why when the two men all in black with balaclavas on came in suddenly and pointed guns in her face, she shrieked and spilt the coffee everywhere, hot liquid hitting her hand and making her yelp.

"Give us the money in the till, bitch! Now!"

She was so horrified that she just stared for a moment, her heart hammering in her chest, her brain in shock; then one of the guns went from pointing at her chest to pointing at her unborn baby.

"Come on! Or we'll shoot! Whether it's you or the baby you'll just have to find out, now *give us the money*!"

The muzzle jabbed at her swollen abdomen. The violence and the threat were too much, the sudden ferociousness of the attack blood-chilling, and she cried, "I can't open the till unless there's a sale rung through!" desperately trying to think, but totally unprepared for what was happening. Her thoughts were centred on her baby, like a mantra – *the baby, the baby* – and she could barely focus on anything else, both arms coming around to cradle her bump.

"Then scan something!" he yelled at her.

"Ow!"

The second of them, who had kept an eye out for other customers and glanced out of the door every few seconds, put a hand up to his head and tested his hair, expecting to see blood.

"What the fuck is it?" the first said to him.

Janice, having seen the can of green beans come sailing over the display aisle and smack him on the head – it had been an excellent shot – suddenly remembered April. *Please don't let her do anything stupid . . .*

"Something hit my head!"

"How can something just *hit your head*?"

He got his answer when two more missiles, in quick succession, hit them each on the head, arms too late to protect themselves because they had been too busy arguing. If Janice hadn't been so petrified that her already under-pressure bladder might give way in terror, she would have laughed it was so comical. The cans made a dull thud when they hit the floor, and the men looked down and read the labels – green beans and processed peas! – and decided that being attacked by cans of vegetables was not how they thought their robbery should go down.

"I'll go sort them out. You get the money."

The man who had been hit twice strode off towards the back of the store, readying his gun, and after turning a few times to look through the aisles – knowing there were no other customers – he was rather surprised to find a skinny blonde girl waiting for him, eyes angry and body tense. He laughed at her and lowered his weapon. Just a kid. But stupid thing to do. Shouldn't have got involved.

"You shouldn't have done that," he told her, stepping forward and slinging his gun strap over his shoulder, intending to smack her around a bit then leave. No point wasting bullets on her or making noise that might alert someone and bring the cops down on them.

"You shouldn't have come here waving a gun," she told him promptly.

She braced herself, not sure quite what she was planning to do, but sure as hell determined that she wasn't going to leave Janice on her own. They had no right to threaten her and the baby. Plus, she hated guns, and hated the ugly balaclava on his face.

The man didn't like her attitude and swung at her. He missed as she moved away, then blocked the next swipe, then the next. Slightly flummoxed he paused . . . and she kicked him hard in the groin, and then in the head when he bent over with a yelp. *What the fuck*? He half stood up, shaking his head, but she was ready: two punches and an elbow in his gut. Then she grabbed his head and shoulder and hauled him over her back, just like Mr Gibson had showed her, using his own weight and momentum against him. His back slammed into the floor and he groaned as she looked down at him, breathing hard. She then bent down and swiped his gun. Just like that.

Anger and determination still guided her actions and she reached out an arm and swept a host of condiment bottles off the shelf next to her. They landed around him and on him, some of them smashing, and he flinched, bringing his hands up to protect his head.-

"Matt? Matt! What's happening, dude? Talk to me! What the fuck is going on?" the guy at the till yelled, his gun still on Janice.

She started back along the aisle, bringing the gun up in both of her hands. It wasn't like the gun the cops had used, this one had two handles. But it looked simple enough to use. Although tall for her age, she was just short enough to walk to the end of the aisle without having to duck, her trainers soundless on the smooth floor. She used the mirror in the shop window to watch him, contemplating her next move. If she ran out from the cover of the aisle nearest, he'd have time to shoot her, but if she came from a direction closer and where he wasn't expecting . . .

She picked up a couple of bags of nuts from the shelf and backed up a dozen paces, holding the gun in her right hand, the bag in her left . . . and she started running, not sure if this was going to work. She tossed the bags so they landed and slid out into the open as a distraction as she jumped, grabbed the top of the aisle shelving and leapt over, landed, rolled, and came up to point the gun straight at his chest.

"Drop it," she spat out, not realising she was so angry until she was there, facing him. Hating him for attacking a defenceless woman. Just like her father against her mother. It wasn't fair, and all the emotion from the times she had been forced to wait until the front door slammed before she could go to her mother's aid, all the times she'd longed to fight back, came to the fore and she let it. "You want me to say it again?" she growled, stepping a little closer.

He dropped the gun, exactly like the one she was holding – or rather that his 'mate' had been holding – and she kicked it away so that it skidded under the freezer that held ice cream.

"Now put your hands up and keep them up."

Janice didn't make a sound. Didn't dare. Her eyes wide.

"You dare come in here and threaten a pregnant woman, you sick fuck." The disgust in her voice clearly surprised him. He was obviously not expecting such language or such condemnation from a mere girl. "Put your hands up."

He did, watching the gun still pointed at his chest, and Janice backed away from the counter.

"I'll call the police," Janice said.

She sounded relieved, but the girl did not want the police. "Call Carl first." Anything to avoid the police.

Where's the other guy?

She didn't dare turn around, and flicked her eyes to the overhead security mirror in the corner: good, he'd stayed where he was on the floor, unarmed and alarmed at the turn events – but not enough to do anything about it. This girl was bloody scary, and he didn't want to be shot with his own gun. Perhaps best to try and creep away out of the door unnoticed instead . . .

Shaken and upset, Janice did as she said, her fingers shaking as she pressed in the commands. A few seconds passed and she cried, "I can't get an answer . . . I'll call the police!"

Oh shit.

Then nature stepped in.

"April!"

The girl looked at Janice's panicked face. "What?"

The guy with his hands held up in surrender looked at her too.

"My water just broke!"

Janice forgot the call, put the phone down and felt between her legs where the wetness was trickling down.

"*Now?*"

A nod.

The girl gritted her teeth. *Great. She's gonna have her baby. Right now. Think, think . . .*

"Call an ambulance, and then your boyfriend." *It might be a godsend.* "On your knees," she growled at the man still holding his hands up.

He paused, not liking the idea.

"Do it!"

He complied, and when he was down, she reached out quickly and pulled off his balaclava, revealing the face of a man with shaggy light brown hair, fair stubble over tanned cheeks and pale eyes, maybe twenty-six or twenty-seven. Old enough to know better. Old enough to get a job and not pull guns on innocent women. She could hear Janice talking on the phone. Now to get these guys out of here.

She put the gun against his neck, pushing his head up, her eyes intense, memorising every detail.

"I know your face, and I will not forget you. If you come to the shop again, or if I see you anywhere near me or Janice, I will finish what I started today . . . and I am a very good shot." An absolute blag: she was sure she would be. She pressed the gun a little harder into his throat, seeing his

Adam's apple bob as he swallowed in panic, his eyes on her, and she saw fear, the same fear he had inflicted on Janice. "Do you understand?" she demanded angrily.

A nod.

"Now get up and go to your friend. I will follow you and keep a gun on you all the way, just in case you decide to be stupid. Then you will pull his balaclava off so I can see his face too. Then you will both leave before I *change my mind* about letting you go. With Janice as a witness we could make a very good case for self-defence if anything should *happen to you*."

Her low voice was dangerous, and the confidence she had gave him no reason to doubt she meant every word she said.

She was worried he might try something, however, but a few shoves of the muzzle in his back and he went to his mate and removed his balaclava, revealing a slightly younger guy, with darker skin and dark eyes, black hair pressed against his thin face. She made sure she took a long look at him, her eyes boring into his as he was helped to his feet.

The girl watched them leave, trying as best they could to straighten up, to appear like two regular guys who'd been to the store for a soda.

She looked down at the gun. Unable to believe she was really holding it.

"April!"

Her thoughts came back to the moment in a split second, and she slid the gun under the freezer with the other one and went to Janice, helping her around the counter just as the ambulance arrived, and her boyfriend, and Carl.

There was a flurry of activity, and Janice was so busy gabbling at Carl trying to tell him what happened that the medics had a hard time getting her to concentrate on getting on the stretcher. April watched, rather dazed by what had just happened. Had she really just done that? Finally, the ambulance doors were shut and it drove away.

Carl turned to April. "Are you alright?"

"Yes, I'm fine."

She shook herself out of it, and as Carl turned to go to the back of the shop, she went to the ice cream freezer, got down on her hands and knees and pulled out the guns – just as Carl turned back to her. His jaw would have hit the floor if it could have stretched that far.

"Where should I put these?"

"April? Where the hell–?"

"I can explain."

"What in God's–?"

"I can explain."

"Put them in my office. I'll deal with them," he answered, utterly shocked, trying to sound like he wasn't, trying to be the boss he was meant to be. "April, what happened here?"

"You take them. I threw some cans of food around. I'll go tidy them up."

She walked to the front of the counter, where he was standing, put the guns down next to the till, picked the three tins of vegetables up off the floor and wandered off.

Carl shook his head in disbelief and shut the door to the store, changing the sign around to 'Closed.' He locked it, then went back to his office, passing a now unarmed April as he did so, picking up the guns on his way. He sat down to view the security tapes.

Twenty minutes later, after watching them three times, he got up and went out to find April generally tidying up, replacing many of the condiment bottles, and wiping up the slick of jalapeno relish and Ketchup that had splattered when the bottles had smashed.

"April."

She looked up, pausing, the blue cleaning cloth in her hand.

"April, I think you can go home now. You must be shaken up. I've seen what you did . . . pretty brave coming to help Janice and stopping them from taking any money. We both owe you." He held out his hand. "Give me the cloth, I'll finish up."

He saw her face cloud.

"You're sure? I'm not in trouble?"

Carl smiled slightly. "No, not at all."

"Are you going to report this to the police?" *Please, no . . .* She handed him the cloth and stood up, brushing her knees off. "I did my best to scare them. They won't come back."

"You suggested that Janice call Carl, not the police . . ."

Her face darkened further.

"Yes, I did."

He watched her. Watched her face become closed.

"No, I'm not going to call the police." Her relief was palpable; though she tried to hide it. "Get your things and I'll let you out. I think we can close for a few hours over lunch. I'll call Lucy and see if she'll come in this afternoon."

She nodded and went as she was told, slipping past him silently. *What a kid. But who was she?* He dropped the cloth, intending to go back to it. He went to the till.

"April." He held out a bunch of notes. She turned and looked at them and then at him. "It's the least I can do considering what you did today. You saved me a load of money, and saved Janice and her baby. I'm sure she'll thank you herself, but . . . you deserve this."

He held it closer to her, insisting as she hesitated. She took it tentatively. Was she being paid off and told never to come back?

"I wondered if you'd like some more hours?"

Her head came up sharply, relief and joy clear to see.

"Sure."

"Well, how about 6.30am to 4.30pm every day, and one day off a week – your choice. That sound OK?"

"Yes, thank you."

"You won't thank me in a few days; you'll be hating me for making you get up even earlier."

"I don't mind."

"Well, OK then. Go grab yourself a bottle of milk from the fridge and a bag of chips or something – on the house."

She smiled and raced back to the fridge, grabbed some chips, and then with one final look which he couldn't for the life of him decipher, she left.

She raced off home, wanting to feel safe and secure. Five minutes later she realised she didn't have a gun anymore . . . and there were two people out there who had every reason to come after her.

Time to set some security measures of her own.

IT WAS LATE and she couldn't sleep. She'd already danced for hours but still she couldn't lie down and get her mind to relax. It wasn't fear, wasn't that she couldn't get the thoughts of the two men out her head. She had largely forgotten them – which was a blessing – and besides, she reasoned she had every chance of being able to defend herself now. So what was it that was keeping her awake? And then she realised.

She looked out of the window and down at the dark ground, judging the distance to be the same as from her bathroom to the driveway *that night*. Dare she? Hadn't she wondered if she could? Hadn't she tried to understand the reason why she was alive and not dead over and over again, not a broken body outside the police station? Wouldn't the best way to find out be to . . . jump and see what happened? She already knew her reflexes were good – hadn't Mr Gibson told her so?

She tried to open it. It was a struggle, and it took some thumping and plenty of heaving, but stocking up shelves and carrying groceries was making her stronger. She climbed onto the sill, her legs dangling over the edge. Her stomach did a little flip. Was she really going to do this? *I need to know.*

She'd been watching the performers in the square. Street artists who were amazing in their costumes and face paints, the fire-eaters and sword-swallowers, tight rope walkers and acrobats, as well as the mimes and human statues. What if she could do something like that? Perhaps she could rope walk as well?

She took a breath, looked down into the dark, trying to judge the distance. She then braced herself on the edge of the sill and pushed, just like she had that night from the bathroom window. She tried to feel every moment, the fall, the drop, the air rushing through her hair, and she acknowledged the ground rushing up to greet her. It was so fast, but she wasn't scared. Instinctively, as if she knew what she was doing, she put her hands out, curling her body, and then she rolled and stood. Painless. Easy. She looked up to where she had jumped. That could have just been luck, right? Was it enough distance to really know?

She headed back into the building and went up an extra floor, running into the room above her own and, again, fighting the window open. This time when she climbed up on the sill, she crouched down with knees bent. She could do this. Somehow, she knew she could. Too curious to be a coward, she pushed off, launching herself into the air, half of her telling herself she was mad, the other…

Time seemed to slow. She curled her body round again, tight, like she did in gymnastics and when she had dived off the high boards at the swimming baths, noted the ground, uncurled, stretched out her hands and bent her arms in quick succession, ducking her head in and rolling.

She stood. Painless. Easy.

She looked up again.

She went in once more, running up more stairs, going to the next floor up of the six. She was on the fourth now, and when she got to the window, it looked one hell of a way down. After all the struggling, finally finding a job, finding this place to call home, was she really going to risk it all by jumping from here?

But what if she could? *I need to know.*

The window was strangely easy to open; if it had been a struggle like before she might have given up, but no, this was an open invitation. She climbed up once again, loving the feel of the warm Vegas wind on her skin, the calm of being poised on the edge. She calculated the fall. She would have time for . . . two rotations?

She looked at the sky, without warning silently praying to her mother, telling her that she loved her, and if she did break her neck she was sorry for anything she'd done she should be sorry for.

She leapt, channelling the energy through her legs like a spring so she flew out into the air, giving her the chance to fall properly, not just drop down the side of the building where she would have no space to turn.

Her body embraced the pull of gravity, curling in tight, knowing she turned once, twice; then she opened up, her arms were ready, and she touched down for the merest fraction before rolling twice and then standing, almost thrown by the momentum and the split-second realisation she had managed it. She crouched back down on the ground, the unkempt grass now a little trampled and squashed. She looked herself over, asking herself if she felt any pain?

No pain. Easy.

How was she doing this? Was she a freak? Was she actually dead and a ghost? She didn't *feel* dead. She went back inside to close all the windows, resisting the urge to jump again. What a discovery. *How high can I go*? Finally, she returned to her room and slept.

DARYL LEANED BACK in the bath, a huge sunken thing more styled on a jacuzzi – but there was a separate one of those. He was in his favourite Washington townhouse, and he was celebrating his birthday, which was why he had all his Cherries there to attend him. He had flown them all out from New York to accompany him while he sojourned in the capital for a month, trying to take it a little easier, despite the contradiction that he would be closer to the White House and inevitably called into yet more meetings.

He relaxed with a glass of champagne in his hand, female hands sliding over his shoulders in a thoroughly enjoyable massage . . . and there was a stream of black hair floating just below the surface of the water over his crotch. This was definitely how to enjoy one's birthday.

Last night had been very . . . interesting. He liked unfair sex ratios and being outnumbered in his bedroom. He had given them all a platinum pendant with his engraved initials, DB, as he was so often referred to. (Everyone knew who it referred to.) Far from deciding to stay out of the public eye after his diplomatically ended engagement – where both parties had had 'a change of heart'; though he'd had a few rumours started just to make sure he wasn't blamed – he had been utterly outrageous. He still smiled when he thought about how he'd turned up with a model in a bikini to a rather exclusive casino last week, where all the women were beautiful and just as well dressed – but dressed, not strutting around, mere wisps of fabric covering their breasts – and yes, she had been worth every cent. And naturally, no one had risked arguing or asked him to leave. Harvey, he decided, had been a bad influence on him; but he was enjoying every second: flaunting rules and daring anyone to contradict him or condemn his behaviour had turned into a new game.

He took another sip of champagne just before he climaxed, letting the bubbles linger on his tongue to savour the taste, and pulled her closer against his chest and let her sip from the glass when she emerged.

Daryl then remembered he was meeting various individuals – all suitably important – for lunch in less than two hours, and there were a number of things to do. He stood up, dislodging Tammy, and stepped out, a naked Leanne coming forward to wrap a towel around him, and he stood for a moment as she dried him, aroused by the way she bent down in front of him (as she meant him to be). So, he took the towel and tossed it aside, pushing her slightly to go ahead of him into his bedroom. He shut the door with a nudge, and Leanne lay face down and grabbed hold of the bedstead and cried out as he rammed into her, loving the force of him as she always did. It was addictive knowing he could do that, knowing what he made her feel. He cupped and kneaded her breasts, and then fingers flickered over her nipples . . . and she climaxed just before he did, a shriek of joy escaping her as his thrust pushed the breath from her body, and in the long panting seconds afterwards, he slid his hand up her back to her hair and tugged.

"As good as ever?"

"Better than ever," she returned whole-heartedly, and flicked a lock of hair back to look at him coyly over her shoulder, knowing he was still inside her, hands now resting on her back as her bottom pressed up against him. She pushed back and ground herself against him as best she could, wanting to see if she could tempt him to another round.

The gleam in his eye told her she could indeed, and she let herself be pulled up off the bed and pushed up against the wall, where a set of handcuffs waited for her.

God, she thought as they snapped on, willingly moving her legs apart, fresh wetness between her thighs. *I love my job.*

THE GIRL WAS standing in the doorway of a shop that was closed, unnoticed by everyone walking down the street. She was waiting for the music store – The Cantina – across the road to open; or re-open, as it closed in the afternoons and came alive again at night, with the shop on one floor and the bar with live music on the second. She liked walking past it at night, hearing the music. She again wished she was older, taller, bigger so that she could. *One day.*

She was idly looking up and down the street. It was fairly quiet. There were vehicles parked on both sides of the street, and she saw a cyclist, a truck, a car moving.

Suddenly a group of men came out of the building just across from her and down a little. They were disputing something, one shouting angrily over his shoulder at the four men behind who were all dressed almost identically. The way the first man walked, and his attitude, marked him the leader. He half turned to shout something else at them as they followed in his wake, heading it seemed for one of the black stretched limousines parked across the road.

His long dark coat flared out as he walked into the wind and revealed a smart suit, his hair dark and cut short, his skin tanned. He was a trim figure – a change from the rather slack bodies of most, and the tourists who exposed too much flesh because of the heat.

He walked confidently, striding boldly, metres ahead of the rest of them – and straight into the path of the truck that had to swerve because the car had tried to pass the cyclist. The blare of horn was too late to warn him, and she started running, not thinking, and her body slammed into his with enough force to send them both flying; but the momentum of the impact meant he fell safely out of harm's way onto the pavement, while she continued to career onwards. . . and she turned, just in time, and her back slammed into the solid wood door of The Cantina just as a huge crash sounded, so loud it seemed to fill the world with noise. Her head snapped back and smacked into it, pain reporting itself instantly, and she fell forward onto all fours as the inertia let her go. She coughed on taking a breath, trying to get air into her lungs, not having felt anything like this since her father had thrown her down the stairs when she was seven. She felt something trickle over her skin and a hand went to her neck, searching in her hair, and she found blood on her fingers. She felt instantly sick at the sight of it, the red glistening and dancing in front of her eyes.

She tore her eyes away to look at the man who was moving slightly, still half-lying half-sitting on the pavement. He looked at her in dazed shock, then back at the delivery truck which had piled headlong into the front of the parked SUV he had walked in front of. The crunch area was impressive, enough force employed to stove in the bonnet and into the engine. He would have been in between the two vehicles, and certainly not in the single piece he was still in were it not for her. All this she could see also. Then he looked at her again.

Her eyes met his.

A fraction of a second that would change their lives forever.

Enough for her to take in the hard eyes, the equally hard lines of his face.

He realised his men were running towards them, and glanced at them, just as she pulled in another breath and pushed herself to her feet . . . and ran. Ran even though she almost fell within five yards, despite the dizziness in her head, her long legs sprinting down the street, ignoring the shouts behind her.

Donatello Raphael Capello, Mafia don and Lord of Vegas, felt arms take hold of his and pull him up on his feet, voices asking if he was alright; but his eyes stayed on the girl as she ran. All too soon she was gone, disappearing around the next street corner. And he knew he would remember her. She was much too thin, but had hauntingly beautiful eyes, a bright lovely face. She looked young, but the eyes were older, wiser. There was something wild about her, her blonde curls dancing around her pale face, her fingers stained red from an injury. And when he looked, there was blood on the pavement where she had landed; her blood spilt instead of his.

"You OK, boss?"

Paulo's voice made it through the fog in his brain as the deafening crunch of the collision worked itself loose from his stunned consciousness.

"Yes, I'm fine." He pushed the hands away that held him and stood alone, though they continued to brush down his superbly expensive coat to rid it of the dust that was everywhere in Vegas. He tore his eyes away from looking after where the girl had gone. "I'm alright, thanks to her! Not thanks to you useless fucking lot! What were you? Asleep?" He turned on them, his face angry and temper hot, and they all looked shame-faced and stepped back from the brunt of his rebuke. "And then you just let her run off? Ah! Imbeciles! Next time you see her you catch her and bring her to me, understand?" He turned and strode past the wreckage, checking before he crossed this time, and went to the car where his driver was waiting for him, holding the door.

Paulo looked at Mario, and Lucio looked at Pepe, who looked at Mario.

Mario and Paulo got in with him a few seconds later; the others got in the second limo. Those in with the boss knew better than to speak.

None of them bothered to check on the driver of the truck. As far as they were concerned, they'd not seen anything.

They drove off. At speed.

He wanted to see the CCTV footage from the street, wanted to see just how it had happened. To think he – he who was so feared, and the master of the city – should almost die because of a swerving truck when he had risked death by so many other terrifying means? And saved by a child? It had happened so fast. How had she done it?

He would find her and he would thank her. Something told him, *instinct* told him, that there was far more to her. What kind of person would do that? Risk themselves to save a life? In his world, where someone was more likely to put a gun to your head and pull the trigger, or at least smash your face apart or chop off some fingers, it felt like even more of a miracle.

Why had she run? The look on her face had been one of pure terror and he could not exactly blame her. She was just a kid. Twelve? Thirteen? Yes, somehow he'd have her found. There was one thing he never did: leave debts unpaid or mysteries unsolved. This was his city; he would have his answers.

DONNY LEANED BACK in the black limo, the inside as impeccably clean as the outside, enjoying the luxury money could buy from the $300,000 ruby tie pin to the bespoke leather shoes on his feet. The one-way tinted bullet-proofed windows still afforded him a decent view of his city at night as he drove home from his club – not too late for once, only 1am, though he suspected he would be up for another hour yet. He was deep in thought.

"Boss."

He looked round at Paulo, his constant companion, his extra pair of eyes, and if need be, a shield for his own body against a bullet.

"Isn't that the girl?"

His mind instantly alert, he leaned over and looked where the finger pointed. There, walking alone, her concentration fixed on the small thin item in her hands trying to read it in the city lights, was the girl. The same thin legs. The same blonde curls spilling over her shoulders. She was concentrating on the item in her hands, weaving in and out of the other people on the pavement without looking up.

"Get her. Bring her to me," he ordered, not taking his eyes off her.

Paulo patched through to the others in the second car as they slowed and then stopped at the lights, and all six men got out, all moving around the other cars and the line of parked vehicles and surrounding her quickly. The other drivers behind knew better than to start complaining: they saw who exited the cars and no horns were blown.

A hand grabbed for her elbow and she twisted instantly, dropping the CD case, ducking under the arm but realising in a split second she was out-numbered and surrounded. She tried to dive past the nearest one, but he grabbed her arm, so she punched his face with her free hand, kneed him in the gut, felt the hold weaken and twisted out of it. She ran, over the pavement to the road, eyes going left to right. She saw the first stationary black limo, and realised it must be their car as she recognised it from that day in the street with the truck. She took a big stride, put a hand out and jumped, vaulting over it. Landing on the other side, she sprinted away, making the traffic swerve and horns blare – though she didn't care. There was no way she was letting them grab her. But why were they grabbing her? She'd saved that man's life, and now they were coming after her, like this?

She looked around as she hit a quieter back street, annoyed that there were three figures still behind her, the fitter of the pack running straight after her. She then ran, not thinking about where she was going, realising she'd run down the worst possible streets. They were mostly dead ends. But she kept going, noticed she was heading towards the railway line . . .

She charged up the slope of the bridge, hearing some shouting behind her, knew if she could just get out of sight for a few seconds, past the bridge, she'd be safe. She could hide, and they'd get bored when they couldn't find her and leave.

Then a car appeared, coming around the corner at the bottom of the bridge at the opposite end with a dangerous amount of speed. Her escape route was now blocked! She turned to look back, still moving, and saw the three figures coming closer. They were tired from the sprint, but they were still alert, their eyes fixed on her . . . and all of them with a gun in their hand. *Why guns? What had she done?*

She came to a halt near the top of the bridge, the car pulling over at an angle to indicate its ability to go either way if she tried to run again. It was a wide bridge, with pavements either side. So much space and nowhere to go!

The girl looked around. Only the wall of the bridge was behind her. And another three men were getting out of the car, leaving the doors open, all of them carrying guns.

"Come on, kid, it's over. You had your run, now give it up."

One of the men came forward, the rest of them creating a semi-circle around her. His voice did not sound friendly. And the hold on his gun was with both hands, and though pointed away from her, it was ready to be used. His face when it was lit by the street light was serious, ruthless, and the hard line of his lips and the blackness of his eyes brought memories back she had tried so hard to suppress.

She did the only thing she could do: she turned, put a hand on the wall and jumped, just as she saw a light flash over her head and felt the low vibration of the approaching train.

"Shit!" Mario swore, and looked at Paulo. They peered over the edge to see her balanced on the safety barrier just below the bridge.

The last thing they needed was a suicide! What had they done?

"Come on, kid, get down, there's no need to go jumping!" Mario cried.

His voice was tense; both of them were tense. They hadn't expected this. They shifted slightly, not sure what to do. They still had both hands on their guns. The others joined them on the bridge and glanced at each other nervously.

The girl stayed completely still. *If they're going to shoot me why not aim at me now? Why are they waiting?*

A seventh figure joined them. She recognised him. It was the man she'd saved . . .

"Jesus Christ!" he swore. He then looked angrily at Paulo, as if it was his fault she was on the barrier, her body in a most precarious position. This wasn't what he wanted. "Did you have to scare her?"

He stood in front of his men, facing her, dead centre. He didn't fear her. He didn't want to scare her. She was unarmed and had saved his life. He had to get her to trust him or . . . he didn't want to think about what might happen if she didn't.

"Kid, just come down, OK. We just want to talk to you."

His voice had an Italian lilt, but it didn't detract from the iron-like command he used: the words were not an offer, they were an order.

"You want to talk when they have guns in their hands?" she asked, her whole body tense and ready to flee, her voice angry.

He found himself drawn to her, able to respect her because she was holding her nerve despite her obvious fear, and though he knew it already, it was clear from her words that she wasn't stupid, despite being so young.

"Boys." He raised a hand, then put both on to his hips, purposefully pushing his coat back to reveal a suit . . . and no weapon. His men slowly put their guns away, not used to weapon-less negotiations, even with girls who were five times smaller than they were. "We're not going to hurt you. We just want to talk." He repeated the words, keeping his voice low and level.

They all felt the increasing vibration on the bridge.

"No. I don't believe you," she replied, her eyes staying on his; but she took a split second to look behind her. She could make it easily. It was just a question of timing. She looked back at him in the long seconds that followed, saw the intensity in his face. But still she didn't trust him. His face was too ruthless, and everything about him screamed danger. "I save your life and this is how you repay me?" she then asked, just as she felt the tremble of the barrier as the vibrations coursed through it.

His reply turned into a shout of protest as she shifted backwards, balancing herself right on the edge . . . any second, any second . . . they could now hear the train, saw its lights.

"No!" Donny yelled, a hand rubbing over his mouth. *Oh good God, no!*

It was all in the timing. She waited. She waited. She looked him straight in the eye, and then closed her eyes and somersaulted backwards off the barrier.

His yell was drowned out by the roar of the train as she disappeared into the blackness, and then his screaming at his guys for terrifying an unarmed kid into killing herself in front of a train.

"Boss!" Mario shouted as the train hurtled under them and into the night. He was on the other side of the bridge, staring after it.

"What?"

"She's on the train!"

"What!"

"The kid. She's on the train."

He looked at Mario's face and saw the disbelief. He was right! There, illuminated by the lights along the track, was a person standing on the roof of one the freight carriages.

"Get me a scope!"

They had sniper rifles in the boot – they never knew when they might need one – and quickly one of the guys fetched him one, putting it in his outstretched hand. Paulo took one as well, both looking, able now to see her clearly. She was staring back at them, no expression on her face at all. And from her pose, she looked completely untouched. How the hell had she done that? After a few more moments, she turned and walked up the train a little, then jumped, arms outstretched, letting her body fall towards the ground, where she rolled and stood and ran to the wire fence and sprang up again, making it over and dropping back down on the other side.

Donny watched her pause, a hand on her side, one against the fence, and she bent over slightly . . . perhaps she was not uninjured as he had thought . . . or was she just catching her breath? He already knew she didn't give in to pain after what he'd seen outside the Cantina when she'd run, despite being hurt. With one more glance at their direction – could she see them watching her? – she turned and ran, the same long-legged fluid stride that had carried her away from him before.

He waved an arm and turned away when she was out of sight, going back to his car.

"Load up. Let's go home."

He *was* going to find her, only next time he was going to have to be smarter. He had the whole of the city's CCTV and innumerable eyes and ears available to him on the ground. And she was resident in his city; there were only so many places she could hide. And when he did finally get her, he had a very long list of questions for her.

IN THE END, though, despite spending hours devoted to the task of finding her, the girl gave herself away quite without wanting to, but it put an end to their frustrated months-long search.

"The girl. We've found her! She's in Palm Square . . . jumping off buildings!"

"What the hell?"

Donny was on his feet.

"You've got to see it to believe it. That thing with the train was *nothing* compared to this!"

Both men hurried down the corridor to their surveillance room in the basement. It contained a dozen computer stations, all installed with the latest technology, and all linked in to the hundreds of city cameras, the same that the police would see . . . and some more they wouldn't. Population had got such that, combined with the government's limited revenue, the police had been forced to admit the need to embrace rather than attack the organised crime lords who, with the right incentives, had then worked to keep crime controlled. This had helped establish relative peace in the larger cities that otherwise would have turned into war zones

– not good for business, politics or tourism – but it was a relationship they did not inform the general public about.

Donny went to the main screen, a montage of all the views around Palm Square. It was large and displayed ten different angles. And each angle showed her, a small figure, blonde hair tied back in a ponytail. How had she kept herself out of sight? Where did she squirrel herself away?

"Get the nearest guys down there to tail her when she leaves and find out where she goes. And get two others on a computer to help guide them in case she makes things difficult. Make sure they know to keep their distance and not give themselves away. And absolutely no guns," he instructed.

Paulo nodded at two of the crew gathered, their earpieces installed, and they moved away, paging the men on the ground as asked. There was always someone somewhere. That was how they stayed in control.

Donny saw the girl gesture around at the square when it seemed a tourist was taking issue with her about something.

"Turn the sound up," Donny said, wanting to hear whatever he could.

"It's got to be a trick," the tourist accused, with disbelief written all over his face, mirroring that of the many people behind him.

"It's not a trick," she corrected calmly, having anticipated that people would doubt her; she hardly dared believe it herself. "Pick another building, and I'll jump again if it makes you happy." She gestured at all the buildings around them again, the crowd watching, waiting to see what would happen next. Her jump had brought everyone over, including the other performers who were amazed, but curious as well.

"That one," the same man said.

He pointed at the tallest, which luckily was only a little higher than the one she'd already leapt off. Somehow she knew he'd pick that one. And she was glad there weren't any bigger buildings. For now.

"Fine."

She started towards it.

"HOW'S SHE GOING to get up there? It's not like they're just going to let her take the elevator," Mario said quietly.

But no one spoke.

AT THE BASE of the building she paused and looked up, planning her route. Then she stepped forward and began the ascent, using the sills and balconies, making everyone suck in their breath. It was only five storeys, so she wasn't too worried, and though she never liked jumping onto concrete, she had trained herself to overcome the fear. This was the first day she'd revealed her 'talent', having spent months practising and perfecting it, turning it into an art form of her very own, going to the swimming baths and jumping off the high boards to learn the distances and how to turn her body.

Finally, she was there, and she climbed over the lip of the roof, feeling a little tired, but used to it – this was how she spent her evenings, after all. She smiled as she thought of the rather surprised faces of the people inside the building as she'd passed them on the way up. One guy had reached for his comms unit – no doubt to call the police. She would have to make a swift exit once she reached the ground again; the police were *not* on her list of people she wanted to make friends with.

She looked over the edge, seeing the crowd gathered but leaving a good semicircle of space below where they presumed she would land. Either in one piece or not.

She backed up, jumped on the spot a few times and rolled her shoulders and shook out her legs, feeling the muscles ripple. She might still be skinny, but she certainly wasn't weak.

THE AUDIENCE IN the surveillance room had had to switch to another camera on one of the high buildings a few streets away to see her, and they could not believe the calm they saw on her face when they zoomed in.

"This is insane. A fall from half that height would kill anyone," Donny said, angry and confused. Why was she doing this? He was irritated he couldn't stop her.

"You'd think," Paulo replied grimly, but not looking away.

Donny glanced at him briefly, surprised by his tone and looked back at the screen.

The girl had backed up from the edge, giving herself a run up . . . and he watched as she swung her arms across herself, rolled her weight backwards and then forwards on her feet, and then started running. She reminded him of a gymnast at the Olympics – only they weren't heading towards a five-storey drop! He had to admire her speed and the acceleration, but he did not like it. She was going to her death, surely. And he'd never get to meet her.

With about twenty feet to go, she raised her hands in the air and flipped twice, before landing on the edge . . . and soaring out into nothingness. Donny put a hand over his eyes, held his breath, but then peeked out, unable to resist looking. It was so beautiful to watch; a precision he could not have expected from one so young.

She controlled herself expertly in the air, arms out for balance, legs together, and then she dropped, arms over her crossed over chest, twisting like a diver, then curling up and turning end over end . . .

Did he really want to see this? It was all happening so fast!

Then she uncurled and stretched out and, in a split second, she rolled, twice, and then stood, arms poised by her side.

The crowd just stared at her for a very long second; then the applause and cheering started. The doubting tourist came forward and offered his hand, looking apologetic, and after a joke or two, pressed a fifty-dollar bill into her hand and backed away, a little unsure of her now. He was awed, like the rest of them, but he was soon replaced by another, and then another, keen to speak to this strange, incredible girl and give her money for her 'performance'.

"How the fuck?" Donny rubbed his hand over his chin, still mystified.

"Exactly."

"Are the boys ready to follow her?"

"All in place, sir."

"Have all that footage sent over to my screens and keep me up to date with progress. Remember, no mistakes. And no guns."

The look he gave Paulo was dark and serious; then he left, going back to his room to watch the madness again from the beginning, wanting to slow it down to find out just how she did it.

She should be dead.

THERE WAS A wail of sirens and she froze, and someone appeared at her side, one of the other performers, his face and body painted blue. He was a fire-eater, and he smiled at her; it looked strange with all the make-up.

"Hey, kid, you might want to make a dash for it before the boys in blue – not me – catch you. Here, use this. I guess you're new to this donations thing." He offered her a strong paper bag for all the notes that had been shoved at her while she caught her breath, and helped her stuff them in and fold down the bag. "Use the crowd, keep your head down and avoid the cameras."

He gave her a friendly push as he told her this last bit of advice, and she ignored the crowd – who were still trying to get her attention and speak to her – and ran, jumping easily over the fountain troughs and bolting through one of the exits from the square and into the back streets which would take her home. She was rather worried by his comment about the cameras, but she couldn't waste valuable seconds looking around trying to find them – it wasn't as if they were in obvious places like on corners or store fronts – so she decided to just go. She had never worried about them before, why should she now?

A squad car screeched into the road ahead and she turned and ran in the opposite direction. She was only fifteen minutes from home. She could do this. She turned briefly, just in time to see a car pull out. The police car smashed into it, and hard enough that pursuit was now going to be impossible. But further up the street an identical car pulled out and drove after her, and she ran, brown paper bag clutched in one hand.

DONNY SWITCHED TO footage of his men after watching the jump again.

His car kept her in sight, and after changing street six or seven times, her pace barely slowing, he recognised where they were. Donny smiled. What a clever girl. She slowed and started jogging, and the car pulled over, silently, still a hundred yards away; but a moment later she was up and over the metal barrier, out of sight of the camera, jogging towards the derelict hotel.

Clever girl, Donny thought again, *the one place no one will look for her.*

"You seeing this, boss?"

“Yes. Get some help. Set up some surveillance and get a team ready to go in – but wait till she leaves and then go in and explore. Take some cameras and get them installed. And make sure you leave no trace of your visit.”

“Sure thing, boss.”

He clicked off the monitor and stood up, went to the window and looked out. He had been waiting so long to speak to her. Now, finally, he had found her, and quite by chance. He let out a breath, put his hands in his pockets and forced himself to relax, trying to assure himself that the waiting was nearly over.

DONNY STOOD BEHIND the comms people that were monitoring the team going into the hotel; they’d waited, as instructed, for her to leave. It was hard though, letting her go, letting her just walk down the street. He knew she would run if she was suspicious, and knowing now what she could do, she could go places his men could not follow – certainly not as fast. No, when he caught her, it was going to be away from open spaces, with as little risk of losing her as possible.

The six men in dark combat gear walked towards the hotel over the uneven ground littered with weathered objects: bricks, large stones, items that had been pulled from the burnt husk and left outside to rot.

“Try and find where she goes in, and check the perimeter for other ways in or out. We don’t want her escaping when she makes it to ground level.”

They spread out, skirting around the outside, using their night vision goggles to see. The time on Donny’s computer said 23.18; where had she gone to at this time of night? Being unconventional and fearless of the night was obviously within her character, but still, he worried for her – and cursed himself for it as well. Why did he care so much?

“I’ve found an entrance on the north side. It’s well concealed, but I can get through if I . . .” Donny watched the scene shown from Mario’s camera on his jacket. “Oh shit.” Donny felt a flash of fear. Had she booby-trapped it? “Oh Christ! There’s something sticky everywhere. What the fuck is it? Oh yuk! These are $500 shoes!”

Paulo's voice patched through: "Mario, you're such a woman. Have you broken a nail as well, *bella*?" Everyone sniggered.

Donny crossed his arms, smiling, anticipating a few more surprises before his guys were out of there. "Hey, fuck off, Paulo, you're not the one with shoes that now squelch. Jesus."

"If you're wearing $500 shoes for this, I'm paying you too much," Donny told him dryly.

"Boss, I can't go in without leaving a real mess that she'll see. I'll stay outside and keep watch," Mario said.

Donny agreed and flicked his eyes over to the other cameras. He saw Paulo go in through the entrance it seemed she used most: the path to it was fairly worn, and the door moved noiselessly as if it had been oiled. The other five went through with him, moving into the building to get to the main staircase, spreading out through the rooms in sweeping progress, leaving no room unchecked.

At the staircase one of them was gestured to wait, and the other four went up. It wasn't long before they found the room that was obviously hers. It was clean and tidy, and had been painted blue. There was a pile of pillows and blankets that constituted as a bed, and a makeshift table where a board had been raised up on top of piles of bricks. There were books on it, and pens and paper. On the other side of the room, there was a huge collection of CDs, and a CD player plugged into a generator, along with a fridge. A box next to the fridge had a selection of food items, and lots of bottled water. Large dark sheets hung down over the window, and lamps were set at various places – although they were turned off. They would brighten the room well, but were directed in such a way as to minimise the light that would show through at the window.

One of them went through to the bathroom – again, pristinely clean despite being outdated. He saw the jug next to the bath, the single toothbrush in a glass with a tube of toothpaste, and he felt something inside him shift . . . but he was too busy to properly analyse the emotion. There was no mirror.

"There is a lot of music here, and so old some of it," Lucio said, and everyone startled, having been quiet, observing the refuge of the girl that had so eluded and mystified them.

"Don't touch anything. Start putting the cameras in place." Donny didn't want to either give away their presence, or disturb her room. It was so heart-breakingly obvious she had so little, had struggled every step to accumulate what was there – none of it valuable, but enough to create a life, a . . . home. The love of music was so touching, the way it was all neatly stacked up, the CD player given pride of place. "What books has she got?" he then asked.

Paulo went over to the makeshift desk-come-table and looked down, half shutting the book that was open so Donny could see the title: Advanced Mathematics in the Physical World. Should he really be surprised she wasn't reading a comic?

"OK, finish up. Leave everything looking as it was, then clear out. Two of you will remain in a car around the corner. We'll watch her for a few days and then make our move – and this time, she isn't getting away."

Donny turned away from the screen, confident his men would do as they were told, finding himself smiling again as he remembered Mario's shoes. *Who wears $500 shoes for such a job?*

He sat down behind his desk and picked up the CD she had dropped in the street. Bon Jovi. How long ago was that album? It was at least as old as he was, if not more and he was twenty-four – but felt about eighty sometimes he had so many concerns, so many responsibilities. He still couldn't fathom his . . . his obsession with this child. So much so that he didn't even like admitting it to himself. It wasn't just that she'd saved his life, it was the determination, the skill . . . and that she was so self-contained.

It had been a relief to find her and discover where she lived, and he now had a perfect plan for repaying some of his debt to her: making her safe, secure and comfortable. He wondered how long it had been since she'd enjoyed a hot bath. Even if the water was still working in that place, it wouldn't be hot . . . And really great food. Had she eaten Italian? He doubted it.

A few days, just a few more days.

SHE WAS WALKING back from work, having done a late shift. She was tired and desperate to go home and sleep. She had a bottle of milk in a bag, as well as big bag of crisps that she was planning on putting in a sandwich – simple food, as she was so hungry. She cut through the alley behind the shop, and carried on walking homewards. She yawned as she got to the last stretch, having walked it so many times before. Sometimes it seemed to take forever.

She spotted an object at the bottom of the fence. It hadn't been there when she'd left; she would have seen it. She approached, thinking it could be a bag of rubbish – it wasn't uncommon for people to launch finished bags of food or drink items out of their cars, thinking it was OK because it wasn't outside their own house and because it was a stretch of wasteland. More than once she'd tidied it up and put it in the bin at the end of the street, and she sighed as she went to do the same . . . except she paused, her hand almost touching it. She froze, not believing her eyes as she saw a tuft of fur. She told herself it was probably an old teddy bear wrapped in a blanket and shoved in a bag. But it was not. It moved.

She crouched down cautiously, opened the blanket a little, reached out tentatively to touch a paw. She grew bolder and unwrapped the blanket. It was a cat. Or was it? The poor thing was a little squashed inside the bag, and she had a horrible feeling it had been thrown from a car – such an easy way of getting rid of an unwanted animal that was unloved or sick and too expensive to treat. She knelt down and put the ties of the bag over her other wrist – she was holding the bag of food with the other – and lifted gently. It wasn't heavy. She couldn't just leave it there, whatever animal it was.

She walked on a bit further, glancing down repeatedly, desperate now to get it inside and see it properly, see what was wrong, feeling a cloak of responsibility fall over her. She tossed the bag of milk and crisps over the fence as gently as she could, wincing as she heard it land, praying the milk bottle hadn't split. She then backed up a few steps, cradling the animal to her with one arm, and ran and jumped, hooking a leg over the fence – which she managed, just – and then slid over to the other side, deciding that that was the most inelegant and poor piece of fence-climbing she had ever done, but with good reason.

Once inside, she placed the bundle on the floor by her bed and pulled back the blanket completely. She gasped in surprise, having thought it might be a cat, but this was . . . a leopard cub? It could also be a cheetah, she thought, but it looked more like a leopard. The pattern of its fur was unmistakable. Where had it come from? Why had someone thrown it away? Perhaps it had been a pet, so wasn't utterly wild or vicious. It certainly didn't behave like it had the desire to attack her, it had barely stirred – which made her wonder if it was ill. She knelt and gently picked it up, cradled it to her, seeing 'it' was a he, and her heart melted as a little head snuggled instinctively against her neck and a soft paw – the nails on which were too immature to be of any danger – lay against the skin below her throat. She stood up, holding him, and found another blanket – the one he had been wrapped in was very dusty – and draped it around her like a sling so he was close to her, so her body could keep him warm.

After struggling slightly to make a sandwich and pour a glass of milk, she sat down on the pillows that made up her bed, and left him to sleep by her side while she ate, reading some more of the massive maths book she had found in a second-hand book store. When she had finished, she put the plate aside and pulled a bowl of milk towards him. She had seen cubs suckle on a nature programme, and human babies drank milk, so why not baby leopards too?

She gave him a little nudge.

"Hello," she whispered, and he blinked and yawned. "I don't know where you've come from, and I don't know anything about leopards, but you need to have a drink of something. So, you see, if you drink this, or the water, I'll get you something to eat in the morning, OK? Unless you'd like some bread soaked in milk? Or chicken? I'm afraid I don't have very much. You definitely picked the wrong hotel; ours is a simple limited menu."

The conversation was totally one-sided, but she felt she should talk to him. He flopped over when he attempted to stand. Had someone hurt him, or was he just weak? But he sniffed at the milk, and with a little help with standing, he tried some . . . and kept going. When he stopped, she went over to the small fridge – she had also found this in a second-hand shop – and pulled out a packet of chicken, already cooked and sliced. It was expensive, so it was precious, but he needed to eat more than she did. She took a piece and broke a little off and offered it to him. It took a moment, but finally he responded to whatever his taste buds were telling him it was, and accepted the food into his mouth. His eyes then opened fully and he looked up at her. She smiled and stroked his head, and fed him some more. She didn't care how much he ate; just so he felt better.

Finally, he seemed to have had enough, or it tired him out, for his eyes closed again and he lay down. She left him and went to wash her face and brush her teeth. Locking the bedroom door, she covered him with the blanket, snuggling pillows around him to keep him warm, and turned off the lamp. Getting into bed, she could hear the little snuffles of his breathing and she smiled in the darkness. She buried her head in the pillow with a newfound sense of happiness. She had always wanted a pet, something to love, and now she had, and felt emotion rise in her throat; but she refused, for the hundredth-millionth time, to let herself mourn for her mother, her sister and her grandma, and held on to the quiet joy of having a new friend. She ignored the tear that slipped out her eye and trickled to her chin as she drifted off to sleep.

THE EYES WATCHING the camera didn't miss it though. And thoughtful fingers rested against pursed lips, and a brow puckered in a frown.

Soon. Soon.

THE EIGHT MEN were as silent as ghosts, leaving another four outside, and another two with the cars. None of them were planning on letting the girl get away. Donny had ordered that all weapons would be left behind – which felt wrong – but they couldn't afford to scare her again.

Seven progressed up the stairs, one staying in the hall by the staircase. They all knew where she was. Information from the cameras was being fed to them through their earpieces. They arrayed themselves along the corridor from her room, with two on the stairs in case she somehow managed to get that far. All of them felt a knot of tension in their bellies; but not because they feared her, just because . . . well, she was so unpredictable. She wasn't like anyone they'd come up against before.

And it felt strange that they were just going to grab her. Wrong even, in a way. But orders were orders.

Mario had not seen the inside of the building before, and he was amazed that such a young girl could make a home in this dump. He wasn't easily scared, but all the shadows and darkness – how did a kid stand it?

He leant his head back against the wall and waited for the signal from the others. Then he felt something else . . . Oh no. Not now. He started to put a hand up but it was too late: he sneezed.

Everyone froze; he froze. She froze too. She had been checking on Lazarus – his name now – and felt her stomach drop into her feet. Pure fear flooded into her. Someone was here, in the dark. She carefully put Lazarus down and pulled a blanket over him to keep him out of sight and stood, listening.

"Who the fuck sneezed?" Donny growled into his comms system.

He'd strangle them, whoever they were. He'd wanted to make this as easy as possible, go in quietly and gently – as gently as was possible when capturing an unsuspecting human being. He saw her stand, waiting for the next noise. Suddenly she moved to the window, and he knew what she was going to do.

"Paulo, go! She's heading for the window."

The door crashed as she perched on the window sill, and then she looked around at the terrifying black-clad figures coming towards her in night vision goggles, looked down and saw the men on the ground waiting for her. It was a trap! She didn't think, just let herself out of the window and grabbed, clinging to the guttering and pushing onwards and upwards to the floor above. A hand lunged for her ankle, but missed.

She wanted to scream. Wanted to shout at them to leave her alone. But she needed all her breath for the climb. She reached the next storey and clambered onto the sill, thanking whoever was up there in the sky that she'd not slammed it completely shut the last time she'd used it. She heaved it up and climbed through, even as she heard feet on the stairs. Not hesitating, the girl ran for the door and headed for the stairs, knowing they would most definitely follow her, gambling she would get to the top before they did. She was right.

They all ground to a halt just below her as she vaulted over the edge of the banisters, and hurled her small body into the darkness.

Donny ordered them to turn around and go back down the stairs. He switched cameras, alerting Lucio, just in time to see her land, roll and stay crouched, like a dangerous hunting cat ready to pounce, unaffected by the long drop through the darkness.

Lucio stepped towards her, but she was up and lunged forward to run past him. He reached for her hair, grabbed it and twisted her around.

"Give it up!" he half shouted at her, feeling the strength in the small frame fighting him. He did not want to hurt her, as aside from the fact he was scared what his boss might do to him if he did, he wasn't good at man-handling small girls. Big men who knew violence by trade, yes, but children? No.

"Fuck you!"

A foot collided with his gut, hard, unexpected, and he realised just how strong she was, doubled over and let her go. He was still down on one knee, gasping for breath, when the rest of the cavalry thundered down the stairs and past him into the darkness to see where she had gone.

Paulo gestured, signalling for them to spread out and sweep through the rooms, to flush her out from wherever she was hiding. Three of them got to what was the ballroom and they crept in; but their night vision did not reach all the way to the end of the room, so they went in further, searching for her, for a gleam of hair or tiny movement.

The girl jumped down from the ledge above the door they had just come through, ducked back out into the corridor and slammed it shut, running back the way they'd come. The shouting through the comms system sent everyone hurtling back towards the staircase, and Lucio was warned she was on her way, so he was at least ready for her when she appeared, hurtling out of the darkness. He managed to make a grab at her, bringing her flight to a stop, sending her tumbling onto the floor hard enough to hurt . . . but within a second she had picked herself up.

Just like before, on the pavement, they surrounded her, only this time they were ready for her. She turned, keeping an eye on them all as much as she could, her breathing too fast, and something in Donny flickered – what? – and he instructed them to go in gently.

"Come on, kid, give it up . . ." Paulo tried to sound reasonable, cajoling.

It didn't work.

"I don't think so!" she spat.

She tensed her arms for the attack she knew was imminent . . . they could only stand so close for so long without trying to grab her. One of them tried, and her hand whipped out and grabbed his wrist and yanked, sending him into one of the other men – another move that Mr Gibson had taught her. Another came forward, and she blocked both attempts of his to reach her, and then stuck out her leg, tripping him over. Another hand grabbed her arm, but she twisted it fast so that she bent his arm back and freed herself in one move, shoving him away from her. But then a large arm went around her chest and yanked her up, crushing the breath from her and lifting her into the air. It was over.

"Get some cuffs on her!"

She fought the arm that starved her of air, kicked hard, but still the arm held her.

"*No! No*!" she yelled.

Her hands were pulled together. She began to weaken as she still could not breathe, could not fight them. She felt the cold steel on her skin and felt the cuffs snapped shut on her wrists. She closed her eyes. Did not want to look at the men now looking at their prize, captured and trussed. Why were they doing this? *Why*? And her fear turned into such a sadness that she thought she might stop breathing entirely.

"Now, we really would like to do this the nice way, not the nasty way. Are you going to behave, or do I need to cuff your ankles too?"

The man who held her waited for her reply as the others looked on. Had it not occurred to him, to them, that this *was* nasty?

"Yes, I'll behave," she said, struggling to speak. It was bad enough that her hands were cuffed.

He released her a little, and then to her relief, he put her back down on the ground, but he didn't let go of her. She managed to suck in a breath, and another.

And then an awful silence, broken only by her ragged breathing. Donny held his breath. They all did. Something stirring in them at the sight of this young girl.

"Why are you doing this?" she then asked weakly, defeated.

"Because the boss wants to speak to you, and when the boss wants to speak to someone, we bring them to him," Paulo answered, quietly. He wished he could take the goggles off. He must look terrifying. But they hadn't been instructed to do so.

"Your boss?"

"You saved his life, remember? When the truck swerved?"

Of course she remembered.

"So, let's get going, shall we? Don't want to keep him waiting any longer."

He tugged her towards the door, the hold on her not painful but still firm. And the others followed.

"Wait!" she cried and he halted, looking down at her. "Where are you taking me?"

"To see the boss, in town."

"Please . . . there's a leopard cub upstairs, on my bed, and I don't want to leave him, he's *ill!* Please can he come?"

Far from being enraged at news of the cub, Paulo saw her distress, saw that despite her obvious fear she cared deeply about it. They'd seen her tending to it on the cameras. Donny confirmed through his earpiece that it was OK to bring the cub, instructing Lucio and Pepe to fetch it from upstairs.

"We'll take care of it."

She was then pulled into the familiar overgrown world outside the hotel, watching the men she'd seen earlier coming forward to flank them. The guys instructed to collect Lazarus appeared, and one of them was cradling him in his arms. Something about his body language told her he would be safe. One of the fence panels had been moved and she was hustled through the gap and into a waiting car – Lazarus was carried to a second car – and three men got in with her. As if by some unspoken agreement, they all pulled off their night glasses simultaneously and folded them away, silently looking at her, contemplating how curious a specimen she was compared to their usual targets. She looked at them, feeling calmer now she could see their faces and their eyes: they were men, not monsters, and in fact had hard, but pleasant faces. But she was still uncomfortable with their scrutiny, not sure what it meant or how to interpret it. She looked away from them, studied the interior of the car instead. Wished they'd take the cuffs off.

"Not used to cars?" said the man who'd held her so tightly as they set off.

His voice wasn't condemning, just curious. They all were. They'd had a chance to observe this unique creature for almost a week, learned where she worked – the most unassuming job one could imagine – and concluded that this was not your normal kid.

"No."

"You're thin. Didn't your parents feed you right?" Mario then asked, rather bluntly.

"No."

She heard an "Ouch!" as Paulo reached over and slapped Mario on the side of the head. And something about that made her want to laugh.

"Why are you so stupid? You think she'd be struggling on her own in an abandoned burnt out fucking hotel if she had a mommy and daddy cooking her homemade fucking meals and reading her bedtime fucking stories at home every night?" Paulo said. It was what Donny would have said, and he watched, enthralled, at the developing exchange in the car.

And again, they made her want to laugh. "It's OK, I guess I'll fill out one day," she said.

She surprised them by speaking, and they quit glaring at each other.

Paulo slapped Mario once more, for good measure, but then said, "Yeah, sure." Then, "You're pretty fast on your feet."

"Guess I've learnt I have to be."

There wasn't much anyone could say to that. It both admitted great sadness as well as being a mild accusation at them for making her run. The girl closed her eyes and tried to relax a little, tried to enjoy the feel of riding in the car. She didn't even attempt to work out what was going to happen to her now.

Finally, the car pulled up, and the guys all jumped out and the cooler night air moved in. She stepped out onto the pavement and stared up at a smart town house; not so showy it screamed for attention, but still very grand. Her face must have said everything, as Paulo smiled at her astonishment and took her arm, more gently than before, and led her up the steps. Mario opened the door, above which was an ornate light. The hallway was beautifully decorated above highly polished mahogany panelling, everything perfectly just so, from the lamps and ornaments to the mirrors and pictures. It made her feel even more shabby, looking at the beautiful things. It was a home, a *real* home, not what she had left behind so long ago . . . *Don't think*. And not the dark horrible place her imagination had concocted for their destination. An elderly man was sitting in an armchair further up the hall.

"Not what you expected? Don't worry, we don't torture people here anymore," Paulo told her in a low voice; then saw her horrified face and realised she'd taken him seriously. "I'm joking," he quickly added. He tickled her under the chin, and nodded at the old guy. "I'm Paulo, by the way. And this is Giovanni. He doesn't really go anywhere; he just keeps an eye on everyone coming in and going out."

The guy looked at her, the wrinkles on his face many and deep; but his eyes were bright as he observed her. She was too scared to say anything, but he said something in fast Italian to Paulo, who shrugged and gestured further into the house.

Paulo led her forward, shadowed by the other two, and the guy carrying Lazarus, past plush carpeted stairs going up to another floor, and another set going down. All along the hallway there were smart painted doors, until they got to one at the end – a deeply polished wood door with a brass knob and various security devices.

"Take the cub to the kitchen and settle him. Get the kitchen staff to give him some milk," Paulo said, and the guy nodded.

She felt her face tighten in anticipation. She knew instinctively who was going to be behind this door. She had not forgotten his face. Had not forgotten the darkness that hung around him.

The door was opened after codes were typed in and Paulo's thumb was pressed to a small, blue-lit pad. He nudged her forward and she went, unwillingly, feeling uncomfortable, especially given her bound hands. She wanted to push the hair away from her face that tickled her cheek, wanted to smooth her clothes, but couldn't. She glanced at the room, a spacious, sumptuous study in dark woods with gold, cream and claret fittings. Bookshelves covered two walls, and there was a big leather sofa in deep cherry red with two matching chairs set on one side of the room, and a huge mahogany desk on the other, with computer screens on it. The lights were soft, making the room seem warm and inviting. There was a doorway in one corner that perhaps led through to another room. It was like something out of a magazine she'd seen at the store: it was beautiful, and she might have enjoyed the experience were it not for the tall, imposing figure standing in front of the desk, his dark hair combed back from his chiselled face. He was dressed in black trousers and a black shirt and had his hands in his pockets. She was walked over and placed in front of him, like a dog being returned to its master.

She didn't want to look at his face, didn't want to get caught in the mesmerising power of his stare. She'd seen it at the bridge, his intense blue eyes watching her, and she knew he had been from the very moment she entered the room. She didn't want to look up. But she couldn't resist. Her eyes met his and held. She was just a few metres away from him.

"Thank you, Paulo."

The large man nodded and backed away, leaving them alone and shutting the door. Once back in the hallway, he shrugged to the boys waiting in the hall. Neither he nor anyone else knew what his boss was going to do now. To a point, it didn't matter. They would just do as they were told, like they always did.

Inside the room, both figures stayed perfectly still and silent for what felt like eternity for her, but a few moments to him. His eyes left hers for a moment, to scan her face, her hair, taking in the dusty blue jumper – far too big for her – and the black leggings, the soft-soled pumps on her feet. She had grown a little.

"So . . ." he said, not sure how to begin, seeing the fear in her eyes as well as the bright gleam of defiance. He knew this was going to need careful handling. He needed her to trust him and relax her defences. "You agreed to come and see me."

"I wasn't given a *choice*," she corrected without hesitation.

She was amazed to see him smile. He couldn't help it. Her response was perfectly natural *and* she was also correct.

"Why don't you sit down?" He nodded towards the sofa just behind her.

"I'm hoping I won't be here that long," she replied firmly, not wanting to sit.

"Well, you might be, so I'd sit if I were you." He used a bit more force in his voice now, and she looked at the sofa nervously.

"But I'm all dusty. I don't want to get it dirty."

His mild annoyance melted away. Everything must feel so very odd to her, and no doubt intimidating, too, including him.

"I'm not bothered. Really. Sit."

He nodded at it once again and slowly she backed up and sat down, having never sat on such a comfortable sofa. She wanted to touch the soft red leather, lie on it. She could hardly take her eyes off it, but she looked back at him, unaware of how innocent, and indeed beautiful, she looked with her dishevelled hair, toes off the floor as the sofa was so big. The dark scruffy clothes did not suit the purity of her face at all, or the depth of her clear, expressive eyes.

He slowly came forward, and she leaned back, away from him. "Now, if I take these off, are you going to try and run, or are you going to stay?" He gestured at the cuffs.

She looked down, rather surprised. This wasn't what she had expected. Allowed to sit down and have the cuffs removed?

"I'll stay," she said, after a moment's consideration. "It's not like I have anywhere to run to anyway."

He smiled again as he reached down and pressed three numbers on the key pad at the centre of the handcuffs and the bands snapped back.

"You can always run, but whether it affords you any freedom is debatable," he said quietly.

She knew that. She went to sleep every night wondering if her father would find some way to get to her. She didn't know if he was in prison, if they'd caught him . . . had he disappeared too, like her? She spent every day knowing what lay in her past. Every day in fear of her future. Was that freedom? . . . As he said, freedom was debatable. She rubbed her wrists, not knowing what to say, sensing he knew about her. But how much did he know? He stepped back, placed the cuffs on the desk and leaned against it, happy just to watch her for a moment, seeing that taking it slowly and gently was helping a great deal towards calming her down.

"I've been waiting for quite a while to speak to you."

She kept her eyes away from his, purposefully.

"What do you want with me?" she asked, unsettled, not knowing whether to feel anger or fear.

"You saved my life . . . did you not think I would want to thank you?" Her eyes almost fell out of her head at that moment, and she looked up, and he could have laughed at the disbelief he saw. "You saved my life at the risk of your own, and got hurt as well," he added.

"I wouldn't have bothered if I'd known I'd get chased and kidnapped," she declared in a low rebellious voice – but that only amused him more.

"I think you would have. I've seen the footage from the street. You reacted instantly to the danger. You didn't think at all, you just acted. It's a miracle how fast you moved."

His voice held a degree of quiet admiration that she didn't know how to react to.

"I don't like standing by while people die. I think that's quite normal," she threw back, not wanting to encourage further acts of gratitude from him if it involved being hunted down like an animal.

"I also heard, and have since seen, that a certain person took on two armed robbers at the shop where she works, and not only stopped the robbery, but saved her pregnant co-worker." Her face froze and her eyes bored into his. "Very brave."

"I was lucky."

"No. I have seen the footage. There was no luck involved; it was all calculated perfectly," he corrected her firmly, and in a voice that didn't invite argument. "You're quite remarkable, aren't you?"

"I'm just a kid." She shrugged dismissively.

"A kid who defies gravity and science by jumping off buildings?" He saw several emotions now. She'd clearly hoped he wouldn't know about that too. "A very exciting afternoon that was, in Palm Square. Did you think I wouldn't see?"

Eyes sparked at him, at the implication of his question. It had been purposefully posed to test how quickly she caught on as to who or what he was.

"Who are you?"

And there it was. Quick as a flash. He sighed. He was worried that the answer might frighten her. And he didn't want to frighten her. Not now he had her here.

"Have you heard of the mob or the Mafia?"

Her face paled and she went completely still.

"Yes."

"Well. My name is Donny Capello. And Vegas is my city."

He watched her absorbing these revelations, and moved slowly to one of the high-backed leather chairs and sat down, reclining like a lord – which he was of sorts.

"So, you're like a king?" she guessed, raising one eyebrow at him in a way that he liked. She seemed more curious than petrified – thank goodness.

"Yes, in a way. I rule – or deputise. This is a big city, and I have many men who are employed to look after various sections, keep things organised. People with businesses in the city pay for the protection on offer from us, and we make sure their interests are secured."

He kept the explanation free of any mention of force or violence, as that was how it worked to a large extent – and it worked well.

"So, Carl, my boss, pays someone who pays you?"

"Yes." He was relieved she'd grasped the point so quickly.

"Does he know you exist? I didn't." Her head tipped to one side as she asked this, making her look wise beyond her years, yet so young.

"Most people know after a certain . . . *involvement* in the urban food chain, if you catch my drift?" She nodded. "Though most people in the city find out one way or the other. If they don't find out from hearing someone speak about me, it'll be because they break rules and need to learn them." He paused and opened a hand in a simple gesture, trying to sound reasonable not ruthless. "My boys help people learn. It keeps the peace."

Attentive eyes blinked at him, the depth of their colour startling, even in the muted light of the lamps. Her face remained passive.

"Is that why Carl didn't call the police after the robbery?" A hint of smile played on her lips.

She's quick, this one. "Yes, I would say it probably is."

He was pleased to see her relax a little more; then the brow puckered and her face fell.

"The people – the performers in the square – do they pay too?"

"Yes."

"So, I owe you money?"

"Technically. But that's not why you're here, and I've already told Rubino – that was his patch you were on – to forget it."

He was pleasantly surprised at her ability to connect the dots; though he wished she'd not picked up on that issue just yet.

"Why? If I owe you, I owe you. I don't like debt," she told him stubbornly – and he had to admire her for that. She was so honest, even if she didn't have much. "I still have the money the people gave me, so take what you want."

"I really don't care about the money. Please, just forget it."

She scowled. He could see that was one argument that wasn't going to end easily, so far better to change the subject.

"How old are you?" he asked. "And I want the truth, not that bullshit you told Carl, or the extra bullshit Carl added to your file to make it legal."

She swallowed and looked away. Was that why she was here? Because she was too young to work?

"Ten and . . . a bit."

He stared at her in horror, thinking it would be more like twelve. She was even younger than he'd thought, and therefore even tougher as well. "Why . . . why aren't you with your family?" He had to ask.

She closed her eyes, knowing that question would come sooner or later; but it was the one topic of her life she didn't want to talk about. Not at all. But she guessed, with him, there was no point in lying.

"Because they're dead," she spat out angrily. *Why did he have to ask me that? Why does everyone have to ask me that? Why does it matter? What does he care? He can't magic them back to life.*

Donny stayed quiet for a moment, having suspected it would be something like that. Something bad enough that had driven a kid so young and vulnerable out into the world to fend for herself.

"What . . . happened?" he ventured.

"I don't want to talk about it, and I'm not going to." Her eyes flashed at him and he saw real distress and anger, and he knew whatever had happened was still raw inside her. He guessed then that she'd had no one to talk to about this. "I'd rather you just shot me," she then said. "It would be less painful. I don't want to remember."

He knew nothing would persuade her to open up, understandably, so he let it be – for now.

"Carl said you had no papers."

Rather blunt, he knew that, but he'd used a soft voice. He wanted to see her reaction.

Her eyes dropped down again. "I was running for my life. . . why would I think about papers?" *What are these 'papers' I'm supposed to have?*

"Why were you running for your life?"

"Because the person who killed my family . . . I didn't know if he'd escaped. And the police were coming after me."

"And now?" Still the gentle voice, drip-feeding the questions.

"Now the police have him. I think. But the police wanted to give me to some social carers or something. But I won't go back, so don't try and make me! I'm fine looking after myself!" *Why am I telling him all this*?

The panic had brought tears to her eyes and she was desperately trying not to let them fall. He could see the tension in her whole body, like a coiled spring.

"I'm not going to make you go back. I don't know where you're from, so I can't, can I?" He attempted a smile and watched her relax again, just a little. "Roughly where are you from? You don't have to be specific. I don't need a name."

"A long way east. It took me ten months to get here."

He was shocked, wondered how she'd managed to travel this far and still be alive.

"Why did you come to Vegas?"

"I didn't plan to. I was just trying to get as far away as I could. Then a man who . . . I met . . . mentioned Vegas because of the hotels and tourists. He said I would be able to get a job here."

Donny heard a voice in his ear and looked away from her for a quick moment, not moving his arms from where they lay along the armrests, or the ankle crossed over his knee.

"No, bring it in," he said.

She looked at him intently, then at the door as it opened. Lucio came in carrying a basket with a blanket-wrapped bundle inside. Donny saw the quiet joy and relief on her face at seeing what he'd brought in.

"Put it next to her," he directed, and nodded at his man to go.

The door shut, and for a few more moments she stayed bent over the basket, checking he was OK. Satisfied, she sat up.

"An unusual pet."

"I'm not sure where he came from. I think somebody threw him out of their car and left him. I'd love a chance to tell them that is cruel. You shouldn't treat animals like that."

She was fierce again. And he liked it.

"*Just* tell them?" His lips twitched into a smile.

"With my fists!" She actually smiled back this time.

"You know how to fight well – for a kid."

"I have to. No one is going to fight for me." She shrugged again, sad now, reminded of how alone she was against a multitude of threats. "I seem to find myself getting into trouble without meaning to."

"That's not your fault. Life's just like that sometimes." He turned a pressed a button on a console on his desk.

She looked up at him and her face cleared. "Maybe."

"Have you had dinner yet?"

"No."

"Are you hungry?"

"I'm always hungry."

He didn't doubt she was, and once more her answer made him smile.

"Then will you have dinner with me? I've not eaten yet either."

"I-I . . ." she stammered, obviously confused. Why was she being treated like a guest?

"You saved my life, so I think dinner is the least I can do," he reminded her gently, not wanting her to think of it as a debt. "Do you like pasta?"

"I've never had pasta."

"*Never*? Dear God. Well, my mother's pasta is the best! Come on." He stood up and motioned towards the doorway, and she eased herself off the sofa, but looked down at Lazarus. "He'll be fine where he is," he said. "But I'll ask one of the guys to watch him, if you like?"

She looked up at him for a second. He'd read her concern for her leopard. She couldn't work him out. He'd arranged to have her trapped and caught, but . . . he seemed so kind. She complied, and he stood back and indicated that she go into the next room with an open hand and smile.

They went through and saw the colours were the same, but there was a table next to the far wall, another two sofas at angles in the rest of the space, and a big screen on the wall she presumed was the television. It was bigger than she was! She didn't know TVs could be so huge!

On the table were two bowls of pasta on placemats, cutlery by the sides, and a steaming garlic flatbread on a platter in the middle. She gasped, her eyes wide, and he pulled out a chair and waited behind it until she sat, enjoying her utter innocence and wonder. How long had it been since she'd sat down to a meal with someone else? He then sat opposite, watching her looking at everything from the white shapely bowls to the shiny fork and spoon, from the crystal-cut glasses of water to the polished wood placemats, and from the pristine white tablecloth back to him. *Wow . . . everything is so beautiful.*

Donny ripped off a piece of the garlic bread and held it out to her, letting her take it in her own time, and then took some for himself.

"You've really never had pasta before?"

"No," she confirmed, and shook her head. Curls bounced, shining brighter gold in the light.

"Don't say that near my mother or she'll try and make you eat everything in the kitchen!"

She laughed, for the first time, and the sound hung between them, and he smiled; but then she remembered her own mother, the kitchen, the lack of food . . . and the laughter drained away and she felt sick. She wanted to be away from everyone and everything. She had no right to be here when her mother and sister were . . .

"What is it?" he asked quietly, sensing her distress, upset that her laughter had died so suddenly – what had she just thought of?

Her eyes dared go up to his. If he was asking, did that mean he cared? Might he understand just a little bit?

"My mother . . . she never had enough money to feed us much, and used to give us more and go without because she knew we were so hungry all the time. She tried so hard. And now she's dead. And it's not fair!"

Twin tears raced down over her cheeks and she brushed them away with her sleeve. *Don't cry!* But the loss was too raw, and the need for her mother so close beneath the surface she couldn't help it.

"Who is 'we'?" Such a softly spoken question with such a hard answer.

A sob. "My sister."

"Where is she now?"

"She's dead, too. I told her we had to go. I told her what he'd done and she wouldn't move, but I ran."

She said the last words as if condemning herself for being alive. More tears fell.

"It's not a crime to survive. It's not your fault she didn't go with you." Eyes finally looked at him, luminous pools of deep blue misery. How did he know that's what she thought? "If your mother could see you, she would be glad to see you alive, and she would want you to grow up and have a great life. You know that, don't you?"

She swallowed, stunned that this stranger, this man who had scared her so much for capturing her, could be so sensitive and understanding.

"Is this real?" she asked suddenly, as if he wasn't there at all.

"Yes, this is real. You're not dreaming." He shook his head once, trying not to smile. "Though my mother would like to claim that her cooking is heavenly. Have a try, tell me what you think . . ."

He picked up his own cutlery, and saw her do the same – and then realised she was waiting to see how he did it. So, with practised ease, he put in the fork and twirled it round to coil the spaghetti with the sauce, keeping it together with the spoon, and then put it in his mouth.

She tried to do the same. And she managed it on the third go . . . and had her first try of spaghetti Bolognese. It had smelt so good, but the taste was even better. And on an empty stomach, it was pure heaven – just like he had said!

"I think your mother is right," she said, and her smile said everything.

He felt so glad to see her eating, had been worried about her not eating enough since that very first time he'd seen her.

"I'll make sure she knows you said so."

They ate the rest of the food in silence, and in the end, she had to admit defeat, and feeling full she leaned back, waiting until he finished, feeling bad her bowl wasn't as empty as his. He used the rest of the garlic bread to mop up the final remnants of sauce, sighing contentedly when he was done.

"So, you like pasta?" He picked up his napkin and wiped his lips and laid it down.

"Yes. Almost as much as pizza."

"You've had pizza?"

"Just once."

"She does good pizza as well," he told her with a smile.

"I bet she does."

It was a lovely smile she gave him, then. She had perfect teeth, he noticed, and the smile was completely genuine. He didn't think she had a deceitful bone in her body, and realised she would rather not answer him at all than lie to him.

He got up and came back with a pad of paper and a pen, and slid it across the table to her right side, knowing she was right-handed, and looked at her.

"Will you write down what you will not tell me?"

Her face paled again and her heart pounded. Why did he have to ruin everything by asking her to do that? She didn't want to do that. She squeezed her eyes shut. But the urge to wipe her soul clean of the pain, of the hurt and the blood, was growing within her. But why here in this room, with this . . . stranger?

"You don't want to know what I know. I don't want you to know." It was a whisper. "Sometimes I wish I was dead too so I wouldn't be able to remember." She shook her head. "I can't write it."

"The man who killed your family, I can make sure he's never able to come after you."

Her eyes snapped open, and despite the emotion they were bright and alert now. "He's in prison. I think he is, anyway."

"Even easier."

She shook her head. "No. I'm not a killer. Though he deserves to die a million times for what he did."

"You're sure?"

"Yes . . ."

It was a shaky whisper. It was clear the idea was tempting, but agreeing to more death was obviously unthinkable for her. And he didn't want her to become blood-thirsty, he just wanted her to feel safe.

"Will you tell me your name?"

"No."

She picked up the pen and wrote the initials of her mother's name very faintly, then crossed them out, not wanting to give away any clues.

"You can't go through your whole life being a mystery with no name."

Absent-mindedly she wrote the word 'mystery', doing an impressive slanted 'M' and two looping 'Y's. She tilted her head and crossed out some of the letters, and then rewrote the word she ended up with. She put the pen down and turned the pad around and pushed it to him.

"Then I'll be a mystery inside a name."

This was no average kid. He was going to have to get used to that.

"Mysty? Two 'Y's? Unusual. It suits you. You're sure?"

She nodded decisively.

"Fine. OK, Mysty, now explain to me another mystery:how do you survive those jumps off buildings?"

He crossed his arms and leaned back, looking at her with eyes that told her he wanted an answer and it had better be honest. Squirming a little under the scrutiny, she fiddled with her napkin while she tried to come up with a good enough answer.

"I . . . don't really know. I'm trying to work out why. I know it should be impossible, but it can't be, else I'd be dead. And I wouldn't even be here, because I'd have died in my hometown the same night as everyone else."

Her answer didn't quite answer his question, but it gave him other information that he could use, and he had already anticipated her not understanding how she could jump the way she could.

"You found out that night?"

"When I jumped out the bathroom window. I should have broken a leg, or both, but I didn't. And the next morning when the shooting started, I ran and smashed through a window in the police station. I should have died on the pavement as it was so high, but I just landed." She shrugged in helpless honesty: she really didn't understand. She looked up and found his eyes still demanding more, and carried on. "I didn't think about it much. I was too busy trying to run away and then . . . something else happened." She shut her eyes again to block out the memories of her grandma's body, and he sensed her skirt around something pretty awful. "I-I was just trying to survive, that's all. I didn't do anything about the jumping until a few months ago, when I was at the hotel, and I decided to experiment by jumping out of the windows."

"Jumping out of the windows?" he repeated, his voice calm.

"I leapt off the fourth floor on the very first night I tried. The sixth floor was high enough to prove it was real, which is why I went higher."

"I saw the jumps in the square, as you know, and you don't just jump, you do all that . . ." He spiralled his fingers – and she smiled shyly.

"I did as many clubs at school as I could when . . . before . . . because it was a reason not to be at home. I've done gymnastics since I can remember. I used the ballroom in the hotel to practice in, and I went diving at the swimming pool to help me get the distances right."

Always finding a solution to any problem.

"What else did you do? Clubs I mean?"

"Dancing, athletics, theatre."

"What types of dancing?"

"Every type I could."

He had already guessed that, as he had seen her lonely dance practices, seen the delicate discipline of her ballet contrasted with the upbeat tap dancing. She certainly could dance.

"You should be in school," he said quietly, not sure how that would be received.

"I would like to go to school. I miss learning things. But it's hard without 'papers' or a parent, and anyway, I need to work to buy food."

She sighed and put both hands in her lap, wondering when she would be allowed to go home. She was tired now, and she'd had a frightening evening riding the emotional rollercoaster of his 'interrogation' – for that's what it was, despite it being kind and quiet – and she just wanted the meagre security of her bed.

"I can get you papers. And you won't need to work so much soon."

"What do you mean?"

"I don't want you going back to the hotel. I've got a small set of rooms you can use, and you can go to school as soon as I can arrange it – if you'd like to? You don't want to get behind, do you?" His voice wasn't harsh, but there was an indication that he would not pay attention to any argument.

"But how? I can't afford it, and I don't want pity, and I don't want to owe you anything! Why can't I just go back to the hotel?"

He didn't respond to her agitated protest.

"You couldn't owe me anything if you tried; you gave me my life, remember? How could I do anything to rival that? And it's not pity. You're not going back to the hotel because . . . I don't want you to."

She shook her head at him, not sure she liked the way he was taking over. She opened her mouth to protest further.

"Why did you save my life?" he asked suddenly, not wanting to let her continue to argue, his voice harder, his eyes stern.

"Because it was the right thing to do."

"Exactly. You did it not knowing who I was. Without expecting anything in return. Fate has dealt you a pretty rubbish hand so far, but it doesn't have to be so hard any more. That is why I'm doing this. I repeat: it's not pity, but because it's the right thing to do. Alright?"

She blinked and couldn't answer. How was this happening to her? It couldn't be. He could see the turmoil, and if he knew her better, and if she trusted him more, he'd have pulled her into his arms and held her. He, who so rarely touched anyone – except perhaps a beautiful woman, and even then briefly until he was finished with her – seemed to know that to hug her would also be the right thing to do. This was something else completely.

"Mysty?"

She forced herself to respond, and managed to nod shakily. "OK." A tiny whisper.

"Good." He relaxed a little, having got her agreement. He knew she didn't lie, and doubted she would break her word. "Now, I have to go out for a while on business, but you are staying here."

She looked at him, alarmed by this new proposal. "Why can't I go home, just tonight?"

"Because it's safer here; in fact, I doubt there's anywhere safer in the whole city. You can watch TV, or choose a book, or whatever, but you are staying here. I'll have some blankets brought in for you, and you can choose whichever sofa you like best, and I will see you in the morning. There is a bathroom through there." He pointed back through to the office and stood up, switched on the TV, punched in a channel that usually had something amusing on, not thinking for one moment it might be unsuitable for a ten-year-old; but then she wasn't an average ten-year-old, she was like a young adult and, like him, had lived so much in a short space of time. He showed her how to use the remote control, then put it down. He then went through to the office and grabbed his black jacket from the leather desk chair. It was the suit jacket to his trousers and showed off the finer silky material of his shirt perfectly. He was just adjusting his lapels when he looked up and realised she had followed him, and was standing uncertainly in the doorway.

"When will you be back?" she whispered.

She observed him, and had she been a little older she would have recognised him as being an attractive man, handsome in a dark, unfathomable way. But right now, all she knew was that she didn't really know whether she liked him or not, trusted him or not. And she didn't want to be left alone in these quiet, comfortable rooms.

He picked up one or two things from the desk and slipped them in his pocket, one of them a small camera so he could monitor her occasionally while he was out – having waited so long to get her here, he wasn't taking any chances. He had also seen her pain, and it brought him comfort to know that she wasn't alone anymore, that he could check she was OK.

He turned and gave her his full attention. "I'm not sure, kitten, I don't know how long it'll take, but I'll be here in the morning when you wake up." He startled slightly at calling her 'kitten'; but it had felt as natural as any term of genuine affection. He searched her face for a reaction, but she didn't seem to mind. "If you need anything, the intercom is here." He pointed it out on his desk. "So just press the green button and someone will answer. And if someone comes in with blankets, don't attack them!" She lowered her eyes bashfully at his last instruction; but they were smiling somewhere behind the look she gave him.

He went to the door, feeling better than he had in as long as he could remember. "Oh, and Mysty?" He turned; her eyes were still on him. "Just so you know, the windows don't open and are made of reinforced bullet-proof glass that nothing will break – unless you've managed to smuggle in a stack of explosives? – so I wouldn't try to get out that way if I were you." A blush raced over her cheek bones. "And Mysty . . ." How could he put this? "I don't know exactly what happened to you, and I know right now the last thing you're able to do is trust anyone, but I promise you, you can trust me." He gave her the benefit of his powerful, dark blue eyes for a few more moments, seeing her own eyes grow intense at his words. The look would not be lost on her. Nothing ever was. "I'll see you in the morning. Don't stay up too late, you're tired."

He opened the door and was gone.

She stood staring at the door for a second.

What on earth had just happened?

It was all so strange. She felt like he actually understood some of what she was feeling without condemning her, without judging her, or treating her like she was just a silly kid. But who was he? His eyes were guarded and haunted, the same kind of look she recognised in her own when she occasionally saw her reflection – she usually avoided mirrors as she reminded herself too much of her mother. What had he seen to make him so unhappy? She'd wished so many times that her life would calm down, that she wouldn't have to live in fear of fate's twists and turns . . . but this? As much as this scared her, it might be good to be here.

She carried Lazarus, still asleep in his basket, through to the TV, sat down on the sofa and pulled him out. Having been fed earlier, he was content and relaxed in her arms, like a baby, and his head nestled on her shoulder, the immature features a promise of something very fine when he was grown . . . just like her.

It was not long before she was asleep, flopped over on the sofa, the cub next to her, shielded by her body. She didn't see or hear the blankets or pillows arrive, and didn't stir as one was laid over their curled bodies, such was the depth of her sleep.

Watching her from the noisy surroundings of the club where he did business, Donny felt a warmth creep through his bones. A little miracle child. That's what she was. He just wasn't sure who was going to benefit most from their knowing each other . . . her, or him.

WHEN SHE WOKE up she had the confusing feeling of being comfortable, and safe, and yet her brain was telling her something was wrong. And then memories from the night before filtered in and she raised herself up on her elbows. She saw the soft cream blanket over her, and Lazarus standing on all fours looking down at her expectantly. He licked her cheek while she stared at the room, at everything, remembering how she had come to be here, and the man who had left her there to go out.

"Good morning."

She jumped, and there he was, sitting casually on the other sofa in front of the now silent TV screen, as calm and relaxed as if he usually woke up with a waif and a stray on his very expensive furniture. He was still wearing the same black trousers and black shirt from the night before, and he looked like he'd been out all night and come back not so long ago. *Has he changed his mind? Is he going to chuck me out now?* She searched his face, but it didn't look angry or annoyed. At all. In fact, if asked, she would have said he looked . . . amused.

"How did you sleep?"

"Better than I thought I would."

"Excellent. Then your subconscious recognises a friend when it sees one. So, you can stop looking at me like you're terrified of me," he chided softly, knowing her disorientated alarm was natural.

"Sorry." She looked away and tried to school her expression into a different shape – a relaxed and calm shape – which wasn't easy. Perhaps he hadn't changed his mind after all? "How was your night out?"

"Busy. I've only been back half an hour."

He rubbed a hand over his eyes. He didn't mind the tiredness. He was often late back, and the extra time last night had been because of her, and he didn't begrudge that at all.

"What time is it?"

"6.30am."

He knew she rose with the dawn. Sometimes even earlier.

"I have work in half an hour," she remembered with a jolt. This room seemed a world away from the Vegas she knew, her hotel, her quiet life working in the store for Carl.

"No, you don't. I had one of my men call Carl and you're taking one of your many days of owed holiday. He was fine about it, so don't worry."

He was glad she didn't argue. He was tired, and perhaps not in the best mood to be diplomatic despite his relief at having her here. She sat up properly and invited Lazarus to sit on her lap, and she stroked him when he flopped down against her chest.

"Don't you think you need to sleep for a bit?" she asked gently, not looking at him.

For a moment he was lost in thought, enjoying the innocent picture they made, the cub and her. It must be a one in a million-billion chance that an abandoned leopard would be saved by a feral girl. But no one else was better for the job of looking after him than her. And now she was worrying about him?

"I'll sleep sometime. I'm used to staying up. Don't worry about me."

"Who does?"

"Pardon?"

"Who does worry about you?"

She looked at him, cradling the leopard on her shoulder, who was happy in her embrace, his nose in her hair.

"I have a whole army of people whose job it is to keep me alive," he replied, but he wasn't sure he liked his reaction to her concern.

"If he was in a zoo, there would be people to look after him, and keep him alive." She nodded to Lazarus. "But none of them would care for him like I do."

He had to admit, it was a good argument. "Are you volunteering for the job, then?" he asked lightly, half teasing; but it wasn't a simple question at all: it was the beginning of a much deeper level of trust, of accepting each other.

"Seeing as you seem to worry about me, I guess I am, yes."

Her eyes turned back to his, bright and fathomless and infinitely beautiful.

"That's a fair deal," he acknowledged with an inclination of his head, and he watched as she smiled at her victory.

"Donny?"

"Mysty."

He liked her saying his name. Still uncertain, but determined nonetheless.

"What happens today? Why did you tell Carl I was having the day off?"

"Because there are lots of things to do – not least going to the hotel and packing everything up. I'm sure you'd rather do that than have me send someone?" She nodded, not sure why she was so accepting of his plan. But if he'd wanted to hurt her, he could have – many times over. "I need to go through a few details with you so when I get papers made for you they make sense and the story all adds up. I also have someone coming to meet you so you go in at the right year group at school. And, lastly, you need some new clothes . . . and a wash." She blushed and looked away, feeling even more of a ragamuffin compared to the suave elegance of his appearance, even after a night out. "In hot water." She hid her face in the cub's fur and prayed he didn't say anything else.

"I was a year ahead at school, so I shouldn't be behind," she dared say when she felt her cheeks burn a little less. "And I did get some text books that I've been studying."

"I saw." She looked round at him sharply, confused. "I've seen inside, Mysty. I had my boys put some cameras in so we'd know when you were there." He had to be honest with her.

"You *spied* on me?" she demanded, horrified.

"Only for a few days. I hoped it would make coming to get you easier. I hoped to avoid scaring you. I really, really didn't want to scare you, and . . ." He didn't know what else to say. He looked at her. Her face was still indignant, but his words had taken the edge off her anger, and she relaxed a little again. It was best to change the subject. "You have lots of old music."

"Old is good."

"Oh! I have something of yours." He reached over and held her CD out to her, and she recognised it instantly. "You dropped it on the pavement. Paulo brought it to me." She took it, remembering when she'd last seen it – her Bon Jovi CD – realising this man really did seem to care about her. "You like music?"

"I *love* music. I learn all the words."

"We will have to upgrade you. You get far better sound from something newer than the CD player."

She knew the 'we will' was 'I will'. "When I can buy one, I will. Please don't buy me anything." There was an edge to her voice.

"We're friends, aren't we? What's a little present between friends?"

"We're friends?"

She was a kid, a runaway. How could he really be friends with her? And how could she be friends with a Mafia boss who was so important, dangerous, and so much older?

"What makes people friends?" he asked; it was time to use her type of argument on her.

"Umm . . . they talk."

"Yes. And?" She didn't respond. "They share a meal, have a laugh, make each other feel better, help each other out, right?" She nodded reluctantly. "So, I guess that makes us friends." The simplicity of his argument made sense. But how had she made him feel better? How had she helped him out? "Except, so far, *you've* done the helping by jumping in front of a truck for me, so now it's my turn. So, don't argue about it again."

He said this last in an especially stern voice, and tried to look at her severely – which was hard because her face was so open and innocent – to get his point across.

"Yes, boss."

She gave him a little mock salute and her impish smile stole his ability to be serious for much longer.

"Right, for that, you can go upstairs and have a bath *before* breakfast," he laughed. "Come on, bring the pussycat as well. What have you called him?" He stood up, wearily but purposefully.

"Lazarus."

"Good name."

She followed as he led her out into the hallway, and up two flights of stairs, then into the spare bedroom. It was so beautiful. She could hardly believe her eyes.

"Now, I asked my mother to get some clothes for a girl of your size, so there should be something for you to wear when you get out the tub." He looked at the assortment of pink and white frilly items on the bed. "But I think I should have been more specific . . ." There was no way this tomboy girl would wear a pink puffy skirt! She would look like candyfloss with her skinny little legs sticking out the bottom!

"I-I would look like candyfloss if I wore that!" she said, looking in horror at the clothes. "On a stick!"

He had to smile at her blunt honesty – and at her reference to candyfloss! How had she thought of candyfloss too? She looked up at him as he looked down, and they both laughed.

And then her face clouded as she realised she might have appeared ungrateful. "I'm sorry–" she began.

"It's OK! I'll send someone for something more suitable. These clothes are . . . well, they're not at all you!" Her face softened. "The bathroom is through there, and the towels are in there." He pointed to the en suite bathroom and a large linen press. "I'll leave you to . . ." He wasn't quite sure where to go with that sentence. He was a little out of his depth, he realised. He turned to leave.

"Donny?" He hoped it wouldn't be an awkward question.

"Yes, Mysty?"

She decided in that very second that she liked her new name. It was better than April.

"Can I wash Lazarus as well?"

"Sure, you can." *Phew.*

He shut the door and walked away, patching through to send someone into town for a new set of clothes.

Whatever happened with her around, he knew for certain it wasn't going to be boring.

SPLASHING AROUND WITH Lazarus in the bath had been so much fun – and in hot, bubbly water! The water had sloshed on the floor as they'd played, however, and she had frozen, wondering if someone would hear them having fun and come in and shout at her if they saw it. But no one disturbed them. She had carefully mopped up the water, anyway, before towelling Lazarus dry and using the hair-dryer on him. And then on her own hair. It had seemed like such luxury, and felt strange, but so nice.

And putting on a simple pair of new black leggings and a blue short-sleeve t-shirt that morning had felt so good too. They were clean, and smelt so fresh, like someone had washed and pressed them – even though they were brand-new – before putting them in her room. And it didn't go unnoticed that he had obviously noted that she liked blue – her old sweater had been blue – and favoured leggings over jeans.

Her worn-out trainers had disappeared from the bedroom, so she wondered what to do about her feet. She wanted to explore, and curiosity and boredom were winning over the trepidation of leaving the room. Donny hadn't said she had to stay in the room, had he?

She rested her hand on the door knob and Lazarus looked at her, clearly ready to follow her wherever she went. She picked him up, determined they would stick together. In bare feet, she crept slowly down the stairs, wide eyes taking in all the door ways and the details of the impressive staircase. She was right at the top of the house, it seemed, as there were no other stairs going up, and when she peeked over the banisters, she could see two, or three floors? Normal human noises were coming from downstairs: voices, footsteps, cutlery, and it all became a little clearer and louder the further she went. Her stomach rumbled loudly.

"Hey, kid."

Swinging around she came face to face with a shirt, and glanced up to see Paulo just behind her, looking amused.

"Donny says you're staying around a while?"

"He told me that too."

"And what he says goes. He also told me you'll need breakfast. You hungry?"

"A little." She downplayed it, blushing because she knew how starving she really was, and suspected he knew it as well.

"You want to tell me what your little shadow wants? We don't usually have such furry house-guests."

"He can eat most things. We won't be any bother."

Apologetic, anxious eyes looked up at him in a way no one ever had before: so vulnerable, yet so humble – and grateful. And she was too overawed and too young to note the effect she had on the imposing black-clad figure of a man who would gladly walk into a gun fight, happily attempt to remove a man's head from his shoulders with his bare hands, who knew every inch of Vegas like it was his own skin, and yet felt humbled himself somehow by this new arrival in their lives.

Someone else arrived to fill the silence.

"You won't be a bother at all. We're used to dealing with much worse." Mario appeared at Paulo's shoulder, also in black. They looked intimidating, despite the smiles on their faces. "Donna Capello has just made some fresh focaccia bread. You want to try some?"

"Is it good?"

"It's the best!" Mario held out his hand to Mysty. "I'm Mario, by the way." A moment passed. And then an uncertain hand reached out and the much larger fingers closed firmly around hers. "What's his name again?"

"Lazarus."

"Good name."

"He's got some growing to do."

"So have you. I could pick you up with one hand!" Mario said, a tease more than a criticism, but Paulo rolled his eyes at him – but refrained from slapping him around the head this time – at his indiscretion, *again*!

"Down here we have the kitchen," Paulo then said as they reached the bottom of the stairs, "where Donna Capello–"

"Donny's mother," Mario interjected.

"Makes the best food in the *entire* world," Mario said with feeling.

It seemed true. The smells enough were amazing. And whatever focaccia was it had to be amazing too!

A shriek made them all start.

A woman with lots of dark hair plaited into a bun on top of her head bustled towards them in a flurry of apron and flour, bringing with her the warmth of kitchen like a homely mist in the air.

"Is this her?" she asked, following up with a steam of excitable Italian.

The girl had no idea what was being said as she was inspected, affectionately, by large blue eyes that reminded her of Donny's. Bending over, Donna Capello was all round cheeks and crinkled eyes, her olive skin healthy, making her seem youthful despite the stoop to her shoulders and the weight of a bosom that obscured the difference between breasts and waist. Mysty was then grabbed and hugged tightly, with Lazarus squashed somewhere in the middle, and his yowl helped save her from another crushing.

"Donna Capello doesn't speak much English!" Paulo laughed. "You'll have to learn some Italian, si?"

But there was no time to answer as she was then led into the kitchen and sat down at a long rustic wooden table with two long benches either side. She took in the hanging garlic bulbs, the herbs, the heat radiating from the oven, was given orange juice, focaccia, cheese, ham, tomatoes and an apple, all the while listening to Mario and Paulo banter with Donna Capello, who bustled around in her element, clearly loving feeding her 'family' – and new guest. The relaxed attitude of the men helped her to stay calm, despite feeling somewhat overwhelmed by all the activity. Is this really how people ate together? Or just Italians? She was mesmerised.

Donna Capello almost fainted when she offered Lazarus a piece of ham and realised she wasn't holding a normal house cat, and pointed at his small, pointed teeth in horror. Dramatic hand gestures followed and much laughter, and then slowly, carefully at first, she began to relax. She'd never heard laughter like it, had never tasted such food – the focaccia was incredible! – or witnessed such natural joy at just being in each other's company. No one there seemed to think anything of it. It was clearly normal to them. But it meant the world to her.

The plate of food was gone before she even realised, and then Donna Capello plonked herself down next to Mysty and put a pastry on her plate. It had some kind of jam inside, and it looked so soft and delicious that she felt her mouth begin to water just breathing in the aroma of it. But there was so much happiness at the table, and such generosity, that it finally it caught up with her: tears suddenly pricked her eyes and the pastry turned into a blur. Donna Capello covered her small hand with her own and squeezed. Then the Italian matriarch winked.

Mario then started complaining that he needed a pastry as well, and the ensuing exchange was fast, colourful and utterly beyond the girl's comprehension. But it was enough. Enough to make her want to understand, to learn, and to embrace these good things that were somehow happening to her. She didn't know these people at all. But she had been brought into this house that was a home for this family, and invited to become a part of it. All the acceptance she had never thought she would find, was right there waiting for her. *Don't think. Just accept.*

"SO, WHAT HAVE you been up to today?"

"Breakfast. With Paulo and Mario and Donna Capello. She fed me so much. I tried not to let my eyes be bigger than my tummy! I would have eaten more it tasted so good, but I would have popped!"

Donny grinned, unsurprised but happy to hear her reportage, amused at her word choices. Her mother obviously had been English. From one look at her, he could already tell that the warmth, rest and food was having an effect. Her cheeks had a little more colour, her riot of curls was even brighter; or maybe he was being fanciful; he liked to think not. The tension in her face had eased, and her eyes were a little less watchful. And the look she had when she was thinking too deeply had disappeared. Thinking too deeply because she had to. Because she had no one to do any thinking for her.

"What else?"

"Mario measured my feet for some new trainers."

Glancing down he saw her bare feet as they went down the stairs to the basement rooms. He walked; she hopped. Full of energy, childish, uninhibited and playful. Inwardly he smiled, not just to see the improvement in her and her innocence, but at the recollection that far bigger, tougher men had walked down the same steps in fear, knowing what reckoning awaited them. She, however, was blissfully ignorant, and that was the way it was going to stay. As long as she was there, no one and nothing business-related was going to be brought into the house. They had other locations. All Donny's boys understood their new instructions.

They had wondered why Donny had gone to so much trouble for her, but they understood immediately when they spent time with her. Even watching her from a doorway, as most of them had after lunch, as Paulo had presented her with a book that would help her take her first steps to speaking Italian, her face had lit up the room. He had spent an hour patiently going through simple words for every-day items with her, and somehow even this low-key event had attracted attention, and soon Lucio, Mario, and Giuseppe had crept in to 'help'.

Donny hadn't anticipated her being quite so popular, however, and word from his mother at what his fearsome troop of cut-throats were up to had both amused and irked him. Why was that?

"We can go shopping for some more clothes. You'll need some things for school as well."

Donny waited for the exclamation that she didn't need anything, and slyly looked round at her: she was frowning, somehow repressing the words she knew he would reject anyway. How strange this must all be for her.

"Which school will I go to?" she asked instead.

"It's the best, I've already checked. Safe. Good reputation. Good results. And it's about a mile away, so you can get there easily on a bus, or you can walk."

They'd now reached the basement, which was different to the rest of the house. It was functional, for business, and it occurred to him that a child might consider it unfriendly.

"One other thing we need to do is get you proper papers. We're going to get all that set up now so you don't have any problems in the future." From her face, he could guess her thoughts. She must know, young as she was, that this was illegal. This wasn't a government office he had brought her down to. "Just think of it as unofficial witness protection, and it's costing the tax-payer nothing."

He was pleased that his optimistic interpretation eased the frown on her face just a little. He knew she understood this was the path of least resistance; legality for her would come with records, police files, social worker reports, and probably a few press releases. This was by far the lesser of two evils.

Leading her into a small office, he saw Fabio, smart in his black suit, fiddling with a piece of equipment.

"Fabio."

The man straightened and turned instantly, having been expecting them. He was of average height, average build, and had exceedingly pale but bright hazel eyes. As one of the tech team, he hadn't been there to witness first-hand their attempts at 'kidnapping' her, but had been keeping watch on her remotely via the cameras.

"Boss!"

"This is Mysty."

"Nice to meet you, Mysty." Crouching down, he offered his hand.

"Fabio is going to take your picture and help make your papers."

"You OK with that, Mysty?" Fabio asked.

She looked at the camera and the plain blue backdrop. "Yes. I had school photos taken like this."

"Great, so you know how it works. Just stand over here for me and . . ."

Gently she was eased away from Donny's side, Fabio telling her every second what he was doing to avoid spooking her – and to keep his boss happy. He gently moved her curls away from her face, arranged them over her shoulders. He then went to the camera and saw intense eyes staring into his camera lens. He took half a dozen shots, removed the memory card and went to his computer and began tapping information into his keyboard.

"How old are you, Mysty?" he asked.

"About ten."

Fabio's eyes flicked to Donny's and back. He wasn't expecting such an innocent-looking kid to play her cards so close to her chest.

"She's going into year six. That's two years ahead of her age group. Bump it up to twelve," Donny said, confidently.

Fabio didn't know about the tests she'd done that afternoon with Paulo. Or the results. Donny might not be a father, but he knew what would happen if she wasn't challenged at school, and he didn't think it would end well. She was a very bright kid. And there was no argument from the girl sitting in the chair next to him.

"Her accent is a bit of an issue."

"She's half-English. On her mother's side. And why?"

"Just thinking about it attracting attention. People noticing. Especially kids at school. But it's kind of cute. Sure, they'll love it."

Fabio continued typing, and a few minutes later a printer whirred into life. He then handed the documents to the girl. She read them, silently, in awe that these men she barely knew could do things she didn't understand. It felt kind of nice. To be looked after.

"This is just a copy that I need you to read and learn all the details. I've sent the file to a place where it will be printed and hologrammed properly. Who you were doesn't matter anymore. This is you now, and you're all set up on the national database." He said all this very gently, aware of the sensitive nature of his words.

Donny took the piece of paper to check it after a few seconds of letting her look, letting her absorb the information.

"Why didn't you put her first name as Mysty?" he then asked, frowning.

"Because it's too unusual. And if anyone's hunting for her, they'll never get anything trying to correlate her name with the name on her papers. Only her friends or real associates will know her as Mysty. Especially with the double 'y'."

Fabio's voice was too calm for it to be a fudge, or a dodge, and his eyes were steady as he waited for judgement. Even Mysty looked up at Donny in those few seconds, awaiting his verdict.

"Fair point."

The papers were then passed back to Mysty, and she clutched them like they were sheets from the original Gospels.

"Anything else today?" Fabio looked up at his boss, ready for the next challenge.

"I'm going to get this sent over to the school and smooth a few things over of an official kind. Could you keep Mysty occupied for half an hour for me?"

"I . . ."

But Donny was already heading out the door.

"Sure." He took a deep breath, not sure what to do with a now ten-twelve-year-old kid, let alone one who had apparently witnessed some shocking events and spent most of a year fending for herself. Fabio smiled. "You want to see where I normally work?"

"OK."

Getting up, they headed out the door to the surveillance room, and

Fabio smiled as various heads looked up from their screens, and then stayed up as they realised who was with him.

"Hey! It's the Butterfly!" they laughed. "Hi!"

Mysty looked utterly confused.

"They saw you jumping of that building in Palm Square, or 'floating' as they called it," Fabio explained."They're big fans of yours. They gave you the name." She nodded, blushing, but Fabio wasn't sure she heard, because she was too busy staring at . . . *everything*. "Have you never seen computers before?"

"Not like these!" Her eyes were huge, skimming over every surface in the room, from the data-logs scrollingon the screens to the consoles, from the giant monitor on the wall that showed the live camera feeds from around the city to the guys themselves. "We had a few at school, but only the older kids could use them. You watched me on that?"

"Yes." Fabio saw the information sinking in, wondered which way it was going to go, like watching a coin spin, heads or tails, either fearful rejection, or keen interest. He hoped it was the latter, so Donny didn't think he'd freaked her out.

When her eyes turned back to his, they were bright with intrigue, but she was too shy to say what she was thinking.

But he guessed. "You want me to show you how they work?"

"Yes, please!" She replied with a fervent nod of her head, both childlike and determined.

"Right well, we'd best get you a chair . . ."

They found a headset and adjusted it to fit her.

"OK, so, you can use this screen." He swivelled her chair. "It'll display what you tell it to. Much of what I do is by voice command because the computer recognises my vocals, but if I don't want to, I can use the keyboard, or the touch screen. It's a very versatile set up. With me so far?"

"Yes."

"So, say for example I want to go to the CCTV feed of Palm Square, on the off chance that some crazy girl is going to jump off a roof . . ." – he glanced at her, but she was smiling, thank God! – ". . . I go here. Here, type it in, Palm Square, and then . . ." Her eyes darted around, trying to keep up with the new information, to see the instructions being typed into the keyboards that Fabio knew blindfolded. "I'll do that again, here, here and here."

The look on her face was enough of a wow. "And that's *really real*?"

Fabio nodded, amused at her incredulity when it was something he took for granted every day. "Live feed."

"Like instant TV?"

"If you like." Her wonderment was the best audience. "How about you try? You can't break it, so go for it." He clicked off Palm Square and the screens restored to the previous views of the city.

She almost didn't dare touch, but doing exactly as she'd been shown she held her breath and, once again, the picture-feed of Palm Square popped up, and a face full of delight turned to Fabio.

He grinned at her. "How easy was that?"

"This is the best thing ever!"

Laughing at her enthusiasm, Fabio zoomed all the way out on satellite, until the view became one of the rotating Earth upon which they sat.

"Oh my goodness!" she cried.

"And we can zoom in using this. Or back out, or to a different location using these commands here. Once you're familiar, when you're really good, you can use voice command, because you'll know the latitude and longitude."

"Wow!"

"OK, time for an educational Google moment."

Fabio pulled up the Earth's gridline information and let her read it. While she did so, he noticed a figure standing quietly behind them and realised it was Donny, eyes amused but approving. Fabio got a nod, and Donny melted away, content to let her enjoy her first computer lesson; she was clearly eager to learn more. Every minute with Fabio, he decided, would be a godsend for her as her young mind clearly yearned to learn.

DONNY LOOKED AROUND the large lounge, with a small open kitchen area, her bedroom and bathroom just off the hall. The door had added security now – the windows too. He'd also had some cameras installed, so they could check on her every now and again, check she was OK.

He'd given up a certain amount of time that day getting things ready for her, and spent some time with her, too, partly to help her feel more confident around people, but also because . . . if he was honest. . . he'd enjoyed it. It was never dull being with her, and she was always so quick to understand everything he told her that it was easy to forget just how young she was. He'd seen her wonder of the surveillance room, and her eyes had almost popped out of her head; he'd introduced her to everyone she'd not met yet, and she'd remembered all their names. She'd spent some more time with Fabio, and she'd loved every minute. And that morning, his mother had wrapped her up in her ample arms and bosom – and squeezed her so tight he had thought she might break! – and all the time thanking her in rapid Italian for saving her boy's life. It had fallen on uncomprehending ears, but it had been good to see her embraced, and although she'd been alarmed, he'd heard she was smiling too.

"Well, here we are . . . your first night in your new place. Do you have everything you need?"

She was standing awkwardly against the counter in the kitchen space, looking at him with those huge eyes – which were filling with tears. She nodded in answer to his question and pressed her lips together, not trusting herself to speak.

"Right, well, a few rules. Number one – no big parties with beer and sex, except at weekends." He saw her start to smile. "Number two – don't go out at night on your own if it's after 11pm." That one was serious and she knew better than to argue. "Three – don't tell anyone where you live, or that you know me." A proper nod. "Four – and don't argue with me because I am trying to organise something! – do not do your building jumping in daylight or in front of people. OK?"

A long pause, followed by a slow nod. She didn't quite understand, but she trusted him – and she'd do anything he asked her to really if she were honest.

"I know you might not like that rule but, believe me, there are people out there who wouldn't hesitate to kidnap you and sell you to the highest bidder, or keep you in a cage so they could make money from making you perform. It is an amazing and unique talent you have, but it is a danger to you as well. Understand?"

He saw her expression darken as she realised the truth of what he'd said. *Shit. I kidnapped her too*. But she seemed to accept what he'd said.

"Yes, Donny, I promise."

"Now. Tomorrow you have your first day of school, so I want you to get some rest. One of my men will drive you and will leave at 7.55am. You can eat breakfast here – I've had the cupboards and fridge stocked – or you can eat with Mother if you get up in time. Please be ready. Your uniform is being pressed and will be brought up to you shortly. If you need anything at all, you can call me on the intercom, OK?"

Once more she nodded.

"And Friday night we are going to eat pizza and start watching all the great movies you've missed, starting with *Lord of the Rings*!"

During the day they had discussed films, and she had confessed she had not seen any of the classics; his secret passion, and one he seldom indulged was movies, and he was, he had to admit, rather excited at the thought of a night off sharing this passion with her.

"Good. Now I must leave. I have business to attend to. I will see you in the morning."

Her smile said it all, and he felt reassured that she'd understood the rules, but also the reasoning behind them. Smart kid.

"HOW WAS YOUR first day of school?"

She was still in her grey skirt and white shirt. It looked strange on her as he was so used to the leggings and t-shirt combination.

"OK . . . it was a bit weird being in a class with the older kids who are all so much bigger than me, but the work was no problem. I even have homework."

Her huge smile was like a sunburst in the room. A small bundle trotted up to her legs and pawed at her to be picked up, which she did, lifting Lazarus up against her chest.

"And did you sign up for any clubs?"

"Gymnastics, ballet, modern, diving, athletics and performing arts."

"Wow! I'm never going to see you at this rate."

Her face fell completely, and he felt bad for having stolen a piece of her joy.

"I only put my name down . . . I can pull out!" she replied quickly.

He shook his head. "No, I want you to do them – *all* of them. Just save one night a week – hopefully Friday night as that can be movie night – or my mother will miss you, and so will everyone else. And who's going to look after me?"

They stared at each other for a few moments; sometimes they didn't need words. He knew she'd realised he would miss her too, and she him.

She smiled. "So, you're just like all Italian men: you like having a woman around worrying about you," she accused.

"Absolutely," he agreed with an unashamed smile. She had obviously been taking lessons from his mother!

"I really want to watch the movies. I'll bring the popcorn."

"That's a deal. If I'm busy, let me or Paulo know what time you're coming over and he'll contact me. You have your new phone, yeah?"

"I do, and I will. I understand."

"But you're always welcome, and if something happens . . ."

"Donny?"

"Yes?"

"I'll be OK, honestly. But if anything happens, I promise I'll tell you. My phone knows your number."

Jesus, he hadn't wanted kids, but this one, she was great. He knew she was now better equipped to live life, to go to school, and come back to a secure home – everything he hoped he could give her – but it was more than that: he'd so quickly got used to having her around, liked having her around.

He drew himself up and tried to look serious, saying, "I'd better go." He smoothed his jacket.

"Try to go to bed before four in the morning," she chided – another sign of her growing confidence.

"Yes . . ." he laughed. "So, pizza on Friday night – shall I tell *Mama*?"

"Si. Bueno. Grazi."

He was proud of her accent, and her quick grasp of the basics of their language. With her hair dyed dark brown she could have passed as a native!

He nodded and started walking to the door, trying to put his thoughts to business.

"Donny?" He turned and she was right behind him, and her arms reached out to him. He responded unthinkingly and held her tight for a few precious seconds, ignoring the feel of her bony back. She'd get there. She was a fighter. He knew she was. "Thank you."

Two words. Whispered, but screamed from the rooftops.

Donny let go, slowly. It was the first hug he'd shared with anyone other than his mother in almost a decade. He wasn't good at emotion, and was unsure how to respond to 'thank you' as mostly the people around him just did as they were asked and had no need to thank him. So he didn't reply, just ruffled her curls. She seemed to understand that too, however, and didn't seem expectant of a response.

He went to the door, more touched than he had anticipated by the simple gesture of a child's hug.

"Friday, don't forget."

She shook her head.

Donny went down the stairs down to the waiting car; Paulo was at the door to shadow him into the vehicle.

He and Mysty. Two lost souls. Where would they end up?

DONNY CLIMBED THE steps of his townhouse without really looking at anyone or anything. He was tired. He'd had a long day and an even longer week. All he wanted was to relax.

"Hey, Gio." He acknowledged the man as he passed by.

Giovanni nodded at his boss slowly from his chair, knowing better than to try to start a conversation with him.

He knew Paulo was behind him and would follow him all the way to his rooms until he was secure behind the locked door. They started pushing numbers into the key pad when the door was pulled open and four-foot-two-inches of school uniform and golden hair looked up at them.

"Donny!"

"Mysty? What are you doing here?"

"Donna Capello taught me how to make lasagne – she said it was one of your favourites! And I've been doing homework, waiting for you to come home." She suddenly felt awkward. It was only the third time in three weeks she'd seen him, and she'd thought it would be a nice surprise, but from the look on his face. . . "You said to come around on Friday again, but I can go . . ." She scuttled off.

Donny's surprise had worn off sufficiently for him to realise his own error, and how his words had made her feel. He nodded at Paulo, who nodded back and retreated. Donny stepped through the door and shut it firmly, tempted to lock it, but decided he wouldn't need to. She appeared through the doorway from the other room, her school bag on her shoulder, and she stopped a few metres from him.

"You made me dinner and you're leaving me to eat alone?"

"You're busy."

"I forgot today was Friday. I've had a really tough day. Don't go . . ." He held up one hand in gentle but effective protest. Slowly, she took her school bag off her shoulder and dumped it on the ground by the nearest bookshelf. "You've finished your homework?"

"I'll do the rest over the weekend."

"Everything OK at school?"

He knew it was. He'd see her grades on the school database.

"Yes. Though no one in my year really likes me. They know I've skipped a year. Thank goodness they don't know I've skipped two." He smiled and indicated they go back in the TV room. "Why was your day so tough?" she asked in Italian, making him smile.

"Too many men all wanting their own way. And too many arguments and not enough reason."

"I promise not to argue with you tonight," she told him firmly, and that made him smile.

"Good, then you won't mind fetching me a beer from the fridge while I rest."

He flopped onto a sofa and looked as useless as he could, despite the fact he looked disgracefully healthy and clearly had toned muscles underneath his fine suit. She laughed and went to the fridge, getting out a bottle of his favourite and a chilled glass.

"How is Lazarus?" he asked when she returned.

"Bigger. He keeps wanting me to pick him up but he's getting too heavy."

"And how are you?"

"I'm fine. I've been asked to join the school diving team." She looked at him for guidance.

"Do you want to?"

"I think so. I'm just a little . . . scared, I guess. I'm not used to doing things with people watching." She looked down at her hands. "And I'm still so skinny. I feel like a twig." She stuck one leg out.

"You can't help being a little twiggy right now. One day you'll stop being a twig and turn into a flower." She looked at him dubiously, amused at his attempt to reason with her. "It doesn't matter how you look. And you're not a *weak* twig – you've very strong! Don't be impatient with yourself." She tilted her head to one side, contemplating his answer, deciding it was a fair point. "I have some news for you that you might just find as exciting as joining the diving team."

"What? Tell me!" She turned to him and her eyes glowed with interest.

"But . . . seeing as you don't like people watching you . . . I guess maybe I shouldn't tell you," he teased, taking a deliberately long swig of his beer while she fumed in anticipation.

"Donatello Raphael Capello, you are mean if you don't tell!" She was on her feet now and had her hands on her hips – and he burst out laughing. "And don't laugh! I'm being stern!"

"I know, I know! *Very stern*!" he said. "So, you really want to know?" She narrowed her eyes at him. "Alright, well . . . I have a friend who works in Cirque de Soleil, you know the place?" She nodded vigorously. "Well, I told him about you and he's very interested in meeting you. He takes in new artists and helps them develop their talents, meet their potential, and build their acts up. He says he's taken on a full quota for this season, but your talent sounds like a chance he'd be a fool to turn down, so . . . he's got you an audition on Sunday afternoon."

He paused and watched her face.

"It's not really an *audition* as such," he continued, worried that the word might have put her off, "because I can't imagine he won't take you, but it's standard procedure so he can get an idea of what you can do. How does that sound?"

"It's amazing!" She suddenly said, so excited that she threw her hands into the air. "Will you be there?"

"I can't, kitten, as it wouldn't be a good idea for you to be seen with me. I wish I could see his face though when you don't go splat." His smile helped her over her disappointment. "I'll have a discreet car take you, and it'll be there to bring you back." She nodded, her mind already racing ahead – what a weekend! "All of which means you're going to have to be on top form, so you'd better have some dinner. Now where's this lasagne masterpiece?"

"I'll go and get it. We did garlic focaccia as well, and a salad, so I hope you're hungry."

She danced around the sofa and went to the cupboard by the table, getting out the tablecloth, cutlery and place mats. She slipped through the hidden door – that was disguised as a wall – that went down to the kitchen. (There was another room down there, but she'd not been in that one. She knew there were underground tunnels, because that was how she went into the house so she wouldn't be seen. Paulo had shown her, and loaded her into the database as she was now part of the 'family'.)

He rose and made his way to the table when she'd finished setting everything out – and stopped short. Everything on the table looked great, pristine, and just where and how it should be. Except the lasagne. *Dear God, what has my mother taught her?*

"What do you think?" she asked, her eyes bright.

What should he say? He arranged his expression to look encouraging, and something less horrified than he felt.

"It looks . . . really great."

He tipped his head back and swallowed the last of his beer, only to see her grab onto a chair for dear life and bend over double laughing

"Might I ask, what is so funny?"

"You! You look so serious. You were trying to say something nice, even though it looks awful! It's the one Mario dropped on the floor when he was trying to help, and I just wanted to see what you said if you thought I'd made it!"

She began laughing again, and Donny couldn't help but join in. When had he felt so carefree? So human? When had anyone ever treated him with such familiarity and lack of fear?

"Oh, I feel dizzy now!" she said, and put a hand on her forehead – and then found herself being lifted up and thrown over his shoulder. "Donny!" she screeched, laughing again, but a little scared. *What's he doing? Is he angry?*

She was deposited at the doorway and directed to go back down and get the real lasagne before he decided to send her to bed. But he was laughing still, and moments later he was presented with a much-improved version.

"You don't want to be a twig, do you?" he said as he loaded her plate up, observing her mock horror at the huge portion – which still wasn't as big as his. "Are you sure my mother didn't make this?" he added, tasting it.

She smiled. That was the best compliment, *ever*.

"Hand on heart. She sat there with her sewing while she told me what to do. Although the flour did go everywhere at the beginning. But I made it myself. All of it."

He could just imagine the mess, but it cheered him to think of it.

"Well, that's kind of good *and* kind of bad." She looked at him, suddenly worriedly, and he wondered if she would ever lose that instant frown when she thought she had displeased him. "It means I'll expect good food like this *every* Friday night from now on." The demand was a welcome one, and they ate in happy silence for a few minutes. "Would you like to watch a film after we've eaten?" he then said.

"I was wondering if you'd teach me how to gamble or play poker."

He looked up in surprise, a bit worried she would get bitten by the gambling bug that infected so many in Vegas.

"Can I ask why?"

"I saw Paulo, Mario and Lucio playing something, and I asked what it was and they said I was too young to understand. Well, I don't think I'm too young, and I'd like to know what people play."

Woe betide any man or woman who patronised this kid. Her IQ was sufficient to keep child prodigy specialists occupied for a long time. He relaxed. It was just her insatiable curiosity. He was used to that.

"Well, I guess I can." He was one of the best gamblers in the city, or the world – though he didn't do so much of it any more, either in the casinos or in virtual competitions. "As long as you promise not to bankrupt me." She rolled her eyes. "How's the dancing going?"

"Oh, fine, though I'm trying to find a club or something outside school for better ballet, and I want to learn Spanish dancing, so that will be a challenge. I definitely can't be a twig to do that."

He smiled as he took another spoonful of lasagne.

"Try to take it easy tomorrow, alright? Sunday's audition will not take very long, but no point in arriving tired."

She nodded. "Are you going out tonight?"

"Yes." She sighed and he added, "Though to save you scowling, I promise to be back by three."

She huffed as though he had just promised to personally make sure the sun came up the next day.

"I will check with Gio next time I see him," she threatened.

"Have I ever broken my word?"

"No, I suppose not," she conceded.

"You want some ice cream or something?" he offered, wondering if he could tempt her to a bit more food.

"I don't really like sweet things." She never wanted to taste sugar again; but she had spoken too fast and too seriously for him to think it was just a taste issue.

"Is it a diet thing? Or a taste thing, or what? Most people love desserts," he asked gently. Seeing the happiness drain away at the mention of ice cream, he knew he'd touched upon something new. "Or is it a memory thing?"

"It's a memory thing." *Please don't ask me anymore.*

"You want to tell me about it?"

"I . . ." She did, and she didn't. "The last thing my mother made was . . . my birthday cake. She died on my ninth birthday. I don't want to eat anything sweet again in my life."

She made it to the end of the succinct explanation and looked down at her lap, trying to push away the images, her mother laughing in the sunshine with the other mothers as the children chased the balloons over the grass. It had been a completely stupid and pointless game, but a lot of fun.

Donny connected the dots. She'd been running since her ninth birthday then, roughly. Nine years old and on the run with practically nothing, and had somehow survived all the way across America to Vegas.

"Will you tell me when your actual birthday is? Is it in April? Is that why you told Carl your name was April?" he asked quietly, wishing he knew how to take some of the pain away, bring back the child who was weak with laughter just a short while ago.

"No, it was just on a sheet of paper listing stock. He asked me for a name, and it was the first word I saw. I'm not good at lying."

He knew that.

"Then, when is it?"

"I won't tell you, Donny. I'm sorry, but I want to forget it. I won't ever celebrate my birthday again. And I won't give you any more information. Who I was doesn't matter anymore."

He hated it when she was sad and afraid; hated the fact she was so young and had such a burden on her shoulders.

"Will you at least tell me when you've turned eleven?"

"Sure."

"Fine, then I won't ask you again. Now, are you ready to learn how to lose money?"

"I was hoping I would learn how to win money," she replied with a shy smile.

"Maybe one day, if you're any good, but I'm merciless with a deck of cards," he threatened her wickedly and stood up, going to fetch the poker set from the sideboard. He settled down at the coffee table, setting it all out. "But, as an incentive, so you don't give up, even when I beat you . .

." – he saw her smile at his arrogance – ". . . if you manage to win, I will give you the amount you win in chips in real money."

"But how is that fair? I can't do the same for you."

"You made me dinner," he reasoned easily.

"Donny!"

"You promised not to argue with me," he reminded her, and she growled at him and sat on the floor opposite him. "I can see Lazarus is teaching you his language," he added.

She grinned at him, and accepted the cards he dealt her. And then Mysty put on her serious face . . . and listened. Fridays were the best day of the week.

SHE FELT THE jumble of nerves in her belly. She wanted to do well. Didn't want to let Donny down for giving her this chance. But what if she suddenly couldn't do it? What if her body had forgotten? But why should it have? She had practiced last night, as soon as night had fallen but before 11pm, and it had been just like before. She wished Donny was there. Wished her mother was there. But that was a futile hope. She was just going to have to make the most of this . . . by herself.

Guiseppe was driving the plain saloon with Pepe in the passenger seat, but neither spoke to her much, though they were friendly when they pulled up and let her in. She guessed they were just a little uncertain how to treat her, knowing she was 'Donny's girl' – an even more confusing position than if she had been a grown woman and his bit on the side. As a child in this family, she was a strange addition.

The car stopped and her nerves were just as taut. Even listening to her favourite upbeat songs to give her confidence hadn't worked. But would she be *more* nervous if she hadn't listened to them? She didn't know.

"Here we are," Guiseppe said, announcing it with a tone of expectation that made her tummy do somersaults. What would Donny say to her if she fluffed it? Quiet, reliable Pepe twisted in his seat to look at her properly, offering her an encouraging smile. He was always more sensitive than the rest, always the first to call time when the banter-factor got a little too much for their little girl and things got out of hand. She'd been glad to see his familiar face in the car as it had arrived; now she didn't want to leave.

"Go get 'em. Just don't break a leg," he said. She shot him a smile before moving to the door. "We'll be parked over there by the palm trees, however long you are, so no rush."

She nodded and slipped out, shutting the door firmly, and at the same time looked up at the huge building – even bigger than the giant hotels. She had seen pictures on the internet and read about the place, but nothing had prepared her for the reality. She put her bag on her shoulder. It contained a Lycra suit and spare pumps she had got from a dance shop on the edge of town. She'd bought them using some of the money she had hidden in a box in her bedside cabinet – leftover from the cash she had been given after her jump in Palm Square.

She walked towards the intimidating entrance, putting her shoulders back and pushing through the door to get inside. The air-conditioned atmosphere was a balm compared to the heat outside, and though she'd learned not to mind it, the cool was welcome. She stopped and looked around. The huge atrium spoke of the crowds that flowed in and out its doors for performances, and the desk at the far side was lined with staff taking bookings over the phone, internet or anyone who came to the counter.

She took a breath and started towards one of the tall desks, which were almost as high as her head. She chose the friendliest-looking person and said she was there for an audition with Mr Chardon. After a look which told her she really didn't look like audition material, a button was pressed and a call put through.

"If you want to wait over there, he'll come and fetch you." The woman pointed with a manicured nail towards the fountain at one side of the hall.

"Thank you."

Her politeness in the face of such disdain clearly surprised the woman – who she'd thought looked quite friendly – and she was glad to walk away from her.

Five minutes after watching the water and admiring the edifice, she felt a presence behind her. She turned and saw a man before her, older than she thought he'd be at about forty, with a lined face. He was muscular, however, and clearly very fit. Keeping in peak physical condition was a way of life here, it seemed.

He looked at her with critical eyes.

She looked right back.

"Mysty?" he demanded shortly, his eyes having moved up and down her body. He found nothing that gave him any confidence.

Mysty saw the look, and decided that his attitude would give her a chance to prove him wrong.

"That's me."

"Mr Chardon." He offered a hand, and she took it. "If you would come this way."

She followed him as he abruptly turned and strode off, clearly trying to outpace her and unsettle her. They went through a set of double doors, and she stayed by his side, having to jog occasionally to keep up.

"Apparently, you're a bit of a miracle," he said.

"Donny said that?"

"Mr Capello did, yes. I hope I won't lose any of the respect I have for him because you are a disappointment." He opened another door and nodded for her to go through. She scowled at him for the words that were practically an accusation. He hadn't even given her a chance yet! He led her backstage and then stopped and pointed out a room. "You can change in here. I presume you have something to do whatever it is you do in?"

"Yes. I do. Where do I go when I'm changed, or will you be waiting out here?"

She raised her eyebrows and saw his snap together. Did he really think she didn't have a backbone?

"Go along to the left until you come to a tunnel leading off to the right with blue lights on the ceiling. That'll take you out into the central performance area. I'll see you there."

She sensed he resisted from adding something cutting like *If that's not too complicated for you.*

She nodded and went into the room, changing quickly before she got an attack of the nerves and changed her mind. She put on the suit and caught sight of herself in the mirror. She wasn't too skinny . . . well, not as bad as she had been. And there was clearly muscle on her legs and arms now. She wished she had a baggy jumper. Self-consciously she hugged herself as she went out into the quiet corridor and along until she found the tunnel, glimpsing a few people, but they were all so busy with their own thing that they paid her no attention whatsoever.

The main arena was even bigger than the atrium, and the ceiling soared so high above the huge circular room that it snatched her breath away. The seating went all the way around and, in some areas, there were exclusive viewing boxes or lounges for drinks and dinner while the show went on. The performing floor was a smooth, vast circle that felt hard under foot, clearly solid enough for all kinds of equipment.

There were some mats to one side, and in various places around the arena there were different groups of people chatting, or people practicing. It was like walking through a circus: contortionists bending in amazing ways over a gymnast's horse with extra handles; someone swinging about on a trapeze; strong men throwing people high into the air so they turned and span like she did, coming down to earth; men walking around on giant balls…

"Mysty."

Her head snapped round and she saw Mr Chardon, looking impatient. Clearly, he had no time for her admiration of the arena.

"So apparently, you can do some gymnastics and acrobatics? Would you like to show me some? Do whatever you need to warm up."

He stepped back and waved her into the space.

"Anything?"

"Anything. Just try not to damage yourself. While you're here I'm liable."

His dry tone irritated her a little more. She jumped on the spot and swung her arms. She had already done some gentle exercises before getting in the car, and she wasn't stiff. She then turned around and walked away, stopped, and turned to face him. She hated the bored expression on his face. She balanced on the balls of her feet, then sprang forward, ten steps, then bounced on to her hands, flipping, twirling and flying high through the air while she curled, and came back to earth, landing perfectly balanced on her feet again. She crouched and immediately jumped back up, flying up and back, rotating once in the air before her feet touched the floor again, then back flipping all the way back to where she started, though with a corkscrew-twist at the end just for good measure. Again, she landed. Going nowhere she shouldn't. Not even a wobble. She let her heels go down, her arms poised by her side, and looked at him.

"He said something about defying the laws of science."

There was a look on his face that could split a mountain in two. What did she have to do to get anything other than a nasty response? She looked up, saw the long metal platforms suspended from ropes hanging high up over the practice area. There were five of them: two together that would give her a nice long run up; others that were spread out all over. The two together were a decent height off the floor, but not as high as she could go. Still, they would do for starters.

"Can I go up there?"

She pointed.

He looked. His eyes went back to her.

"Sure. Can you climb a rope?"

He waved her towards the ropes that dangled from the undersides in invitation.

She gave him a look which expressed some of her disgruntlement at his attitude and strode off, caught hold of a rope, tugged it to make sure it was secure, and then began climbing. A minute later, she got to the top, and pulled herself onto the platform. Without looking down at him, she walked to the end. She thought about warning him to watch out . . . but decided not to. She stood on the very end, her heels actually over the end, balanced on her toes, pushed off and then ran. She launched into the same handstand flip and then went over and over, soaring into the air, turning, curling, and rotating all the way down. She heard a shout of protest, and then she uncurled, and her hands went out instinctively. The reflex worked and there she was, standing, completely unhurt, completely balanced. She took in a breath, feeling everything become very still around her. When she opened her eyes, she saw that everyone else had stopped and were looking at her. It was almost funny. Everyone looked so horrified.

She looked round at Mr Chardon. His face was just the same.

"Fuck me," he then said.

She crossed her arms. Waited.

"How the hell do you do that?"

"I just do. I'm working on the maths."

"Shit."

He rubbed a hand over his face as if he couldn't believe he was seeing her.

"How high can you go?"

"I've done seven storeys so far."

"*So far*?"

"It's hard to find the buildings to jump off. The bigger they are, the more security they have. Getting arrested by the police isn't on my list of life goals." She saw he was still processing all of this and wasn't about to speak. "You want me to do it again?"

"Sure."

She turned around and ran, flipped and landed ten feet up the rope, hands finding it in the air easily, and she carried on climbing as it swung under her weight. Performers moved from their statue-like poses and came forward, standing around next to Mr Chardon. Even they hadn't seen anything like this. She got to the highest platform and looked down, judging the distance. She didn't have so much of a run up, but never mind. She took four running steps, jumped to the edge with her feet landing together and bounced up, turning onto her front and curling into a ball like she did when she dived. Three rotations later she twisted over, round, and then landed, standing again – but this time to the sound of applause. Clearly the other performers weren't as mean with praise as Mr Chardon.

"In all my life . . ." He couldn't finish, could barely take his eyes off her.

"Maurice," he then said, "we're going to borrow your horse for a moment." He beckoned her over to the gymnast's horse and gestured to it. "Now, I want to see how flexible you are. Bend however you can, but don't do anything that hurts, even a little. You've already impressed me, so you don't need to push it."

Mysty nodded and hoisted herself up. The design was made for someone bigger than she was, but no matter. It required a lot of strength in her arms to balance, and she had to stop occasionally, but he didn't mind. When she was poised and balanced, he would let her move and then direct her, doing the splits first in both directions, then seeing if she could bend so her back was curled, her foot pointing past her ear.

"Maurice is out of a job," he commented dryly – for the first time offering her a small smile. She almost fell off she was so amazed. "OK, enough." He offered an arm to help her down, knowing it was the awkward, short distances that usually caused the most problems, and this was a girl who he didn't want to see injured. "You alright?" he checked.

"Fine."

She wasn't sure how to really react to this change of attitude.

"Is there anything else you'd like to show me?"

"Not really. Though I can tightrope walk, as well. Can I try one of those?" She pointed up at the trapeze that hung motionless, everyone standing around debating what she might do next.

"I'm not sure . . ."

"Please?"

He was too tempted to see how good she was . . . and those eyes. Why not? He could lower it down so she was nearer to the ground.

"Patrick! Move the trapeze frame down to forty feet!"

He led her over as the contraption was lowered. It was still a decent height off the floor, and was set up for basic practice and technique perfecting.

She waited for him to nod and then backed up, flipping to bounce up and grab the waiting bar, four others hanging motionless for her as well. She swung to and fro, letting the momentum carry her, feeling the speed through the air, enjoying every second. She would need much stronger arms, she decided.

Mysty swung once more, brought her legs up, turned her body, and recaught the bar, gliding back through the air, letting go, rotating once in the air and catching the next one. Again, she built up some real momentum, and this time let it go to fly up, rotating, twice, and then catching the bar as it swung back. She almost missed, but just made it. She decided not to push it. She swung a little more, let go, flipped and landed without rolling.

"And you've not gone on a trapeze before today?" Mr Chardon asked her quietly.

"No. It's not as easy to set up as jumping out of windows." She said this as if it were obvious.

"No, I can imagine it's not."

It was the best reply Chardon could get past his lips. He gestured for her to go with him, clapped his hands, and yelled for everyone to get back to work.

"Why don't you go and get changed. There's a shower in the room if you want it. Then go back the way we came, out through the double doors, and we'll go into the restaurant and have a chat. OK?"

She nodded and walked away, confident strides carrying her quickly to the corridor with the blue lights.

He pressed a finger to his earpiece and looked up at the director's room high up above. "You saw that?"

"Yes. Pretty good for such a young girl," Craig Roberts replied, his mind already working out the kinds of revenue possible from an act like that . . . though she would have to be a little older.

"I think she will do very well."

"Very well indeed. Get a coaching schedule worked out with her."

Mr Chardon nodded and strolled to where he would meet her, in no rush at all. For that girl, he had all the time in the world. But how would she react to an audience, he wondered, remembering her awe at first seeing the hall. Then he remembered her spark of attitude towards him, at his unfriendly, impossible-to-please approach . . . and he smiled. With the right preparation, she'd be fine. She was a natural performer. She hadn't worried about him watching her, or the other performers, had she? What a chance! She was going to be a sensation.

MYSTY HURRIED TO get into the house. Pressed her thumb to the pad and let it scan her eyes, and the door swung open. She shut it and carried on towards the rooms where the boys usually were, and sure enough she found Mario and Paulo in a doorway discussing something with lots of hand gestures, but they stopped when they saw her. The place smelled of the fantastic pizza Donna Capello made. Today had to be one of the best days ever!

"Hey twiglet! How'd it go?"

Mario turned around and his smile, along with Paulo's grin, was enough to tell her they'd been waiting for news – everyone knew where she'd gone that afternoon.

"I'm in! I have my first practice on Wednesday!"

She was grabbed and thrown in the air, and five others came in from the room they were playing cards in, all bets forgotten, all more interested in her. It was like she was there kid sister, and they were really proud of her.

"You'd better go upstairs and tell him, he's waiting for you." Paulo gave her a nudge towards the stairs and she smiled, retrieved her bag that had fallen from her shoulder in the celebrations and started towards Donny's room. They followed her. His door opened, and he was there, in his usual black. He looked so serious that she skidded to a halt and her smile faded instantly.

"Well?" he demanded without any greeting.

"He didn't want me," she told him seriously, stealing herself to keep the smile from blossoming on her face again.

His face clouded with disappointment, and she was aware of the huddle behind her. "What?" It was barely a whisper. He couldn't believe it.

"I'm joking!" she shrieked. She couldn't manage it any longer and she grinned broadly. "I have my first practice on Wednesday! I have a training schedule in my bag!"

"You little…!"

He reached forward and grabbed her and threw her over his shoulder, making her laugh and gasp for air, his grin of happiness making everyone relax. They'd never seen their boss act like this, but it was so natural.

"So, what happened? Tell me!"

He took her into his TV room and set her down on a sofa, waiting while she caught her breath. She was used to being manhandled now and thrown around by a dozen or so men who were all strong enough to snap her in two, but treated her with easy familiarity. The days of never being touched in her desert of human contact were gone.

"Well . . ." Everyone else had come in now and was sat or perched on the furniture. "He was really rude to begin with, and then I did some floor work and he sort of liked it; but it was only after I did one of my non-splat jumps that he really reacted. Then I did another, and his attitude was way more friendly. He looked a little scared, actually, and . . . disbelieving. Then he tested my flexibility and balance on one of the horses, and then I had a go on the trapeze. That was fun. I need stronger arms, though," she finished, smiling.

"So, when are we going to see your name in lights?" Lucio teased. Like everyone else, he was pleased for her and also quietly proud. They knew where she had come from, how all she'd had was this talent – and guts. They respected that.

"Mr Chardon says I probably won't do any real shows for about a year, because I need to work on my routines and my strength, but after that..."

"Well, this calls for a celebration. Luckily we just happen to have enough pizza for an army – if you're hungry?" Donny took charge again and she smiled shyly. "What do you think?"

"I'd say that was a yes." Donny smiled back. "Boys – you want to bring up the pizza and some beers? Let Mysty sit down for once?" So Mysty found herself allowed to stay enthroned on the sofa while everyone else, except Donny, went to help. He then plonked himself next to her and put an arm around her shoulders, giving her a squeeze. "You did really well. I'm proud of you."

"Thanks, Donny." She looked up at him. "You know I'd never let you down."

Such a solemn, yet open face. All the goodness a person could possess shone back at him, and he knew she was one of the best things that had ever smacked into him and thrown him over. Considering everything he'd done in his life, he didn't really know quite how he deserved her.

"I don't think you ever will," he told her, just as solemnly, and then tickled her under the chin and took his arm back as he heard the clump of feet on the stairs. "Do you want a film on?" he asked her as the pile of plates and the different pizzas were loaded onto the table, glasses of beers poured. Someone had remembered to bring her a glass of water: Donny had strict ideas about when she should be allowed to drink and it was only after she turned twelve, not before.

"Only if everyone else is OK with one?" she checked, not wanting to ruin the fun if no one else wanted to watch a movie; but she just got nods from happy faces eating pizza that was so good it was wrong. There wouldn't be any left.

"What do you want to see?" Donny took a huge bite of pizza.

"Well, I was thinking . . . *The Little Mermaid*?"

He choked and so did at least six other people. She would have fallen off the sofa laughing, except it would have dislodged her plate of pizza onto the floor, which would have been sacrilege. She managed to stop laughing, and said, "No, really, can we watch *The Bourne Trilogy*?"

Her suggestion won some approving cheers from around the room, as they were film buffs themselves, having been inculcated about the greats by Donny.

"We can certainly see one of them, at least, but you have school tomorrow, and I doubt you'll stay awake longenough to watch all three," Donny told her with a knowing smile.

She rolled her eyes and snorted – though she knew he was probably right. In a few moments, the TV was switched on and the lights off.

AT SOME POINT, after the pizza was finished, and all the plates were back on the table, Donny's arm went back round her shoulders and soon after that she fell asleep, despite the on-screen excitement. At the end of the film, gentle hands picked her up and put her in the car.

Donny watched the car leave, wishing he could take her home himself rather than stay indoors for security reasons. Or that she'd stayed the night in one of the spare bedrooms – not like there wasn't enough of them. Perhaps he'd have her over on the weekends. It would be good for her, too, after being in the flat all week on her own. He'd suggest it, somehow, and he doubted she'd say no, just as he'd suggested that she move into the quiet safety of the flat in the first place, away from any scenarios that could develop at his home – scenarios that may scare her, or worse, endanger her. She'd agreed, understanding the reasons. The last thing he wanted was for someone to try to hurt her to get at him. That was something he could not bear to have on his conscience. Not for anything.

"DONATELLO CAPELLO! DON'T tell me you're going out now?" One very enraged face and fierce eyes, hands on hips, stood before him in the doorway. She was a very determined sight.

"Mysty–"

"Don't try sweet-talking your way out of this, Mr Capello! You almost fell asleep with your face in your pasta bowl three times in fifteen minutes! Now you're telling me you're going out again for half the night? I don't think so!"

The tirade was even more impressive because it was in perfect fiery Italian, and he enjoyed seeing her concern for him demonstrated so well.

"It's business."

"It can *wait*! You need some sleep. You've not had any for almost three days now, and it's not good! You'll end up looking like you're a hundred not twenty-five if you keep going on like this!"

She crossed her arms and so did he, his head tilted to one side, admiring her for arguing with him. He wouldn't let anyone else.

"Oh, compliments now?"

"Make the most of it because you'll not be getting anymore if you walk through that door!" she flung back with as much menace as she could muster.

"Mysty…"

She saw the tiredness rise in a wave again as he tried to argue and her concern melted away her anger, her tone softened.

"Donny, please, just have a sleep until twelve, then I promise I'll wake you up and you can go to the club then. You've told me before most of the important people don't get there until later anyway. If you don't turn up as early it'll just make you look more important and so busy because you had such terribly pressing matters to see to that kept you away."

Her argument was pretty sound and she did have a point. He'd just got into a habit of going to the club earlier than necessary when she wasn't visiting because his rooms seemed a bit . . . lacking without her. It was so tempting. He did need sleep. Exhaustion would make him vulnerable to mistakes, and he could not afford to make one. Could never afford to make any.

"Fine, I'll sleep till twelve."

"Good. Now go back and lie down on a sofa. I'll tell Paulo about the change of plans and get a blanket for you."

She didn't budge from the door until he'd turned and taken his jacket off again and gone through to the other room.

By the time she got back, he was already asleep, though she lay the blanket over him anyway, sighing as she watched him for a few moments, wondering how on earth she came to be here in the house, in the inner sanctum of this Vegas mobster. The Donny she knew, wasn't the one the world knew. But she couldn't imagine him any other way. He was the best thing that had happened to her in her whole life. Where would she have ended up without him? Realistically, she knew it would only have been a matter of time before someone had discovered her in the hotel – and God knows what might have happened to her then. And she couldn't have gone to school without him. She might be smart, but you only get so far in the world without real qualifications.

She'd not let anything happen to him, not if she could help it. She'd wanted to protect her mother and been too afraid, and paid the price for it. She'd never make the same mistake again. Even the burden of sadness that he carried around inside himself seemed to have eased over the last six months, and she was glad of it. He smiled more too, and she could not imagine being closer to another human being in the world, even though she didn't see him every day, and sometimes barely in a week. But their time together was always so good, and she never felt like it was for any other reason than because he wanted to be with her.

She sat back down at the dinner table and carried on with her homework. It was Sunday night and she'd spent most of the weekend either dancing or at Cirque. After she'd woken him at twelve, she'd go to bed.

"DONNY – ITS TWELVE o'clock." She bent over him, feeling tired herself having stayed up to wake him, and she wished she could dare to leave him. He looked so peaceful, not the devil she once thought him to be, just a dark, sleeping angel. "Donny." He stirred and murmured. She reached out a hand and stroked his hair back from his brow, "It's twelve o'clock – are you going?"

"No."

It was a sleepy murmur and it made her smile. He didn't open his eyes.

"Are you sure? Don't be angry in the morning when you wake up and realise you didn't go out."

He sighed, his eyes still closed, and pointed to the other end of the sofa. She thought about refusing, going to her room, but then she smiled, and crawled under the blanket and snuggled down. Their toes barely even touched the sofa was so long, and it felt safe to be there. Maybe she would sleep and not have nightmares if she stayed here. . .

Within minutes, they were both asleep.

PAULO CREPT IN at 12.15am, concerned, as neither Mysty or Donny had appeared, and came up short when he saw the sleeping a pair. Considering what he'd seen his boss do – kill at point-blank range and in cold blood, order rivals to be executed in ways that silenced other dangerous men – to find him asleep under a blanket with that little bundle of attitude at his feet was rather endearing. He looked at Lazarus, who blinked back at him calmly, sitting comfortably on the other sofa, tail flicking, guarding them.

Paulo left and shut the door, deciding to leave them sleeping and not move Mysty to her bed.

MYSTY WOKE TO the sound of buzzing: the intercom. She raised her head and saw the time on Donny's clock on the desk: 7.05am. Wow! She'd slept all night! *They'd* slept all night. And she'd not had any terrors in her dreams. She felt annoyed that it was Monday and couldn't just lay on the sofa some more. She got up and hit the button to answer, not wanting its buzzing to wake Donny.

"Donatello Capello's office." She flicked her hair back, trying to stifle a yawn.

"This is Don Salvadore of Boston," came a rather terse voice with an Italian lilt she knew so well.

She smiled and switched over to Italian, hoping that might soften him. If he was someone Donny was meant to have spoken to at some point last night, she felt she should do what she could to stop him getting into trouble.

"Good morning, Don Salvadore," she said.

There was a pause. He hadn't expected such a lovely Italian voice.

"And who are you?"

"I am Don Capello's secretary. He is unavailable at the moment."

"And are you as lovely to look at as you are to listen to?"

She knew men liked to say things like this, and composed her reply: "I'm afraid so. I'm a six-foot redhead and I'm only allowed to work wearing my underwear." She thought this was outrageous enough.

"Well, that is an incentive to go to work. I trust you will tell him I rang and I need to speak to him urgently?"

"Of course, Don Salvadore, I will do so as soon as he is available." She took a breath, needing to end the conversation before he asked her any more questions that meant she had to lie. "I'm sorry, I have another call coming through. Have a good day, Mr Salvadore, sir." She pressed Disconnect and flopped back down on the sofa. It was way too early for phone calls.

"Six-foot redhead and I make you work in your underwear?"

She saw Donny looking at her with laughing eyes. She blushed and giggled.

"I thought you were asleep."

"Do you have any idea who that was?" he said in mock-horror. "And do you know that it's going to be all over the west coast of America that I have a secretary parading around in skimpy underwear at 7am!" He couldn't supress a grin.

"It made his day, and you've started the day smiling – it could be worse! Anyway, who is Don Salvadore?"

He threw back his head and laughed. It seemed it didn't make any difference to her who rang, or who she spoke to, she dealt with them all in the same way, with her simple, unaffected confidence.

"Don Salvadore is my mother's cousin, a very wise man, and our 'eyes and ears' in Boston."

The buzzer went again and he waved at her to answer it, sure it was going to be Paulo or someone ringing to see how he was and if he wanted breakfast – especially after his no-show last night. Had he really slept the whole night? God, he'd needed that sleep.

She pushed herself up on her elbows again and pressed the button.

"Donatello Capello's office."

Donny smirked and put his hands behind his head like some kind of king who didn't need to do anything in his life. He looked exactly like she liked to see him: without the dark weariness or lack of expression from exhaustion.

There was a pause. The caller clearly hadn't expected a female to answer.

"Who is this speaking?"

It was a hard, authoritative voice that had a hint of accusation as though she was in the wrong – and she didn't like it.

"I'm Donny's secretary. Can I ask who's calling?" She gave up referring to him by his full name.

"Tell him it's the man from New York."

What an arrogant tone!

"Hey, Donny, it's *the* man from New York. The *only* man!" She put the intercom next to him on the sofa. "If he's the only guy in New York then you should definitely move there! You might even get a date."

Donny just smiled at her, recalling their conversation a while back about the fact he never went on dates. Trust Mysty to think of that now!

"Go and make yourself useful, like finding me some coffee, you minx."

She gave him a haughty look and swept from the room with far more poise than an eleven-year-old – yes, she had announced that she was now eleven – should have to check on Lazarus. Donny shook his head. Trust Daryl to rub her up the wrong way in less than ten words.

"Daryl. Good of you to call."

"Who on earth was that?" Daryl's voice was torn between disbelief and amusement.

"Apparently, my six-foot redhead secretary who I insist works only in her underwear." *Dear Lord, this kid gets more outrageous every day.*

"That's the kind of thing I would do! But why 'apparently'?"

Donny enjoyed the curiosity in Daryl's voice – the man who thought he knew everything.

"Because she's just a kid!" He really hoped that didn't sound patronising, but Mysty smiled. She got it. And then went off to get ready for school.

"I didn't know you had kids."

"She's not mine." Donny knew how he felt and what his relationship with her was. It was something, but it wasn't fatherly. He wasn't, however, about to try and explain that to Daryl. "So, what can I do for you this morning?"

"You remember I sent you the details on the new Cirque de Celeste?"

"Of course. Very impressive, big investment. Sounds like an amazing show you're planning on putting on." (Donny didn't let on he knew one of the acts who would be staring there.)

"Indeed."

"A very large building you're wanting to build in my city . . ." Donny added carefully.

And so commenced the verbal fencing.

"A very large source of tourism and revenue for your city."

"True, though we're not doing too badly at the moment. As you know."

"Accepted."

"And you would want to have all planning permission as soon as possible, without any hold-ups of any kind . . . the traffic issue might be a big concern. I would need to speak to lots of people to smooth the way."

"I would like to get the groundwork started within a fortnight, if that is at all possible?"

"Then name me a figure."

"Ten million."

"Fourteen."

"Done." Donny raised his eyebrows. Clearly, he should have gone higher.

"Not feeling like arguing this morning?"

"I'm distracted by a six-foot semi-naked secretary. Considering the overall investment and the turnover, I expect when it's finished, that really is a drop in an ocean."

"Excellent, then you won't mind throwing in a private viewing box for myself when it's done."

"I think I can manage that."

"Send over the plans and I'll look them over. Seeing as I know this place better than you or your exceptionally over-paid architects and planners, it might be worth a check."

"Granted. Will there be a charge for that?"

An amused voice. Donny smiled too. He really was in a good mood this morning.

"No, consider it a gesture of goodwill."

"You must be distracted as well."

Donny looked up as he heard the door open. Mysty's hair was wet from her shower, her school uniform was on, and she had a tray for him.

"Oh, you angel. Orange juice, coffee and a bacon sandwich. I am definitely marrying you when you're old enough."

She set the tray down on the coffee table and gave him a brilliant, if cheeky, smile.

"Oh, you are, are you?" she responded insolently. She went to the table behind him and packed her school bag.

"Shouldn't you be on your way to school already?"

"There are eighteen minutes left, and I can make it easily in twelve. I can annoy you for another six." But she was already heading for the door. It shut behind her.

"Hold on, Daryl, I'll just get the screen on."

A few button presses later and they were revealed to each other: Donny having moved to his desk in the other room with the tray of food, busy biting into the delicious bacon sandwich; Daryl leaning back in a very expensive leather office chair at his pristine desk in his pristine office, with not even so much as a crumb in sight.

"Great, now I have breakfast envy, and right after you've swindled me out of fourteen million," Daryl groaned.

"It's worth every dime and you know it," Donny dismissed nonchalantly, deciding Daryl was perfectly right to envy the sandwich.

"Same account?"

"Same account."

"She's pretty brave if she bosses you around," Daryl needled, an amused smile on his lips, yet feeling somewhat jealous of his business associate and friend, of sorts.

"I boss her around enough; it's a mutual thing. She's a great kid, but she'll be an exceptional woman when she grows up. And I intend on being there to see it happen."

Donny's certainty made Daryl feel an uncomfortable emptiness. Someone he had thought himself akin to had something he did not, and it changed his view of Donny completely. He was a man he had thought more lost and alone than even himself, and he had found something to put a real smile on his face. Daryl wished he could see this wonder-child for himself; the child who had managed to win the good favour of this ruthless individual. Donny was someone he didn't want to get on the wrong side of, not because he couldn't handle such a situation, but simply because it would involve too much effort, time, money, blood – and God knows what else; besides, Donny was a man he liked . . . as much as he liked anyone.

"Donny!" The voice was strong and not at all childlike.

"I thought you'd left for school!" Donny replied, slightly exasperated by her rather authoritative tone of voice!

"I was putting my shoes on and eating toast. I just wanted to say don't forget to call Don Salvadore, and Paulo told me to remind you that you have the meeting at the office at Westville at ten. And don't forget to feed Lazarus something before Lucio takes him home."

"I will, now go! You've got twelve minutes!"

"I can make it in ten! And don't forget Wednesday night or I'm never cooking again!"

The door slammed shut and Donny looked back at Daryl, who was having a hard time keeping a straight face.

"Never a dull moment," Donny commented dryly. "Take it from me, avoid children with an IQ above Mensa, they're high maintenance!"

Daryl wasn't sure whether to believe that comment. "How old is she?" he asked.

"Not as old as she can think, and not as old as she looks." Donny finished the sandwich and licked his fingers with obvious enjoyment, then swallowed the last of the orange juice. "She was looking through college-level math textbooks when she was ten, teaching herself, and she actually understands it all." He shook his head and then reached for the coffee, enjoying the smell and taste, not just gulping it down for the caffeine fix that would wake him up.

"What's happening on Wednesday?"

Daryl despised himself for asking. Why did he care?

"A high-diving competition. She's quite brilliant at it, though she only started it as practice for something else." Donny spied something on the tray. "How perfect, a toothpick! She knows me so well." He smiled and sat back, contentedly poking at his teeth. "How are things with you?"

"Busy. As always."

"Hence the need to divert yourself with *lots* of very beautiful women, no doubt," Donny responded, making it sound grand and heroic.

"Of course," Daryl replied, not really wanting to agree, but such was the image he had chosen to employ, the life he led. Trying to explain how different the reality was, or how contrary and confused his own feelings were, was something he didn't want to attempt. He feared what might happen if he started questioning even the fundamentals never mind examining his soul. He was not sure what he would find it had gone ignored so long. Best to stay ignorant, stay with the moment, always look forward, never back.

"Must be awful for you. Have to say I've not seen anything too scandalous in the news about you recently."

"One can't be scandalous all the time, otherwise it becomes . . . normal," Daryl replied easily.

"There is that." Donny sobered slightly. "I know I've not spoken to you for a while – things have been busy for both of us – but I was sad to hear about the 'thing' with whatever her name was. I know you wouldn't consider marriage lightly."

Daryl's face became serious. "No, well, best I found out what she was before I'd put the ring on her finger. An unpleasant lesson for the greater long-term good," Daryl replied philosophically, not having expected any such concern from Donny, who had already vowed never to marry or have children – which Daryl now thought showed remarkably good sense. But what had this kid done to him? Who was she? He hoped he wasn't losing his touch. Any weakness would be exploited and picked apart within days in the shark-infested waters of organised crime. "I had better go. Enjoy the diving competition," he concluded.

"Oh, I will."

"That good?"

"The best." Donny's confident grin made Daryl want to punch someone. "Take care, Daryl. Don't work too hard."

Fat chance of that, though – and they both knew it.

The screens disconnected and Donny paused for a moment, then stood with new energy and strode out, intending on having a run and then a shower. He really had needed that sleep, and he'd made $14 million before finishing a bacon sandwich.

Daryl sat back in the chair, rested his head and closed his eyes. He could still hear that voice: '*Hey, Donny, it's the man from New York . . . the only man! You should move there then you might get a date!* How old was she? Hell, it had even made him smile and he was having a dire morning.

"Mr Blackmoor, sir, the secretary of state is on line one for you," his secretary's voice buzzed, and he used voice recognition to connect the call as he sent a message to get $14 million transferred to Donny's account.

You don't need anything or anyone, Daryl reminded himself firmly, even as his voice greeted the new caller. He knew from experience that work was the best distraction he could find.

"DONNY?"

HE WAS working and she was doing homework scrunched up in the chair in front of his desk. It was Sunday night again, a long three weeks after she'd managed to get him to sleep the whole night – and he'd promised to do the same again tonight after she'd caught him asleep on the sofa when she'd arrived. She knew something was worrying him, but as a rule, he never discussed business with her, partly because he didn't want her to know what kinds of things he got up to, but mainly so she would never have anything to confess – which was a scenario that tortured him in his quiet moments.

"Yes, kitten?"

"Where can I learn how to fight?"

"*Fight*? But you can fight." His brow instantly knotted together.

"Not really. I just fumble my way through and manage things because I'm so quick, but I want to know what I'm doing."

"Has someone at school been picking on you?"

She smiled at his instinctive concern.

"No, I just. . ." She signed and scowled. "I don't go looking for trouble but trouble seems to find me, so when it does, I just want to be as prepared as I can for it. I'm not going to pick fights, but you, or the boys, might not always be there to pull me out of a scrape. You see?"

He looked at her for a second, relieved to find it wasn't anything to do with her growing physical strength, or that she was suddenly going to turn into some attitude-strutting punch-slinger.

"Yes, I see."

He leaned back in his chair and looked at her, realising how she had changed subtly: there was a little bit more shape to her face now – but she still had those high cheek bones and cute little nose – and her legs were now even stronger, with some shape to them. Her arms too, from the swimming, were showing more muscle definition. She was coming along nicely, and she was not as fragile, so he guessed it would be safe enough. It might even, as she implied herself, save her one day, especially if she turned out to be as beautiful as he suspected she would be – the kind of beauty that men would do stupid things in order to possess. He had seen it happen before.

"The best boxing club is the one all my boys go to," he said. "That is where I would send you. But it's boys only, and the guy – Sid Hooch – who runs it is a real stickler for that. No wives, no girlfriends – they're not even allowed to sit in the car park and wait. However, he owes me a least three big favours, so I'll send you with Paulo, and you tell him you're from me and he's to train you, show you the ropes etc., but take it easy on you, alright? I don't want you getting all mangled because there's too much ego flying around."

His stern tone did nothing to dim the delight on her face and she threw her book off her lap and ran around the desk, to squeeze him around the neck. And then a kiss was planted on his cheek, and she was gone, twirling out through the doorway.

"I'll get you a coffee! Decaf!"

He stayed perfectly still, not sure how to feel, or if he should let himself feel it at all. God knows it was hard enough that she was so grown up already, despite being so young . . . but they shared a bond so close, and not for the first time he wished she was older, more able to be in his world without him fearing for her every day. She made him want to be a better person – the person he was for her – and actually made him think about how he could extricate himself from everything he knew. He wondered what it would be like to take her away from the danger and power and live a life in the sun, not in the shadows, be a family, give up everything he had shed blood for, sold his soul for . . . it felt like she had given life back to him, but with an altered perspective.

"Here you are." She breezed back in, and a stylish coffee cup and biscotti on a matching plate were deposited next to him on the desk. He smiled as she sat back down, knowing he was a lucky son of a bitch.

"You know, one of these days I'm going to get you one of those outfits the other maids wear, seeing as you cook now and bring me coffee."

She looked up at him with fire in her eyes, saw the wicked gleam in his eye, and something inside her fluttered – what did it all mean?

"You do that, and you're going to wake up with something rude tattooed across your forehead in permanent marker pen."

Donny threw back his head and laughed. She was so wonderfully defiant. No one else in the world would get away with saying that!

She grinned at him and silence fell as Sunday night homework resumed.

Monday always came too soon.

MYSTY COULD SMELL it before she got through the doors: male sweat. She looked up at Paulo, who looked back down at her, rather uncertain how he felt about their little girl going into this testosterone-packed room. He knew also, from having sat next to her in the car, that she was less confident than she had let on to Donny. Paulo knew from experience that acting on instinct and just flying by the seat of your pants because circumstances dictated such was one thing, but knowingly going into a tough situation that would involve fighting was something else. He was under strict instruction from Donny to pull her out if he had to. None of them wanted her to get hurt. This was a faster, better way of learning how to fight than just sending her on a self-defence course, then a ladies' boxing class, but it came at a price – and they wanted to avoid her paying too highly.

"Sounds like it's pretty busy," he said.

The music could be heard through the doors easily, and the din added to the whir of gym machines, shouts of instructions, punches hitting bags, yells of encouragement, and dozens of feet stomping around.

"Great," she murmured ruefully, comforted only by how fit she felt in herself, never having felt stronger. The months of practice and exercise and proper food was working the miracle it needed to, and she had even noticed something happening to her chest which she didn't quite understand, and that she really hoped would stop.

Her training at Cirque had made her realise just how amazing her body could be, and what it was capable of, and it was the most precious thing to her, the one thing she valued far more than anything she might own. It was a simple realisation that most people forgot: her body was God's gift to her and she was going to make the best of it.

Paulo pushed open the doors into the main hall. Thursday night, it seemed, was a busy night.

Mysty found herself standing in a room very much like she had imagined, like Mr Gibson's boxing hall only bigger, more modern, brightly lit up and full – as her nose told her – of aggressive, athletic, sweating males. Most were bare-chested, skin gleaming, muscles rippling, wearing shorts or jogging bottoms. A pair were in the main ring, people watching. And around the room men were sparing or training.

Some girls her age might have found it intimidating because of the amount of naked flesh on display, but she barely noticed, she was used to it from Cirque, where a certain degree of nakedness was usual – and the skin-tight costumes didn't hide much anyway.

But it was really hot in there. And in leggings, a sports t-shirt and a baggy hoody, she was sweltering. No wonder the rest were wearing the bare minimum. She pushed the hood back off her head and revealed her face and mane of long gold curls that were plaited out of the way. She was now very obviously female.

"*What the hell do you think you're doing*?" The enraged shout from the fully-dressed man brought everyone to a standstill, and fifty-odd pairs of eyes turned on her. He strode towards her, cutting across anyone in his path as if they didn't exist.

"Not much of a welcome," she replied, wondering why she always seemed to find herself dealing with unfriendly males.

His red face almost exploded at her calm response. "*Not much of a . . .*! Did you not see the signs outside clearly stating this is a *men's only* gym?"

"I did, but I thought they were very sexist and unfair. And I haven't come here for the gym, I'm here to learn how to fight. I'm fit enough already."

She insolently glanced away and back again, wondering how on earth she held her nerve; but it was partly because she knew he wouldn't touch her while Paulo was standing just behind her, and even if this man, Mr Hooch, could beat him in a fight, he'd still get hurt.

"Oh, you are, are you?" he scoffed in angry disbelief.

Jesus Christ, he couldn't believe his own ears, let alone his eyes! This four-foot-something kid looking up at him as though she was taking a walk in the park, as if she was judging his gym and finding it wanting!

"You came recommended," she told him seriously, crossing her arms over her chest, not moving an inch.

"You with her?" Hooch demanded of Paulo.

"He's with me," Mysty corrected, knowing he was about to tell Paulo to take her out.

Hooch's eyes came back to hers. Paulo resisted telling Hooch just who had sent her, and why he couldn't throw either of them out. He knew Donny was listening to the exchange and watching from the camera Paulo had on his jacket in a button – quite standard issue for them.

"Well, seeing as you can't read: I don't have *girls* in my club, and I *don't teach girls* in my club. So why don't you just turn your little self around and *fuck off*."

Mr Hooch clearly wasn't in the mood for being polite.

It didn't bother her; neither was she.

"I can see your language might put gentile and polite people off, but I'm not *fucking polite*!"

It was the first piece of emotion she'd shown, and the fierceness of it surprised him.

"Tell me," she continued, "is it because you're scared of girls, or because you're scared they might put one of your macho boys on their arse?"

Donny would have cried with laughter if he hadn't had perfect view of just how angry Hooch was. He was worried, chewing a finger nail, breathing slowly to hear every word.

"Tell you what, how about we have a little bet?" Mysty then said when Hooch, too stunned to answer, just stood and shook his head in utter disbelief. She took two steps towards him, her arms crossed in imitation of his, her eyes intense. Neither were sure where this would end, and Hooch was certainly not used to people standing up to him, let alone with such conviction – and female. "I go for five minutes in the ring with anyone you choose. If they manage to touch me, I lose, I go. And if they don't," she concluded, "or if, by some miracle, I win, I stay. And you apologise. What do you say?"

The whole room held its breath; so did Donny, waiting, but knowing what Hooch would say. The pause was due to the veteran fighter getting over the nature and delivery of the straightforward challenge. From a girl. In his club. God knew, he never thought he'd see the day.

"I'd say you have a mighty pretty face to risk losing it, but that's your choice. You have a deal."

He held out his hand; her grip was stronger than he expected.

"Excellent."

Her smile stunned him. She was so pretty. Who was this little hellcat throwing insults at him? And now she wanted to go in the ring? What the hell was she doing? Still, sooner it began the sooner it was over, and she would leave. Hooch stepped back and waved an arm for her to go forward.

"Darius! Why don't you tape up your hands and get in the ring for a quick dance with this . . . little madam?" He realised he didn't know her name, but was rather reluctant to ask. "Free membership for a year if you get her in less than two minutes."

Mysty walked towards the ring, feeling Paulo shadow her.

"Are you sure this is a good idea?" Paulo asked her in a low voice – the question Donny had demanded of him. She held out her hand and he passed her some tape, having brought some with them. "Why don't you just tell him Donny sent you?"

"Because Donny has done enough. Because I don't want to be here as a favour. Because I want that sexist man to respect me or I might as well not bother. If I lose, I'll cook you whatever you like; if I win, dinner is on you when we leave. Deal?"

She wrapped the tape around her knuckles with a practiced ease – that Hooch didn't fail to see; who had taught her that? – and she bit the tape to cut it and passed it back to Paulo. She then pulled off her hoodie and he took that from her too. She didn't know what effect that had had on everyone else, as she neither looked up at them or glanced in the mirrors.

Hooch looked at Darius, a six-foot six-inch muscled giant. And the girl. David and Goliath. And he looked at Paulo, saw the rueful smile. Now, why would he just stand there as she went into the ring to get the shit kicked out of her; unless . . .

She climbed into the ring without any hint of nerves, as if she did it every day.

"Mr Hooch?"

Here it was, the *I've-changed-my-mind* moment. Hooch sighed audibly, already rolling his eyes in disgust.

"Yes?"

"If I knock him out in less than two minutes, do *I* get free membership for a year?"

She didn't bother looking at him, she was busy sizing up her opponent, who was doing his best to intimidate her with his size. He had huge biceps and very broad, powerful shoulders. *Just more to aim at,* she told herself.

Paulo hid his smile behind a hand, unable to resist a snort at the gall of the girl. She pushed, and then she shoved her luck right out there.

"Sure. Make it two, in fact," Hooch scoffed.

"That's very generous of you. I'll try not to make too much of a mess."

She saw Darius' eyes narrow and lips purse in anger, and his bouncing stance told her he was ready to fight.

"Are we ready?" she asked.

Darius nodded, impatient to wrap her face round his fist. And the audience that had gathered around the ring braced itself.

"Time!"

Someone started the clock. Every pair of eyes was on the ring.

But she didn't put her hands up. She wanted to lull him into thinking she wasn't ready for him, or had lost her nerve. She felt cold, hard defiance well up, the same instinctive defensiveness she had unleashed in the grocery store. It had surfaced, just as she knew it would. She imagined her father's face on the man in front of her . . . that was all she needed.

His fist went straight at her face, and there was a collective gasp; but she wasn't there. She'd stepped calmly to the side and watched his hand whiz past. He tried again. Same thing. And again. Hooch shouted at him, but she was just too quick, and her smile was infuriating the giant, who was unable to move any faster, frustrated because he really wanted to hit her now! He was the best in the gym and this *girl* was making a fool out of him! She ducked under another potentially chin-breaking strike, and turned to face him, leaving a little distance between them.

"Time?" she called.

Hooch wondered why she was bothered about time when she was doing perfectly well!

"Fifty-eight seconds gone," someone shouted.

Hooch then realised the guy with her was standing next to him, arms crossed, holding her hoodie, eyes on the fight.

"She yours?" Hooch asked without looking away from the ring.

"Hell no. Though I wouldn't mind it if she were," Paulo replied calmly, admiring her as she side-stepped two quick punches in succession.

Hooch was just about to ask another question when he noticed her stance change: her hands came up, her fists bunched, and for the first time, she actually looked like she was going to fight. The audience cheered.

She ducked another punch, but moved closer and her first fist caught him on the cheek, the second in his gut, and the third across his nose. She stepped back, composed herself. He shook his head, felt blood trickle from his nose. She might be small, but *shit*! she could punch.

"Shit . . ." Hooch said softly as the audience jeered, watching her face, her body, the poise that stayed with her every second, perfectly balanced. Her face was fierce, her eyes hawk-sharp, picking weaknesses, missing nothing.

Darius moved in, determined to make her bleed as well, but she was too quick and two more punches landed on his face – and for the first time in a long time he felt himself falter as his body struggled to absorb the sharp, hard impact. It wasn't like being punched by a guy. Her hands were smaller, the point of impact more concentrated and somehow far more painful. And he felt cumbersome, wieldy, while she was agile and whip-sharp.

The jeering and cheering had stopped. Now there was silence, interrupted only by the sound of Darius breathing through his nose as he pulled air in through the blood. For a split second he seemed to lose his bearings.

"I'm really sorry, this will probably hurt," she then told him suddenly, her eyes narrowing, as she made the most of his single moment of distraction and slammed her left fist into his gut with all the force she could, and then her right fist flew up perfectly into his jaw, snapping his head back, and his weight went back with the strike.

The world seemed to slow down as everyone watched his body hit the deck, his arms flailing as if trying to catch himself. And then he lay still. It was the outcome only one person present had believed possible. And the silence expanded as they observed who remained standing in the square of canvas.

"Time?" Her eyes on Darius.

She stood perfectly still, aware of her breathing, monitoring how her body felt. She could feel her pulse, could feel muscles in her belly move as she breathed. She felt so alive.

"One fifty-five."

"Super."

She stopped staring at the fallen giant and fixed her piercing eyes on the coach. "Mr Hooch. I think you owe me something."

She started taking the tape off her knuckles, and then vaulted easily over the rope to land beside him.

Behind her, two older men, friends of the groaning ex-champion, jumped into the ring to help him up and get some ice on his face. Hooch was aware that Darius's recovery would be far less about the physical. This defeat would be a knock to his confidence.

Hooch looked at her, seeing her afresh, experienced eyes now noting the long clean limbs with a critical eye, and finding only positives. "What would you like me to apologise for? Being sexist or being rude?"

"Both. And for swearing at me. I did try to be polite, after all," she added cheekily, with a smile so winsome that Hooch unwillingly wanted to like her.

She had guts, lots of guts, and plenty of control – all of which he could respect. Just why had God chosen to give it to a *girl*?

"Fine, I apologise for all three. And you have your two years of membership. But why did you say you wanted to learn how to fight when you clearly already can?"

"I just know I can be better – and I want you to teach me how," she answered simply, as if it were obvious.

"Fine." If she wanted to learn, he was going to make her work for it. "I hope you don't mind a bit of sweat and hard work?"

"No, I'm used to it." He clenched his jaw. She was a tough one, alright, and infuriatingly, nothing seemed to shake her. "You want to start now, or you got to get off home and paint your nails?"

She was amused at his attempts to rile her, so she stayed smiling, relaxed now the fight was over. "Now is fine. I don't paint my nails on week nights."

He glared at her, then at Paulo, who just looked amused – he was listening to Donny laughing in his earpiece.

"Do I know you? You look kind of familiar," Hooch then said to Paulo.

Paulo turned calm eyes on Hooch, not offended that his old coach didn't remember him – it was nearly twenty years ago that they'd met. He was no longer a floppy-haired boy with a lot of aggression.

"I work for Donny Capello, who I believe you know." Hooch's face froze at the revelation and drained of colour, despite his tan. "He recommended you to her, and asked me to bring her."

So little said, left unsaid. Alarm bells rang in Hooch's brain.

"Oh shit. You mean I just had his daughter fighting in my ring?"

"Does she look like his daughter?" Paulo reached out and lifted Mysty's golden plait off her shoulder.

"Then who is she?" Hooch demanded, confused.

"That doesn't matter. What matters is she's here to learn, you're here to teach, and I'm taking her home at 10.30pm. So, I'd hurry up and make a start, because my boss is going to be asking me how she got on today and, so far, I don't think he'd be too impressed by you."

Hooch looked like someone who'd just had something sharp shoved somewhere personal. He then composed himself, not liking threats in his own hall. "Right, you, over here," he said.

He pointed at Mysty and then indicated she follow him, his attitude authoritative again. She didn't argue; she was used to it from Mr Chardon. She looked at Paulo, who smiled and winked, then retreated to the edge of the hall by the door, content to watch. Everyone else went back to what they had been doing, and the noise levels resumed.

"SHE'S UNBELIEVABLE SOMETIMES," Donny remarked, almost sad the excitement was over – once he'd realised he didn't have to be fearful of watching it. It was amusing, too, to see the way she handled herself. She reminded him a bit of himself, when he was much younger, and he liked it. Liked that the contrast of her attitude to her size was bridged by her talent.

"Sometimes? You alright if I take her for a pizza afterwards?"

"Sure, I'll be leaving soon, so no point bringing her back here. Take her to Manny's. It's quiet in there and you won't get any hassle. You want any of the boys to come and meet you?"

"No, Lucio's in the car – though he'll be pissed to know he missed that performance. I'll catch you up at the club as soon as."

"Tell her well done from me."

"Will do, boss."

Donny disconnected, and sat back to replay the whole lot again. He wished she was there, he was so proud of her, remembering the scared, if defiant, collection of skin and bones that had sat on his sofa and glared mutinously at him, even as she'd worried she'd dirty it. He sent the film file down to the surveillance room for the rest of the boys to see, knowing they would enjoy her victory as much as he and Paulo had. She was exceptional, and he wouldn't have her any other way. But thank God, she had the brains to go with the ability.

MYSTY APPROACHED THE building, not sure if it was wise to do this without telling anyone, but fairly certain she would have come up against numerous arguments as to why she shouldn't go. She was curious. And she wanted another challenge.

She pushed the lattice-weave door with a dragon on the front. She liked it. It was unusual, just like the reed matt floors just inside. This place had been recommended to her by many people, but it was apparently very exclusive. Her only hope had been that Hooch had told her if anyone had a chance of making the grade, it was her, despite the fact that they too didn't accept female members.

She felt like she was entering a film set of one of the Rush Hour movies. There were more rush mats on the floor, and she observed all the people in cotton suits, most in white, some in black and one in red. Traditional dress. Everyone was barefoot, with no jewellery. The one in red looked Korean, was about five-nine, with smooth, timeless skin and a trim figure underneath the garments. He had a black sash around his waist. She liked the way he carried himself, walking through the grid lines of people practicing moves. Her eyes moved on to watch them, hoping to see at least one woman. No. Only men between the ages of eighteen and forty, all fit individuals who stared straight ahead. She removed her shoes.

"You." She looked at him, knowing he had spotted her by the door. "What do you want?"

"I want to learn Kung Fu. You were recommended."

"I don't teach women. There are no women here." An elegant hand gestured at the roomful of males, demonstrating his point.

"Why?"

She took a pace forward, pretty sure she might be letting herself in for a thorough beating, but determined not to just let him throw her out without trying. She didn't have time to waste. She wanted a teacher, and a good one.

He turned fully to face her and walked towards her. Everyone froze.

When he was only two feet away, he stopped, his eyes fixed on her.

She was taller now, not so childlike, and there was nothing childlike about the fiery determination in her eyes, nothing immature about the firm tone of her voice. She knew that.

"You have a very young physique and a pretty face. You are not so strong. Are you sure you want to do this?"

"I'm here, aren't I?"

Why did people always have to mention her face?

"Fine. When I've finished with you, you can crawl out of here and leave me alone. I have a class to teach. Of men."

She smiled. But it was with menace.

"Why don't we just see what happens?"

"You have the smile of a tiger. I wonder if you have the heart of one," he remarked.

She liked that. Her hair was tied back again, but the gold and blonde streaks still shone, and some were darker now, some even red. She felt tiger-ish.

He ordered everyone from the floor and they went, moving back to clear the area. The man, whose name was Choi – as far as she knew – went to stand in the middle of the rush mats. She tossed her bag to the side of the door where her shoes were and pulled off her jumper and added it to the pile, realising that her small collection of things was the most disorderly part of the room. She then walked forward, in a cropped sports top that left her midriff exposed, and jogging bottoms hugged her hips but fell loose around her legs, concealing the muscles. But still, her upper body revealed her strength, and she saw his eyes focus on it, saw the spark of surprise.

"So, the tiger has a few claws?" he mocked gently, and put his hands together and bowed in a formal gesture before they engaged.

"She has plenty of teeth as well." She imitated his gesture, both of them keeping their eyes on each other, not looking away.

"Have you any idea what you're doing?"

"Not really, but I'm a fast learner."

"I won't apologise if anything gets broken."

"I wouldn't expect you to."

She sent him another tiger-smile. He narrowed his eyes at her and took up his stance, his body sideways on, one foot and arm forward. She did something similar – what felt right – one arm gracefully poised out to the side, as if beckoning sunshine down from the sky. She breathed in and out, trying to focus in a similar way to how she had been coached by Hooch, but knowing this was going to be far faster and more furious than anything she'd done in the boxing ring.

He moved, jumping forward, and there was a quick succession of blows aimed at her . . . and she blocked all of them in imitation of his own movements, moving back step for step, then crossing her arms and catching his next blow, ready to twist, but he had already moved back. She thought he would move back, but then a foot came in, aiming for her belly, and she let herself lean away to the side, avoiding it and blocking the next blow from another arm. Sweet lord, he was fast; but luckily, she was fast too despite being unused to this type of fighting. Another half a minute of the same and he paused and stepped back again, returning to the centre of the room. She was so far untouched, except where their bodies had met when blows were parried.

After a moment of suspicion, Mysty followed, not sure if it was a move to try and launch a sneaky attack when she was not expecting it; but he took up his pose again, and she followed suit. This time she was a little more ready, and didn't move back in the same way, catching one of his arms and throwing it off so that he had to rebalance himself. His legs came at her, and she had to jump back; and he jumped and aimed a double-footed kick at her head. She reacted instinctively and back-flipped one handed out of the way, going back to a fighting stance the second she landed, seeing his expression change.

Then he attacked again, and this time it was even faster, feet and hands coming at her from all directions, and she had to use everything she had to keep up. She felt like she was drowning under the rain of his blows, not sure how she kept passing them off, everything alien still, her body not having learnt the moves or the actions yet. He took a swipe at her head and she knew she needed space, so back-flipped, again and again, twisting to land, and then she stood, breathing hard, like he was, taking up her pose.

"Running away?" he mocked, refusing to follow her.

"Never."

She let her arms go gracefully out to the side and ran three steps, then flipped back towards him, bounced high in the air, twisted and aimed a kick at his head that he had to fall back and roll to avoid, rising to his feet quickly to find her just there in front of him, her arm already coming in to smack into his chest. He was forced to block and fight to stand his ground.

They gave and lost ground for a few minutes, and she knew she was tiring fast. He grabbed her arm and twisted, slamming her back against his chest and putting an arm around her throat. She elbowed him as hard as she could, not caring if it was not Kung Fu to use so crude a strike, and as she felt herself released a little, she broke away from his hold, running straight at the wall, bounding up, pushing off and flipping over to fall, roll, and stay crouched, one hand down, one hand behind her. She felt properly attacked, the force of her breath in her throat, all her defences alive with adrenaline.

He came for her, running forward to try and kick her in the face, and she was up and blocking, having to dance back, trying to get a bit of force back into her fight, demanding her muscles obey her. She blocked, two hands and then a leg, and then somehow his leg came out and hooked round hers, pulling them out from under her. He then spun her around and slammed her hard on the ground. She realised that the move had only been achieved because he had sacrificed his own balance to use both legs so quickly. Choi, however, was far more used to hitting the ground than she was, and she'd only just turned over when she felt a hand on her. It grabbed her wrist, twisted her arm back and round in a hold that forced her to obey or else her arm would break. She closed her eyes and flinched with the pain, angry her tiredness and her ignorance had let her down.

She looked up at his face, realised how hard they were both breathing.

"And you came here to learn Kung Fu?"

Choi looked at her with serious eyes but a smile that changed his face. He then released her arm and she jumped to her feet, hands going to her hips while she recovered, feeling a little bruised from the smack on the floor, but otherwise fine.

"I will teach you, tiger, but on your own. No one else here is starting, and you must start at the beginning. Come back tomorrow night at nine o'clock, when everyone else has left, and we will start."

He wiped the sweat off his forehead and nodded at her with approval.

"I'm not sure I can afford private tuition."

"There is no extra charge. You think I would let money make me turn down talent like yours?" He stepped up to her and took her chin in his hand, not unkindly, and tilted her head to see her eyes, realising how unusual they were. "I have waited my whole life for someone to walk through those doors and challenge me. I am glad you found me."

She was drawn by the intensity of his eyes, knowing he meant what he said, and she felt a strange sense of . . . solidarity, despite knowing they would throw their worst at each other.

He let her go, stepped back, and again, pressed his hands together and bowed with his heels touching. She mimicked it, and this time they let their eyes drop, both trusting that neither would attack now the fight was over, their peace made.

She straightened, letting the tension ease from her body.

"Where do I get the clothes? Do I need them?"

"They are not important straight away. I will get you some when you are ready."

He stood still, waiting for her to go, and let his class back onto the floor.

She grabbed her jumper, pulled it over her head, reached for her bag and shoes, and then slipped out of the door. She stopped just outside and took a deep breath. Wow.

"MYSTY?"

SHE LOOKED up from the computer parts she had in front of her on the kitchen breakfast bar. It was Donny's voice.

"Donny!"

He looked horrified.

"Who the hell hurt you?"

He marched forward and lifted her bare arm. A large and nasty-looking purple bruise and was visible on the smooth skin on her shoulder, and there were two smaller ones on her wrist.

She was taken aback by the suddenness of his appearance and his anger, and looked up at him in dismay. "No one, Donny. They're from my Kung Fu class. Really, I'm fine," she told him quickly.

He let her go.

"Kung Fu? Since when have you been learning Kung Fu?" he asked, frowning and crossing his arms.

"Um . . . well . . . for a few weeks. It's going really well."

She thought that might please him but, no, his scowl only got worse.

"So I can see. It's making you very . . . colourful."

"Oh, Donny!" She hopped off the bar stool and stood in front of him. "They're bruises. They're not so bad. Please don't be angry."

"I don't like you getting hurt," he growled back at her, refusing to be swayed by her bright eyes.

"It's making me safer. Choi says I'll be unbeatable. I could get a job protecting you at this rate," she told him seriously, ending with a hint of a smile.

He felt his anger melting away. "Hmm. I'd rather just keep you safe, thank you very much," he told her sternly, then let some of the tension go.

She responded by uncrossing his arms and hugging him, and quite without thinking he picked her up and spun her in a circle.

"You're getting heavier," he observed.

"Good! Not quite such a twiglet?"

She tilted her head to one side, and a strand of hair fell over one eye, and he realised just how much she had grown up, right under his nose. She had the body of an athlete, but, if he were not mistaken, a young woman too, and he had felt the press of small breasts against his chest only moments ago – when had that happened?

"No, quite definitely a flower," he answered, reminding her of their past conversation.

She smiled shyly, never sure what she should say or feel when he complimented her in those subtle ways. She liked it. She loved it. But this was Donny? Her best friend, like an uncle or a guardian.

"Would you like a drink? How come you're here?" she asked suddenly, before she lost herself in the blue eyes that seemed to look right into her soul. Could he see her confusion? He was so much older and wiser, and she felt sure he must see the feelings written on her face.

"I finally found I had some spare time after the most gruelling week, so I decided to come see you. I needed some twiglet-time to help me relax."

She smiled in pleasure at being wanted.

"Well, I'm glad you came." She paused, then looked up, wanting to say the words but not sure she should. "I missed you," she finally said.

The words that brightened his day.

"I missed you too." He touched her nose with a forefinger. "You want to go grab some dinner? I know a place we can go where it's safe to be seen together." He made the suggestion, but he kind of knew where she'd rather go.

"Can we go to your house? I feel like I've not been there for a *year*."

He smiled at the exaggeration, liking that she wanted to go home with him. He prayed that would never change.

"Sure we can. Shall we grab a pizza on the way?"

"Yes!"

"What are you doing with all this?" He nodded at the computer parts and leads and connectors, at the moment a complete mess. He knew she had a computer that worked, and a handheld, and a new phone – all of which she had paid for herself from the money she'd been given after jumping in Palm Square.

"I bought these bits from a second-hand shop. They were dead cheap. I'm experimenting," she said, as though it were a perfectly normal thing to do.

"Oh. To do what?"

"Just a few theories I have. I want to play around with some stuff, but I don't want to risk breaking my main machine."

"You're just too smart sometimes," he laughed. "Anyway! Let's go get pizza!"

DONNY DIDN'T KNOW what to expect. He'd seen her regularly, every weekend, but she had lots of commitments now, and he'd not exactly been idle either, so it had somehow been over a week since he'd seen her. His guilt had worked to her advantage, however, because when she'd told him she was in the high school talent show, and asked him if he'd go, he couldn't think how he could justify disappointing her again by saying no.

So, despite Paulo and the rest not being happy about the security, they had all put on disguises for their trip into the huge school auditorium, keeping as close together as they could. Two guys stayed with Donny all the time; the rest were scattered through the audience nearby, all of them connected with their earpieces. No one was taking any chances.

She'd refused to tell him anything about her act, and he was dying of curiosity, just like everyone else. He also knew she was forbidden by Cirque to do anything involving her skills from there outside the arena, so he didn't know what she was planning.

They settled into the crowd, surrounded by glowing mothers and fathers, all exchanging stories and news. Paulo, Mario and Donny just talked among themselves, not wanting to give anything away. The main floor of the auditorium was completely full of students – and what looked like most of the school to his eyes. Clearly this was a big event, as the posters, banners and excitement buzzing around him indicated.

The show began, the principal greeting everyone and thanking them for coming, before leaving the stage quickly as he felt his audience rustle with impatience for the entertainment to begin.

Donny had to admit, there was some talent: cheerleaders doing a routine – two different groups of guys and girls doing a dance piece – but none of them got his vote. There was one rather novel juggling act between three boys, seven more singers, two guys and five girls . . . and Donny had just become thoroughly bored by the mediocrity when she appeared, and the moment she came into view, he was wide awake again. He couldn't get over how she looked.

She was wearing black skin-tight trousers that clung to every toned curve, and a pair of sexy-looking heeled boots. On her top half, she wore a simple black halter-neck top that left her back bare, and showed the curve of her breasts. But the most beautiful thing was her face. Even from a distance – and he had a scope with him, Paulo's idea because they'd chosen to sit at the back – she was stunning, her hair loose so that it flowed over her shoulders, all the colours in it adding to its magnificence. Usually tied back or plaited, he'd never seen it so wild and free.

There was little wonder there was an appreciative selection of catcalls when she emerged from the back of the stage, and Donny ground his teeth just imagining all the young guys at the school who eyed her up on a daily basis, and would do so even more after tonight. Her walk forward, composed, with catlike easy grace – he didn't know she could wear heels – was a work of art. She definitely didn't look twelve years old – more like seventeen!

She stopped a few metres back from the front of the stage, a small smile on her lips, not shy, but not arrogant. Two pairs of girls came from the sides to stand by microphones – the old-fashioned stand up ones – at the sides of the stage a few metres behind her. She raised a hand up to her face and Donny realised she was holding an also-dated cordless mike. Even he, a non-performer, knew the usual thing was to use a digital earpiece. Somehow, though, it suited her to have the older-style microphone which took skill to use.

He could feel the interest around him from everyone. Somehow, she was different, and they'd realised it too. He held his breath, waiting for her to speak.

She eyed the crowd for a moment, sensing the collective anticipation. "Well, I'm very glad you didn't all give up and decide to go home," she smiled. There was a hint of humour with the implication, because it was late and she was the last act. And Donny felt a twinge of guilt, because he had contemplated leaving the room too. He wondered if she'd spied him and watched his growing impatience; it wouldn't surprise him to know she had. "The good news is, I'm going to try and make your patience worth it."

Classic Mysty style: the quiet promise, that brilliant smile, the one he knew so well – or thought he had until he'd seen her tonight. He'd always known she'd end up performing with Cirque, but this . . . this was different.

She looked round and nodded at someone, and the music started, gospel music style: 'Makes Me Wanna Pray' by Christina Aguilera.

It was pure joy. Her voice rose, the power huge so that it filled the room: "*What is this feeling coming over me*? . . ."

He began to smile, and couldn't stop. How had she managed to hide this from him? All this time, and he never realised she could sing too? This was like the artist herself come to life. Even better, she danced too, to some bits; in others she just stood tall and proud, eyes closed, hand held out, completely lost to the music.

"*Life with you has been a blessing,*" she sang, and he knew in that one beautiful moment she was singing for him, hitting every note, wholly competent and completely fearless.

"*You got me thinking that I'll be alright and you're the reason. Makes me want to get down and pray . . .*"

She glided down on to her knees and raised a hand, then rose up, and he realised everyone around him was clapping, the kids in front of the stage dancing around, the force and passion in her voice totally infectious.

"*Makes me need to . . . pray . . .*"

She was the artist, the performer, the controller of the stage. But she had the voice of a woman. Not a schoolgirl. A voice rich, deep, strong, expressive, reaching up and soaring through the long notes. He would have closed his eyes and just listened, but he didn't want to miss a moment.

Too soon the song came to a climactic end – he didn't want it to end! – and she gave a little laugh, her own happiness unashamed and shared with the crowd. She acknowledged her backing vocalists, who laughed and smiled too, waving to the audience.

"Alright, that's it," she said, and put a hand up in farewell, turning to head into the darkness at the back of the stage.

The applause escalated. But she hadn't sung one note for the applause, Donny knew that, because she wasn't that kind of girl. She did it because she clearly loved singing. That first morning, he remembered her saying, '*I love music, I learn all the words.*' And she did. By God. Every word and every tiny inflection.

He looked at Paulo and Mario, who were clapping just as hard as everyone else and they grinned at him like monkeys. She'd done it again, in her own naturally outrageous style!

The principal appeared on stage again.

"Wow," he said. And there was a huge smile on his face that hadn't been there before. "Was that worth waiting for?"

Donny laughed with everyone else as he heard someone shout, "Let her go first next time!"

"So, as everyone knows, there can only be one winner and our judges have made up their mind – though I'm sure we would all like to congratulate all our acts from tonight, because it takes a lot of courage to come out here and perform." He put his hands together and everyone gave another round of applause. "However, I think we all know what song we're going to remember from tonight . . . and with such talent, I don't doubt she'll go far. The winner, if she would come back out on stage, is . . . Mysty!"

The cheering started and the principal clapped, even though the audience needed no encouragement to start doing so again, and back into the light from the darkness appeared his little girl.

She was smiling, but embarrassed, and she was a little shy of the volume of the audience, who were all too happy to demonstrate how much they'd liked her performance. She gave them a bashful wave.

"Now, Mysty, I believe this is yours." A student brought on a cushion with a crown resting on top of it, and it was placed on her head. A sash was added, going from hip to shoulder, and she accepted a kiss on the cheek from the principal. "Now, do you think you have one more song you could do for us tonight, send us all out on a high?"

It was tradition that the winner did another piece, which was why everyone was always told to have two acts ready. Someone ran on with her microphone and she took it, feeling a lot better for having it back in her hand.

"Well." She cleared her throat, wanting to laugh at the question. Did she have a song? *She had a thousand*! "I think I could manage that. I think the music guys know what to play."

The principal backed off out of sight, and she looked around for a second, as if trying to get her bearings again after the surprise of winning, and then the notes began, and Donny recognised it from having heard it somewhere – somewhere related to her no doubt. It was another Christina song.

He then worked out why she'd chosen it: it was *Soar*, about self-belief and determination, the encouragement to '*. . . spread your wings and soar*' perfectly encapsulating Mysty the girl, and now, Mysty the woman. The lost child that had had the guts to take on the world, to dare to throw herself out of windows for proof, the girl who saved his life, who challenged gunmen, who took herself off to learn Kung Fu.

Will she ever stop amazing me?

It was so beautiful, and he was silent, along with the rest of the crowd, the music and power of her carrying everyone high with the emotion. There was no question she believed what she was singing.

When it ended, when she sang, "*What you waiting for*?" it was like she was asking each and every person in the audience . . . and with her eyes on the crowd, her voice dropped to a husky tone as she sang her last notes. She then raised both hands and gave a bow, a wave, and finally retreated to the back of the stage and disappeared to uproarious applause.

THE CAPELLO TRIO made their way to the parked limo, the rest of the boys appearing out of the crowd as people filtered back to their cars. Donny watched, waiting for her to join them, and just when he thought he would send someone to find her, she appeared, coming down the steps, crown gone, a pair of very cool shades pushed up in her curls instead, with that jaunty gait that now had a new feminine swing to it that he was going to have to pretend he couldn't see. People congratulated her and cheered a little as she passed, and there were some admiring shouts along with it, but she didn't stop, just waved, and kept heading for the car. Mario got back out to open the door for her, and she was immediately yanked over to his side for a warm hug of congratulations.

"You little minx! How did you keep that voice of yours hidden for so long?"

"You put me in a block of flats where nearly everyone is a hundred, so no one complains about the noise because they're deaf!" she replied. "I didn't mean to hide it, it's just . . . well, you're very busy, and how did I know you'd be interested?"

He knew he'd been busier than she deserved, than he'd wanted to be, and he hadn't spent as much time with her as he should have. If she'd felt more confident in him she would have told him sooner, and not surprised him with that big-bang wake-up call.

"Good God!" he cried. "Know that I'd have been *very* interested in the fact that my little girl is a reincarnation of Christina Aguilera! With a voice that . . . it's just too good, kitten." His voice had softened, seeing the relief in her eyes that he was proud of her. And with all the emotion that came with going on stage and winning, there were now tears on her cheeks. "You've got one bright future ahead of you."

"I'm never going to be famous, Donny, you know I can't risk that. But tonight was great, and it was good to see so many people enjoying it."

He sobered, realising she wasn't the giddy, head-over-heels, I'm-going-to-see-my-name-in-lights girl most would be after a night like this. Her past haunted her still, and the spectre of her father still burned bright. She would not give up her anonymity for fame or riches, not if it brought her fear and horror.

"You never know what might happen, sweetheart, don't ever say never."

She smiled sadly. He understood her words and was trying to give her some hope. She leaned against him and his arm went around her, the smooth skin of her back beneath his hand.

"You want some dinner?" he asked.

"Yes! I'm starving!"

She usually was. Not surprising, given everything she did. Her metabolism must be through the roof.

"Paulo, swing us by Manny's, would you?" She grinned up at him and then rested her head on his shoulder. "It's Friday – you have a whole weekend to sing songs for me," he then said.

She snorted – though he could tell she was smiling from her voice. "You haven't asked how much I charge."

"Whatever it is, I'll pay it."

And he sealed the promise with a kiss on her temple, breathing in her scent, not perfume but a feminine fragrance that was natural, and sweeter. He loved it because it meant he was close to her, and he would never forget it. Just like he would never forget this night. If only they could live every day as close as they were tonight.

MYSTY LOOKED OVER from where she was watching Donny talking and playing cards with some similarly dark-suited, dark-haired individuals. Occasionally ripples of laughter reached her where she sat on the grand piano with a microphone, now allowed to sing at Donny's club on Friday and Saturday nights. She was loving her new role as entertainer. She could do any song she liked, but she knew the kind of thing that went down well. She did requests, too, and then she usually got a $50 note or two pressed into her hand, as well as getting paid $200 by the club. Donny had tried asking her what she was saving her money up for, but she remained elusive; in part she didn't know, but she had seen a motorbike she loved and hadn't managed to shake it from her mind. She would love a chance to try one out, but she wasn't sure how well the idea would go down with Donny.

She remembered how nervous she'd been the first evening – which had been silly really, because she was there with the most powerful man in the city, who owned the club, and she'd known about the club for years now, and about the people there. Still, one mobster – who was gentle and kind around her – was one thing; a room full of them was quite another. But she knew the only way to win them over was to pretend she wasn't bothered. But having a pretty face and a new set of curves helped. And being protected by Donny.

Now she was a recognised performer, not just 'Donny's girl', she felt as at home there as he did. The bar staff brought her drinks; she could take a break when she liked; and people would come and chat to her. The musicians were good fun too, and loved and respected her talent. They enjoyed having a voice that made them the centre of attention, after playing background tunes or jazz like they did the rest of the week.

And Donny liked having her there, knowing she was with him, a part of his world – and it was also a chance to show her off a little. He hoped, very much, that he wouldn't regret it, and that everyone would remember their place. He didn't know what he would do if someone overstepped the mark with her.

He looked up from the game of cards, stakes high, to her and smiled as he watched her, leaning back on one arm while sitting on the grand piano, the other holding the microphone, the magic of her voice. It didn't matter what the song was.

She sensed his eyes on her and looked over, and her lips curved into a smile as she sang. She winked at him and he grinned, realised he probably shouldn't let his affection for her show too obviously. It wouldn't help either of them.

He looked away and tried to ignore her for the next half an hour, knew she understood why and wouldn't be worried. They would have time enough to themselves later on.

"TIME TO GO, kiddo." Paulo touched her shoulder where she now sat at the bar. She was waiting to go home, which was whenever Donny finished. She didn't want a special trip made to take her, and she wanted to stay up as late as he did. Weekends were the best.

She smiled sleepily and pushed her glass towards Tommy, who'd kept her company by polishing glasses near her, telling her all his new jokes. He gave her a nod, and she let her feet drop onto the floor from the bar stool, allowed Paulo to guide her to the exit, where Donny, Lucio and Pepe already stood, all tugging jackets or cuffs into order. Donny had that swagger she knew so well: he must have won. He answered a few more shouts of goodbye with a raised hand, and then turned his attention to the figure beside him who looked so tired she could have slept standing up.

He put a hand on her back and gently brought her forward next to him, and they went out into the balmy night air.

"I thought you were getting used to these late nights, kitten, you clearly need more practice."

She blushed and looked up at him as they walked to the waiting car, the door already open. By pure chance, her eyes caught on something shiny as she glanced up. She could see the irregularity in the roofline of a house on the street that ran perpendicular to theirs, only forty yards away, and whether it was pure instinct or not, or if it triggered a memory or not, her actions once again saved Donny's life.

She grabbed him while the thoughts were yet registering in her brain and pulled, yanking him and sending them both against the car in a tumble, just as a shot rang out and took a chunk out of the pavement somewhere near them. More shots were fired as the world span around her, all of the boys pulling guns from under their jackets, aiming and firing at the figure on the roof, whilst taking cover.

Paulo grabbed Donny and pulled him over, shoving him through the open door, and Mysty knew he was going to reach for her next, but she didn't want to get in the car. How dare someone try and hurt Donny? Why did everyone she loved have to be taken from her?

She reached forward and took Paulo's other gun from his back holster – she had seen it hundreds of times before and never thought to touch it – as he was bundling Donny into the car, shouting at his boss to stay there. It was all happening in slow-fast clarity, and she focussed on her destination, rolled back around the car and started sprinting, past where Pepe and Giuseppe were firing from behind the open car doors.

She heard shouts and ignored them, cocked the gun as she ran and kept it trained on the roofline as she started climbing one-handed up the drainpipe, thanking God she was strong enough now. Near the top she paused, ready to spring over, and she noticed the shots had stopped . . . were they afraid they might hit her? Or had the guy on the roof retreated? She listened, heard a footstep or the sound of weight moving as someone shifted. She took a breath, imagined it was her father on the roof, and her heart hardened. She would love to put a bullet in him. A little of the payback he was owed.

She pounced, launching herself up over the edge of the roof, gun ready. Then she saw him, a dark shape huddled by the chimney stack. Instinctively she aimed and fired, felt the recoil and almost dropped the gun as she fell back down to the ground and rolled, keeping low with the weapon ready. She listened, and when she glanced left and right she realised the sniper rifle and the stand were right there next to her unmanned. She heard a rustle and a scurry and knew he was getting away over the roof. She didn't really want to follow him, but watched him head to another roof, fifty feet away . . . she'd never make the shot. Her hand was shaking and muscles twitched in her shoulder from the shock of the first blast, the sound still ringing in her ears. Holding a gun and firing a gun were two very different things.

Mysty turned around and looked at the instrument of death, crouching down to inspect it. She then picked it up and lobbed it over the edge of the roof, not wanting to leave such a deadly weapon up there. She heard it clatter down into the street, three dark figures running towards it, guns pointed to the sides.

Mysty looked back at where the weapon had been, furious at the way it had been so well positioned to get the best angle, the best shot to kill the man who meant the world to her, who had turned her life around. He was her whole family, her most precious friend, her confidante – everything. She spied a pair of gloves – probably used to help him climb up to the roof, and prevent leaving prints. But he had left something else, too. Bending down, she picked it up. It was a bracelet with a metal plate in the chain that had snapped. The initials GH reflected up at her in the moonlight.

After another quick scan of the flat rooftop, she took a few steps and then jumped without hesitation, landing for once without rolling – perhaps it was her anger – but she didn't feel any pain for the difference. She started striding back towards the car. She didn't look at anyone, even though there were three of them on the ground near the house who walked back with her. She held out the weapon to one of them and they took it. She didn't want to touch it any more, hating it as always, despite its use.

She saw Paulo standing by the open car door waiting for her, not letting Donny out, everyone's faces as grim as death; exactly, she realised, as hers probably did. Paulo stood back to let her get in the car. She ducked as she stepped in and sat on the opposite seat to Donny, who was looking as angry as she'd ever seen him.

"Just what *the fuck* did you think you were doing?"

The raw vehemence of his voice was like a slap. He had never used that tone with her before. Ever. Somehow it didn't surprise her, and she wasn't cowed by it: the adrenaline in her bloodstream had prepared her for any attack, including verbal ones. And yet still it shocked her.

"After I saved your life?" Mysty threw back, not reacting well to his fury when hers was burning bright and indignant. "*Again*?"

"*For fuck's sake*! You're not meant to run into a gun fight, you stupid girl!"

She felt the urge to slap him, hating being called a stupid girl, and by him of all people – the person who meant the most to her in the whole world. *Didn't he understand why she'd done it*?

"So stupid that I might be able to tell you who sent him?" She reached over and took his hand where it sat clenched on his leg, opened his fingers and slapped the bracelet into it, her eyes still fixed on his, daring him to push her a little more. "Fuck you, Capello. *Next time they can have you.*"

She didn't know how she'd dare say those words; she'd never said anything like it before. She moved to the door, seeing Paulo's body still blocking the doorway, voices going on outside – clearly the alarm had been raised inside the club and others had come to help, although it was now unnecessary.

He reached and grabbed her with one hand and dragged her closer, and with his other he took a fierce grip on her hair and pulled her head back, his face an inch from hers. Long seconds passed, his eyes on hers, their breath coming hot and angry. She grabbed his suit lapel and held on, and it grounded her as the world disappeared in the heart-pounding moment of pure fury . . . and . . . what else? What was this?

He let go and crushed her to him, and she put an arm around his neck as he pressed his cheek to hers, placing a kiss in her hair as he held on, as if for dear life.

"You don't mean that," he whispered, and she squeezed her eyes shut. She hadn't. Not one bit. Not ever.

"I know."

She nuzzled her head instinctively closer to his and moved into his embrace just a fraction more than she was – not that there was far to go, his arms were so tight, but he felt it all the same – and he felt the wetness of her tears on his cheek.

"You're not stupid. I didn't mean that. I . . . what if you'd been hurt, or? . . ." His voice was tortured and she let some more of her emotion go, stopped trying to be strong, and let her body relax. He relaxed his arms a little, too, and moved her so that he could cup her head in his hands, forcing her to look up at him. Her beautiful, expressive eyes were swimming with tears.

"It's alright, kitten. I promise, it'll be alright. OK?" She nodded and he held her again. "Paulo! Take us home," he then said, handing him the bracelet. "And get this bracelet and that gun to forensics."

The door shut and his hand went to her face, her hand still holding his lapel like she might tumble away if she let go.

"You're insane. I couldn't believe it when you ran at the house with a gun," he murmured, replaying the horrible moment in his mind. There was something both incredible and terrifying about the vision she'd made, a dark shadow darting towards danger. Paulo had been forced to slam both doors on him and lock them to stop him getting out to go after her But, somehow, she'd made it. Partly due to her speed and the fact the shooter would never have thought someone would be so . . . crazy . . . or bold.

"No one shoots at you while I'm around," she growled defiantly against the smoothness of his black jacket, thankfully free of any blood, just wet from her tears.

"No. I realise that now."

He held her close. He was alive once again *because of her*. Somehow she'd seen the danger and done the only thing that could really stop the shooter from picking any of his boys off: created a distraction.

"You definitely owe me a pizza this weekend," she murmured.

He hoped he'd have the chance to enjoy it with her. Someone had just tried to kill him, which would mean a number of other people would be hunted down and possibly killed in retribution. He would need her after it was all dealt with to make him feel human again. Once he hadn't cared, but now . . . now he didn't want to be involved in any bloodshed or brutality if he could help it. But if he were to stay alive, and stay in power – which was one and the same thing – he would have to mercilessly crush whatever upstart had thought he was an easy target. He was in too deep now, had made too many enemies, had too much history, that that dream of living in the sun free of it all, with her, was exactly that – a dream. Tonight had brought that home. At some point, too, he realised, he was going to lose her – or rather he would have to say goodbye to make sure she was safe. She had seen enough, been through enough already . . . she didn't deserve to be drawn any further into his world.

He would just have to make sure she was kept as far away from it as possible, for now. He wasn't sure for whose sake that would be, hers, his, or whoever made the mistake of pissing her off. He knew she could fight, and with her other talents she was particularly lethal and strong. This weekend, he would have Mario take her to the gun range and get her practicing. It wouldn't hurt. But then he also knew that she hated guns . . .

He had heard the shouts of the boys as she'd run at the house, knew they'd been scared for her too; but they were all rather impressed with her fearlessness. Rightly or wrongly, whatever had happened to make her run away when she was nine, had also made her rather impervious to the danger of death, which told him it had been something truly awful. He remembered his own moments of madness, taking on five men armed only with one gun, emerging covered in blood and none of it his own, throttling a man to death with his bare hands in a desperate fight . . . just imagining what her experience could have been made him hold her tighter.

"As much pizza as you like," he replied belatedly, not sure if she was asleep.

"Will you be able to find them and make sure they don't do it again?"

"Yes, of course I can."

His lips grazed over her temple. Had she felt what he had felt just minutes before, their faces inches from each other? Or was she scared of him, of his anger? She was already old beyond her years, and in that split second, he'd seen her as the woman she would become; but how did she see him? As her protector? A father? Or did she see him as more? . . .

He silently carried her in and up the stairs, wondering if a mob boss had ever carried a twelve-year-old child up to bed before. Had ever had their life saved, twice, by a kid.

He stopped at the edge of her bed and she looked up at him, her face now so gentle, all the fierceness gone.

"*Fuck you, Capello. Next time they can have you,*" he repeated.

No one had said that to him in his entire life.

She blushed.

He dropped her abruptly on the bed and she bounced on the mattress.

"Yes, if you call me stupid!" she retaliated and grabbed a pillow and launched it at him.

He took the hit, snatched it away, chucked it and grabbed the duvet and rolled her up in it till she couldn't move, only her head peeking out at the top. She glared at him.

"That should keep you out of trouble for five minutes at least!" he told her with an infuriating grin.

"Four and a half, if you're *lucky*!" she growled.

"See you in the morning, kiddo."

She huffed as the door shut, and then relaxed. She trusted him and was glad she was here, not at her flat. She liked hearing the sound of voices downstairs; liked knowing she would wake up to company; liked that the windows were bulletproof. She was tired, and knew she wasn't processing the danger she had just been in very well, but she couldn't just then. In the morning it probably would hit her like a sucker punch to the gut, but at least tomorrow morning she wouldn't have to wake up to the truth that Donny had been . . . she couldn't even think the words.

DONNY WALKED SLOWLY down the stairs and looked up and saw Paulo waiting for him; both remained silent as they walked down the corridor to Donny's rooms. Paulo pulled the bracelet from his pocket and held it up to see the inscription: GH. Gino Haberman. Known hitman and rarely in Vegas. Good friends with Carlos Labaro, one of Donny's first lieutenants who had gone rogue. Had decided he wanted to be his own master, rather than answer to one. This didn't come as a surprise.

Inside, Paulo closed the door and sat down in the chair in front of Donny's desk. Donny held out his hand and Paulo tossed it over to him. He leaned back, the bracelet in one hand, the fingers on the other pressed to his lips, contemplating how to proceed, the violence that would be necessary; but he was struggling to concentrate, unable to stop himself revisiting the fact he could have been shot dead.

"She found it on the roof," he finally said.

"I had three of the boys go back and check the roof. The shot she got off managed to damage him enough to leave a blood trail. We have a blood sample and some prints being processed, so we'll get something. Is this what I think it is?"

"Yes. We both know whose initials they are. And who will have paid him. Why he would be so stupid as to try this when he must know how weak his position is?"

"Do you think it's because . . .?"

Paulo looked away, not sure he wanted to say it, knowing better than anyone else how Donny felt about Mysty. He didn't want to be the first one to voice criticism.

"Say it."

"Do you think it's because he thinks you've gone soft over the girl?"

Donny grimaced at having to hear his own thoughts spoken to him by another.

"Well, he might think that, but he's soon going to see how wrong he is. Sending a gunman to pick me off outside my own club? Jesus. Fucking coward," Donny replied dangerously.

Why couldn't he have something wonderful to care for? Why must he be a monster only in order to retain his authority? Imagine how distraught she would have been to have seen him shot dead.

"If she injured this shooter enough to leave a blood trail, get some boys round to all the places he might try for medical help. He'll then try and leave town," Donny instructed. "Get Surveillance to do a sweep. The roads were pretty empty as it was so late, so we should get a plate for his car. We can wait until it gets picked up on the system tomorrow morning – if he makes it that far – and pull him over. Then we get some answers. And depending on those answers, we'll then proceed as seems best."

"And you are going underground until we have this a little better covered. That was without warning, and we'd had no intel to indicate anything. Not even a whisper. This had been kept well hidden. God knows how she saw him in time . . . just be glad she has the reactions of a jungle cat."

"Oh, don't worry, I'm fully appreciative of that," Donny confirmed ruefully, not pleased at having to spend his weekend in their secret underground chambers. "Have Mario and Giuseppe take her to the Matrix tomorrow, before dropping her off at Cirque. And try and get her to handle some guns and practice. Don't let her outside if you can help it, and keep eyes on her. I know they're after me but . . . I wouldn't put it past them."

Donny got up and poured them both a brandy. It was going to be one hell of a weekend.

"You want her to go to the *gun range*?" Paulo asked in disbelief as he was passed the glass.

"If she knows how to use one it could save her life. She's a smart kid, we both know that, and we both know she's as gifted as a person can be. I've no doubt she'll prove as competent with a gun as everything else."

Paulo sat looked at his brandy, not drinking it. He had grown to love that kid – not like Donny; he didn't quite know what Donny felt – and he didn't want her hurt, endangered or dead. She was too pure and innocent – despite the swearing and the fighting – to live amongst such raw danger.

"Paulo, she can't stay for much longer . . . I . . . I know that." Donny knew his men; but knew the man sitting opposite him like a brother. There was over two decades of history between them. "But until she goes, I want her to be safe. I'm hoping to see her career launched at Celeste, and then life will take its natural course for her. She won't like it, but she'll move on. If she stays it could kill her, and none of us want that."

Paulo looked up and saw the sadness in his boss's face, relieved that there wasn't going to be an argument about the issue; but they'd all miss her so much, and the realisation hit him that his formidable boss must actually really love the kid to accept her leaving for her own good, and not risk keeping her with him just because he wanted her there.

"I understand. Sure will miss her though."

"Yeah. I can't even remember what life was like . . ." Donny caught himself before he started reminiscing on things that would only make him feel worse. "She can always visit."

"Of course," Paulo agreed, knowing it wouldn't be the same, not at all.

"She mustn't know anything of what goes on this weekend, clear?"

"Of course. The boys all know that." Paulo knew the rules, knew like Donny that whatever was going to happen was not going to be pretty in the slightest. He paused and swirled the amber liquid. "Did she really say what I think I heard her say in the car back there?" he asked tentatively, looking at Donny a moment later, trying to gauge his reaction; but his dark eyes were gleaming with amusement.

"Yes, it was something like 'Fuck you, Capello. Next time they can have you!'"

Paulo couldn't help laughing. "She's unbelievable." He shook his head when the laughter receded to a chuckle. "Naturally, I won't tell anyone she said that."

"No, because anyone else but her would get a bullet in their ass," Donny confirmed menacingly, remembering the bright glint of determination in her eyes, her beautiful face contorted with anger. *Why do I have to give her up?*

"You want to leave now or in the morning?"

"Give me an hour, then have a car ready. How badly was that one hit?"

"Not so bad. There were enough of us to keep him busy. Her approach clearly put him off staying." Paulo finished the brandy in one swig and put the glass down. "I'll come get you in an hour."

He knew when his boss wanted some space. He left the room.

Donny rubbed his eyes and groaned. This was not how he had planned the weekend.

MYSTY WAS NOT happy. Only last night he'd almost got killed and now he had just gone, leaving her a message saying he would see her as soon as he could, and they would definitely have pizza and a film. How many times had she heard that before? And where had he gone?

She pulled out a screwdriver she'd borrowed from the tech guys. She had a feeling this was not going to be as straightforward as she'd hoped it would be. Whoever had put Donny's computer together had not done a very good job; it was running too slowly, and waiting to see if something was wrong with it was annoying because the configuration was poor.

The intercom buzzer went. She looked at it, not really in the mood to talk to anyone at the moment. And besides, she only had ten minutes and then she had to leave because he wanted her to go to the gun range and practice handling them. Did he not remember that she hated the things?

Impatiently she hit the button. If it wasn't Donny she might as well take a message for him.

"Donny Capello's office." She knew her voice was less than friendly, and she started typing commands into the computer.

"Ah. The six-foot redhead secretary in underwear."

She groaned mentally. It was The Man From New York.

Daryl was secretly delighted. What a bonus getting her on the line again!

"What underwear are you wearing today?"

She was amazed at his cheek. He didn't even know her name! But luckily, being around lots of over-sexed Italians who all thought themselves something rather special had made her immune to flirtatious overtones.

"Who said I was wearing any? I could be completely naked on Donny's desk, handcuffed so I can only answer the intercom." She heard a splutter as if he had choked on something. "How is New York?" she then asked calmly.

"Hot," Daryl managed to say as he mopped up the mess from his coffee.

"Not as hot as Vegas, I'll bet. If you ever come here you might understand why we don't wear much." She typed in one last command, sighed and slipped under the desk, taking the screwdriver with her. "You want Donny?" She raised her voice a touch so he could hear her.

Daryl couldn't work out why her voice was different. The typing he could fathom, but now it sounded like she was in a cupboard. "Yes, I take it he's not there?"

"That is definitely one way of putting it."

"He run out on you?" Daryl teased wickedly.

Something slammed.

No answer. Nothing that was audible anyway. And just as he was trying to think of another way to get her to speak, she answered: "He's not here is all I can tell you. And I don't know when he'll be back. Perhaps Monday." It was like she was answering but really concentrating on something else entirely. "What the? A 7290 with a RT60 couple link and SSDT5? Who the hell put this together?"

Her disgust was obvious; he had to agree that was a bad combination.

"What are you doing?"

"I was upgrading Donny's computer with some software, but it looks like it's going to need a complete overhaul." There was a big sigh, and another slam.

Daryl was amazed. She must be what – twelve, thirteen? And she knew things he would expect his technical team to know. The things he knew because he'd designed some of it.

"Do you actually know what you're doing, or are you making this up as you go along?" he then asked, with a hint of impatience, not liking the idea of some kid pulling apart an associate's computer and making a complete mess of it.

"I admit, sometimes, I do make things up . . . but I promise you, right now I know exactly what I'm doing." She didn't seem offended; more amused at his doubting her.

"Hey, kiddo!" Another voice.

"What?" A yell from beneath the desk, half-muffled.

"Five minutes, then we're leaving. You got your stuff ready for later?"

She peered out from under the desk and saw Mario looking down at her, typically handsome and debonair, as Mario always was. But he had a soft side too: after forgiving her for his 500-dollar ruined shoes, he treated her like a kid sister.

"It's in the hall. I'm good to go. If I leave a list with the boys downstairs, do you think they can have some parts ready for me when I get back?"

"Sure thing, twiglet."

Daryl was aghast at the natural trust the two speakers had for each other, and the mutual respect for their absent boss: she was clearly completely accepted by everyone, even Capello's notoriously loyal and brutal bodyguard . . . how bizarre.

"Mario, do we really have to go?"

"You know we do. Boss's orders."

"But I *hate* guns."

"You used one last night just fine."

"Exceptional circumstances for expedient measures," she growled back, looking out at him from under the desk.

Daryl smiled. This was not the talk of a regular child.

"Well, just pretend this session at the gun range is exceptional. And expedient. It'll be fun, you'll see."

"Hmm." There was no other reply to such a poor argument in her opinion.

"Three minutes," Mario said. Like the rest of the boys, he was rather proud of her, and rather pleased to be the one who got to take her to play with guns. It wouldn't be anything less than interesting, not after what she'd done last night.

"Get out of here then and let me finish."

Mario left.

"You still there or have you gone?" She didn't sound bothered either way.

"I'm here. What happened last night?"

"Putting it bluntly, someone tried to put a bullet in Donny's head outside his club at 1.27am."

"Do you know if he's alright?" Daryl felt his blood freeze. Surely she wouldn't sound so blasé if Donny had been hurt, or worse?

"Do I know?" she snorted in disgust. "I was the one who pushed him out of the way. He's fine." He heard more computer tinkering. "Was there anything else?" she then asked.

"Pardon?" Daryl was still getting over the fact that this kid was clearly a . . . very unusual kid. Why was Donny taking her to the club with him? Would she ever stop surprising him? And the cheek of her!

"I said, was there anything else? Did you want to leave a message for him?" she repeated.

Daryl shook his head in disbelief. *How had he let this kid lead the conversation?* "No, it's not urgent. It was of a more frivolous nature really." *About Donny's private box at Cirque de Celeste.*

"That's good. He does far too much work as it is."

He was half-amused, half-jealous by the affectionate frustration in her tone, and once again struggled to reply.

"By the way," she then said. "What underwear are *you* wearing?"

His chin nearly hit the desk. This was not the conversation he'd anticipated having today, particularly not with someone he'd never met, and who was definitely way under the age of consent, but so . . . sassy!

"Who said I was wearing any?" he returned, thinking it was a clever retort, echoing her own.

"Of course you are." She made it sound like it was obvious and he was really pushing his luck thinking he could fool her, thinking he could be clever. "You're sitting in your neat, pristine office, in your neat, pristine suit, doing work on a Saturday morning, so you're hardly going to be doing that without wearing underwear – just think how it would shock your neat, pristine secretary. I bet you're even wearing a *tie*." She made it sound like he had committed an awful sin.

"I am." Daryl scowled. She was smart. And he got the impression she was mocking him a little – a lot? Perhaps she didn't like neat or pristine; but in his world, he couldn't have it any other way.

"And it's . . . erm . . . dark blue," she guessed, interrupting his thoughts. He looked down, and sure enough, his tie was blue: dark blue. "Well?"

"Spot on." It sounded like she'd emerged from under the desk.

"What a guess." She brushed herself off. "So. Underwear. Or are you too shy to say?"

Her voice was teasing. What on earth did she look like? He couldn't even conjure up a guess she was so unusual.

"It's my own brand."

Did she honestly expect him to tell her what type of underwear he preferred? Boxers or Y-fronts, or what? Like he, *he*, *Daryl Blackmoor*, would answer such questions from a woman – who was probably not even a woman!

"Is that in case if you forget your name and need to check, or in case someone else runs off with them?" she asked.

The insolent reply was just typical, perfect, and hilarious. Daryl struggled to keep himself in check. He wasn't going to encourage her.

"Because it's the best."

"Ah, of course." She didn't sound surprised or impressed; but if she'd known who he was it would have been obvious: he only ever had the best, no expense spared. "Well, do try not to work the whole weekend. Why did God give us sunshine if not to enjoy it? I've got to go."

Despite the fact that she'd irritated him, she had amused and intrigued him far more. He didn't want the call to end. She was the most interesting person he'd spoken to all day – all *year* in fact.

"Kiddo!" It was Mario again.

"I'm coming!"

"Don't make me come in there and get you!"

"You manhandle me and I'll put your nose where your ear is!"

She was smiling as she said that, Daryl could tell.

"Threats now, is it?"

"Promises, Mario, as you know."

There followed some Italian in both voices that Daryl could not understand.

"Goodbye, New York!"

The Disconnect button was pressed and she was gone.

Daryl and stared at the intercom, fingering his tie. Abruptly he pulled it off, tossed it on the desk and swung his chair around to face the window. *What underwear was he wearing*? Dear God, she couldn't possibly know who she was speaking to. But then again, he was glad she didn't. He'd rather hear her unaffected, honest chatter any day. She hadn't really spoken to him with even a modicum of the respect he was used to, and certainly none of the crawling reverence he received from so many. And he absolutely didn't care.

He looked at the brightness of the sun beyond the windows of his office suite. What kind of kid stays out at a club till the early hours, gets into a gun fight, saves someone's life, decides to overhaul their computer the next morning, and then gets taken to a gun range? Was Donny utterly insane to teach this child how to shoot or? . . . He couldn't even imagine. He then looked around his orderly office – pristine as she had guessed. Was she incredibly clever, or had Donny told her about him? Somehow, he didn't think so, not from the nature and tone of her questions. She was so confident; nothing threw her. It was rather interesting that he was so intrigued by someone he'd never met. Indeed, it was quite the most interesting thing that had happened to him for a while. A *long* while.

He looked at the clock. 2.45pm. Another half an hour, then he was leaving. He didn't know what for, but he wasn't going to spend all day in a suit. Perhaps he'd let someone else find out what underwear he was wearing.

DONNY SAT DOWN in his chair. It felt like a year since he had. He rubbed his eyes, knowing even as he did so it wouldn't clear some of the horrible images that played through his mind, or magic Mysty onto the chair in front of him.

He sighed. What a weekend. Monday night and it felt like a week had gone past. He'd overseen the interrogation of the sniper, who Lucio and Pepe had caught up with in his car trying to leave the city with a bullet in his shoulder. Lucio had helpfully tipped some alcohol onto the raw wound as an opener, and then yanked his arm out, forcing bullet and bone to grate. But even that hadn't been enough to get an answer, so they'd brought him in, and he must have known he was a dead man. It was just a case of how. No one took pot shots at Donny Capello and lived. Certainly not if they missed.

It was a long time since he'd had anyone *encouraged* to share information, and the screams still echoed in his head. He longed to hear Mysty's laughter instead, that chuckle when she teased him, or fits of giggles at something on the TV. There hadn't been enough of that of late. And there wouldn't be much more of it either. He'd had time enough over the last seventy-two hours to realise that his attachment to her was unfeasible. He had to try and distance himself.

He switched his computer on and noticed it fired up much more quickly. He also noted there were some video messages waiting for him and he clicked on them, hoping one was from her. It was and his spirits lifted. He felt so bad he hadn't seen her at all that weekend, or been there the morning after the attack. She gave so much, and he let her down in even the simplest ways – all because of the demands of his lifestyle, because of who he was.

'Hi, Donny,' the message began. She was sitting in his chair, and he smiled before she even got any further, because her face was kind of shy, kind of playful. He knew she hated being on camera . . . ironic for one so beautiful. 'Erm, well, I didn't want to have to leave a message, but I've been told you've had to go somewhere safe, which is OK, but . . .' She looked down into her lap. 'It just feels wrong being here without you, so I just thought I'd leave you this so you had something to cheer you up whenever you come home. I won't ask questions and I don't want details, I just hope this weekend isn't too . . . horrid.'

She then looked back at the screen, her eyes piercing. 'I see it in your eyes sometimes, a sadness, like a memory, so I hope it hasn't made it worse, that's all.' Donny couldn't have said anything if he'd wanted to. His throat closed up. 'I really don't like seeing you unhappy – aside from the fact it'll make you go all wrinkly because of too much frowning, and I know how vain you Italians are.' A hint of a smile around her mouth; he rubbed his hand over his. How could he tell her the things he'd seen that cast a shadow over his soul? 'Anyway, just before you think I've gone all soft on you, you probably noticed that your computer started much quicker. I've upgraded the firmware and some software, so it's all a lot better put together now so it'll be faster. And I've added an extra firewall too. I'm thinking you definitely owe me pizza until Christmas by now." That smile again. 'You're probably tired. And I really hope you go to bed, but I guess you won't." She rolled her eyes. 'Lazarus says hi too.'

The leopard pushed his head up against her chest and she rubbed his fur. He was growing up as well. Donny could see how large he was now in comparison to her, and properly sharp teeth were peeking out as the big cat enjoyed her fuss him.

'So, that's it, except to say I completely surprised the guys at the gun range and . . . I missed you. I couldn't believe you disappeared on me.' A ferocious scowl. "You're lucky I still like you, Donny Capello!' she added with a smile that told him she didn't mean it. She reached forward, pressed the End button, and the picture was gone.

He wanted to watch it again, but he clicked on the file marked Matrix-She's-Got-a-Gun. He realised what it was immediately, but it cut to Mario's face first: 'Hey, boss, just thought you might like to see how she got on at the gun range. After showing that she had no problem hitting the targets we put her in the Matrix . . . it's worth a watch, boss. I don't think she's someone you'd want after you, if you know what I mean, so thank God she's watching your back. Hope to have you back with us soon.'

Mario gave a little salute and he disappeared, then the video started to play again, shot from cameras inside the Matrix – a four-storey building converted to a practice ground for shooting in enclosed spaces, with multiple rooms, doorways and a main staircase. The guns were handgun-sized, and they sent electric shocks like a tazer, but were more accurate. Contenders wore suits and helmets so the electrical charges were picked up and also felt. This meant the computers knew who'd been hit and where, so people could be wounded or killed, depending on the shots received.

She had been pushed through a door in the corner of the room and almost immediately a shot was fired through the doorway in front of her that almost hit her leg, but she moved aside. Somehow. She went quickly to the doorway at one side then and peeked round, and immediately there were shots.

"Come on out, cupcake, we'd sure love to see you."

She clearly didn't like the patronising tone, or the mocking words. *Cupcake*? She clocked him lurking in a doorway at the far end of the room.

He could see her thinking, looking round the room. She was pinned unless she found a way out. And there were about twenty others against her. She suddenly dived across the doorway, and the guys taking shots missed. She then ran two steps, cart-wheeled and then flipped, loosing shots as she went, and relieving one guy of his gun as she did so. She then used both guns to take him out and the two guys who'd been covering him. Their cries of astonishment did not go unnoticed by Donny.

She kept going, dropping and rolling to a crouch the moment new danger was sensed in each room. Those she found were dead within less than a second of her detecting them. But the guy she clearly wanted was Cupcake Guy, and the look on his face was priceless – even through his visor – when she caught him by surprise and ended him with one shot to the heart. Donny actually threw back his head and laughed when the cameras picked up her voice: 'Nobody calls me cupcake, you dick.'

He could see the timer running: seven, or eight down in less than three minutes? She hunted her way through the rest of the floor, despatching with another guy; his buddy hurtled up the stairs and disappeared. She followed, ducking and weaving, both guns ready, firing instinctively it seemed as her brain registered movement – and on target, killing everything she hit. Pausing for a second, completely still, and listening in silence behind a pillar, Donny held his breath. Had she seen him? Sensed him? She suddenly swung round and fired straight at his chest. Had he let her watch too many movies? Obviously not!

The next few minutes passed in a similar fashion, and soon she was up on the top floor where the exit button was. She saw the button on a table, with a large leather chair behind it, and again she paused, safe for a moment behind another pillar. She then raised both guns and fired at the chair, and Donny nearly jumped out of his. 'Like I'd be dumb enough to fall for that!' she laughed as she heard a loud groan, the guy behind the chair very much feeling the impact of her shots through his suit. She then sat down in the chair and leaned back, put her feet up on the table. She looked at the watch she had been given to check how long she'd been in there, tossed one gun on the table and waited with the other in her hand, resting it on her thigh.

And waited.

'Hey, sugar.'

The voice was as clear as a bell, and the sarcasm biting. But the direction was unclear. She didn't move. Neither did Donny, his eyes glued to the screen. This was as good as any movie he'd seen. Long seconds passed, and somewhere in his head he imagined her shot at, and suddenly this was deadly serious. *Mysty, what are you doing? Are you ready?* Silence again. And her still, hardly breathing as she listened.

And then she raised the gun on her lap and fired, hitting the guy who appeared around a doorframe to her right straight in the head. She then got up, pressed the button and walked out, tossing the gun on the table with the other, and stepping over the guy holding his head and shouting something she couldn't make out. She walked down the stairs, elegant as a queen, got to the third floor, got bored of the time it was taking, vaulted over the edge of the stairs and dropped to the ground floor.

Suffice to say, she did not appreciate being called 'cupcake' or 'sugar'.

She was met by an exultant Mario and Guiseppe, who'd found the whole thing highly amusing – unlike the five other men who'd been watching, and who took it as a personal slight that she had succeeded to wipe the floor with their best guys. They owned the building, and they'd designed the layout of the rooms to be difficult; but she'd made a mockery of it – and with far too much style!

Mario watched her unzip the jacket of the suit and remove her helmet. Donny did too. But she looked far from happy, despite all the monitoring screens showing the defeated picking themselves up and spilling down to the lounge rooms, looking demoralised.

"Well, I guess that's $400 you owe me, Mark!" Mario said to the approaching manager who'd been watching in his office. Not only did she win, but she did it in less than ten minutes. I think that must be near the top of the leader board, right?"

Mario had a bet on her?

"She didn't even get hit once! Who the fuck is she? You said she was thirteen fucking years old, and she's gone in there like she's some goddamn marine?" An accusing finger pointed at her. "How the fuck did she *do* that? She–"

"Why the fuck are you swearing so much?" Mysty cut in angrily. Tossing the suit back on the pile, she glared at the manager. "I just did what I had to do; no more, no less. And I'd be happy to go back in there and settle it with you if you have a problem with that, or my age. And the next person who calls me 'cupcake' or 'sugar' or a 'marine' is going to get a busted face, you got that?" She took her jacket from Mario.

"And she means it, too," Mario added with relish, seeing the looks on the guys' faces. They'd wanted some juicy entertainment, not this unashamed battering of their egos.

Mark came forward and got out his wallet, eyeing Mysty suspiciously. He slapped the notes into Mario's hand.

"Are we done?" Mysty snarled.

"We're done," Mario replied.

He gestured towards the door, but she was already on the move – and the men around her stepped out the way.

"You OK, kiddo?" Mario asked gently as they stepped into the fresh air.

In his own heady sense of success and pride, he hadn't been paying close enough attention to her real feelings, so had completely misunderstood the reason for her fury only moments before. She looked away from him, the camera above the door showing perfectly how awkwardly she was standing, hugging herself. Gone the easy, fluid steps that usually carried her along.

"She doesn't like guns . . ." Donny whispered to the screen.

"I-I just don't like guns." She turned slightly and it was obvious to Donny from her voice that she was trying not to cry. "I *really* don't like guns."

The first tears slid from her eyes, and she started for the car, slipping a pair of impenetrable shades on, leaving Mario and Guiseppe to follow, his face showing just how surprised he was at the intensity of emotion.

The film ended.

Donny felt terrible. Clearly whatever had happened to her all that time ago had involved guns, and she'd seen someone, or more than one person, get shot. And in his great wisdom he had instructed Mario to take her to the gun range. Paulo had told him she'd not been keen on going, but he'd assumed it was more nerves than anything; but had it been simple nerves, she wouldn't have got so emotional. If only she'd tell him what happened back then, but then why should she bare her soul when he kept so much from her?

He switched off the computer and went upstairs to bed, her enraged face still in his mind. He'd just wanted to know she could handle a gun, keep herself safe; but at what cost? He was now safe in the knowledge that those who had ordered his death were no longer a problem; but again, at what cost? Which households were this night mourning their losses, not sitting down to an evening meal, not able to imagine life without the men he'd had killed?

What he wouldn't give to have her there with him. His ray of sunshine. The question was, would she still feel the same about him?

MYSTY SIGHED AND looked around her. *I shouldn't be sad. My home has everything I ever dreamed of.* She had her own bedroom with soft covers and pillows. Fully stocked cupboards of all the food she could eat and more. There were proper curtains and thick carpets under her feet. Not like . . . A door inside her mind slammed shut. Saving her. Keeping her in the present.

I miss Donny. And I miss Fabio and Lucio and Mario. And Guiseppe. And Donna Capello. I miss all of them. She thought of Donna Capello's garlic bread and focaccia, and laughing around the long table in the kitchen. Donny had become so distant. Maybe he'd got bored of her. She was just a kid, after all. Perhaps his being so busy was just so he could avoid her, or . . . maybe he'd met someone.

Closing her eyes, she could easily remember the alien sensations she had encountered waking up to her new life in the Capello townhouse. How nervous she had been of making a mistake and them shouting at her. But they never did. They just seemed to love her, accept her. Then a little while later, Donny had told her he had a little place she could make her own, where she could have more space and do her homework undisturbed. But she could read between the lines. In that month amongst the black suits she had become aware of the coded messages used to avoid saying certain words, or the way people discretely left the room to speak to Donny out of her earshot. She knew there were things they kept from her – not that she was made to feel in the way, but somehow she knew she was – and she honestly didn't want to know what they were. But she missed them all so much.

Guiltily she rebuked herself for her ingratitude. She was going to the best school, doing sports, dancing, singing, learning languages . . . but she was lonely, she had to admit that.

She sat down in front of her computer. Her first. The one Fabio had helped her build from scratch, getting in trouble a few times because he had spent so long with his avidly keen protégé. The hours spent with him had been some of the best of her life. Second to those spent with Donny. Sitting with popcorn and bottles of water the hours had slipped by as knowledge had been transferred, exploring everything and anything, her hunger for knowledge sated by a willing teacher who nurtured her ambition. She had more than caught up with her peers, and was now learning things that wouldn't be taught in the classroom. She knew much of it was illegal, but if it wasn't used to hurt anyone, then was it really so bad?

Looking at the screen, Mysty contemplated messaging Fabio, asking if he was free, but knew that wasn't fair. It wasn't fair to risk him getting into Donny's bad books just because she wanted his company. Plus it was Saturday night – always busy for the Capello boys.

She logged into her Facebook account and scrolled. She didn't really have any friends. And she'd lied about her age to get her account – not that that bothered her at all. It was a minor deception compared to stuff other people did. Updates about some of her favourite musicians, sports people and the environment made up her news feed. Clicking on a new report out about how global warming was affecting the water levels in Alaska and ruining precious habitat, she pulled a foot up onto the chair so her chin could rest on her knee.

She found it difficult that she'd lived her whole life, until now, so ignorant of the world. She'd not even known Vegas existed, for goodness' sake! Her days had been taken up by simply surviving from one sad event to another. She had a lot of catching up to do. She started to read the article. Lots of people seemed to know about this, but no one was doing very much. She read about a whale with hundreds of plastic bags in its stomach and other rubbish in the seas that was killing the fish, and she felt sad – and helpless. Perhaps she could volunteer, like the people who'd written the article, when she was older? That thought cheered her.

The adverts and popups around the article changed and one caught her eye: Facebook was offering her the option of joining a group named 'Plan A: Save the World'. *Wow.* What Fabio had told her about algorithms was true. The search engine has reacted to my preferences. Clever. Sneaky though.

Clicking on the link, feeling like she had nothing to lose, a little frisson of excitement tingled through her veins. The page loaded and she saw the mission statement of the group: 'Sharing ideas and motivation to help save our beautiful planet. We believe if enough people want to make a difference, we can make a difference. Join us if you want a better world!' *Wow.* Clicking to join she waited, wondering how long it would take. About to skip away to look at the article again, a notification flashed up:her request to join had been accepted by Andy Telleman. And now the posts loaded for her to see.

Someone had shared the exact same article she had been reading, and below was a discussion about how best to de-plastic the oceans, theorising a new invention that would make it quicker and easier to clean up the decades of trash that was ruining such a precious resource. There was also a petition to get a bill passed to get micro-beads in beauty products made illegal worldwide so they didn't find their way into the water system. A video appeared on the screen, something about something called Greenpeace, and then a maths challenge. But it was posed as a conundrum to do with the theoretical number of acres of forest needing to be planted over the next decade to stop, then reverse, the process of global warming given the rate of gas production and respiration of carbon dioxide. *Wow.* It was a maths challenge and then some, requiring the calculation of numerous factors, and research to get accurate figures, considered concurrently, before any final sum could be reached. It was exactly the kind of problem she loved and so far hadn't found in her maths classes at school, where she spent most of the time holding her impatience in check.

Pulling a notepad across and beginning to scribble, she started creating figures. She rechecked the details: for the sake of simplicity, the 'forest' was meant to consist of only three main types of tree, and the relevant details of their consumption of carbon dioxide and production of oxygen were also stated. The rest of the figures were down to the individual to find. Whoever did this really must love his numbers, she thought. Typing 'climate change figures' into Google wasn't what she'd imagined she'd be doing that night.

People were coming up with answers and commenting, the list getting longer. No one, so far, had got it right. She scrolled to the original post, which had been put up by someone called Raju Khan, who was informing people of their erroneous answers with a brutal straightforwardness. She instantly liked him. He must be a number geek like her. She was loving this. They didn't get proper questions like this at school.

Scribbling away, crossing out, drawing lines, multiplying, adding it up and then going back to double check her answer, she smiled. Fifty-two minutes later she held her fingers over the keyboard, planning to type it in. *What if I'm wrong? Everyone else has been wrong!* She typed, making sure every number and word was copied over correctly. After hesitating, again, she hit the Enter key and her answer was posted.

Her post was instantly liked by three people and then two things happened: first, she got a friend request from Raju; then a message popped up from him as well.

'Hi, Ecce.' Mysty realised how odd her chosen online name was seeing it typed by someone else. 'Congratulations on your answer. You're the closest by a long way! My own answer was only 232 out of your calculation! It's so great to talk to someone else who can do maths like this! Where are you from?' *Wow.* How on earth was she supposed to respond to that?

She typed: 'Hi, Raju. I'm in the US. West Coast. Where are you? And yes, I love maths. The harder the better!'

He sent back some laughing emoticons that made her smile, and: 'India. South-west.' Worried the conversation might stop, Mysty tried to think of what else she could ask that would be OK. Talking to strangers was so weird! Luckily Raju saved them from awkward virtual silence: 'You care about the planet?'

'I wish there was a thousand million of me so I could make the difference I want to. The more I read the sadder I become.'

'I know. Humans have ruined so much. But I won't give up on the hope we can turn it around.'

Unconsciously, she was drawn to his optimism and determination, but typed: 'Some scientists say it's too late.'

'No. Life can't and won't be sustainable in the same way as we have it now, but we can save ourselves from complete disaster. If we act soon that is.'

'But how? How can we get enough people to bother, and governments to get on board?'

'Well, that's the challenge, isn't it?'

'Have you sent your tree-growing idea to anyone?' she then asked.

'I've thought about it.'

A pause. *Gosh this is hard. This guy seems really cool. What can I say to him?* 'The group seems really great.'

'It is and it isn't.' His comment made her frown, so she sent back a question mark, surprised by the semi-negation. 'People share a lot of info and agree that so much needs to be done, but none of them do anything. Not really. One person can't do a lot on their own.'

'Well. There's two of us now. Who want to make things happen. That's two more than nothing.'

'I guess you're right. I like that kind of maths too.' She was sent a fist pump. 'How old are you?'

'Probably not as old as you are.'

'I'm 17.'

'I'm at school.'

'I wish I was at school.'

'Why aren't you at school?'

'I'll tell you one day.'

She wasn't one to judge, or push. The fact he had stuff he wanted to keep private made it easier. 'Thanks for the friend request. I don't have many right now. Least not my age.'

'How come?'

'I'll tell you one day. It's not a great story. I've moved cities, so I know almost no one right now.'

'You seem cool. Whatever happened you seem to have survived pretty well.'

Mysty grimaced as she read the words, feeling they were as premature as they were encouraging. *Am I? Have I?* 'Some people go through crap late in life, some of us get it early on. I got my share early.'

'Ha! Me too!' Suddenly she found herself smiling. 'You can message me. Anytime. I don't go out much. I'm usually online if you need to chat.'

'Thanks. I've never had a long-distance friend before. That would be great.'

'And we can save the world.'

'From itself.'

'From ruining the planet.'

'That too.'

A whole line of laughing emoticons and high-fives followed and Mysty grinned, amused by their overuse, and unexpectedly buoyed up by the exchange.

'I better go.'

'Your parents yelling at you?'

'No.' *I don't have parents.* A catch in her throat put a pressure in her chest. *Get used to it. People are going to ask.*

'My parents are always yelling at me.'

'I'm sorry.'

'Don't be, not your fault.' The sadness and resignation practically leapt off the screen. How had he been so upbeat and determined if his depressed him so much? 'You go get some sleep. I'll message you tomorrow.'

'Start coming up with A Plan.'

'You can be the Robin to my Batman.'

'I could be Batgirl instead?'

'Yeah OK' More laughing emoticons. It felt good to end the conversation on a happy note. The thrill of making a friend, of finding someone she seemed to get along with, however far away, put a buzz in her head that she hadn't expected. 'Well done again on your maths! Impressed!'

'Not your fault you got your answer a bit wrong!' The most daring thing she had ever typed, she put some tongues-out emoticons after it so he knew she was joking. Still, it took him a few seconds to answer and Mysty began to worry she'd over-stepped the mark.

'Fighting talk. I like it. I'll come up with something even harder for you for tomorrow, Ecce!!!'

Laughing out loud, partly out of relief he'd taken it as she'd intended, Mysty put a few waving hands and thumbs-up and closed everything down. She needed to go to bed. To think most kids had their parents send them to bed, and she had to send herself, was hard sometimes, no matter how tired she was.

Somewhere, thousands of miles away, however, was someone she might call a friend one day. And that made her smile. It was pretty amazing. Pretty cool too.

She brushed her teeth and got into bed, Lazarus following. She could hear cars on the road outside. Water trickled in a drain to her left somewhere inside the building. Lazarus yawned. She did too.

She thought about tomorrow. Would Raju message her? Feeling a new excitement, she slept.

"HEY, SIS?"

The bedroom door was pushed open to allow Alexander Huntley just enough room to enter and then shut again. His entrance was like a rock being thrown in a pool; it disappeared beneath the surface and the motionlessness resumed.

She didn't return his greeting; the familiarity fell flat. She just continued to stare out of the window. As she had been doing for far too long. Lex had heard all about her silent, thousand-yard stares, her days spent in her bedroom, days spent not communicating. Hence why he'd come back. He should be in Oregon finishing a business deal worth $46m, but his mother's shrill tone on the phone had convinced him.

That and his deeply ingrained dislike of Daryl Blackmoor. Born in Texas, raised in Texas, and proud of Texas, he had no time for the rich city-boys who thought anyone not from their Manhattan social circles was a hill-billy, particularly one who had just broken it off with his sister after barely two months. Feeling the rejection on her behalf, he had taken the news of the ended engagement in silence, well aware of his parent's happiness at its inception – second only to his sister's. She had glowed like a prom queen, bursting with the pride and joy that had come with netting the richest man on Earth without barely doing anything. She'd been chosen. Selected, tested, and chosen.

She wasn't glowing now. She had been chosen, tested and rejected. What had gone wrong? What had Blackmoor found fault with? His sister was beautiful, dignified – everything a man could want! Both of them had known it wasn't a love match. It had been politic, smart, beneficial – everything many marriages were not. The questions had only grown bigger since her surprise return to Texas, and the Blackmoor press machine had churned out some pitter-patter about a mutually agreed split and a 'change of heart' by both parties: a flowery collection of bullshit.

"Rachel, I've come quite a way to see you. Not even a hello for your big brother?"

"I suppose mother called you."

"Are you surprised?"

No answer. Just a huge inhale and a long, long exhale. Lex resisted doing the same, hands shoved in his pockets, hoping his relaxed attitude might rub off on her so she might drop her crossed arms from her chest at least and turn to face him.

The silence became awkward but he could tell she didn't care. She'd already had similar stand-offs with her parents.

"Are you going to tell me what happened?"

"I really don't want to talk about it."

"OK, well, either you talk to me, or I'm pretty sure Mum and Dad are going to get a shrink involved. Your choice."

There was no mention of Sophie, their younger sister. She wasn't even considered as an appropriate confidante. She was too young and too naïve; too wrapped up in selfish ambitions of beauty and popularity to have time or the attention span for her sister. Her only contribution had been at the breakfast table the morning after Rachel's abrupt return to the ranch, bemoaning the lost chance to be part of the second most important family in America, second only to the president. No one had had the heart to break the awkward silence by pointing out that, in reality, first and second were probably the other way around. Rachel had stood and walked out. And hadn't come to any other family meal since.

"I've been sent home," she finally murmured. "The engagement is over. He's now carrying on as if it never happened." A hand flapped. "As if I never existed."

"I could get that information from a newspaper," Lex said, struggling to control his frustration. After some thought he then added,"You're my sister. I care about you. I cared about you just as much before you were his fiancé as I do now. Fucking talk to me, Rachel, or I can't help." He put his hand on her shoulder.

"I don't want to talk about it!" It was almost a scream. And Lex registered the tears on her face, and she went stiff, shuddering at his touch, almost panicking at the contact. She thrust his hand away.

"Whoa! Jesus, Rachel I'm not going to hurt you! Calm down!" Shocked at her panicked response to his concern he tried again. Why had she shied away from him, like she didn't know him at all? Her brother? Her partner in crime for over twenty years, since the cradle. "What the hell? Did he hurt you? Is that it? Did he hit you?"

Her eyes went heavenward, trying to avoid answering, but he was there, her big brother, who wouldn't leave her alone until he had answers. But she daren't give them. If she told him the truth, if anyone knew the truth, she'd lose all sympathy. Lose their respect. Lose even more than she already had.

But her evasion of his questions was interpreted as affirmation. The way her head hung and her rejecting him only confirmed his suspicions. "He did, didn't he?

"Lex…"

"Goddamn! You should have called me! *Why didn't you call me*?"

"I . . . he's very important. He's not someone to argue with!"

"When did it start? In all the press photos, you looked so happy, so gorgeous. I never saw any marks?"

"He never hit me where anyone would see." Her eyes stayed on the floor, like a whipped dog, and while her brother processed this bombshell of news, Rachel found she was warming to the idea. How easy would it be to adopt the role of the abused? Far from being sent away in disgrace, she could become the victim, to be treasured and cosseted: she was forced to make the brave decision to leave the man with the big name and the money in New York for the sake of her health; anyone would have made the same decision. "I had to look good for the cameras or it was worse for me when we got home. I endured as much as I could but then . . ."

His arms closed around her, pulling her up and against his solid familiar chest. Her big brother. By three minutes and twelve seconds. Twins were always so close. And for them, the bond had always been remarkably strong.

"I always thought he was an asshole but I never thought he'd be the kind to do that."

"Neither did I." Rachel closed her eyes, imagining, mentally rewriting those nights in his penthouse to include a slap round the face, a punch in the stomach, and a kick in the ribs. *If I can believe it, I can make anyone believe it. There's no way anyone will tell I'm lying.* "I thought it would just be the once. Because he was angry. But it kept happening. Again and again." He hugged her even tighter; ironic that hugs from her brother were more heartfelt than a single touch from Daryl.

"Why didn't you tell Dad?"

"It was such a great connection for the family. They were so happy I was chosen. I don't have a career, Lex, I'm not smart like you, and I thought I could make them proud. And they were. Plus, Dad does business with him."

"Oh, Rachel."

"And now I'm here, back in fucking Texas, with the whole world knowing my face, knowing who I was, who I won't be, and all because of him! I fucking hate him!"

"Do you want me to deal with him?"

"You can't do anything, he's too protected, too important."

"We can press charges. Go to the police. Go to the papers. He'll have to answer to the law."

"I don't have any proof. I never took any photos. His staff watched me like hawks."

"Did you tell anyone else? Did anyone see anything?"

"No. It only happened when we were alone."

"God, Rachel, I want to shake you! You're an idiot for not taking any pictures!"

"I'm sorry! I was scared he had a track on my phone. It would have been impossible."

"It's OK, I'm not angry at you, just . . . Jesus! Fuck! You need to get out of the house, Rachel, you–"

"I don't want to go out because I can't stand the gossip! Everyone knows I'm the one who got dumped by Daryl Blackmoor, no one will ever look at me again–" She pushed him away.

"Oh bullshit, you're still the most beautiful woman in Texas. Of course all the guys'll be after you again. Probably even more so now!"

Images flashed through her mind of Harvey, that room, that sofa, of her legs spread across his belly as she plunged herself up and down, his hands on her breasts, such an uncontrolled, inelegant coupling that had cost her so much. So much it made her want to vomit with regret.

"I don't *want* anyone from Texas!" she shrieked. "I want to be in New York, *engaged*, with the world at my feet!"

"Rachel–"

"No! I know it's stupid, but *I still want it.* And you can't criticise! You have no idea how it felt to be by his side. The fame, the money, the *influence*. It's not like here. Father is *nothing* compared to him."

"Rachel, he abused you! This is for the best!"

"He *humiliated me!* He used me and treated me like his whore, and I never once complained, and yet now the world will think *I* failed! Because he's such a *god*! Because Daryl Blackmoor is nothing less than perfect! And I'm just some girl from Texas! He picked me up, Lex, bought me clothes and jewellery, and then dropped me! And he's just carried on like I didn't exist. I do exist! How can I do this? I am I supposed to carry on?" A little spittle flew from her shapely lips and she ran out of breath, her eyes wild, her hair loose.

Lex could feel the pain emanating off her, stronger than before. "Whatever pain you feel, I'll make sure he feels, alright? I'll make this right, Rach, trust me. You're not alone, you're never alone, you know that. You've got me, your big useless twin brother. Nobody hurts my sister and doesn't pay the price."

"I wish I'd called you." She slumped back in the chair by the window.

"I'll speak to Mum and Dad. Make sure they back off a little."

"I don't want them to know about–"

"They need to know. At least enough so they can understand."

Silence.

No one could claim to be better friends, or closer than they were. Losing her to Blackmoor had been a loss accepted invisibly, a smile pinned to his face, towing the family line with the usual patter of blithe congratulatory words. But he hadn't wanted her back like this. He spotted a stack of magazines by her bed, showing them hand in hand on the cover the night their engagement had been announced. The world press had done somersaults. So much glamour, such glittering promise, so much champagne, and flashing of perfect white teeth in huge smiles. How had it ended like this, with Rach hiding out in her room like a depressed school girl?

Daryl Blackmoor, you absolute bastard.

BOUNCING BACK FROM school, Mysty bounded up the stairs, burst through the front door and headed straight for the kitchen. Bread and peanut butter were combined and shoved unceremoniously into her mouth. Lunchtime seemed a long time ago and she almost groaned with relief at eating!

Another day at school survived. No major dramas. No new insults from the 'cool kids' that didn't like her because she seemed so content by herself. No new levels of boredom. And in an hour, she had two dance classes back to back across town. Tuesdays were a good day.

Logging in, she grinned to see Raju was online – and that she had new messages.

'Hey dude! Thanks for the new challenge! I'll take a look at it when I get back later tonight.'

'Ecce! Good day at school?'

'Not bad. Got 98% on my chemistry test. The cool kids, and the geeky kids, hate me more than ever.'

Lots of laughing emoticons. 'What happened to the other two points? Try harder next time!'

'Come on. 100% would have got me lynched!'

More laughter. Even if it was just symbols on a screen, and she'd never heard him laugh, it made her grin: it was good enough; it felt like they were sharing the moment. 'Where are you going tonight?'

'I have some dance classes. Do you have any clubs you go to?'

'No. I don't really leave the house.'

Mysty frowned, surprised and saddened. She couldn't imagine staying in the house all day. She wondered why he didn't go out. 'If I ask why, will you tell me?'

'It's not important. But I am jealous of you!'

'You're the maths genius. I'm jealous of you!'

'Come on, Ecce, you're as good as I am. Don't be kind.'

It was just words. Just marks on a screen. But still, she could feel the sadness again. It crept in every now and again, whenever they stopped talking about the planet, or pollution, or society, or how to get people inspired to do more for the world not just themselves, or what they'd say if they got to speak to the president. But whenever this happened and the focus fell on Raju, or his life, there was this same drop-off of conversation. Like running up and finding a cliff-edge, leaving them nowhere to go. She respected him too much, however, to push for answers that might upset him. But it upset her too.

She looked at the Call button. She'd contemplated it before. Wondered why they hadn't used it already.

Maybe today?

Hitting the button, she held her breath, wondering if he'd pick up.

And then he did.

"Hey."

"Howdy from Vegas." *Wow. We're actually speaking.* "Gosh, this is weird."

"You don't sound American." Was there slight suspicion in his soft Indian voice?

"My mum's English. I speak like her."

'Oh. Is your dad American? Why do you live over there?"

"We moved here." *Let's move on now.* "Your English is so good."

"My accent is bad."

"No, it's really not! Imagine how hard I'd find it trying to speak . . . what language do you speak?"

"Punjabi." Raju helpfully filled in the blank.

"Exactly."

"I guess. But I bet you wouldn't."

"Raju." It was the first time she'd said his name aloud. "I really didn't mean to make you feel sad."

"You didn't. and anyway, it's not your fault."

"But–"

"Really, Ecce, don't worry about me. Things have always been like this. I'm used to it."

What are you used to? What have you always been like? "You don't have to tell me anything, just . . . if you ever want to, I'm here. Miles away. Would it change anything if I knew anything?"

"I err…I don't talk like to about myself."

"I get it. Neither do I, but–"

"I'm glad you rang. It's great to hear your voice. I know you're definitely a girl now."

"I thought you knew!"

"I wasn't sure. Your profile is pretty vague. But I've been trying to build a picture of what you look like in my head."

"You don't give anything away either."

"What a pair we are," he laughed.

"This is so cool. You're so far away, and we're just chatting like . . ."

"Like friends."

Raju said it so she didn't have to. She'd been so used to being alone. Donny and the boys were great, but they weren't really around so much anymore and they were all so much older. She had come to love their gruff, big-brother like protectiveness and affection, but none of them talked about maths puzzles or the environment. This was a different kind of companionship; a faceless acceptance of each other.

The moment of silence extended as they both took a second or two to enjoy it.

"How hard is the maths challenge you sent me earlier?" Mysty then asked; she spotted it in his messages.

"Pretty tough. It'll take half-hour at least."

"Did you look at the website I sent you?"

"Yes. I sent them the forest-planting proposal but nothing yet. They probably won't reply."

"Well, if we have to send it a thousand or ten thousand times it doesn't matter so long as someone helps us make it happen."

"I like your optimism."

"We have to try, right?"

"Of course." A pause, both of them aware there was so much to be done, and they didn't know the first thing about how to make it happen. "Don't you have dance classes to go to?"

"Yeah. I've got to go. I'll be back online later, OK?"

"Go have fun. For both of us."

"Send me some Punjabi words I can learn."

"OK, I will." He laughed. "Thank you for your call, Ecce."

She pressed End.

"I think I have a friend," she said out loud, turning to Lazarus, who bounced on the spot. "And I wish I didn't have to leave you here. I'll buy you some dinner on the way home."

How mad life was. She was living in a city of hundreds of thousands of people, and the person she felt the most affinity with, of her age, was thousands of miles away. Swallowing the lump of emotion in her throat, she felt almost too sad to go dancing, but she knew wallowing about how stuff had changed with her and Donny would get her nowhere. When she danced she forgot everything, and she couldn't wait for opening night. She'd finally get to see him, and he'd promised she could stay at his house for the weekend. Maybe he'd plan a big surprise for her. Maybe he wouldn't. Either way, all she wanted was his company.

IT WAS THE biggest night for years in Vegas. The world's media had descended on it – not least for the grand opening of Cirque de Celeste, but because *the man himself* was going to be there. There wasn't anything that they didn't want to know about or take pictures of. All day, people had been running live reports from in front of the massive 100,000-seat circular arena, and broadcast ratings were sky-high. Some members of the Celeste board had been interviewed, as had some performers, adding to the speculation about what the show would involve, as everything had been kept firmly under wraps. Security had been out in force, and already there were a dozen incidents of reporters trying to get in before they were meant to in order to land a massive scoop from the inside.

Which was why, when Daryl Blackmoor stepped out of his armoured Bentley outside the main entrance where the red carpet was laid out for him, he knew it was going to be sheer chaos. Lines of security guards held back the crowds and the press, cameras flashed, and there were a thousand voices talking at once, excited, emitting shouts and screams as news reporters attempted to provide live updates. Daryl – as if there were maybe three or four rather than hundreds of journalists and photographers outside the arena – stepped out, looked around casually, thus treating the sea of people like small tea party, and gave a satisfied, imperceptible nod and strolled towards the great doors, Mac and two others in his wake.

He was pleased so far. He had only visited the building once before completion, the rest of the time observing virtual camera tours and constant updates from trusted managers in the field; after all, he was too busy to keep making the trip to Vegas, even for a project so important.

He was greeted by a line of board members, all very important in themselves, but nothing to the man that now stood taller than they, every bit as handsome and as composed as ever. He accepted their congratulations on the design, and even beating the schedule for completion, and assured them he was going to have a very enjoyable evening. He damned well hoped so.

Daryl let it all flow around him. He was used to being made a fuss of, used to champagne on trays and the brimming excitement that came with grand events; but he was glad when, two hours later, he went to his private viewing lounge, dead centre from floor to ceiling.

The highest arch of the roof was over three hundred feet, and the diameter of the performing area one hundred feet, with an apron for props and storage and for performers to wait before coming on. The steep-sided bowl of seats was impressive, the interior kept dark rather than have bright light permeating every nook and cranny. Some of the items that would be used were easy to see – a trapeze, a giant ball, metal frames.

High up there ran a corridor, the complete circumference of the arena. It led off to other private viewing rooms, and the hotel. Also up there were bars and restaurants, and seating in open spaces where visitors could go to indulge and also view the show, the platform edges extended so they stuck out over the seats below. It was truly magnificent in conception and design, ambitious but dignified.

Daryl was suitably proud, and knew it was a sell-out show – in fact, it had sold out only two days after the tickets had been released. From this first night alone he knew the take was almost $5 million. He watched as the huge audience found their seats, milling around purposefully, chatting and laughing in anticipation. Not long now.

He looked over at Harvey, already on his third glass of champagne and chatting with Robbie and Guy, who had also come for the amazing night – at Daryl's expense. They were his chosen group of bachelor roués, and a reliable source of companionship, but obviously contrasted sufficiently with himself as to preserve his utter superiority. When the world remembered him, they would remember Cirque de Celeste very soon afterwards; his superbly orchestrated marketing and publicity campaign would make sure of that.

He picked up his viewing glasses and searched for Donny, remembering where his private box was. Had he brought the red-haired Girl Wonder, he wondered? Would he finally see what she looked like? He found Donny, that familiar debonair dark hair cut in a timeless style, his Italian features handsome and his face tanned. He looked very well. His men were sitting around him – that bulk of a man Daryl remembered as Paulo, and some others. There were two women: one blonde with large breasts, and another brunette with a Spanish look about her, lush lips and dark eyes, both quite definitely in their twenties. Why hadn't he brought her? He felt the disappointment keenly. He'd been looking forward to having his curiosity satisfied.

He looked at Donny again before he looked away, saw the complete lack of real emotion. The girls either side of him were smiling at a conversation they were having, but Donny was not partaking and his face looked irritated, and just a tad bored. Daryl knew what that felt like. How many times had he taken women to events simply for show and not cared two cents who they were or what they said? They were just there to look good. Interesting.

"Did I hear rightly, Daryl, old chap, we get to indulge ourselves after the curtain falls with the performers in the after-show party?"

Harvey's voice drew his attention back to the room and Daryl tossed the viewing glasses aside and looked round at his friend. "You did indeed. Indulge as much as you like. I've heard the Flying Tigers have some particularly interesting specimens that might be worth a try. I'm sure those jungle girls know all kinds of tricks to keep even you amused," Daryl replied.

"I admit I do fancy getting a little mauled," Harvey replied, his wicked grin infectious, the gleam of anticipation in his eye apparent at what the night would bring.

Daryl was saved having to answer because the lights changed, dropping down and focusing on the vast stage.

Let the show begin!

It began with an explosion of music, a rain of bodies abseiling from the high ceiling at breakneck pace, somehow exchanging ribbons and banners so that when they reached the bottom, there was an amazing knot of colour in a perfect cylinder which then fell slowly down to reveal lines of fire reaching all the way up to the ceiling, which then burnt out, leaving everything in darkness.

Everyone was silent, in anticipation of what would happen next.

First, a glow, a mere dot of light, shone in the centre of the stage; then a dozen, then a hundred, and it became obvious each light was held by a person because of the way it moved. The first central light then whizzed upwards, growing and expanding, but so the person with it was obscured completely, until it reached the top where it burst and sent a massive explosion of fireworks and light out and down, illuminating the arena in that second in beautiful blue-silver glow.

The people weaved around each other on the floor, the music building until it reached a climax, and abruptly the arena was flooded with light, revealing the ropes that had been used to abseil down. The performers moved in every direction and then skyward, where their lights burst in a staggered array of colour, their own magical supernova. No dancer remained in the arena as once more they were plunged into darkness, and the audience broke into rapturous applause.

Daryl leaned back in his chair. That was good. What followed was good. Better than good. It was exceptional. Wild and bizarre. Contortionists, rope-walkers, fire-eaters, sword-eaters, muscle-men performing incredible balancing acts, all in stunning costumes and accompanied by music. Everything was perfectly done with no mistakes, everyone performing out of their skins. The fact it was opening night created its own magic, and he could feel it.

He knew from having glanced at the programme, about twenty times already, that the headline act was next, and he hoped it was something that fulfilled expectation.

The lights went to the stage. It was empty. There was a low rumble of music. And then it was alive! Bodies came flying in from the sides, flipping and jumping and bouncing, each in a skin-tight gold body suit with black tiger lines, faces painted in gold and black paint, hair pieces in red and gold and black flowing down their backs. They threw each other up in the air, grabbing the trapezes, then flying through the air to catch each other, both in the air and on the ground.

It was frustrating in a way that there was so much going on, and Daryl wished they would do their parts separately so he could see everything rather than have to divide his attention and therefore miss different parts of it; but then that wouldn't have achieved the whole mesmerising effect! The beauty and elegance of the flying – so practiced they made it look easy, and fearless – was the kind of risk-taking that Daryl could envy. These were skills he would never have, never experience, because he wasn't permitted to risk his neck to even perform a handstand, let alone throw himself around with the glorious vitality these people did! He'd even been pulled out of the Harvard football team in case he got injured, which had annoyed him no end. And then assigned a bodyguard – Mac – which had seriously cramped his teenage style!

Anyway . . . he noticed one dancer move to the edge of the circle and stop, turn around and pause. For a moment Daryl thought they might have been injured . . . but no, a second after the thought went through his mind, they raised up on their toes, braced themselves and then pushed off. The slender body moved so fluidly. It jumped, bounced on hands, flipped, again and again, one last time, and a push . . . and the small curled body flew through the air high above the heads of their fellow performers and caught hold of a trapeze sent their way. The grab was perfect, and after a few flips and tricks that captivated because of the height and speed, the lithe body then moved and twisted, swung forwards and back, and then released and grabbed hold of another, higher trapeze.

Daryl picked up his viewing glasses, wishing he'd done so sooner, and trained them on the flying gravity-defying daredevil who was progressing higher and higher. His eyes focussed on the shimmering material of the costume, admiring the long strong legs, the slender curve of hips and tiny waist, and then the breasts that confirmed what he had already surmised: a girl. And a girl with the most beautifully shaped body he had seen for a long time. He loved the ripple of muscle beneath the thin material of her costume, the mane of golden hair flashing with bright highlights of red and black. Something about her was coltish – she must be quite young – and he couldn't take his eyes off her.

He had been so fascinated with the sight of her he had not paid attention to how high she was going – until Harvey remarked upon it. He looked down at the ground: it was a long way down, and she was now way above where they were sitting. Was this really safe? There was no net.

Unworried, it seemed, she flew around between two trapezes with a fearlessness that made Daryl hold his breath. He was just beginning to relax, feeling more comfortable that she knew what she was doing, when she released her hands from her bar . . . and simply dropped!

He took the glasses away so he could follow her progress, not believing his eyes. What the hell was she doing? She hadn't missed her catch? . . . Had she? . . .

She fell earthward, then halfway down two trapezes swung towards her with men at the ready, and at the zenith of their swing, one held out a bar, the other took the end and they held it firm just as she reached them. Somehow, hands reached out, and then she was flying back towards heaven – how the hell had she managed that? What kind of reflexes must a person have to make that grab and swing up? But it wasn't over, as flying upwards, she turned and rotated in the air, reached her peak, elegantly raised her arms out like a bird, hovered for a split second, then dropped, diving down through the air from a break-taking height. *Oh dear God.*

Daryl, and indeed the entire audience, took in an audible, collective breath as she turned in the air, curling around just as she did during her diving competitions, spreading her arms and hands as the ground approached, and landed, rolled twice, and then stood.

Daryl breathed out slowly, asking himself if he had actually seen what he had just seen. How had she done that? It had to be a trick!

The music built again as the performers once more entered the arena, hand-springing and building into a pyramid of people, men first, followed by the women. A larger man and another – the girl – stood poised in front of them. He recognised her instantly from her shape and the hair – which he liked to think was real, but was probably a wig – which shone under the lights.

The girl ran to the edge of the arena. Clearly she was going to run and be thrown to land on the top – a feat in itself – but would she really make it? He noticed something as she ran: she turned and waved at the larger man to move, before disappearing past the glare of the lights into the darkness. Had she bottled it?

He didn't believe she had, but there was a tense fifteen seconds as the rest of the Flying Tigers waited, trying to hold their positions, confused as to why she had gone off-stage. (No one had heard the terse words exchanged between the girl and Mr Chardon.) Not a single person in the building was breathing when she emerged from the darkness, sprinting with a speed that amazed in itself, before bouncing and flipping, heading straight at the tower of people. Just as Daryl thought she must be insane, she sprang, legs pushing off, whole body moving in harmony, curling into a tight ball, uncurling, stretching, and then there she was, feet touching down on the shoulders of the performer she landed on. Hands reached up to grab her ankles, but she was perfectly balanced. She then straightened and raised her arms just as those on the edge of the tower flung out their arms.

The applause was phenomenal, and Daryl almost clapped himself, except he never did, for anything or anyone. It was that good. What kind of power must she have in her legs to get so high? And to do it so . . . perfectly.

"Fucking hell. I want to get mauled by that one," Harvey said with heartfelt appreciation of her superb body and unmatchable skill, as aware as every other male in the room how that would translate in the bedroom. Daryl raised his viewing glasses, annoyed he could not see the face behind the stage paint, satisfying himself with the gorgeous curves, astounded that those slender legs could do so much. "She might just give me the ride of my life," he added, and nudged Robbie, who laughed with him and then raised a finger to signal more drinks.

The tower broke apart, led first by her as she pushed off, tucking herself up tightly and rotating three times, before landing with feline grace, and moving forward as the others tumbled groundward in a waterfall of gold and black. The clapping and the cheers continued.

Daryl watched them run from the stage, like a pack on the hunt, towards the tunnel that led to the dressing rooms and practice warm-up areas. He saw a good number of the others run up behind her and reach out to ruffle the curls . . . perhaps it wasn't a wig. One of them put an arm around her shoulders and hugged her as they ran, all congratulating their star for pulling off not only her part in the act, but the whole act. It surprised him they were so nice to her, having thought they might be more jealous than admiring; but he wasn't a performer, and maybe those thoughts were more a reflection of how he felt. He tried to ignore the second niggle of envy at such skill. He'd never know what that felt like. Money couldn't buy everything, despite what people thought.

He relaxed back into his chair, comfortable in the knowledge that the evening had, and would continue, to be a great success.

MYSTY WAS TIRED, but she obediently followed the rest of the troupe; she wasn't sure where they were all going, but it was the first night and everything had been a little different from rehearsals. She felt another hand on her shoulder, and turned and smiled at Tanza – and received another congratulation for her part in the performance. She was a little blown away by the whole evening. Performing in front of other artists was one thing; a 100,000-strong crowd was something else . . . and the applause! She'd hadn't imagined it would be so deafening, so intimidating.

They all filtered through the doors to a larger suite in the upper echelons of the arena that had been fitted out with luxurious sofas, chaise longues and chairs, big tables, even some large cushioned stools that looked rather like beds. She stayed next to Tanza, one of her closest friends from the troupe. She was older by a good five years, but had been supportive rather than jealous of Mysty's talent, won over by the younger girl's daring, good humour and relative humbleness given her abilities. She'd never done anything to show off, and never minded listening to suggestions or criticism – not that there were any serious ones – and that had made a difference, earning her the respect of fellow performers who had been a team before Mysty had joined them. Mr Chardon had insisted she become a Tiger because she had so much to add to the act, and all initial reserve over the interloper had been forgotten as the talent spoke for itself. The youngest at thirteen by four years, she was the baby of the troupe, and all of them felt proud and protective of her – especially when they'd recognised her abilities would alter their fortunes as her star rose.

They spread out through the room, all still in costume, grateful for the chance to flop down and relax.

"Why are we here, Tanza?"

Tanza looked at Mysty in surprise as she let herself drop into a chair.

"This is where we earn our extra pay, sweetheart," Rucho answered for her, as he walked past and patted Mysty's head.

"Yeah, as if we should have to," Gillian muttered, sitting herself down on the sofa just across from Mysty, who had yet to sit down. She really wasn't sure if she wanted to; her instincts were telling her this was not a place she wanted to be.

"Oh, come on, it can pay really well. They're usually pretty grateful and tip well – I made $5000 one night," Bryony said and sat next to Gillian. "Be bold and pick a good-looking one."

"Yeah, it's all very well if you're beautiful, Bryony, like you are," Gillian threw back, knowing beneath the costume and the face paint, her best feature was her extreme healthiness, that her face wasn't anything special. The one saving grace was that if the guests were drunk enough, it didn't matter.

"I don't understand . . . What do you mean?"

Bryony looked at Gillian and then at Mysty, her smile sad.

"Girl, when you're a celebrated performer, when you can do things that few people in the world can do, men and women pay very well to have the pleasure of your body to finish their evening off."

"She shouldn't be here," Aaron said tersely, hands on hips, looking down at Mysty from his six-foot-five height. He had the broadness to proportion the height, and he was not someone anyone argued with, being a lynchpin of the troupe and full of strength and experience. "She's too young. God knows they're probably breaking enough rules allowing her to perform. No doubt they've got enough money to make it legal, but she's too young for this."

Mysty looked at Aaron, deciding he was very much right, and for once felt completely out of her depth.

"Chardon said she wasn't to come up here, so why is she here? Did no one tell her? Why did you let her?" Monique joined their little cluster and spoke angrily, without waiting for a greeting.

"No one knew – or at least we didn't think about it." Gillian spoke for everyone there, all sharing the guilt from having forgotten just how young their Tiger star was.

Aaron turned to Mysty. "Kid, get out of here and go enjoy your evening someplace else . . . unless you want to stay?"

Mysty shook her head, still not fully comprehending what would happening if she stayed. *No one has ever mentioned this part of performing before. Why do people do it they don't want to?*

"Oh shit, they're coming in – go!" Monique hissed. She was the leader of the women because of her experience on stage and her natural authority, and gave Mysty a little shove towards the door at the side of the room, just as the dark-suited gentlemen came in – with a small selection of ladies as well; ladies who would pay well to be serviced by a handsome muscle-bound giant such as those their troupe included. All the super-rich that had come were invited to this private 'party' through association with Mr Blackmoor – and for being suitably deep in the pockets. Was there nothing their money could not buy?

Mysty glanced once at the fate she'd hoped to avoid, curious if horrified, and then walked as quickly as she could towards the door, praying she got away unseen, the threat so unexpected and horrible that it made her feel sick and shaky . . . she just wanted Donny. Just wanted to go home and have a rest. Aside from anything else, she was starving hungry, had been surviving on energy drinks for the last five hours.

"Don't tell me you're leaving the party before it's even begun, my little pussy cat?"

A hand grabbed her wrist with some force, and as she turned to the danger he pushed her back, holding her against the wall by the door . . .

so close and yet so far. She used her other hand to push against his chest, but it was a hopeless task as he was using his weight to keep her still. She could feel his body pressed against hers, and it made her want to retch, especially when she could feel how excited he was by that simple contact. She might be young, but she knew enough about men to know that's what happened. Nor was this the first time someone had tried to force her.

She was too frightened to speak, and angry to be accosted by this stranger in a place she considered safe; she spent half her life at Cirque, knew it like the back of her hand. It had been a home in a way, and this was a violation of everything she associated with it, again. The safety of its walls now proved paper-thin, again.

A strong hand forced her head up and she had no choice but to look up into his face. He had brown hair and blue eyes, and might be considered handsome had he not looked so leering and hungry. She could smell alcohol on his breath . . . the same type as her father used to drink . . . she'd never forgotten that smell. The urge to throw up contracted her empty stomach; she could feel the pulse of her heartbeat in her head.

Harvey found himself looking into the most beautiful eyes he'd ever seen in his life, eyes that were both angry and scared in bright indigo, her face still painted but the delicate features wildly attractive. She was everything he'd hoped and more.

"Come on, sweetheart, I pay well, and I can promise you a good time."

He pushed himself up against her a little harder and she winced.

"Get *off* me!" she growled angrily, knowing if she really had to she could move him, but it would hurt him and get her in trouble . . . and she didn't want to lose her position in the troupe for this.

"That's not very friendly, is it?"

She leaned her head away as he brought his lips down close to hers, knowing he was going to try to kiss her. Then he shifted his weight to get a better grip on her . . . and she made the most of it, managing to slip a fist in between them and ram it hard into his stomach. The grip on her instantly loosened and she reached for the door handle.

But a hand pulled her back and she was slammed up against the wall again, and this time she was facing it, and he used his full weight against her, making it hard to breathe. In desperation she reached out a hand, clawing along the wall for anything to grab hold of, but there was nothing. His hands slid over the silky-smooth fabric of her costume and cupped her breasts. Then one hand then slid down and reached between her legs. Her gasp of shock and involuntary jolt made him laugh in her ear, and she felt bile rise in her throat.

"Come on, sugar, it'll be a lot easier on you if you stop fighting me."

His words were like poisoned honey in her ear.

"*No!*" *Make his hand stop! What is he doing with his fingers? Oh please stop!*

"Monique! He has her!"

Gillian's voice cut into Monique's brain as she was being drawn closer into the charming smile of Mr Blackmoor – *the* Mr Blackmoor himself, could you believe? At least this was one lay that might be worth it and pay well! But she couldn't ignore the plight of the child. She'd been young once, and she'd had to fight to remain unmolested as well – though not always managed it, which was why she wouldn't let Mysty share her fate. Her head snapped around, and she saw Gillian, who pointed . . . and then she saw the large figure in a black tuxedo, slender golden legs somewhere behind him, and one arm stretched out in desperation, hoping for something to pull on to get away. His hands were roaming in intimate places, telling her everything she needed to know.

Others had heard Gillian's shout, and Aaron stood up from where he had been reclining on a sofa with some woman who'd been happily feeding him grapes and touching whatever part of him she fancied.

Daryl looked around as well, irritated that something was interrupting his very entertaining after-show show. He had a woman astride him, sadly still clothed, but who knew what might happen next, and he could feel the muscles in her body, knew the strength she might employ . . . *Delicious.* But he couldn't help wondering where the star of the show, the golden-haired wonder girl, was . . . That was the girl he wanted. He would find her by the end of the night, he was sure. He wanted her body to bend just for him, to feel those magnificent muscles ripple under his hands.

"He's got to let her go!"

There was genuine panic in Monique's voice, mirrored in the face of the friends who had all turned to watch.

"Why? If he wants her, why can't he have her?" Daryl said in a bored tone, picking up his champagne from the table next to him, wondering how quickly this might be over. He knew Harvey. Once he caught the scent of a woman that was usually it until he was worn out or tired of her.

"She's thirteen years old! She's a *child!*" Monique told him in a low angry voice.

"How is it she's performing at Celeste then?" Daryl returned, unconvinced.

"Because her talent is too good to go to waste!"

Ah-ha, so Harvey has found the golden-haired minx before me – how irritating. And he had a perfect reason to stop him having her: possessiveness and jealousy were an awful combination when combined with arrogance and an ingrained tendency towards self-serving gratification.

"Harvey, let her go, she's too young!" He raised his voice a touch, sure his friend would hear him now the room had gone so quiet.

"You said we could have whoever we wanted – what if I want her?" Harvey answered, not looking or moving away from his prey.

"Well, you can't. Anyone else but her. She's thirteen and not for the having. Aren't there enough amusés to choose from?"

Performers around the room looked at each other under lowered lids as they heard the words, disgusted at the utter and complete arrogance in his referring to them in such a way, as if they were a collection of toys.

"She doesn't look like a thirteen-year-old," Harvey murmured, his lips so close to her neck she could feel his breath.

"You take this any further and I swear you'll never have an anything-year-old again in your life!" Mysty spat, trying to stop herself from giving in to the urge to panic and struggle, which would only wear her out and not get her very far if she needed to fight him; but she knew she couldn't fight him, and the panic built again.

"I like them feisty, you know, a bit of fight, a few claw marks . . . I'll enjoy every second."

His lips found her neck and she cringed away from the bite, squeezing her eyes shut.

"He's got to let her go or he's going to get hurt!" Monique whispered urgently to Aaron, who nodded and started walking towards them, Rucho getting up to go with him.

"What do you mean?" Daryl asked in surprise, annoyed with Harvey for creating such a combustible situation; everything else this evening had been so seamless and smooth.

"The last guy who tried this ended up with three broken bones and fifteen stitches. The kid has had to get good at defending herself," Monique told him, without looking at him, too afraid of how this was going to end, convincing Daryl to insist using a harder tone.

"Harvey, let the kid go! Choose another woman to enjoy your evening with. There is nothing that exceptional about this flying freak that you can't find with another, for God's sake. Let her go. *Now.*"

Rucho and Aaron stopped, waiting to see if the commands would work. As much as they resented Blackmoor referring to her in such a way, if it got her free, it was worth it.

"But Daryl, you really should see her eyes – they're beautiful. She's *utterly* perfect."

Harvey's praise was revolting to the girl suffering at his hands, and she was not sure where her breaking point was, when the coiled spring of panic and anger would let loose.

"You cannot have her, Harvey! She's underage! Let her *go*!"

"She doesn't feel underage. A little small-breasted, I guess, but . . ." His hands on her breasts again.

"Harvey!" An infuriated voice now. Patience gone.

Harvey sighed. Ah well, at least he'd enjoyed her a little. He could always hunt her down at a later date. He wouldn't forget those eyes. He could drown in them.

The pressure went and she let herself take a deep breath. She pushed away from the wall and turned around, bright hot anger just beneath the surface. Her eyes seared into the animal that had trapped and humiliated her. How dare he touch her? Defiance had renewed her strength and every inch of her was poised. She surprised him by stepping up to him, her face so fierce he wasn't sure what she would do.

"You're lucky I don't want to get blood on my costume. If you *ever* try that again, I swear no amount of money will put you back together, *sugar*."

She wanted to punch him just for good measure, but she was satisfied with the rather humiliated look on his face that somewhat dissolved his arrogance – and his desire.

A second later she was out the door and gone.

Two girls approached the rather rejected Harvey and led him to a sofa where they helped him get over his loss . . . such good friends of Mr Blackmoor were sure to pay well, weren't they? And he was rather handsome.

Daryl looked back at Monique who was so relieved she could have cried.

"Well, I believe you have what you wanted. Does that mean I get what I want as well?" he asked pointedly, a little impatient after the tension of that unpleasant kerfuffle. Thanks to his friend's broad shoulders, he'd not even had a chance to see the girl, and he would rather have liked to judge her for himself rather than take Harvey's opinion on the matter.

Monique smiled and leaned down, using her body with feline flexibility to arch along him . . . this could be a very memorable night. "I think so. Would you like to accompany me to my private room? I promise I don't bite. Not too hard, anyway." Her eyes flicked up to his, a challenge and an offer all in one. Daryl liked her boldness. She would do. At least for starters. "I'm sure there's something I can do to keep you . . . entertained." He was given a brief demonstration of the litheness of her body, and decided she definitely *would* do for starters!

"Do you have others that might join us?" he asked. She didn't bat an eyelid; she'd been asked that question many times before. "I don't want the evening to be too tame; after all, *tiger*, it's been a memorable night so far, and I want that to continue."

"I should think so too."

Daryl smiled and let her fingers ease his bow tie off and start on the buttons of his shirt.

This was how to celebrate success.

MYSTY HURRIED DOWN the corridor, wanting to put distance between herself and that room, and that man. How disgusting! She needed to wash herself all over. How intimate had his hands been? And that sickeningly arrogant voice, calling her a *flying freak*? She felt pain ball up in her chest. She wanted a dark room to hide in, wanted to disappear. She ignored the other people that she passed in the corridor, all of them going in the opposite direction, unaware that they had all paused, wanting to ask her for an autograph.

"Mysty!"

She heard the shout the third time and span around. *Donny! Thank God!*

She tried to steady her nerves, not wanting him to get angry if she told him about the man. He would probably, definitely, be furious and want to find him, and she wanted to go home. More than anything.

She turned, smiling broadly, and it made him smile. She was still in costume and make-up, and she made a very good tiger, her bright eyes gleaming from the gold and black-painted face.

"Hey, kitten, how's my superstar?"

He reached out a hand, not sure if he should hug her as he might end up covered in paint! She seemed a bit nervy – but that was not surprising considering what she'd just done, and all the build-up, and no doubt she'd been at the arena for the whole day. At some point the adrenaline and euphoria would wear off and she'd be exhausted.

"Hardly, I just did a few jumps." She shrugged and her arms tucked around her body, hugging herself in an unconscious attempt for comfort, to hold the distress inside.

"You were brilliant! Even I was impressed and I know you!"

She smiled shyly and wished he'd hold her, make her feel safe like he always did. She was disappointed, however, as he hung back slightly, keeping some distance between them, as he had done when they'd been together for a while now. She wanted to ask why, but . . . didn't think she'd get a straight answer.

"Donny, can we go home? I'm really tired and I-I really need to leave now." Her eyes implored him, and he sensed there was something wrong but did not know how to ask. "Can we go and have dinner and a film, like you promised? Please?"

He felt his insides churn, and he knew he was a bastard for doing this. Knew it was selfish. Knew it was also because he was too gutless to be honest with her about how he felt.

"I'm not going home yet, sweetheart. I'm staying out with friends for a while – you know, a few drinks, a bit of poker. It's a big party night and I need to be here."

He watched her take in the words, saw the disappointment in her eyes.

"But, you said–" she began softly, confused and lost, only to have a harder, firmer voice cut her off, the tone and the way he spoke not like him at all. It stunned her.

"Well, things change," he snapped. "I can't just go home on a night like this. I have to be seen, talk to my associates, play my part in the social scene, you know how it is. I have friends with me. I can't just leave."

The big mob boss was out. He was not her friend, not her Donny. How had she been so stupid?

"Oh, yes, your friends, I've seen them – a blonde with big breasts and a brunette with more lipstick than brain cells. I thought you had better taste."

Her words were like ice around his heart, and he knew he deserved it. What was she if not his friend? She was worth a thousand of them, so why was he doing this to her? Pretending he'd rather mingle amongst men like himself with those two hired escorts on his arm than be with her? He *had* promised, and that was what he really wanted to do: take her home, listen to her tell him about the show, eat pizza and crash out on the sofa until she fell asleep.

"A man is allowed a woman, Mysty. Christ, I'm not a saint!" His own guilt was making him angry.

"No, no you're not. But I didn't think you were such a . . ."

She couldn't find a word that fitted, for once. Perhaps it was the tiredness, the shock, the disappointment, but she took a step back, not wanting to be near him. Being near him saddened her now, and she despised the need for him that she felt was trying to consume her. She felt tears in her eyes, and an awful sense of loneliness too. So many different things were gathering together in her heart and her mind, and she was helpless against the despair that rose up. His anger made it worse. It was so uncharacteristic, and it made her feel even more alone, like she didn't even know him. Had the world gone mad? *Had he*?

"There's a car waiting to take you home," he said to fill the silence, sad at the look on her face, sad that she'd stepped away from him.

"I don't want to go home in one of your cars, Donny!" She imagined the car ride on her own, going to her empty flat. What had she done? "If you'd changed your mind, all you had to do was say. You didn't have to leave it till now to tell me," she then murmured.

Behind her soft voice was a very hurt girl, he knew that, and saw the tears slide, creating streaks in her tiger stripes. He also knew she was right, and was speaking a truth that made him a coward.

"You know . . ." She waved a tired hand towards the arena. "All of this, tonight, was for you. I thought it might make you proud of me. Or happy. That you were looking forward to celebrating this with me. I don't even know what I've done wrong. Is it because I'm a freak because I can jump? Because I'm still a *child*? Are you ashamed of me?"

She looked up at him, knew those blue eyes so well, and usually loved seeing them; but now they only brought her more heartache. She had denied the glaring truth and now it crashed home like a tidal wave on a sandcastle: he'd got tired of her; he didn't want her around anymore. She was alone again. Utterly and completely alone. In a world that wanted to crush the life out of her, one way or the other.

Mysty turned away. And a hand went to stop her, but she evaded it easily and held up her hand to ward him off. "*Don't touch me!*" Angry words thrown at him hard enough to make him flinch.

In a moment of horror, Donny could see the lost child was back, could see the haunted expression on her face. And the reality of his treatment of her became clearer. How had he thought he could treat her with such distance without her wondering why? Of course she would think it was her fault.

"Mysty, sweetheart–"

"Don't call me that! Don't *ever* call me that!" she snarled. "And don't pretend to care, Mr Capello, it doesn't suit you to lie! Don't worry, I'll leave you to enjoy your evening with Tallulah and Marilyn. I hope they give you your *money's worth*."

He was helpless against her fury. There was no defence against such righteousness. And like the coward he was he hung his head as she turned on her heel and walked quickly away down the corridor. He grasped the railing and looked down on the almost-empty arena, gripping it tightly as he grappled with all the pent-up emotion inside him, wishing he'd managed to make her stay so he could comfort her in his arms. What had happened to her today? Why hadn't he asked? Was he afraid of the answer? *Brow-beaten by a thirteen year-old kid in my own city . . . what the hell are you doing, Donny?*

He didn't see the view, didn't see or hear any of the parties carrying on in the upper echelons for the rich, famous and debauched – where he was meant to be. He saw nothing but her. Those eyes he loved so well, so full of pain. This had been the greatest night of her life so far, the beginning of a sparkling career, and he hadn't kept his promise to her . . . even his congratulations had been poor. He should be taking her home and celebrating her success . . . but no, he'd just made her feel worthless and unwanted. And he'd also underestimated, due to his own stupidity, how much he clearly meant to her. She who'd risked her life for his?

Damn it. He was a fool. He, Donny Capello, Lord of Vegas, was an utter fool.

He groaned and heard footsteps . . . was she coming back? Even just to punch him? He wouldn't have minded. Was it Paulo coming to check on him, knowing he wouldn't be far away? No, it wasn't either, it was someone else in a gold costume and tiger paint, a six-foot-something giant who must be part of the troupe.

"Have you seen her?" the man asked urgently, more concerned about the girl than who Capello might be, but knowing he must be fairly important if he was on this upper level, in a tuxedo, and looked exactly what he was: an Italian mobster. But he had to take the risk and ask.

"Who?"

"Young girl, tiger paint, loads of curls!"

"Mysty? Why?" Donny reacted immediately. Why was this guy looking for her? Was he hassling her?

"You *know* her?" Aaron asked in surprise.

"Yes, I'm her . . . guardian." *I was her everything and now she hates me.*

"Is she alright?" the man asked.

"A bit tired, but . . . why wouldn't she be?" The inflection of the question implied he knew she might not be.

"She . . . she didn't get out the room before the VIPs came in for their after-show party, and one of the guys with Blackmoor grabbed her and . . ." Aaron wanted to look away from the piercing eyes that demanded the truth from him, unprepared for the commanding nature of the man he had chanced upon; but he'd started now so he may as well tell the whole story. Who knows? Maybe this man could do something? "He . . . held her against the wall and groped her. She was petrified. Monique – another performer – managed to convince Blackmoor to call his friend off, but I don't know how much he, erm . . ." The face in front of him had twisted into an expression of pure rage. "Well, she's only just got over that last guy's attempt at forcing the issue, so to have another try again, so soon . . ."

"What? *Who*? And what *other guy*?" Donny demanded instantly, horrified.

He hadn't known? Of course he hadn't! He'd been doing such a good job of distancing himself, trying to protect himself from how he felt about her, that he'd let her down and she'd got hurt, scared and almost raped!

"You don't *know?* What kind of guardian are you if you don't know what happened three weeks ago?" Aaron demanded instantly, his bluntness shocking Donny. This guy obviously either didn't know or didn't care who he was. Or both. But the accusation was accurate, and it stung.

"I've been out of town." It was the best excuse he could come up with and testament to his failings as her friend, and everything else he wished to be. In truth, it was pathetic.

"Well, someone tried to . . . have her when she was leaving one night, trapped her in a dressing room and even tied her hands, only he didn't account for who he was taking on. Luckily, she fought him off, but it could have ended very differently. She was shaking so much when we got the ropes off. Rucho and I found her when we were leaving and turning out the lights. We heard her screaming. He already needed an ambulance or we might have hurt him more than she did." Aaron shook his head at the memory.

"And tonight? Who was it?"

"Blackmoor called him 'Harvey'. He told him she was underage and to pick another one. I wanted to hit him when he called her a *flying freak* – she's amazing, not a freak. Any one of us would give five years of our lives to have her talent." Aaron looked closely at Donny, who had closed his eyes as her words came back to him and started making sense. "Anyway, I just need to know she's OK. I didn't want to take part in that orgy. I'm worried she might have had a bit too much to handle tonight; she's just a kid, after all. So, you saw her? Is she heading home? I want to make sure she gets back safe . . ."

Dear God, this man was a better friend to her than he was. Donny felt sick with shame, and rage. What had been an awful exchange between the two of them was now worse because of his utter selfishness.

"Paulo." Donny raised a finger to his earpiece and clicked through. "Tell the boys with the car to look out for Mysty, and get the boys in Surveillance to keep eyes on every exit – she probably won't want to go with them, but don't give her a choice. Take her back to mine and feed her something, then get her to bed and tell her I'll see her tomorrow morning. Whatever happens, don't let her disappear off into the night, clear?"

He received an affirmative and looked back at Aaron, who was looking at him strangely.

"Who *are* you?"

"Donny Capello."

Everyone knew that name. And the realisation hit Aaron like a punch to the gut: he was talking to the most dangerous man in Vegas.

"Holy shit."

Donny Capello was Mysty's *guardian?* Mysty hadn't breathed one word. Had never said anything to anyone about that. In fact, thinking about it, no one knew anything about her except what they saw with their own eyes during practice.

"Yes, now where might she have gone?" Donny demanded urgently, aware his heart was pounding.

All plans for the evening were now dropped. He needed to find her, even if she swore at him and thumped him. He needed to ease the pain and fear he knew she was carrying around inside herself, needed to bring her back, needed to hold her in his arms and kiss her hair. He knew her well enough to know that when she was angry and hurt she was at her most defiant and outrageous. No wonder she'd got so upset. It was a front to keep the world from her, to hide how she had needed him! And he'd failed her! His little girl, his most precious girl, who'd never let him down in her life, and he'd failed her!

"There are a number of places she might have gone to from here, but right now, there's one place she is, and it's really not good."

Aaron's gaze was fixed somewhere over Donny's shoulder and he slowly turned . . . and saw a familiar figure running towards the railing at the far end of the viewing balcony, level with them on the upper corridor, a hundred feet away as a crow would fly, and quite a bit more going around the edge like an earth-bound human.

"*No!*"

Donny's cry of protest was unheeded, and Aaron began running down the corridor to try to get to her . . . but she kept going. In a sequence he knew so well, she jumped, bounced off her hands, flipped and flew, landing with brilliant precision and balance on the metal railing. Donny breathed out again. He had thought she was going over the edge!

He hurried along the corridor, keeping eyes on her as much as he could, willing her not to move until he got there. His eyes flicked for a second to the arena floor beneath her, the drop huge. She couldn't make that. Even with her skill, it was death.

Mysty took in a slow breath, trying to balance herself inside, unafraid of the huge height beneath her and, strangely, not afraid to die. She had been here before and stared it straight in the face. Part of her would be glad, finally, to go and be with her mother again. In that moment it was all she wanted. Her mother had never let her down, had loved her so much, had made her feel so safe in her arms, despite the demon that haunted them both. She felt so alone in this world, she might as well see what there was in the next. She'd had enough. She didn't care if she made it or not. Her body would decide. Just like it had the first time.

She heard the shout but didn't look round. She straightened, lifted her arms out to the sides, took a deep breath, exhaled and then pushed off. To feel the air all around her was beautiful. It was not a bad way to die. Better than her father finding her when he got out of jail.

"Sweet Jesus!" a voice declared in horror, and those of the troupe who were not already drunk or in the private rooms with their admirers, turned to look. Some of them got up and went to the edge of the room so they could see.

"She'll never make it!"

"Oh my god!"

Some people looked away, hands clutching at each other, not wanting to see her die.

Donny covered his mouth to keep the scream that rose in his throat silent, watching her drop with the incredible precision that had always amazed him. But he waited for her to crumple, his breath trapped, his heart pounding.

Those able to watch saw her finally stretch her arms and turn, twisting and curling to break her fall, and then land, roll, stand. For three heart-stopping seconds she paused to look back up, intact if not a little surprised. The next moment, she began jogging to the exit tunnel, ignoring the people that ran after her.

Donny rubbed his face. *Dear sweet God.* She must be in a bad way to have done that. She hadn't acted with any jubilation at the bottom, not rejoiced in her feat, or her survival. No, that had not been an exercise of ego; it had been an expression of despair.

Aaron appeared round the curve of the corridor and his face was a mixture of relief and worry . . . and admiration. "She's unreal. She doesn't need the troupe. She's an act all on her own!"

"She's pissed off," Donny muttered. He was still furious with himself for being one of the reasons she'd been driven to act so recklessly. She couldn't have known she would live. She had taunted death. Perhaps even wanted it. All the hope and faith he had given her he had taken away. He knew in that second why she had jumped. "Really pissed off."

Aaron shook his head. "I'm going to go after her and see if I can calm her. You . . . you want me to give her a message?"

"No, don't mention me; it'll probably get you a broken nose." Donny replied, now exhausted, but wanting nothing more than to see her. He wasn't going to know a moment's peace until he had spoken to her, and he knew relying on the boys to grab her would be a slim hope after that demonstration: she would realise he'd sent them and would simply evade them. But right now, and with a heavy heart, he had business to attend to.

Aaron gave him a strange look, not sure what to do with this man, who he should fear, but who clearly cared a great deal for her. And cared even more than he was willing to admit judging from the distress on his face.

Aaron didn't speak again, but left, running down the corridor, hoping he would find Mr Chardon somewhere, knowing of all people, Mysty might listen to him.

MYSTY WENT INTO the dressing room and slammed the door, throwing the security lock, knowing the people following right behind her wouldn't leave her alone even if she begged them.

Now she could hear them banging on the door. Wanting to get in. Wanting something. Always there was something. She just wanted to be left alone. So she wouldn't have to face being disappointed. Again.

She opened her eyes and moved forward into the lights around the wide mirror. Stuff was everywhere – make-up, costumes. She shared the room with two other women, but there was little of her own there. She stared at her reflection, the gold costume, the way it clung to her, the stripes, feeling like the *freak* she was called. She looked at the face that got her into so much trouble. It reminded her so much of her mother whom she loved and had failed to save that she thought her heart might break all over again. She moved suddenly and her fist smashed into the mirror, the crash loud in the room, the Perspex shattering. Shards and light fell about her, bouncing the chaos off the dimly lit walls. She didn't feel any pain as blood seeped from her knuckles; the pain was in her chest and her head, so full she could burst . . . and yet it was empty, like a vacuum.

"Mysty!" A voice she recognised. "Mysty, what was that? Don't hurt yourself, child! *Please!*"

Mr Chardon.

She drew back from the broken mirror, glad that her face was once again in the shadows. She picked up a pot of cream and a cloth and began wiping the stripes away. Then she pulled off the costume and got into the shower, but the water did nothing for her brokenness. The performance seemed so long ago. Had it really only been a few hours? Why had everything between that moment and this descended into sadness? She had been looking forward to this night so much. How had it ended in such tatters, just like her birthday party? Despair gripped her afresh as memories crowded in, making her weak.

Another set of bangs on the door brought her back into the moment.

She stepped out and pulled a towel from the shelf.

"Mysty, kiddo, please open the door!"

Stuck outside, Chardon was furious she had taken such a risk with that jump; but had also been blown away by her pulling it off. But why had she done it? Something had to be wrong for her to be behaving like this. She wasn't a show-off. What had happened a few weeks ago . . . well, he'd been praying nothing else like that would happen again, that she would get her equilibrium back. He'd thought she was OK. He was obviously wrong.

"She locked herself in?" Aaron asked quickly when he got to the scene, finding the space outside the dressing room crowded with people.

Chardon regarded the door impatiently, worried he was getting no answer. He didn't know how to override the high-tech locks on the doors, didn't know how long it would take to find someone who could.

"Yes. Do you know why?"

"You saw her jump?"

"Yes. Why would she do that?"

"She was upset. No one passed on the message about the after-show party, that she shouldn't go. Monique sent her out but she didn't make it before someone with Blackmoor grabbed her and had her up against the wall. Luckily Blackmoor told him to stop, and eventually, after scaring her stupid, he let her go. After what happened before . . .

"The fools! Rich idiots who have no idea. No idea at all, damn them!"

Aaron stepped a bit closer to the door, trying to think what might get a reaction from her.

He leaned in to Chardon. "Mr Chardon, sir . . . did you know Donny Capello is her guardian?"

Chardon turned his head slowly to look up him.

"Yes, he was the one who contacted me about her in the beginning. It is a closely guarded secret, however, so I suggest you tell no one." Chardon's eyes bored into Aaron's, who nodded solemnly. He got the message. "How did you find out? Did she tell you?"

"No. I met him when I left the party to find her, check she was alright. I think they must have had some kind of argument. He was . . . angry and upset. I imagine she was as well."

"Which combined with Blackmoor's guest was just one 'event' too much. Jesus." Chardon leaned his head back against the wall.

Suddenly the door opened and there she was, dressed and clearly ready to leave, her face tense, but sad, make-up and costume gone.

"Mysty–"

"Please don't speak to me," she said in a voice that did not invite discussion.

She did not look at anyone. Not Chardon. Or Aaron. Or any of her fellow performers. Instead she walked through them, looking straight ahead.

No one could think of anything to make her stay. Even Chardon, who thought he knew people well enough, did not think he could reason with her. She was not an average person. She was unique. Unparalleled. And if he was honest, he didn't really know her at all; they had been united in the progression of her talent not the exchange of small talk.

Mysty kept going towards the backstage exit, not hearing or acknowledging the further congratulations or admiring shouts, the wolf whistles or catcalls. She pushed the door open and stepped out into the cooler night air and immediately saw the car. Inwardly she sighed. She was exhausted and didn't want to deal with any more obstacles this night.

Lucio came forward with Mickie, Giuseppe and Roberto – Pepe stayed by the car – creating a funnel towards it. Roberto reached forward to open the door. In their identical, sharp-fitting black suits they looked like something out of a movie, or some sort of agents; but she did too, in her tight black trousers and jacket, black shades hiding her eyes . . . not that she realised or cared.

"Mysty."

"Lucio."

She stopped a few metres from the backstage door, a few metres from him. She stood calmly, quite unworried by the force sent to snare her.

"Donny wants us to take you home now."

"Really? That's nice. But, you see, I don't give a *fuck* what Donny wants, and I don't want to go home just yet."

She was furious, and she saw Lucio flinch at her vehemence.

There was a long pause.

"I'm not going with you, so you really should leave."

Lucio shook his head, remembering the wild child that had challenged and defied him in the hall of the derelict hotel. She was still there, but older, wiser, stronger and more confident. Far more able.

"No. I have my orders, kiddo."

His attempt to appeal to her by using that pet name made her grimace, remembering too easily Donny's cold-shoulder treatment less than an hour ago.

"Well, it won't surprise you to know I don't give a fuck about those either."

She smiled as she stepped forward. Her walk was so nonchalant, so relaxed. It fooled them all into thinking she'd given in and decided to comply, despite her words. She kept going, past Lucio, past the first pair, then in the final two strides, bounded forward, put her hand on the roof of the car and leapt, sailing over it as she had done before, but this time with greater ease.

She was exhausted, but the anger gave her a cold, hard energy, drawn from reserves of endurance. The same energy and endurance that had kept her alive before.

"*Shit!*" A single word uttered by all. How easily they had been duped!

She ran off across the street, fleet as a deer, easily avoiding traffic. Two of them started after her; the others got into the car . . . but she was gone. There was nothing to follow.

"Where the hell did she go?" Lucio demanded.

"Hey, Surveillance! What happened?"

"She grabbed onto a truck heading south on the 303, looking quite happy, just holding onto the side," came a voice in all of their ears, sounding impressed with her flight, and amused at how easily the team of five had been evaded. But this was not funny.

"OK, we go after her," Lucio snapped.

He waved the driver on, and he had just started accelerating when the voice patched through on the earpieces again: "Erm . . . guys . . . got some bad news. We lost her. She's gone."

Great. The boss was going to be furious.

"*Fuck!* How does she do that?"

Everyone looked grim; Lucio speaking for all of them. They turned the car around and drove back, parking up not far from where they'd started.

Lucio patched Paulo. "Paulo, this is Lucio."

"Please tell me something I want to hear." It was a growl.

"She got away, Paulo. Even the boys with the eyes in the sky have lost her."

"*Shit!*" Paulo rarely swore, and everyone flinched, waiting, all very glad to not be as close to Donny as Paulo was at that moment, but knowing their time would come and their failings would be addressed. "He's already fit to shoot someone! Goddammit!"

Paulo wanted to shoot someone himself, preferably that Harvey bastard who'd dared touch her! *Why do I always have to be the one with the bad news?* He shook his head and rubbed a hand over his chin, glancing round at his boss, who was doing a sterling job at pretending he was utterly fine, champagne flute in hand, talking with three other mobsters from other cities. It seemed serious business had largely been put aside to enjoy the evening; though some subtle negotiations were being made during the mingling. Everyone else was having a pretty good time, it appeared, unaware of the drama.

"Surveillance must keep looking for her. Call Fabio and get her heat signature loaded into the database – that'll work for about fifteen minutes if she's on the move as she'll be respiring enough to show up on satellite scans. Once she stops somewhere we've lost our chance. She's tired enough, so I don't think she'll go far. If she's located, you go again, understand? But no threats, as little force as you can. Poor kid's been scared enough this evening as it is."

"We understand. I'll keep you informed," Lucio confirmed.

Lucio's clicked out, and Paulo pressed his own earpiece and patched through to Donny, who was now looking at him across the room. He had been waiting for news and seen Paulo talking to his boys. Conversation with his associates was proving a painful experience as he held all the frustration inside.

"Paulo."

"She bailed, boss, eyes in the sky lost her as well. They're still searching, but . . ."

Paulo was glad Donny was somewhere public. He couldn't explode like he might have done in private.

"God*damn*." Donny looked away as he swore under his breath, afraid for her, afraid for what she might do, and so angry at himself, because he couldn't make it right. "Have a car go wait outside her place. Lazarus is there, so she won't leave him. She must be exhausted and probably starving hungry, so she will go home at some point. I want to know the moment she does, clear?" He was banking on it.

"Yes, boss."

"And Paulo . . ." That tone Paulo knew: it was when his boss was planning something less than savoury.

"Yes, Donny."

"Have two boys watch Mr Harvey Lincoln. I have a feeling I'm going to be doing *business* with him soon. Find out where he's staying, when he's meant to be leaving, etc." Donny felt part of him contort and twist, wanting to get his hands on that son-of-a-bitch who touched his girl. He'd seen the man before, with Blackmoor. He was tall, handsome, and strong, with a reputation to make most women flush with anticipation. Harvey hadn't known she was a child, and they all knew she didn't look like one, but he should have known better, should have left her well alone. "And, Paulo, apparently there is another man who tried it on with her three weeks ago. Ask one of the performers for his name and find him. If his legs aren't already broken, see that they are."

"And if they are?"

"*Break something else.*" Paulo nodded calmly, having anticipated that answer and the deadly tone in which it was given. "He tied her up, Paulo. She was screaming for help. Make sure he screams." Paulo clenched and unclenched his fists, angry, like his boss. It was going to be a real pleasure fulfilling that part of his job. He knew Donny wouldn't mind doing it himself, but he had to use some discretion. "Keep me informed."

Donny clicked out and turned away, going back to his associates, all of them accepting his presence back into their circle seamlessly, deferring to his greater importance. Being called away to deal with things was a natural part of their world; keeping fingers on pulses was a way of life, or you risked ending up dead.

Paulo started relaying the orders.

Donny glanced over and up at the shiny glass that fronted the room he knew Harvey was in. It was as much as he could do to not walk up there now and throw Mr Lincoln off the balcony, see how well he could fly.

Goddamn rich kids; no fucking idea. But he will be made to learn.

PAULO DIDN'T KNOW it, but someone else was on the war path to the same room.

Mr Chardon was incensed after hearing what had happened, and what his performers were being inveigled into partaking in. He knew them, knew some of them were inured to it; but there were others who would not want to, younger women who should not have to share their bodies. What happened to Mysty just typified how wrong it was. What did Blackmoor think? That he owned them? Having an after-show party was one thing, but inviting the Tiger troupe and using them for some free-for-all orgy was disgusting! As if these people who risked so much with every performance were merely objects there for his and his friends' amusement.

Chardon pushed open the door and strode in, forcing himself not to react to the partial and complete undress, the abandonment of bodies in various positions and on different seats or sofas or cushions.

"Rucho."

Chardon saw the dark-haired giant with a well-manicured woman sitting astride his naked chest, clothes half off. Rucho was clearly embarrassed at seeing his manager and blushed; but the woman looked around at Chardon with angry eyes at the interruption.

"Who was it who hurt Mysty?" he snarled with barely restrained anger, and Rucho knew there was little point in saying anything except the truth. Any attempt to defuse Chardon's rage wouldn't work. He knew his boss, had known him for years. He was as hard-headed and stubborn as a mule.

"Harvey Lincoln . . . he's over there with Lena and Ira."

Mr Chardon looked over to where he pointed and nodded, moving swiftly between the rows of bodies.

"What the hell did you think you were doing assaulting a thirteen-year-old girl?"

Chardon didn't bother with introductions, and Harvey's head snapped up from where two delightfully naked tigresses were laying each side of him, fondling different parts of his anatomy alternately, feeding him food from the platter beside them.

"I didn't know she was thirteen," Harvey answered simply in a low voice, not really wanting his actions broadcast in such a way, despising this man who stood so tall and angry before him. Who the hell was he to talk to him like that? Even more irritating, the two girls had rolled away and sat apart from him with their costumes clutched to hide their nakedness, embarrassed and uncomfortable with their boss so close. The indulgent, sensual mood had been ruined completely. How tiresome.

"What the hell did you do to her?"

"For God's sake, I only touched her – it's not as if I got any further, is it? I let her go; no harm done."

Chardon couldn't believe the arrogant dismissal of his victim.

"*No harm done?* Have you any idea how frightening it is for a young girl to be violated by a complete stranger?"

Chardon's words would have triggered a normal man's conscience, but not that of Harvey, who was used to being allowed to do as he liked, women having only one purpose to him – and to think that they might not want to fulfil that was wholly unthinkable, especially when he'd had a little too much champagne. Being asked if he knew what it was like to be a young girl brought an unfortunate, amused smile to his lips.

"No, strangely I don't. And she has little to complain about anyway . . ." Harvey paused, taking a sip from his drink, unworried and still relaxed, making Chardon more incensed. "I don't quite understand what all the fuss is about, anyway. A girl like that will be fucking everything in sight in a couple of years' time."

Chardon thought he might implode he was so angry. He wanted to reach down and shake this insolent fool until his neck snapped.

"If you knew the girl, you'd know you were utterly wrong, you arrogant–"

"What is going on?" Daryl's voice cut through the argument that was beginning to attract the attention of the whole room, and had indeed distracted him from where he reclined on a sofa with a topless Monique and two other semi-clad performers. "Who are you to come in here like this?"

Mr Chardon turned his head towards the voice and marched over to Daryl. "I'm Mr Chardon. I manage the acts you saw tonight and these are my people. I presume you are Mr Blackmoor?"

Mr Chardon's hard-lined, moralistic approach appeared intransigent to Daryl, and he scowled. "Yes. However, I prefer to think that they are *my* people, considering *I* pay their wages . . . just like I pay yours. What business have you got with my friend?"

"I take issue with his conduct towards my youngest performer, and I am disgusted he shows no comprehension or regret for what he did!"

Harvey appeared unworried, if a little irritated himself at the interruption. And faced with such rudeness, Daryl was only ever going to come out on the side of his friend.

"I think Harvey comprehends quite completely what he did, but why he should regret such a brief fumble, I don't know. Have you tried it, Mr Chardon? Look at these women. I'm sure being a performance manager must be a very hands-on job. If you let yourself try it for once, you might understand." Daryl let his hand slide up from Monique's backside, up her flank to cup her firm, rounded breast, his eyes staying on Chardon, his lewdness designed to shock and infuriate. "Do feel free to join us. I'm sure someone could be found to suit your tastes. It is first-night celebrations, after all . . . why don't you go out with a bang?"

Daryl's mocking smile and Harvey's snort of laughter was too much. Chardon felt his fists clench. How he'd love to punch this son-of-a-bitch!

"I don't need to force or pay a woman for such an experience; I have a *wife*, Mr Blackmoor, something I know you lack – and seeing you now, I should say that's a very good thing indeed. No woman on this earth would marry you, or your disgusting friend."

Monique felt the hand on her breast tighten: Daryl was clearly furious at the insult.

"If you find me so unappealing, you won't want to remain in my employ, will you?" he snarled.

"You're not firing me, Mr Blackmoor, *I quit*! I may not have billions of dollars, but at least I have some goddamn morality!"

Chardon heard the intake of breath from the troupe around the room, who all knew he was brilliant, they relied on him, he was their rock, he was the architect! How would Celeste cope without him?

He turned on his heel and headed for the door, slamming it behind him, leaving silence in his wake.

"Now, where were we?" Daryl breezed; though his good humour had been soured. His patience had worn thin now. He wanted hot, mindless sex to stop him thinking about business or responsibilities . . . and he wanted it now. "Let's find a room."

His hand closed over Monique's breast again and squeezed, just on the side of painful, and she got the message. She got up, the other two following her lead, and they made their way to a private bedroom suite. Daryl took hold of Monique's dark hair and held her head while he kissed her neck, biting into muscle, the hand on her buttock gripping hard. She responded to the silent demands, arms wrapping themselves around him tightly, fingers feeling the ripple down through the muscles in his back, realising he was as superbly fit as any of the men in their troupe. He rammed into her with enough force to throw her head back and she gasped at the sheer lust, felt her body coming alive. She dug her nails in.

"No marks, tigress, keep your claws to yourself," Daryl growled in her ear, and she shivered and eased her grip.

Moments later, he left her alone and turned his attention on Abbey – their only English girl. She was nineteen and fresh, and Monique watched with frustration as he spread her legs and slid his hands up her back, then back down, pulling her hips up. But she felt herself get wetter watching him push into the girl, and the way she arched and cried out; but she was angry he hadn't finished what he'd started with her, nor directed her in how to please him. After a few minutes, however, he released Abbey and left her in the same way – hot and wanting.

Monique realised what he was doing. Taking Trudy's hand, all long blonde Swedish hair and blue eyes, he pulled her towards him and lay her back, drawing one of her legs up so she was almost doing the splits. He then leaned over her and started the same nerve-tingling journey with the third female, just the right side of pain, body stretched to accommodate and please, wanting to curve around his magnificent body.

Daryl pulled back and watched the woman beneath him, blue eyes bright in the painted face, alive with passion, and he was satisfied they were all now sufficiently in the mood to make this a little more memorable. He watched the disappointment on her face as he pulled out of her and sat back on the pillows. The three lithe, naked women then crawled towards him on the bed, hair loose, faces half-disguised by the gold and black.

Monique straddled him, her eyes closing in pleasure as his whole length slipped inside her again, strong hands on her thighs; Abbey allowed her lips to be guided to that sensitive part of his body between his legs, her body curving around over one of his thighs; Trudy was then directed to satisfy Abbey with a soft, gentle tongue, while one of Daryl's hands slipped between Trudy's legs and found her spot, fingers working their practiced magic.

Daryl looked at Monique, eyes hard and critical, insisting she do her best, demanding her best. He was too experienced to come quickly, and she knew it. Knew he was a master of women's bodies like they were masters of their own art. The litany of moans and whimpers, to which hers became a part, but to which he never contributed, was part of the haze of the passion that had taken over the bed where they were, all moving and writhing as one, and there was something sinfully glorious about it.

Trudy came and Daryl removed his hand, putting two hands on Monique's hips, enjoying her strength, not at all disappointed, so far. Trudy moved up over Abbey and concentrated on her task, a hand creeping up to fondle her friend's breasts, and Daryl felt the mouth on his falter, followed by hot panting breaths and a low cry . . . a few seconds and she was back, her head bent over his legs, teeth nibbling the insides of his thighs.

It was a suitably wild climax, all the more decadent for the minimal effort he had had to use, acting merely as the conductor of the instruments at his disposal. He knew Monique had held out, pushing and riding harder to make his own release that bit more intense, and when he had some control back after the rush of orgasm through his body, he rolled her over and pounded into her a final few times as her hands braced on his shoulders, her face strained with passion, begging him for an end to it. Her scream of pleasure was pleasing in itself, and he even paused for a moment inside her, something he did not normally do, enjoying the throb of her around him.

Not bad. But he would bet his life and his fortune that that little golden-haired tigress would be better one day. Knew that the passion and fearlessness that made her so unique would make her spectacular company in bed. She was utterly remarkable – and he had seen a lot of women – but he didn't want her as a shy, inexperienced virgin. That would just irritate him. No, he would wait. He knew where she worked, after all. And that thought almost made him smile. And made him hard.

He pulled out of Monique and sat back, three pairs of female eyes watching him. He told one of them to get him a drink and they did, obediently leaving the bed and coming back shortly after. Daryl watched the gorgeous backside of the girl as she'd walked across the room. He then looked up at the wide, solid headboard of the bed, painted an ornate gold and white.

He knew what he was going to do next.

An hour and a half later he left the suite, fully dressed and fresh, giving instructions for three cash cards to be given to them: two for $20,000; one for $30,000. Largesse was a mark of greatness, and paying well always paid dividends to one's reputation, plus, it would silence any lingering protests.

Mr Chardon would be replaced within a week.

IT WAS FOUR in the morning when Mysty finally gave up her vigil on the top of the huge advertising tower. She'd discovered it months ago. It was one of her favourite places to be on her own. She knew the four sides of moving pictures and words were so bright that no one would be able to see her – not unless they were very high up, and even then there were satellite dishes and air-conditioning units all around her, so she would be well obscured . . . even from Donny's satellite boys.

She ached at the thought of him, having tried so hard not to. But try as she might, the thoughts just kept crowding back in on her. It was such a lonely place to be safe, and she desperately wanted her mother. Wanted what she knew she could never have – not in this life anyway – and so much that she'd doubled over as the sobs racked her tired body. There was never going to be a substitute for her mother's love and the comfort of her arms around her.

She went to the edge, looked down at the ground. Knew the space at the bottom of the tower was flat and debris-free. Usually she climbed down, but now . . . now she knew she could jump from such heights, why not? It was exciting, she had to admit, knowing her ability was so much greater than even she had imagined.

Half a minute later, she was strolling down the street. There were a few people about, in twos and threes, on their way to a different club, casino or to their hotel, and a good number of cars still. Vegas was like that. It never really stopped or slept, and it wouldn't tonight, not with the grand opening of Celeste. She'd accepted the place, in a way, even grown to like it, yet everything she felt for it was tainted now. As much as she loved the jumps, the flying, the trapeze, she hated the arrogant fools who thought they could do what they pleased with her, the way people forgot she was a person when they saw her face, her eyes.

Something smelt fantastic, and suddenly she remembered just how hungry she was. There was a pizza place just across the road! And it was open! Normally she was at home asleep at this time, not out on the streets, so this was a discovery to her: could she *really* buy a pizza at four in the morning? It smelt like heaven!-It looked Italian and authentic, and she stepped through the door, hoping she wouldn't get shouted at if someone had left the door open by accident and they were really closed.

She saw a head bob near the counter, as if they were bending down sweeping. She then heard a shout in Italian to someone else in the back room, saw the big stone oven with flames at the back taking central position behind the counter.

"Hello? Are you open?" she called, speaking Italian, hoping that might please them enough not to shout at her.

"Si! We're never closed!" the voice shouted back.

A head popped up, and then a body. He was forty-something, tanned and definitely Italian, and when he looked her up and down and smiled he had one of the cheekiest smiles she'd ever seen in her life.

"Can I get a pizza? Will it take very long?" In Italian.

"No, not at all! This is the best time of the day to get one if you want to know the truth! Everything is so fresh right now because we're prepping. I can promise you the best pizza of your life!"

He was clearly so proud of his shop and his food that it made her smile.

"Good! Because *I'm starving*." She sat up on one of the bar stools in front of the counter, put there for those getting takeaways to perch on.

"What would you like, bella?"

"I don't mind, as long as it doesn't have any anchovies. You choose! Surprise me!"

He clearly liked the challenge, and smiled even more as he turned to begin twirling the dough expertly on fingers and hands.

"What are you doing out at this time of the night – or morning – little one?"

"I work at Celeste. I'm sure you know it was opening night last night?" She'd just managed to get the words out when she was overtaken by a huge yawn, which he saw as he turned around to look at her with admiration.

"You are one of the performers? An *artiste*?" he said.

"I'm a freak who has my face painted, if that's what you mean," she muttered dryly, watching the flames in the oven.

"No, bella, who said that to you?" He tutted at her and turned back to the pizza. "Jealous, no doubt, who wouldn't be? Aside from how pretty you are, what is it you do?"

"I'm with the Tigers." She was hoping her short answer might put him off asking any more questions. No such luck.

"The Tigers? Oh my god! Really? They're amazing! I've seen some of the shots on TV tonight. This one girl – I was stunned! I almost burnt every pizza in the oven! She made this drop! From a height you'd think she'd break her neck, but no! Rolled and ran off! And then she did this jump–"

Mysty purposefully looked away. "Yeah, I know, amazing," she managed to respond, and then realised he had come to stand right opposite her.

"You know her?"

"Yeah, I guess so . . ." she hedged, badly, so tired her brain wasn't up to a convincing evasion.

"Bella!" He reached over and took a piece of her hair and pulled it out, admiring the colours. "It was you, wasn't it?" The voice was gentle, a little awed.

"Does it matter?" She gently retrieved her hair, not wanting more attention, just wanting to eat something and go home and fall asleep, leave the entire world, even the universe behind for a few blessed hours.

"You're not a freak," he told her sternly, going back to add the final pieces to the pizza, before putting it on the board and shoving it into the oven. "It is a gift to be able to do something no one else can do," he continued. "How many thousands of people make pizza in pizza shops? How many people can do what you do?" He brushed away the flour and cheese, and when it was all clean again, he turned around, not really expecting her to have answered. "Would you like a drink?" He wiped his hands on his apron.

"Have you got any milk?"

He raised his eyebrows and smiled. "For you, bella, of course."

He went to a fridge and pulled out a bottle, poured a big glass of milk, put it on the counter and pushed it towards her. She pushed a $100 bill towards him, and his face fell. "I don't have change for that, bella, I'm clean out of change until the banks open. Tonight was our busiest night ever and everyone came in with big notes."

"I don't want any change, I just want a pizza. Keep the rest, really."

He raised his eyebrows at her flippancy at giving away eighty dollars."They must pay you freaks really well," he said, with a smile that told her he was teasing.

"They just don't feed us anything, and I'd choose food over a piece of paper any day. Especially pizza."

"I like you, you can come again. And you can keep your money, bella. Thanks to you, Celeste is going to bring plenty of business my way, and I won't overcharge you."

She scowled at him, reached over the counter, hit a button on the till, put the note in the drawer, and shut it with a decisive click.

Something about her prevented him arguing or attempting to stop her.

"Like I said, it's just a piece of paper, and I'd really like you to have it."

He shook his head and pulled out her pizza, sliced it, and then slid it into a box, which he left open and presented to her just as she finished the milk.

She looked at it. It looked good – pepperoni, ham, onions, peppers, a few olives – and she looked up at the creator and smiled. He was waiting for her verdict.

"Looks good."

She took a slice and tried it. Nothing had ever tasted so good! Her mind practically sang at the taste of it! She closed her eyes and enjoyed every flavour, her whole body reacting to the smell. It was just what she'd needed, and it was such a relief to eat!

"This is awesome pizza," she told him when she had swallowed, and she leaned on the counter and devoured the rest of the slice. He took her glass, grinning, and refilled it.

"You can come again, bella. And the next four are free."

Her wide, beautiful smile was the best thing he could have seen that morning, and even with the slightly red eyes and the wildness of her hair, she was perfect. His favourite customer of the night.

"No. This is worth a hundred dollars, trust me," she told him seriously, and polished off a second slice, not sure how much she could eat but definitely nowhere near full yet.

The guy came and sat next to her with a bottle of beer in his hand. He took off his apron.

"I will tell my brother, Raffi, you said so. He has a pizza restaurant in LA. He is very upmarket though, charges big prices, not like me, with my humble pizzeria, but still, we both love what we do. I will enjoy telling him of my superstar customer – normally he's the one telling me!"

She laughed at his compliment, enjoying his story, the freely given information.

"I'm not much of a superstar."

"Maybe one day you will be."

"No, I don't . . . But thank you for making me feel so welcome."

"You speak Italian, bella, very well, but you are not Italian?"

"I learnt Italian when I got to Vegas. I have friends who are Italian, like you."

He nodded, storing away the information. She had a perfect accent, perfect diction.

"I'm Marco, by the way." He held out his hand and she put down the third slice to shake it.

"Mysty."

"Ah. Mysty. Well, pleased to meet you." Marco enjoyed watching her eat for a few seconds, then took in the shape of her. Even sitting down, the curves and the fitness were obvious. "Pizza, eh? The new food of athletes?"

"I'm not very conventional, and I'm always hungry. I promise, I burn it all off," she told him in a pause between taking a gulp of milk. "You know, I've not eaten anything since . . . eleven o'clock this morning, actually . . . yesterday morning. Nothing but water, water and more water, with dextrose complexes thrown in."

She threw him a look which told him she didn't like all that running around and no food for so long.

"Sounds mad I know, but . . ." she continued, and took another bite, "we can't afford to have anything inside us to weigh us down." He nodded, and she sat back, replete after four slices. And he was content with her satisfaction. "If I eat anything else, I'll go pop," she then said.

He had heard his daughter – now grown up – say the same thing many times when she was young. How old was this girl?

"That was great." Another yawn, and she blushed. "I should go home."

"If you ever go to LA, you go to Raffi's, tell him Marco sent you, and he'll look after you." He stood up and reached for a bag from behind the counter for her pizza box. "When you're rich and famous, of course."

She smiled, finished the milk and stood up wearily, her energy now diverted to digesting pizza.

"I don't think that'll happen, but if I go, I will try and visit."

"But you come back here, any time you like. I'm always here, bella, and I'll feed you." He patted her on the shoulder and handed over the pizza box.

"You'll see me again," she promised, and with a handshake, he watched her go.

He leaned on the doorframe and stayed until she was out of sight. She was quite something. More than she thought she was, obviously, but time would tell. He met lots of people, talked to many and liked very few; but she? It was the way she met everything head-on, the simple approach she took, the way she'd reached over in defiance of his offer and put the money in his till. If she was young, she certainly wasn't stupid or weak; but in the world she was in, she couldn't afford to be.

"BOSS."

DONNY CLICKED in his earpiece and looked away from the gaming table. He'd wanted to leave for hours, but didn't want to go home to the emptiness that would just make him feel even more lonely, where his mind would taunt him imagining where she was.

"She's home."

It was the only news he had wanted to hear from Fabio, who had been monitoring everything like a hawk. He pulled out his handheld and pressed in the channel, matched the bet just raised, and then watched her, relief and joy bursting in his chest just to see she was all right. All of her there, no blood, nothing broken.

She got through the door and immediately had a leopard launch himself at her. She let him pull her down to the floor and lick her face, teeth grabbing onto her wrist playfully. She stayed on the floor, using a quiet voice to reassure her furry friend, his familiar smell and warmth a balm to her. He calmed eventually and lay still.

Donny stayed watching, and then realised she was asleep, curled on the wooden floor, her arms wrapped around him. His tail was draped over her thigh, the end flicking occasionally.

He breathed out.

Thank God.

It was tempting to send the boys in now, grab her and bring her in, but that wouldn't have been fair. He had no right to make such claims on her after what he'd done, and she'd never trust him again if he did that. This time he was *really* going to have to make it up to her for his failings, and an apology was just the beginning. He had every expectation of her making it very difficult. Not that he didn't deserve it.

He sighed, imagined how exciting it would be to be married to her. Every day would be unlike the last as she grew into her emotions and talents, and herself. But thoughts like those would have to wait. Perhaps always now.

Paulo appeared by his side, and Donny passed him the handheld without a word, sharing the image, knowing the sense of frustration and worry had affected them both all night.

"Poor kid must be completely whacked. You want me to–"

"No. Leave her be. Just have someone keep an eye on her, and make sure the boys in the sky don't lose her again. And have the car ready in half an hour. It's time to go. Mr Lincoln will keep until tomorrow night."

"The other matter you mentioned, sir?" Donny nodded but did not look around, threw some more chips in without looking at his cards, musing on tomorrow when he would be playing for different reasons and for far higher stakes. "I will be making a visit tomorrow morning. Let me know if there are any other instructions."

"I give you carte blanche, Paulo. I think we feel the same about the issue."

Donny smiled a particularly shark-like smile, and Paulo couldn't resist responding with an equally evil smirk.

"I'll get the car organised. Here, I think you need this more than me."

Paulo passed him the handheld and Donny took it without a word.

Tomorrow he would take revenge on Mr Lincoln, and tomorrow, somehow, he would start trying to repair the charred bridge with Mysty. He hoped the fires had burnt out by then.

DONNY WAS WORRIED; in fact, that was a total understatement. Considering no one had tried to kill him, no one had stolen from him or killed one of his boys, he was feeling remarkably pissed off.

He had been checking on Mysty every so often. After she'd woken, about 9am, she'd fed Lazarus, drunk a litre of water, and just gone into her bedroom. And after Lazarus had joined her, she'd slammed the door and there she had remained. For the entire day. She was probably sleeping, or thinking, and there might have been some tears, but it was so unlike her to be so stationary and he was now in a state of mild panic. And when she missed the start time of the show that evening, he thought he might go mad.

He rang in to speak to Mr Chardon, but apparently he was unavailable, and would be from now on because he'd quit last night after an argument with Mr Blackmoor. He was almost glad, but then annoyed. Who would replace him? He had trusted Chardon with Mysty.

He sat at his desk watching the screen, and then the bedroom door opened and she wandered out, still dressed, stretching her arms. She went into the bathroom, emerged fifteen minutes later in a towel, and went back to the bedroom. Three minutes later she appeared, dressed again, and wandered to the fridge, drank half a pint of milk, munched on a biscuit, tossed a biscuit to Lazarus who had jumped up to sit on a bar stool, and then gestured to the door. Ten seconds later they were both on their way down the stairs.

Donny did not like the lack of expression on her face. Did not like the darkness in her eyes, the way her lips didn't go anywhere near a smile. He patched through to Mario and Pepe in the car outside and Surveillance to warn them she was on the way down. At street level, after walking down the steps, she stopped, put on her shades, despite it now being night. She raised her watch on her wrist, pressed some buttons, shook out her legs . . . and Donny half knew what she was going to do. Wanted to see it. Wanted to see proof of her vitality.

She dropped her wrist, looked down at Lazarus, inclined her head, and then they moved, both sprinting off down the street. He followed them on satellite, their speed impressive, like the hounds of hell were after them, working as a duo, never far from each other, splitting to go over or around cars, jumping obstacles and barriers and moving back together, Lazarus' bounding legs mirroring Mysty's as she leapt and ran with glorious precision.

Donny knew from where they were that Celeste wasn't far away, and they were heading for the main road, which was fairly quiet now as most of the traffic was parked up for the performance. As they sped on, Donny saw a truck coming, and he wanted to shout for her to stop but she didn't. Even with the shades on she hadn't missed it, but jumped up onto the partition in the centre of the road in one bound, pushed off again, put a hand on the edge of the truck, and sailed over, landing safely on the other side.

She turned back to look at Lazarus, who was looking accusingly at her for having taken the aerial route, one that he couldn't follow. She smiled slightly, beckoned him over, and then they ran the rest of the way together, heading for the backstage area.

Donny sat looking at the screen, feeling a little stunned, even though he knew what she was like. But this had been different. Unemotional.

Calculated. There was no joy in her journey. No joy in her. That was what Daryl and his disgusting friend had taken away. And set the scene for his own misjudged actions.

He, however, intended to make his own mistakes right – if she would let him – but from what he could tell from speaking to Aaron, neither Daryl nor Harvey thought they had anything to repent. He was going to have a very busy evening.

He wouldn't know the jubilation of the Flying Tiger troupe when it reached them she had arrived. She was surrounded, berated, welcomed, congratulated by her fellow Tigers, all so relieved to see her. But she would not remove her shades. She did not want the world to know her feelings. It was easier that way. No one said a word about them. And no one dared argue with the arrival of her leopard, who further underlined just how exceptional she was.

"Give me five minutes, I'll be ready. I'm already warmed up, please, just five minutes?" she asked.

She shut the door to the dressing room once Lazarus was inside, leaving the stunned group of men and woman standing in the corridor. They looked at each other. She seemed to be in control. Almost *too* in control. Aaron looked at Monique, who looked back and shrugged. They had to trust her. She hadn't been there at the usual time, but that wasn't such a bad thing as long as she'd done the preparation, like not eaten a four-course dinner and warmed up. They all knew if there was one person there who could magic something sensational with apparent effortlessness, it was her.

DONNY SIPPED HIS Martini and glanced around, knowing his main prey was arriving with his patron just across in the main room in one of his own casinos. It was the best, the most exclusive in Vegas. It also boasted the best security system to avoid cheating – and to protect some of its clientele who were somewhat of a darker shade of grey, like himself.

He had everything ready, had the dummy players there to sit in, had given them copious amounts of his own money to play with. Seeing as he was going to win, it didn't matter if they lost; it would get back to him anyway.

The Blackmoor foursome strode in, like a set of sleek wolves, smart, well-groomed, all attractive young men who all enjoyed every advantage money could buy, and did so with an aggressiveness masked by the suave, charming exteriors – which was why they were all so arrogant. They gradually filtered through the room, stopping to talk with those that greeted them, already being eyed up by the beautiful females employed to entertain the casino's guests however they wanted to be entertained. But each was a woman who knew the job description and had applied willingly, and not a frightened young artiste who should not be touched. Donny knew after this night Mr Harvey Lincoln would know the difference.

"Donny!" Daryl greeted him.

Donny turned, putting on his most charming face as he held out his hand in welcome. They exchanged a firm handshake. Donny resented the fact Daryl had another two inches on him in height, and was, if Donny was honest, better looking – divinely so – as well as younger by three – or was it four? – years. Youth had never bothered him before, as passing years meant he was older and wiser . . . and still alive. But that was before he'd taken guardianship of a kid who he wanted to spend as much time with as possible, and who was over ten years younger than he was.

"Daryl. Enjoying Vegas I hope?"

"Yes, very much. You enjoyed the show?"

"It was superb." Donny forced out the words as if he didn't want to punch Daryl's handsome over-confident face to a pulp. They had deliberately not spoken before or after the show; in fact, seemed to avoid each other despite making eye contact a number of times. Daryl because he'd wanted to observe Donny to see if his 'secretary' turned up; Donny because he knew that.

"Where's the redhead? I had thought you'd bring your little secretary last night, but I didn't see anyone in skimpy underwear with you."

Donny knew Daryl would ask tonight. He just couldn't resist it, could he? But Donny was more than happy for Blackmoor to remain ignorant. And given the choice, he would rather keep Mysty five thousand miles away from him.

"She was busy. Had a night of entertainment planned of her own." Daryl couldn't hazard a guess at what Donny might mean, and his face didn't invite him to ask. "I heard your after-show party had a few fireworks? . . ." he then asked with incredible nonchalance, and Daryl had no idea of danger of his next few sentences, or how they would be judged.

He picked his drink up off the bar, and turned to lean on it like Donny, on his elbows, both the superior specimens of power and stature in the room; others there weren't quite sure whether to be glad they were together, or worried as to what they might cook up between them.

"Oh God, yes, not that I want reminding. Harvey wanted this girl . . . turns out she was only thirteen . . . how was he to know? Frigid little thing. Don't really know what all the fuss was about. Even had the performance manager come storming in to berate Harvey. All he did was touch her up a little. I honestly don't know why she argued quite so vehemently, it won't be long before she realises she could earn an easy fifty thousand from the likes of Harvey, when she's older, and learns how to behave herself. He was so very taken with her. Never mind, maybe she'll learn her place in time."

Daryl was too busy explaining the situation from his elevated position of hindsight to notice the twitch of fury that momentarily twisted Donny's lips; then it was gone.

"You mean she didn't want handsome Harvey?" Donny forced himself to smile, and Daryl turned, and his eyes met Donny's.

"No. He caught her by the door as she was making her escape. He likes them a little feisty, so her fighting him wouldn't have done much to encourage him to stop. He was hard to dissuade. No doubt he'll attempt another conquest of her at a later date, if he gets a chance."

"Pretty brave of their manager to go to her defence," Donny replied, casually, his head thumping with rage, trying not to imagine punching Daryl in the face. Repeatedly.

"Very irritating. I fired him; or was about to when he quit. An inconvenience, but not one I can't work around. Apart from that minor trifle, for a first night, everything went rather smoothly." Daryl's smug smile of self-congratulation was too much. "I should be in profit in ten months. Possibly eight."

"More riches . . . what will you do with it all?" Donny really didn't care, but he knew how to flatter Daryl's ego, it was almost too easy.

"Who knows – build on the moon, perhaps?"

Daryl smiled at that thought, and his eyes wandered across the room, picking out people he wanted to talk to, trying to find a woman who might do to entertain him later that evening.

"I'm trying to find a fourth for a game or two of poker – can I interest you, old chap?" Donny asked.

"Not yet, Donny. Thanks all the same. Maybe later. I know Guy and Harvey are after a bit of a challenge though; they are rather notorious in New York."

Donny smiled in anticipation. "I'm sure I can make it interesting. I'll see you later, Daryl."

Daryl inclined his head as Donny moved lazily away, totally unsuspecting of the brooding anger in his apparently relaxed 'friend'.

Donny nodded at Paulo who waited across the room, all the boys versed on the order of events . . . and closed in on his intended prey.

"Harvey, good to see you." Donny offered his hand and Harvey looked up, mildly surprised at the familiar greeting; but in his own arrogance, and knowing who Capello was, it wasn't something to take issue with. "Enjoying Vegas?"

Harvey shook the hand and smiled. "Yes, all in all. The show was pretty good, wasn't it?"

"I hear you had an even better after-show?" Donny forced an intimate, conspiratorial smile onto his lips – and Harvey answered it with one of his own.

"After a brief false start, and then a later dressing down by the performance manager over some stupid little piece in a costume – she didn't *feel* like a thirteen-year-old, if you catch my meaning."

Donny smiled again, wondering how he was managing to restrain himself from shoving the broken stem of a cocktail glass into Harvey's throat and watching him choke on his own blood. His fingers twitched at Harvey calling her a 'stupid little piece'. *Soon. Be patient. Hard to say which of them is worse; Harvey or his more famous friend…*

"Certainly had a temper on her as I remember," Harvey then added. "Although I wasn't really interested in what she was saying, to be honest, just those nubile breasts and young, firm buttocks."

Harvey's lewd smile almost got the better of Donny's control.

"How irritating for you," Donny consoled. "I wonder, would you like a hand or two of poker – it's quite high stakes? I asked Daryl but he declined, but said you might fancy it."

Donny tried to sound casual, included the implication that Daryl thought of Harvey as his second, but also managed to infer that the high stakes might be a bit much for someone of Harvey's lesser standing. Which made it instantly irresistible. As he intended.

"Splendid, why not?"

Harvey allowed Donny to lead him to a private room, finding nothing amiss in the charming small talk, nodding to the two other players who would be joining them, unworried by the presence of four identically suited men in the room, along with two waiters. That wasn't so strange or unusual when one was playing high-stake poker with a mob boss. Especially in his city. Within minutes, Harvey had his details pulled up on the computer and could designate whatever sum he liked. Virtual chips piled in front of each player, easily going into hundreds of millions.

The first game was just a warm up to Donny, who tossed chips in, almost without a care, happy to lose the eight million to Harvey, knowing he would get it back and then some . . . and very soon. Just let the rich kid find his comfort zone.

Harvey was amiable, in truth, and Donny could easily see how – the incident with Mysty aside – he could be the kind of man he would happily pass an evening playing poker with, having a drink and a chat. Harvey was a sociable chap. That was how he lived his life after all; being sociable, treating life as one long party, just the dress changing depending on the time of day and the location. He could also see how he charmed his way into women's beds and into business. It sickened him to think that once he might too have turned a blind eye to Harvey's behaviour. Might have let the violation of innocence pass without a second thought because it would require too much effort to care. But fate had stepped in, and he did care. *He cared a whole damned lot.*

"How do you feel about going a little higher, Harvey, old chap?" Donny caught the young man's attention as he finished his drink and the dealer was shuffling. "This is Vegas, after all, and I trust you're not afraid of numbers?"

"Not at all. No limit?" Harvey offered nonchalantly, not intending to let this Italian get the better of him. He was having a bit of luck for once, why not risk a little. About time his luck ran in his favour after last night!

"Certainly. Naturally my credentials and those of Carlos and Thomas are unquestionable. We are regulars here. I will take your standing with Mr Blackmoor and your reputation in good faith."

Donny implied he was doing Harvey a favour; the other two players stared at the young man with eyes that didn't blink.

"Run all the checks you need. I assure you I have plenty to throw around."

Donny inclined his head in graceful acceptance of Harvey's assurance, already knowing full well what his financial status was. His boys had been busy gathering information about Mr Lincoln for over a day.

Minutes later the cards were dealt. But unlike the game before, there was less talking, Donny making one or two comments to his associates in Italian, to which they smirked. A few words were exchanged between Donny and Harvey also; but the atmosphere in the room had definitely changed, dropping down a few degrees.

At $60 million, Thomas dropped out; at $80 million Carlos dropped out.

"Just us two," Donny remarked as he raised the bet to $85million, quietly nodding to his friends either side, then looking at Harvey who was sat directly opposite, his replenished Martini now ignored as he concentrated on the game. "I've always thought poker is a little like sex."

Harvey's eyes rose to look at the piercing blue ones of the Italian across from him, seeing nothing friendly. Seeing something unforgiving. Harvey was thrown, had been for the last half an hour when the charming man had disappeared and this dangerous shark had appeared, reminding him of Daryl when something had seriously pissed him off. He exuded restrained, malevolent energy. A silent force in the room. Making anyone in the vicinity afraid when it would unleash itself. Like waiting for lightning to strike.

"Each player trying to push the other a little higher, both aiming for satisfaction," Donny continued. "But like *bad* sex, it only, eventually, pleases one person. The other is left feeling . . . empty, robbed, *violated* even."

Harvey didn't know how to respond. Where was this going? Warning bells were going off in his head the moment Donny had said 'violated' – the very way he had said the word, with that terrible curl to his lip, making him wish he had left after the first game.

"I only like good sex; perhaps that's why I don't always win at poker," he offered.

Donny raised his eyebrows as he contemplated the answer, twirling the only ring he ever wore on his right hand as he did so. It was a one-of-a-kind platinum ring, engraved with DC in elegant italic script, gifted to him by his father only weeks before his passing – a father who would more than approve of what Donny would do in the next few minutes.

The bets went up to $95 million.

"Are you feeling lucky tonight, Mr Lincoln?" Donny then asked, as he pressed the bet up to $105 million, daring Harvey to match it, knowing he was going to win, having known since $40 million was on the table. He also knew Harvey was bullshitting. "Luckier than last night, perhaps?"

"I don't believe in luck."

"No. Neither do I. I believe in choices. I believe in making the right ones at the right times, bringing their own rewards. Conversely, wrong decisions at the wrong times, lead to . . . consequences."

Donny said the last word so lightly; but it held all the ominous potential of a sword hanging over one's head.

"Shall we end this?" Harvey said then.

"Pushed you as high as you think you can go?" Donny asked with a wicked smile, knowing he was about to *violate* the smug, rich puppy in front of him. *And I'm going to enjoy every second.*

"As high as I want to go. I don't think I get as much of a kick from poker as you do."

"No, though you do prefer those you have sex with to have a bit of a kick though, do you not?" Donny asked, and he tossed his cards towards the middle of the table so Harvey could see them, keeping his eyes on his opponent, watching his face drain of colour before he'd even looked down to see he had lost. Could Harvey see the fury in his eyes?

Yes, he could, and he felt fear creep down his spine . . . and in that moment, he realised just how carefully crafted his entrapment had been. He wasn't quite sure exactly what the issue was, but he was damned sure it had something to do with that girl. And he was damned sure he didn't like being in this room any longer, without a single friendly face. In fact, they were decidedly unfriendly. Even Carlos and Thomas were staring at him with dispassionate eyes, as if they knew his fate, and knew why.

"It seems your luck is most definitely out at the moment, Mr Lincoln."

Donny's soft voice drew Harvey back from his thoughts, as he tried to piece it all together.

The Vegas boss then raised the little finger and first finger on the hand that rested on the table. Carlos and Thomas got up without a word and left, the waiters going with them, their pace just fast enough to convince Harvey that the poker had merely been a punishing and expensive prelude to whatever was coming next . . . to whatever Donny Capello had planned for him.

The virtual funds disappeared and he knew they were being transferred into Donny's account. Knew he would feel the loss of such a sum. Not desperately, but . . . it wasn't insignificant. Usually he would be angry about such a figure because he had high standards of his own in a poker game, and rarely lost, so when he did it rankled . . . but right now? Right now he had more to worry him than money.

The game over and the danger becoming more apparent every second, Harvey went to get up, deciding to risk making a move for the door, but Donny's voice stilled him.

"Going so soon, Mr Lincoln? Is that how you treat your women after sex as well? Leaving as soon as the fun is over? Is that why you have to pay them so much?"

The taunt forced Harvey into keeping his mouth shut, not wanting to make things worse by losing his temper. He realised that two of the four men with Donny were in front of the door, even though, as he suspected, it was locked. On the other side, without his knowledge, Paulo and Giuseppe stood guard.

"Donny? . . ."

"Mr Capello to you, Mr Lincoln. I do not count you as a friend. Or an associate. In fact, I did not want you in my casino, except it suited me to have you here tonight, as much as you repulse me."

Two bouts of insults. And testament to how badly his weekend in Vegas was going. He was not used to such abuse.

"Mr Capello, I really do not see how I have so offended you, but if I have, I will apologise." Harvey's attempt at civility, even a hint at humility, was grudgingly delivered – and it was not welcome.

"Apologise? Do you think everything you abuse can be fixed by an apology?" Donny asked him with measured disgust.

"I understand this is your city, Mr Capello, but with all due respect, do you have any comprehension of who I am? I do not appreciate this game you are playing at all."

Harvey regretted the words the moment they left his lips as he saw the tightening on Donny's face: that really had been the wrong card to play.

"And who are you? *Really*?" Donny mocked, not sure how he was maintaining control of his rage. "One of the yuppies who runs after Daryl Blackmoor? A rich kid used to having his own way?" He tilted his head to one side, enjoying Harvey's intense discomfort. Poor Harvey, he really wasn't used to having anyone speak to him like this. "You think this is a game?" Donny stared hard at Harvey. "I don't play games, Mr Lincoln. Have you no comprehension of *who I am*?" Donny snorted in disgust as the young man's hands clenched and unclenched on the smooth table top. "You don't know what it is to struggle, to fight, to kill, to torture . . .

to hold a life in the palm of your hand with the choice of crushing it. Do not lecture me on *who you are*!"

The vent of fury told Harvey how precarious his position was.

"As I said, Mr Capello, if you would tell me what it is I have done, I will gladly apologise."

Donny paused, knowing his men were ready. Knowing he could have this man killed and floating in the river in less than half an hour if he wanted; but that would be too messy in more than one sense of the word.

OUTSIDE THE ROOM, Daryl had noticed the other two players leave, and then Paulo and another guy step in front of the doors, pressing a button to lock them. How odd? Why were Donny and Harvey still in there? He made his way across the room until he reached the imposing figure of Paulo, who matched him in height but definitely outweighed him.

"Why are the doors locked?" he asked.

Paulo remained staring forward, hands clasped calmly in front of him, as with Giuseppe, stances uncompromising and solid.

"Mr Capello and Mr Lincoln are having a chat," Paulo answered with a practiced lack of emotion. "A private chat."

"About what?"

"That really isn't for me to say."

Daryl didn't like this one bit. What was Capello playing at, holding his friend hostage in a room?

"I'd like to see Harvey."

"I'm sure you can, Mr Blackmoor, when they leave the room."

"I'd like to see him now."

"Mr Blackmoor." Paulo finally turned his eyes on the tall man and looked at him with a chilly coldness that Daryl rarely saw: he had forgotten the type of men Capello employed; had no doubt this man was a trained and professional killer, if instructed. "I'm aware of who you are, but I point out to you, with the greatest respect, that this is Vegas, and Vegas belongs to Mr Capello – every single part of it. And most particularly, this casino, in which we are currently standing. I would ask you to remember this because these doors aren't opening for you, or anyone, until Mr Capello tells me so. Is that clear enough for you?" Paulo's tone was so reasonable, as if explaining to a child that he needed to wait till after dinner to eat ice cream; but he might as well have drawn a weapon and pointed it at Daryl's head his face was so hard, uncompromising.

Daryl bit back his anger. No one denied him anything, and he did not like his friend being behind these doors and quite possibly facing an unpleasant fate.

Several long seconds later, spent glaring at Paulo, he walked away. There was nothing else he could do. He didn't believe Donny would kill him, but he felt an unsettling menace.

INSIDE THE ROOM, Harvey stood up, having not received an answer to his repeated offer to apologise. With one more look at Donny, he went for the door.

The two men at the door didn't move; but the other two did, and Harvey suddenly found himself forcibly thrown against the wall. Between them they pinned his arms, and pushed his head hard to one side. It occurred to Harvey that these plush surroundings and luxurious furnishing were pure veneer, disguising the savagery of the man who owned it all.

"Sadly for you, I'm not interested in an apology." Donny stood up and walked towards the man who struggled a little, quite ineffectively, and then gave in to his captors, but remaining tense, in anticipation. "The fact is, it would be meaningless, because your very own words have made clear to me you do not regard your actions as a crime, so I repeat: I do not want an apology. Instead, I want you to learn a lesson that you should have already learned during your life, but clearly one all that money has robbed you of with respect to some essential aspects of humanity."

Harvey really did not like this. He was at the mercy of one of the most powerful figures in America, who was notorious for his ruthless elimination of anyone who opposed or offended him. It was like a gangster film where he had a lead role, only he hadn't known he'd been auditioning.

"Ironic, I think, the way you are being held right now." Donny walked slowly backwards and forwards, silently, behind Harvey. "I should imagine how you're feeling right now is very much like how my youngest performer was feeling last night when you grabbed her. What do you think?"

Harvey closed his eyes. Tried to remember the words he had spoken to Donny about the girl. *Shit!* Why hadn't he just kept his mouth shut? What was she to Donny anyway? Why did he care?

"Quite possibly." Harvey forced the words past his lips, not really wanting to speak, sure every word only condemned him more.

"Luckily for you, all my boys are red-blooded *straight* Italians, so we're not going to grope you in the same intimate fashion you touched her, and though it was tempting to arrange, I'm not quite the animal you are."

Harvey felt a tiny bit of relief . . . perhaps Donny was just going to scare him, not hurt him?

"You just won a great deal of money from me, isn't that punishment enough?" Harvey exhaled the words in a rush of barely restrained fear, a flutter in his belly.

"I couldn't care less about the money, Mr Lincoln. But I'm deciding whether your money is all I'll take from you this evening." Donny paused from his meditative strolling behind Harvey and picked up his Martini, biting the olive from the stick and chewing it contentedly, enjoying the waver of panic in the man's voice. It was a start. "How much would you have given her? . . . if she had let you have your way? Apparently, you *pay well*?" Donny knew he was toying with Harvey, torturing him by asking questions that would require dangerously incriminating answers.

"Thirty, forty thousand?"

"Such is the price of innocence?" Donny asked softly, and pulled out a sharp Italian stiletto knife from his suit pocket, stopping close to Harvey, close enough for him to see him . . . and the knife. "Your hands touched her where she should not have been touched. Maybe I should cut them off so they do not offend anyone else."

Donny pressed the knife against the wrist bone of the hand Mario held flat against the wall, and drew the blade down, not needing much pressure, watching blood well and run along the cut, not deep, but deep enough to hurt, to scar, and remind Harvey of these moments chatting with Donny Capello.

"Mr Capello! That really isn't necessary!" Harvey's voice was high-pitched with pain and fast with panic.

"I really don't think you're in a position to tell me what is and what is not necessary; but do not worry, I detest making too much of a mess." Donny then flicked the knife, and carved 'DC' into Harvey's arm above the wrist, where his shirt and jacket sleeve was pulled back in the hold against the wall. Donny was aware of the pain he was inflicting, knew Harvey was forcing himself to stay silent and breathe hard through his nose, not trusting himself if his mouth opened. "If you ever forget, may that remind you," he snarled. "You offended a number of people last night, and you must understand that I could not let that go without dealing with you. Mr Chardon was a particular friend of mine, and he, amongst others, is not happy."

Harvey stared in horror at the blood gleaming on his skin, chilled by the calm on Donny's face, as if they were exchanging betting tips on the horses, but also as though he was a delinquent child being reprimanded by the school master.

"A child, despite the fact that she is exceptional, is still a child, and you should have let her go the moment you knew. I trust you will not make the same mistake again?" Harvey shook his head as well as he was able. "This is *my* city, and as much as I know such things happen every day to some unfortunate child somewhere, I would have thought you, with your Harvard education and your cultured parents and your moneyed lifestyle, would not have stooped so low as to get your pleasures from an unwilling, underage girl."

Donny nodded to Mario, and turned away as the punches were launched into Harvey's back, at the unprotected kidneys. They were hard blows, knuckles meeting muscle and soft tissue, as Mario sought his revenge for Mysty's treatment too. Donny heard the force, almost wishing he could do it himself; but that was not the way it was done, as it was the detachment that made him untouchable, and powerful.

After another minute, he held up a hand and Mario stopped, going back to holding Harvey against the wall, though now he sagged gasping in their grip.

"You are due to leave in a few days, but it is 1am now, so you will be leaving no later than 8am this morning. I suggest you make your arrangements the moment you are allowed to leave this room. I do not want to have to send men to bring you back to me if I find you are still in my city. I know you have your private jet, so you will have no problem complying. Unless, of course, you are still stupid enough to think you are someone, and this is a game?"

At Donny's look, and for good measure, Mario hauled Harvey back and slammed him into the wall, bruising his chest and temple.

But Donny had not finished, and took another sip of his drink.

"You will not come back to Vegas for any reason in the future, unless you have first asked my permission. And I will grant permission only on the assurance of good behaviour. And, should I ever have to trouble myself to summon you for a further *private chat*, you will not walk again because your legs will have been broken or removed. Is that clear?"

Harvey nodded, desperate to collapse on the floor and let his bruised body recover. He was struggling to breathe, aware still of the hovering danger.

"Yes." It was a croak.

"Good. That wasn't so bad, now was it?"

Donny nodded to Mario and Mickie, who let Harvey go. They stepped back, but not far, ready to beat him again if he did anything stupid. But Harvey turned around slowly and leaned on the wall, his back and head pounding, fear in his eyes. He looked at Donny, who was just as composed, the knife gone, Martini glass held casually in his hand.

"I would make the most of my current good mood and leave before I indulge my impulse to have *a certain part* of you removed. I'm sure you think of it as quite priceless." Harvey swallowed, and tensed as Donny's hand reached out towards him; but he merely straightened the lapel of his jacket with a fastidious hand, then patted Harvey's smooth-shaven cheek, the most patronising gesture he could have made, denoting which of them was the adult, and who was the unruly idiot. "It is up to you if you tell Daryl or anyone else what happened in here tonight. I, for one, am happy to keep it a closed matter; no one will speak of it. Do not make the mistake of underestimating me again, Mr Lincoln, for I am not merciful, as the dead will testify by their absence."

Donny's face was as hard and formidable as granite. Blue eyes glittered with a deadly intensity. Harvey really wanted to leave. Bile rose in his throat.

Donny stepped back and waved an elegant hand towards the door, a mocking invitation that was really a merciful dismissal, and they all knew it. Harvey went, unsteady for the first few steps, pulling his jacket and bowtie back into some sort of order, tugging his shirt and jacket sleeve over his blood-stained arm, running a hand over his hair, so that by the time he got to the door he almost looked normal; though he didn't feel normal at all.

The door was opened by one of Donny's boys, and then he was back outside. He had never been so glad to leave a room. He went immediately to the bar and ordered a large brandy.

"Harvey."

Daryl was there by his side. He'd been waiting for his friend to leave the room.

"Ah, Daryl."

Daryl was the last person Harvey wanted to see just then, and he tried to hide his distress behind a smile of greeting.

"You alright? What was going on with you and Donny?"

"Yes, I'm OK, no problem, we were just talking, playing." The lies twisted his gut. Luckily the drink arrived in front of him, and he took a large swallow.

"Did you win?"

"No."

Harvey looked away. Away from Daryl's impeccable appearance, the usual impenetrable look in his green eyes, everything screaming success and authority. He was always Daryl's shadow. Never even close to his equal. Then again, no one was. Still it rankled, as his own failure and humiliation taunted him. Harvey put his hand deep in his pocket, praying no blood was visible on his cuff, and turned around again, picking up his glass with his good hand.

"How much?"

"I won eight then lost. One hundred and five."

"*Million*?" Daryl was rather horrified. Even he wouldn't want to lose that much playing a card game.

"Yes. Donny is rather good at cards."

"So it seems. Perhaps I will decline any further invitations from him."

"Not like you couldn't afford it though, eh, Daryl?"

Harvey's tone was just a little too pointed, and Daryl frowned. He never made comments about his wealth, and Harvey didn't usually make any either. What had Donny said? Or was it just the losing that had irritated him? And on top of the incident with the girl the night before, he could imagine Harvey was feeling rather hard done by.

"Still, never nice to lose, old chap. Have another, I'll join you."

A minute later they both had a fresh glass with the strong amber liquid in it, and Harvey swirled and drank with the concentration of a man trying to forget, and Daryl swirled and held back, not really wanting it, feeling concerned.

"I'm leaving earlier than expected. Something came up, business, so I'll be flying out at seven," Harvey threw into the silence between them, like a rock into sea shallows. It got swallowed up by the waves, but it still made an entrance.

"That is a shame. I hope it's nothing serious? Usually it's me who has to run out on you and the boys for business."

Harvey forced a smile to his lips. He realised Daryl was trying to make him feel better without actually knowing what was wrong. And for Daryl, that was remarkably sensitive.

"No, nothing too terrible. I just don't trust anyone else to sort it out without me. You know how it is."

Harvey's tone was relaxed enough to be convincing, the very real wish to be far away from Vegas helping him.

"Oh yes, I know how it is. Better than most." Daryl smiled. "How about we finish up here, find ourselves a club, work up an appetite for breakfast, and then retreat for a feast before you head off for your flight – and tonight's on me, by the way, you've lost enough for one night's entertainment."

Harvey kept his own smile pinned in place while his mind screamed at him at how he was paying for last night's entertainment! Nor was it over. As now he had a mob boss in his social orbit who very much disliked him. It was like living knowing someone was carrying a gun with a bullet saved especially for him.

"Excellent plan," he replied jovially. Rather too jovially. Anything to leave this club. "Where are Robbie and Guy?"

Soon all four were heading out the door and into the waiting Bentley that roared off in an arrogant declaration of its power.

DONNY STOOD IN his upstairs office by the window having watched the four leave. Paulo was sitting in the chair by his desk, waiting.

"I take it the other was dealt with?"

"Yes."

He turned away from the view, knowing the skyline of his city so well he did not need to look; though it calmed him slightly to see his domain laid out beneath him. He thought of the $105 million . . . not bad for one night's work. If only he could give it to Mysty. But she'd never accept it.

He pressed a few buttons on his computer and got the view of her apartment up, knew she had returned because the boys had reported her back. They'd spotted her strolling along the road with a bag of groceries, Lazarus by her side, eating something and chucking bits to him every now and again. They were both so similar it almost made Donny smile; both instinctive survivalists. She was hungry, she ate; she was threatened, she fought, or ran. Just like a wild animal, tamed to a point. It was the very reason she was alive. The very reason, in fact, he was alive. Was that why they felt such a bond? Were interdependent upon each other's instincts?

He was glad to see all the lights off, the bedroom door shut. He left her alone. Tomorrow perhaps they could talk.

"She asleep?" Paulo asked.

"Lights are off, so I presume so. The show OK?"

"Fine. She got there, did her thing, and then left. Seems she's getting a bit of confidence back."

"Yes. Or cynicism."

"It had to happen."

"It didn't have to happen like it did." The correction was immediate, in a firm tone.

"No," Paulo agreed, remembering the man's screams as his legs had shattered, any future as a performer gone forever. He had shown Donny the video. He had been satisfied. They had left the man on his own living-room floor, and called an ambulance half an hour later. They weren't totally heartless. If they'd wanted him to die, they would have arranged it.

"Have some roses organised. Leave them outside her door. She'll know they're from me."

Paulo was momentarily thrown: his boss, sending flowers? *Roses*? He did his best to not let the surprise show on his face.

"How many?" *I don't know. When do I ever send roses to anyone?*

"Thirty? Fifty?"

Paulo smiled, seeing his boss flounder for once with such a simple question. He wasn't a natural romantic, or very experienced in such gestures; but there would be fifty roses.

"Make sure they're the best." Paulo grinned and Donny, too, allowed himself a small smile. "And get something for the boys back at the house . . . champagne, beer, whatever they want. And have the car brought round for me in half an hour. I'm going home."

"Sure thing, boss."

So the reparation had begun. The easy parts – the reprimanding of Mr Lincoln and the chastisement of her first attacker – was over. The hard part – the winning back of one amazing girl, and getting her to believe in him again – well, that felt like climbing Everest. But he had to believe she felt enough for him to give him the chance.

MYSTY GOT UP, gulped down some orange juice, tied her hair back and pulled on shorts, a t-shirt and running shoes. She looked like something off a Nike advert, not that she realised. Most girls her age would have stopped to take a selfie for her Instagram account; she just headed for the door. With her iPod in her hand – her most prized possession – she whistled for Lazarus. She had bought it from a second-hand store, and not only had it come with 2,000 songs, she had added hundreds more, so now she had everything she wanted at the press of a button. It went with her everywhere.

She whistled again for Lazarus, and pulled open the door . . . to find the most beautiful bouquet of dark red roses she'd ever seen. She stopped short. Glancing into the corridor, she saw no one, heard nothing. These had been left as a surprise. And she knew exactly who they were from though she could see no card. It was an unwelcome surprise. Did he really think he could win her over with a huge bunch of flowers? *And roses*? Like she was his *girlfriend*?

She picked them up; she had to really as they were blocking the doorway. She walked two doors down the corridor and knocked.

"Mrs Cavanagh?" she called gently, knowing the old lady didn't like opening her door, especially early on a Sunday morning. But she did, eventually, after five different locks, bolts and chains got thrown back.

"Mysty?" The shrunken elderly lady peered up at her from behind very old glasses, her dressing gown done up neatly with buttons and waist cord. Even her hair was all in place. She was a stickler for appearances, even at unexpected moments.

"I just wondered if you'd like some flowers. I know how you like the ones in the park, you told me."

"My dear child, wherever have you got all these from?"

"It really doesn't matter, Mrs Cavanagh. I'd really like you to have them."

The old lady looked at Mysty, and then at the roses, admiring the soft petals. "Not won over by flowers, are you? Whoever they are from clearly doesn't know you very well."

Mysty smiled ruefully at the woman. She was spot on. Age had made her wise and perceptive.

"No, I guess not."

"Well, if you're sure you don't want them? Not even a few?"

Mysty shook her head firmly. The woman invited her in, to help find a vase, and after arranging them, Mysty said goodbye. Moments later she was on the streets, heading for the park, running fast, Lazarus by her side.

Donny watched the satellite view of her progress. He'd seen her reaction to the flowers. Seen the look of pure anger on her face. Now she was running, her beautifully smooth gait, graceful but strong, so recognisable. God how he wanted to see her in person. See her eyes again. Hear her laugh.

He had hoped she'd like them. Well of course he had. He'd never had the desire to work as hard in his life for a second chance before; actually, he'd never wanted to. And now that he did, he didn't have a clue how to go about it, clearly, as she'd given the roses away, and gone for a fast, furious run.

He watched her run back along the road towards her flat, wondering what on earth to do next. Should he try calling her? He really wanted to go over there and pin her down until she stopped fighting this fight, let him talk to her; but he had no right to use force on her.

Suddenly she darted across the road, still a hundred yards from the door, and he realised why: the parked car that was stationed to watch her house. Why had he thought she wouldn't notice? He was too late to stop the inevitable, and the two in the car, Lucio and Pepe, were too busy discussing breakfast and keeping eyes on the front door to suspect a visit from their target. Windows open, they were sitting ducks.

Pepe's coffee went into his lap as Lazarus' head and paws appeared in passenger window, and Mysty bent down and leaned her elbows on the door, breathing fairly hard.

"Lucio. Pepe." She smiled.

"Mysty."

She was being dangerously polite – just like Donny did when he was really pissed off.

"Isn't it a coincidence? Of all the streets in Vegas, I find you two, breakfasting right outside my building."

The sarcasm was superb, and Donny knew it was all meant for him. He could hear every word as clear as a bell on the car's security system.

"Listen, Mysty . . ."

"No, Lucio, you listen. And you can pass this on to your arrogant, selfish mafioso boss as well: I do not want to be spied on, *as he very well knows*, so if I find you or anyone else in a car watching me, I will disappear properly, and he won't see me for dust, because there is *nothing* to keep me here anymore. Got that?"

Lucio knew his boss would be listening; he didn't need to remember a word of it. Not like he could have got the words out anyway . . .

"He hasn't had the time to ask what has been happening to me for months, so why should he care now? I don't know what has got into him, but I sure as hell don't care." She reached in and started the engine, the eyes that bored into Lucio's angry and unforgiving. "You have one minute to drive away. Lazarus!" The leopard jumped down from breathing hot breath on Pepe who was attempting, but failing, to attend to his steaming-hot lap, as she vaulted over the car in that way she liked to, and then sauntered across the road.

Jesus. When did this girl get so determined, so angry?

DONNY JUST STARED at the screen as she disappeared through the door. *Arrogant and selfish . . .*

"Boss?" It was a nervous voice.

"Come home. We can still see her with the satellites. I won't risk it," he replied.

He was so tired. Things were not going well. Not at all.

Goddammit.

MYSTY WAS INCREDULOUS as the very next morning there was another bouquet of flowers on her doorstep. She bent down, fuming, and was about to hurl them against the wall when she noticed the card: '*Mysty, my belated congratulations, Mr Chardon,*' it read, and on the back was taped a small memory chip . . . she knew what that was. She picked them up and brought them inside, detached the chip and inserted it into her computer. She had just enough time before leaving for school to upload the contents, and watched as the face of her old teacher popped up. He looked uneasy, stern too, and just as she remembered him.

'Hey, kiddo. Look, I'm not good at these . . . so, just bear with an old man, would ya? So erm . . . I'm sorry I wasn't there the next night. I had a run in with the man at the top, as you probably know, and he would have fired me but I quit, so . . . But it's fine. I've already got a new position, sadly not in this country, but anyway . . . What I meant to say was a really big well done for your first night. You were brilliant. I know I never praised you like I should have, and I'm sure I seemed utterly impossible to please most of the time, and I guess I just assumed there'd be more times to say those things, but . . . Well, life never turns out quite the way you think sometimes.'

He paused. Mysty was barely breathing. This was a proper message, and he meant it, which was why he was so uncomfortable. He wasn't used to talking about feelings, just technique or choreography.

'I know what was said that night,' he continued, 'and that someone had the arrogance to call you a freak, and I know it hurt. I know because anyone doing what we do gets called all kinds of things and, sadly, your ability will always be questioned and picked over because it's so exceptional. You, Mysty, are exceptional, but it's brilliant, it's not something to ever be ashamed of. Don't let anyone *ever* make you feel bad.

'The rest of the Tiger troupe, and me too, we can't know what it is to be you, to know what it is to fall so far, to be so at ease with those heights, to have the power you do. The world will envy and love you. Don't think your part in the Tigers is as far as it goes . . . you have a whole world of discovery to enjoy with your ability, and you don't need a troupe with you. Despite what you think, you are going to be a star, perhaps one of the biggest of the decade, and you'll deserve every second of it. And I'll be watching. I only wish I could be there to help you, but I think you'll do just fine on your own. Like when you snarled at me to piss off on opening night because you knew you could make that jump without Rucho throwing you. You knew. You have all the instincts you need, and I believe in you, if that means anything.'

There was another pause, his face more relaxed, as though he had given himself up to the emotion he was expressing and didn't see the point in hiding it anymore.

'The only thing, I will ask of you, Mysty, and this is so important, is don't let it go to your head. Enjoy your skill, enjoy every second, but don't go crazy. Don't do anything stupid, even if you get upset. Anger and hurt . . . they fade . . . as much as they feel like they won't while you're feeling them. But you have to trust yourself to deal with it – whatever *it* is. Don't ever do something that will kill you. You're amazing, but you're still human.

'I want to see you on screens and in newspapers for years to come, not end up as some headline tragedy. I know you're not driven by ego, but I know your temper, and I know the passion that drives you. Fearlessness is admirable, but not if it gets you killed.'

She found she was smiling, touched he had taken the time to try and understand her so well.

'I don't doubt there are things you'll be able to do that will leave me – and everyone else – utterly speechless, and I can't wait to find out what you discover. I've spoken to the director at Celeste, and the guy coming in to replace me, and I have asked them to make certain things available to you – not least practice time in the arena to use all the space and equipment you need. There are some particularly interesting additions arriving soon that I think you'll find very useful . . . and no, I won't say what they are, you'll have to find out. I have also put my contact details as a file on the chip, so if you ever need me, for whatever, just call. And you never know, one day I might just come back for a visit and enjoy a live performance.'

A smile then, a real smile in a face that rarely did.

'Well, that's it. It's probably a good thing I'm not there in person because I'd have never got all of that out. You were the biggest surprise of my whole career, on and off the stage, so keep doing what you're doing, and you'll be just fine. Take care, Mysty. Trust yourself.'

The film cut and she just sat for a second getting over the emotion, suddenly realising there were tears on her face.

She'd never known he cared so much. It was advice and praise – everything she'd never had from a parent – and she would remember it, treasure it. She saved the file and the contact details, and put the chip in her locked box of precious things in the kitchen drawer.

Slowly, she picked up her school bag, ruffled Lazarus' fur in goodbye. She'd never dreamed he'd say such things. Did he really think so much of her and her ability? What was the new equipment?

DONNY WATCHED HER make her way very slowly down the stairs, feet landing on every step rather than vaulting down six or seven at a time. He had heard the recording too, and felt glad Chardon had said what he had . . . but it saddened him that he hadn't been the one to give her the praise she so deserved. Flowers had been rejected. Phone calls ignored. Six days had gone by and he had made no progress. What was he going to do?

Once again his thoughts returned to her first night at the house, and he remembered the rebellion and the fear; and yet, she'd so desperately needed someone to trust, even if she hadn't been aware of it. He'd taken it slowly and gently with her. Had earned her trust so carefully. So how was it that he'd wrecked it so totally, and in such a relatively short space of time? Why hadn't he realised just how fragile she still was? It wasn't too late to fix, though, was it? If she really hated him she'd have already left Vegas, right? He wouldn't let himself believe she didn't still care. Somewhere inside he knew this wasn't what she wanted – this distance from him. She'd wanted the same accepting love she had taught him from the first morning, not estrangement and anger. Everything had always felt so natural between them – the laughing, the pizza, the movies, not to mention the way she cared for him, making sure he slept and ate . . .

He swore softly. He couldn't see anything but that delicate, beautiful striped face looking at him, but so lost. Couldn't he go back to that fateful night, stand with her on the balcony, realise her distress, take her home – after punching Harvey hard enough to break more than his ego – and just get it right? What would work now? Did he need to answer fire with fire? This was by far the hardest thing he had ever had to deal with.

PAULO SAT TO one side of the counter, happy with a slice of pizza and a cold bottle of Coca Cola. He didn't normally eat out, certainly not at eleven at night like this, but this was no ordinary pizza parlour. Or rather it was, but the clientele was not.

"Mysty! Bella! How you doing tonight?" Marco's greeting was friendly and his smile, Paulo noticed, was genuine, not leering.

"Not too bad, tired though."

"You? Tired? What happened? Someone take your energizer batteries out?"

Paulo knew she must be tired not to have noticed his familiar bulk at one side of the counter, and he covertly looked round as she climbed onto one of the high stools. It had been a long week, but finally it was Sunday night, and she would have Monday, Tuesday and Wednesday off from performances at Cirque as headline acts only did Thursday through to Sunday. With school, exams, and all her other commitments – including a musical she could not remember signing up for –she was a busy girl.

"Something like that," she said, as a glass of milk and the bottle was put on the counter for her. Marco's smiling face at least made her want to stay awake long enough to feed herself.

"What would you like tonight, superstar?"

"No anchovies, as you know. Other than that, have a ball."

Marco laughed and turned away to create a masterpiece for her, with no anchovies.

"Hey, Mysty."

She went perfectly still but did not look round.

"Paulo."

He judged it was safe enough to move a little closer, and pushed his bottle of Coca Cola along the bar and took the stool next to hers, still leaving some space between them.

"How does this stuff rate up against Donna Capello's?"

"I wouldn't know. I can't remember what it tastes like."

SITTING AT HOME in his office staring at the screen which showed the camera view from Paulo's jacket, Donny winced to hear her reply. Helpfully, Paulo had sat sideways onto the bar towards her so he had a good view of her. Her profile, at least.

"How you been?" Paulo moved on; no way of arguing that pointed comment.

"How do I look?"

"Well, you look as gorgeous as ever," he dared to tease, "but that only tells me half the story, as well you know. So?" he prompted, demanding a better answer.

She finally looked around and he saw that her beautiful eyes were huge, and hurt and lost. "I'm miserable. Are you going to leave me alone now?" she demanded bluntly, unprepared for his presence in the small pizzeria.

Marco looked over briefly, concerned. He'd never heard her say she was miserable before.

"Kiddo, I just came here to talk, I don't want to upset you."

"You know I look at you and I'm just reminded of the one person I'm trying not to think about. You want to talk, please talk, then just go."

She looked away, not wanting to see Paulo's familiar Italian features, or remember all the times they'd laughed and teased and joked around in the kitchen, not wanting his face to conjure up that of his boss. She'd tried to give up caring or thinking about him . . . but it hadn't happened. Time didn't seem to be making much of a difference. It was only two weeks, but it was all so raw still. She wished she had more control over her feelings, but she didn't.

"You know he's miserable as well."

DONNY HADN'T GIVEN Paulo permission to say that; though it was completely true. He'd been as grumpy as sin, had been snapping at everyone. He's also raped a number of people's bank accounts at the casino, and dealt ruthlessly with anyone who made a problem of themselves.

"WHAT? YOU THINK hearing that is going to make this OK?" She turned disbelieving eyes on Paulo.

"No, it's just so you know you're not the only one feeling like shit."

"Well, it's not my fault, and it's not for me to fix."

"Why don't you give him a chance to fix it, kiddo? He really wants to, but you've not answered any of his calls."

"The phone is broken."

"How did that happen?"

Paulo knew. Donny had shown him the moment when his call had rung through. She'd been on the sofa, curled up with Lazarus, and the buzzer had gone six times. She'd sat up and lobbed a cushion at the intercom unit, knocking it off the table top. It had smacked onto the floor, the smash accompanied with 'I do not want to talk to you!"

"It had an accident . . . with the floor."

"Oh, really. Did it have any help?"

"It got attacked by a cushion."

Paulo wanted to laugh, and even Donny found his face cracking into the first smile for a long time.

"You want me to have it replaced?"

"I'll fix it sometime."

"You want me to get it fixed?"

"*No.* I'll fix it when I'm good and ready." Her eyes flashed around again. "He's the only one who calls me on it, because no one else knows the number. Or at least, he used to call me. It had a good layer of dust on it before it had its accident. I think that says everything."

"No, it doesn't," Paulo corrected gently; but she just snorted and looked away, unconvinced. "He does care, kiddo, he just . . . went the wrong way about it."

"Care? Don't bother, Paulo, you shouldn't be here making excuses for him. He's a grown man. I think he can speak for himself."

"I know, I just . . . don't want you to hate him for something he didn't mean to do. A misunderstanding . . . of sorts."

Paulo was fudging his way through this, hoping if he got her to admit some of her emotions, it would at least give them something to work with to win her around. Paulo could feel the tension in her. She was hurting as much as Donny was. And both of them just as stubborn.

"I couldn't hate him if I tried, Paulo. Maybe it would be easier if I could," she then said – and Donny felt some kind of relief. "Whose idea was this? Yours or his?"

"His. Only he knew if he came himself you'd make a bolt for the door or rearrange his nose. Neither of which were outcomes we really wanted."

"I wouldn't hit him," she growled back, offended. "I might want to, but I wouldn't."

Marco chose that moment to present Mysty with her pizza, and she took a long swallow of milk before attacking it.

"You want some?" she asked – and it was a relief to both men that she was just as sweet as ever in offering to share.

"No, kiddo, I'm OK, but thanks."

Paulo watched contentedly as she ate the first slice, having been concerned, like Donny, that she hadn't been eating properly. And she had been eating less, missing meals completely, or just eating an apple, not a sandwich as she normally did. A sign, they were both convinced, of her unhappiness. She was as lean as a hunting cat, her high cheekbones just a bit more obvious.

"How's everything else going?" Paulo asked.

"Fine. He cares so much he asked you to ask me?"

"He cares enough that he arranged to get that cu . . . that bastard from the opening night in a room with him and four of the boys and beat the shit out of him, after stinging him for $105 million. So yeah, I'd say he does."

Donny hadn't been sure if it would be a good idea to tell her that, but Paulo thought she should know that Donny was fighting her corner even if she didn't ask him to.

She was silent for a moment.

"That's almost rude. *I* wanted to beat the shit out of him."

Paulo saw the beginnings of a smile on her lips as she navigated the pizza box to extract another slice.

DONNY SMILED TOO; this was his Mysty alright.

"I'LL TELL DONNY to let you join in next time."

She sobered again, chewing quietly, as if wondering whether to say something. Half-guessing what that something was, Paulo kept silent, waiting for it.

She swallowed and then looked round at him. "I heard . . . I heard on the grapevine that the guy who tried it on, those weeks ago, I heard he was attacked at his home, had his legs broken and something rude carved into his forehead with a knife."

Paulo didn't enlighten her as to what else they'd done to him. She was a child still, and did not need to know that he would remain childless for the rest of his days on Earth.

"You want me to sit here and tell you we had nothing to do with that?" Paulo asked gently, not sure how she would react.

"No. I suspected, but you've confirmed it. I suppose that is something I should thank him for."

"He didn't do it to be thanked, Mysty. He did it because he was fucking livid, and so if anyone else connects the dots, it might make people think twice about touching you. Whatever you think him guilty of, whatever he did to upset you, he would never let anyone hurt you. Not if he could help it. He's on your side, you know?"

Her face darkened as she obviously went back to a place in her past where she hadn't had anyone on her side, and she stayed quiet.

"Pretty good job you did, busting his jaw and his shoulder," Paulo then added.

She choked, half on emotion and half on pizza.

"The dickhead made the mistake of tying my hands. Big mistake. My legs are the strongest part of me."

Paulo tried to ignore the tug inside his chest as she tried to shrug it off. He thought of his own sister, who was beautiful, classically Italian, and who had been attacked when she was sixteen. He knew the terror of it, having heard her weeping upstairs while his father had imparted the news, his world tilting to encompass the shock of it. He had never forgotten it, despite what he had seen and done since. Paulo made sure the bastard had paid the price. He'd had that small satisfaction at least. But he knew it didn't undo what had been done to her. It made a hell of a difference when you knew the person, you could practically feel the pain in them. And Mysty hadn't had a family to run to, a mother to cradle her as she wept. Somehow, she had dealt with everything on her own. Independence was a sad trophy, and a burden to bear, as much as it was admirable.

"Everything OK at Cirque? At school?"

"Yep."

The short answer didn't invite further questions, and from the look of her, Paulo judged it was because she was too tired for more in-depth conversation. Her eyes were closing and she had slumped on her stool.

"You want a ride home? I promise no diversions, just home."

Paulo held up his hand to forestall any protest. As tempting as it was to ferry her over to the townhouse and lock the two of them in a room together until they sorted out their differences, he knew he owed her more than that – respect for one. At least if she trusted him a little, she might start trusting Donny again. He could see she half wanted to accept.

"Come on, kiddo, you're beat. Take the easy road for once."

She looked round at him for a second, analysed his face and saw no deceit. Plus she wanted to trust Paulo, it felt normal to, and completely wrong to keep everyone at arm's length.

"Alright."

"You want to bring that in the car? You can ride up front with me?"

She closed the box, finished the milk and slipped off the stool.

Marco looked round from where he was cleaning and gave her a wave, and Paulo gave him a look which looked vaguely approving – perhaps for treating her so well? he hoped so – and shepherded her out the door and into the car. Marco wondered how on earth he was going to keep all that to himself! But he would, if he didn't want to get his legs broken! *Donny Capello? And Mysty? What was the connection there?*

She was asleep by the time the car pulled up and Paulo hated waking her up. He touched her shoulder, and with gentle words, she managed to sit up.

"It was good to see you, kiddo, don't forget to fix that phone sometime."

She looked at him with unreadable eyes, every bit as vulnerable and young as a kid could be, and got out.

Paulo waited until she was inside the front door before pulling away. He smiled, pleased with the minor triumph.

"So she doesn't hate you, and she wouldn't hit you," Paulo summarised, the connection through to Donny still open.

"We're practically married," Donny replied blithely, pleased none the less, and glad she was safely home and not trekking across the dark city late at night.

When would she fix the phone?

MYSTY REACHED INTO the cupboard above the stove and pulled down a few stacks of notes. She shoved the money into her bag and did it up, then glanced once more at the magazine on the breakfast counter. Pausing, deep in thought for a few moments, she then reached up and grabbed two more bundles. Each had a thousand dollars in it, and with her money from various performances, as well as Cirque and playing at the club, she had accrued quite a small fortune – not like Donny's fortune, but considering what she'd had, she was rather proud of it.

Never would she have guessed that Donny was paying her rent. She'd thought it was his flat. She knew he owned buildings and property all over the city, and at the time she'd not thought to question it, but now that she knew she planned to do something about it.

She took the bag and strode out the door, Lazarus hopeful of coming with her but forced to stay at home. Usually he came with her, with a little scarf tied around his neck so people would know he was owned, not a runaway from a zoo. In the neighbourhood, most people were used to the sight of them together, though to begin with there had been a few instances when someone had taken fright to the leopard, quite naturally, and particularly as he was full-grown now. Today however, she was doing errands in different parts of the city, and she was going alone.

Ten minutes later, she knocked on a door to another house, and it was answered. After a short conversation, Mysty left the man with four of the bundles and left, ignoring his protests and the panic on his face. She wasn't taking no for an answer, and if that didn't send Donny a message, then nothing would. Really she should find somewhere else to rent. She'd look into that another day.

Next, she headed to the bike shop. She'd been putting this off for . . . how long? She admired them through the window, and then went inside, a little uncertain, a little overawed by the shiny gorgeous machines. If there was ever an incentive to earn lots of money, it was this.

"Can I help you?"

She swung around to look at the man who had appeared from a doorway she hadn't seen. Small wonder. She'd been too busy admiring everything around her.

"I hope so," she managed to say. Finally there, in the shop she had walked past a hundred times, it was all so much better than she had expected. "I'd like to buy a motorbike."

His face split into a big smile, and he walked forward, wiping his hands on a cloth. She could see oil on them, his check shirt old and torn, rolled up to his elbows and tucked into jeans that were also covered in oil. She loved the smell of the place, and she dearly hoped she wasn't going to have to argue her way past deep-seated sexism.

He took a few steps towards her. She looked like a biker already with the black leather jacket and black jeans, but she was slender with it, and mighty pretty. "This a new bike, or a replacement?"

"I've never been on one before." She rested one hand on a bike.

He looked back at her face. Beautiful, very beautiful, but innocent, he could see it in her eyes, guileless and honest.

"Right. And you're how old?"

She'd been waiting for that question, and she had the perfect answer that didn't even mean she had to lie. "I'm taking my exams for my college place at the moment."

"OK. So. First bike. I take it your parents aren't going to make you bring it back?"

"I don't have any parents. I've been on my own since I was nine."

"But you have a guardian, right?"

She ground her teeth, not wanting to use his name, but accepting it would make things a hell of a lot easier. She really wanted a bike. "You know who Donny Capello is?"

His face froze. She was used to that reaction.

He thought a moment; she waited.

"Are you the girl who saved his life? Twice?"

She didn't know anyone who knew that. How did he know that?

She shrugged. "Someone had to."

He saw her discomfort. Didn't see a boasting loud-mouth tearaway. He didn't like selling bikes to those types. He thought they would end up killing themselves.

"Yeah, I guess they did. What would Vegas be without Donny Capello keeping an eye on it?" She smiled, caught for a moment in his good humour, her feelings about the man a little confused. "So, do you have an idea of what you want, or a budget?"

"I've had a look at some magazines, but I'd rather have a recommendation. You're the expert, not me. I have $3000 to spend. I don't know what that would buy me."

He nodded, a little cautious of her now he knew who she was. But there was nothing threatening about her. In fact, if asked, he would have said she was as lovely as she was to look at.

"That's a perfect sum for a first bike. No point blowing $20k on your first machine when you'll probably drop it, chuck it down the highway – all sorts. It's a learning curve, you and a bike. You have to work together, in harmony, learning what you're both capable of and where your limits are." He beckoned her down the rows, the floor just as shiny as the bikes, all lovingly polished and perfect. It was heaven. "That make sense?"

He glanced round at her; but her silence was because she was busy looking around, not because she hadn't paid attention.

"Yes, completely," she answered, meaningfully, and nodded.

A real bike nut in the making. He could remember when it bit him, all those years ago.

"Right, well, the one I would recommend for you, is this one here." He stopped next to a great-looking machine, a Kawasaki Z250SL, all black, as she would have wanted, the handlebars just inviting her hands to hold them. Everything was sleek. Not as amazing as the ones further up the shop, but far better than she'd imagined she'd buy. "It's a 250cc, got some kick, but nothing you shouldn't be able to handle with a bit of practice. Top speed 110mph – but if you squeeze you might get a little bit more out of it . . . though I don't suggest you try. Already has Bridgestone tyres – his hand patted the rubber – and a light body, so it won't be too hard to move around. They're heavier than they look."

"I'm stronger than I look."

He smiled at her quick response. "Well, you'll be even stronger after two weeks on this baby. You want to try her?"

"I always thought of them as 'him'."

"Well, that's up to you, obviously." He patted her shoulder. "I'll roll her out and get you a helmet. I'll call Greg down. He'll come out with you for a quick practice spin."

Her mind flipped over – wow! She was actually getting on a bike!

Greg joined them on the shop floor and the boys exchanged a few words, and then she was outside, seated on the bike, helmet on. Greg showed her how to select neutral and start the bike, explained the clutch and gears, the front and rear brakes, how to lean a little into the corners, and then got on his own.

"You OK?"

She heard the voice in her ear, rather impressed with the comms system in the helmet.

"Yes, fine. I think."

He laughed, a strange muffled chuckle inside the helmet. He then flicked his visor down, and she copied him, and he fired up his own bike: a glorious monster with a deep throaty rumble made her shiver. She loved that sound!

"Ready?" She nodded. "Just stay behind me. Any problems, you give me a yell, OK? We can stop any time."

Dropping into first, releasing the clutch, smoothly as instructed, her feet coming up to rest on the pegs, she tested the feel of it, the power at the twist of her wrist. He sped up a little, and she copied, flicking up into second, and they went a little faster down the street. She heard him throttle back to turn the corner, saw him nip the clutch an inch, and she copied exactly, moving with the bike. Straightening out he turned around and looked at her, nodded, and turned back. A couple more streets at that slow pace, and then they got to some back streets, empty and gloriously open. He moved up through the gears, and she followed, enjoying the push of air on her, the growl beneath her, aware his bike could do more, but grateful he was respecting she was a newbie. This was the best thing she'd *ever* done – next to Cirque!

"How you doing back there?"

"All fine!" she answered, smiling, hearing the smile in his voice.

What a feeling! It would be worth every cent of $3000 to be able to do this every day! And there was no way she wasn't going to test the top speed!

He eased them down to more moderate speeds as they worked their way through some traffic, and then they were back at the shop. They rolled slowly into the yard, and she slipped into neutral and put the stand down. He did the same and they cut the engines.

"Well, what do you think?" Greg asked, smiling as he removed his helmet.

"It's fantastic!"

"You wait till you're a little older. You can get something really amazing, something that'll really get your heart racing." He was pleased for her, and impressed. He'd been watching her in his mirrors, and she'd not faltered once, or wobbled, or done anything stupid. She was a natural. Balanced and confident. He had no worries selling her the bike. "You did well, but remember to take it all fairly slow and steady to start with, just like learning to walk." She nodded, knowing she was probably going to ignore that advice completely. "You happy?"

"Very."

"You're almost too easy to please," he laughed, and dismounted.

She did too, but did not want to leave the bike. She wanted to go again.

"You need anything – road test, service, any kit – you come to me."

"I don't think I'll ever go anywhere else."

He held out his hand and the firm handshake was exactly what he knew he'd get. He liked this kid. Whatever she was to Donny Capello – David had whispered in his ear to take care of her, *especially* take care of her – she sure had turned out alright for herself.

"Right, now the important stuff before the fun starts. I just need to check your licence. You got it there for me? And you'll need to insure it."

"I forgot my licence, but you can look me up. Here's my ID card. I'll make the call to my insurance company when we've done this bit."

She handed over the ID Fabio had presented her with during her first month in Vegas. It had been necessary to do a little hacking, and well, the ID was fake anyway, she'd figured, so what difference did it make to tweak the dates a little? To add that she had passed a bike test?

"Well, that's all good. Thank you. I'll need to just save a copy, if that's OK?"

She nodded. He could do whatever he liked. They were bits of paperthat opened doors. Waiting patiently, it started to sink in that she'd pulled this off. On her own. Without Donny, or Paulo, or any of the boys.

"All copied. You want to call your insurance company?"

"Sure."

She stepped outside, pulled her phone out and dialled a takeaway Chinese. She'd memorised her fake driving licence number and pass certificate number, and gave these to the very confused man on the other end of the call who kept calling her 'ma'am'. She then told him what bike she was buying. Lastly, she charged the insurance, to commence immediately, to her fake Bank of America account, and thanked him for his help.

She went back into the shop.

"All sorted. Do you need the insurance reference?"

"No, we don't need that, just make sure you keep the certificate safe somewhere when it arrives. Right! Now some important stuff: helmet and leathers and boots! Let's go and see what we have for you, and then we'll agree a total price. OK?"

Half an hour later, with her own super-sleek black helmet with black visor, gloves, boots, and proper leathers, she slung her leg back over the bike. She had happily parted with $2950, knowing he had given her at least $300 off with all the kit as well. And with a year's warranty, it was a great deal. Her rucksack on her back, with a security chain inside.

She fired the bike up, and eased away, taking it very slowly.

In the shop, David held his breath, Greg did too. Would she be OK? But moments later they watched her move off down the street, picking up pace. Greg heard her change up a gear, and then negotiate the corner, just as they had done before. He kept listening, didn't hear a crash, just the gradually receding sound of the engine.

She was going to be some rider, and he had a feeling he'd be seeing her again.

"DONNY!"

"WHAT?" HE replied, rather curtly.

It had been a month now. He felt he might go insane. He'd had the conversation with her a thousand times in his head: the one where he apologised and tried to explain and she forgave him.

"She's got a *bike!*"

Mario half fell through the door in his haste, and Donny went from the window, where he had been glaring at the world, to his computer to pull up the satellite visuals. Mario came to stand behind him, joined by Paulo.

"What the hell?"

Donny saw the black shape zoom along the street, then pull up in front of the building. After a second, the engine was cut, she kicked the stand down and sat up straight. She swung her leg over and stood up, pulling her gloves off and then her helmet, shaking out her curls. She secured the bike, saw the electric pad on the chain flash blue to tell her it was armed – as Greg had showed her – and then backed up a few steps to look at her new machine. *She was in love.* She then pushed her gloves into her helmet and went into her flat.

Sweet Jesus. Donny shifted uncomfortably, totally taken aback. Mysty? With a motorbike? How sexy did she look in all that black leather, and pulling off her helmet, all the hair tumbling out . . .

"Fucking hell." Mario summed it up succinctly for all of them.

"Yes," Donny managed to say, backing up the clip and watching it again.

"Holy Mother of God," Paulo added.

They were still trying to put the astonishing into words, but only managing to swear.

"Yes," Mario said.

"She looks . . ." Paulo breathed.

"*Yes, I know*," Donny snapped.

Donny wished they would shut up. His bad mood had abated somewhat, and was now tempered with pride, but also a sense of possession – the very emotion he had tried so hard to squash: she was not his possession; not his in any way.

"Boss!"

All three looked up to see Lucio looking nervous in the doorway.

"Yes?" Donny asked.

"Mr Benito is here. Mysty went to see him this morning and gave him $4000 for rent. He says he tried to refuse but she wouldn't give him a chance. She was apparently rather pissed off."

"Shit." Donny put a hand to his face. Another declaration of independence.

"Mr Benito has brought the money over. He doesn't want to be paid twice. What shall I tell him?"

"Tell him if she brings him any more fucking rent, he is to bring it to me and I will see she gets it back. I will continue paying the rent *as before*."

Donny's voice was thunderous, like a proclamation from God, and Lucio nodded and backed out the door, glad to shut it firmly behind him.

"How the fuck did she find out?" Paulo asked, both he and Mario feeling rather uncomfortable in the presence of their now very angry boss.

"Does it matter?" Donny demanded, no longer surprised by what she got up to, pushing up and pacing to the window. "Why does she have to be so stubborn?"

It was not a question he did not already know the answer to: this was his fault. He alone had made her feel she must now reject all help from him.

He wanted to go and strangle her for being so damned proud, wilful . . . honourable.

"What would you like us to do?" Paulo asked tentatively, aware it might get his head snapped off.

"Wave a fucking magic wand."

He knew they were missing her too, that they felt as helpless as he did. Paulo was disappointed that his chat with her as she ate pizza had borne so little fruit. He looked so lost, and they honestly didn't know what to say. They were trained fighters, killers, thugs, but faced with the conundrum of this girl, they were flummoxed.

"Just put the money somewhere safe, and do nothing. We'll just have to wait it out, see what happens. Maybe once she's used up all her anger she'll calm down a bit."

"We can hope," Paulo muttered, wishing he could think of something to bring this impasse this to an end.

Hope. It was all that was left. But it was fading.

Mysty logged into Facebook, knowing she'd been putting it off, knowing Raju would have been worried about her. She was conscious she had become something of a hell-raising teenager while the heat of her anger still roiled inside her.

She knew part of her hesitation to speak to Raju had been because she wanted to share her feelings with someone, but Raju and she still kept so much about their personal lives to themselves. Which was strange, and they both knew it, but it meant there was a mutual respect for each other's privacy.

She saw that she had fifty-four messages waiting for her from Raju. They started off normal, then more worried, asking how she was, if she was OK, and then more panicked. He'd even tried to call her.

As always, he was online.

'Hey,' she typed,'sorry for not replying for so long. Some stuff happened and I . . .' What could she say? That she'd been attacked at work? That the guy who'd rescued her, turned her life around, had kind of dumped her like a pair of shoes that went out of fashion? That she'd jumped off a top-floor balcony not caring if she died? No. she couldn't say any of that stuff. '. . . I've just been having a hard time dealing with it. It will sound mad if I tell you. I'm sorry for worrying you so much.'

She could see him typing. *Please don't be mad at me.* The typing stopped and she held her breath. She couldn't really even tell him about the bike, with its carbon footprint. She felt like she couldn't say anything at all.

'Hi. I admit I was worrying about you. But it doesn't sound like what happened was good. Are you OK?'

Oh thank you, Raju. I don't think I could handle it if you got mad at me too. 'I'm better than I was last week. Thank you for caring,' she typed.

'If you ever want to talk about it...'

'I know. How are you?'

'Same. You going to be around more now, or . . .?'

'I hope to be. I have a favour to ask actually. More of a challenge.'

'OK. Tell me?'

'Can you try and hack past my firewalls for me? I have something I need to do and I need my system to be as unbreachable as possible."

'Impenetrable.'

His correction made her smile. She'd missed his intellect. 'Yes, sorry. Impenetrable. Exactly.'

'Sure! What's the thing you need to do?'

'I'll tell you one day.'

'Oh, now this sounds interesting!'

'It's illegal. One more on a list of illegal things I've done recently.'

"I've missed you, Ecce. Don't disappear on me again.'

'I won't. I promise. I missed you too.' *I really have. I've missed me too. Nothing feels normal.* 'I'll be back online tonight. Catch you later, OK?'

'Yeah that's fine, I'll be inside your system nosing around your files.'

The tongue-out winky-face emoticon made her grin so she sent one right back, then, 'Good luck!'

DONNY HEARD THE beep in his earpiece and took the comms: "Boss, it's Fabio. Mysty has been putting some new computer equipment together. We saw her bring it to the flat. We tried to get in to find out what she was doing but she has some pretty impenetrable firewalls in place. I don't know how she knows all that shit because it's far more sophisticated than what *I* showed her . . . anyway, we managed to pick up this conversation with someone on an old phone. Number is untraceable. Thought you should know."

Donny leaned in and clicked on the file he sent over. She was at the breakfast bar with her school books, her handheld and computer, everything spread out around her. What had she done now?

A phone bleeped and she picked it up: a phone, but not the one she had broken. That rankled.

"Frisky."

She put the phone to her ear, held it using her shoulder so she could continue what she was doing. It was not a new model. It was old-fashioned, and huge compared to the earpieces the guys used. But because it was so old, it meant they could hack into it, so they heard the other side of the conversation as well.

"Trinity." The voice was confident but not deep, not manly.

"What can I do for you? I thought our business was complete?" Her tone was not friendly. She didn't stop pressing buttons on her handheld

"I have business for you, sweetness, business that pays well."

Donny wanted to punch the caller. What right did he have to call her 'sweetness'? What kind of *business*?

"I told you before, I'm not interested. Doesn't matter how well it pays. After I put the phone down I will turn this phone into melted plastic and there is no way for you to contact me. All the details you have for me are already deleted. You really are going to get nowhere."

"Have you any idea what people will pay for safe access into the FID?"

Donny's brain nearly imploded. *The Federal Identity Database*? What the hell? Had he heard that right? It was the most sensitive government database in the world. Even he didn't mess with that . . . unless he really had to, and usually that meant paying someone somewhere high up a vast amount of money to get details changed, because people like this 'Frisky' were so unreliable at getting the job done without leaving a trace.

"I really don't care. I'm sure they won't want access for the same relatively innocent reasons I did. I'm not a criminal, so don't think you can pay me to be."

That was reassuring. But what had she been doing?

"But, sweetness–"

"Don't call me sweetness. I am not sweet."

Her voice was hard and it made Donny smile.

"Fine. Look, you know how long it took me to work out how to hack into this even for a few seconds. And I'm afraid the Feds are going to be knocking on my door anytime. I don't know how you did it, but I want to know!" there was frustration in his voice, and not a little anger.

"I'm not telling you. You'll use it for all the wrong reasons."

"Just give me a clue then."

She sighed and swivelled on the bar stool.

"The way in is not the key, but the keyhole."

"Oh *great*. That really helps."

"I'm not going to just lay it out for you. It took me four months."

"I've been working on something better than the usual hack I use for over a year!"

She grinned at his outrage. "Life's tough like that."

"Trinity please…?"

"No. I've told you at least twice already, and I don't like repeating myself: I am not helping you, so just drop it."

Silence. Then, "It's really not fair, you know. And you're a fool for not making the most of this. You could retire by the time you're twenty-five if you would just accept some of the offers I've got."

"I'm not interested in money."

Donny was enjoying himself now. He was intrigued and amazed, and not as angry as he might have been. He didn't want her stooping to the darker shades of grey, making a living like he did, didn't want to be responsible for her choosing to live life on his side of the tracks; but God, she was smart.

"I went into the database in an attempt to save a life – my life, as it happens – and then I got out," she continued. "And compared to your machete-type butchery, my work was the delicate mastery of surgeon's scalpel. They cannot trace me; they cannot find me. And if they knew I was there at all, I'd be very surprised. That is the way it is going to stay. Is that clear enough for you?"

"Trinity–"

"Another time, Frisky. Try not to get caught."

She ended the call and got up. She turned the oven on, put the phone in an ovenproof dish and put it inside and turned the heat up to max. It would be a lump of melted plastic soon enough. Calmly she sat back down, flicked her hair from her face and carried on studying.

Donny was incredulous. Since when had she become some hacker ace? Had Fabio shown her how to do that? And who was this 'Frisky'? Had they ever met? Thank God she'd kept her tracks covered.

He needed to speak to her. Properly. And soon.

He zoomed the camera in and saw the intercom phone system was back on the table, and it looked fixed. The red standby light was on. Did that mean she was ready to talk?

He sat for a moment, resisting the urge to call her immediately. Give it another day or two.

DONNY CLEARED HIS day. Sent everyone away and made sure there would be no interruptions. He didn't want anything to distract him during this call. How strange it would feel speaking to her after so long, after their last conversation had gone so horribly wrong. But would she take the call?

He pressed the button and sat down in his chair.

THERE WAS ONLY one person it could be and she knew it. Five rings and she didn't move. Seven. Then she reached over and pressed the button. The connection was made but there was silence.

Let the battle commence.

"MYSTY."

"MR CAPELLO."

He hated it when she called him that. How he longed to hear her say 'Donny' like she used to.

"Not forgotten how to answer the phone then?"

"Not quite." A pregnant pause. Donny held his breath. "Not forgotten who I am then?"

"Not quite."

"I might ask why you called. I am rather busy."

If he had not known her so well, he might have fallen out of his chair. He, Donny Capello, feared mob boss, being told by a thirteen-year-old she was a 'rather busy'.

"Yes. I had noticed. Coming in late – even on non-show nights. A motorbike. I'd say you've been very busy indeed."

She snorted in derision. "What's it to you, *Mr Capello.*" She was glaring at the intercom as if she might turn it into a melted mess of wires and bent plastic like she had the phone. "I am preparing for my college entrance exams." She was not about to discuss her late hours or her beloved bike with him.

Donny was quiet for a few moments. *Mysty going to college?* He hadn't even thought of that. Couldn't really even process that. How had time flown by so fast? So he said instead, "I hear you have decided to pay the rent?"

"Yes."

"Why?"

"You really need me to explain? You said the flat was yours. It isn't. Paying my own rent is important to me."

"I really don't know why you have to make everything so hard." Donny rubbed his eyes. "Mysty, rent or no rent, it doesn't matter – would you rather I bought the flat off Benito?" He tried to sound conversational, reasonable.

"No!" He saw her hand go to her forehead in frustration. "I don't want *anything* from you! Don't you understand? I don't want anything from you because you feel some sort of misguided obligation to me, because . . ." She was on her feet, knowing he would be thinking *because you saved my life*, like it made all this OK. But she didn't give him a chance to say it, and yelled, "I don't do debts, you know that!"

"What price do you think I put on my life?" She felt like screaming. "And how much do you think Paulo and the rest get paid to keep me alive? You think the rent on the flat even comes close that?"

"I didn't do it for money or reward. When are you ever going to understand that?"

"No, I know. And I do. But do you have any idea how important it is for *me* to know you have a home, somewhere you are safe?"

"Safe? So, you do care about my safety? After treating me like I'm cross between . . . some unwanted cousin twice removed and someone with leprosy!"

He knew what she was implying, and he was glad he wasn't in the same room because her eyes would have scorched him raw.

"I didn't want you to feel like that. I didn't know what happened to you. And I didn't mean to be so dismissive of you that . . . that night. Why didn't you tell me, Mysty?"

"Well, you were dismissive. And I couldn't tell you. It . . . it . . ." *It hurt too much. So much.* She flopped down on the sofa in defeat.

"Kitten . . ."

"Don't call me that!"

"I won't *ever* stop calling you that. And you won't ever be able to push me away far enough, because *I will always come back*!" His own frustration and anger blasted right back at her and he saw her face crumple. A moment of weakness. He was getting somewhere. "I know I let you down, and I know I've hurt you . . . but, Mysty, I never meant for any of this to happen. God knows I want to make it right. Please, Mysty? I need to tell you . . . something."

The emotion in his voice silenced her angry retort and there was silence. She couldn't ignore the sincerity in his voice, and Donny knew this was what she really needed: the truth, from him.

He stared at the screen, suspected she was holding Lazarus so tightly because she had tears in her eyes. "Kitten, please, I hate you being upset." His hand moved, instinctively wanting to reach over and hug her. He knew her so well. Knew why she'd put this distance between them.

"What did I do? Why . . . why didn't you want to see me anymore?" Such quiet questions, full of confusion, feeling she'd done something wrong and didn't know why. "Ever since that night with the shooter outside the club, you've just . . ." She waved one helpless hand, and words failed her.

She didn't need to say them. They both knew what she meant. He could see tears on her face. How was he going to continue this conversation? Where were all the words he had had prepared in his head? Did he dare tell her the whole truth?

"Kitten, you didn't do anything wrong, I promise you, it wasn't *anything* you did."

"Is it because I'm a freak who doesn't die?"

"You're not a freak, so don't ever say that again. I couldn't care less if you could jump off the moon and land, or not manage to jump off a box without spraining your ankle. That has nothing to do with this."

"Then *what?* I *don't understand.*"

Donny paused. It would either mend all or break all.

"Mysty, you know I'd do anything to keep you safe and well and happy. But I don't think of you as a niece, or a sister, or a second cousin twice removed – with or without leprosy – or even my daughter. . ." He sighed. This wasn't making much sense. Even to himself. He was making a complete mess of this. It was time for the truth. "The reason I tried to distance myself is because I don't see you as a daughter, or any of the things I said before. I-I see the woman you'll be when you're older. The beautiful, strong woman I know you're going to be. I distanced myself to try and protect you, so my feelings wouldn't scare you. I realise now, while it made perfect sense to me, it wasn't at all fair on you, and I just hurt you. And . . . well, perhaps you don't understand what I'm saying . . . and I don't know what you think of me. Am I just the guy who took you in, took care of you, or? . . ."

He couldn't see her face because it was hidden behind Lazarus. What was she thinking? Did she know what he meant?

"I am a woman now if that makes any sense to you."

As usual she'd floored him completely.

"No, yes . . . I mean, are you? Oh wow. Oh, Mysty. Are you OK? Do you need anything? I . . . I can get my mother to…"

"I'm OK, really."

The significance of her words settled between them, and he smiled. She was a woman. His little girl was a woman. He swallowed the lump in his throat.

"But you still have to be old enough to know what you want. Enough people have tried to take your innocence from you already. I don't want something bad to happen to you. I want you to grow older and . . ." Why was he making such a terrible mess of this? "If one day, when you're older, and you think might see me as a man you might want to . . . well, be with . . ." He ground to halt. Had he just made things a hundred times worse?

Mysty took in a deep breath, not sure if she was really hearing this. Was this why he'd treated her like he had? Kept away from her because he didn't want to confuse her? Because maybe, if she was older, he'd like her to be his girlfriend?

"Why didn't you just tell me, Donny? It would have made more sense than . . ." The words were a whisper but the comms unit picked them up.

He closed his eyes in relief at not hearing any anger or shock or outrage. And she'd said 'Donny'. Like she used to.

"Because I didn't know how you would react. Because I didn't want to lose you when what we had was so good already. I didn't want to scare you. There were so many reasons." He paused. "But I was wrong to have ignored you. I was so concerned about hiding what I was thinking that I didn't think enough about your feelings."

"My feelings?" she said in amazement, the hands coming away from her face; he was right, there were tears. "Donny, I would die to keep you safe."

He didn't have a reply to that. She still took his breath away with her care for him. And he knew she meant it. Had seen her sprint towards a sniper rifle without so much as a second thought.

"Why the hell are we having this conversation half a city apart?" she then asked.

It was exactly what he had been thinking. He should be there.

"Because after what you did to the roses, I figured I might end up getting marched round to Mrs Cavanagh's for a telling off if I came over in person." He heard a choked sob and a laugh.

"How do you know?"

"She's a friend of Mario's mother. They go to the same hairdressers. I found out." Donny heard a groan that only made him smile wider. "You want me to send a car round? I am not busy. In fact, I'm never going to be busy ever again in my life." *Please come over. Half of me is missing and I need her back.*

"No, it's OK. I can be there in the time it would take to get a car ready and over here."

He wasn't sure he could handle biker-Mysty. Bikes were dangerous, and the thought of her riding one across the city . . .

"I'm sorry about the flowers, Donny," she then said. "They were beautiful, but I just couldn't–"

"It's alright, kitten, I understand. If I were you I'd have done the same thing. I'm not so arrogant I don't realise that. But you must know I'm sorry, even if you blame me."

She closed her eyes, knowing she was going to go over there because that's where home really was – with Donny. The comfort he brought her was like nothing else in the world. All the time she'd spent telling herself she was fine and didn't need anyone was a complete lie. And now she felt only relief that the gaping wound between them might be healed.

"You want me to get some dinner organised?"

"I don't think I could eat anything."

"What? I thought you were always hungry!"

"Some things are worth starving for."

JUST AS SHE got to the front door it opened and there he was. Just as handsome as she remembered. How could this be? That this man whose authority was absolute, whose reputation was so feared, could really feel the way he did . . . about her? His confession – because that's what it had felt like – echoed her own thoughts. She'd never even looked at another boy at school, or at Cirque, or anywhere, because she'd already decided who she wanted, and no one else measured up. How could they?

Seeing him in person was strange after so long, and she was too stunned to move; but then he reached forward, took her arm and pulled her inside, and then she was in his arms. She breathed in the smell of him: so familiar, so loved. She would have stayed in that embrace forever if she could.

Then went to his rooms, as hushed and safe and familiar as ever, and he kicked the door shut.

His hand cradled her cheek and he tilted her head up to look at him, wanting to see her eyes, reassure himself she was still in there. Finally, he could stop lying to himself, to her. But her innocence was a fragile thing, something he was determined to protect. He would wait for her, and never let anything happen to her again. He pulled her close, and she wrapped herself into him, just like she always used to, trusting him, safe with him.

"Do you have any idea how much I've missed you?" she whispered.

"Hopefully as much as I missed you."

Their tentative words were as determined as they were uncertain. Why did this still feel like a confession? Donny had heard many and offered few in his life; this one was, by far, the most memorable. How was it that she always made everything right, made him feel so good? So *loved*. Was that what this was? There were no doubts in his mind; indeed, he suspected he had always loved her in some way from the very moment she'd arrived. But he was fourteen years older than her, and she still had so much to discover and learn. Would she still feel the same when she reached eighteen? That was five years away? Life with him wasn't simple, wouldn't be easy; but then he knew she knew that, and he didn't want her to commit to that, or any of this, just yet. She had known enough violence already.

Despite this grounding thought, he basked in the warmth of her just being there. They didn't need words. And then he felt the guilt again of not having protected her from hurt and humiliation.

"I am sorry I wasn't there. I'm so angry I didn't protect you like I should have."

She knew that he knew, and for him to openly apologise and to so obviously mean it stole her breath. It felt wonderful to know he still cared so much, and barriers she hadn't even realised she'd put up turned into dust and were lost as a wave of happiness carried them both, making them feel closer than ever.

"It's alright, Donny, I'm alright. We're alright. That's what matters."

He didn't deserve her softly spoken forgiveness; but it was so precious and so beautiful.

"I'm here now, kitten. I'll always fight for you if you need me. There is *nothing* I wouldn't do for you."

The words wove them together, like invisible lace, as their emotions welled up inside. It was a promise that there would not be any space between them anymore.

She slid her hand into his hair, feeling the smoothness of his dark locks, searching, testing, everything a new discovery. There was such innocence in her touch. On the rare occasion he had been with a woman, nothing had ever felt as pure as this – besides, it had always been a function, just a release. But this he understood as a beautiful fusing of minds and souls, and one day, a few years from now, he hoped and prayed their bodies would fuse as effortlessly as well. She leaned against his shoulder. Where she belonged.

Donny heard a long, contented sigh and smiled.

"You think you can cope with a few more Italian mobsters? I know the boys want to see you too." She seemed reluctant to move, and didn't answer, so he didn't push it. "I meant what I said, kitten. I'll wait until it's your choice, and not a moment before."

"And how ancient do I have to be to make my choice? Can't I decide now?"

"You can decide how you feel, yes. And if you still feel the same–"

"I'm only thirteen. It will take so long to be eighteen."

"I think you mean twenty-one?"

"Donny!"

He grinned at her. "What's wrong with twenty-one?"

She narrowed her eyes. "Eighteen." Her face became defiant and he knew there was mischief afoot.

"No, I think even twenty-one is a nice number. That's nearly a decade. I think you can wait that long."

"*Eighteen*!"

"Mysty–"

"Why do I have to be so young? I don't feel thirteen! It's not fair. Don't make rules!"

"Talking of rules, we're going to have to have some, OK? So, number one rule: outside of this room, no one is to see anything between us. Not even a look. You understand? This is deadly serious. It doesn't mean I'm ashamed of you – how could I ever be? – but I will not give anyone even the slightest excuse to judge or hurt you, or me, because they've seen a look or a smile they don't understand. Got it?"

She nodded solemnly; she completely understood what he meant.

"Second rule: if anyone ever tries anything again, whoever they are, you tell me, and *I'll* deal with it. *No one* touches you."

The wrath of God himself was imprinted on his face as he contemplated someone daring to lay a single finger on her.

She nodded again.

"Right, let's get the boys in before they break down the door. They've all missed you like crazy."

He opened the door and called to them, and Donny smiled as she got hugged, picked up, had her hair ruffled, and was generally teased and told how glad they were to see her. They still treated her like she was ten and a cross between a basketball and a kitten!

"Do you think next time you have an argument with him you could still come over and play cards?" Lucio asked.

She dared look at Donny, who was aiming a ferocious scowl at Lucio that would have been scary were it not for the hint of a smile. "*Next* time? One argument is plenty thank you!" he responded.

"I'll go with that," Mysty added.

Everybody was relieved at the pair of them sparring again. Seeing their boss relaxed and smiling was a long-forgotten sight, and a welcome one. But they still weren't quite sure what was going on; they'd always been close but . . . the look in Donny's eyes told them he was more than just relieved she was back.

"Right, let's get some food and get a proper celebration organised. Boys!" Paulo said and herded them all off to go and start planning a feast – whether from downstairs or somewhere outside, it didn't matter.

Donny shut the door again and turned to her.

"There is something I need to talk to you about," he said as they sat back down on the sofa. He couldn't completely relax until this was resolved, and he didn't want it to be dealt with at a later date. If they could get all the fireworks out the way in one day, then they could move on. Together.

"What is it, Donny?"

"Mysty . . ." He took a breath. "Who is Frisky?"

He watched her face, so open, become instantly guarded. She really had not expected that; why would she?

"How the hell would you know about Frisky?" She was on her feet, eyes blazing indignation. "Of course! How could I have been so stupid? I should have remembered your love for cameras! What have you been doing? *Spying on me*?"

Her voice was so accusing, and he fought to keep his own voice level.

"I only put them in to be sure you were safe, in the beginning . . ."

"Then they just stayed there because you enjoyed watching me!"

He could see how angry she was. She like a tightly coiled spring. This was exactly what he had feared would happen.

"No, I just liked being able to *check* you were alright when I didn't see you very much. The cameras only show me the two main rooms and the entrance, not your bedroom or the bathroom. Nothing intrusive." He knew it was the wrong word the moment he said it.

"Not intrusive?"

"It was just so we could make sure you were safe!"

"So that makes it OK? *And who's the 'we'?*" She couldn't believe he'd been spying on her? For three years! Who else had watched her? "I hope it made a good movie and that you recorded it all, because *that's all you're ever going to get*!"

She turned on her heel and launched herself towards the door.

Donny panicked at the thought of losing her. There was no way he could survive her walking away from him again. He grabbed her arm and swung her around, caught the other hand that tried to push him away and manoeuvred her so her back was against the doorframe. He forced her hands up and against the wall, using his body to hold her still, not giving her a chance to push him off. She was caught, trapped in a matter of seconds.

It took him one more second to realise this had happened to her before, that she had been pinned to a wall by someone who wanted to destroy her innocence, and he felt instant and intense disgust; but he couldn't let her go.

Her huge, furious eyes glared at him; but there was something else: surrender. She didn't want to go. He knew that, like he knew her heart would be beating just as hard as his. He could feel her pulse jumping in her wrist from the pressure of his hand as they both breathed into the same small space.

"*Don't you ever* walk away from me again. *Ever*. You got that?"

"Yes."

"Don't you understand what you mean to me?" He released her. She didn't move. "If I hadn't had those cameras, I'd have sent the boys in to bring you here months ago, as much as I knew you'd hate me for it. Just because I didn't see you for those weeks didn't mean I didn't *care*, didn't mean I stopped thinking about you. I was there, watching over you, *every day*. And I'm sorry."

"OK," she whispered, just wanting this to stop.

"Now will you tell me what I need to know, or have I got to hang you upside down?"

"Only if you promise not to hand me over to the Feds."

"I promise."

"I . . . I wanted to go into the FID database to erase myself – not that there was much on me, of course, being such a child when I . . . ran. But I still didn't want there to be a trace for anyone to follow. I was recorded as 'missing' and they clearly haven't given up trying to find me because there were updates and active enquiries from just eight months ago. I don't know if my father might someday come after me if for some reason he is released early from prison. He was insane enough to raid a police station to kill me, so there's every chance he would do it again." She paused. Donny didn't say a word; just filed the information away. "The only people that cared back then are dead. I can't risk the police or him finding me."

"So how did you get into the database?"

"I found a way past all the firewalls and security. But I didn't want to get caught, obviously. As seamless as my hacking in was, I didn't want to waste time once I was inside or leave any unintentional trace or some piece of information undeleted. Frisky – as you will have gathered from the conversation you apparently heard – makes a living from hacking into sensitive databases. He had got into the FID before, so I just wanted to know the structure and any procedures it used – like encryption, automatic copying over of files, logging changes etc. Thanks to that, I developed a means by which there is literally no trace of me having been there."

Donny was captivated. She explained it so simply, laying out her logic. She was so, so smart.

"How did you do that?"

"I created a new person, wholly fictitious, created by organically developing algorithms I designed, so to all intents and purposes she will appear to be real as far as the FID is concerned. She will get a job, have a life, get ill, go on holiday, and at some point – probably long after I do – she will die. But she's not at all real, so no one is paying any attention. They'll never realise." She paused, a frown on her beautiful face. "The database keeps a tally, so it's no good just deleting an ID, as that would be noticed at some point and create an error report that someone – an actual person – would look into. So by creating a replacement, there is no discernible change. I have no intention of going back into it again, once was quite enough."

That was what he wanted to hear. He could breathe easier now.

"You're just a bit too smart, aren't you?"

He was full of admiration, but concerned too. It had been fear that had driven her to it, not fun. But the Feds wouldn't have been too understanding. He wondered why she hadn't come to him. It would have been much quicker for him to pay someone to do it from the inside. But then he knew exactly why she hadn't come to him.

"I don't mean to be," she said with an embarrassed half-smile. "I just . . . really don't want him to find me."

"Give me a name and I'll have him dead within a week. Inside or outside."

"I'm not a killer, Donny, I've told you that before. I can't do that."

He'd already known she would say that, and he loved her for it, but still wished she'd let him erase that ghost from her past.

"Good job you've got me, then."

"A very good job."

"Come on, kitten, time to relax. You've been through enough, thanks to me, and a number of other arrogant individuals, so let's have a great evening and then get you home. When are your exams?"

"First one is in two days; then they're spread out over the next two weeks. Final one is on Friday the 22nd – hurray!" It was a muted cheer, however, as the work was still ahead of her, and that wonderful day felt an age away.

"How do you feel about them?" Donny got them a beer each out the fridge, opened them and passed her one.

"Fine. I'd do them all tomorrow if I could, as I hate all the waiting. I'm holding off on some of my projects for the college stuff, though, because I don't want to confuse myself with what won't be on the papers. My coursework is all handed in, so, it should all be OK."

"What projects are these?"

He loved the way she lounged back against the sofa opposite him, arms spread along the back, beer bottle casually held as if she did this every day, one ankle on a knee.

"I'm writing a program for my Cirque stuff. I'm getting an act on my own, can you believe that? Some new equipment is arriving, the very latest technology, and I debut in six months, after the Tigers finish headlining and Cirque closes for two weeks for a refurb, so I need to get familiar with it. I'll make sure you know the date, then you can make sure that night is free." She looked at him with eyes that warned him this was dangerous territory. "Obviously bring Tallulah and Marilyn, if you're feeling *really* brave." She didn't tell him she'd come up with a beautiful stage name based on the boys' very first nickname for her: The Butterfly. She wanted to keep it all as a big surprise, especially now he obviously knew even more than she thought he did thanks to the cameras.

He threw back his head and laughed, seeing the gleam in her eye.

"I can't remember their real names, if I ever knew them at all, and I don't think anyone except Paulo and the boys will be going to Cirque with me from now on, so you can put those claws away, Tiger." She smiled; Choi still called her that. "What will you be doing? Travelling at the speed of light, perhaps? Or turning water into wine?"

She shot him a killer look, and then removed it because his boyish grin was just too irresistible.

"I started ice skating a while ago. I'm actually quite good now."

He held his amazement in check, asking, "And anything else?"

"I was in a musical at school, and a ballet performance over at the Stratosphere."

One of the biggest hotels in Vegas. How much had he missed?

"Wow! You have been busy."

"So, what you've been up to? You can make something up if you'd rather?"

He saw her insecurity surface, not sure how much she was allowed to know or ask, but wanting to know because she cared about him. She knew he couldn't discuss his life, and he hoped she remembered why.

"Kitten, you don't really want to know what I've been up to. It's just business, and not half as pleasant or interesting to talk about as you. Please don't get upset if I don't talk about it."

She looked up at him and tried to smile, unsure how she dared say the next words. "I don't care. It's a part of you. I don't want you to feel you can't talk to me, even if you think I wouldn't like it. There's nothing you could tell me that would change how I feel . . . And I am old enough to *know* what I'm saying," she added before he could say anything.

How well she knew him. How well she loved him, even if she didn't say the words.

"I don't doubt you. I never have. Knowing that means so much."

The most perfect moment of peace descended between them. How he had missed this. How much better it was now that he had made his confession.

The door banged and many voices broke the silence as Paulo led the troops in and food smells came in with them.

Soon everyone had a beer and the room was full of noise. Mysty had a hard time dividing her attention between everyone, but she held her own, enjoying the banter, always giving as good as she got. He was proud of her. She'd earned their respect – and their affection as well – so it would always be like this between them. And then there was this precious gift:

their total acceptance and awareness of each other's feelings; a bond so deep it only seemed to get stronger.

DONNY WAS EXCITED. He glanced at the clock again. Not long now.

Because they never celebrated her birthday it was hard to find the right time to celebrate anything. But today he had the perfect reason to treat her and he wasn't going to let her argue. He knew everything was ready, had thought it all through to the last detail. He opened the drawer next to him and looked at the small box, checking it was there, and that he hadn't moved it in a moment of distracted over-preparation.

The intercom buzzer went and he was too impatient to look at the ID before pressing the button. Had he done he might have changed his mind.

"Donny."

His good mood wavered slightly: Daryl was the last person he wanted to speak to.

"Daryl, what a surprise."

"How are you, old chap?"

"Absolutely fantastic. How are you?"

Donny was determined to irritate Daryl by being superlatively happy. Which he was. He had an afternoon and an evening with his girl planned.

"Wow. Somebody's in a good mood. Dare I ask if it has anything to do with your fiery little redhead?"

"I'm afraid so." *Fuck you, Blackmoor.*

"Where is she? I expected your extraordinary secretary to have answered for you."

Donny heard the touch of pique in Daryl's tone and grinned, thoroughly enjoying the opportunity to wind the world's most powerful man up.

"She's not here at the moment, otherwise she would have, and wearing only her underwear, of course."

"So, where is she?"

Donny felt like telling him to piss off, but decided to indulge him. Why was Daryl so curious about her?

"She is currently finishing her last exam, and then she'll be heading back here." Donny could hear the pride in his voice and didn't care.

"Celebrating?" Daryl wasn't totally stupid.

"Exactly."

"What have you got her? A poodle? Jewellery?"

Donny almost laughed.

"She's not really a poodle kind of girl." *And Lazarus would eat it for breakfast.*

"Then what?"

"A Ducati 899, a gorgeous new set of leathers, and a new helmet designed just for her. She's going to love it. I can't wait to see her face." He refrained from telling him the plan he and boys had devised in order to present her with it!

"Fucking hell, Donny, she's a kid! And you're giving her a superbike? Are you insane?"

Donny just smiled. Daryl didn't know what he was talking about, and the outraged astonishment in his voice was so satisfying. Since when was Daryl Blackmoor such a responsible adult? The guy who would turn up at Monaco's casinos in a Bugatti with a nearly-nude girl in his passenger seat?

"She's perfectly capable of handling it. I won't tell you any of the other stuff she does, you might spill your coffee on that terribly tidy desk I'm sure you're sitting at."

Daryl didn't appreciate Donny's sarcasm. It was reminiscent of someone else.

"Jesus, last time I spoke to her she was being taken off to the gun range – on your orders – even though she doesn't like guns, and now this? What are you doing to her?"

Daryl's information caught him off guard, and his hackles rose defensively, not liking the accusation.

"When did you speak to her?" He tried to keep his voice from sounding sharp, not wanting to give away the surge of possessiveness that made him want to reach for a loaded gun. Blackmoor and his ilk were the last people Donny wanted near Mysty. He would not lose her again.

And certainly not to someone as unworthy and shallow as Mr Rich-Boy of New York.

"It was the morning after someone tried to shoot you and she *apparently* pushed you out the way."

From his tone Daryl clearly anticipated Donny correcting him and telling him someone else had saved him; but he was disappointed.

"Oh yes, of course."

Daryl kept poking. "She was rather pissed off to find you gone. I rang about your private box at Celeste but, obviously, you weren't there. And by the time you returned, I'd had to leave for a business trip and passed the matter over to one of my secretaries – who are, sadly, far less interesting than yours."

Donny smiled. Even over the phone she had the capacity to intrigue, despite being in a bad mood. He would find that call. They were all logged and recorded.

"Well, she's not really your average girl, as I've said before, and she's rather spectacular with a gun in her hands as it happens. It was for her own safety. Don't fret, I'm not setting her up as an assassin – though she would make a very good one," he expanded, jerking Daryl's chain a bit more.

"But a *superbike?*"

"She's the safest thing on the road. Though I suggest if you know anyone in Vegas you might tell them to keep off the freeway this afternoon. I'm letting her loose with Mario in tow, and I can imagine it'll get a little fast."

"You're insane."

"No, I just trust her."

Donny could just imagine the look on Daryl's face. He didn't trust anyone; he didn't like knowing other people did, so it would really rattle him to hear those words.

"And her exams?" Daryl was determined to find something to disapprove of.

"Oh, she'll ace them all. She could do them in her sleep; she's three years ahead of her age group."

He lounged in the stunned silence on the other end of the line, thoroughly enjoying himself, brimming with pride for her.

"And what is this genius-speed-demon going to do with her life? Apart from save yours?"

Donny knew Daryl liked to think of himself as the only one particularly gifted in the intelligence department; the boy who was accepted to Harvard early, and graduated early with a first-class masters degree in business and finance.

"I don't know. I think that's up to her. She has many talents from which to choose."

"If she doesn't kill herself on the freeway first."

"She'll be fine; though I'm sure she'd be really touched to know you were concerned for her."

"Yeah, I'll bet. She has a rather wicked sense of humour, as I remember. I really cannot imagine this person you describe, Donny; she doesn't sound very feminine, at all."

Donny's laugh was instantaneous. Mysty unfeminine? She was Venus-incarnate.

"I can assure you, Daryl, she is unmistakably feminine."

Silence.

Donny could practically hear Daryl thinking this over, trying to add all the pieces up and coming up with . . . nothing. He could sympathise. If he didn't know her, he wouldn't believe half of it himself either.

"So, she's pretty."

"Traffic-stoppingly beautiful," Donny corrected, unable to resist. Daryl's weakness was beautiful women. Trouble was, none were beautiful *enough*, so never lived up to expectation, hence the high turnover rate.

"You should send me a picture." It was a testament to both his arrogance and his weakness that Daryl made the suggestion, giving away his interest, unable to stop himself.

"I don't think so. Moreover, for your own sake, I wouldn't let you within a few thousand miles of her."

"Why's that?"

"She'd punch you within three minutes of meeting you. I don't think she likes you very much."

"Oh, thanks. I'm so flattered."

"And she can punch quite well."

"Is there anything she *can't* do?"

Donny was silent for a moment. *Yes. She can't tell me when her birthday is or what her real name is, where she is from or what happened to her family. She won't eat anything sweet and she is petrified of guns.*

"Not really."

"How was the upgrade she did on your machine?"

"Perfect. She could have done it with her eyes closed. I think I have a firewall protecting my system that even God couldn't get through."

Daryl scowled ferociously. Knowing about computers was one thing, but for anyone to be good at software and programming was coming close to stepping on his toes. Even if she was good, she couldn't be *that* good.

"I think you're making her up."

"She's just a little different from the society women you have flouncing round in New York, Daryl, that's all. I don't think she's ever painted her nails for one. She's quite, quite different."

"I should say! How the hell did she save your life, anyway?"

"The second time? She saw the shooter, quite by chance, but managed to pull me down fast enough that the bullet missed. She's got reactions like no one else on Earth. And if that wasn't enough, she then took one of Paulo's guns and headed up to the roof where the sniper was." Donny paused at the memory, at the fast ghost sprinting away into the shadows, uncaring of the bullets, his shout of protest unheeded from inside the car.

"You're both mad." *So she has saved his life twice.*

"No. Maybe you just don't have any conception of danger, of what it is to have your life or that of someone you love threatened. People do amazing things when pushed to it."

"You're right. I have never known that . . ." Daryl paused. Donny had used the word *love* . . . *Change the subject.* "I wonder if you remember, Donny, months ago, the game of cards you had with Harvey . . . why was it that your men stopped anyone going in the room while you were in there?"

Donny attempted to sound surprised, and said, "Did they? Well, they can be a little protective of me. I'm sure Mac is just as protective of you."

"Yes, I'm sure you're right. Do you remember what you talked about?"

Donny analysed Daryl's tone, finding it genuinely curious, not testing.

"No, can't say that I do. Can't have been very important. I know he wasn't too happy about the $105m, and he'd had a call from someone needing him back home, but apart from that . . . no. Is he alright?"

"I asked him to come to Vegas with me this weekend but he declined. Gave a rather poor reason. I wondered if there was something else . . . something preventing from visiting the city?"

If you had a conscience you wouldn't need to ask me. "Vegas isn't going anywhere. The excitement will be waiting for him another time."

"True."

"And there's $105m up for grabs, if you fancy a game while you're visiting?

"No, thank you. Anyway, you're going to need all the money you can get to buy presents for your little redheaded protégé. You don't want to be losing it all to me."

Donny laughed, but not for the reason Daryl thought. *Like I would lose at cards to Daryl Blackmoor? Not in this lifetime.*

"Why did you call, Daryl?"

"To renew the agreement at Celeste."

"Ah, yes. Well, the price has gone up, sadly. Next time don't tell me how much money you're making."

"Very funny. How much?"

"Twenty-five."

"She must have expensive tastes. Or she gets through a lot of bikes."

"She probably would if she let me buy her anything, but she's rather awkward like that. She'll try and refuse the bike, but I know she'll want it too much. She bought her first herself."

"Eighteen."

"Thirty-five." Donny leaned back and smiled. He was going to sting Mr DB for everything he could from now on.

"We're obviously in a negotiating mood today?"

"Yes. You drop, I'll increase. Plus, I feel I was far too generous at the outset of this business arrangement on account of a particularly good bacon sandwich."

"Very well. Same account?"

"Same account."

"Fifty if you send me a picture."

An extra fifteen million to find out what Mysty looked like? A picture that would have Blackmoor sniffing around her like a stallion on a spring filly? There wasn't a figure on God's earth that Daryl could offer to make that acceptable.

"No."

"You have got it bad."

"I would rather have it bad than not have it at all," Donny replied honestly and without hesitation. He had something priceless that Daryl would never understand.

"Do I at least get an invitation to the wedding?"

"Maybe. I'd have to ask the bride. But at the moment I think she'd probably say no." *And not very politely either.*

"I really do wonder what you tell her about me."

"I've told her nothing, Daryl, truly."

Mysty thought Daryl was an arrogant son-of-a-bitch just from speaking to him on the phone. And if she knew he'd been at the after-show party, had witnessed what Harvey had done to her, and had called her a 'flying freak', she would probably fly to New York and punch his self-satisfied face to smithereens. It was so tempting to tell him what she thought of him, but it would reveal too much about her, so he stayed quiet.

"Donny!" He heard a shout. It sounded like Lucio. A head poked round the door. "Donny, she's here! In tight black leathers! You have to see this!"

"Got to go, Daryl. Have fun doing whatever it is you're doing. I'm off to see someone test a Ducati and then head off to the ice rink."

"*Ice rink?*" Daryl made it sound like Donny had said the moon.

"Did I forget to mention that? Goodbye, Mr Blackmoor."

Donny hit the Disconnect button and hurried after Lucio, a smirk on his face.

DARYL LEANED BACK in his chair. Fifteen million, for a single picture, and Donny didn't even hesitate to decline. Either he was insane. Or the Vegas sun had gone to his head. Or both. Or he really did have something rather special. From having spoken to her, he rather suspected it was that. And he would be wise to keep Daryl away from her. As a proud man, a mob boss and an Italian, there was one thing Donny would never compromise over and that was a woman he loved.

Tight black leathers? (He'd overheard that bit.) Traffic-stoppingly beautiful? Was Capello bullshitting him? Making it all up just to tease him because he'd shown an interest? Somehow, he didn't think so. Aside from the pride in Donny's voice, he had spoken to her himself, and whichever of Donny's men had interrupted the conversation about the leathers confirmed the bit about her being a biker. His mind boggled.

Daryl had never contemplated women being anything other than the well-groomed ones on offer in his own elevated social circles, who wore stylish outfits, not a hair out of place, jewellery that told of their family's wealth, and who led respectable society-centred lives, accepting one day that whatever job or career they had chosen would give way to marriage and bearing an heir. Or, of course, his Cherries, who generally didn't wear very much at all, and whom he'd never really seen outside of his rooms. The prospect of an outrageously hot biker-chick with a sassy attitude was like presenting snow to someone who lives on the equator: a wholly novel and enlightening experience.

Daryl pressed a few buttons to see if there was a satellite over Vegas he could use to have a look for her on the freeway – he didn't know where Donny lived, otherwise he'd have looked there first.

"Mr Blackmoor, your plane is waiting."

His secretary's voice came through on the intercom and he saw Mac's shadow outside the door. Sighing, he cleared his screen and switched it off, resigning himself to having to wait. But all the way down in the elevator he was silent, trying to imagine her. But he couldn't. But he knew what he could do instead.

"Mac, have Clarice brought to the plane. I'll take her with me."

Donny Capello, he thought as he stepped into the waiting car, *you're one lucky son-of-a-bitch.*

MYSTY STEPPED OFF the bike and heard the shout as she pulled off her helmet. Lucio came down the steps, smiling in greeting, looking very happy.

"Hey, kiddo! I'll put the security chain on. You go see Donny. He's been waiting for you for an hour at least."

She rolled her eyes and grinned at him.

"You didn't take the exam wearing that, did you? How was that fair on all those guys sitting in the same room?" Mario joked, making her blush.

She strode towards the open door, through into the shade of the hall, and smiled at Gio. She realised Mario, Paulo, Pepe, Giuseppe and Mickie were all there too, obviously waiting for her, along with the most important person, who was striding towards her.

"Well, kitten, how did the last exam go?"

She grinned. Just seeing him made her smile, but to share today and the relief of all the exams being over made it extra wonderful, especially compared to the distance and sadness that had consumed her a month ago.

"Breezed it. I had to spend half an hour staring at the ceiling before I was allowed to leave – and I'd checked it all three times. I'm free!"

Her smile was utterly gorgeous, her relief at finishing her exams tangible, and he would have kissed her on the cheek had the boys not been present.

"Well, definitely time to celebrate. Come on."

He pulled her after him, not giving her a choice, and everyone followed. The champagne was opened and glasses poured. She'd never had champagne before and he allowed her to try it; but he only let her a have one mouthful, considering what she would soon be doing.

Everyone was in a good mood and full of questions as they'd not see her for a while, but the chatter was interrupted when Lucio came rushing in, making everyone look round.

"Someone's taken your bike!" he cried.

"What?"

They all saw her face drop, and Donny felt a twinge of guilt for making her panic, despite knowing it would be worth it.

"They just left the chain on the floor!"

If she had been thinking logically, she would have worked out the numerous flaws in the announcement – the most obvious being that no one in their right mind would take anything from outside this house unless they had a death wish!

She ran from the room, everyone following, all of them wanting to see her face when she opened the door.

Mysty stopped. It was true her bike was gone, but what was that? She knew exactly what it was; she had been looking at pictures of them and daydreaming about them for months. *What the hell was a red Ducati 899 doing outside Donny's house?*

She slowly walked down the steps, vaguely aware of the guys behind her. Approaching the bike, she scanned every beautiful part of it, the sleek lines, the deep Ducati red. Her eyes spotted something on the paintwork, and she crouched down and saw what the marks were: a paw print had been air-brushed on in silver, and she knew it was a tiger print. Donny had done this for her. He had wanted to surprise her. Her finger touched the paw print. *Was this real?* She knew how much this bike cost.

She stood up and looked around, seeing the faces watching her from the door. They'd all been in on it and she couldn't help but laugh! Even Lucio coming out to offer to put the chain on so he could take her bike away! She thought her heart might burst she loved them all so much . . . but one in particular.

Where was Donny? She ran back into the house, the boys laughing too, and parting to let her through, and kept going, all the way back to his room. He was standing leaning on the desk, the same place he had stood all those years ago when she had first been brought to see him, legs crossed at the ankles, hands in his pockets, that familiar slouch across his shoulder blades. How different things were now.

She stopped in front of him; he didn't move. So, she did the only thing she could think of. She reached up, took hold of his tie and pulled to bring him down close enough for her to reach her arms over his shoulders. His arms then moved around her, pulling her closer, holding her like the precious thing in his world that she was.

"You," she said seriously, foreheads resting against each other, "are a very bad man."

He laughed without meaning to. But it was true: he was a very bad man, and not just because he'd bought his best girl a red motorcycle.

"I know."

"That is the most amazing present in the world. I will never be able to thank you enough."

"You don't have to, you give me everything I need by being you." He stilled any further argument with a finger on her lips. "Plus, as you never let me treat you on your birthday – understandably – I'm doing it now." He looked into her open, happy face. "Do you like it?"

"It's *beautiful.*"

He heard the catch in her voice.

"No, sweetheart, you're beautiful." A thumb stroked over her cheek. "Don't cry, kitten, you are allowed to be happy. It's not a crime." He let her cry for a moment, and then said, "There's a new set of leathers and a rather special helmet on your bed upstairs. Put them on and then take that bike for a spin. I've been waiting all day to see you on it. You don't want to disappoint an old man, do you?"

"*Old*? Donny Capello are you fishing for compliments again?" she accused, standing away from him.

"A few never hurt," he grinned unashamedly, and she laughed.

"I didn't know that feared, handsome Italian mobsters had such fragile egos," she teased.

"Now, two things," he said, changing the subject. "One – that bike has plates that are known to the traffic cops, but they know who you are and will allow you, today, to break the sound barrier riding it. Two – as much as I want you to have fun, and I know you know what you're doing, please don't do anything too risky. I'd never forgive myself if you got hurt, alright?"

"Donny, I promise I won't be stupid."

"OK, well, you go try on those leathers and we'll see how you go. Mario is all set to ride with you. And then . . ." He paused for effect. "We're going to the ice rink so you can show me your skating."

"*What?*" Her face lit up. "You mean you're actually going, in person?"

He rarely went anywhere like this because of security reasons.

"Yes."

"Wow!"

"When you get back from your ride you can shower, then we'll swing by your place and you can grab your skating stuff and anything else you need for the weekend. Deal?"

"Deal!" *This is going to be the best weekend ever!*

"Are you really still here?"

She laughed and ran from the room, returning in an expensive set of armoured leathers and boots that fit perfectly. She held the helmet in her hand, in black, with the same silver paw-print. He admired her new kit, admired her in it, and then followed her to where Mario waited with the bikes, his 1299 Panigale parked alongside hers – why had she not known that Mario rode too? Donny would have given anything to have been the one riding with her, but hadn't even bothered suggesting it to Paulo because he would have received a resounding 'No': the security risk would have been far too great.

After a playful round of wolf whistles that made her laugh, and blush, she pulled on the new helmet and gloves and threw her leg over the bike. She fired it up. The roar as she flicked the throttle made her heart beat faster, made her tremble with anticipation! Mario then started his bike, and the combined sound filled the street.

"How does it feel?" Donny's voice then sounded in her ear, and she looked up. They were commed-up!

"It's amazing! And you can speak to me!"

"Yep. This helmet has a LT fitted, so we can talk if you need to. It also has a music function so you don't have to be without your tunes. It's all controlled through Bluetooth on your dash. I did ask, but they couldn't fit a cassette recorder." She laughed loudly at the reminder of her decades-old sound equipment. "You go now and have fun. Give Mario a run for his money! I'll patch him in so you can throw some insults at him if he slows you down."

"Will do, boss."

She looked round at Mario who gave a thumbs-up. "You ready?"

"I'm always ready!"

"Yeah, yeah! We'll see!"

He turned and roared off. She took a moment to adjust a glove, leant forward, revved the engine. The bike leapt forward, a swirl of dust rising up, and she caught her breath. It was fast! Then bike and rider as one, she leaned into the curve of the tank. Donny and Paulo exchanged looks. A smooth twist of the throttle and she was away. Should they have expected any different?

In the surveillance room, everyone crowded around the screens to watch; they might as well have had buckets of popcorn as if enjoying the latest blockbuster they were watching so avidly. They saw her zoom up behind Mario and then go straight past, skilfully gliding through the traffic, unworried by the narrowness of the space, and in moments they were on the freeway. Threading through she moved into the outside lane. Mario was hot on her tail, but she was still ahead, her body crouched low and perfectly balanced over the bike.

Donny enjoyed the verbal banter between the two riders, loving her confidence. When the traffic was too concentrated, Mysty took Mario's suggestion and scooted over to the hard shoulder. A driver who had pulled out forced Mysty to swerve around the car and a truck who was stuck in the inside lane, and just at that moment everyone took in a huge breath. She didn't think; just moved instinctively through the gap. Her subconscious knew when to save her and, as she always did, she trusted it completely. She then sat up, her heart racing a little faster, the adrenaline rush making her feel she could ride until she ran out of road. It was the same rush as standing on one of the top platforms at Cirque; like she couldn't die; like she was safe, even from her father.

"Jesus Christ!" Paulo exclaimed for everyone when the moment passed.

"You alright, kiddo?" Donny asked, his heart having just stopped dead in his chest.

"I'm fine. No sweat."

There was an exchange of looks.

Mario had gone around the other side of the truck and now caught her up. "We have roadworks ahead, and they've blocked off the road. Everyone's filtering off. Let's try another route," he said.

Mysty followed where Mario pointed, both of them disappointed by the traffic. The gloriously empty road was so close but out of bounds!

"How well do Ducatis move, Mario? Shall we find out?"

Mario didn't like the way Mysty said that.

"Mysty, I don't think . . ."

But she had already twisted the throttle and was rapidly approaching the barrier, aiming for the gap that led to the freeway.

She looked back, saw Mario still on the wrong side of the barrier and smiled, then accelerated. The whole road was empty for her, three beautiful lanes empty of traffic, and she rolled on the throttle, a little more, and a little more. The needle on the speedo climbed: 80mph . . . 100mph . . . She knew the top speed was 133.38mph . . .

But at the next exit, she decided to turn off, weaving between the cones. She then headed back into the city using the smaller roads where she could really take the corners, bike leant over, using her body and momentum as naturally as breathing. This was something she wanted to do every single day.

She spotted a red bike and pulled over.

"You took your time! Where have you been?" Mario teased.

"I took the scenic route – or least I think I did! I didn't *see* much of anything!"

"Let's get back. The ice rink is booked for between 5 and 7. The bikes and the roads will still be there tomorrow."

"The rink is booked?" she repeated in disbelief, the comprehension a slight struggle after her brain and body had been channelled into riding at breakneck speeds.

"Yeah, the whole thing, just for you. I'm not sure there's anything Donny wouldn't do for you. You'd better be careful, there'll be a ring on your finger before you know it."

Mario was half joking, but she knew he was right, and for once she didn't have a reply. She was actually a little stunned. But then why should she be? She knew now how much Donny cared for her.

"That's not something that scares me, Mario, you should know that," she finally said.

"I know, nothing bloody scares you, kiddo. Get that monster in gear. $100 if you beat me back!"

She grinned, not sure if Donny would have heard that last exchange. Perhaps Mario had deliberately muted their comms.

Approaching the big junction not far from Soleil and Celeste, she eyed up the traffic and the lights, judged her timing. She heard Mario throttling back to slow down . . . so she opened up the 899. She heard a shout in her comms system, but in defiance she zoomed through the four lanes of slowing cars, her timing perfect, and reached the emptiness of the road in front, Mario now waiting with all the traffic at the lights.

"I think that's $100 you owe me, dude," she told him, before turning into the last but one turn.

The door opened and Paulo stood there looking equally angry and impressed. She pulled off her gloves and then helmet.

"If you were my daughter, I'd ground you for five years for that stunt!" he said.

"Which one?"

Her voice was genuinely curious, and Paulo burst into laughter, beckoning her up the steps. Lucio stepped outside to put the bike away.

"Donny is insane to trust you on that thing," Paulo answered.

"Far from it," Donny replied, now standing in the hall, and her eyes rose up to meet his. "How long do you need to get ready, kitten?"

"Ten minutes."

"Sure. I'll get the cars ready."

They heard another bike, and Mario rode around the corner, also pulling up outside the house. He flicked his visor up; his eyes were laughing, shaking his head at her skill and her daring. Mysty went to him and they gripped hands, like bikers do after a fine rideout, and bumped helmets when Mario removed his. These were good days to be in the Capello family.

THE ICE RINK felt strange. She was used to the movement and flow of people, even though she came late in the evenings when it wasn't so busy. Occasionally she'd had the place to herself, quite by chance, when the guys who managed the rink let her stay an extra half an hour after chucking everyone else off the ice, but mostly there were other skaters about.

She waved to the girls behind the desk and they waved back, and then froze as they saw the group with her. There were twenty of them in total: two had stayed with the cars, but the others were securing the location. Paulo, Mario and Lucio stuck like glue to Donny, who had Mysty by his side. After they had done a thorough search and satisfied themselves there were no dangers, they returned to Donny.

Mysty certainly stood out amongst her gang of dark-suited protectors, who looked particularly imposing in their three-quarter length black coats; but she felt proud of them, of the way they served their boss. Donny was a fair mob boss, and that fairness was testament to the length of his reign in Vegas. Violence was a last resort, and not used with wanton abandon, and those who knew him also knew that not everyone with his power shared that philosophy.

"You get changed. You know what you're doing. We'll go and sit down," Donny said.

She smiled and disappeared into the changing room – once Pepe had emerged and nodded, telling them it was clear. Mysty respected the paranoia. One gun fight was enough. She knew how real the threat was and just let them get on with doing their jobs.

A few minutes later she passed the recording she'd made to the guys in the office, who took it and promised to put it on when she gave them the signal. With nimble, practiced fingers she laced up her skates; old-style ones as she hadn't yet bought the newer ones that had used a mesh-like fabric to keep them on.

Stepping out onto the ice, she felt the familiar thrill, the chill and rush of the air around her. She spied some of the guys on the far side and pushed off, gliding over to them, hair loose around her shoulders as she liked it, her costume a shimmering blue leotard with sequins and a silky-smooth train that flowed from the shoulder over her right arm. The long sleeves finished over the backs of her hands.

"Jesus Christ," someone said amongst the group of twelve males, all sitting in the rather old-fashioned pull-down plastic seats. It made Mysty want to laugh; it was not quite what Donny was used to, and was probably the most uncomfortable seat he'd ever sat in – certainly in the last decade of his life. And none of the men stood less than six feet tall, with muscles to match, and they did not fit easily on the seats either.

She pulled up to the rail, smoothly, with a little twirl, and looked at them.

"Wow." Donny was the only one who spoke.

"I've not done anything yet."

"I'm impressed already."

She laughed, a little embarrassed. His eyes were so warm it was making her uncomfortable.

"I've given the guy the music I warm up to, but it all runs in one sequence – is that alright? There are six pieces in all, and the last one is the piece based on the competition rules. Shall I just do it?"

So organised, Donny thought. Everything done logically and nothing left to chance. But would it really be any other way when her performances at Cirque also had to be perfectly orchestrated?

"Sure, we're in no rush. If you need to have a break, that's fine."

Donny thought of the coming evening, the dresses he had waiting up on her bed, the bracelet, and the dinner out at the club. This was going to be a night she would remember. And for once she was not the entertainer, nor the performer, which would give her a chance to relax. He wanted to help rid her of the memories of that night when he had so disappointed her. If she did go to college somewhere, if he did have to lose her to a career, then so be it, but he would make the most of his time with her now. It was time to make her feel as special as she was.

She smiled and glided off, her confidence on the ice surprising him.

She signalled for the music to begin, and so the magic unravelled, the first two pieces slow – the 'Flower Duet' – and more about stretching and warming the muscles, getting her body used to extending and retracting with the music. With some Tchaikovsky from *Swan Lake*, and 'In the Hall of the Mountain King' by Greig, she amazed them with her jumps and the leaps – and the speed. And during the footwork of the overture and 'Chanson Bohème' from *Carmen* they were too absorbed to speak.

There was a five-minute pause after the fifth piece of music, and it was obvious how hard she was breathing – Donny could see the stretch of her ribcage under the material of the costume – and as she gathered her breath he considered her moves. He'd occasionally seen the professional skaters during the Olympics and admired their immense control and strength, and he saw this in Mysty, her head going all the way down to her ankles, the flexibility and strength to do so *and* keep her balance *and* do it at high speed was just stunning. Each nuance of the music was expressed, her hands beautifully poised and expressive, flowing in a fluid, seamless sequence of moves. She wasn't just good, she was spectacular. And he knew from the spellbound silence around him that everyone else was thinking the same.

He knew watching her that she could become famous with this talent, just like her singing. But he also knew she wouldn't take that chance. Could he change her mind? Should he try to?

She kept moving slowly around the ice, weaving her feet in and out, turning and gliding, not letting cold get into her muscles. She then came to a stop in the centre of the ice, and he knew the last piece was about to begin: 'Waltz of the Flowers' from *The Nutcracker*.

Starting off slowly, with no element of the music left out, no detail avoided because it was difficult, she moved beautifully, expressing the joy and the distress of the music in turn, jumping from foot to foot, every second graceful, controlled. The number and size of the jumps were astonishing, and the crescendo perfectly timed with a sequence of triple jumps that culminated in a spin so fast that she was a blur. The music ended and she was still. Long seconds passed and then her hands went to her hips and she hauled air into her lungs.

She then leant forward as she pushed away, gliding slowly over to the barrier again where she stretched out her back and her legs, her breath still fast. Eventually she looked up, eyes searching, wanting to know if it was really any good or if she was just kidding herself.

"That was . . ." Donny tried to find the words, cursing himself for not asking one of the boys to video it, wishing he could watch it all over again. "Absolutely . . . amazing." He stood up and went to her, covering her hands with his. "I don't know how you did that. You should be in competitions! You'd win hands down!" She lowered her eyes. The praise was good, so why was she so uncomfortable with it? "Boys, piss off somewhere, would you? Show's over," he said over his shoulder. He wanted some time with her. "Where did you buy this costume?"

"It was left behind by someone who fell three times in a competition and she decided it was unlucky. She managed to rip it and left it behind. Doug – he's the caretaker guy – gave it to me and I sewed it up. I also added the train." She did a twirl to demonstrate the point and he smiled.

"Not unlucky on you, though."

"Not one bit. I've not fallen for months. I did in the beginning, when I was learning, but you end up hating falling on your arse coz it hurts, so it makes you try even harder to get it right." She smiled shyly, and he found it hard to imagine her falling. There was a long pause and then she mustered the courage and said quietly, "Will you skate with me?"

"I can't skate."

"Neither could I the first time I tried it," she countered easily, wanting to share this with him, make him stop being a mob boss for a moment and just enjoy himself. He so rarely did anything just to relax: couldn't take a walk in the park; couldn't go for a run. What was power was also vulnerability. Here they were safe, so why not? "Come on, Donny, just a few minutes. I won't let you fall, I promise."

He wasn't sure if it was her eyes, or her smile, or the words that persuaded him. He just knew he wanted to say yes, to step onto the ice, to do something different. His life was so penned in. But with her? With her he had a chance for something more.

"I don't have skates."

"I know your size."

She quickly skated over to the racks where they were stored and grabbed him a pair, then sat him down and helped him get them on, lacing them up tightly, aware this was going to be a real test for him. Once on, she pulled him up and helped him make it the two metres to the edge of the rink where he grabbed onto the wall. She could see him thinking this was not a good idea, but went ahead and opened the door for him to step through. Like a toddler just beginning to walk, he did, clutching onto the rail with every step.

She held back a laugh.

"Don't you dare laugh!" he growled, seeing her twinkling eyes even as she fretted over him, wanting to help more but not wanting to seem patronising.

"I won't laugh."

His coat was in the way.

"Take off the coat and your jacket. It's not that cold once you're moving. Then you'll look more like a man learning to skate than a mob boss with skates on."

He did, laying them over the wall, and she held out her hands, positioning herself so that he had room to move away from the rail. "Come on, Donny, trust me." He looked at her, then the ice, then the hands. He then took one, then the other, and she pulled him very gently. "Don't look at your feet. You can make them do what you want them to do without looking at them. And don't let your toes go together." She kept her voice low and steady, remembering what it felt like to feel totally out of control on the slippery surface.

Mysty put his hands on her hips, held them there and pushed backwards a little more. She encouraged him to move with her, with her feet, left, right, left, right. Donny was seduced by the feel of the air against his cheeks, the smoothness of the ice, of her control, of being dependent on her. There were so few people he trusted . . . but her? He could trust her with anything. Could let his guard down, let her take some control knowing he didn't have to give orders. He didn't have to be the boss with her. They were equals, as crazy as that might sound to anyone but himself.

"OK?" she asked after half a minute of silent progress.

"Err-yes." *I think.*

She tilted her head back and smiled, making him smile too. It was so pure, so full of goodness and joy. "Do you trust me?"

"You know I do."

She pulled him a little closer, telling him to keep the same smooth rhythm with his feet, to relax his shoulders.

"I never expected to find you," he suddenly said.

"I never expected to find you," she answered. "I guess sometimes you don't know what you need until you find it."

"I'm so glad you found me."

"I think we found each other, Donny."

They skated a slow arc around the rink, and then she said, "You cannot possibly know how much you mean to me." She didn't look away, kept her eyes on his as she said it, not denying him the truth. "Even if I die, I won't mind, because I know what happiness is. Thanks to you. You've given me so much."

His grip tightened on her. He hadn't expected that statement. Had something happened to make her afraid? So melancholy?

"You're not going to die. I won't let you. Who would worry about me if you don't?"

She smiled but had no answer; somehow there wasn't one. They both knew he'd never let anyone get as close as she had.

After a minute, she let his hands go, but kept close to him so she could grab him if she had to. He was very unsure, but he looked so handsome, his black shirt and black trousers tailored beautifully to fit. If he could learn to skate it would be so magical. Perhaps she'd try and get him to come with her occasionally, it would be something they could share? . . .

A VERY CONTENTED girl leaned against Donny as the car sped from the rink, watching him turn the platinum ring on his middle finger. She knew his initials were engraved into it. It was the one his father, Gianluca, had given him before he died. Paulo had told her about it, along with the unspoken rule never to mention it. What a day. She wouldn't mind having exams more often if she got to enjoy moments like this afterwards.

"How do you fancy going out to dinner tonight?"

"What?" She looked at him, surprised: they never went out for dinner!

"I'm taking you out for dinner. Only to the club, but still, I thought it would make tonight a bit more special. We can eat in over the weekend."

"I've never gone out for dinner before; well, apart from pizza," she laughed.

He enjoyed the excitement in her face.

"It's OK, it's all perfectly safe," he said, and she laughed again. "There are some dresses up in your room, try them on, choose whichever one you like best. There are shoes too, so I expect you to come downstairs looking like a million dollars."

She looked completely surprised. Clearly she couldn't believe how much thought and effort he'd put into today – and it still wasn't over.

"Only one million?" she managed to say after a few seconds.

"OK, ten," he replied, glad she didn't seem to mind that he'd chosen clothes for her. Dressing up for a night out was not something she'd ever done – costumes for her performances didn't really count.

"How do you know my size?" she asked slowly, trying to get her brain round his thoughtfulness.

"I know your size," he answered smoothly, his eyes staying in front, focussed on where the car was going.

"I hope none of it is pink."

"No, I decided you wouldn't want to look like candyfloss."

She burst out laughing, remembering their last conversation about candyfloss – it seemed like forever ago.

MYSTY TUGGED AT the dress again, asking herself for the hundredth time if she'd chosen the right one. She wanted to look beautiful, like all the women she'd ever seen in the club and at Celeste; but they knew *how* to wear a dress, and she felt totally odd. Gym shorts, leotards, costumes, leathers she could do . . . dresses, however . . . She looked in the mirror again, and decided that where the dress clung to her was . . . where it was meant to cling, and there wasn't much she could do about it. It was 7.57pm; they were meant to be leaving at 8pm. She didn't dare keep him waiting when he'd gone to so much trouble. Neither did she want to waste any more time fretting about her clothes when she could be with him.

She slipped the white heels on, took one last fleeting glance in the mirror and headed out the door. If she looked really awful he'd send her back upstairs to change. Maybe even let her wear her smartest biker trousers instead.

She had no idea that the man who had bought them for her had had an equally confusing time trying to choose from all the colours and styles in the prom dress shop across town, and all via video-cam with Mario and Lucio, who confused him further with their input – and made the bemused shop assistant smile.

"Mysty!" She heard the call as she reached the top of the stairs. "Do you want my mother to . . ."

She paused, and everyone turned and looked up.

Oh Christ, I knew choosing the white dress was a bad idea. I should have gone for the black . . . they always wear black! And I like black! Why did I choose white?

Donny's eyes swept up from the white heels, followed the split that ran all the way up the side to the top of her thigh. He saw the way the fabric held her hips and breasts, cut away at the front to her navel. He took in the subtle make-up, her hair pinned up and held with a white flower . . . and held his breath.

She felt self-conscious, and a little out of her depth when she regarded their serious faces. Should she take the flower from her hair? Did it look childish? No one spoke as she descended the stairs, and when she reached the bottom her heart was pounding.

"If you don't like it, if you'd rather I put the black one on . . ." she began, wishing she could hide behind her hair – hide behind anything.

Donny recovered sufficiently to step forward. His stare was intense; but there was also soft light in his eyes.

"No, kitten, you definitely picked the right dress," he whispered. He took her hand from where it tugged nervously at the white cloth. "Paulo, get everyone loaded up, we'll be out in a moment."

They moved down the hall and emptied out into the street. Even Gio got up from his customary seat and followed.

"I was right, you know, you have turned into a flower. An incredibly lovely flower." He smiled gently, saw the nervousness, realised how alien this was to her. Unaware of her natural beauty, not yet sure what to do with her curves and femininity, she blushed. She'd never known how to accept compliments, but especially now, when they were delivered in such a serious voice. "I have one last gift for you; something I would like you to wear. Not just tonight. Always. But . . ." he hesitated . . . "only if you want to."

He reached into his pocket and pulled out a slim, black box, opened it. She leant closer to him and saw a bracelet comprised of three closely woven platinum chains, the initials 'DC' in diamonds in the centre. Donny took it in his fingers, slid the box into his pocket and laid it over her wrist, doing up the clasp. He lifted her hand to his lips, kissed the back of it. She wore no other jewellery, never had, and the effect of the piece with the white of her dress was stunning. "One day, I hope to give you a smaller piece of jewellery to wear forever, but until then, you'll always have me with you."

He wasn't surprised when her arms went around his neck, and he thought she was going to cry; but when she pulled back and looked up at him, she looked so happy. She had once been so desperately sad, so scared, and so alone . . . and now? Now she was safe. She still hadn't spoken, but she didn't need to – the happiness in her eyes was all he needed to see.

He did the only thing he could do to change the intensity of the mood, of the feelings stirring in his soul: he stepped back and teased her, saying, "$200 says you're asleep by 1am." He knew her, and today had been a long day – she would be tired by midnight and want to go home!

"Ha! I'll just drink lots of espressos."

"I'll tell Johnny not to let you have any."

"I see you like keeping the odds stacked unfairly in your favour, Mr Capello."

"Of course."

She glided past him and down the steps, not realising what a sight she made. He enjoyed watching her. He had never been prouder.

Lucio opened the door for her, and she slid into the waiting limo with a glance over her shoulder and a smile that Donny would never forget. So bright; so pure. And although she was surrounded by men whose trade was brutal, she remained untainted by it, like a ray of sunshine, and gave out a light that touched them all.

ON THE WAY home, at 2.30am, after she had managed to stay awake past the end of the bet, she fell asleep on his shoulder. Donny smiled to himself, watching the twinkle of diamonds on her wrist.

It had been a fantastic day.

A most perfect evening.

But his face clouded with sadness as he admired the long eyelashes against her cheek, the peacefulness of her, knowing such wellbeing could not last.

The sun doesn't shine forever.

Even in Vegas.

MYSTY WAS LOOKING forward to tonight as finally, after a very busy week, she would see Donny and the boys. Cirque, and all the different classes she went to, as well as her projects, had kept her very occupied, and it would be so good to see them.

She pulled up in the back street two blocks away from Donny's where she now parked the bike, not wanting to be seen as a regular at the house. After the dinner at the club she had gone back to being inconspicuous, not going anywhere with him, and she understood why. She never wanted to risk his life by creating a tempting target whilst indulging in the high life. Things were good, challenging and interesting, and her relative freedom allowed her to explore being herself. There wasn't anything she would change . . . except perhaps being four years older so her handsome Italian could finally take her upstairs.

She sighed as she pulled off the helmet, and let the scanner read her retina ID and her thumb print. The rather dirty, unappealing door led to the underground tunnels that ran like a rabbit warren under the streets in that area of the city. She knew her way around as the boys had shown her where to go, but didn't like the darkness . . . it was too easy to imagine things that weren't there.

She walked down the steps, for once not vaulting or rushing. She was relaxed and looking forward to a bowl of pasta, a beer, and lots of laughter.

She was so busy thinking about what was to come she didn't see the body until she was right on top of it. She instantly knew the face: it was Pepe, tall quiet Pepe, who had more sensitivity than most of them – or at least chose to show it more often. She also knew he was dead. No living person would be laying that still, in that twisted position, with their right hand cut off and an eyeball taken out. The small bullet hole in his forehead was also an indication. A thin black dribble of blood ran into his dark hair.

Mysty registered all this in less than a second, her heart stopping. The dim light didn't spare her the horror or mitigate the shock. She closed her eyes, trying to block it out, not wanting to see him, not wanting more death. Why was he lying there in the dark tunnel and not safe and alive inside the Capello stronghold? In a few seconds the world shifted, crumbled and reformed into a far less solid shape than it had been moments before. The foundations had been rocked by one bloody discovery . . . and all that it meant.

What had been removed was not lost on her: an eye and a hand – both required for scanner identifications. And Pepe had clearance everywhere . . . even Donny's room. A chill ran through her body as the implications sank in.

She stepped over the body, knowing in that single moment what was taking place: behind the door before her there was a takeover afoot. She hesitated before pressing her thumb to the pad. Instead, she went back to the body and laid her hand on Pepe's chest: it was still warm. She felt tears on her face then. But now was not the time for emotion. She had to get to Donny. It would be him they were after.

Carrying her helmet in one hand, body now alive with adrenaline, she stepped through the door after peeking round and seeing nothing but the empty tunnel that led to the surveillance and weapons rooms. And she knew that tonight she might have to change her view of weapons, for the last thing she wanted was to be ill-equipped to defend Donny. She felt bile rise in her throat at the thought of him injured . . . or worse.

She crept forward, and reaching the door that led up to the ground-floor rooms, she slipped through.

"Hello? Yes, they're all secure. Made a mess in the surveillance room . . . shot out quite a bit, so that's inoperable at the moment . . . yes . . . for fuck's sake, it's not a walk in the park! They had guns, we had to shoot back . . . no . . . Paulo's not among the ones we have locked up, but there are others I know you'll want for a little *special treatment* . . . yes . . . well, just hurry the hell up. I won't be comfortable until the bastard's dead, alright? . . . Yeah, I'll let you know if anything happens, just *do what you have to do*."

She held her breath, rooted to the spot in the middle of the corridor. It wasn't a voice she recognised, and it had been speaking Italian with an accent she wasn't familiar with . . . but she grasped every horrible word of it.

A man dressed in black combat gear appeared from one of the lounge rooms, and she saw the gun immediately, her stomach turning over a couple of times as she realised how unprotected she was. She had biker leathers, a helmet . . . and her wits. But if she could just get close enough, she could deal with him, regardless of the gun.

"Hey, how's it going?" She said the words with as much friendliness as she could, trying to sound relaxed, and strolled forward as though she had just come through the door. She shook out her hair so it fell over her shoulders, covertly watching as his head snapped round. He instinctively tightened his grip on the gun but resisted raising it. She saw his face, but did not recognise it. "You new? I haven't seen you here before?" She said it with a little smile, a smile of invitation and interest. She was three steps away from him.

He smiled a slow smile in return. *Who is this foxy little thing*? "Yeah, I'm new. Do I get a special welcome, *bella*?" he smirked. His eyes feasted on her hair, the young, beautiful face, her curves under the leathers . . . and she let him; she wanted him to.

"Of course you do," she purred, her voice luring him to think she was up for a rather more intimate greeting.

He scanned her body again, his eyes resting on her breasts.

She was two steps away from him.

The arm holding the gun dropped a fraction, and her hand shot out and took hold of it, pinning it against the wall whilst with her other hand she brought her bike helmet up and smacked him round the face. She watched the glimmer of surprise just before impact, it being too late for him to move, and she paused for a split second before then backhanding him with the helmet. This time he crumpled. His face was a mess. Plenty of it was broken, and blood started to appear in the wounds. From the way he lay, he wasn't going far. One more thwack to the head and he was out cold. She pulled the gun away, slipped the strap over her head and dragged him into the room from where he'd appeared, leaving him behind the sofa where he would be obscured if someone glanced into the room.

God, he was heavy, and breathing hard from the effort, she went to the door and brought the gun up front, listening. Leaving her helmet just inside the door, she eased along the corridor. She saw most of the doors were open, including the one to the gun room. She carefully checked there was no one in there and then crept along, surprised there weren't more men down there . . . and then found one. It was a hard call as to who was more surprised.

Luckily, she was always going to be quicker, and her hand lashed out and hit him hard in the throat, compressing his windpipe and instantly making him choke, knowing it was painful, and not a move to be used at will – something she'd learned from her training with Choi; but this wasn't usual fighting, it was survival. Now, she meant to hurt, and she wanted to.

Her knee went into his groin. And then she grasped his hair as he lurched forward, bringing her knee up hard into his face. He fell choking to the floor, hands going to his throat and groin, his grunt and struggle for air the only sound. She paused for a second, and then leaned down and smacked the butt end of the gun into his head. She could have just pulled the trigger and blown his head off, but she couldn't quite bring herself to do so, even as adrenaline, and now rage, pounded fast and loud in her veins; besides she didn't want to alert anyone to her presence. But she couldn't take the risk of this intruder recovering too soon and coming after her. This was not playing fair: this was invasion; this was war.

She watched for a second, listened as he attempted to draw breath into his lungs through his shattered throat. She then pulled the earpiece from him and put it in her own ear, wishing she'd thought to do it with the first guy. She might as well know what was going on.

Standing up straight she continued on her hunt, as swiftly and silently as she could, gun poised, eyes darting everywhere, into every shadow, every space. She found a locked door – which was unusual as most were open or ajar – and this one showed on the keypad that it was locked . . . but a bullet had been put into it to keep it jammed and unopenable.

A sudden thought shot through her mind.

"Guys!" she whispered as loudly as she dared, conscious of the fact she was in the corridor with the stairs not that far away, and if someone suddenly appeared, she had no cover.

"Mysty?"

She heard a scuffle as bodies moved across the room and then someone leant against the door, obviously trying to get as close as possible. She knew that voice, knew it from him teasing her a thousand times and trying to persuade her to explain her firewall programming.

"Fabio, what happened?"

"Guys in black appeared, guns blazing, took over the downstairs. We're locked in, but they're after Donny. You gotta get out of here, kiddo, these guys mean business . . . we're all dead men."

Like hell she would clear off out of there. With Donny at risk? And so many other lives at stake?

"Like fuck I'm leaving! Is there any way I can get the door open?" she hissed.

"It's designed so that only we can get in here, but we're locked in here, and I heard them put a bullet in it."

She paused, thinking."Is there a panel on your side?"

"Yes, but–"

"It's better than nothing. Hold on." She hurried back along the corridor, jumping over the second body, grabbing a small tool kit from the armoury and running back. It was kit for fixing computers, and the parts were small. She crouched down and poked them under the door. "Look down. Have you got them?"

"Yes . . . thank you."

She could hear other hushed voices, seven or eight of them perhaps. If she could free them it would swing the balance in their favour.

"Thank me when you get the bloody door open, Fabio. And hurry up, I could probably do with a hand shortly."

She didn't know her terse reply made a number of the people on the wrong side of the door smile.

"Mysty, what are you planning?"

She was already eyeing the rest of the corridor, and stood with her back to the door.

"When I've worked that out, I'll let you know. Get to work, the clock's ticking."

She then worked her way along the corridor, shutting doors and locking them, making it harder for any rogue individuals to hide . . . unless they were still carrying Pepe's hand or eye.

At the surveillance room door she paused. Did she really want to see this? She knew she didn't, but she had to see it, had to know, had to know how real the threat was. She glanced around once more: everything around her was perfectly still. She pushed open the door.

A room she had spent many happy hours in, joking, learning how to work the systems, watching people, was now largely without lights as they had been shot out, which was a mercy, as it hid a great deal of the gore. Screens mangled by bullets were dark, reduced to piles of plastic and glass. Blood dripped from the desks onto the floor where there was a pool of slick blackness that merged with the shadows. She could see it gleaming, saw that it was dark red, not black. She felt sick, felt memories rise up and almost claim her, almost make her run for the door. But she forced herself to finish looking. To confront the proof of the many-headed monster that had invaded this home.

One body had fallen to the floor, an arm outstretched as if in supplication, and the angle of the arm and head told her they were dead. The men in combat gear would have made sure of that. Another was thrown back in his chair, the wires still running to his headset. She couldn't see any faces, thank God. Someone would had pressed the alarm button, but then have been quickly overwhelmed, and now everything – all the security and cameras – were rendered useless until someone repaired the control units in this room.

She turned away and headed up the stairs, dropping down and creeping up step by step, her gun ready, accepting she really might have to pull the trigger. But these were men who knew death and deserved it . . . what she had just seen confirmed that.

She peeked over the top of the stairs, saw the polished wood floor that ran the entire length of the hall from the front door.

And then she saw Giovanni. The pool of blood around him was beautifully smooth, like someone had emptied a large pot of red paint across the floor. Her eyes widened in horror, her body unconsciously rising up to see him, not wanting to believe what her eyes were telling her. The old man who'd always had a smile for her, who everyone treated like an uncle, the guardian of the front door . . . was dead. Bullets had cut into the cloth of his suit and the black fabric was stained with red, his jacket open as he lay on his back, the white of his shirt splattered too. The cream-painted walls of the hall were also decorated with his blood, the ghastly patterns testament to the violence of his death. The only blessing was that his face was turned away, so she could not see the expression of his last moments as one of the living.

She wanted to be sick. It felt like one of the many nightmares that haunted her, and she felt herself sliding back . . . but a sudden voice snapped her back with a jolt.

"Hey, you heard from downstairs?"

She ducked down instantly, the voice so loud, so close. She held her breath, prayed the stairs didn't creak.

"No, I bet they've got their feet up already."

"Lazy bastards. Bet you any money they complain we take too long."

"Sure wish the boss would hurry up, though. Until Capello's dead, my finger ain't leaving my trigger."

"You heard any shots yet?"

"Nope. Then again, you know how the boss feels about Capello . . . might just take his knees out or something first. Make it hurt. Until the boss walks outta his room, it ain't finished."

Mysty contemplated launching herself from her hiding place at hearing mention of Donny, but knew from the angle, and the fact there were at least four of them, she would instantly be gunned down – and then all would be lost.

She crept back down the stairs, her mind trying to grasp what she had heard. *Torture* Donny? Wasn't killing him enough? Who were these people and why did they want him? At least she now knew where Donny was: in his rooms.

Within moments she formulated a plan. There was only one other way into the room, but it was rather difficult for the very fact that the windows were so damned strong, designed, like the doors, to be safeguards, to not be broken in from the outside.

She got to the corridor and bent down by the door.

"Fabio!"

"Kiddo? What's happening?"

"Whoever they are, they're in with Donny, in his room, and they're going to kill him." Her heart ached and her voice cracked with the words. "Are there any explosives in the gun room?"

"Erm . . . probably. I'm not too sure . . . I'm a satellite boy, not a gunner."

"Shit. Do you know where Paulo is?"

"He was out on a visit – thank God."

"How are you getting on in there?"

"We've broken into the control panel, but it's completely disabled."

Mysty got up and left without another word, going to the gun room and properly investigating it with desperate need rather than scant attention and huge distaste. In a box, she found what she wanted. She also found plastic explosives in a locked cupboard which her thumbprint allowed her to open. She grabbed a bag from the rails where the protective clothes were – the room was literally full of anything you might need to attack or kill in any terrain, any situation – and saw racks of automatic weapons. She felt a shudder run through her, but then looked at them with new appreciation: *what could take a life could also save a life.*

She knew the glass in Donny's room was bulletproof, but there were bullets . . . and then there were big fat awful bullets that could rip into the side of an armoured truck like it was paper – and those might be what she needed.

She shoved the explosives in the bag, took detonators too, knowing how to work them – it was amazing the things you learnt over games of poker when the bets were a bit slow and you were playing with five guys who liked showing off how much they knew *and* had drunk a few beers to loosen their tongues. She grabbed rope and then one of the automatics and ammunition, dropping the one she had taken off the guy in the corridor. It was heavy, really heavy, but she loaded it up with the round of clips and headed for the door, putting the strap over her head like before. She could do this; she had to do this.

Almost out of the door she paused and picked up a smaller gun – a mean-looking automatic pistol. She knew how to use this one, too, as it was the same as the one Paulo carried on him.

Pulling the door shut, she retrieved her helmet, wanting whatever protection she could get. Then walking back the other way towards the stairs, she got to the body in the corridor and paused, looking down. Still out of it. She kicked him. Got no reaction. She walked on. Hiding in the surveillance room she opened a channel on the earpiece and let off two shots, closed it and waited.

Sure enough, ten seconds later there were footsteps on the stairs. Plenty of them. She saw them run past with guns. Then pulling on her helmet and her gloves, she slipped out and up the stairs, finding it a little harder with the weight on her back. She made it past the body of Gio, avoiding the blood, and out of the front door before two pairs of footsteps were heard at the top of the stairs.

Her stolen earpiece crackled and she heard, "Did you just hear the front door?"

She held her breath, body pressed against the door, praying they didn't open it, praying they weren't smart enough to have a car out front waiting to shoot her.

"Maybe it was Giovanni's ghost finally getting off his ass and leaving."

They laughed at their own joke; she wanted to punch them for their disrespect.

"Better let the boss know we've got company."

"Yeah. Keep your eyes open. I'll go check upstairs again. How long till the next team arrives?"

"Should be any time soon."

She didn't mind that they knew someone was about. It meant they were distracted searching inside. Mysty jumped up onto the railing that ran along the steps and caught hold of the top of the stonework around the doorway.

Trust Donny to be in the back of the house.

She kept climbing, and had just reached the third floor when she saw a car sweep around the bend at the end of the road at high speed. She looked down at the number plate – *shit*! It was Paulo returning with one of the drivers. No doubt rather worried when he'd got no response from Donny, the surveillance boys, or anyone . . .

She pulled out the pistol from inside her jacket, flicked the safety off and reached out with one arm – and shot in front of the car. She had no other way of warning him. If someone shot at him, at least he'd know there was a threat, and not just walk through the front door and end up like Gio.

The brakes were slammed on. Then the car was reversed back up the street to a safer distance. She saw one window open slightly, put the gun inside her jacket and tried to wave. She needed to get to the roof. And her arm was going to give way.

She prayed one of them had seen her and realised she'd fired the shot, and why, and why the hell she was climbing up the building.

The gun was heavy, so heavy, and she finally clambered up onto the tiles, went to the other side of the roof and looked down. Thank God she wasn't afraid of heights. Trying to ignore the slight tremor in her hands, horribly afraid she was going to hear a voice in her ear telling her the worst had happened, she tied the rope around the chimney stack. It was an old but well-kept house, and the chimney, although a defunct feature, was sturdy all the same. She began working her way down, glad of the biker gloves or her hands would have been badly chafed, listening to the black combat boys trying to work out what was happening after hearing the gunshot outside.

She kept her ears open, wondering what Paulo would do. He would probably go in through the tunnels like she had. And see Pepe.

At the balcony on the second floor she paused and dropped the excess rope, letting it stay in a pile. She then pulled out the plastic explosives and stuck in the detonator sticks. She looked down. Through the flooring of the balcony she could see the lights on in the room where Donny was. *Let him live; please let him live.*

She climbed over the edge of the balcony, after swapping the gun for the plastic explosives, and dangled over, still out of sight from the light that spilled from the window.

Peering through the blinds into the TV room, she was relieved to see Donny, and her heart sang that he was still alive; but he had a gun to his head and she eyed the man holding it, taking in his size, his age – he looked older than Donny – and his weathered, harsh face. She pulled out one of the explosives, and slowly moved sideways to fix it to the window of the next room, where his desk was, wincing at the low thump it made. And then she moved back to the other window, attaching an identical device to the glass, in case the first didn't detonate.

She saw both men freeze at the sound of the thumps on the window behind the blinds. Saw the flicker of fear – or was it hope? – on Donny's face. But he remained still.

"WHAT WAS THAT?" the man with the gun said.

"Could have been a bird, or a bat. They often fly at the windows – the light and the glass confuses them," Donny answered calmly, silently praying for a miracle.

The hold on the gun didn't falter, and the eyes that stared at him were full of hate.

Where the fuck is Paulo?

"By the time I've finished with this place, there won't be any windows. Your time is finished Capello. And your finish is long overdue."

Donny was tired of the man's words. It had been a tedious, drawn-out half-hour of verbal assault, as he'd attempted to get passwords and business information from him that would aid the takeover; but Donny hadn't felt in a giving mood. He knew Ericson wanted the pleasure of killing him alone so he could emerge victorious from a one-on-one with Donny Capello, but also that he wasn't really up to beating the shit out of him to get the answers he wanted. He wondered several times why he had been chosen to do the interrogating, as there was no doubt who was the superior specimen, both mentally and physically: Donny was younger, stronger, wiser; however, all that mattered very little when a bullet would silence him forever in a single second.

Although he'd faced death numerous times before, none felt as real as this threat. Today there was no get out, no possibility of escape. It was sobering really. This could be it. In a few seconds, he would be nothing. A life finished. And the idea of not being in charge, or what would happen to those he cared for and lived with . . . Thank goodness his mother had gone to stay with Don Salvadore, and that Mysty would be warned to come nowhere near the house. His heart ached when he thought of her; of the evening they'd had planned.

The muzzle was moved forward so it pressed into his forehead, and he knew by the time he'd snatched a hand up to push it away the bullet would already be passing through his brain.

"Won't you beg me for your life, Capello? I might be feeling generous," Ericson smirked, and Donny wanted to smash the look from his face.

"I don't beg."

"How about I get your little blonde number in here . . . maybe she'll beg me for your life?"

Donny felt a tremour of fear pass through his gut. How did they know about Mysty? Not for himself, but because the idea that even after he was dead she might be targeted, and thoughts of the horrors they might put her through before finally killing her, were too much to bear.

"She doesn't beg either."

"She will by the time I've finished with her. She'll beg me to kill her. She's young isn't she, Capello? And very pretty, I hear. I bet she's nice and tight, ain't she? And she's fit so I hear, so she'll give you a good ride, I'm sure. Do you think she'll do the same for me? She must be rather good to keep you so interested."

"She'd spit on you and pull the trigger herself rather than let you touch her," Donny told him with a confidence that infuriated the man in front of him, whose demeanour spoke of a victory not yet secured.

"Feisty? I like that. I'll have my boys hunt her down after I've finished with you. Keep her for a while, until I'm tired of her. Show her what a real man is."

Donny held his fists down by his sides.

At the sound of the first bullet, they both looked round, and both pairs of eyes focussed on the impact mark of the slug into the glass. They then saw the strange object on the outside of the window. Donny forced his consciousness into a higher gear, trying to work out what was happening. More bullets hit the window, every one making a huge thud into the glass, which turned white-grey under the force but still held. A ring of bullets then circled the object and he realised exactly what it was.

He looked at the guy with the gun, saw the fearful surprise. The gun was still against his head, however, so he paused, knowing what was going to happen next. But so did Ericson. His mouth opened to tell Donny to move away just as the world exploded, and noise, heat, air and glass hurtled through into the room at the mercy of raging elemental physics. There followed several seconds of complete chaos, and all of Donny's senses were assaulted as he was thrown backwards; but as he fell, he saw a pair of feet appear through the swirling mess of smoke and flame, and to his utter and eternal disbelief, a slender black shape in bike leathers emerged. Colliding with the coffee table as he hit the floor, in the most inelegant landing of his life. His only thought was of her: *his miracle.*

He righted himself and lunged forward through the debris to look for her, not thinking about himself. He saw her leaning over the man on the floor, one knee on his chest, a gun pointing at his head. He felt weak with relief, with amazement; but horror too: *Why is she here? She shouldn't be here!* She reached up, pulled off her helmet and dropped it on the floor. The man beneath her was dazed, coughing – and not fighting her.

Looking around, she saw Donny, and felt a sweet dizzy moment of joy, her heart beating so hard inside her chest it hurt. He was alive.

"*Jesus Christ*," he breathed, unable to move for a second. It had never felt so good to be alive.

She kicked Ericson's gun across the floor to him and he picked it up, attempted to stand up, to go to her, but he felt unsteady, like a ragdoll pulled apart and re-sown hurriedly. He crawled instead, wanting to be near her, not wanting her to be alone with a would-be killer.

He had almost made it to her when a bang made him turn, and she instinctively raised her gun and fired at the figures in black combat gear coming through the door.

Six shots later there was silence.

They all slumped, falling backwards and downwards, and she stared in the aftermath of the noise, her gun dropping. She felt her body go weak.

Donny watched her face pale, and then looked back at where she'd fired, saw the bodies, and knew what was wrong. He saw them move slightly. He couldn't see any blood on heads or faces. They were disabled and bleeding but not dead.

He went to her, put an arm around her, and she slumped down in shock.

"Oh God. I shot them. Did I kill them?" Her horrified voice was that of a frightened child.

"No, no, you didn't kill them, you did nothing wrong. It was us or them, and you'll be OK, I promise."

It was then that the man Mysty had pinned to the floor drew in a huge breath, his face red and contorted as he started thrashing and groaning on the floor.

"What's wrong with him?" she asked in confusion.

The man put one hand on his throat, the other on his chest, his mouth trying to shape words that wouldn't come.

"A heart attack . . ." Donny muttered.

She instantly dropped to her knees and went through his pockets, wrenched open his jacket and searched until she found a small bottle of pills and opened it. Donny hesitated in telling her there was little point, he was a dead man anyway. Perhaps it would be better dying at nature's hand rather than Donny Capello's? After attempting to get the man to swallow a couple of the pills, she seemed to know, and hung her head. She then went back to pointing her gun at the dying man's head. Just in case he was faking.

Donny quickly checked the three prone men for weapons, removed everything from them, including their comms equipment, and went to the door. They would be on the move soon enough, and he would happily have put a bullet in each of their skulls but for Mysty. He didn't want her to see him do that.

He listened, closed the door, and strode back to her. Her knee was still on the man's chest, but the gun was lowered. He was still. She was still. Her eyes were as huge as saucers in her pale face.

He took her arm and pulled her up, realising she was going into shock. But those memories, and this, would drown her and make her vulnerable. She had to come back to him. He forced her to look at him, his hands on her face, breaking the awful stare.

"Mysty." He felt so many things in that moment, wanted to say so many things, but he had to finish this and make them safe. "I want you to stay here." He eased her down onto the floor behind the sofa as gently as he could, going down with her. "You're going to stay here until I come back. I'm going to check on everything and make it safe. If anyone who isn't me or Paulo comes through that door, you shoot them . . . as much as I know you don't want to, *you have to shoot them for me*? Promise?"

He shook her slightly until she responded, her eyes going to look at the gun he pressed into her hand, wrapping fingers round so one was on the trigger. She nodded vaguely, her eyes rolling up to his, so blue in the pale of her skin.

"Gio's dead, Donny. He's full of holes . . . there's blood everywhere. Don't slip. In the hallway. And the guys in the surveillance room. And Pepe's in the tunnel, with his hand cut off and his eye . . ." He realised she wasn't rambling, but relaying what she had seen. He listened carefully as she continued. "Paulo arrived outside, in a car, so I shot in front of the car to make him stop or they'd have got him too. Fabio and some others are locked in a room downstairs. There were four men in the hall, Donny, not three. . ." She glanced at the men on the floor. "Please be careful."

"I will. I promise. I'll be back soon. Keep your head down and the gun close."

He pressed a kiss to her temple, briefly, as much for him as for her, wanting to reassure her, feeling her trembling beneath his hand, underlining how urgent his next task was.

Every part of him knew this was life and death. A fresh rush of adrenaline kicked in, and the cold, hard rage of the predator in him that had seen him through so much, took over. Moments ago, he had been facing death; now he had the chance to salvage his invaded home and reclaim his life, in every way.

Donny got up, satisfied she was low to the floor and as safe as she could be for now. One by one he dragged the injured men through the door and into the corridor, and Ericson too. They would all be dealt with, but now he needed to contact Paulo. His earpiece had been removed and crushed under Ericson's foot, and he had to locate another. He closed the door, securing Mysty inside the room.

He made his way quietly down the hallway, and around Giovanni's body, curbing the impulse to drop to his knees and mourn. Now was not the time. Gio would understand.

Creeping down the stairs with gun poised, he reached the bottom step, but unable to see left or right, he shifted, leaning so that he could scan the corridor.

The step creaked.

Fuck.

He heard a click as a gun was readied.

Donny knew it was fifty-fifty; friend or foe. His gun firmly in his hand, he took a step . . .

A figure swung around and for the second time that day a muzzle was pointed at his forehead; but abruptly it was pulled up and he saw Paulo's hardened face then break into a grin. Relief ran through him as they embraced, a nervous laugh breaking the silence, guns still raised in defence over each other's shoulders.

"Jesus, Donny, I almost had you." Paulo was not a little shaken at how close he'd come to killing his own boss.

"I knew it was you," Donny scoffed, trying to take the edge off the intensity of the moment.

Mario, Lucio and Giuseppe stepped out of one of the room, and behind them a further ten or so gathered; thanks to Mysty having the sense to slide the toolkit under the door, they'd eventually managed to get the door open.

"What's the count? I know Gio is dead." He sighed deeply.

"Five lost in the surveillance room. Pepe is outside in the tunnel . . . he . . . was how they got in."

Donny nodded. He knew. And he felt deeply saddened that it had been Mysty who found him.

"How in God's name are you even *alive*? I thought they had you." Paulo then said, thinking the unthinkable, thinking about their lost comrades too.

They stood silently for a long moment, and then Fabio stepped forwards and asked, "Is Mysty OK, boss? She was here . . . she . . ."

What would they say when he told them what she'd done?

"I'll tell you what happened later, but suffice to say, whoever told her how to use plastic explosives, I'm really fucking glad you did . . ." Donny paused, not wanting to go over any of it just then, but saw their astonished faces. "There are four men upstairs, one dead from a heart attack, but the others need dealing with. Are there any more?"

"We found one trying to get out through the tunnels but he's a little past conversation now. There was another two with serious head injuries

– I'm guessing Mysty dealt with them when she came in – but they've been moved," Mario answered. "She got three of them?"

"After blowing up my windows and flying in to stop Ericson putting a bullet in my head, yes. Not dead though; just seriously injured and disarmed. I want them taken care of, Paulo." Paulo nodded. Like the others, he was grateful to be alive, unharmed, and ready to start reasserting Capello dominance. "And Paulo . . ." Donny paused, half-turned to go back up the stairs, "I'm not sure you know, but it was Mysty who shot at your car to stop you coming into the house."

There was another moment of silence, everyone realising just how much they had to thank her for. There were no words. It was one thing to feel the euphoria of being alive, but to be humbled by the bravery of the person responsible for making it so was another.

"Start getting the mess cleaned up," Donny then instructed. "Get the bodies to the undertakers – the families can be notified in the morning. Get the surveillance room back up and systems online as best you can – call for back up from our boys in Langton. No one is going to sleep tonight until we've secured this place. Let's go."

They prepared to move.

"One more thing," Donny said, and they paused as one. "I'm going to take Mysty upstairs where she'll stay tonight while we get everything sorted. I'll be back down as soon as I'm sure she's OK. I don't want her to hear any gunshots or screams or see any blood. Clear?"

"Clear," they repeated.

Three of the men disappeared up the stairs with guns poised, as silent as panthers in the night. Paulo and several of the others remained in the hallway as watchmen. The rest made their way to the surveillance room.

Donny went in to Mysty. The destruction in the room was significant, but it was a small price to pay.

"Mysty?"

"I'm here."

It was a whisper, but he heard it, and he went to her and knelt down, taking the gun from her hand and tossing it away. Tears had run down her face, making tracks in the dust. She was still very pale, but still the most beautiful creature he had ever seen, and the most precious.

"I'm going to take you upstairs. You can have a long bath and a rest while we get everything tidied up," he said softly.

She wasn't up to arguing and only flinched slightly when he took off his tie and tied it over her eyes, wanting to blindfold her to the sights outside the room. She looked so terribly vulnerable in that moment, and his heart swelled with tenderness as she put her arms around his neck, trusting him, despite everything. He picked her up, one arm round her back, one under her knees.

Mario led the way upstairs after exchanged looks confirmed it was clear; Lucio followed behind.

Donny carried her into his bedroom, saddened that he was taking her there now, not as an excited young woman in love, but as a frightened girl who had again, somehow, defied all odds to save his life – their lives.

He laid her on the bed, sat next to her and removed the blindfold. He didn't bother with lights; the darkness was somehow calming. She looked at him with eyes that begged him to make it all better. He wished he could; wished he could take away what she'd had to do and what she'd seen.

"Is everyone downstairs OK?" she asked slowly, fearfully.

"They're all fine. Paulo too."

"I didn't kill them, did I?" she asked again.

"No, you just winged them."

"I feel so cold."

It was shock, he knew, and he was not surprised.

"Why don't you have a hot bath and then curl up in bed – whatever makes you feel better – but I want you to stay in this room tonight. I need to go and help straighten everything out downstairs, but I'll be back, and when I do, I want to find you here waiting for me, alright? Don't go anywhere."

"Yes." Followed by a shaky nod of the head.

"Good girl. Do you need anything? Are you hungry?" He leant down and kissed her forehead, and for a long moment she clung to him, making it harder for him to force himself to let go. She shook her head. "I'll come up later," he said, wanting to stay and comfort her, but aware of what awaited downstairs and the orders he would have to give.

She nodded again and released her hold.

But if the world thought Donny Capello had gone soft, they were about to find out just how wrong they were. Having something – someone – to live for made a man more dangerous than any other being on Earth.

DONNY WALKED THROUGH the front door at 2am, quite literally feeling like death. The last four hours had been spent on a hunting mission through the city, leaving rooms and doorways stained with blood. Wives, girlfriends and mothers screamed as they watched their men die. Some made it into the street or their garden or a back street, but they were all shot down as a stark warning to the living, a cull of all that was connected with Ericson, reminding those left what it was to fail against Donny Capello.

He knew there had been six teams out – he had been with Paulo and his closest boys – and the body count was rising. It wasn't the first time, nor would it be the last, but it had been the first for a very long time – years, in fact. Was that why it felt so bad? Or because he knew the ending of lives also represented the ending of something that meant more to him than riches, than his house, his cars – any of it?

He was relieved to find Gio gone from the hall floor, the dark polished wood absorbing most of the stain, but he knew the whole area would have to be redone, a new watcher found for the front door. One of the many ways that life would change in the Capello household, but not the most significant . . . one particular way was weighing him down like lead through his veins, making every step harder to take.

Continuing down to the basement, he could see progress had been made in the clean-up, and all the camera screens but two were working, the remaining satellite boys helping the teams still out track down their prey. There was a small cheer as the they saw him return to their midst, and he managed to put a smile on his face. It was a relief to be alive.

"Mysty OK?" he asked, surveying the room.

"Not a sound," Giuseppe replied.

"Anything else I need to know?" he asked as Paulo walked over to him.

"The two Mysty dealt with down here – they're alive and awake. One is very messed up. You want me to deal with them like the rest?"

"Yes. Find out who they are and have their bodies delivered back to their families." Donny looked round at Giuseppe, not wanting to open his mouth and say the words, but he didn't have a choice. "Giuseppe, book a flight for Mysty tomorrow, late afternoon, going to LA. One way. Book her into a hotel, nothing too flashy. And get a call put through to Francois for me. I know it's late, but he'll take it if he knows who's calling."

Giuseppe stared at Donny for long seconds, and then looked down and started punching details into his computer, not asking questions.

"*LA*?" Mario finally said, his voice barely audible, asking the question for the entire room.

Everyone stopped what they were doing and looked at Donny, apprehension stamped on every face. Paulo stood quietly behind his boss, knowing they'd discussed this in the car, and Donny looked sadly at the shot-up comms desk, reminding himself why he was doing this.

"Mysty's leaving. It's not safe here. Last night Ericson made threats against her, threats because of association with me, with us. I don't need to tell you what kind they were, but you know as well as I do that they weren't pretty. I know Ericson is dead, but we have no way of knowing who else is out there . . ." He turned and faced the room, seeing on each face a sadness that mirrored his own. "She fights for us, and we trust her, but she's not one of us. She's not a killer. She never will be and she doesn't want to be. And I have no right to endanger her by keeping her here with us any longer. Last night proved that. I don't think any of us want it on our conscience that she got tortured, raped or killed because . . . because we wanted her to stay."

It was a brutal truth that each one of them believed but didn't want to accept. No one moved or spoke. They had all been to glad to survive, to celebrate their victory despite their sad losses, but this was the last thing they wanted. Any sense of elation was now shot down like spring flowers killed by an unexpected frost.

"She has to go now, while she has a chance at a life away from this," he continued, and waved a hand at the dried blood and broken glass. "If, one day, someone gets lucky coming for me, I don't want them going after her and no one being here to even warn her. She deserves better than a life in the shadows because of us, so no one is to argue with me, or encourage her to argue because I'm really not in the mood to hear it."

He glared at everyone, utterly distraught at the idea of losing her, and not because she didn't love him, or he her, but because of this world of guns and men and power and money; because he was so deep in it that nothing could get him out now. He had to accept that or it would cost him more than he wished to even think about. God knew he'd seen enough blood. None of it would be hers if he had breath left in his body.

He stepped back in the vacuum of silence and took the earpiece offered to him by Giuseppe.

"Francois?"

"Donny, lucky for you I wasn't in bed!" The friendly jovial voice he knew so well.

"I appreciate you taking the call, Franny, really."

"I'm assuming it's fairly urgent. I know you're usually a decent man who leaves business to at least ten, and after a delicious breakfast and a good coffee. What can I do for you?"

There was genuine concern under the layer of friendly banter. Franny was always reliable, always ready to do what had to be done – two of the many reasons they got on so well and trusted each other. Donny could think of no one better for the responsibility he was preparing to entrust him with.

"I need a favour. Quite an important one."

"I think I owe you more than a few, Donny. Whatever it is, just say."

"There's someone I need to be safe. I'm sending her to LA." Donny said that purposefully. Knew Franny had lost his first wife to gunmen; knew he would be sympathetic.

"I didn't know you were . . . with someone?"

"I'm not. She's . . . well . . ." Donny was a little past cogent explanation.

"I get it. Too goddamned precious to risk losing. OK. When is she arriving?"

Donny let himself relax a little, glad Franny understood. It somehow made everything feel that much less impossible hearing that simple acceptance; made things feel just a fraction simpler than the complicated mess they really were.

"This evening. I'm putting her on a plane late afternoon. I shall send her stuff after her. She's just finished school and is about to go to college, but she's fourteen, and too smart for her own good, really, so she's years ahead of her age group. She's . . . pretty tough, and doesn't need babysitting; but I want to know someone's keeping an eye on her while she's not in my city. I also want her bike plates flagged as an Untouchable to the boys in blue. Apart from that, she'll take care of herself."

There was a long silence.

"What has happened to make you send her away? Doesn't sound like you want to."

That was Franny: gone 2am and still as sharp as the stiletto knife that lived in Donny's jacket pocket.

"I was seconds away from getting a bullet in my head this evening. Ericson decided to try a takeover. Thanks to her, he failed." Donny didn't want to go into long explanations; it was all Franny needed to know for now.

"Thanks to her? Fuck me, Donny, are you sending some assassin to take me out?" Disbelief there may have been from his LA brother-in-arms, but it was also a subtle way of asking for more information.

"No, Franny, she didn't kill anyone, just dealt with everything as she had to. Saved a hell of a lot of us, including me. Even tried giving Ericson his tablets when he started having a heart attack – though he was a dead man the moment his gun pointed away from my head."

"I think this is a story I want told in more detail."

"No problem. But not at this moment."

"You want me to find her accommodation?"

"I'll have a hotel booked for her for tonight, but if you know somewhere out of the way, not flashy, not big . . . and she'll insist on paying the rent herself."

"You not paying her way, Donny? She's your girl, right? Don't tell me you're turning mean in your old age?"

"Hell, I'd pay everything that needed paying if she'd let me, but she's independent like that. She's had a job since she was ten."

There was a long pause as Franny digested this.

"I can't wait for her to step off that plane. This is going to be interesting."

"Yeah, well, just remember two things: one – she's mine and she knows it; and two – she's got an attitude like you wouldn't believe when she's pissed off, and she's going to be *very* pissed off, so she might be a little . . . prickly to start with. I haven't even told her she's going yet. I might survive, though it'll be a close-run thing." Donny heard a snort of laughter. Understandable. Franny didn't know the whole story. But it was hard to hear. "Franny, this is going to be one of the hardest things I've ever had to do."

"I hear you, Donny. Seems like life might just get a whole lot more interesting in LA. But you have my word: she'll be safe."

Franny was married and had kids of his own, and that was the reason why Donny trusted him, despite the nights out when his wedding ring was ignored.

"She's beautiful, Franny, so make sure people understand that it's hands off across the board. She's already been attacked a couple of times, and I don't want that happening again."

"I get it. A few broken legs here and there – job done. You let me know the plane time and I'll pick her up – that OK? Make sure she knows she's among friends."

"Sure. I'll give you a call later today, about midday, tell you what happened tonight. There'll be a hell of a lot in the news, no doubt." Donny rubbed his eyes, imagining the headlines, knowing he was going to have to have a big chat with the police chief tomorrow, too, to make sure no one panicked.

"A bad one, huh?" Franny knew those.

"Yeah, but luckily most of us are still here."

"That's good to hear, Donny. Now, go tell that girl of yours she's coming to the best city on the planet."

Donny smiled, despite a big chunk of him not wanting to. Franny was a real friend; a brother in the trade; had walked the same road of blood and bullets to get to the top of the tree on his own turf. Nothing would make them turn on each other, neither would they ever have need to. They could respect each other from their own city kingdoms.

"Good to talk, Franny. I'll call you midday, as I said."

"Sure, Donny, good luck."

"Yeah. I need it."

Luck and courage. She was not going to be happy. In fact, he had a feeling that his estimation of 'very pissed off' was going to be an understatement.

DONNY PAUSED OUTSIDE his room, knowing nothing in his life had prepared him for this conversation. He then opened the door and looked towards the bed, hoping she would be asleep.

She was lying on her side facing away from him, long legs stretched out on the dark green satin coverlet, wearing a black shirt he recognised as one of his own.

He closed the door and it made a soft click. Instantly she stirred, turned and look at him. The fear was still there.

He slowly walked over to her and sat down beside her, pushed his shoes off. She shifted to make room and he leaned back against the pillows.

She sat up, curled her legs under her and watched him, the light from the bedside lamp shining through her hair.

"I'm disappointed my shirt looks better on you than it ever has on me."

"I . . . everything smelt of smoke and . . . my leathers are ruined. I didn't think you'd mind."

"No, not at all. How do you feel?"

"I don't know. I can hardly believe it all happened."

"No." He took hold of her hand and held it gently. "I thought I knew what you were capable of after that shooting outside the club; but tonight, you proved just how wrong I was."

"What else was I supposed to do?"

"I know, kitten. You seem to have a habit of saving my life."

"Guess I just can't imagine life without you in it."

He felt his heart squeeze. Soon she would have to.

"I'm sorry you saw what you did tonight, and I'm even more sorry you were put at risk."

"I accepted the risk, Donny, please don't worry about me."

He shut his eyes, knowing he was about to cause both of them a great deal more distress than the scenes they had witnessed tonight.

"But I do. I do very much, which is why . . . Mysty, kitten, you can't stay here. I'm . . . I'm sending you somewhere safer."

He had anticipated the lurch of her body and his hand tightened around hers, always surprised at how strong she was.

"*No!*" She rose up like a wild animal, desperately trying to wrench her hand away, but he held on, trying to grab her to hold her still. "*I won't go! It's not fair! I don't want to leave you! How can you send me away?*"

"Because . . ." He finally getting a hold of her as she bucked and flailed to escape. The accusation in her voice cut him to the heart. He was already hurting at what he had to do, what he would lose. "Because tonight you almost got *killed* because you got involved in my world! Because you took insane risks to save *my life!*"

"*And I'd do it all again*!"

"*But you shouldn't have to*! Tonight I heard threats made against you because of your association with me! I watched you swing through a fireball at an armed gunman! I promised I'd keep you safe, don't you remember? How am I keeping you safe? By putting you in danger! It was worse than having a gun pointed at my own head – *don't you understand*?" She still fought him, but her strength was weakening, and holding her to him he said, "I love you too much to have you live with this risk," his voice breaking with the words.

Her face lost the fierceness when confronted with his broken voice. She went still and tears glistened and her lips trembled.

"I would give everything to keep you here, if I could be sure you were safe. And I would give up everything to take you away and start over, but I *can't,* sweetheart. I can't ever walk away from the world I'm in. It's a one-way street: no going back; no getting off. The only way I can protect you is by keeping you apart from me, and keeping my authority to use for your benefit."

Her eyes dropped down, but he saw the flash of anguish before they closed. She knew he was right. Because it was all true. They both knew it. And she sobbed.

"I need you to be safe, Mysty. I could never live with myself if you got hurt. You're so young, and you have so much ahead of you, so many talents. You should be happy, not living afraid of the next bullet. I don't want that for you." His words were tender whispers in her ear, and his breath was warm on her skin.

"But I want to be with you. I don't care about anything else. *Please*, Donny, don't send me away."

Sobs wracked her body and he rocked her backwards and forwards. He knew she would say that. Knew that his reasoning wouldn't change that beautiful light she carried for him, and her conviction that if they could just be together nothing else would matter.

"I don't want you to go, sweetheart, more than you could understand. I want to hear your voice in the house, feel your hand in mine, have your shoulder against me when we sit together. But it can't be now. It will have to be in the future. I have to do this, for both of us, but most of all for you. You are too young to make these choices. Trust me, darling, I wouldn't lie to you. You know I only want the best for you."

The ache in his heart was unbearable, and he could imagine the pain in hers.

"So, it's not forever?" she said, in between the sobs.

"No. And it's not like I won't ever see you again. It's just until things calm down."

This hadn't been part of the plan. It was meant to be forever. But somehow he knew if he'd told her that, she'd have done something crazy.

"What about tonight?"

"Tonight you sleep here. I don't want you anywhere else. This house is not secure yet."

She quietened down, too exhausted to reply.

"Where are you sending me?" she finally whispered.

He closed his eyes with some kind of relief, even though he felt like his heart had been wrenched in two. Her question was acceptance of sorts.

"Los Angeles. Not far. Far enough. I have a friend there, Franny, he's a really good guy with a wife and kids, and he's going to look out for you."

"When am I going?"

"You fly out late this afternoon."

"*Today*?"

He heard the distress clear as a bell.

"You have to go today, kitten, before any more damage is done. This attempt was a big one, and things are going to be unsettled for a while. I don't want you involved."

"Can Lazarus come?"

"Of course he can. You have today to pack everything up. You can fly out with just a few bits, spend a night at a hotel, and then everything else will arrive tomorrow and you can move into your new home," he said quietly, quite aware that he was breaking her heart.

He could feel the wetness of her tears through his shirt. Oh God, he wished he could spare her this. She then wept like he'd never seen her cry before, hurting with every new sob that wrenched from her lips, her hands clinging to him like she was drowning. This wasn't just upset, this was pure grief, loss and despair that she had to leave everything and everyone she now loved and held so dear: a home, a family, a sense of belonging and security. Starting over on her own again was the last thing she needed or deserved. If only he could take this away.

Eventually she went quiet again.

"Did tonight bring back memories of . . . before?" *Please give something away so I can kill the bastard.*

"Some. It's the blood. And the sound of the guns. I've seen enough blood . . ." There was a long pause. "I can't believe I carried that huge gun over the roof. I should be put on the payroll."

He had to smile at that; and she'd said it with a half-smile.

"You carried it over the roof?"

"Well, you had to be in the room at the back of the house, didn't you? The one with unbreakable glass as well! I had to climb up with it – that's when I saw Paulo coming back and shot at the car."

"I apologise. Next time I will insist on getting almost shot in a much more easily accessible room with normal glass."

She hit him playfully on the chest and the arms around her tightened. "Don't joke. I never want to touch a gun again."

He didn't argue with her; but he knew it was possible she would have to . . . and he was sending her to LA with one.

"I'll take you to the airport, alright?" he said softly.

She nodded, not wanting to speak, not wanting to acknowledge something that hurt so much.

"God, I wish this evening had gone as it was meant to."

"Me too."

"Do you want to have a shower? It'll help you relax."

He looked down at her, saw her concern, knew he would miss that as well as the thousand other things about her he had got so used to and cherished.

"You promise not to move off the bed?"

She smiled. "Yes, I promise to stay on the bed."

MYSTY WOKE UP slowly, aware of the sensation of not being alone. And it wasn't because Lazarus had climbed on the bed during the night. She looked at the arm that stretched out above her head, felt another over her body, her back up against Donny's chest: she had spent the night safely within the protection of his strength and warmth. How strange it felt, yet so natural. And the trust between them only added to the love as she lay listening to his quiet breathing. She snuggled back against him, happy to stay there for as long as possible.

She must have gone back to sleep, for then she heard, "Good morning."

She turned her head, saw his face and smiled.

"Do you remember the first morning I was here?" she asked. "You said good morning then. I wasn't sure if you'd changed your mind and decided to throw me out."

"Never. You were mine the moment I looked up and saw you after you saved me from the truck," he teased.

"Bloody typical Italian male." She rolled her eyes in mock disapproval.

"Absolutely."

"I love the way you swear when you pretend to get angry," he teased again.

"I am absolutely *starving*," she suddenly said, and he could have laughed: it was so welcome to hear something so normal!

"I thought you might be which is why I've ordered breakfast be brought up at 9am. Breakfast *in bed* no less."

Her big smile didn't hide her sadness. It was obvious she knew why she was getting special treatment. Donny could see her thoughts colliding and felt sick. This was the morning of the day the countdown had begun. But until she was on that plane, he would spend as much time with her as he could.

Setting her head back down, within five minutes they were both asleep again.

DONNY WAS DOING his best to stay composed, trying not to give in to any emotion that might make him weaken and change his mind. That would make it harder for her.

He wanted to make the most of these last precious few minutes, wishing it was a longer journey, wishing he'd been able to spend more time with her. He knew every morning and night would be accompanied by memories of her. How on earth was he going to let her get out of the car?

He'd had phone calls and people to deal with the moment they had finished breakfast, using one of the other upper rooms to conduct his business while he listened to the work being carried out in his rooms to repair the damage. Mysty had helped with some of the repairs on the computers, and created a new computer system to go in his room, and when she'd finished she'd gone back to the flat to pack, Mario and Lucio in tow.

For once she seemed thwarted: she didn't know where to start, her energy silenced, like someone had unplugged all the slot machines in Vegas.

"Hey, kiddo, you want us to help?"

Mario came in with a handful of boxes for her to use, followed by Lucio, both of them looking concerned.

"No, I'm. I'll . . . put some music on . . . it won't take me long," she smiled.

Her false cheerfulness didn't fool them.

"Well, there's no rush. You take your time. It's not surprising you're tired after last night." Mario came up next to her and dared put a hand on her shoulder, looking at Lucio for some help as to what to say. "When you finish we could take the bikes out? A little spin somewhere before . . ."

He ran out of words and she threw herself into his arms, the first proper hug they'd had in months. They'd spent so much time together since she'd arrived in their lives, and any contact with her had been play-fighting . . . it hadn't been this. He was taken aback, and put gentle arms around her, not used to a Mysty that needed comfort.

"Hey, kiddo, it'll be alright. Donny knows what he's doing."

He could feel her crying into his chest, and knew his boss was right: she wasn't like them; she never would be.

"*I don't want to go!*"

It was a fierce declaration that made words even harder to say and, in a rare moment, Mario felt his heart squeeze with affection, the poignancy of the emotion so beautiful, so sincere.

"I know you don't, kiddo, nobody wants you to go. But . . . well, sometimes you gotta do the thing you don't want to do."

That was as philosophical as it got with Mario, but it worked. She looked up at him after a few seconds of quiet, worried he might be annoyed at her weakness, but his face wasn't angry, or scornful, just concerned. She would miss them so much. They were like brothers to her; all of them a family. How could she just *go* after four whole years of their company, their friendship, and the trust she had in them?

"Hey, how come he gets a hug, and I don't?" Lucio laughed. She smiled through the last tears and went to Lucio, who lifted her off the floor, squeezing the breath from her lungs. "You ever need us you give us a call, OK? You know there isn't a single thing we wouldn't help you with." He sat her on the breakfast counter, got her a glass of milk and put it in her hand.

"We'll be outside if you need us, and we'll bring you up some lunch at 12.30. Don't worry about moving any boxes or cleaning, just pack it up and get yourself a bag together for tonight. OK?"

She nodded and they each gave her a long look, checking the tears had stopped.

Once the door had shut behind them she looked at the glass of milk in her hand, put it on the table and lay back on the breakfast bar. Lazarus jumped up and stood over her. He snuffled at her, sensing her sadness, trying to give her some comfort. Several minutes passed, and then she sat up and jumped down, went to the sound system and punched in what she wanted, turned the volume up, and began packing. And singing. Drowning out her misery in tunes that lifted her spirits. But she still couldn't stop the tears from falling.

"YOU SURE YOU got everything you need for tonight?" Mario asked when she called him to say she was done and was on the way down to the car.

She was in black trousers and her black leather biker jacket, an overnight bag on her shoulder. She was glad she'd put it on. It was a message to herself that she was going to be fine; that she was a fighter; that she'd be OK.

"I travel light."

Lazarus jumped in next to Paulo as though he rode every day in a limo. Mysty sat with Mario. It was obvious her mood was dark.

"Franny's a good friend of ours. He thinks you sound great, you'll be fine," Paulo said. *She doesn't even know who Franny is. What is she supposed to say to that?*

Silence.

He tried again: "I've sent a whole load of information to your handheld – you have it?"

A nod. She closed her eyes.

"It has your hotel details, address of the new apartment, picture of the guy who'll meet you in the airport – everything. You need anything else, you just say, OK?"

No response.

He looked over at Paulo who was doing his best, as only a rather large man can, to remain inconspicuous on the other side of the car. He looked back with an expression of hopeless sadness.

"You got your bank card?"

"Yes."

"You need any money, you just say, alright? I'm docking Paulo's pay for being out last night, so it's only right you should get it."

Paulo grinned at the attempt to lighten the mood, and she opened one eye to look at him.

They pulled up at the town house and Donny got in on the other side of Mysty.

"Paulo better get his backside in gear 'cos next time I might not be there, and if anything happens to any of you, I'll kick his arse. Hard."

Paulo grinned. But she descended into silence again.

"I have a theory on a systems upgrade for the door locks. I'll send it over as soon as I have it finished," she suddenly said.

Donny was struck afresh by her intelligence, but was so choked he didn't know how to reply.

"Thanks. You let me know when you get your exam results, OK?" he said, for want of anything else to say. "I might need an excuse to treat you to something."

"I'd rather just stay here."

He felt the thwack of the anguished reply, knowing she was panicking because the car ride was almost over, could feel how tense she was in anticipation of having to leave the vehicle.

"I'd rather you stayed here too," he whispered, and finally she moved closer to his side, allowed him to put his arm around her shoulder.

The car pulled up. Donny closed his eyes; he didn't want to let go.

"Guys, would you give us five minutes?"

They understood. Lazarus jumped off the seat and followed. They stood up front, standing guard, not really wanting to talk, knowing exactly what was happening inside the car.

Mysty looked at Donny, saw the guarded expression on his face, but also the emotion.

"Kitten, I'm not changing my mind. You're getting on that plane, so don't try and persuade me to let you stay. I love you too much to risk you."

"I'm not. I will get on the plane"

She shifted, and pressed the side of her body into his, as if in defiance of her words, as if she would happily climb inside him if she could. He felt her warmth, her strength, her vulnerability. What should he do? She needed to get on the plane, and soon. If he moved her would she take it as rejection? He couldn't bear it if their last few moments were filled with more hurt.

She reached into her pocket.

"We have five minutes to listen to one piece of music, don't we?" she asked.

He knew the piece she meant: a powerful, heartbreakingly beautiful piece of music by Andrea Bocelli, 'Canto Della Terra'. And he knew why: it was the first Italian song she had ever heard, way back when she had first arrived as a scared kid. He'd found her sitting listening on the stairs outside his rooms, tears in her eyes, as he'd played it. She'd said she'd never heard anything so beautiful. It had become a tune they shared together in snatched, precious moments that had become a catalogue of memories.

"Hold me like you won't let me go," she whispered with tears shining in bright indigo eyes.

He crushed her in his arms. If this was how she wanted it to be, then yes. She always managed to find a way of getting him to express his emotions by offering her own. He felt muscles in his face and throat and chest constrict as the music played, carrying them along.

"I love this music. I'll always think of you when I hear it. Think of me when you hear it," she whispered.

And then hands clasped at faces, eyes locked, joined by the music and the minutes that held them together. He could not imagine how this felt for her, having lost everything in her world once already, only to have to say goodbye to him like this. How the hell had she ended up meaning so much to him? He vowed he'd make it up to her. Every tear. Every second of this heartache. He hoped and dreamed he get that chance. Prayed he deserved it.

The music soared to its climax, and he put his hand in her hair, held it tight.

"One day, when the time is right, we'll play that music again, I promise," he said, the words choking in his throat.

She stared at him for one single second more, the music ended, and she was gone.

Donny didn't move, couldn't move. This was a love so perfect, so painful, and it hurt worse than any knife in his chest. The most he could do to was turn his head for those last few moments she was in view.

Through the glass he watched as she gave Paulo a hug, let him brush away her tears, accepting the words he spoke to her without argument. Mario got one last hug, too, and then he watched her sling the bag up onto her shoulder, pull out some shades and start walking. Back straight, head up and shoulders back, the long strides of a graceful, powerful tiger, just like always. Away from him. Without looking back.

It took everything he had to not call her back. He knew nothing would ever be the same, that he could only pray that fate would be kind enough to give them another chance. She glided through the doors, and he saw people turn and stare, not just at her but at the big cat by her side. He had pulled some strings, *many* strings, to get the animal on the flight, he'd had to for her sake. The leopard had been there when Donny had failed her, and he didn't want her to have to live without him too.

And then she was gone, swallowed up in the building and the people.

The car doors opened. One look at Donny told the guys not to say a word.

PART III

MYSTY KNEW SHE was in one hell of a bad mood. And didn't care. In fact, she didn't care about much right now. The whole flight she'd spent with Lazarus lying across her lap, half out of his seat. She'd kept her shades on, iPod on in an attempt to soothe her, stoically ignoring the looks from other first-class passengers who eyed him suspiciously. The flight attendants had been wide-eyed and curious, but nervous enough of them both to leave them alone. She hadn't even put her seatbelt on. And no one had dared try and break through her wall of ice to tell her to.

Everything felt unreal. The whole day had been unreal. *How am I supposed to do this? Just start over again?* All she wanted was to get to her hotel room, fall on the bed and weep. And even though she was hungry, she just didn't care enough to eat.

Part of her knew she had changed. That she *was* changing. That the attempted coup just hours ago was just the start. The fallout was going to be so much bigger than the actual event. Like a butterfly flapping its wings on one side of the world causing a hurricane on the other. Cause and effect. Causality. *What on earth is going to happen to me now?*

The people around her were happy to have arrived in LA and set about grabbing their belongings from the overhead lockers, and thanking the stewards and stewardesses; she would rather have been sucked into a black hole. She walked down the airport terminal corridor, the same direction as everyone else, swept along by their combined momentum. But people gave her room. Aside from the big cat that strolled by her side, her ice-cold face and customary black attire – when had that happened? – she gave the impression that any contact with her would end badly.

They weren't wrong.

She spotted the guy waiting to escort her to the car. It wasn't hard. He was the tallest person she'd ever seen, looking serious and uncompromising in a white suit perfectly tailored to his giant physique.

She saw his eyes find her, look down, back up.

She stopped two feet in front of him.

"Mysty?"

She raised one hand and lowered her shades to look at him, somehow managing to look down at him despite his being so high up.

"You see anyone else here with a leopard?"

The insolent reply only made him smile.

"Donny said you had an attitude, and that you'd be pissed off."

The shades went back up. "Understatement. Are we going somewhere? Or are you setting down roots?"

He stepped back, inviting her to go with him. She fell into step with him – had he slowed his pace to match hers, or had she sped up to keep his? – and she did not see his sideways look of amusement that she was clearly not intimidated by his size, height, or obvious strength.

Without saying another word, he led her through the bustle and out through the main doors. An immaculate stretched white limo waited for them, a man, also in a white suit, poised to open the door. Clearly white was trademark for these guys.

She paused for a fraction of a second before stooping to step into the vehicle, Lazarus right behind her. She flicked back her hair and leaned back, looked at the ivory leather interior and neat gold detailing.

Goliath stepped in, the car tilting, and sat next to his boss, also wearing a white suit, again superbly tailored. She stared at him for a moment from behind the shades, deciding to keep them on so that he, and the world, would not see what she was feeling. She took in the crossed leg, ankle casually on one knee, a cane with a silver top in one hand, another hand lazily propping up the chin of a face that was fairer than Donny's, older, but still handsome, clean-shaven, dapper. Fine eyebrows. And he was smiling, lips curved in delight and eyes twinkling with amusement as he took in her beauty, despite her hiding behind her shades.

"Donny wasn't lying then."

As openers went it was intriguing, with a touch of subtle flattery.

"Donny doesn't lie." For a single second she flicked up the shades, to emphasise her point – and he visibly startled when he saw her eyes. She flicked them back down.

"No. You are correct." He leant forward and observed her closely.

After five long seconds, he sat back. She was not pleased about being examined like some circus curio, but endured it because he was Donny's friend; and it seemed genuinely admiring, not lecherous. She knew the difference.

"I am Francois Laperta. Franny, to my friends. LA is my city. I'm sure Donny told you."

"Yes, he did. As you know, I'm Mysty. To everyone." She offered her hand, deciding to play nicely, at least on the surface, and he took it, resisting the urge to kiss it rather than shake it. She was allure and innocence all in one; fire and silk combined. It was no wonder Donny did not wish to part with her.

Franny could sense her mood easily: she was pissed off, just as Donny had warned him she would be. But she was being civil, despite the tension and even distress in her face. He had made a career out of reading people, working out their feelings and making the right choices; making the right judgment calls and trusting the right people. She wasn't hard to read: she was hurting.

"Donny must love you very much to send you away."

"So he says."

He had to admire her nerve, sitting in his limo, exchanging words like this; but having grown up and lived among the Vegas mob, should he really be surprised? From what he'd seen on camera – Donny had sent him a couple of clips so he knew what to expect – he knew she could handle herself.

"And, Donny doesn't lie." He repeated her own words, meaning them. "We are good friends, so anything you need, you only have to ask."

"Thank you. I don't usually need anything. I'm very good at looking after myself."

Franny paused, remembering what Donny had told him about her past, and the plenty that had happened since.

"Yes, Donny mentioned that as well, but still, the offer stands. I assure you, you can trust me, just like you trust Donny."

Her face was expressionless as she contemplated his answer. But then she smiled. "I think I do. And if he trusts you, that's good enough for me."

How crazy was it that she'd been involved with one mob boss, and was now making friends with another?

"Will you introduce us?" Franny gestured at Lazarus who had been watching him intently with unblinking eyes, clearly protective of his mistress.

"This is Lazarus." She signalled to the cat and Lazarus offered a paw to Franny, who took it tentatively, shook it, and carefully sat back, rather in awe of the animal. Only having seen a leopard in a zoo, he'd never dreamed he get so close to one, nor see one so tame. "He's four years old, nearly." Franny could hear the affection in her voice, the quiet pride. "He's just a big kid."

"He's rather something. How did you get him?"

"He was thrown from a car and left for dead when he was a cub. I took him in, and we've been together since. He's perfectly tame. He doesn't eat people, and he wouldn't hurt anyone unless they hurt me, so you don't need to worry." He got the impression she'd had to explain that a good number of times – little wonder. He watched them a moment longer. "Where are we going?"

"I thought it would be wrong to take you to an empty hotel room for your first night in LA, so we're going to my house. We've got a barbeque going, and you'll meet my wife and kids – and you can ask us anything you like about LA. Afterwards, Giles will take you to the hotel."

She tilted her head to one side. "What's a barbeque?"

"Jesus *Christ*, has Donny never done a barbeque for you?"

Mysty was amused at his horror; Giles silently so as well, watching without a word. Even though his eyes had drifted to the window twice, she knew he'd been listening intently to the conversation, storing the information away, just like Paulo would.

"Before I knew Donny I'd never eaten pasta," she told him with a shy smile.

"I bet his mother put that right!" She couldn't help but laugh at that, because he was right. "Well, it's cooking outside, with either a coal fire – rather old-fashioned but fun – or gas fires. Spicy chicken, kebabs sticks, burgers, sausages, chops, then salads and garlic bread. Felicity – my wife – she always does a great spread, so I leave it to her. I know my place and it's not in the kitchen. So I'm told." His tone told her his wife was not a meek woman and she grinned, amused to find this mob boss also had a soft side as far as his family were concerned. Somehow that made him seem a little less dangerous, or at least, more likeable. "Sound OK?"

"Sure."

Franny smiled, glad to see she had lost a bit of the tension. The best thing she could do was keep herself in good company, not wallow in loneliness. He then let her enjoy a time of silence, without any more questions. It wasn't like she needed to be interrogated.

A short time later the driver turned the car with practiced speed round a sharp angle and went through two imposing pillars, the gates shutting after them. She admired the expanse of garden and palm trees that lined the drive up to the house. There was a vast lawn, overflowing flowerbeds and big shrubs around the edge. There was even a fountain and a small stream. It was beautiful.

"One benefit of not being in a desert. And there are the beaches," Franny said quietly, not bothering to look out the window. He knew what it looked like, and knew she was admiring it.

"*Beaches?*" She looked round at him sharply. In her sadness at leaving Vegas, she'd never really thought about the geography of LA; it wasn't Vegas, and that was really as far as she'd got.

"You know, waves, sand, sea, sunbathing."

"I've never seen a beach, except in photos." She felt so instantly stupid saying the words, and two pairs of eyes nearly fell out of their sockets.

"You've never seen a *beach*?"

She shrank back from them, not comfortable with the acute surprise, the disbelief. How different her life had been to everyone else's. How small, and closed. Her blighted childhood was blighting her still.

"No."

Franny shut his mouth, remembering what Donny had said. There'd not been enough money to feed her properly as a small child, and her mother had been physically abused by her husband . . . of course they'd never been a normal family who went on holiday. Suddenly he had doubts about how brilliant an idea it had been to invite her for a family barbeque when her family had been brutally murdered. It was only his surprise at her vibrant appearance in his car that had made him forget these rather salient details. He silently cursed himself. Sure, she had an attitude, had courage by the spade-full; but she was also scarred and fragile.

"Well, all the beaches are within easy distance. You can make up for lost time. Lots of people go running on them, surfing, all sorts. You can enjoy exploring."

She nodded, for a moment struggling with the gorgeous garden. It was like a paradise . . . but it reminded her of her grandmother's garden. She wondered what it would look like now. What had happened to the house? Would whoever had bought it love the garden as much as she had? Too many thoughts crowded in on her, and she ran out of time to process them as the house was in view, and she did the only thing she could do: push them away and deal with what was happening right then.

The limo pulled up and the door was opened. Giles, the big guy, got out first, followed by Franny, who turned to offer her a hand. She took it after a little hesitation, not used to such courtesies, and uncertain about touching him. But his grasp was firm and gentle, and he let go the moment she was standing. Lazarus jumped out and sat next to her as she looked around, amazed at the spacious bright-white mansion, the lights that would illuminate the grounds at night, the grand doors . . . and the five white-suited men that stood on the steps staring at her.

"Chez moi."

Franny gestured grandly with his hand and drew her forward, enjoying the reaction to his home, touched even. She had been exposed to Donny's vast wealth; but this was a little different. And then there was the reaction of his men to her. He'd seen the looks they exchanged, even if she hadn't. *Issue number one to deal with right here: I don't want to have to put a bullet in someone's head because they get infatuated.*

The White King of LA led her up the steps of his castle into the cool interior of the hall. A hand took her overnight bag from her hand – another white suit who tried to give her a smile of reassurance. It was just like Donny's house, superbly decorated and impeccably clean, but lighter, and she was glad this time she didn't look like a complete ragamuffin.

Franny had a beautiful garden, a beautiful house, complete with a beautiful wife – was this who was strolling over to greet them with a wide, welcoming smile, two children holding her hands? Mysty went completely still, and her face paled to chalk-white. The children were young, only seven or eight years old. She saw herself and her sister; saw her mother how she had been, before it had all gone so wrong. It wasn't a reaction she could control. It wasn't one she had anticipated.

"Mysty." A hand touched her arm and she jumped, brought back to the present with a jolt. She turned sharply to the man who had spoken, saw Franny's face, looking worried. "Are you alright?"

"Yes."

The word was a complete lie and he knew it. She'd said it too quickly, and it belied the detached expression on her face.

"My wife, Felicity, and the children, Marguerite, and Nathan."

She tried to smile at his wife, who was looking concerned but who offered a hand. She was slender, but with full breasts, and had rich chestnut hair, cut in a bob around her heart-shaped face. She was wearing a colourful floaty silk top and long white trousers. She looked stylish, complementing her dapper husband. Mysty took the soft, manicured hand, screaming inside to stay in control of her emotions.

The children looked up at her with wide eyes, thinking she looked like a superhero off the television . . . and at the leopard.

Oh God. I can deal with plastic explosives better than I can deal with this. What do I say??

"Hi." She knelt on one knee and pulled Lazarus under one arm, seeing their curiosity, hoping this would bridge the gulf between her lack of experience with children, and the children themselves. "Would you like to shake his paw? He's very friendly; he won't hurt you."

They came forward together – a glance was exchanged between the parents – and each successfully shook paws, then moved forward, a bit braver and touched his fur with tentative hands. Both children then lost their fear, and Mysty could not resist the bright smiles when Lazarus responded by licking their hands. She smiled back. But she needed air. She stood up.

"Do you mind if I just freshen up?" She had never felt more awkward in her life. Well, apart from once before.

"Sure, sweetie, I'll show you where to go," Felicity smiled. "Franny, why don't you take the kids and get some drinks going?"

Felicity stepped forward to take her hand, another going to her shoulder, instinctively wanting to ease the distress of the young, gorgeous girl who had just arrived. She knew from Franny that she'd had a rather tough start in life, and that she'd just had to give up everything in Vegas because she was in danger . . . because of the man she had grown to love. She could sympathise better than most where that last matter was concerned.

Mysty let herself be led away, Lazarus following after her obediently. She didn't see much of the splendid furnishings that graced the wide-open spaces; she was just aware of Felicity's heels clip-clopping along on the polished wood floor.

"Just in here." Felicity stopped at the door and the light came on automatically. "When you're done, just head back that way then go right, you'll end up on the patio somehow – we'll all be there, OK?"

Felicity smiled, and turned and left her.

She stepped into the bathroom, amazed at the size. There was enough polished marble and porcelain tiles to keep a Roman emperor happy. Perfectly appointed fixtures and fittings gleamed brightly under the concealed but effective spotlights. This place was a palace!

Gratefully she shut the door, locked it and sighed. She looked down at Lazarus, who looked back with intelligent, soulful eyes. She hugged him, removed her shades, and then went to the sink and splashed cold water on her face. She unzipped her jacket, slipped it off to reveal a simple black lace vest, and smoothed water over her bare arms and neck, concentrating on the simple physical relief, but not sure how to rid herself of the emotional turmoil.

Finally she looked up and looked in the mirror, bracing herself for what she saw.

She thought of Donny, remembered his words: *"It's not a crime to survive. If your mother could see you now she would want you to be happy, want you to make the most of your life."* It might not be a crime to be happy, but it sure as hell hurt. What had happened had devastated her, nearly broken her, but because of it she'd met Donny, and Mario and Paulo. If it hadn't have happened she'd have never gone to Cirque, raced around on motorbikes . . . life had not turned out as she might have wanted, but it wasn't so bad, she knew that. Or was it?

She felt like she was suspended from a trapeze in Celeste and it was spinning so fast she couldn't get down. In a few hours, she would be alone in the hotel. And it would be quiet. Too quiet? She knew she could do this; get out there and be sociable. They were good people. She could sense it.

She put her shades into her curls – yep, she could survive a barbeque without them – and took her jacket and bag, heading back the way she had come. She felt the warm evening air on her bare skin, saw intense eyes watching her, let it go over her. She turned towards the sound of laughter and found herself on the patio.

Franny and Felicity turned away from the playing children to welcome her to the gathering. Giles was there, and a good number of suits – just like at Donny's, but the suits were white not black.

"Mysty, what would you like to drink? Wine, beer, orange juice? We have almost everything . . ."

Franny was playing host and enjoying it, white jacket off, standing in trousers and shirt; he was so like Donny it almost undid her all over again.

Had Donny mentioned she occasionally drank alcohol? Is that why he'd offered it?

"Orange juice would be great, thank you."

Someone took her jacket and disappeared; another brought a chair forward for her and she sat, put her bag at her feet, feeling suddenly tired. She knew it was the emotion making her weary: heartache sapped energy worse than anything else she could name.

"Et voila!" Franny presented her with a tall glass of orange juice. Real, fresh orange juice. It smelt and tasted so good. "Are you hungry?"

"Didn't Donny tell you, I'm always hungry?"

"He did mention it."

"I might wonder what else he chose to tell you in his eternal wisdom."

Her hint of mockery was delightful.

"A fair few things." Franny sat down next to her and watched Felicity take the children off into the house – probably to wash their hands. "That you like fast motorbikes and have no fear of speed. Or heights. That you can fight. You dislike guns, but you love music, dance and singing. That you can high-dive and ice-skate. That you are a little bit of a genius when it comes to computers. Though naturally, I'd rather hear about these things . . ." – he looked round with knowing brown eyes – "from you."

Mysty was well aware she had the attention of the entire patio. Having her interests listed so eloquently made her realise what an unusual fourteen-year-old she actually was. Surely she should just be into make-up and boys, right? But if it needed confirming, here she was, having a barbeque with a mob boss's family, dressed in black in the City of White, with a leopard as a best friend, never mind the rest of the stuff.

"Did he mention I work at Celeste?"

"He did, but he did not elaborate."

"Did you go to the opening night?" She suspected he was important enough to go.

"Yes, Felicity and I both went. It was fantastic."

"You remember the Flying Tigers?"

"Of course."

"You remember the Tiger who did the high drop and was the last to join the human pyramid at the end?"

"That was *you?*"

She smiled at his disbelief, realised she was enjoying it a little, saw the glance between him and Felicity, saying something words couldn't.

"That was *nothing* compared to what you will see in two months' time. Donny can get you seats if you want to go? He has a private box."

"Really? Wow!"

She blushed and looked at her glass, now a little uncomfortable under his appraising eyes. Perhaps she had said too much? What else did he know? That she had climbed a four-storey town house with an assault rifle; that it was the reason she'd been sent to LA?

"You want to say hi to Donny? There's a comms console just inside. I'm sure he'd like to hear from you, know you're here and everything."

"No, thanks, I don't think I could right now." Her face lost its relatively relaxed look; the tightness came back instantly.

"No problem. I've sent a message anyway, so he knows you arrived safely."

"Thank you."

Felicity returned with the children and she was invited up to the long table, the children deciding they wanted to sit either side of her, captivated by her. Perhaps they sensed she was actually still one of them: just a kid really. Whatever it was, they seemed to like her already, and didn't consider her a threat.

She coped well, considering, and Franny smiled at Felicity, deciding that the exposure was the cure, letting the children touch her hair – that was bright gold under the garden lights – and admire her shiny black trousers and boots. They offered her pieces of food, recommending their favourites, and she let them even if she didn't want to try them, all the time accepting them with gentle patience.

Lazarus was the grateful recipient of anything that was thrown towards him, and the children squealed with delight when his quick jaws would catch a piece of food from the air.

After the meal, the children clamped hands on Mysty's wrists and pulled her off to the grass, deciding she was the perfect new playmate, and despite being completely out of her depth, she enjoyed it. They were used to adults not knowing how to play simple games, used to making up rules at the drop of a hat, laughter the vital ingredient. She was pulled to their climbing frame (a huge contraption) that had a rope walk, slides, cubby holes and ladders – big enough for at least ten children to enjoy. The part she was most interested in was the bar over the rope walk, and she swung up easily, surprising both children by walking along it perfectly calmly. How she missed Celeste. Wished she could be there, knew she would have to spy out the city for some taller buildings, just to feel the thrill, the freedom, the release.

She let her boots drop the twenty feet to the floor, the children calling at her to walk along it again while they danced beneath her, safely on the ground. She smiled at how easily pleased they were, stood up, stretched her back, walked to the end and then flipped back, an intricate set of moves that brought her to the other end, the children clapping and shouting for her to do it again. So she did. Entertaining them, looking down at their avid faces.

From the patio, everyone watched in silence as she then dropped to the ground and lifted Nathan up. And even though his parents would not usually have let him be so high up, she had demonstrated how competent she was, and they relaxed. She climbed up to the bar with him on her back, and then walked him along in front of her, safely within her watchful reach, keeping him steady and level, her hands on his shoulders, all the way to the end – when he turned and waved at his parents. His pride at his achievement, at his daring, was rewarded when they clapped, watching as she carried him safely back down.

Marguerite then took her hand, and Mysty lifted her up, the smaller of the two. With slower, smaller steps the child walked the bar too, her brother holding his breath, as she was also guided to the end.

There was another round of applause as the girl gave a little wave for her audience, and made a little curtsey as suggested by Mysty. Marguerite was then carried back down.

Then glancing at the ground at the end of the rope walk, Mysty strolled to the climbing tower that had a room at the top as a den for the children. Two excited voices called for her to do some more jumps. She turned with the poise of an Olympic gymnast, pointed one bare foot, stretched, breathed out, and took two steps, launching into a beautiful sequence – one of her favourites from when she first started at Celeste – landing the end perfectly. It felt good. As familiar as breathing. And she knew that however upside down her life was, or became, she could still turn herself upside down and round and round and enjoy it.

Marguerite jumped into her arms and she carried her back to the patio, Nathan skipping along beside them.

"I think we'll definitely have to make that trip to Vegas," Franny said as they reached the table, Nathan running over to his father to grab his arm, bouncing up and down until he was allowed into his father's lap.

"It'll be like nothing you've ever seen before," Mysty promised with a quiet smile, a strange sense of wellbeing coming over her as the little girl clung to her and rested her head on her shoulder, sucking her thumb. "Oh, and I did tell them they must never ever do that on their own," she said, referring to the bar-walking, realising that it might not have been something they'd approve of even if they had clapped. "They wouldn't be able to get up there on their own, anyway, if that helps."

"I don't think they will," Franny smiled as his son snuggled against his shoulder, and his hand went to his wife, who took it, both pleased to see their young guest having found a way to overcome her sadness regarding children.

Mysty yawned and raised a hand to cover it.

"Would you like to go to the hotel? You must be tired? It's gone ten, and the children will be going to bed now. They were obviously so excited to meet you," Franny offered, seeing the yawn.

"I think that's a good idea. I'm not as good as Donny and the boys at being up so late."

She stood up and Felicity did too; Franny still had Nathan on his lap.

"It was lovely to meet you, Mysty. The kids and I would love to see you again."

She placed a kiss on Mysty's cheek, the soft, feminine warmth and perfume bringing back a sudden memory of her mother's touch. She remembered Donna Capello, too, as she had hugged her in the warm kitchen in Vegas. She didn't know what to say. Or do. Whether to return the kiss. But Felicity made it easy for her by leading the children away into the house with a wave. Franny then stood up and invited her to follow him.

At the door she was passed her jacket. She zipped it up, flicked her hair over her shoulders. They went out to the car and Giles opened the rear door.

Her piercing eyes turned to Franny, who was quiet: they didn't need many words to say the many things they were thinking. Maybe it was the foundation of trust between them because of who they were to Donny, but there was a bond between them already. New certainly, but definitely strong.

"You have a wonderful family. If ever you need me . . ."

She didn't need to say anything else as he smiled, and she knew he knew. She offered her hand and he took it silently. She already had a mobster's talent for saying so much with few words, and he knew she meant them.

"Thank you."

He rarely thanked anyone, but he felt suddenly honoured. She was exceptional, and it was the greatest sign of friendship that she'd offered her skills should he need them.

"Thank you for dinner . . . for the barbeque."

"You're always welcome. My boys will be outside the hotel with the car at ten to take you to your new place; everything will arrive at eleven. As I said, anything *you* need, you just say. We very much look forward to seeing you again." He gestured, and she knew he meant his family too.

He watched her get into the limo with easy grace, the leopard after her like a shadow. He gave Giles a nod; the big guy got in, the door was shut and the car moved off.

A mystery and an enchantment. What a girl.

DONNY FINISHED HIS coffee and put down the cup, the taste bitter on his tongue, knowing he'd have infinitely preferred a cup of coffee Mysty had made him; knowing it was just another cup of coffee on another day in which he wouldn't see her, and it felt like poison in his stomach. Franny had given him access codes to one of his cameras, so occasionally he saw her on screen, but how could it ever be the same? She wasn't here, and it was driving him insane.

He knew he had been as angry as hellfire lately, had ruthlessly thrown himself into his work in the hope it would distract him sufficiently not to notice her absence so acutely; but no one and nothing pleased him.

The intercom buzzer went. He hoped it was Franny. He wasn't surprised that she hadn't called him yet, so to hear from his friend would be most welcome.

The screen didn't display the name he wanted, but it wasn't one he could ignore. *Just get it over with*, he told himself.

He took the call.

"Daryl." He noticed his voice was flat. His face expressionless.

"Donny, how are things?"

"Real great. What can do for you?" Donny didn't even try to be friendly. He didn't owe Daryl anything. 'Real great' was complete bullshit; but he didn't care.

"What happened to 'absolutely fantastic'? Where's your girl?" Daryl was confused. Last time they'd spoken Donny had been full of the joys.

"She's gone."

"Gone?" Daryl's face actually twisted into concern, or was he merely crestfallen due to his own self-interest? "Don't tell me something happened to her?"

"No. I mean *she's gone*. I've sent her away."

"Why would you do that?" Daryl's face was a picture of confusion.

"Because there was another attempt on my life and . . ." He paused, and raised a hand in a hopeless gesture. "She almost got killed. There were threats made against her too. I won't have her hurt in any way because . . ." Donny faltered, again. "I was seconds away from getting a bullet through my head, and then the world explodes and she appears." He shook his head, then turned to look at the now fully repaired windows and room, everything almost exactly back to what it had been. Except one.

There was a long silence, and then, "Why are you so worried when she can clearly take care of herself?" Daryl asked slowly, this not being the way he imagined their conversation would go. Also, he realised he was disappointed that he wouldn't get her smart-arse replies again when she answered Donny's calls.

Reluctantly, Donny brought his gaze back around, pinning Daryl with a look that was full of loaded resentment, frustration . . . and misery. Sadness might as well have been tailored into his suit; it felt like he was wearing it.

"Despite what you obviously think and have wrongly concluded, and despite being remarkably capable and thoroughly lethal if pushed, she's completely innocent. She's never been involved in anything illegal, wouldn't touch a gun except to save a life, and has never killed and never would. She's already been through so much just to survive this far, and I won't have her go through any more. Certainly not for me. I know you think she's some gun-toting hell-raiser, but you couldn't be more wrong."

Daryl digested all of this, including the anger in his friend's voice. What did Donny mean? *Been through so much just to survive this far*?

"Where has she gone?"

"Far enough. She's with friends, and by all accounts she's doing very well."

"You should have said; she could have come to New York; I'd have looked after her for you." The words were lightly said, trying to bely the interest beneath them.

"I wouldn't trust you with her," Donny replied without hesitation, knowing exactly what would happen if Daryl so much as saw her for a second.

"Why not?"

"Daryl, she's an innocent fourteen-year-old. But she's so smart, and talented. Has this energy . . . I wouldn't trust her with you, as I said, but you also wouldn't know what to do with her."

"Well, I'm damned sorry, Donny. I realised you two were . . . close."

"Yeah. That's an understatement." Donny looked down at his ring, wishing he could have put a ring on her finger.

"So, the wedding is on hold."

Donny didn't acknowledge the half-joke; there was no joke. "It'll be on hold until she's eighteen. I hate her not being here. It's like someone took the sun away." He despised himself for even saying the words, admitting to emotions that he should just keep to himself . . . but he wanted to say them.

"Sounds like a long time to wait."

"I'd wait ten years. Twenty."

"You think she'll wait?"

Donny could see disbelief imprinted all over Daryl's face.

"If you knew her you wouldn't bother asking that question. She's more loyal than . . ." He didn't even know how to express that loyalty. "Seeing her fly through a fireball at the man holding a gun to my head was . . . enough."

Daryl didn't know what to say.

"After climbing a four-storey house with a bag of plastic explosives and an assault rifle."

Daryl still didn't know what to say.

"After dealing with two of the intruders in close combat."

"Let the military clone her; you'd make millions," he then said.

"No, Daryl, she's priceless. She's worth far more than mere millions. Things that kid can do would make your eyes fall out your head."

"Are we talking–"

"Don't you dare go there. She's under the age of consent. As you well know. Does *that* answer your question?" Perhaps he should have taught Daryl the same lesson Harvey had enjoyed so thoroughly.

"Fine, just checking."

"Well, now you know, you don't need to check again."

"Understood." Donny's defence of the girl made Daryl feel lacking in a way he hadn't expected, but brushed it aside quickly, despising the fact he'd proved Donny right not to trust him with her as he'd said so emphatically a few moments ago.

"Why *did* you call? Aside from hoping to talk to my secretary?" Donny then asked.

"It's about Cirque de Soleil, actually. Now Celeste is such a big hit, it's largely defunct. I was going to suggest two possibilities. I know you have a forty percent share in it, as I have bought up the other sixty, so we're partners . . ."

How nice. "What were you thinking?" he said.

"Either turn it into real estate, some luxury apartments, or maybe a hotel – you know, the sort of place we like. Or turn it into a rather superb concert hall for music performances, as there isn't one in Vegas."

"I'd go for the concert hall. It would complement Celeste perfectly, especially with them so close. Add another hotel as well, and it's a no-brainer."

"Exactly what I was thinking. Shall I get some architects to draw up some plans? Send me anything you think is relevant, anything you'd specifically like including, and I'll get some quotes for conversion."

"No problem."

"You're coming to the re-opening of Celeste in a month's time?"

"Wouldn't miss it for the world."

"I assume another incredible show is planned?" Daryl asked.

"Yes, but it's under wraps; even I don't know what's in it. I've received numerous assurances I won't be disappointed."

"I don't think you will be, even by your standards."

"Do make sure Harvey comes, won't you? It would be wrong for him to miss it." He knew there was one thing Mysty would enjoy: pay back. And he would arrange it for her. Allow the fool back into his city so that *she* could have a personal 'chat' with him.

"I have invited him, and he said he would let me know. I'll tell him you asked after him. I trust you aren't looking to leave him penniless again?" Daryl joked, hoping to cheer Donny with a little levity.

"Ha. I'm wondering if you'll dare have a game or two with me, Daryl . . ."

"Maybe . . . though I haven't been inclined towards cards for a while. Not sure why." Daryl hadn't been inclined towards much lately; even his Cherries hadn't managed to excite or interest him particularly, and it was worrying him.

"And how is your love life? Found any exciting 'secretaries' of your own yet?"

"Yes, but I get bored in about a week so they have to go. I don't suppose the redhead has an older sister, does she?"

Daryl honestly meant it as a joke, and didn't expect to see Donny's face darken so quickly, and he didn't reply immediately. Daryl's attitude was enough to make him want to disconnect the call; but then he didn't know Mysty's background.

"Yes, she does. Or rather she did."

"Did? What happened?"

"That's how she ended up with me. Her whole family is dead, Daryl, all murdered, including her elder sister. It was not pretty."

Once again there was silence, and then Daryl said a slow, "Oh . . ."

"Yes, quite." Donny watched Daryl's expression cloud as the impact of Donny's words hit home. "So, she's rather special, in many ways, not least in her ability to survive." He knew Daryl had lost both of his parents; but they hadn't been murdered in cold blood, and he had most certainly not been left entirely alone and penniless.

"She's very lucky to have you, then." Daryl recovered some of his composure, but remained sobered at the shocking and horrible revelation.

"No, Daryl. I'm very lucky to have her." Another silence hovered between them, and then Donny said, "I shall look forward to welcoming you to my city in a few weeks."

"Yes. I've already told my driver to stay off the freeway, just in case she's visiting."

"You do that, Daryl. I was tempted to upgrade her, but she loves the 899."

"Upgrade her? More exams passed?"

"She got two scholarships – one of them to somewhere I know you know quite well." Donny smiled with pleasure at relaying the news. He couldn't help himself. Talking about her achievements was lifting his spirits.

Daryl paused. *A scholarship to Harvard? When she is how many years too young? Shit!* "Wow. Tell her well done from me! If she ever needs a job, I'd be happy to find her suitable employ."

You already employ her . . . only you have no idea, Donny thought, a wry smile on his lips.

"I think she'll be just fine." *A long way away from you.*

"I'll catch up with you at Celeste, then. Stay away from armed gunmen, they're not good for your health."

Donny half-smiled. "Yeah, I had noticed. Goodbye, Daryl."

Disconnect.

DARYL TURNED HIS chair away and stared out of the window – as he had that time after being interrogated about his underwear. What a blow! She wouldn't be there again to answer the phone. No more sassy comebacks. Sent away? It was insane to think he'd ever meet her, but he sure as hell wanted to – and before she became Mrs Capello. Seducing any mob boss's wife was suicidal, particularly Donny Capello's future wife. Doing anything associated with insulting Donny Capello, in fact. Daryl had seen the news. Seen the reports about the dead found gunned down across the city in 'gang-related incidents' a few weeks ago.

Her family dead? All of them? It must have happened when she was very young, as she'd been with Donny for four years now? It made sense that she hadn't hesitated to save him: he was her family now.

What did she look like? What was she like to talk to, in the flesh? Would she still surprise him? It was madness to think so much about someone he would likely never meet; but she was so intriguing. Irresistible. An enigma. What he wouldn't give to meet this girl . . .

Not long till he would be in Vegas. But this mystery girl wouldn't be there, would she? Donny mentioned the 899. But that didn't mean she'd be in the city. And even if she was, he'd probably keep her hidden away. That was just too bad.

WHEN DONNY DISCONNECTED, he gave into temptation and punched in a call to Franny. If he couldn't speak to Mysty, then at least he might be able find out if she was doing OK. The call was connected and the screen came up, and he saw Franny's torso.

"Mysty, are you sure it's safe to take the call?"

"Yes, it's fine. I'm working a different chip set and it doesn't have any voltage. Just don't make it buzz again because I hate that sound."

The voice was half-muffled, and Donny guessed she was under the desk. Franny sat down, the impeccable white suit as pristine as ever, and looked at the screen properly, his face breaking into a big smile when he saw the dark-suited individual leaning back in his black leather chair looking rather intrigued.

"Donny! Hello!"

"Mysty under your desk?"

Franny held up his hands in admission. "She's doing something to my computer! Apparently, it's not up to scratch."

"Well, don't worry, she did the same to mine and now it's vastly improved. She knows what she's doing."

"Yes, I gathered that." Franny's rueful smile told Donny quite a bit. "How long you think you're going to be, Mysty?"

"Oh, I'd say at least another three years."

"Not long then," Franny joked cheerfully and smiled, quite used to her responses by now.

"What the hell is she doing?"

The new voice was outraged and upset, and Franny looked up at his (also) white-suited technical guy who had obediently brought up the pieces requested.

"Ricky, it's OK She knows what she's doing," Franny replied.

"Like hell she does."

Donny saw some golden curls but no more as she looked out from under the desk to face her accuser. He almost smiled in anticipation. He had missed her so much. Would she turn around and say hi?

"Hey, Ricky, calm it down. Don't get that white tie of yours in a twist. I know what I'm doing, alright? In case you didn't know, I got offered scholarships to Harvard and MIT for computer science, and I'm three years too young to go, so why don't you just pass me those bits you're holding and relax?" She reached up and the parts were passed to her, leaving poor Ricky feeling rather dressed down, and a little impressed – although he wouldn't have admitted it.

"And she hacked into the FID when she was thirteen," Donny threw in happily.

Franny looked at him sharply. "The FID?"

"Yep. Completely untraceable as well. She could have made millions." Donny failed to keep the pride from his voice.

"Jesus Christ."

"She's also just here and she didn't want to mention that," came the voice from under the desk.

Donny grinned.

"So how are things?" Franny was still processing the revelation about the FID and smiled at his caller, glad to see Donny looking happier.

"Busy, but fine. All that mess with Ericson and the fallout has been cleared up so things should go back to being relatively peaceful again."

"Does that mean I can come home now?" Again from under the desk.

Franny almost laughed; Donny was secretly pleased she still thought of Vegas as home.

"No, it doesn't, though I wish it did. It just means, hopefully, that you're completely safe where you are." Something then got said that was inaudible to Donny; but Franny laughed. He guessed it hadn't been very polite. "So, how are things in LA?"

"A bit of funny business to handle with a couple of new drug gangs trying to make themselves top dog, and all the usual stuff on top, but can't complain. We're just killing time before a family barbeque. I can't believe Mysty had never been to one before she arrived! Shame on you Donny!"

"Well, I hope you've suitably impressed her," Donny replied easily. "But I can't believe you're making her work for her supper . . . really, Franny, I thought I knew you better than that."

Franny grinned at him, knowing Donny was purposefully trying to get a reaction from under the desk by talking about her.

"Not guilty. She heard it running and was horrified. Apparently, it's much too loud. And then, upon inspection, she was even more upset and set to work. I'd be happy for her to be sunning herself outside with the kids. How you doin' down there?"

"Almost done."

"Good, then you can come up here and talk to Donny."

Donny heard a snort. *Boy, was this going to be interesting.*

"How is she?"

"She's fine . . . well, almost no problems, I just need to make sure she and Giles don't end up in the same room at the moment."

"Giles? Giant Giles?"

"No less. They had a little scuffle, and he's still a bit touchy about it."

Franny was trying to be diplomatic, but the voice under the table spoke again: "Hey, the guy asked me to step outside, what was I supposed to do? Like I was going to walk away from that invitation!"

"Well, exactly," Franny agreed, glad Donny was in Vegas and couldn't strangle him judging by the look on his face.

"Can you press the green button? In the middle on the screen? Don't touch anything else." The picture at both ends disappeared for two seconds, and then came back. "Can you hear that? Almost nothing. Perfect. You might want me to upgrade your firewalls; they could probably do with it if that configuration was any indication."

She crawled out and stood up at Franny's side.

"After dinner and after speaking to Donny. Come on," Franny said, and got up and manoeuvred her into the seat in front of the screen, where she sat, one leg coming up to her chest, her head looking away. She didn't really want to talk. "Ricky, come on, give these two some space. Mysty, do you want a juice?" She nodded. "Orange or pineapple?"

"Pineapple sounds great."

The footsteps retreated and the door shut and there was utter silence.

Donny waited, hoping she would look at him, trying to ignore the jealousy that ripped him apart after seeing the easy friendship between her and Franny, wishing it was him getting her a drink and having a barbeque. What he wouldn't give for five minutes alone with her, let alone a whole evening.

"So." *Where to begin?* "How are you? You OK?" *Please talk to me.*

"Well, if being shipped off to another city where I don't know anyone and away from all the people I love constitutes as 'OK', then sure, I'm peachy." It was rapier-sharp and he took the cut, knowing she was hurting more than she was pissed off. "How are you?" She was still staring at something away from the screen.

"About the same. Moody, angry, pissing everyone off . . . Paulo wants to strangle me. You know . . . peachy." He knew saying 'peachy' might win him a smile, and he saw her eyes flash, despite her head still being turned away: finally, some emotion. "How's LA?"

"Not Vegas."

"Apart from that? Not too hot? Tried the beaches?"

"No, the heat's fine. A bit fresher without the dust and with the sea breeze, and the beaches are great. I go running on them sometimes."

"Only sometimes?"

"Guys try and chat me up and it's annoying. They don't take 'no' very well, either, so I just speed up till they can't keep up. I feel like a gazelle being hunted down sometimes."

"But no one's . . ." He held his breath, instantly worried for her.

"No. I'm too fast for that. Donny, do you think it will always be like this? With men? Will they ever leave me alone?" She really was the complete opposite of every other woman on Earth.

"I'm afraid that is quite unlikely, kitten, as I think you're only going to get more gorgeous."

"It's not very fair." Donny muffled his laugh and her eyes glanced angrily at him for the first time and then away. "It's not very funny either."

He guessed it didn't feel very fair, and wasn't funny; but the way she said it was so typically honest and open.

"What happened with Giles?"

"Oh, he decided he wanted to see what I was made of. He managed to split my lip a little. He's still got a black eye." Donny's eyes immediately went to her lip, but it looked OK so he held back from telling her to be careful.

"And how's Lazarus?"

"He's got a willing fan club out in the garden, so he's happy as pie."

"I . . . the boys miss you like crazy. They'll be jealous when they find out you're barbequing with the Los Angelians!"

"Well, I'd much rather be in Vegas eating pasta on your sofa."

"I'd much rather you were too, sweetheart."

"You're a mean, cruel, evil person for sending me away!" Two hands came up to cover her face. Donny waited. Finally, her hands lowered and she wiped away the sudden tears, and at last, she looked at him with the blue-blue eyes he knew so well, her curls tumbling over her shoulders framing her face. "And I'm not taking either scholarship, by the way."

"What? Why?"

He'd heard a report from Mario and Lucio. She'd taken a three-day trip to Boston and stayed with Don Salvadore and visited both institutes. But her radio silence had meant that this was the first time he'd spoken about it to her.

"Do you know how expensive it is to go there? Even with a scholarship?"

He should have known that was the issue.

"You know I'll pay. If it's what you want to do, I'll give you all the funding you need."

"And I love you for that, but I can't accept it." They were simply-spoken words, and the animosity crumbled away. This was his Mysty alright, just as sweet and loving as he remembered . . . and just as stubborn. "Aside from how far it is from Vegas. It would be way too much flying for me to keep up with Celeste, which I don't want to give up. I love doing Celeste, especially now I have my own act."

She paused and he didn't speak; had a feeling there was more.

"Going there was a real experience though," she continued, suddenly forgetting her reluctance to talk to him, now happy to be able to tell him what had happened. "Thirty seconds after arriving at Harvard I had one chief jockstrap giving it some with his little pack of wannabe friends. I just looked at him, and I knew in ten seconds I could have laid him out on the floor . . . but it wouldn't have made any difference . . . they don't have a clue, all those rich, pampered kids who think they can do what they like. It would never change. Fight one argument out, and I'd end up with another just as quickly. I wouldn't fit in and I knew it. I felt like a tiger walking through a field of pedigree pussycats. And what would I do about Lazarus? Going there would be a mistake."

She paused, took a deep breath and looked up at him again with a little gleam in her eye while trying to look vaguely innocent. "And quite pointless," she added. "I've hacked into both databases and looked at the curriculum. I'm already way beyond what they think they could teach me, so it would be a big waste of time."

He smiled, unable to help himself. She was so smart, but so sensible. But it wasn't easy. Being different never was. It could be lonely. She almost smiled back at him but looked unsure, and he realised she was afraid he was going to be angry with her.

"Well, Salvadore is going to be disappointed . . . he has already asked me twice when you'll be going back to visit."

"If someone had told me I'd one day be in love with one mob boss and friends with two more . . . I didn't even know what a mob boss was!" She shook her head and looked down at the bracelet on her wrist, not realising how much her words meant to him.

"Do you know what you are going to do?"

"I've applied at an LA college to do Law. I want to be a criminal defence attorney. I'm going to send as many people like my father to jail as I can, and I don't care about money. I'll take all the pro bono cases. I just want to make a difference."

Law? It made sense. She was certainly smart enough, and it would be a proper career.

"Do you need any help with the application?"

"No, they practically locked me in the room until I was enrolled once they saw my record. They couldn't believe I was turning down the scholarships. But it's the right decision; I'm doing a part-time course in the first year so I can do all my other stuff. I'm still young, after all, and taking it more slowly is better. There's no rush."

He nodded. He had to agree with that.

"How is all the other stuff going?" he then asked, so glad she was now talking, not wanting the conversation to end.

"I have an audition for a Thursday night slot at a big hotel in two days. I've found classes for nearly everything, and I've got a job at the ice rink in return for time on the ice. And the guys at the airport are so used to seeing me they're teasing me about where my cat is."

"You alright with things at Celeste?"

"Yes, I want this first debut performance out the way, so I can get started on the next ones. We had a practice set up last weekend, and it was amazing – even the director came down and shook my hand."

"I can't wait to see it. Not long now – two weeks?"

"I know! Have you spoken to Franny?"

"Yeah, he's coming. It'll be good to have someone to share my private box with seeing as I'm not allowed to bring Marilyn and Tallulah." She laughed at that, and he felt some part of him relax to hear the sound. "Mysty, I have some news for you, something I'm arranging

. . . though it doesn't have to be this performance . . ." He wasn't sure how to phrase this.

"Donny, come on, what is it? Do I get to see you?"

He felt his heart squeeze at the hope that shone in her eyes.

"Not this time, but soon, I promise, as soon as I can be sure you'll be safe, I'm going to kidnap you in my limo for a bit!" She grinned, not at all worried at the prospect of being kidnapped this time by Donny. "No, seriously, there is someone you might want to see . . ." He paused, saw the intrigue in her face. "How would you like a few minutes alone with Mr Harvey Lincoln, he of the after-show party and wandering hands?" He held his breath. He watched her absorb the words, assess the offer and the implications.

"The one you robbed of trillions of dollars? The one who you . . .?"

"Indeed."

"Five minutes?"

"Ten?"

"Five is fine." He watched a tiger-smile appear on her face, and her eyes glittered dangerously. "I only have one thing to do to him anyway. I'll make sure it's memorable."

He felt proud of her. Never a coward, she was now even more confident, secure in her own strength.

"Excellent. You tell me when would be best to have him made available and I'll make it happen."

She knew she could rely on him to keep his word; knew his word was law.

"Good." What an interesting proposition! She'd never imagined she'd have the chance to exact revenge on that loser of a man! "Did you get my software upgrade for your door security? What did Fabio think?"

"He thinks you're a genius."

"Yes, but does it work OK?"

"Perfectly. He's getting more done, so soon we'll have every door fitted with the same. I owe you pizza until at least 2040!"

He resisted telling her he was patenting it for her, and already had a long list of customers waiting for her newly designed retina scan and thumb print software. After Pepe's fate, she had developed a system that made it pointless trying to use the body parts from unfortunate victims, as the computer would only accept both eye scans, and only if it could detect normal movement from the retinas and a heartbeat. Anyone dead or being coerced would be rejected, and there was nothing that could be done unless the system was overridden from the inside. The thumb scan also required middle finger recognition, and rejected them if there was a lack of pulse. He didn't know how she'd managed it; he only knew it would make plenty of money that he could surprise her with, as she deserved. And he was certainly going to be selective as to who he offered it to, and definitely not share the mind behind the software.

"You owe me way more than pizza," she countered, interrupting his thoughts.

"Agreed, no arguments from me." He basked in the beauty of her smile. "Are you going to ring me now, so I don't have to hunt you down or ring Franny to find out how you are?"

She had the grace to blush. "Yes. I'll call every day if you want me to."

"That would be nice."

"Nice?" she repeated, insulted at such a poor word choice.

"Wonderful. Is that better? It would be *wonderful*!" he laughed. "It might help me return to being vaguely sociable."

"How are they all? The boys?"

"They're good. I might have to send Mario and Lucio over to you sometime as I think they want another bike race. Call the surveillance boys one day, I know they'd like to chat to you. All the firewalls and security is in place, thanks to you. How is the new flat?"

"Great. Really. I even have a *plant*."

She was clearly proud of the achievement of owning a plant; it was obviously a sign of maturity!

"Wow. An actual plant!"

"I love Franny's garden – have you seen it? It's like heaven."

He smiled. Since when did Mysty like gardens? Maybe he should do something with his garden, surprise her when she visited.

"I have. It's beautiful. Which reminds me – you're meant to be having a barbeque. You'd better go or there'll be nothing left."

She was as lean as her leopard.

A few long seconds of silence passed, and then with a small wave and a smile, they disconnected, and Mysty went to join the barbeque in the garden, quietly assured she was still very much loved.

LA REALLY WASN'T a bad place to be, especially, since she had discovered strawberry milkshake. She was sitting in her favourite little café just a few streets away from her home, reading law stuff on her handheld, with a sandwich in front of her. She'd discovered the place when she'd run past it one morning and decided to try it. It had been an excellent decision and she understood why so many people also went there. The area wasn't rich, and the seats weren't new, and it could do with a lick of paint, but the portions were generous and the prices reasonable – and everything had tasted great so far. It was in a street that had all kinds of businesses on it, and all sorts of people came in, from guys in fluorescent work jackets to men in shirts and ties. She'd seen someone enjoying a strawberry milkshake on one visit, and wanted to try one – and that had also been an excellent decision. She hadn't wanted the ice cream or marshmallows or whipped cream on top, but had decided she could happily drink strawberry milkshake every day for ever now.

Mysty looked at her watch: in two hours – 4pm – she'd be at an audition. She'd seen the advert for it by chance, and she loved the look of the hotel, and longed to be back on stage. She judged it would be relatively safe. There were so many hotels in LA, and how many performers? She would be one in a crowd. A big crowd of hopefuls, all hoping to make it big – except her. She just wanted to stay small.

She just taken another slurp of pink heaven through the stripy straw and reached for her sandwich when she heard a loud, unattractive voice cut through the quiet chatter in the café.

"Hey, sweet cheeks! I've been looking for you."

Covertly Mysty turned her head. The voice was directed at a very pretty brunette sitting at table with three girlfriends. Everyone had frozen, including the girls at the table, and the speaker was a tall, butch-looking muscle-boy with tattoos on his arms wearing a black t-shirt and khaki combat trousers. He was big enough for most people to feel it was best to let him win an argument. But then six guys piled in after him, taking up enough space in the café to make people want to move away – except they were scared of attracting attention by doing so. The girls were all late teens; the guys a little older. They were rough around the edges, like a bunch of unkempt Rottweilers turning up at a poodle party.

The alpha dog leant over the brunette, using body language to intimidate as much as his voice: "You left the party last night without giving me what I wanted. I'm here to collect," he sneered.

The girl looked horrified to see him, and scared too, despite being in the safety of a public place.

Mysty's hands gripped the glass of milkshake in front of her. Her eyes went from Alpha Dog, to the brunette, and then to her girlfriends – who all looked like frightened sheep confronted by a hungry wolf. None of them dared move. They had no idea what to do.

"But I told you no," she said in a small voice.

"I don't care what you said, *stupid girl.* I know what I want and I don't take no for an answer." He reached out and took hold of her wrist and pulled her up out of her seat, her resistance nothing to his strength. "You can come blow me off now. And if you're lucky, I'll let you off being so rude, making me drive all the way here to fetch you. Let's *go.*"

His face was twisted with intent, and Mysty's eyes narrowed, his words hammering into her brain like a scene from her childhood. He had the same cruel voice as her father, the same selfish arrogance.

He yanked her through the door, and she cried out in protest, her bag left on the floor by her chair. His minions followed, and once outside they formed a group around the leader who had captured his prize. Mysty watched the girl struggle, trying to wrench her hand free, and in one easy motion, the guy turned and backhanded her across the face hard enough to send her stumbling, held up only by the grip on her wrist. He started to drag her away, his crew following.

Something in Mysty snapped. She'd seen this before. Too many times.

She stood up and moved towards the door, the only person who had dared move despite the malevolent force having left the room. She pulled one of the leather strands from her leather jacket. She flexed her arms. Man, she was going to enjoy this.

"Hey, ugly!" she shouted, stepping out onto the cracked asphalt of the street. They were making their way towards an old but pimped-up SUV. "Yeah, you, with the dodgy haircut."

They all stopped and swung around as a pack, full of aggression. The girl was handed to one of the guys, and for a moment her face showed relief that someone had stopped their progress; but then she saw Mysty and it was obvious she didn't much like the look of her rescuer. Alpha pushed his way through his guys to face the blonde girl in black jeans, biker boots and white t-shirt.

"Who the fuck do you think you are, bitch? You want to suck my dick as well?"

"Hardly. And that's the whole problem, fuckwit: she doesn't either. And I understand her point of view. You're not much of a catch. Let her go, and this doesn't have to go any further."

She saw his face redden. He really wasn't good at opinions that varied from his.

"Are you *threatening* me?" he asked in disbelief, turning to glance at his boys – who were sniggering.

"No, arsehole, I'm promising you a world of pain unless you let the girl go. So, you decide. One. Or the other."

Mysty saw his face tighten as he realised she was serious. She had insulted him. And she'd meant it. He knew that his boys and everyone in the café – who were now watching closely from the doorway and windows – had heard too. It was the kind of disrespect that couldn't go unanswered, and she had banked on it.

Mysty raised her hands and tied her hair back with the leather strand with quick hands.

"She's leaving with me. You can leave in a goddamn body bag, bitch."

"Is that so?" She stepped forward.

Alpha came forward to match her, bunching his fists up, rolling his shoulders and his head, psyching himself up for busting the gorgeous bitch down to size. It was a shame, really – she was really pretty.

"How do you fight?" she asked.

"What do you mean, *how do I fight*?" he threw back, angrily, not wanting to talk, wanting to punch her instead.

"Jesus, you really are as dumb as you are ugly, aren't you?"

Her voice was mock-sad, and he didn't see the fist that came out and smacked into his face, the left hook that followed, or the upper cut that threw his head up. A foot then collided solidly with his groin, then his gut, then the top of his chest, throwing him backwards and he landed on the gravel with a thud. She lowered her leg slowly and straightened, settled back to a strong, two-feet-on-the-ground pose.

He groaned, but didn't move. There was blood on his face, but she wasn't interested in that. She looked at the six boys who were now looking rather more curious than before.

"You want to fight too? 'Coz I can keep going all day." She walked towards them, opening her arms in invitation. "Let her go. Now."

The girl struggled, but hands held her firm as she was shoved around and then pulled back, as if they didn't quite know what to do with her. Then one of them pulled out a knife.

"You're going to regret this, blondie," he warned her, his face just as nasty and sneering as Alpha's had been.

"Nope, I don't think so," she corrected calmly, placing one foot behind her, taking up the pose she used when fighting Choi. *Bring it on.* Her hand beckoned them, and they ran at her. Hands and arms moved to block the blows and the slashes; powerful feet collided with soft unprotected flesh; bodies hit the deck and blood started dribbling from noses. It was fast and furious, but she was used to that, wanted it, enjoyed it. She was merciless. Just as they would have been with their chosen victim. As they'd tried to be to her. But they were clumsy, untrained boys who knew nothing of skilled fighting.

Karma is a swift and humiliating mistress sometimes.

Mysty then walked over to the last guy who held the girl and he quickly let her go and held up his hands wanting to avoid the fate of his friends. She ran back to the café, straight into the arms of her friends.

She felt something on her arm and was surprised to see a blood coming from a cut – obviously from the guy with the knife. She was slipping, clearly. She saw it on the ground, glinting in the sun, and picked it up. This boy was another monster in the making. As was Alpha. She went over to him.

"Next time you think you can hit a girl without any consequences, think of me and remember how hard I hit you. And if I ever see you doing that again I'll break a bit more of you. Now, get in the car with your fuckwit mates and drive away. But I have your plates, and I know people in this city who'd run you off the road just for the fun of it, so you'd better drive carefully . . . you never know who might be behind you."

With that she bent down and sliced through the waistband of his jeans so that they would fall down when he stood up. He flinched violently, but didn't move and didn't speak.

She then stepped back, the knife still in her hand, and crossed her arms.

"I'd leave now if I were you."

Seconds later they were all stumbling back towards the SUV, Alpha clutching his jeans. They drove away fast enough to make the car complain and the tyres screech.

Sighing, she returned to the café and found herself face to face with the four girls, the café staff and the other customers. She ducked her head, embarrassed at the attention, pulled the piece of leather from her hair and tried to hide behind it.

She looked up at the owner and said, "Do you think you could get rid of this for me, please?"

She held out the knife and he took it without a word.

The people then parted as she made her way back to her table, with quiet murmurs of amazement – and thanks. Gratefully, she sat back down in her seat and took a sip of milkshake, hoping everyone else would sit back down again as well. They did, and took their places, sipping their coffees and soft drinks. Such excitement was not usual at lunchtime; and for a known and feared bully to get his just desserts was something that made every mouthful taste just that bit better.

She didn't look up, even though she just about glimpsed some guys arrive at the front of the café, crowding around the girl, talking in loud voices. She tried to make herself invisible; didn't want thanks or attention.

Then she got both.

"Hey."

The voice was deep, male, but not aggressive . . . a little uncertain in fact.

Here we go. Just go through the motions. Thanks. No problem. Bye.

"Hey," she replied without commitment, looking up at him, seeing a deep LA tan, dark hair with blonde highlights that actually suited him pretty well. He was wearing jeans and a t-shirt, both stained with oil, and had a physique that told her he was far from weak. A couple of artfully designed tattoos did not hide the muscles in his arms. But he wasn't there to fight.

"I . . . I just wanted to say thanks. That's my sister you just saved from Troy and his thugs. I work at the garage down the road. I saw some of what you did, but I wasn't quick enough to get here before you . . . well, you handled it."

He wasn't sure how to talk to the slender, beautiful girl whose eyes were so captivating; but he couldn't look away. Normally it was him watching women getting nervous chatting him up, trying to impress him, but she . . . she was in a league of her own . . . and not that he'd intended chatting her up but . . .

"It's no bother. Really."

Such a calm but uncommunicative response. What could he do with that? From her competency and control, he didn't doubt it had been 'no bother', but what was he supposed to say next?

"Well, maybe . . . but still, you didn't have to, so . . . just thank you."

"You ever heard the phrase, *'The only thing necessary for evil to triumph is for good men to do nothing?'* I couldn't have sat there and just watched what he was doing, not unless I was dead."

That wasn't the reply he'd expected; but this was no ordinary girl. And those listening who had done nothing felt a twinge of guilt and inadequacy.

"Selena is so grateful, and so am I. He's been bothering her for a while, despite my attempts at putting him off, but I don't think she has anything to worry about now."

"He comes anywhere near her, you just tell me, and I'll happily kick his arse." She shrugged and almost smiled, feeling glad to have done something that meant something to someone.

"Again."

He smiled, and Mysty couldn't stop the blush, and the ice was broken.

"However many times it takes."

"You've got some moves on you, haven't you?"

He could fight himself, or had thought he could until he'd seen this girl take down that group with such professional composure.

"I know what it is to be in your sister's position; if you learn to fight back, and fight back hard enough, they leave you alone. Permanently."

He nodded, still smiling. He really liked this girl. She was intelligent, and had obviously had to learn some tough stuff about life, but she wasn't a cold, hard bitch. No one with a melting smile like that could be a bitch.

"How old are you?" he asked.

"Does it matter?"

An evasion that gave something away, but he wasn't sure what. Maybe she just didn't like too many questions from a stranger; that was fair enough.

"Just curious. I've not seen you before and if I had I definitely wouldn't have forgotten you."

She blushed again and ducked her head. His appraising eyes made her feel a little warm. He then perched on the seat next to her, and she felt a little nervous. She'd come back to finish her milkshake and lunch, not have a conversation with a rather good-looking stranger.

"I go to college. I've not been here long. Less than two months."

"Where you from?"

"Vegas."

"How'd you like LA?"

"It's not bad, nice beaches, plenty of freeway."

She smiled. She had promised herself a fast ride later, depending on how well the audition went.

"*Freeway?* You like watching cars?" he asked in confusion, and she laughed.

"No! I like motorbikes, and I can hit higher speeds on the freeway, especially at night."

Motorbikes? Was she for real?

"You have a *bike?*" His face lit up like Xenon headlights.

"I have two."

"What do you have?"

The automatic question that she'd known was coming: any bike-nut would be the same.

"My first – a Kawasaki 250, and a Ducati 899."

"Jesus. That's awesome . . . how can you afford those?"

"I saved up and bought the Kawasaki. And . . . I saved someone's life . . . it's a long story, and I passed all my exams, so he bought me the 899."

From anyone else it would have sounded like a boast, but from her it was obviously just the truth.

"You been to the Indi-bike racing yet? We go," he said, and he gestured out of the window at three guys who were standing with the girls, clearly talking, but also waiting for the outcome of his chat with her. "There are more of us, and we're all bikers when the working day is over. You want to come with us one night? It's pretty wild! Sounds like your kind of thing if you like speed? . . ."

She could see he wanted her to, and . . . she wanted to. It really sounded like fun. And so far in LA biking had been a singular experience. She liked to be around other bikers, and actual racing sounded even better!

"Erm, sure. Why not?"

His face broke into a smile.

"Great! We meet up out the front of the Dancing Mermaid – you know it? Downtown, near the big fountains? 7pm on Saturday nights. Biggest night is the third Saturday of every month, but still, it's always worth going. I'll look after you, I promise."

Mysty smiled slightly, resisting the urge to remind him she was pretty good at taking care of herself; now was not the time to put off potential friends with overstated independence.

"OK, that sounds good."

"And if you need anything done on your bike, just bring it in. We're half a block down. That way" he pointed. "On the other side of the road. It'll be on the house. It's the least I can do considering you busted Troy's ass for me."

"I usually like to do all my own tinkering, but I might need an expert opinion, so thank you."

His eyes widened again just a touch: a girl who looked like something off a magazine cover, who could fight like no one else he knew, liked motorbikes and knew mechanics! *He was in love.*

"So, you'll definitely come?"

"Sure. I wear all black. The bike's red. What colour are you? In case I get there and you've got your helmet on?"

"I've got a black and green Kawasaki ZX10r and leathers to match. My helmet is black with silver lightning. My friends call me Slick."

He offered his hand, and he'd given her his bike name. She liked his style. Straightforward and honest.

"Mysty."

She shook his hand and got an oil smudge on hers for her troubles, and he apologised. She waved it off, not bothered.

"Awesome. I'll introduce the rest of the guys on Saturday; they'll all want to meet you." He stood up, reluctantly, but knew his friends and work were waiting for him.

"No problem."

"I'd better get back. Good to meet you, Mysty."

"Yeah, you too, Slick."

Slick walked away and she smiled, not sure what had just happened. He was genuine, and his being tongue-tied at the beginning was amusing considering he was old enough and attractive enough not to be. She watched them all head over the road, the four girls and four guys, all probably asking him questions about her. She sighed. Her milkshake was warm. So was her sandwich. But she'd made a friend and discovered Indi-bike racing. Something told her that was worth her ruined lunch.

She glanced at her watch. She had fifteen minutes and then it would be time to go.

BENJAMIN MORRIS RAN a tight ship, and his ship was the best hotel in LA. Best in terms of standards, size, attractiveness, menu, parking, valets, beds, sheets, flowers – you name it, he made a point of making it superb. He didn't do sloppy, didn't do shabby, and certainly didn't do average. He knew it was because of his sky-high, cast-iron standards that his boss left him alone to run the hotel as he saw fit, and that was the way he liked it. Which was why, when he walked down the grand marble staircase with red carpeting, past huge flower displays tastefully positioned in alcoves and plinths, to find the front desk unmanned, three bell hops and desk staff standing by the large open door with poses that suggested they were admiring a particularly nice car, he wasn't at all pleased.

Striding up behind them he opened his mouth to say something sharp to make them jump when the words stilled on his tongue.

He could understand what they were staring at. He hadn't seen any famous names or rock stars on the check-ins . . . was it a walk-in? He'd missed the bit when she'd cut the engine, put down the stand with a casual flick of her heel, and swung a leg over and stood up, every inch of her clad in black leather; and he missed her pulling off her helmet and shaking out a mane of blonde hair. But he didn't miss the groan from one of the men next to him as she looked around, and then bent to put some kind of security device on her bike, and then climbed the steps, the fluidity of her hips and shoulders quite something to behold.

"Boys, that's enough staring for one day. I don't pay you to gawp." Benjamin's voice cut into the air and they scattered, not realising their boss had been right behind them.

She took the last three steps slowly, not sure how to approach the guy who was looking at her so sternly, knowing he had authority but, was it the authority she was meant to speak to? She didn't know much about hotels; indeed, the one she'd stayed in on her first night in LA had been the only one she'd ever stayed in, and it wasn't anything like this. It had been comfy, low-key and quiet. This hotel was like a palace, proclaiming its grandeur from every inch, with huge marble columns at the front like the great edifices in Rome she'd seen in pictures. She could see the inside was just as impressive as the outside; did she really belong here?

"Can I help you?"

Benjamin enjoyed seeing her reaction to his hotel, but hot biker chicks weren't his usual clientele, and he didn't like the fact that his staff had ground to a halt when they'd seen her. Girls this beautiful were trouble.

"I hope so."

She smiled, her voice softer than he expected, nothing coarse or unrefined about her, despite the type of transport she'd arrived on. "I'm here for an audition, at 4pm. I'm really sorry, I've never been here before . . . do you know where I should go?"

Perfectly polite; well-spoken in fact. Not at all what he'd expected. She didn't even sound American. More . . . English. *In black leathers and riding a motorbike?* Was he dreaming this?

Benjamin was not sure whether this was a good idea, after all. A girl like this was either going to be a total hit or a complete disaster. Did she think her pretty face would win her the job? He knew plenty of girls who would.

"Yes, I do. I'm Benjamin Morris, and I'll be conducting the audition. I am the manager of the hotel, but I also take personal control of all our entertainment, as it is so important we have the right shows for our guests. You want to go ahead with the audition?"

"Why? Do I look like I've changed my mind?"

She looked meaningfully back at the bike, which was being admired by the valets, then back at him. His eyes told him she was young, but she wasn't stupid. She wasn't like anyone he'd met before. Inwardly he rebuked himself: he should have guessed that thirty seconds ago.

"Fine, well, I'm a very busy man, as you can imagine, so let's get this done, shall we?"

Abruptly Benjamin walked off and left her to follow, which she did, enjoying the cool of the reception atrium that reached up to painted renaissance-style ceiling. They walked across a dark red, spotlessly clean carpet, then along a long corridor with cream-painted walls, plaster architraving and chandeliers. It was like a fairy tale, and she spent as much of her attention looking around as she dared without falling behind.

"Where have you performed before?"

"I did some shows in Vegas." He looked round at her sharply, and she caught the look, realising how it sounded. "I *come* from Vegas, and the shows were musicals, or opera, not *those* kinds of shows."

He nodded, giving her the benefit of his doubt, and pushed through three sets of double doors into the lower section of a two-tier concert hall, the stage wide and curving. There were a good few hundred round tables, all set up with silver cutlery and crystal glasses and intricately folded white napkins on white tablecloths. Ruby, gold and cream were the predominant colours, and it reminded her of Donny's rooms and made her smile. The size didn't bother her at all, and the current emptiness didn't feel wrong. It was a place that belonged to music, song and laughter, and that was something that she felt instantly at home with. The whole room felt like it was waiting, poised for someone to light it up and bring it to life.

Mysty turned to Benjamin. His height was level with hers; his age she had judged around fifty-something; greying hair that was probably as much to do with overwork than age. He was clearly a man with high standards as she had seen with every step through the hotel, and was wearing his finely tailored suit so well she couldn't imagine him ever wearing anything else – except to sleep. And then it would probably be in pyjamas ironed with military precision.

"This is where you would be performing, so this is where we will do the audition. Any problems?"

"No."

"Good. I'll take a seat. I'm not sure what you have to show me, but the sound system is at the side of the stage to the left, with the lights. The stage is yours; impress me."

She looked at him, saw the challenge, knew he was judging her biker clothes, her face, her looks. They weren't why she was here; he would soon find out why she was.

"Sure. I prefer being left to do my own thing. Peachy."

She loved using that word. It usually threw people. It was cute and sweet, and sounded a bit clueless, and she really wasn't.

Calmly she pulled down the zip on her jacket and strolled down the central runway towards the stage, leaving him to admire her but also wonder what the hell he had let himself in for. She vaulted casually onto the stage, not bothering with the steps, and disappeared stage left. Brains and beauty were a fatal combination, but could she really do anything to impress him?

He sat down at one of the tables in the centre, not wanting her to see his reactions. He settled, waiting patiently, and even undid the buttons of his jacket. He glanced at his watch. He'd give her ten minutes of his time and then shake her hand, tell her thanks but no thanks, and send her on her way. She couldn't possibly do anything to . . .

The lights were adjusted on the stage and she reappeared, wearing a black halter-neck top with a trail of diamantes around her throat. The curls glowed a fiery gold under the lights, blondes and reds glinting at him, contrasting with the smooth creaminess of her face and arms. He followed the slim waist down to long black satin-clad legs and biker boots that on her were somehow perfect. His poise was balanced, her grace catlike. He held his breath. She *belonged* in a concert hall.

She moved to the middle of the stage, holding an old-school microphone which he'd left there on purpose, knowing it would highlight any faults in her voice rather than cover them up. She raised it to her lips and looked down at him.

"I would just like to point out that I usually have backing vocals for this first song – you'll understand why when you hear it. And I don't know quite what you want to hear, so I've compiled a mixture of tunes for you. Anyway . . ."

She stepped back a little, pressed a button on the remote control for the sound system, and then ramped up the volume. She had prepared the music herself, and knew it all backwards, sideways and upside down. And she had space to fill, so she would make the most of it.

She flicked back her curls and smiled; she loved this song.

'Make Me Wanna Pray' she could sing in her sleep, and she let her voice go, soaring to the rafters. Then she went through short sections of her whole range: 'Respect' by Aretha Franklin; 'Nobody Does It Better' from Carly Simon; 'So Emotional' by Whitney Houston; 'Another Suitcase in Another Hall' by Andrew Lloyd Webber; 'On My Own' from Les Misérables; 'Halo' by Beyoncé; and ended with her favourite from Sia with 'The Greatest', singing them all as if it was Donny sitting on that chair in the dark. Wishing he was there. Wishing so much.

She got to the end. He'd not said anything. She could barely see him. Just knew roughly where he was. She pressed Stop on the remote control, backed up and flicked the lights so she wasn't blinded and could see beyond the first few feet of the stage. And realised he wasn't alone.

Benjamin had been aware of people coming in through the doors but hadn't wanted to look away or waste breath telling them to leave, and she was clearly a little surprised to see so many faces looking back at her.

"Mr Morris . . . I just wondered if you wanted me to do anything else? Because I guess if you don't like me now, I don't think you ever will."

She stood there, completely comfortable with the old-fashioned microphone that he had watched her use with consummate ease, leaving it up to him to make the call, a hand on her hip.

He stood up and walked slowly down towards her, seeing her watch him, her face a little nervous . . . why would anyone with talent like that be nervous?

"I liked you in the first twenty seconds, I just didn't want to stop you." He let himself smile, saw the joy on her face. "Turn the lights off and grab your stuff. Let's go and have a chat. Everyone else . . ." – he turned around abruptly to face the various members of staff who must have heard the amazing voice through the walls and come to investigate – "go *back* to work. Show's over."

They headed for the nearest exit. They were now alone. He looked at her again, trying to find a fault. He'd been in this business a long time; no one ever had it all. There had to be something wrong with her.

"This way," he said, and led her to a plush bar. With her leathers and helmet in her arms, she could have looked out of place. Any woman not in a cocktail dress would have. But somehow, she looked at ease, and he admired that. "What would you like to drink?"

He waved her to a sofa but stayed standing, ready to go to the bar where his smartly attired bar staff waited to serve him, looking very alert . . . and he knew it was more to do with his stunning female companion than himself.

"Water would be great. No ice."

"You can have anything, you know."

"Thank you, but really, water is great."

He gave her a funny look, suspicious of her undemanding nature, and sat down with her a few moments later. A waiter came over and placed a glass of water with no ice but a slice of lemon on the table for her, putting a coaster down first, and then a cup of black coffee for him, before retreating silently.

"You don't think I should have asked for water, do you?" she remarked quietly, trying to work out why he was so determined to disapprove of her, despite liking her voice.

"Given the choice of the whole bar, I think most people would have grabbed at the opportunity to avail themselves," he answered simply, curious that she'd challenged him without being confrontational.

Her reply was similarly blunt but gently put: "I don't drink many things, and I rarely drink alcohol – particularly not when I am riding my motorbike. Room-temperature water is the best at re-hydrating the body and for the voice. Aside from singing, I do various things which require me to be in perfect physical condition. I am not 'most people'."

It was a subtle way of telling him she knew what she was doing and didn't want to be questioned or patronised. He also realised he didn't have to worry that she'd turn up to work late or drunk or hungover. And clearly, from the look of her, her body really was in superb shape.

"And what are these 'various things'?"

"I'm a dancer, amongst other things."

"Ah. That would explain a good deal. What kind?"

"Ballet, modern, tap. I can do break-dancing, but rarely do. Spanish, ballroom, Latin. A couple of others."

Benjamin stared at her for a long second and then took a sip of coffee. He would have struggled to name any others. He had a feeling she was going to be one big bundle of surprises. Her voice was just the tip of the iceberg, clearly.

"And would you be able to use some of those talents in your performances here?"

"Of course, if you want me to. I would have demonstrated, only I didn't know whether you'd be interested."

"You have an exceptional voice," he then said. "Some of those songs – and they're classics, and for one so young I'm surprised you know them – you sang better than the original artists, in my opinion." She stayed silent, not sure where this was leading. "You could have a very interesting future with a voice like that; are you *sure* performing at a hotel is what you want?"

"I don't want to be famous, Mr Morris, but I love singing. I love music and I love dancing. I can promise you'll never see a bad show as I will give everything to my performance. Does that answer your question?"

He smiled slowly. She was remarkably quick on the uptake and remarkably astute at answering questions. She put her money where her mouth was and gave rather firm assurances without being asked for them. He liked that.

"Yes, perfectly. Now, when can you start?"

"This week if you'd like me to."

In her mind, the sooner the better: she wanted to sing again, wanted to get back on the stage.

"I see. And what do you think you'll sing?"

"Whatever you want me to sing – it's your hotel, and your guests. I can sing pretty much anything." She wasn't bragging, and he realised that as he looked at her open expression: it was a statement of fact. "I can do a pretty good job with songs usually sung by guys too."

He didn't doubt that.

"Right. Well. How about we choose some together for this first week, and next week you'll have more time to work on backing vocals and dancing etc. We do have a live band – even an orchestra some nights – so it obviously helps if they have the playlist beforehand to practice. You understand?"

Her calm absorption of the information told him she did.

"Will it mostly be guests from the hotel? Whose shoes am I filling?"

Two very good questions and he found himself respecting her even more. He still couldn't put her age much above seventeen, if he were honest, despite the bike and the leathers and her composure; but she had all the innocence of a child in some moments, and her voice during some of the songs had been both that of a young girl, sweet and soft, and a mature woman, with resonance and power.

"It's about fifty-fifty really. The woman who did Thursday nights got married and decided to have a family, so for the last two months we've been hiring some fairly decent acts but nothing permanent. I would rather have something permanent – and fantastic. Thursday nights in LA are as big as Friday nights really, so having a good show is a priority for me. It doesn't have to be a huge show, but something that people will enjoy while having dinner, and something reasonably spectacular they will talk about it with friends and feel they won't find anywhere else. Having listened to you sing, I think you can do it, if it's not too much for you? How old are you?"

"Old enough." *I could do it blindfolded and on my head.* "What if . . . when people buy tickets for the night, they get to nominate a song? And all songs from tickets bought a week in advance go into a draw and five or six get picked out. Provided they're not insane choices, we could go with those, and then people have a vested interest, because it might be their song they hear. People could also do dedications for special occasions. Naturally it's too late for this week and maybe next but . . ." She paused, waited for his response.

Benjamin nodded, understanding and instantly liking the idea. It was novel, fresh, and would demonstrate her talents perfectly.

"Once people know about it, it will gather momentum. And once word gets around about you, I'm quite certain it'll get booked out pretty quickly." Benjamin's look made her blush. "I'll talk to the web guys, get something added to the website for you so we can take bookings that way and help get you noticed. I'll have some sample clips put on there, too, to listen to and explain the song nomination idea. Sound OK?"

"I can do the website pages if you like?"

"Ah, just another little thing you happen to be good at?"

She looked away uncomfortably. "I'm quite good with computers."

"What can't you do?"

He had been utterly wrong about her. She was as competent and smart as he could wish for, and a born professional, nothing left to chance, nothing not thought out.

"Wear pink."

Her answer and grimace made him laugh loudly, and he had to admit he couldn't ever imagine her in pink either.

"OK, now, wages. Per performance, taking into account time spent in rehearsal, preparation etc, I can give you $600. The show starts at 7pm every Thursday, and finishes whenever it finishes. I'll leave you to organise the music, the people you need – I'll give you all the names of course – and the dancing, the lighting etc. I will require a run-through viewing the first couple of times. Is that a problem?"

"No, I have no argument." That was her rent covered!

"Obviously, depending on how things go, that sum may go up, so it's all there for you . . . so you go work your magic."

"Cool."

"You want a bite to eat while we choose your songs for the first night?"

"Erm . . . Yeah, sure."

"Right, we'll go and steal a table in the restaurant in a discreet corner and make a start. I'm Benjamin, by the way."

He offered his hand before they stood up – a handshake that sealed the discussion.

"Mysty."

He smiled, having anticipated something unusual. It suited her image. It would have been rather a disappointment for her to have had a name that didn't capture her so perfectly.

"What do you fancy to eat?" he said, as they walked to the restaurant.

"Anything, I'm not fussy . . . except raw fish actually."

"Sushi?" he prompted helpfully.

"Yes, that's it. I'd rather swim with sharks."

He laughed and held open a door for her and followed her in.

Thursday nights would never be the same again.

DARYL SIGHED AND glanced covertly at his LT. At awards ceremonies, it was rather frowned upon to be keen to leave, at least before the main prizes had been awarded. But he had been there an hour and a half, and was bored, irritated and tired. And he shouldn't be. Most of the acts receiving the music awards were signed up to *his* record label, were managed by *his* performance companies, doing shows in *his* concert stadiums making *him* money. And he was a feted attendee to the affair, acknowledged as the architect of so much, and given due respect in every possible way – except with an actual award on stage. He sat apart, alone, and regally aloof at his table, champagne flute barely touched, with eyes that saw everything and rested on nothing.

What was it he was missing in his understanding or outlook that meant he could not find any joy? Was he missing something? Was this it? Was this the best life had to offer? He was uniquely placed to have done and seen so much, despite his relatively tender years – though he sometimes felt much older – so was this the natural result of such knowledge and experience? Could anyone understand what it was to be him? He thought not. And they never would either, blissfully unaware as they were in their cosy little bubbles of minor achievement.

Which was why he chose to sit alone. Away from the pointless flirtatious advances of countless women, and men, who usually wanted something, or wanted to discuss business, which he only did when he wanted to . . . if he could help it. God knew it took over enough of his life.

It was diplomatic that he attend tonight, given his connection to the artists being celebrated. His absence would have been detrimental. His face would be on magazines and web pages covering the event, on the news, and his presence had the effect of no other celebrity on Earth. But it brought him no satisfaction.

He took a sip of the champagne and glanced down at his handheld, seeing it flash up some new alert: a news story about the awards ceremony he was sitting at. Could he not add a filter to the news feed to avoid headlines about himself?

He looked back at the stage, not particularly impressed. Despite owning most of the winners – body and soul, considering the investment put into them and the help they received to make them what they were – he didn't think much of any of them. His attempts at finding new talent had found some interesting specimens for the fame-train, but nothing that really shone. And the latest batch were sufficient fodder for the masses to scream and cheer at for short periods of time, guided to do so by clever marketing, and trained to do so by the three decades preceding this one . . . And all the while Mr Blackmoor himself had been disappointed with all of it. He wanted something to surprise him. To amaze him.

He was even bored with his Cherries. Leanne had been a Cherry for a couple of years and earned her place; Clarice had been most disappointing in her attempts at being a biker chick . . . and he had to admit to a desire to match the excitement of Donny's enigma, the girl who so intrigued him. He would hire a couple of new Cherries at the weekend – once they'd passed the health checks – and send someone to break the news to Leanne and Clarice.

"Mac."

"Yes, sir?"

"Have my car brought round in half an hour. I've had enough."

"Of course, sir."

Daryl heard orders being relayed and watched one of the divas of the moment take the stage – a tall woman, five-eight perhaps, her Caribbean skin gleaming under the lights, and wearing a dress designed to show off her cosmetically enhanced cleavage. She looked like she had gained a little weight; he must have a word with her personal trainer about that. And no doubt she thought she had 'made it' because of her 'amazing talent'. But no. He was just making the most of what moderate amount of ability she had, and that, with plenty of costumes, make-up and PR handling, had helped make her the 'star' she thought she was.

But it wouldn't last. None of them would, and that was the problem. Which was why the talent hunt was an ongoing process. Every week he had new acts put before him, but few made it through the first thirty seconds before he crossed them off the list.

He sat calmly for the remaining half an hour, and then stood and headed out of the door at the back of the private seating area and into the corridor.

"Do you know what the Yankees score was tonight, Mac?" he asked.

"No, sir, but I can find out for you."

Why had he asked that? He could find out in a moment just by bringing it up on his handheld? Perhaps it was simply the need to discuss anything other than the evening's events. To talk, like one person to another, about a triviality, just for once in a day.

They all turned down the stairs, five of his guys in front, then Daryl and Mac, and five behind, all serious-faced individuals, fast feet on the steps.

Rounding a corner, the front boys stopped, finding a female in their path. Daryl looked over their heads.

Dear God, it was the overly made-up Caribbean woman with thighs that could crush coconuts. He smiled for a second, wondering if he could pay her to do that instead – it might be more entertaining than her predictable caterwauling.

"Mr Blackmoor, I'm so sorry to see you're leaving," she purred, trying to be sensual and provocative.

Daryl was sure some men would find her attractive, tempting; but he found her utterly undesirable.

"Ms Tyler." He couldn't bring himself to use her stage name.

"You work so hard, Mr Blackmoor, could you not be tempted to play just as hard?"

Surely, she wasn't propositioning him? But her pose said she was. One hip a little forward, head tilted up, breasts pushed out and a length of leg showing. What on earth was she thinking trying to seduce her boss?

"I play very hard, thank you, but not with . . ." What could he call her without being sued for insulting her? "Employees. If you'll excuse me."

"I like to play very hard as well, Mr Blackmoor, are you sure you won't change your mind? I'm sure I could make tonight *very* memorable for you, if you gave me a chance to . . ."

To his horror, she clearly thought he was playing hard to get and took another step closer. He could smell her sweat, stale perfume and stage make-up. Alcohol too. It was most unpleasant, and his guts turned at the thought of this invading the tranquillity of his penthouse.

Mac inclined his head, and Daryl caught the movement; but he was more than capable of handling this woman alone.

"I suggest you return to the hall and enjoy your evening however you see fit, Ms Tyler," he snapped, his voice so cutting it might have been sharpened on a whetstone. "Do I make myself clear?"

She took on the look of a woman who'd been slapped, and she turned quickly, realising, even in her alcohol-fuelled state, that she'd made a fool of herself. She fled back down the stairs.

"Jesus *Christ*. Let's get out of here," he said. "And Mac, get Lorna over to my apartment."

Mac saw him safely into the back of the Bentley and climbed in the front with Geoffrey, exchanging looks that said everything. They were used to their boss being sullen and displeased most of the time. Jokes were unappreciated, conversation unwanted.

Twenty minutes later, Daryl finally shut the door and pulled off his bowtie, pulled off his jacket and undid his shirt cuffs. God, he was sick of wearing tuxedos.

"Good evening, Mr Blackmoor."

He didn't look around immediately; after all, it wasn't a surprise she was there. But when he did he saw the long legs of a gorgeous platinum-blonde in death-defying black heels, stockings and a thong. A black patent-finish bustier hugged her belly and breasts. In one hand, there was a riding crop, and she bit the end with her white teeth, looking at him intently, hair resting on her shoulders in a wave of contrasting colour.

"I'm afraid I've been very bad again," she told him seriously, sliding the crop over her body so it ended up between her legs.

"Really? How bad?" Daryl let his jacket and bowtie fall to the floor. *This looked like fun.*

"Very, *very* bad."

She turned and stretched herself against the doorframe, her eyes staying on him, one leg coming up to hug the wall. Her naked buttocks were displayed beautifully, and a pair of handcuffs dangled from the top of her thong. It was textbook wantonness, coy, enticing – and very attractive. His hands went to his shirt buttons and he kicked his shoes off, and she moved, going down onto her knees to remove his socks, hands smoothing up his trousers to his belt and undoing it. After a tantalising pause, she took him in her mouth and sucked, sucked so hard he caught his breath, and he put one hand down to cup her head against him. She was very good at this.

She slid his trousers down and reached around his legs to clasp his buttocks, pulling him closer, taking him into her throat, trying to please him the best way she could. Perhaps she'd heard that Leanne and Clarice had been dismissed just before receiving the message to go to him and didn't want to share their fate. Daryl hadn't initially factored this into the equation, but he smiled at the unforeseen bonus to this evening's entertainment.

She swallowed his climax, felt his hand release her head and delicately licked the last drops from his swollen tip, looking up at him while she did so, letting her hands retract slowly, telling him she wasn't finished, knowing he wasn't either.

She picked up the crop from the floor next to her and held it up to him, watching him take it. Daryl stepped out of his trousers and underwear, reached down and pulled her up with a hand on her arm, turning her to lean against the back of the sofa, silently instructing her to bend over, trailing the crop up the back of one of her legs. Lorna obeyed, feeling a tingling anticipation send a quiver through her, and after a gentle caress over her buttock she received a sharp thwack, which drew a surprised cry from her. She felt herself go wet, knew her employer was the master of pleasure and pain, knew he was going to make her feel all kinds of things before the night was over. A sharp tug and the thong snapped, and then she felt the cuffs fasten around her ankles. The soft, leather end of the riding crop was eased between her legs and flicked over her, and she gripped the sofa as she felt his hot skin near hers, making her want him, want the ecstasy, however he made it happen.

A hand pushed her head down so her weight was steadied on the sofa, and another slid down the inside of a thigh. He parted her legs as far as the cuffs would allow and pushed into her, reached round to continue flicking the end of the riding crop. It was what she wanted, being at his mercy, letting him take what he wanted, knowing he was giving her what she needed as well. Her ecstasy rose until she could hardly breathe, and with two more quick thrusts Daryl let go with her, feeling a moment of sweet relief, sweet abandon, mindless and simple. It was the one moment when he didn't, couldn't, think or feel anything else. One moment of freedom from his world. The entire world.

And then it was gone.

He let her go.

Walking over to the kitchen he poured a drink of juice from the fridge, finishing the glass and then pouring another. He then strolled back through the lounge heading for his bedroom. Time for a massage.

"Take them off," he demanded, indicating the cuffs.

She nodded.

The night had barely begun.

THOUSANDS OF MILES away, another evening was coming to an end.

"Hey, kiddo."

Mysty turned and to her surprise saw Benjamin at the dressing room door. Last time she had seen him had been hours ago when he'd come backstage to ask if she could she do a few more songs. The audience hadn't wanted her to stop. She had hundreds of songs, so sure, she could do more.

"Please don't ask me to sing again?" she said. Once the adrenaline and buzz of the stage had worn off, once the music had ended, she was always so tired.

"You mean I've actually managed to wear the Human Jukebox out? I promise, nothing till next week," Benjamin replied.

He looked at her for a moment, proud of her. It had been a brilliant performance, and then she'd gone above and beyond to keep the patrons happy. He'd ended up captivated himself, watching it for the sheer pleasure of it. So had a good number of staff, and he was horrified at the number of posts obviously left temporarily unmanned, but he couldn't really blame them.

"Is there something else you need me to do or can I go?" She looked a little worried; was obviously not expecting him to come and see her.

"No, there's nothing else. I just came to check you were OK and to say well done. You did brilliantly."

She gave him a lopsided smile. "I'm really pleased you're pleased, but I'm afraid I'm far too tired to say any more."

He laughed, used to her honesty by now. He picked up her bag as she grabbed her helmet and gestured to the door.

"You need to get home and get some rest, especially if you're flying out to Vegas tomorrow morning."

"Don't remind me." She tried to stifle a yawn and failed.

"What performance is it?" He was rather curious, and hoped while she was tired she might let her defences down a bit.

"It's a rehearsal. New equipment; new show. My act is like nothing done before, so everyone is paranoid, even though I'm fine with it and I'm the one doing it."

"Aren't you worried at all?"

"No, because I designed it and I've done all the arranging. But I do understand that others feel my life depends on getting it right."

"Your *life?*"

They started walking.

"Kind of. People think that, but it doesn't really, not unless I fall badly, which has never happened."

"When is the actual show taking place?"

"Next Friday – finally."

"So, you're at Celeste?"

She realised how she had been gradually lured into giving away information. "You OK with that?"

"Yes, of course. I don't see that your work here will be compromised by whatever you do in Vegas, I'm just curious. I get the feeling you're keeping quite a lot of what you can do under wraps." They paused as they stepped outside at the back of the hotel where her bike was parked. "You will get paid double for tonight, by the way," he then said. "You would have been justified in saying no to a longer performance, but you didn't, so thank you."

"Aw, Benjy, like I would ever let you down. You have way too much else to worry about, so don't waste any new grey hair on me."

Her winsome smile was adorable, and he couldn't reprimand her for the familiarity. No one had called him 'Benjy' before – well, except his family – and no one *ever* commented on his hair. But it was a friendliness that typified her, and had won her tonight's crowd. Eighty percent of the audience had rebooked at the desk on the way out. He was going to need more tables.

"Come in on Sunday or Monday and we'll go over the new stuff – and dinner will be on the house. I know you didn't get a chance to have anything tonight."

"That would be great." She sighed, thinking back over the evening, how it seemed like a dream really. She really had enjoyed every second.

"OK Jukebox, you get on home." She grinned, liking the nickname. It was appropriate! "And here's tonight's performance in case you want to watch it yourself."

She took the disc from his hand, knowing she wouldn't watch it. She didn't want to see herself; but she knew someone who would.

"Do you usually record shows?"

"Depends. I thought tonight it'd be useful for you to know how it looks and sounds to the audience; though I admit I have no complaints. Do you object to recordings?"

"No, I can use them on the website, if that's OK? And I was just thinking, if they're recorded, why not offer them as downloads that people can buy? Or if it's a live recording, people who couldn't get tickets could pay to view the performance anyway . . . if you get what I mean?"

"Do you ever switch that brain of yours off?" He handed her her bag. "And I do understand. We'll talk about it next time I see you. It's a good idea. Now, home before you fall asleep standing up."

She smiled, took the bag.

Ten minutes later she was home, and then the intercom buzzed. *Oh man, I really need to sleep!*

She hit the button, unable to resist the chance of talking to Donny, and flopped into the chair sideways on, hearing her tummy rumble as it demanded food.

His face looked back at her on the screen and he smiled, tilted his so it was at the same angle as hers as it rested on the arm of the chair, and laughed.

"Wow, someone is tired."

"That, is an understatement. Hold on."

She ran to the kitchen, grabbed a bowl of cereal and returned to the armchair.

"Hungry?"

"Would you believe I've not had any dinner?"

"Bloody hell. What happened to stop you?" It was one o'clock in the morning!

"Well, I finished my songs, and then Benjamin – the manager – came down and said that the guests wanted more. There were some pretty important people in tonight, so I think Benjamin was afraid of upsetting them. Anyway, I ended up doing a whole load more, so I've literally just got back in."

She munched on the cereal, and Lazarus came over to lick her arm; but he knew better than to interrupt her when she was eating.

"A success then by the sounds of it."

"Yep. And I have this." She pulled the disc from her bag.

"And what's that?"

"It is a recording of tonight's show. Benjamin gave it to me as I was leaving. I don't want to see it, but I thought you might . . ."

"I can think of nothing better. Send it over. I'll watch it while you sleep. You've got a busy weekend ahead."

"I know, and I have Indi-bike racing on Saturday. I can't *wait*."

She drank the last of the milk out of the bowl, and then put it all down and leaned back.

"One week until the big day."

"I'm so excited – and I know Franny and Fliss are as well." She looked up, to study his face properly, feeling bad she hadn't checked he was OK. He looked tired. "How are you Donny? There's nothing wrong is there?"

"No, nothing, I just . . . I miss you."

"I miss you too. Every day. I wish I could see you tomorrow. Are you sure I can't, even just for five minutes? I could wear a disguise?"

"No, sweetheart, when I see you I need it to be for more than five minutes. I don't think I'd be able to let you go so quickly."

"I could bring glue. Then I can superglue myself to you and you wouldn't be able to let go if you tried."

He burst out laughing at the reply. "No, kitten, but I'm trying to arrange something."

"Promise?"

"I promise."

She leaned forward and slotted the disc into her computer, pressed some buttons and started sending the recording across.

"Will you promise to get some sleep tonight, not just watch me prancing about on stage?"

"Depends how good it is . . . did you sing out of key or anything? Then I might turn it off."

It was her turn to laugh. "I don't think I could if I tried," she said, and he knew she didn't mean that in an arrogant way; it was just the simple truth.

"I'll call you tomorrow when you're in Vegas, alright? Your flight is at eleven, isn't it?"

"Yes, I touch down 12.15, and I'll be at Celeste by 12.45. Any time before 2pm or after 8pm is fine. I should be done by then. Another day of being starving hungry and just drinking water!" Her head fell dramatically to the side in frustration as if she was so wasted away she could no longer sit up.

"It's tough being a star," he mocked gently, proud of her.

"I'm *not* a star," she corrected stubbornly.

"You will be soon enough, which is something I wanted to say to you, and I'll say it now because the sooner the better. I know you're tired, and I wish I didn't have to say this, but afterwards I promise I'll go and let you get some rest." She sat up, wondering what was wrong. He did look rather serious. "Do you remember in the beginning when I asked you not to do your jumps in daylight or in front of people?" She nodded. "And do you remember why?" She nodded again. This didn't sound good. "Only, as much as it's all under wraps, certain information is always available at a price. I have many eyes and ears in this city, and some in others as you know, and . . . I have heard that there are some rather . . . unsavoury individuals interested in your abilities. I'm concerned for you."

Mysty didn't know what to say. She hadn't anticipated this. Donny saw the colour drain from her face.

"I just wanted you to be aware, so if you see anything suspicious, you call me or Mario or Paulo, or any of the boys, and we'll help. I know you're smart and know what you're doing, but be careful who you trust. Your unique talent is about the explode onto the world stage, and don't think that people won't do crazy things to own that. I will have the satellite boys watching over you the moment you get here, but I can only do so much."

He could see she realised the full import of what he had said, which was why she was now staring at him, her eyes huge.

"I understand. I'll be careful, I promise. I'll bring Lazarus for extra protection."

"Good idea. I'll get his ticket sorted and send you the details. It'll be fine. Whatever happens we'll deal with it, alright?"

"Yes."

"Now, this has downloaded all fine, so I'm going to get it on the big screen and pretend I was there while you go to bed." He didn't tell her he'd probably get the boys in to watch it as well!

"Yes, boss." She gave him a little cheeky salute, which he loved.

"Right, now sweet dreams. I shall speak to you very soon."

"Good night, Mr Capello."

He reluctantly reached for the disconnect button.

"Good night, sweetheart."

And then was gone. But he felt OK. Felt OK because she always made him feel so secure in her affections. Because he could now sit back and watch her sing. How he was looking forward to having her back in his city. He just wished he could be sure she wasn't in danger.

MYSTY APPROACHED THE Dancing Mermaid, aware of a number of things. Firstly, that there were a lot of bikers there already, almost too many, so that it was a little intimidating. Secondly, she couldn't see many girls in the crowd. Thirdly, even if she did find Slick, she needed at some point to make it clear to him that she didn't want a boyfriend.

She thought about the projects still incomplete and waiting for her at home, the most complex of her new security systems yet to be finalised, and felt a pang of guilt she was taking the night off to burn some rubber. But she also needed some friends. And biker friends would be a great start. Raju would want to know why she hadn't been online, but she could catch up with him later. Sometimes it felt like he was trying to control her a bit, but she knew he didn't mean it like that.

She changed down the gears and cruised slowly, looking for the green and black helmet with lightning stripes. A figure walked of out the crowd and waved to her, and inside her helmet she smiled. Phew, Slick had seen her, his handsome boyish face smiling, helmet in one hand. Gone were the oil stains on his hands and the raggedy clothes. And the strut of his walk told her he wasn't a newbie in whatever 'crew' he was part of. She had guessed they were like a gang. Did she want to be a part of that?

She turned her bike into the car park, aware she was new girl on the scene, but also knew she looked good on the 899, with its distinctive tiger prints, and all dressed in black. And when she stepped off the bike, there wasn't a head that didn't turn and stare, making her feel the usual discomfort at being observed.

"Jesus, I . . ." Slick was looking at her like she'd just emerged from an alien spacecraft. "You look…"

"Like me. I'm afraid I usually do." She looked a little embarrassed, and he guessed she was not good with such open admiration. "So, how have you been?" she then asked, hoping to distract him from staring at her so intently.

"Oh, busy, yeah, real busy this week, been looking forward to the weekend . . ." he blustered.

"And Selena? Is she OK? Has Troy been back?"

"Nope, I think one ass-kicking was enough for him."

"I'm almost disappointed."

"Hey, Slick, you going to introduce this girl or what? You keeping the hottest chick in LA all to yourself?"

Slick looked round as his best friend strolled up, slapped him on the back and held out his other hand to her. His leathers were dark red and he wore black boots.

"Hi, I'm Rusty. I keep Slick out of trouble and jail, and I run the security company above his garage. Heard what you did for Selena – you need anything, you just say."

Mysty smiled, liking his wide genuine smile. His fair hair was cut short, but was long enough that when he took his helmet off it all fuzzed up. His LA tan was deep and his blue eyes were bright and friendly.

"I'm Mysty, and thanks. And any aggressive guys start hitting on you, you just let me know. Dealing with them is a speciality of mine."

Rusty laughed, the idea of men hitting on him rather amusing, as she'd intended, and his eyes scanned over her. She looked like something from a movie.

"Slick says you're new in LA?"

"Yep. I've been here just a couple of weeks, killing a bit of time before starting college."

"Awesome, what you studying?"

"Law."

"Oh no, you're some law-bird? You going to run to the cops if we break the speed limit?" Rusty rolled his eyes and looked at Slick as if to say *why the hell did you invite her*?

"Hell no. I've broken more speed limits than I can even count, and I don't like cops. I'm doing Law to make a difference, to make sure the real bad guys go to jail, no other reason."

Rusty looked again at Slick, intrigued by her honest refute of his accusation, and her swearing.

"What's your top speed?" he tested.

"Well the top speed is 160 now I've made some after-factory tweaks, and I've been close enough."

"No fucking way!"

Instant denial. She kind of expected that. She was a girl, and if they knew the bike they'd know she'd pushed it to the red line.

"Yes fucking way."

"In Vegas? How come you didn't get your ass busted for speeding? That wouldn't look too good on your record when you're a lawyer."

"I . . . I have special plates. I'm an Untouchable."

"A *what?*"

Both guys looked at her like she was insane.

"The police know to leave me alone. Hands off. I know people who can arrange these things." It wasn't such a secret, and she was surprised they didn't know about it happening, especially if Rusty was in security.

"Fuck me, who *are* these people?" Rusty was in awe.

"The kind of people who most people don't want to know."

"But you do?"

"Yeah, I know lots of them." Mysty looked at each of them, not sure if they believed her or not. "They're not police . . . they're far more dangerous and powerful than the police."

"Are you saying what I think you're saying?"

"Probably, yes."

"So, are we going to have? . . ."

Rusty looked at Slick. This was way worse than a law-bird.

"Look. They're friends, OK? I do my thing; they do theirs." She looked at their faces, knew they were still apprehensive. She didn't need this. "Slick, good to see you again. Rusty, nice meeting you. Enjoy your night." She went to put her helmet back on.

"No, don't go! I guess . . . we just weren't expecting that. You're rather a lot to . . . take in," Slick said.

She lowered the helmet, not really wanting to go. "You haven't even seen me ride yet."

"You want to give us a little demonstration?"

"Not much point unless you can keep up. Hold on for a second." She pulled her earpiece from the pocket inside her jacket and put it in, voice dialling Fabio. "Fabio." She didn't bother moving away. Hearing the conversation might convince them she was for real about her 'friends'.

"Mysty! How you doing? LA OK?" It's good to hear your voice."

"Yeah, it's good. You still slaving away?" She smiled, glad to hear his voice too.

"You know us lot! No rest for the wicked."

"Yeah, quite. Listen, how easy would it be to get two sets of bike plates upgraded to Untouchables?"

"Vegas?"

"LA. Even just for tonight?"

"Can do. I'll just patch over to our LA brothers. If I tell them it's for you, that should swing it. You out making friends?"

"Trying."

"I thought tigers walked alone."

"This one does, normally."

"Except around a certain person."

"Of course. How is he?"

"He's OK. At the club at the moment."

"Tell him I'll have words for him if he drags his arse through the front door at gone three."

Rusty and Slick exchanged looks.

"Yes, ma'am. I'll make sure I use your words, to the letter, and get a cap in my butt for the trouble. You want to tell me the plates? I'll get you a twenty-four-hour upgrade for your buddies."

"That would be great. Rusty, Slick – what are your plates?"

Both plates were relayed over, and all three of them stood in silence for a few moments.

"All done. Yours is cast-iron as always. Theirs will expire by this time tomorrow night, so make sure they don't do a Cinderella and end up standing next to a pumpkin."

She laughed. "I won't. Thanks, Fabio. I owe you."

"No, you don't, that's just one less I owe you. I can't do this all the time, I'm afraid, but have fun, and don't go crazy."

She snorted in disgust. "You've forgotten who you're talking to clearly?"

"Oh shit, of course! What was I saying?"

"Have a good night, Fabio. Tell you-know-who I'll call him tomorrow."

"Will do, kiddo."

She disconnected the call.

Mysty looked up at her captive audience and slipped the earpiece back into her pocket.

"Well, you boys ready or what? The freeway is waiting."

She pulled on her helmet and fired up, the other two fetching their own bikes as quickly as they could, pulling up behind her as she waited on the edge of the car park, face invisible behind the visor. She nodded once and roared off, leaving them to follow . . . or stay behind. They followed, zooming after her as fast as they could, finding it rather nerve-wracking riding so fast and recklessly through the traffic.

She led them out to the freeway, looked round at them, smiled inside her helmet and twisted the throttle. The world turned into a wonderful blur and she focussed on the road, knowing they would either catch up or give up.

After an exhilarating few miles, Mysty throttled back and pulled over on a slip road, intending on meandering back. She looked back to see if she could see the guys. After a few moments they spotted her and pulled over.

"Sweet Jesus!" Rusty exclaimed after pulling off his helmet, hair everywhere, his face a little flushed. "You weren't lying!"

"I don't lie. Ever," she answered calmly, pleased, however, to see them enjoying themselves. Slick pulled up next to Rusty and took his helmet off. "You enjoy it?" She raised an eyebrow at Slick, who looked just as flushed as Rusty, and was staring at her again.

"Hell, yes! Felt kinda bad, but so good! You just disappeared!"

"I did warn you! I'd like to get a bigger bike and be faster by the time I'm eighteen." She said it without thinking and watched them look at each other. *Shit.*

"You said you were going to college?"

"I am."

"But you're not eighteen."

"Not just yet."

"How old are you?"

"Old enough. Don't worry yourselves."

Rusty liked her, admired her, and to be honest, thought she was the hottest thing he'd ever seen; but now he recognised the innocence that shone in her eyes: she was just a kid, really. *How old was she?*

"Mysty, I just want to know the truth. Not because it'll mean we don't want you in the crew, and not because it'll change anything, but just so we know, alright? We both have younger sisters and we're used to looking out for them, even though they think they're plenty old enough for everything. Including people like Troy. How old are you?"

She looked away. Should she tell them? Could she trust them? It was a fair argument. And they sounded like they were offering her protection of a sort.

"I'm not sixteen yet."

"Oh *hell!*" Rusty said and looked at Slick, and Slick returned the look, clearly shocked.

"You really don't need to worry about me. I'm not an average kid. My papers say I'm old enough to go to college, and I've just turned down scholarships to Harvard and MIT. I've dealt with gunmen, snipers, all sorts. I'm smart enough to take care of myself. I *don't* need babysitting."

Slick ruffled a hand through his hair.

Rusty just stared at her. "Oh *hell.*" he repeated.

This was the kind of shit he dealt with on really bad jobs when the security he'd arranged went south – not that that happened all that often.

"Please don't ask me anymore about me. I'm just a girl who likes bikes, alright? The rest doesn't have to matter. If that's too much for you, then I'm going. I don't want to ruin your night."

The guys exchanged looks.

"No, we're cool. It's just . . . you just seem older. But it's not a problem. Clearly you can handle yourself, and you know what you're doing."

"I've known what I'm doing since I was hauling my beaten-up mother into a taxi when I was seven years old. I know how to handle myself better than people three times my age. I'd like to be friends, but not if you won't trust me."

There was a long pause, and she could practically hear them weighing things up. She didn't know if admiration or curiosity would win over prudence.

"You're pretty assertive, aren't you?" Rusty said suddenly, grinning broadly.

"So, you noticed?" she returned blithely, eyebrows arching with the question.

"Well, you have my vote." Rusty offered his hand again.

"Yeah, mine too. Though I can't promise not to worry about you, just a little."

Slick's face was more relaxed than before, but also a little disappointed. She was too young for him. And from the conversation into the earpiece, it sounded like she had someone anyway. Not a big surprise. She was absolutely stunning.

"You think it's time we caught up with the rest and went to the Bowl?" Rusty asked Slick.

"Yep, I think so. Oh man, do you hear that?" Slick said. All three of them paused. "No cops!"

Rusty cuffed Slick round the back of the head and then they all pulled their helmets back on, Mysty dropping back to follow this time, letting them lead her to the Bowl, memorising the route so she knew it for next time. Wherever it was, it was away from the main retail centre and residential areas, as they were heading towards the outskirts of the huge mass that made up LA. They rode towards a monolith of a building lurking in the shadows of the approaching night, surrounded by other bikers and parked up.

Inside, it was a world half on its feet, half on wheels. The track was easy to see, and there were hundreds of people there (mostly men!), all with bikes, all in leathers, congregating in groups. The building was huge, with different levels running up the sides around the track, and space around it for people to gather.

"What the hell is this place?" she asked, following them up the ramps to get a better view.

"It was an old utility complex, but they went bust. No one took it over, so we started using it, and the authorities . . ." – there was a snigger in Rusty's voice – "know that if they tried to stop us it would be way too much hassle coz we'd all end up riding like madmen in LA central, not to mention all the fights and disturbances that would come with it. So this is a convenient place, in their eyes, to let us do our thing and no one else needs to be involved."

"So how does the racing work?" she asked.

"The track runs through the building on ground level. And the basic rules are that riders are divided up into categories based on the CC of the bike they ride, and they race each other – it's as simple as that." Rusty looked at Mysty. "Slick said you got the 899 as a gift for saving someone's life. Is that someone one of those people who you spoke to?"

She knew he phrased it vaguely enough to tell her he wasn't meaning to pry, but just wanted to know a little. She could understand that.

"Fabio's boss, yes," she said. "He's rather important in Vegas. Though I saved Fabio as well." No more needed to be said.

Rusty just nodded and looked away, and she was glad he didn't ask anymore.

"Well, there are times when the track is open to anyone so people can practice, without actually competing. It's all pretty well set up now, as it's been here for five years at least. We even have a speaker system for music, as you can hear. And the massive screen is for watching what's happening on the track – which is as much about excitement as it is safety, as some of it gets a bit . . . competitive sometimes." He didn't elaborate. Usually it was old rivalries that got out of hand, but he didn't want to scare her.

"Who is allowed to race?"

"Anyone, as long as they have a bike."

He knew what question was coming next, and Rusty looked over at Slick as they reached the rest of the crew, who were all having a beer in their usual spot on the second tier.

"So can I race?"

"Sure, though you might want to watch a bit first, see if you think you can handle it. First, however, you should meet everyone coz they sure as hell want to meet you! Races start in ten minutes."

Mysty stayed between Rusty and Slick, aware they were being quite protective and, in a way, she was glad, as the noise and the press of people was intimidating. It wasn't like Celeste, where it was orderly and official, and she was known. This place was lawless and wild, where tempers could flare, and it was strength or friends stepping in who decided the winner. No security, no rules. An oily, roaring, leather-clad jungle of energy and intent. She loved it, despite not feeling like she quite understood it yet or fitted in . . . but she knew she wanted to. There was a buzz in her bloodstream just breathing it all in.

She was introduced to the rest of the crew, called the Pirates, hence the skull and cross bones etched onto their leathers – some of them even had tattoos of the logo on their hands or neck. From what she could gather, Rusty and Slick were two of the top dogs, particularly Rusty, who she realised wasn't as young as she'd thought, probably nearer thirty than twenty – there was no one older than early thirties in the crew at all. There were two other girls in the thirty-strong group, but the rest were guys and, to be honest, they were all friendly . . . and very interested in her. For the moment though she was relatively safe, because it was supposed that Slick had first claim on her, and Rusty was his sidekick. She guessed they'd all heard the story about her and Troy, so she had a bit of street cred to see her through the experience, but she knew she'd have to earn her place at some point. A pretty face only got you so far.

She got handed a beer by Rusty, who smiled and led her over to the railing where she could watch, Slick standing on her other side.

The first race was about to start.

And she only had to watch one to know she absolutely wanted a have a go.

She watched the screen avidly, learning as much as she could, seeing and feeling the mood of the crowd from their vantage point, observing the different huddles, easily fifty different crews spread out over the stands.

"Are you sure I couldn't race tonight, Rusty?"

He had already guessed she wouldn't be happy until her tyres had tasted the track. And after watching her disappear towards the horizon on the freeway, he had anticipated as much.

"What do you think, Slick? Let her go for a spin?"

"Why not? I think she knows what she's doing," he replied.

The gratitude in her gorgeous eyes was enough to make him glad he'd said it.

"Fine, we'll go down and register you."

She nodded, perfectly happy.

"Well, grab your gear and we'll come with you, show you how it all happens."

A few minutes later she was track-side and the smell was heady, the noise even louder, the volume of bike engines added to by the hundreds of voices, some loud, some aggressive, some laughing, and all trying to be heard over the background of the thumping music. She could hear Offspring playing, and she approved.

They cruised along until Rusty parked up, gesturing for Mysty to follow him. And then Slick watched as they emerged from the race room, Mysty's smile revealing that she had been accepted. But as a first race, it was madness. Most riders built their speed up as their skill improved, upgrading their bikes along the way, but she was going straight into the 1000cc class – a newbie *and* a girl – and he could sense the testosterone as she kitted up.

"Ho, mama! If that ain't one I'd like to jolly roger." Everyone heard the catcall, designed to attract attention, to humiliate and belittle. "Hey, Rusty, I see you have yourself a new pirate there. How about I show you my cutlass, darlin'?"

There were louds laughs and whistles.

Oh shit. Perhaps this wasn't such a good idea.

Mysty's head came up and she looked over at the speaker. If there hadn't been quite so many of them, Rusty would have pulled her away and told her he was a jerk, Russell Bruce, leader of the Vipers, a notoriously aggressive speed-obsessed gang of bikers known for their disrespect of women: there were no females in the Viper gang. She clearly didn't like what she'd heard from this arrogant male in black and yellow leathers. And she didn't like the way he was clutching at his groin and thrusting it at her.

"Come on, sweet cheeks, you know you want something with real turbo between your thighs," he shouted, before draining the last of his beer. "Oi, Stace, Twinkie, get me another!" He slapped the arse of a woman next to him, dressed in heels and short denim skirt, large breasts barely restrained by a tight vest top, and obviously his 'bitch'. She obediently took his empty and wobbled off on her heels.

Mysty walked over to him. In his arrogance, he didn't really think he was in any danger.

"Who the hell do you think you are you?" she asked him with obvious disgust.

"Oh, cool! This Twinkie's got attitude!" he crowed, his friends grinning around him, enjoying the entertainment.

"I've got a whole lot of something else too, which usually lands people in hospital so I suggest you quiet down."

He didn't speak; instead he reached forward and cupped her buttock in his hand, giving it a hard squeeze. And Mysty felt something spark inside her, bright and hot. Everyone went perfectly still, sensing even if he hadn't that he had seriously crossed a line. Slick and Rusty didn't know how to step in, and just watched in horror as it unfolded.

"You will let go, and you will apologise," she said, looking up to stare him straight in the face.

"The only thing I'm gonna do is give you my dick to suck. I've got a race to win, though, so you don't have long, sweet cheeks." He gave her butt another squeeze.

She tilted her head to one side, as if amused, curious even; but inside she was smiling. He was going to end up hurt. He just didn't realise it.

Suddenly, she moved, tossed her helmet high into the air, stepped back and jumped. She completed the rotation and slammed her foot into side of his face, snapping his head to the side. With astonishing precision, she then reached out and caught the descending helmet and swung it ferociously into the other side of his head, sending it back the other way.

One more kick to his chest and he was sent flying backwards into his bike, man and machine a tangled mess on the ground.

With a face as grim as death, sensing the fear in those who had laughed with him – and realising they weren't going to step in and defend him – she walked over and stood on the fairing of his fallen bike. She then crouched down, grabbed his hair and yanked his head up, repulsed by the smell of sweat and beer.

"If my boyfriend were here, he would cut your hands off for touching me, so you should count yourself lucky. Your card is marked, *Twinkie*."

She let his head fall back to the ground. His eyes rolled. And he made no attempt to wipe away the blood that was pouring from two very nasty-looking injuries. She stood, took the fresh beer from the bimbo who'd just returned to the scene, and who looked on with a mixture of horror and admiration, and insolently took a swig. Thirsty work, beating up scum. She glanced at the motionless figures of the Viper gang who all looked ready to throttle her – or else run away.

"Ease up, boys. You got issues, I suggest you save them for the track, else you'll end up like him." She took another swig, tossed the bottle over her shoulder so it smashed against the bike, and went back to her own.

She smiled at Slick, who looked like he'd just swallowed his exhaust.

"Holy shit," Rusty said, before composing himself and saying, "Now they're going to get nasty. They weren't going to be friendly before, but . . ." He glanced over his shoulder. Three guys were picking Russell up off the ground and righting his bike; another four were kitting-up to go into the next race – the race she would be in. "Mysty, they're going to be vicious. They will cut you up, they will crowd you and try and run you off the track. They will try and wreck you *and* your bike. You're gonna have to do everything you can to stop them, OK?"

"Aye-aye, captain." She gave a mock salute. "$100 says I win."

Rusty thought for a second. He'd never met anyone like her. "Fine, I'll accept the wager – but any expense required to scrape you off the track I'll charge you for."

"Accepted." She winked at him and put her helmet on, throwing Slick another smile before her face disappeared and the gloves went on.

She fired up and moved away, following the other riders down to the starting line.

Rusty looked at Slick, and then they both watched her ride away. Rusty got a call and took it: Russell's spectacular humiliation had spread through the crowd. Slick nudged his arm and pointed up. Someone had captured it on camera, and the replay of Mysty having her butt groped, then her superb jump-kick-helmet-slam combo was being shown to the whole crowd, and a huge cheer went up from the girls – in fact from anyone who didn't like the infamous Russell Bruce. It was well known that he'd landed a good number of people in hospital through reckless riding, turning races in to a gauntlet between life and death by changing the nature and purpose of them. The unwritten code was clear: hurt one person, offend ten; offend ten, you offend a gang. All for one and one for all. Just like this next race. As the newest Pirate was about to find out.

Rusty and Slick looked up at the line-up: there were four Vipers, two either side of her. *Shit.* The crowd went quiet. The lights came on. The red went to green, and the rumble of engines deafened as they screamed away.

Somehow, she managed to get clear of the four so they couldn't crush over in the early seconds of the race, her acceleration sending a squeal and a plume of smoke up in the air as she went. Her weight to power ratio was her advantage, and her strength and agility. After that, Rusty and Slick, like everyone else, had to rely on the camera footage to tell them what was happening, and it didn't look good. Unused to the track, and having to get used to the light and dark – some parts were well-lit; others were plunged into blackness – it was making her slower than she would really have liked and the Vipers caught up, surrounding her and penning her in, making it impossible to accelerate or pass them.

When the first lap was over, she was nowhere near the lead, just surviving near the middle of the pack. She gritted her teeth. One on one, she could deal with; one on four was just unfair . . . and one thing she didn't like was unfair. It was tantamount to bullying. She suddenly leaned her bike at the guy on her right, making him swerve; then she dived left, doing the same to that guy. Then she braked, just enough, so that they shot ahead as she dropped back. She saw the approaching corner, but didn't follow the race line like the rest; instead she aimed for the edge of the track, like an Olympic cyclist sweeping away, working on a theory in her mind that she now had a nano-second to execute.

"What the fuck is she doing?" Slick murmured, staring like everyone else at the huge screens.

"I hope to God she knows!" Rusty replied, rubbing a hand over his eyes but not looking away.

And then Mysty went for the apex, slicing across the riders and diving in just behind the leading group. Rusty laughed in surprise and slapped Slick on the back, relieved, and the whole crowd gasped. The commentators voiced what everyone was thinking: how the hell did she pull that off? The leaders realised they had company, and swift backward glances were seen as they disappeared into one of the darkest sections of the track. Slick held his breath. They wouldn't run her off in the blackness, would they?

But once more they emerged, the Vipers swerving, riding like fools trying to reach her; but she had other ideas, and once more performed a wide arc away from the race line and ducked into the straight that fed into the final corner and the last lap. She felt the whoosh of air over her back as she rode, chest-to-tank, the Ducati screaming as she passed one, then two of the lead pack. *Just two more to go.*

"I don't believe it," Rusty said weakly as he watched her zoom past in person, the two enraged riders she'd passed almost riding piggy-back.

Slick just shook his head.

The riders all sped past, including the four Vipers who had ruined their own race by trying to ruin hers, and didn't have the skill to make up the time and distance. They saw her position on the board and aborted the race, egos and bikes battered.

The final lap was a blur of the roar of engines and crowd, as she passed the rider in second, slicing under him on a left-hander and blocking his immediate attempt to come right back at her. She made short work of the leader, as at half his body weight the final grunt of the 899 saw her gain enough of an advantage on that beautiful straight to dive past him and take the lead into the final bend and the finish line. She didn't hear Slick and Rusty's shouts, or the crowd that yelled and cheered and stamped as she crossed the line; she just heard the rush of blood in her ears, and then a deep, calm peace as time and the bike slowed.

She spotted Rusty and Slick, headed towards them. The first thing she noticed when she took her helmet off was the noise. They were cheering for her! She looked at the nearest screen and saw replays of her first swerve, her diving back into the pack, her passing the first two leaders . . .

She blushed and Rusty reached out and ruffled her curls and she playfully swiped his hand away. "Jesus Christ, you're going to give me a heart condition!" he cried.

"I don't like losing bets I make," she shrugged, trying not to appear too exultant.

Guys with cameras came up to her.

"Wow! Venus on a bike!" they laughed. "This doesn't get any better!"

The crowd cheered.

A microphone was put in her face and she looked uncertainly at Slick and Rusty.

"What's your name, beautiful?" one of them asked.

"We've been told this is your first night here at the Bowl? So that was your first race?" asked another.

"Yes, it is, and yes it was."

"*You won your first race*! How does that feel?"

"Pretty damn good, to be honest." *Please leave me alone now.*

"I see you're with Rusty and Slick – does that mean you're joining the Pirates?"

At that point, there were numerous catcalls inviting her to join other gangs, and she smiled and looked over at Rusty – who was warning her with his eyes to not even think about being anything other than a pirate.

"Yes, it does."

"Well, I'm sure they'll be mighty proud of you! You've just bumped them up the score tables into fifth place – not bad going for one night!" She hadn't even been aware of score tables? "Looks like we have a Pirate Queen in the making!"

There was another raucous cheer from the crowd.

"I see you didn't appreciate Russell Bruce's advances before the race. . .?" asked another photographer after his flash bulb went off in her face.

"Who? Oh, *Twinkie*?" More cheering, and loud applause at her referring to him with the same derogatory nickname he used for women. "That would be a no, and I hope he takes the hint as I'm not usually so gentle." She really wanted to leave now, but knew it would seem rude, and she took a deep breath, not liking the attention at all.

"And I saw the Viper team didn't really want to let you race?" another guy said, a video camera running on the shoulder of the man standing next to him.

"No. And any further issues they have, I'll happily discuss off the track. Let racing be racing."

That resulted in a huge roar from the audience.

"Well, that's a message and no mistake – and this is a girl to watch out for! What a night! I'm sure we'll be seeing you soon," the same guy said, and turned to face the camera himself. "And I'm sure we'd all like to wish Mr Bruce a not-so-speedy recovery from such poetic justice. Looks like it's all catching up with you, Bruce – or should I say Twinkie?"

The feed was cut and the video guy shook her hand and wandered off, ignoring the shouts of abuse from the Viper gang.

"I owe you $100," Rusty said to her. "And a beer."

"You sure do. And yes, I need a beer after that!"

"*You* need a beer?" Slick laughed. "I need at least two stiff whiskies to get me over that!"

"Aw, Slick, come on, that was just my first run . . . imagine what I might do next week?"

It had been an unexpectedly great night. If only she could get Mario and Lucio here . . .

DARYL BLACKMOOR HAD a sense of déjà vu as he stepped out of his Bentley onto the red carpet. The crowds were just as huge – bigger even – and the noise and cheering just as impressive. The press coverage was intense, and he could even hear helicopters overhead recording footage of the crowds outside Celeste.

Heading coolly through the vast glass doors opened for him by liveried doormen, and into the marble atrium, he was greeted by the new director, Craig Roberts, other board members and key personnel. Polite handshakes, reverent nods, serious faces, nervous eyes followed.

He knew once he'd endured this he'd be able to relax in the dark of his own private box, knowing Harvey, Guy, Robbie, and Zack too this time, were probably already there; they didn't have to make the grand entrance like he did.

"I can assure you, Mr Blackmoor, that tonight has . . . certain acts that will be worth coming all the way to Vegas for," Craig gushed.

"I hope so, Craig. That's what I'm paying you for," Daryl replied dryly.

Champagne found its way to his hand and he socialised with the big names, and greeted some of the notables in the VIP suite where they were all hobnobbing away in half-hushed conversations.

The selling line had been that the show would include something 'never seen before';the debut of '*La Papillon de la Magie Noire*' – The Butterfly of Black Magic'. He liked the sound of that. So had many others. And there were many theories on what it would consist of.

What he did not know, as he contemplated the building and the world stage he had created, that the world and he were never going to be the same after this night.

Daryl looked down at the eerie grey-blue light of the pre-show arena as the seats were filling around him. The whole area was coming alive with thousands of people, and a hubbub of noise filled the space.

He spotted Donny, looking as handsome as ever, a broad smile on his face as he held his Martini glass and chatted with someone in as white a suit as he was in black. A woman in a sleek white dress stood with his companion, and they all laughed at something that was said. Daryl recognised the suit trademark instantly: Francois Laperta from LA. It was Mob Bosses' Night Out clearly. Interesting.

He decided to have a little chat, try to find out how Donny's mysterious girl was before heading to his private rooms. He glanced over at Mac, who nodded silently.

But Donny was laughing with such good-natured ease that Daryl was irritated before he'd even got to them. Weren't mob bosses meant to lead terribly serious lives? When had he last laughed that much?

"What the hell happened next?" Donny was demanding, looking askance.

"Giles turned his back, she leapt out of the pool . . ."

"Utterly soaked!" Fliss put her two cents-worth.

"And grabbed two jugs. The first she upended over his head; the second, of cranberry juice, she hurled in his face." Everyone was smiling and Donny's shoulders were shaking with mirth. "Honest to God, I didn't know if he was going to throttle her or what."

Shaking his head at the memory, Franny was the first to notice Daryl's presence, and then the others spotted the tall figure. Space was made for Daryl to join their circle by unspoken agreement.

"Donny."

A cool handshake.

"Daryl. You know Franny and Felicity, I'm sure."

Donny gestured towards the white-clothed couple, beautiful both of them, and clearly very happy together.

More handshakes.

"Of course. You both look very well. LA clearly suits you."

"Certainly can't complain, can we, my dear?" Franny turned to his wife and she smiled in agreement, content to let her husband speak for her.

"How are the children?"

"Growing fast, and getting more precocious," Franny answered, a little surprised Daryl remembered they had children.

"Speaking of precocious, how is your redhead Mensa-level-secretary, Donny?" he asked, decided to quit with the small talk and cut straight to the chase. Donny had known this was coming, and waited for the green eyes to swivel to his, expectant for an answer. "I can't believe you would be so cruel as not to bring her again? Do you ever take her on nights out?"

"She's busy tonight, I'm afraid, though I will tell her you asked after her." *Like hell he would.*

"How is she?" Daryl couldn't stop himself asking, irritated that Donny always hedged around any information about her. There was nothing more irresistible than a defiantly-kept secret.

"Doing very well; exceptionally well, in fact. One never knows what she might get up to next."

Donny let his eyes settle on Franny for a split second . . . and almost gave the game away. Franny decided to play it safe and politely excused himself and Felicity. He didn't need to be told who the redhead was, or why Donny wanted her kept well away from Blackmoor. The start of the show was not far away, and they were guests in Donny's private suite, so they promised to meet him upstairs.

"How old is she now?" Daryl persisted. "Any closer to being legal on that Ducati?"

"Fifteen now, looks like eighteen. Brain like a wise centenarian and acts like she's going to live forever but die tomorrow. Who cares about legal when ability counts for so much?" Daryl would never get a straight answer out of Donny. "Enjoy the show, Daryl . . . even you might be impressed."

A hand slapped him on the shoulder and Donny walked away, taking a casual sip from his Martini, looking pleased with the world.

Daryl stared after him, incredulous and stymied. The experience was not appreciated. He then finished his champagne in one swallow without tasting it then handed the glass to a hovering waiter, and strode to his private box.

Tonight had better be good or someone is going to get fired.

HE WAS ON the edge of his seat. Not literally, as outwardly he looked as relaxed as if he were on a sun-lounger by the pool sipping a cocktail. But inside he was teeming with anticipation. He desperately needed something to inspire him. Something out of the ordinary.

The lights went out, and an announcement was made that this was the debut performance of the *La Papillon de la Magie Noire*.

Spotlights came on that sparkled like small stars on the ground, and another light went on, illuminating what he thought was an iron girder, but then realised it was part of the new equipment he had heard about – that had been a considerable financial investment. Developed by military sound and movement engineers, it had a powerful system of energy generation on the underside of the beam that enabled it to remain suspended in the air at any height. Unlike the platforms used by the previous performances, it needed neither ropes or wires to hold it up and was far more mobile. No doubt, Daryl thought, as he eyed it curiously, it would be technology transferred onto cars at some point, depending on how cost effective it was to adapt the energy source into a vehicle.

Such logical thoughts were left far behind, however, as spotlights then focussed on the bar, revealing just how high it had been placed.

And then there was movement as a dark object fell from the very top of the ceiling, a black cloak shrouding it. Music filled the auditorium at the start of the descent, and the line '*Now I will tell you what I've done for you,*' from Evanescence's 'Going Under' was timed to perfection as the figure landed on the beam.

The cloak fell away into the nothingness below.

Daryl stared. And his lips parted in a way they had never done before.

The moment of revelation of the figure wasn't long enough; he wanted the lights to stay on her so he could admire the skin-tight white body suit covering everything but her fingers and feet, that shimmered with diamantes. A cascade of bright golden and red curls tumbled away from her face down her back, with white extensions that had been cleverly woven throughout. Her face was hidden behind a white mask, with curling feathers that arched up over her forehead.

She was sensational.

He raised his viewing glasses and looked down.

There was no safety net.

She was over a hundred and fifty feet off the floor!

She danced, no hint of fear or panic – '*Fifty thousand tears I've cried . . . Screaming, deceiving and bleeding for you*' – and the first flip caught everyone by surprise – '*and you still won't hear me . . .*'

And then she moved, *really* moved. Feeling the music, using it to shape the ballet-like steps that were a little more aggressive in places, with a hint of flamenco. She worked the suspended beam effortlessly, fearlessly, perfectly, until she suddenly launched – to a resounding and collective gasp from the audience – from one end, backwards, arching her body into a graceful fall to the words '*going under . . .*'

Her body at first outstretched, then curled and unfurled – *'Don't want your hand this time, I'll save myself!'* – and twisted . . . and from the dark a trapeze appeared, and she caught it mid-flight, soaring upwards again with the trajectory to the beam.

And it just got better. The power of her dance and movements mesmerising as she used every inch if the beam – '*always confusing the thoughts in my head . . . I can't trust myself anymore . . . I'm going under*' – and once more, with the grace and precision of a swooping eagle, she leapt.

Daryl realised he was barely breathing, aware of the knot of fear in his stomach as he watched, afraid she would make a mistake and fall to her death . . .

This time there was no trapeze, she just kept falling, the downward sequence of twists and turns exquisite, captivating – '*I died . . . I'm falling forever*' – until her arms went out, and the cameras focussed in, showing her on the screens that had now lit up.

He longed to see the face behind the mask. Who was she? His eyes flicked from her back to the screen as time seemed to slow. The dive was breath-taking . . . how would it end? He gripped the edges of his seat.

But once more from the darkness a trapeze appeared and she grabbed it, faultlessly, effortlessly, allowing it to launch her into her final descent – '*I won't be broken again*' – and still falling, faster, faster, turning, curling . . . until, music at a crescendo and audience in a state of breathless shock and admiration, she unfurled and rolled, in perfect control, and stood, and the song ended in a final burst of violins and vocals . . .

Silence.

Daryl slumped back.

And then the audience erupted as a soft smile appeared on the lips of the girl in the white mask. She walked gracefully away into the darkness beyond the arena floor. Everyone was on their feet, the cheers and the clapping deafening.

Wow. Daryl had never seen or heard anything like it.

A glance around at the private boxes, especially the Capello box, revealed that they too were standing. Daryl then looked at Harvey, finally able to remove his gaze from the arena now she wasn't there.

"Holy fuck," he muttered.

"That was . . ." began one of his friends.

"Dear *God*," said another.

Daryl didn't say anything.

"That's the girl, isn't it?" Harvey said slowly . . .

"What girl?" Zack managed to say.

"The girl from before . . . the one from the after-show party." He omitted to add *the one I pinned against the wall.*

Again Daryl said nothing, his mind spinning. He'd not caught a glimpse of the girl that night. Surely it couldn't be . . . *could it*?

He looked down at the programme. She would be performing another act later on. Dear God, he couldn't wait. This was a miracle. She was a miracle. She was the something that had finally surprised him.

THE ATMOSPHERE WAS even more expectant than it had been before. The arena was once again completely black, until a single spotlight picked out the lone figure, high up and suspended from silken ropes.

The white costume had been replaced with one swirled in white and cobalt-blue so the two halves of her body were symmetrical, like the sides of a butterfly's wings. The mask too was blue and white, and this time was decorated with gold feathers. Her hair was woven with blue.

Her hands were bound by the silken ropes that held her, held out to the sides, her body extended in a full stretch. She started to spin, turning into a blur of white and blue and gold, just as the music began . . . '*How can you see into my eyes like open doors, leading you down into my core where I become so numb . . .*'

It soared into its first crescendo, and she was released, dropping into nothingness, to the collective gasp of a mesmerised audience. A trapeze appearing as before, and she caught it – '*your spirit's sleeping somewhere cold...*' – flying through the air from trapeze after trapeze, working her way all around the circle of space until she reached the beam that dropped down from the ceiling, launching herself through spot-lit space to execute an effortless landing.

She moved effortlessly along and over and around the beam, before plummeting again to dance among the trapezes, seemingly weightless, causing the audience to hold onto hands and seats as, as if flying, she traversed the arena – '*I've been living a lie, there's no faith inside . . .*' – and back to the beam in what must have been a fifty-foot leap.

Daryl suddenly realised a part of him, somewhere deep where he hadn't been before, was stirring, feeling the music, empathising with the lyrics. It felt uncomfortable. He was reluctant to acknowledge it, but there it was, a connection inside him that made him nervous. He was barely breathing. Hardly blinking.

The acceleration of her moves matched the increasing tempo of the music, every second fluid and smooth, as she flipped and spiralled, until she paused in the very centre of the beam . . .

The audience fell silent. Long, baited seconds passed. Hearts were in mouths. '*Bring me to life . . .*' And she stepped back into the darkness.

Once more a single spotlight picked out her death-defying fall, but this time she didn't unfurl. She dropped like a lead arrow. And as one the audience cried out, some on their feet, some with hands over their eyes. Daryl couldn't move. *Oh God, no . . .*

In the final seconds she threw her arms wide, and with the grace and strength of an eagle, but the softness of a butterfly, landing with effortless precision, coming to rest on one knee, head bowed, arms outstretched, as if offering herself, her performance, to the world.

This time the reaction from the audience was instantaneous, and they rose in waves of roaring and cheering and applause, so loud if felt like the building might lift from its foundations. Which was appropriate. Something fundamental had just shifted, never to be the same. Not just in the world. But in that cold, dark place that felt untouched: Daryl Blackmoor's cynical mind.

Daryl took in a huge gasp of air, could see she was breathing hard, head still bowed . . . and then she rose, her face perfectly composed behind her mask, to acknowledge her audience with a graceful bow. The camera closed in on her face, and he caught a glimpse of deep-blue expressionless eyes.

This had been unmatchable.

This had been the act to end all acts.

And then the lights went off, leaving everyone with thoughts awhirl with the spectacle now firmly embedded in their minds.

"Well. It was worth coming to Vegas for that. Wouldn't have missed it for the world! Thank you for talking me in to coming, old chap," Harvey concluded with uncharacteristic generosity, relieved that he'd been permitted to revisit the city. Clearly Donny had decided to forgive him. Then he put down his glass, reached into his pocket and pulled out his phone. The screen lit up as a call came through. "Excuse me, boys, I'll be back shortly," he then said.

They thought nothing of it, and Daryl turned to the others, who were smiling broadly, stunned by what they had just witnessed.

"Wonder what price she is," Guy murmured, before taking a sip of his Martini.

"I doubt she has one," Daryl replied, annoyed that Guy was thinking the same thing. There was no denying that his mind, his body, *his very soul,* was attracted to her like nothing else he'd ever felt. He wanted to get close to that brilliance, feel her body arch against his, look into those eyes.

AS THE BANTER continued, he couldn't help wondering how he could orchestrate a chance to meet her. He stood and, hands in pockets, scanned the darkness. He thought he saw a flash of white in the unlit arena – was she still out there?

Sure enough there was a body, flying with practiced ease – in almost pitch-black – upwards. The lights from high above in the viewing balconies caught her as she swung from the trapezes, hand to hand, higher and higher. Then, at the peak of the upward swing, she released the bar and floated, allowing the trajectory to carry her. He automatically held his breath . . . would she fall again? She was as high as the upper private boxes. But she dropped down, landing cat-like on the safety rail.

What was she doing? She moved from the rail, smoothly, stealthily, just as another figure walked into the scene.

Harvey.

MYSTY STRAIGHTENED UP, seeing the shock and surprise on his face. The face she remembered so well. It was handsome, she admitted resentfully, with the dapper haircut and soft blue eyes. But he still had the same arrogant expression.

She regarded him, like a predator, motionless, fearless, knowing that in that moment of recognition he knew he was the only item on the menu.

Harvey stopped and stared, eyes fixed on hers.

"Good evening, Mr Lincoln." Her voice was unexpectedly seductive, luring . . . calm. This was no longer a girl panicking at being pinned against a wall; this was a woman in complete control and it was unsettling him. He had every reason to be nervous. Aside from the memories of a blade carving letters into his arm, he'd just witnessed her almost-supernatural abilities, and didn't dare take his eyes off her. "I do hope you haven't forgotten me." She smiled suddenly and, unnerved, he took a step back. She took one forward. "I know I haven't forgotten you."

"I know who you are."

"No, you don't," she corrected him in a tone that implied he was foolish to even make such a claim. "You never even knew my name. But then again, I'm sure that wasn't important to you was it, Mr Lincoln?"

An eyebrow raised to mock him, and he felt a flush of shame at being so boldly confronted about his behaviour. She held her hands behind her back and walked a slow circle around him, and he froze, captivated by her but rather fearful of what she might do next.

"I believe my . . . crime . . . against you was dealt with," he said quietly.

"To a point. He was fairly generous with you, though. You still have your hands, do you not?"

He looked up at the ceiling. Why was she so calm? She was just like Donny had been . . . Who was she to Donny that gave her licence to act like this? For him to have cared so much about her that he had been subjected to nothing less than torture?

"He did take rather a lot of money as well . . ." he offered. Try as he might, he couldn't keep the resentment from his voice about that. But they fell to the wayside. Why in God's name was he was trying to reason with her?

"You think he or I care about money? We are not so easily bought."

She continued her nonchalant stroll around him, regarding him as one might an intriguing animal in zoo. But then her lips still curved into a smile. She seemed to be finding this encounter truly amusing.

"Then I will willingly apologise, if it will make you happy."

She turned abruptly in front of him, her beautiful eyes so angry that he felt himself shrivel before them.

"Make me *happy*? What an interesting phrase, Mr Lincoln. It would have made me *happy* if you had removed your hands from me the moment you were asked! What gives you the right to treat a girl the way you did?"

There was no answer to that.

"Tell me, how much you would have paid me if I had allowed you to continue?"

"Thirty . . . or forty thousand . . ." he answered, sticking to the amount he had told Donny, in case she knew, in case she was trying to catch him out in a lie.

"I could make *millions* using a few hours of my time merely pressing buttons on a computer. Do you think I care about your thirty or forty thousand?" The anger in her voice made him flinch. He'd suffered abuse from two individuals acting in her defence all that time ago, but nothing compared to hearing it from the girl herself. She was terrifying and he honestly wondered what she had planned for him. "There is something, however, I believe I owe *you*," she then said. "Can you remember what it is?"

Harvey struggled to remember; truth was he'd deliberately tried to forget the events of that evening, and he'd been more than a little drunk, and some of the details were a little . . . unclear.

"No," he answered finally.

She then reached out and with delicate fingers began caressing the lapel on his jacket, sliding her hand further and further up. The physical contact was as potent as a magnetic charge, as hypnotic as a cobra's stare as it began its deadly dance, and he floundered, his heart hammering in his chest, his knees weakening as he become hard.

"Would you like me to remind you?"

His eyes went from the hand to her eyes to her lips and then her eyes again. He was enchanted without wanting to be. Her beauty was disarming. What was she up to? She slid her hand around the back of his neck, holding him, her touch gentle yet firm. Lulled into thinking the minx was perhaps going to seduce him, or . . . he just didn't know what . . . he foolishly let his guard down. And she slammed her knee into his groin. Then she let go and stepped back as delicately as a fawn.

Not that Harvey saw.

The world had disappeared in a haze of pain. Agony lanced through him and he was unaware he had fallen to his knees until his eyes opened to see two shapely feet in front of him. He sucked in a breath, his hands cradling that which had been so mercilessly crushed.

"Do you remember now, Mr Lincoln? Do you remember what I said that night? I said: 'You take this any further and I swear you'll never have an anything-year-old again in your life'. But you did take it further, didn't you, even when you were called off? So, I guess this is what they call 'justice', wouldn't you agree?"

He gasped like a landed fish, in no way capable of answering. The pain was not lessening as the seconds passed, but growing, expanding, choking him. All the power he had felt holding her against the wall had been turned on him, and he felt every bit of it. He was in no position to appreciate that this was justice. The only thing he would appreciate was morphine, or a bag of ice right now.

He felt her close, forced his eyes open again and saw her next to him, squatting down looking down at him pityingly, her voice measured and composed like she was addressing a child. Just like Donny.

"The score between us is now settled, and I speak with the same authority as he who put his initials into your arm. I hope I never have to speak to you again. Do try to remember the lessons you've learned in Vegas, Mr Lincoln."

She looked down at him for a few more seconds, before jumping up onto the top bar of the railing again in one effortless move. She stood for a moment, closed her eyes and raised her arms. And then sprang off into the darkness.

DARYL WATCHED HER reappear and dive with practised ease through the emptiness, saw the moment she paused between each trapeze, down and down before landing silently, a whisper of white in the blackness of the arena.

His eyes then went back up to the corridor. Where was Harvey? They had disappeared into the covered section of the walkway shortly after she had landed on the rail.

He rang him and got no answer, and Guy, Robbie and Zack looked anxiously at Daryl.

"Mac?"

"Yes Mr Blackmoor?"

"Go and find Harvey. He was in the corridor up there." Mac looked where Daryl was pointing. "And could you let me know when you've found him."

Mac knew better than to question his employer's orders, but did wonder why he was being sent to find a grown man. Surely Harvey could look after himself?

Mac nodded, turned abruptly and left the room, taking two men with him. They made fast progress, up the private lifts and along the corridor. When they spied Harvey they ran the rest of the short distance to him and knelt down, glad to see no blood. But the man was clearly in great pain.

"Mr Lincoln, sir, where are you hurt? What happened?"

Mac didn't really know how to approach man who was pretty high up the food chain and best friends with his boss.

"Is it not fucking obvious, Mac?" Harvey snarled, his torture worsened for being seen like this.

Mac took a closer look and realised Harvey was clutching his groin. Ah.

"Mr Blackmoor." Mac patched through to his boss, staying by Harvey's side, gesturing for his two companions to back off a little to save the young man his blushes at his . . . predicament.

"Mac. Have you found Harvey?"

"Yes, sir, he's mostly alright, just . . ." Mac didn't quite know how to phrase it.

"Just what?" Daryl demanded, wanting to know what was happening.

"Just got my wedding tackle crushed by that flying-trapeze-wonder-girl! Argh . . . *Jesus*!" Harvey groaned, trying to get to his feet.

There was silence. That hadn't been what Daryl had expected to hear. And Harvey wasn't sure what was worse – the pain or the shame. At least it had been Mac who'd found him, not someone who'd spread tales of this ignominious moment to all his social sphere.

"Mac, bring him back here." Daryl almost felt himself smile: it was kind of amusing. "I'll get some ice brought up."

Daryl patched out and stood overlooking the arena, hands behind his back. He then relayed the information to Harvey's friends, who went to get ice and help their comrade back into their midst.

IT WAS A slow and ignoble return to the private suite. And he lowered himself, carefully, into a chair, where he was handed a large drink – and an ice pack. Why did he always end up in trouble in Vegas?

"Who was it who rang you, Harvey?" Daryl asked.

The wounded man looked up at his best friend and saw the seriousness in his green eyes; knew Daryl would want to know who *and* why. An attack on one of them was as serious as an attack on him. They had a code of solidarity. His friends took their seats and looked at the pair of them, watching the scenario unfold, knowing Daryl was the leader and would naturally take charge. In their elevated circles, they were protected, and this was, quite literally, below the belt.

"It doesn't matter, Daryl."

"Yes, it does. I saw her swing up there using the trapezes. She attacked you."

"It's payback, Daryl! Don't you get it? It's her revenge for what I did at the after-show party. No more, no less." Harvey desperately didn't want Daryl to take this further, and he certainly didn't want Donny coming after him again. "Don't think any more of it."

"Who rang you?" Daryl repeated, not giving up and not intending to.

"It *doesn't matter.*"

Daryl felt a twitch of anger. His friend was being rather uncooperative. He wanted to fix this gross insult, so why was Harvey acting so defensively? As though he was afraid of getting his own back?

"Mac, bring me Harvey's phone."

Harvey shook his head, tried to fend off the big guy; but it was no good, Mac's hand easily found it in his jacket pocket.

Daryl scrolled down the incoming calls after demanding the password, and saw his own missed call and then a 'unclassified' number. The only people who had unclassified numbers were those outside of the law. *Which meant the mob.*

Harvey was watching Daryl closely, knowing he was connecting the dots.

The phone was tossed back to Harvey, who caught it, knowing it had given him away.

"Daryl, please don't take this any further. This is the end of the matter. It's finished. She said so."

"Jesus wept! Who the hell has put this fear of God into you, so much so that you don't want this settled?" Daryl demanded angrily, even though he knew the answer.

"This could get a lot worse, so please, Daryl, just *let it go*." Daryl saw the distress in Harvey's face, could see fear in his eyes. Harvey was no match for someone like Donny Capello.

But Daryl was.

"Can you walk?"

"Yes . . . slowly."

"Then get yourself back to your room and rest. We can postpone our celebrations until tomorrow when you're up for something more than cradling a bag on ice against your nuts."

Daryl's words represented the voice of authority, and he straightened and did up his jacket, preparing himself for a chat with a certain someone. A certain someone he was happy to create a bit of trouble for, especially after witnessing his extreme happiness earlier. His party mood was completely gone.

"No, really, you guys go and have fun, I'll be fine on my own. I'll join you tomorrow," Harvey told them, not wanting to be the reason they missed out on whatever they had planned. The last thing he wanted was to see any beautiful women. He only had one on his mind and, despite the battering, he still wanted her. He was haunted by her mysterious, fiery perfection . . . and by the danger she posed. "I'll sit for a little longer then go back, if that's OK? You boys just go." He waved a hand at Guy, Robbie and Zack, who looked at Daryl.

"Guy, let me know what you boys end up doing, I'm going to have a chat with someone," Daryl instructed, and without giving Harvey a chance to argue, he strode to the door, Mac at his shoulder.

"YOU WERE LYING on a grand piano?" A pause. Daryl watched with interest as Donny leaned casually against the railing in the corridor outside his private box. He'd anticipated encountering a little more difficulty in finding his intended target, so to see him just along the corridor was a surprise. He was also rather intrigued and hung back, wanting to hear more of the conversation. "What do you mean at least you weren't naked? Don't tell me that's next week's show? You take off an inch of clothing more than I'd like and I'll have Paulo pick you up and hang you upside down by your toes until you . . . So, I'm jealous of the grand piano? You get more outrageous every day! . . . No, you were great . . . yes, they liked it too. . . Soon, I promise."

Daryl started to venture into Donny's peripheral vision, and he looked round and then away, drawn by whatever was being said on the other end of the call.

"What do you mean you've got company?" The tone of his voice had changed completely from jokey to hard and serious. "Chinese? *Go!* Get out of there!" Donny ignored Daryl completely and strode forward to bang on the door of the private box. Paulo appeared immediately. "Paulo, she's got company."

Paulo's face clouded instantly, darkening like Donny's. Another voice patched in on Donny's earpiece.

"Boss. She's got . . ."

"Company. Yeah, I know she has. Send the satellite through to my handheld and Paulo's." Daryl couldn't leave or interrupt, and watched the drama unfold. He was curious; especially as the 'she' mentioned was most certainly Donny's girl. "Jesus Christ, how *many* of them are there?"

"I've pegged twenty-one so far, and they have cars that they've exited and are pursuing her on foot whilst the drivers negotiate the traffic."

Daryl couldn't see what was on the small screen they were all staring at, but could see the rapt attention on their faces.

"Come on, kitten, *move!*"

"Donny, she is moving. You have any idea how fast she's going right now?"

"She just needs to get on that plane," Donny replied grimly.

He watched Mysty catapult through the traffic like some chase scene from a movie, Lazarus at her side. He couldn't look away. Not until he knew she was safely at the airport. Fabio switched from camera to camera to keep as close a watch on her as possible, not wanting to miss her for a second.

"Fuck, she really is moving." Paulo agreed, wide-eyed.

"Thank *God*. Fabio, you have someone to intercept?"

"I have Mario on a bike at the next major junction. He can pick her up and get her to the airport. Guiseppe and Mickie have a car moments away to grab Lazarus."

"Well done. How long?"

"Just less than a minute."

"*Shit!* There's more of them." Paulo's exclamation came as they saw another pack of fifteen come out from a side road and join the chase, running and jumping over cars like panthers. "If we had a goddamn bird I'd go get her myself."

"I have one. Use it," Daryl found himself saying.

Both Italians looked round at him, surprised he was there – even more surprised by his offer.

"Fabio, a chopper any good?"

Donny let his eyes settle on Daryl for a second, then looked away.

"No, by the time it gets there it will be after the event. She's covered enough ground. Twenty seconds to intercept."

"If she pauses they're going to get her anyway. Keep moving, *keep moving . . .*" Fabio urged.

There was no answer to that truth. It all depended on the girl.

They saw her point to the black limo one lane away and Lazarus bounded over and disappeared into the back of the car, the door held open by Mickie, who was tempted to get his gun out and shoot the bastards chasing her, but there would be too many witnesses – and too many innocent victims if bullets started flying around. The Capello boys were ruthless, but they weren't stupid.

Daryl was counting down in his head, too, inextricably involved in the events now, despite having no real idea of what was happening.

"Holy Jesus! Did she just do that?"

They watched as she glanced over her shoulder, saw the dark suits behind her, looked left and right at the junction and the traffic running across her path in four lanes, and then jumped. She first landed on a five-foot power cable box, which she used to launch onto a street light, and then landed on a passing truck.

But she didn't stop for the ride.

She pushed off again to land on a second truck, cart-wheeling on her hand on the edge of the vehicle to the third, and onwards across the four lanes until she dropped to the pavement on the other side, landing and simultaneously pulling knives from her boots and holding a fighting stance.

"Christ Almighty," Donny murmured. And since when did Mysty carry knives?

Daryl was dying to know what was happening, and why they all looked so dumbfounded. To his living memory, he couldn't recall ever seeing anything that interesting on his handheld.

MYSTY'S HEART HAMMERING in her chest, her breathing almost hurting. She threw back her hair and faced the approach of the men she knew were still there, smiling in anticipation. But then she spotted Mario on his bike. She had never been so glad to see anyone!

She flicked the knives closed and slotted them back into her boots, running to him as the traffic continued to flood past. She accepted the earpiece from him as she jumped on behind him, and one arm wound round his body as he roared over the pavement, leaving it for pedestrians to get out of his way, then back onto the road to head onwards to the airport.

"Mario, you got her?"

"Yeah, he's got me."

She was still breathing hard, but there was detectable relief in her voice . . . humour too . . . and it took Daryl only a second to recognise her voice, even from a handheld.

"Kitten? You alright?"

"Me? Oh, I'm just peachy!"

Donny laughed in relief, and Paulo grinned at him.

Daryl wanted to smile as well. Well, how very interesting. It was clear that whatever had happened to Donny's 'kitten' hadn't been good, but she'd brushed it off with amazing good humour.

"You sure choose your words. Mario, get her on that plane and let me know the second she is. Kitten, there'll be people to meet you the other end, clear? Don't argue. Lazarus is on the way with Mickie as you know."

Who is Lazarus? Daryl thought, completely thrown.

"I can't bring him again, Donny. If they were smart they'd have tried to take him down first to bring me to them. I can't let that happen to him."

"This isn't happening again. Call me later." Donny's voice was stern and authoritative; exactly what she needed hear to reassure her.

"That's if Mario gets me to the airport – he's not even hit 100mph yet. Mario, you ride like an old woman."

Daryl wanted to smile. Donny and Paulo already were.

"Hey, kiddo, you just remember who just saved your ass!"

"Saved? In your dreams! I sure hope you haven't broken a nail or anything, or scuffed your $500-dollar shoes!" Paulo laughed; Daryl was almost there; Donny was fighting it.

"Hey, you just–"

"Children, children!" Donny understood the euphoria of survival, knew that what he was hearing was the normal banter between Mysty and Mario, but there were important matters to complete. "Airport!" he said.

"Yes, boss."

"Take care." He patched them out, not wanting her to hear the next orders. "Fabio, what units have you got?"

"I have five, aside from Mickie heading there. You want more?"

"I want every single one of those Chinese fuckers in a basement having their bones broken by midnight, so you pull everyone over from our boys in Westville you need, get every car plate, every face you can, pass over some of the surveillance to our Langton office. I want to know who sent them and I need to make an example. Got it? This isn't happening again. Not in my city."

Daryl had to admire the command, the sheer ruthlessness of it. This was a man who protected his own, nothing held back, nothing spared to achieve his ends.

"Sure thing, boss. Reports in say we already have three of them in the bag."

"Keep me posted. Paulo will take over." Donny nodded to Paulo. "Paulo, let the boys at the other end know. Have her taken underground until tomorrow at least, when we'll have answers. I don't want her safety compromised outside Vegas."

Paulo gave him a solemn nod back, and after one look at Daryl and Mac, walked away, already barking orders in angry Italian into his earpiece.

"Daryl." It was a greeting, but Daryl knew it was reluctant.

"Donny." A measured tone. He had not come here to be friendly. "Your secretary really is rather interesting, isn't she?"

"Sometimes I'd rather she wasn't," Donny admitted, smoothing a hand over his hair and slipping the handheld inside his jacket.

"I trust you enjoyed the show?"

Such pleasantries. Daryl knew they were largely pointless. Donny knew why he was there.

"How could I not?" Smooth, slow reply. Ever the Italian charmer.

"Yes. Quite. Must be some cabaret act she does if they're still hoping to get to you through her."

Donny looked at him like he had no idea what he was talking about for a split second; then smiled brightly. Cabaret? Ah yes, Daryl had overheard the conversation about the grand piano. But had he joined any further dots? One glance at the screen as they were tracking Mysty across the city would have revealed her identity as this evening's 'act' . . .

"Oh yes, very annoying. But she's a tough little thing, as you know. Takes a bit more than being hunted by thirty-odd armed Chinese men to worry her." There was a prolonged pause, and then, "So, Daryl, what do you want to see me about? I presume you want something as you've waited a while to speak to me."

"Oh, nothing very much. I just wondered whether you might know how my very good friend Harvey ended up unable to stand, and now making best friends with a bag of ice? . . ." Daryl began, his voice pleasant enough, but his eyes deadly serious.

"What makes you think I would know?" It was a predictable evasion.

"I know who did it, Donny. I saw her swing up to the corridor. Last year, after Harvey's 'indiscretion' with her, you decide to help him lose a significant sum of money. And now he is accosted when so conveniently lured to an empty corridor after taking a phone call from one of your boys?"

Donny didn't really care what Daryl had worked out. His bone of contention wasn't with him.

"Can't stand up, you say?" Donny said.

"No. Can barely walk."

"But nothing is broken?"

"No. Should it be?"

"It usually is. It sounds like Harvey got away fairly lightly."

Daryl was flabbergasted by his tone; it was as though they were exchanging stock market tips not discussing his best friend's assault.

"Jesus Christ, Donny, what game are you playing? I do not appreciate my friends being beaten up by vicious little girls."

Donny's anger rose at Daryl's exasperated tone and his description of Mysty, but he maintained an outward appearance of perfect nonchalance.

"Two points before I address your question: firstly, she's not vicious; she was the victim, if you remember, not dear old Harvey; and secondly, she's not so little anymore. Have you ever heard the phrase 'never kick a pup because when it grows up it might just remember you'?" It was Daryl's turn to curb his anger. Mac appeared and stood behind Daryl, and Paulo took up position behind Donny. "Did Harvey send you to speak to me?"

"No, he told me to leave well alone. Why the games, Donny?"

Donny smiled. He'd anticipated as much. Daryl obviously thought he could take this little matter into his own hands.

"Well, Daryl, I'm sorry that I must even answer that. I would have thought you'd know that I don't play games. This is a simple case of natural justice. Do you think you and your rich friends can continue to run amok in this world, doing what you like, offending who you like, and that there will be no consequences? That no one will ever stand up and fight back? Harvey Lincoln is lucky I was so lenient. I might have done a lot worse. So might she. So, at which point will you and your friends realise that you cannot always have exactly what you want?" Donny explained in a calm, even tone, watching Daryl's face tighten with barely restrained indignation.

"Harvey said she told him the score was settled. Is that true?"

"If she said so, then I guess it must be. So Harvey can now rest knowing his 'debt' is paid. He is free to come and go as he chooses. I have no issue with him, provided he does not abuse the hospitality of my city or its people again."

"I'm sure he'll be relieved to know that."

"Sometimes I think Vegas is a bit much for you New Yorkers. Seems we play a little too rough for your liking."

"Is that a threat, Donny?"

"Not at all, Daryl. It was merely an observation." Donny glanced at Paulo, who told him with his eyes there were things to discuss. "I'm sorry, old chap, I need to go. Was there anything else? . . ."

"No. I think we've covered everything."

"Excellent. Well, enjoy your evening. Best regards to Harvey. Having seen her when she's riled, I'm sure it must hurt quite a bit." Donny turned away for a second so that Daryl would not see his smirk. "Oh, and Daryl." He turned back briefly. "Thanks for the offer of the chopper; that was much appreciated."

"No problem. It would have come with a price . . ." Daryl replied, pleasantly surprised his offer had not gone unnoticed.

"A picture?" Donny remembered.

"Something like that." Daryl replied dryly as Donny turned and strode away.

Daryl looked round at Mac. "Have my car out front. I'm going back to the house."

Mac nodded as Daryl started walking back the way he'd come, pausing by the rail for a few moments to look down at the arena. It was cavernous. Standing there, he saw once again that the drop was massive. He was not afraid of heights, and yet he felt his stomach turn over. But she had stood on the rail and leapt off into the darkness, knowing, trusting herself to catch that first trapeze . . . as light as a butterfly, yet dark: black magic dark.

He couldn't wait to get home and watch a replay of both acts. Zoom in on her face and try to fathom what she looked like without the mask. He remembered Harvey's words about her eyes, and he wanted to see them – and not just the expressionless ones he'd seen today. He had always used eye contact to read people – their emotions, truths, untruths – and how he wanted to see hers. She was without a doubt exceptional, and that was something he always liked to possess. He didn't like average, or good or even excellent; he liked the very best in all things. And she was the very best.

He was silent all the way down in the lift and into the car, glad to feel the night air on his skin. He caught sight of Donny getting into a sleek black limo accompanied by two more just along from his own cavalcade. They were so similar in many ways. But Daryl so much richer; Donny so much happier.

He rang through to Harvey, and this time got an answer.

"Daryl."

"Harvey, how are you doing?"

"OK, I suppose. Did you . . . erm . . . speak to Donny?" It was a tentative question.

"Yes. He has confirmed what she said. It's finished. You are free to come and go in his city, and there will be no more . . . reprimands."

"*Reprimands*? Right now it feels like castration."

"Shall I send a doctor?"

"What? So he can tell me my manhood is crushed? No, I think I've worked that out. Thanks all the same."

Daryl couldn't stop the grin, knew Harvey was smiling through the easing pain. It was a most apt punishment, they both had to admit that.

"Is the ice helping?"

"I can't feel much, so it must be. I think everything is frozen. That and the four brandies the boys tipped down my throat, I'm actually feeling quite jolly." Daryl couldn't hold back the chuckle. "And any jokes at my expense I will pay back with interest at the earliest opportunity."

"Like any of us would dare say anything *below the belt* while you're temporarily *unmanned*?" Daryl replied calmly, hearing the groan of frustration at the other end at his terminology.

"Daryl!"

"Alright, keep your ice pack on." Another groan. "What's she like?" He tried to keep the question casual, but it was anything but, and it elicited another groan.

"Oh God, like an angel. Sweet Jesus, she's so beautiful, even behind a mask. I couldn't walk away, even though I knew she meant trouble. I'll never forgot her eyes, Daryl, they're stunning. So blue. And her smile. I didn't see what was coming I was staring at her so hard." A deep sigh. "Guess I've burned that bridge good and proper. She is incredible, like no woman – or girl, or whatever she is – I've ever met . . . and I've met quite a few. As you know."

She was also going to be the hottest asset on the planet by tomorrow morning. No country, no media station, no company had anything to rival such a bombshell of brilliance. He could practically see the news headlines. She was what he had been looking for in all his talent-hunting, and she'd been there, right under his nose!

"You've seen her up close. You're one up on me. Twice over," Daryl said, trying to sound jovial.

"You can *walk*, Daryl."

Daryl smiled. He had a point.

"I'll see you tomorrow. Take it easy."

"I haven't got much choice. Night, Daryl. Awesome show."

"Yes, indeed . . ."

Disconnect.

Harvey had done nothing to ease the obsession in Daryl's mind. In fact, he'd gone and shone a torchlight on it! *An angel? Stunning eyes? So beautiful he couldn't walk away? And this was Harvey Lincoln? A fastidious and practiced womaniser for over a decade?*

Daryl stepped out of the car and climbed the steps to his mansion, went straight into his den to watch her in peace, leaving orders that he wasn't to be disturbed. He shut the door firmly behind him and instructed it to lock: voice recognition was such a wonderful thing, and something he had helped develop over the last couple of years. One more success amongst a number of such achievements. And something Donny didn't have. As far as he knew.

He flopped onto the black leather sofa and in moments had the recording of the performance up – as owner he had complete access to all files and recordings. Skipping forward, he turned all the lights off and sat in the darkness watching, admiring, wondering. Watched her three times over. This was something he could not fathom. Not her, not the skill, not the landings. Something else. Finally, something had stirred his mind and his blood. How he had waited for this feeling. It felt like a vindication just knowing it existed.

Yet his soul now hungered for more, something undefinable, unknowable. It wasn't just that he had been captivated by the visual aspect of the performances; the songs she had chosen had created emotions in him he could actually identify with. How long had he prayed to be 'brought to life' by something, rather than drowning in the monotony of endless responsibility? How long had he felt the intense frustration, yet remained mute, at the lack of acknowledgement for the lengths he went to, and the hours of his life he spent on endeavours that were so important to so many? How much silent sadness, even emptiness, had he carried around and never given expression to because he always put work, business, reputation and appearance first? Had he ever given in to expressing those emotions? No. Did he wish he had? Yes. And now, tonight, he had seen and heard something that made him feel like there was someone who understood, someone else who might just feel like he did . . .

When he analysed this, he felt just a fraction less alone than he had before he had seen her. Yet still he was trapped behind the mask of the controlled, powerful man the business world relied on. How he longed for the freedom of expression and passion he'd heard in that music tonight and, oh, how she had brought it to life so perfectly with every movement of her body.

He paused the recording on her face at the end of the first act and zoomed in. Damn it! The mask and the lights made it impossible to see her eyes.

Firing up a computer, he went through several databases trying find her, typing in 'tiger performer' and 'tiger troupe' – and came up with nothing. He typed in 'the Butterfly' and still got zero hits on the search. Who was she? What was her name? He'd understood the secrecy before the performance, but there was literally nothing available on her now.

He rang a call through to Craig Roberts.

"Craig."

"Mr Blackmoor. How nice of you to call." Daryl could hear the background noise where Craig was currently celebrating with Celeste's VIPs and press. "You enjoyed the show?"

"Very much. Tell me, why is it I cannot find anything on our new star anywhere in the system? What are the media going to use if they have no information?"

There was a sigh from Craig. He had anticipated this conversation.

"I'm afraid that is rather up to her, Mr Blackmoor. She doesn't want to be famous. She insisted on confidentiality, so an anonymity agreement, also a non-disclosure agreement, was signed to protect any information about her. That is why you only have a stage name, and why she will only ever appear in a mask."

Daryl sat for a moment, his mind thinking a hundred new things. Didn't want to be famous? With skill like that? She could make millions!

"But I *own* Celeste. I am her boss, am I not entitled to this information?"

"The agreement specifies only the bare minimum of people have access to her details, and everything on a need-to-know. You aren't named, I'm afraid, and there are only two people on it."

"Who are?"

"Me and her."

"I see."

"It's a very well-drawn up document and legally binding. I can show it to you if you wish."

"Who is her agent?" *Because he and I are most definitely having words.*

"She doesn't have one."

"What?" *This is getting more bizarre by the second.*

"She doesn't have one. Never has, since the beginning. She does everything herself: the music, the set-up, the whole act . . . every calculation down to the tiniest detail. I wouldn't be surprised if she'd written the agreement herself. And considering how low maintenance she is, and what she'll bring to Celeste in terms of revenue, she's an absolute bargain."

"How much are you paying her?"

"For tonight, $8000."

"Is that *all?*" Daryl was utterly amazed. He'd estimated at least $40,000.

"I'm sure her price will go up. I think she knows she's worth more, but wants to continue to prove herself. She loves what she does, Mr Blackmoor, and it seems that and not money is her driving force."

"How long is she contracted for?"

"She's not contracted."

Craig waited quietly for the explosion.

"*What?* Are you *insane?* Talent like that and *you haven't got her signature?*"

"It's her way of making sure I keep to the agreement, Mr Blackmoor. Don't you think I would have got her contracted if I could? She's not stupid, by any stretch of the imagination. If it's any consolation, I have a personal assurance from her that she has no wish or intention of leaving so long as her identity is kept secret and we want her to perform at Celeste. She has never missed a deadline, never broken any rules, never given a bad performance . . . in fact, she's only ever exceeded expectation. I have no reason to think she does not mean what she says. She has the self-discipline of a professional and I trust her."

Daryl thought this over. It was all very admirable, but it simply wasn't how he did business. *Trust*? He wanted a contract, in black and white, signed and witnessed.

"I think I'd like to meet this mystery of yours, Craig."

Craig, Daryl mused, might acquiesce. A few minutes with Mr DB himself would surely set her straight.

"No can do. She doesn't do interviews. With anyone. Even me. Most things are discussed over the comm. If I ask her, she'll refuse, and if you push the issue, she'll walk. I know she will. And that's a couple of hundred million thrown away. *Billions* even, if this takes off like I think it will."

Daryl could have growled in frustration. None of these were answers he wanted to hear. How could he be refused a chance to meet her, damn it? He owned her as her employer, for God's sake! This was ridiculous.

"And what about the media, the press?"

"They're getting fed all they need to. But no names, no history, no age, no details."

"She's young, isn't she?"

"Very, considering. But she has never acted her age. I remember first seeing her arrive for the audition, and even then there was something about her."

Daryl envied the man. He had met her. Spoken with her.

"I'm going to appoint some specialist PR guys to help you. I don't want this screwed up any more than it has been."

"With all due respect, Mr Blackmoor, I don't think anything has been screwed up. She is an entity unlike any other. Forcing any of the issues wouldn't have worked. In entertainment, you either give all or give nothing, and having her remain a mystery is no bad thing, in fact. The media will go berserk trying to work her out and, believe me, they'll get nowhere."

"Well, there's not much that can be done about it now. We will just have to make the most of the situation as it is."

Daryl heard a sigh on the other end, as if Craig was frustrated by his attitude. Daryl didn't care. How could Craig be such a fool and not get her contracted?

"Tell me, Craig, what's the trick?"

"Trick? What trick?"

"For God's sake . . . she falls over a hundred feet and walks away? What is the trick?"

"There is no trick, Mr Blackmoor. She's unique. She is quite . . . unbelievable. Even she doesn't quite understand the maths, or the science – and she can do calculations in seconds, in her head, that would take me a year. She says she has some theories, but hasn't quite cracked it yet. And you know the most exciting thing?"

Daryl was busy chewing over the answer, and the question took a moment to process. How was it not a trick? Craig had to be wrong, didn't he?

"What?" he finally asked.

"This is just the *beginning*. Her talent has grown. Is growing. Giving her an act of her own enabled her to develop moves that I can see even she is surprised by sometimes. She likes nothing better than to experiment, and I know she's already got things planned for at least three new performances. She's so young, and has so much potential. God knows what she might be able to do when she's a year or two older and stronger."

"She seems pretty strong already." Daryl remarked wryly, remembering Harvey's pain. "How often is she performing?"

"Friday nights and Tuesday nights every week, and after four shows of the same pieces she'll change to the new one."

"That's not very much."

"Early days, Mr Blackmoor, and she's young. She's studying, too, and has other commitments. The worst thing I could do would be to overload her now and end up with a tragedy in six months' time. She should reach her physical best in about eight years, we're guessing, so there's no need to burn her out in the meantime, particularly if this talent of hers is going to evaporate. She makes it look effortless, but it's not. I've seen how tired she gets after rehearsals. This was her first performance on her own, and she carried it off in breath-taking style and composure. Limit her exposure and those nights will be sell-out shows every week, in-house and subscriptions. Downloads and broadcasting will bring in tens of millions more, and you know it. When the time presents itself, maybe I'll take it up to three nights a week."

"True."

"So, you're happy?"

Since hearing he wouldn't be able to meet her, Daryl was never going to be happy with anything Craig had to say. "Whatever she asks for in money terms, let her have it. I doubt she'll ask for anything stupid, but I don't want her to take her talent elsewhere, do you hear me?"

Only a deaf man would have missed the dangerous menace in Daryl's voice at that moment. The idea of losing her was unimaginable. She was his. His star, his mystery. And she was damn-well staying.

"I hear you."

"In fact, insist she gets $20,000 a performance when she starts on the new one. Make sure she feels appreciated."

"Will do, Mr Blackmoor."

"Fine. Well, enjoy your night, Craig. At least you have something to celebrate."

"The greatest show on Earth?"

"Not getting fired," Daryl corrected with such acerbic dryness there was no reply forthcoming. "Have that agreement sent over to me. I want to see it. Tomorrow morning."

Disconnect.

Daryl sat back and leaned his head against the sofa. There was so much information buzzing around his head about her it was making his brain hurt.

When he closed his eyes all he saw was her, her beautiful body so strong and sure. He knew his new girls, Roxy and Lily, were upstairs and would be ready and willing at the click of a button, but he didn't want them. In fact he was worried how much he didn't want them.

This was not what he needed: a fantasy, an obsession about someone he couldn't meet, couldn't talk to, and definitely couldn't sleep with now he knew how young she was, when all he wanted was fast-forward and capture her in a room and satisfy his curiosity about her from the top of her head to the tips of her fingers and toes. To see what her face looked like as she fell into ecstasy, to feel the strength of her legs around his hips, to understand the mind that jumped so fearlessly through the darkness. Even if it was a trick, it was still superbly done and required huge amounts of skill.

He didn't move. Felt his erection ache. Damn it.

He reached over to the comms unit and pressed a button. He'd never go to sleep if he didn't do something about this, and he was paying them after all.

Moments later he strolled into his bedroom and found two sex kittens in delightfully skimpy underwear on his bed, one leaning on the pillows, one draped further down the bed, lying on her front, showing off her ample cleavage and the smooth curves of her backside. He pushed the door closed and pulled his shirt over his head as they smiled in welcome . . . and moved to help him with the rest of his clothes.

One day, he promised himself, as the wrong hands fluttered over his skin and red lips descended on him, one day he would have his illusive *Papillon* and he would find out what lay beneath that costume. Again and again and again.

If she had a price, he would pay it.

He was rather afraid, however, that she was priceless.

MYSTY HAD BEEN picked up from the airport in an unmarked car driven by a guy in plain clothes and escorted by three others. She was taken to Franny's own 'bomb shelter' where he went if he had to disappear.

It was odd not having Franny or Giles there, but she knew some of the boys, and after polishing off a pizza they'd grabbed on the way back she had fallen asleep, Lazarus next to her. By 7am the next morning, they received the all-clear from Donny and took her home in a very ordinary suburban car.

She had just walked in the door, when the intercom buzzed. She guessed who it was and pressed the button.

"Donny!" The happiness in her voice made him smile.

"Kitten! You're home alright?"

"Absolutely one hundred percent." She flopped into a chair. "Is everything OK now?"

Donny heard the slight waver in her voice, knew he'd never tell her the gruesome details of what took place when the chase had eventually ended.

"Yes, all fine. I took care of everything. No one will try anything like that again."

She paused before answering, knowing there was plenty he wasn't telling her. There was only one way a mob boss would take care of a situation like that.

"Thank you," she simply said.

"You don't have to thank me. You know I wouldn't let anything happen to you."

Her throat closed up. His soft-voiced assurances were exactly what she'd wanted to hear since finding Mario waiting for her on the bike. Just because she had been able to run didn't mean she'd enjoyed it. It was only after the buzz of the day and the adrenaline had finally faded away that she found herself trying to hold back sobs as she lay in the dark, Lazarus licking the salt from her face. How close had she come? She was overwhelmed by the stone-cold reality that even now, years later, she was still having to run to survive, to save herself.

"I know." She was quiet for a long time, and then she said, "I don't want to be here. I want to be with *you*. In *Vegas*."

He squeezed his eyes shut. "I know, sweetheart. I wish you were here too." He gave in. "In just over three weeks – after your Tuesday performance – you're coming home to me, OK? Just one night, and we can't go out. You can catch a flight the next day."

"You mean it?" she asked.

"Unless something drastic happens, yes. And it'll be here before you know it. You can cry on me, try and gamble money off me, tell me all your news . . . I'll even get you a grand piano you can lie on and sing," he teased. "Anything you like."

"You're a cruel and mean man sometimes, Mr Capello, making me wait three whole weeks."

"I know. It's a wonder you love me I'm so nasty."

To the rest of the world he was cruel. Some called him a monster. But to her? To her he was her dark angel.

"I'll pre-warn Marco to make extra pizza." Mysty laughed then and he chuckled, glad to hear the sound. "Kitten . . . Mario said you had a bit of a problem at the airport."

She had known this would come up. That Mario would tell Donny that she'd slumped against the wall suddenly, and then fallen to the floor, barely able to move. She'd had to tell him to get the energy sachets from her bag.

"It was just low blood sugar, Donny. It's happened before, in practice. It wouldn't have happened so soon or so bad except for the chase. I'd burnt up so much energy in the arena and was running on empty, anyway, because we only drink water and energy drinks for so long before the shows. And I had to leave so quickly that I forgot to take one of the extra sachets before heading for the airport. I won't do it again. It was horrible."

"Alright . . . but make sure you always have something with you. God knows I worry about you enough."

"I will, I promise."

He relaxed a little, knowing she meant it, that she wouldn't make the same mistake twice.

"So, how does it feel to be famous?"

"Famous?" She sounded incredulous, eyebrows leaping to her hairline.

"Haven't you seen the news? Any headlines? You're on every channel, kitten, did you not realise?"

"I slept right through, and then I was brought back here. I've not seen anything. And I don't have a TV . . ." She paused. "There's . . . nothing actually about me on there, is there? I have the rights to anonymity with Mr Roberts, and if he's screwed that up I'm not going back."

"No, they're just raving about your performance. Apart from your stage name, they have nothing else about you, so you're all safe."

She breathed out. "Good."

"So how did you feel after the show?"

"I don't know how I stayed so calm. It should get easier though."

"You made it look like a walk in the park," Donny told her, smiling, having watched it all again plenty of times. "You get some rest and take it easy today. Any problems, you let me or Franny know. He'll be back today, so no doubt it'll be a barbeque by the pool tomorrow night."

"Jealous?"

"Insanely. If I didn't like Franny so much I would punch him."

"I'll make it up to you on Tuesday night."

"That sounds good to me. You were brilliant, sweetheart, but you take care, alright?"

"You know I will. Same goes for you too, remember? Get that grand piano organised and I'll do an out-of-key song for you."

"Like hell you will."

Donny pressed Disconnect after listening to her infectious laugh.

So, the butterfly had spread her wings. Where would they take her next?

MYSTY LEANED BACK in the cab. The buzz from performing was like nothing else, and she felt she was still riding a wave of excitement, but sitting alone in the back seat she also felt a little sad. Tonight had been the last performance of her two debut pieces, and she recalled how impatient she had been to get them over with to move on to the next, but now . . . *now* they felt precious, four stellar performances that had broken records for broadcast sign-ups and ticket sales, and had got the media so wound up that all kinds of crazy stories were making the rounds.

She remembered the conversations with Raju, who had been exclaiming about the Butterfly, and was now reeling off theories of how it could be a trick, or if it was real, and what it meant for human evolution. But she didn't want to be discussed alongside human evolution. That made her feel like an experiment. To perform in front of an audience of over one hundred thousand and be watched on screens by millions more was one thing, but that made her feel like a lab rat. And it made her feel lonely. There were so few people she could actually share this with.

As usual, she had taken her route from the back of the hotel roof as unobtrusively as possible, and with the stealth of a ninja, had dropped down into the tastefully landscaped gardens and picked up a taxi from those lined up for hotel guests, merging seamlessly into the ebb and flow of people. There was no point trying to leave by the front or usual stage exits. Mr Roberts had offered to arrange something for her, but she much preferred to handle it herself, and she knew the boys were only a call away if she needed them. Thankfully for the last two nights, she had been unmolested – which was not surprising when she found out what had happened to her pursuers from her debut night. It made her proud to know Donny cared so much for her, and was so fiercely protective; but she was glad to be on the right side of him. He certainly wasn't the kind of person you'd want as an enemy . . . but being enemies with Donny was unthinkable. That would never happen.

The cab door was opened for her by one of the parking attendants and she got in, throwing him a smile, shades and trilby on.

"Where to, beautiful?" *She has to be the hottest chick to ever set foot in my cab*!

"Airport. And you'll get a $100 tip if you get me there in less than twenty minutes."

The driver looked at her in his rear-view mirror. She had the confidence and poise of . . . somebody. And it was usually VIPs or celebrities who offered a tip like that and meant it – and she looked like she meant it.

"Sure thing. Don't tell me you're leaving Vegas?"

Driving but half watching her, he pulled out into the traffic, unworried by how busy it was, part of him trying to think how best to get some distance covered, planning his route. He watched her lips twitch into a smile, wishing she'd take off the shades so he could see what she really looked like. Shades at night? Hey, who was he to judge . . .?

"Oh, don't worry, I'll be back soon enough."

"Glad to hear it. You had a good night?"

"Not at all bad, how about you?"

She eased the shades down just a fraction to look at him over the edges into the mirror, so captivating in that split second, he completely forgot he was driving, came off the gas without realising and drifted a little – until someone honked their horn at him.

She pushed them back up.

"Oh, you know, staring at the back of the car in front . . . I know how to lead an exciting life," he grumbled cheerily as he manoeuvred his way through the cars.

Mysty pulled out an energy sachet and took it, then swallowed down the last of her water. She had already taken one, but knew from that slight tug in her muscles she was still struggling.

"Trust me, sometimes things can be too exciting and you'll wish you were just staring at the back of the car in front."

Her answer intrigued him, and also delighted him. She clearly wasn't some stuck-up bitch who thought he was too low down the food chain to speak to – a lot of people treated cab drivers like crap, especially from the top hotels, even though his cab, his license and he were smart and spotlessly clean.

"Really? So, you see quite a lot of excitement then?"

"You could say that. Or rather excitement seems to find me," she said, staring out of the window now at the traffic, the car having ground to a halt in the main street. They weren't far from the exact spot where, on her debut night . . . she noticed the people moving towards the car.

"Speaking of excitement, looks like someone's about to get some. A whole load of suits are heading up the road through the traffic."

Oh shit. Not again.

"They look a bit like Feds, you know, in those grey suits," he continued.

He turned to find his passenger clipping the straps of her backpack across her chest, pulling them tight so it was like a parachute pack on her back. She glanced up at the open sunroof. "I'm really sorry about this but I've got to go."

She slapped a $100 bill over his shoulder and then reached over and opened both doors – at least that would block two avenues.

"What? W-who *are* you?" he gabbled as he realised she was leaving.

She braced her hands on the edge of the sunroof and looked at him, smiling broadly, and left him spluttering on his incomprehension, his eyes wide and mouth open as he realised her intention to climb onto the roof of his cab. Sadly, she didn't have the time for the rest of that conversation; besides, she was happy to live up to her namesake and remain a mystery.

Mysty pulled, and in a moment was standing on the roof. She looked back at them. Counting fifteen, she pulled her earpiece from her pocket and put it in. For a long second she looked at them, watching them watching her, none of them quite sure what to do. One of them took a few more steps; he was now just over a car's-length away from her.

I guess it would be a shame to not show them what I'm capable of. At least a little.

She knew she was ready, was glad she'd had the other dextrose sachet. She reached up, staring at the guy closest as she did so, seeing he was giving some kind of instruction to someone through his comms system. She looked straight at him and smiled the smallest of smiles, and then took off her hat. Even as it skimmed through the air heading for his head, she was already leaping away, landing five feet in front of the taxi, then up the street.

"Fabio!"

"Kitten! You got admirers again?"

"Very funny! Can Mario meet me like before?"

"I'm afraid it's double-trouble tonight. You have Mario *and* Lucio on their way. I sent them as soon as I saw the suits. I've been watching you since your feet touched pavement, kiddo."

She smiled as she pelted full speed up the road, glancing behind her to see the suits trying very hard to catch up, but not getting any closer; in fact, they were falling way behind. She saw four moving towards her when she turned back, having entered the main road from a side street, and without hesitation she sprang up onto a car roof, then the next, and again, so they were given no chance to grab her. She was gone and out of reach within seconds.

She hurdled over another car, oblivious to the audience gaping through their windows around her, quickly gauging her next move. *One day, I will have an easy life.* She pushed off again with everything she had, jumped casually onto a truck, and with a smooth somersault, landed on the ground in a crouch.

Casually she stood from her crouch, hearing the motorbikes not too far away.

"Boys, I'm honoured! Two of you? Where's the red carpet?"

They chuckled inside their helmets, glad to know she was fine and in high spirits – but then she had just completely out-manoeuvred her would-be captors. Most of them had already disappeared into cars, and it had not gone unnoticed by the surveillance boys that none of them had held guns, which was curious. Did they think she was going to stop for a friendly chat before they captured her, or did they have weapons concealed to be used only if they got close?

"Only the best for you, kiddo," Lucio told her, smiling broadly, sitting astride the yellow Ducati that matched Mario's red.

He held out a helmet for her, and she slipped off her shades and put it on. Mario nodded behind him and pulled his visor down, and she saw him smiling before he did so. It was good to be with them, even for a short time.

One arm went around his body as he twisted the throttle, Lucio doing the same a moment later, threading between the traffic, safely en route to the airport.

UNBEKNOWNST TO HER, Donny was ninety-nine percent sure he knew who had been behind the chase. Someone who moved in different circles, so they would not know about the example made of the first attempted kidnap. Eyes narrowed on the camera feed as Fabio replayed the chase, happy in the knowledge she was perfectly safe, but baffled at the shambolic attempt. Paulo glanced at Donny, his look speaking volumes. They both knew. Only one man would be so arrogant as to take on the mob boss of Vegas.

TWO MILES AWAY in his Vegas office, Daryl scowled at the satellite feed and the camera reports from his boys. *Jesus Christ, they hadn't stood a chance. Not against that.* He'd seen her acts dozens of times over, but he'd never really thought about how such energy, strength and ability would translate in the world outside the arena. That had been nothing short of eye-opening.

"Boss."

"Mac," he responded automatically, fingers reversing the feed, knowing it was pointless following her once she was on the bike.

"I'm afraid–"

"I know. I saw. If it's any consolation, I don't think you could have got her."

"She is something else, boss. I've chased a *lot* of people in my life, but she . . . she was just gone. I couldn't believe it when she stood on that cab and looked at us all."

Mac was rarely impressed by anything. Neither, usually, was Daryl.

"Yes. Quite impressive."

Damn it. A total failure. And worse – a humiliation. He had been hoping for success; had hoped to spend his evening prising those dark glasses off her face and getting some conversation out of her, but no, he was going to be left to his torment. He looked back at the image of her on the screen as she had stood, motionless and poised, at the beginning of the chase. That tiny hint of a smile, reminding him of the Mona Lisa, not overtly arrogant just . . . assured. Knowing you can do what she can must give a person that. He saved the image of her, sent it over to his printers to be reproduced on canvas, as he had of the stills of her performance. Pictures were all he had, until . . .

Friday night couldn't come soon enough.

THE WORLD HAD turned its attention on Vegas. Downloads had already earned Celeste almost $80 million from across the world as everyone and anyone wanted to see the unbelievable *Papillon*. And broadcast subscriptions by viewers booking to see it live from their homes were up fourfold, so it was with a light step that Daryl entered into his private box, finding Harvey and the boys waiting for him. He had been surprised Harvey had come back so willingly; but not surprised either, such was the attraction of her act. And after all, the debt was paid, as she had made quite clear, and Harvey need not fear any more retribution to his private parts, or his wallet.

He didn't pay much attention to the other acts. They were entertaining – mildly – but in comparison to her? Nothing. It wasn't just history that had been made here, by her, but a new pre-occupation had been born. A new standard; a new bar of excellence. One people could not quite believe was real, but couldn't get enough of anyway. There was so much speculation in the headlines and press, and he could hardly have asked for a better start to the re-opening of Celeste. Profits were already off the chart from predictions made the previous year.

Money, however, was not what he was concerned with. Far from it.

He sat, once more in intense anticipation, just as the lights dropped and the music started. And once again, the poetry of her moves, her rising and falling with the music, her precision and timing, had him frozen to his seat. He almost cried out with the audience as she rose and plunged, the lights catching the black sequins on the black mask and costume as without effort, it seemed, she traversed the arena.

All too soon the music ended.

The lights went out.

And she was gone.

But before the audience had time to respond, the music started once more. He glanced at his programme: 'Tourniquet' by Evanescence. They were clearly her band of choice at the moment, but hell, it suited her. Dark. Passionate. Defiant. Raw. And again, he felt something stir in his own being; something undefinable.

Then she appeared and he held his breath. Was unable to breathe, in fact. In a pale gold and white mask, her costume almost transparent except for strategically placed sequins, she shimmered like something ethereal.

And so deep in a trance was he by the time she finished her routine that he barely noticed the uproarious noise of an entire arena on their feet. He didn't want to move; didn't want to wake up.

Nothing had ever impressed him as consistently as she did.

"So, Harvey," he eventually said, as nonchalantly as he could muster as the applause subsided, "it was worth running the gauntlet of coming to Vegas to see her again?"

He turned to look at his friend, who was staring at the now empty space, one finger over his lips, head balanced on a hand, elbow on the arm rest.

"I would be a fool not to, Daryl. She's out of this world. Even you know that." His smile was genuine and Daryl looked past him to the others, all of them similarly quiet in admiration, in wonder.

"It is interesting that she just . . . leaves. That she doesn't make a big show at the end, doesn't seem to care for the applause. Someone with her talent, you'd think she would be, would want the acclaim, but. . ." Robbie commented, trying to fathom her.

Daryl knew precisely what he meant and the rest nodded as well. All of them roués and practised lovers, never had any of them been so enraptured, or confused, by one female.

He still had the image of her standing on the taxi fixed in his mind, the way she'd skimmed her hat at one of Mac's guys. That hint of mischief and amusement. It was the behaviour of someone who knew she was in possession of a gift, and knew just how to use it.

They left the room, off for excitement in the casino and wherever the night took them, but their esteemed leader knew one thing, even as he smiled and responded to the easy banter: he would not be happy until he had met her. No woman he saw tempted him in the slightest; no one even came close. He knew it was time to make another move.

PHEW, ANOTHER NIGHT done. And another $20,000. How did that happen?

She was pleased with her strength, with her progression as a performer. The hard work was paying off, And Donny hadn't changed his mind about her visiting, and she hugged herself in the taxi, remembering how good it had felt to hang out with him again.

They'd had a whole evening and night and morning together, and stayed up until three, eating dinner, talking, catching up on all the details missed while apart. And then she'd dropped down on her old bed, not really slept but lain in the quiet of dawn pondering him. Finding it amazing, knowing his ruthlessness, that with her he was just a man, boyish almost, and in good humour. She trusted him so much, felt such affinity with him, that time together was effortless – although there were obvious moments when she knew she was unequal to him in experience, or knowledge. But he never made her feel stupid. Never disregarded her feelings. He was her haven. His townhouse her safety net, despite what had happened there. *Does he know how precious all of this is to me?*

How little she had wanted to leave him. How had she? Yet here she was in a taxi, again, heading to the airport. She had tackled him about this as tactfully as she could, and seen the sorrow in his face at having to reply the only way he could: things had to stay the way they were. She remembered how his hand had lain against her cheek, trying to get her to understand why and how much he wanted her to be safe. As if she didn't already have a pretty good idea.

She opened her eyes behind her shades, hadn't realised she'd closed them, and saw the cabby look at her in the rear-view mirror.

"What's wrong?"

She felt instinctive fear in the pit of her stomach. One glance through the back window and she was strapping on her backpack again. Who were these guys? Who was sending them? *Would they ever give up*?

The second she put her earpiece in Fabio patched in, but she had a plan before she took off across the city, and after thrusting a bunch of $20-dollar bills at the driver and apologising, she launched herself through his sunroof.

She then somersaulted to land right at the feet of one of the guys – a tall, black guy – and it took her a single second to strip him of his earpiece and shades – perhaps they would offer some clues – and then she was gone; but not before saying, this time: "I just want you to know, this isn't personal," and administering a lightning-fast blow to his solar plexus.

She was gone before the pain had registered on his face.

Who would be so arrogant and so stupid as to try this again?

NOT SO FAR away, Daryl watched the satellite feed, saw his man go down. He brought his fist down on the desk. His attempt at capturing her had been an *abject failure. Again.* And all over in a matter of seconds! Mac had suggested tranquilisers this time, but he couldn't risk her falling and hurting herself. He needed her undamaged. And knew she had to perform, loved to perform. He couldn't do that to her. Despite his desperate sense of failure, he couldn't help but be intrigued that she'd taken the earpiece, and shades. Why would she do that?

"Boss."

"I know, Mac." He leant back in his chair, closed his eyes and ran his hands through his hair.

"I'm sorry."

"How's the guy she hit?"

"Sore, but not too bad."

"Good. Get everyone back. We'll fly out in an hour."

No point staying in Vegas. He would return to New York and wallow in his frustration. He'd be back in a few days to see her new performance. Just like so many millions of others, he couldn't wait to see what she would do next. But goddammit. *Goddammit.*

MYSTY HAD A happy spring in her step as she walked back from the airport. Sticking it one to the suits had been fun. And later she would try and crack the coding on the earpiece, hack into the frequency they were using. Donny would take care of the rest. Fliss had called to invite her for a barbeque tomorrow night, so that would be fun. But right now, it was time to grab a pizza and soak up the LA sunshine.

She looked round casually, taking the time – which was rare – and it put a whole new perspective on things. Freed her up a little to just . . . be.

By chance she saw a sign, liked the rich-brown painted building, the canopies out the front with olive trees lining the outside seating area. It had a red carpeted walkway up to the front doors, which were open. It was Raffi's! Instantly she smiled, remembering and missing Marcos and his excellent pizza and happy company. Why hadn't she seen this place before?

She crossed over. Italian music was floating out into the street, along with laughter and the clink of glasses and cutlery. She strolled in, looking forward to dinner in a proper restaurant. Did it matter that she was alone? She was often alone. Had met Marcos alone. No, it didn't matter at all.

There was a dispute occurring in the centre in the restaurant, in front of the bar, and it caught her attention.

"But I'm telling you, I deal with *Franny Laperta.* I pay *him.* I don't know your boss," the Italian of the threesome protested, dark hair slicked back, a few lines on his tanned face . . . the resemblance was astonishing: he had to be related to Marcos. The other two, the heavies, one much heavier than the other, were light-skinned, had brown hair, and wore black suits with pinstripes. She really didn't like pinstripes.

"Well, our boss sent us here to tell you that Franny is on the way out, and we want to get paid too. Looks like your money is paying for shit if there isn't someone here *protecting* you, would you agree?" the heavier of the two heavies said.

"And you wouldn't want anything to happen right now, would you? Tuesday night? Lots of happy families coming in for dinner?" She saw the lighter heavy push back his jacket and reveal a gun. Her mind flipped over, imagining the carnage. "Things could get messy, and then there's the fallout . . . who's gonna to come here after that? You'll be closed down within a week," he added, with relish, designed to intimidate.

"Look, I can give you free food, free drink, but I can't pay you. You can't come in here making those kinds of threats!"

She heard the panic in the Italian's voice, his accent getting stronger in his distress. She noticed the customers at the nearest tables begin to realise the nature of the altercation; the staff too. And a quiet anticipation descended on the room.

"Well, that's funny because I think I just have, Mr Pizza-man. So why don't you just go open up your cash register and hand over the money, OK? Taking longer is only going to make me want more. So. Are you going to give me some money?" He closed his jacket, but slowly tapped the bulge of the gun.

"I think he's already answered that question."

All three looked at her in surprise, the two heavies moving their hands to the weapons on their hips. The Italian looked at her in horror and amazement. She was used to looks like that.

"*Who the fuck are you?*"

They didn't like not being able to see her eyes, which were still behind the shades. And she was a girl? *What kind of girl would come up to them*?

"Who the fuck are you, more to the point?" she answered calmly, looking from one to the other. *Threatening innocent families and a business man? Not a good idea.* "I think it might be a good idea to leave now."

"Why? You going to make us?" the heavier guy mocked; but there was hesitation in his voice.

"If I have to."

They both reached for their guns.

"Really? You need your guns to deal with an unarmed woman? How . . . pathetic."

They paused. A long second. The scorn in her voice did not match her body. Was this girl for real?

That long second cost them dear.

It took her just a few seconds more to lay them out on the floor, disarm them, and smile down at them and say, "Franny Laperta isn't going anywhere. Except here. And to pay your boss a visit. I'd make the most of the time you have left, if I were you, and put some distance between here, this city, and wherever you end up next. If you get out of here at all, that is. Understand? Laperta's boys will be here in five minutes." She removed the clips from the guns as she spoke.

She then turned to the Italian – who must be Raffi – and in fluent Italian apologised for the slight disruption and asked if she may still eat in the restaurant. As the heavies began to move, he flinched, but one look from her made sure they went quietly and quickly, scuttling on their hands and knees from the room. A slow cheer worked its way around the restaurant as the patrons witnessed the enemy leave in such style, and Mysty felt a blush on her cheeks, wishing they hadn't.

It seemed to rouse the Italian, though, who then said, "Do *what?*" Eat here? Jesus, girl, you can have any table you like!" He gestured her forward, took her to a table for four with a plush bench against the wall on one side and two chairs on the other. She chose the bench. Laid the guns down on the table, and the clips. "I'll get you a menu, bella. What would you like to drink?" he said, giving her his whole attention. Who was this? How did she know Franny?

"I know it sounds strange, but do you have any milk?"

"Milk?" His face suddenly split into a big smile of recognition. "It's *you*! Marcos told me about you! Why has it taken you so long, bella, to come here? He's been missing you for months, and you only just make it here to see me?" The rant was delivered in true Italian style, plenty of hand gestures, all reserve gone, his tone full of warmth – and mock annoyance.

"I'm sorry, I erm . . . guess I've been busy . . . moving cities, you know." She laughed; she hadn't expected such a welcome.

"Yeah, I guess I'll let you off!" he teased and turned away. "I'll be back, give me a moment."

She breathed out as she watched him walk away, hearing him shouting at the boys in the kitchen and the bar staff, telling them in Italian who their rescuer was. She put in her earpiece and called Franny.

"Mysty? You OK? Donny said you had another race to the airport tonight."

"Oh that. Yeah, well, nothing I couldn't handle. Listen, I just arrived at Raffi's. Found two dudes in ugly pinstripes trying to hassle Raffi for payment. I have their guns if you want prints off them. Send some boys if you need to. They were saying all kinds of crap about you being on the slide, and their boss etc. They didn't mention any names, though, so it could be–"

"Well, aren't you just worth your weight in gold?" he interrupted, and she felt honoured by the quiet appreciation in his voice. "Sure, I'll have some boys sent over, sort this out. Nothing unusual, but best to stamp it out early. There's always someone – as you know with Donny."

"Yeah, I know," she agreed, no stranger to tiresome problems that seemed to arrive in a never-ending stream.

"I'll send Giles with them. I think I can trust you two to behave in a restaurant."

She laughed and he chuckled. Then looked up as Raffi approached the table with a tray and a glass of milk, carried with flair and deposited with a flourish. She sensed she was getting special treatment, that he wouldn't normally bring drinks himself.

"I promise we'll behave, Franny."

"Hey, Franny, you sending beautiful young girls to do your work now? Shame on you." Raffi winked at her.

"Mysty, you tell that cheeky Italian to feed you right or I'm doubling his rate card."

"Will do. Let Giles know I'm at the back to the left, on the bench against the wall."

"See you tomorrow night? Fliss did ask you, right?"

"She did. And yes, I'll be there."

"Enjoy your pizza and get home safe. Giles will give you a ride."

"Thanks, Franny."

"No, thank *you,* Mysty."

Raffi was standing by the side of the table listening to the exchange, hugging his tray against his chest, his eyes practically glowing with interest at his new, gorgeous customer.

"So . . ." he said slowly, and she looked at him patiently. "You really are who Marcos says you are." As though he just had proof she was the Virgin Mary reincarnated.

"I guess so."

"You and Donny Capello are friends? And now friends with Mr Laperta? You sure know how to pick–"

"I don't think I picked them, it just kind of . . . happened."

"Yeah well, you're part of the *family* now. Now, here's the menu, so you just tell me what you want. You're hungry?"

Mysty took the proffered menu, beautifully handwritten on cream sheets of paper and slotted into a leather holder which opened out into two pages. Which, right then, felt like way too much choice.

"I'm *starving*. I'll have *everything*," she replied, without looking up, not realising she made Raffi smile again. She was clearly not one of the half-starved beauties that he so often saw. He had to admire a woman with a proper appetite. But that figure . . .

"Yeah, Marcos told me that too. That you're always hungry. You been at Celeste tonight?" Her head snapped up with a speed that took him aback.

"I don't mind you knowing, but it goes no further, understand? *No one* must know."

Her seriousness was obvious, and he was surprised at her tone, but didn't argue. He wasn't about to go complicating things for her; especially not when he knew the men who watched over her. Raffi liked having a pulse and unbroken legs.

"Sure thing, bella, you can trust me. You trusted Marcos, didn't you? And I owe you now. Relax, I promise, my lips are sealed."

She nodded.

"The steak is really good," Raffi threw in, wanting her to have the best.

Initially she had wanted pizza, but steak sounded great. "OK. You swayed me. A steak, with a tomato and onion salad, and some breads with dips. And a glass of water please." She had switched unthinkingly into Italian again, his appearance taking her to another time, place, and certain set of people.

"Excellent. If it were not for your hair, I would say you were a native."

She blushed a little. "So I've been told."

He walked away to give her order to the kitchen, just as she saw Giles arrive, the man-mountain moving fluidly through the tables to hers. He sat down, dwarfing the chair.

"Hi, Giles."

"Hey, tiger."

She pushed the guns and clips over to him. "Did you get them?"

"Yep. They'd managed to crawl a little way, but certainly weren't up to much else. We had them on satellite anyway. I'm sure we'll have some answers soon enough."

"Good. Have you eaten – do you want to order something?"

"Sure. Jeez, kiddo. You look tired. You make sure you finish your food before you fall asleep or you could get barred, you know."

The playful reproof made her smile, and yawn so wide, it made her laugh. Giles' laughing eyes caught hers over the top of the menu. Sometimes, it was easier to forget she wasn't in Vegas . . .

SOMETIME LATER, GILES hustled her gently towards the door, her attempts at paying falling on deaf ears. Raffi refused point-blank.

"You make sure you come back soon, bella?" Raffi told her sternly, standing at the end of his red carpet as the car pulled up.

"I'll try. I promise."

Giles opened the door and looked back at Raffi with a smile that the Italian had rarely seen on the big guy's face, then disappeared inside with her.

Neither could imagine the unrest of a man, once again thousands of miles away, who was having a great deal of trouble accepting failure.

"HEY, M. WHERE are you? I'm outside."

"Oh hi. I'll open the doors. I'll see you in two seconds."

Slick relaxed. Despite her kick-ass attitude to life, there was something secretive about the golden-haired girl he'd met in the café. She rarely talked about herself. Questions about her childhood, parents . . . they all seemed to end in dead-ends and then silence. But he never once got the impression she was doing it because she wanted to, but because she felt she had to. Her fairness, kindness and forthright nature made it impossible to think bad of her though, and despite the fact she was young, he hadn't lost interest in her. There was just something about her. An energy. A buzz. Time spent around Mysty was never dull, and when most of her age-group were smoking weed, sponging funds off their parents and watching endless boring videos on YouTube, she was always busy. And when he'd got the surprise invitation to go over and help her with her bike, there had been only one answer – once he'd got over his shock.

He waited by the garage as instructed, and stepped back when the doors opened outwards instead of rolling up, revealing an Aladdin's cave of treasure! But the treasure was wearing a pair of black leggings and a black cropped top. He'd seen it once before at the Bowl. He knew most of her wardrobe; realised she probably owned less clothes than he did – which was unusual for a girl. She looked gorgeous, but the best thing about her was there was already an oil smudge on her cheek.

He took in the mounted screens, the serious piece of computer kit, the tools arrayed on the wall, the workshop bench, a winch screwed into the ceiling, and the bike clamped still, taking pride of place on the floor on its stands.

"Impressive set up." His wide, admiring eyes rolled around to her wide, expectant ones. "For a kid."

"I put all the play dough and jigsaws away before you got here."

Upstairs, she ate, slept and watched movies – occasionally – but her garage was her playroom, her pride and joy, where she explored all the ideas her hyperactive brain came up with, and where she and Raju could talk and debate as she worked as she'd installed a second computer down there. In here, no one could tell her that she was too young or inexperienced to attempt all the things she wanted to do, wanted to achieve, or wanted to invent. It was in this small garage where she'd already managed to make things to keep herself safer that weren't available on the open market. She wasn't doing it for the money, she just wanted peace of mind. And all the above were reasons why she rarely invited anyone here. She'd debated with herself about Slick, but knew it would seem odd if she never extended the same gesture of friendship he had to her. She'd been to his place for pizza, beer and a movie before the Bowl plenty of times, either alone or with friends, and he'd never done anything to make her doubt him. And she knew he kept an eye on her, even amongst their close group of friends, to make sure she was OK and that no one overstepped the line.

"I thought I was coming here to teach you something," Slick laughed. "Now I think I'm about to be amazed."

"I barely know anything. And I probably make loads of mistakes. I've never had a teacher. I usually just . . ." – Slick watched her glance away, thumbs hooked in her waist band – "make things up and clean up the mess when it goes wrong."

"How often do things go wrong?"

"Not so much, but when they do it's *pretty spectacular*."

"Is that why there's a line of fire extinguishers over there?"

"My contribution to being a responsible one-day-adult."

Slick stepped further into the garage and put his helmet down on the bench top, trying to get his brain into gear because, just then, it was having a hard job trying to work out what all the things around him were.

"I think," he said, glancing over at her as he took his leather jacket off – in a way that most women would have swooned over but she barely blinked at – "you have too much time on your own. You need to get a boyfriend . . ."

"Slick!"

He accepted the punch in the arm with a grin, then gave her bike his proper attention, aware she was awaiting some kind of expert opinion.

"The bike looks good. Your first rebuild?"

"Yeah. I got most of my parts from Trickshots over on the Bay."

"Best place for them. At least none of them will have been lifted. You want to show me your tool selection, and I'll make sure we're not missing anything before we get stuck in?"

Nodding, she pointed behind him and pulled out the top drawer of the bench. Then the next drawer, and then the bottom drawer.

Slick tried to keep his face neutral. *Jesus.* He'd expected a few things scattered on the floor – which was what he'd had at her age!

"You want a beer?"

"Sure."

"Do you think we've got everything we need?"

"Yeah, should be fine."

"Great! I spent ages selecting what I thought were all the right tools."

As she turned away, Slick finally let the disbelief show on his face, watching her bend down to get two beers from a fridge. Of course. Why wouldn't she have a fridge in her garage? She was cooler than some of his mates!

"How much beer have you got in that fridge?"

His question made her pause, and an uneasy look dimmed the brightness of her face for a second as she worried she'd done something wrong.

"Only six. Usually there's only water or juice. Saves me going upstairs when I need a drink. I got some beers for us yesterday." Looking at him for an extra few seconds, she tilted her head. "I don't drink beer all the time, Slick. And definitely not when I'm riding. It's just that it gets really hot in here when I have the doors shut. I do know how to look after myself."

"I know. I just . . . worry about you . . . a little."

"That's sweet, but you don't need to worry about me that much."

He relieved her of one of the beers and gave her a look which said *I kinda can't help it.*

"So, you want to tell me what's first on your list?"

"It's only a small list."

"That's perfectly cool. I see this as training you up so you can come help me in the garage at weekends." His eyes teased her, having already toyed with the idea. Seeing her set-up had already convinced him she would be more than capable after some training.

"Could I?"

"We'll see." Slick felt like a bit of a bastard for dangling the prospect in front of her and then putting a question mark over it, but he was a tough teacher when it came to the greatest love of his life: fixing bikes was serious. "Now, you going to put some tunes on and we'll get to it?"

His beer was put down, and he bent down to start checking the bike over. His toned biceps appeared through the thin ripped t-shirt that hugged his muscular torso, but as usual, when he flicked his eyes up to her, she didn't react. It was so frustrating that she didn't!Most girls giggled, or blushed, or at least sent him sneaky looks. Did she not even have an in insy-tinsy little girl-crush on him? And who was this guy she'd mentioned the first night at the Dancing Mermaid? She'd never spoken about him again and, as far as he knew, he'd never visited her in LA. But then would she even had told him if he had? She was such a private person in some respects. He just hoped, whoever he was, that he was worth the waiting. He guessed he might find out eventually. But for now, there was a bike to play with!

DARYL SAT BACK and scowled with displeasure at the paperwork and the multitude of screens around his desk. He had accepted years ago, with his parent's death, and without argument, that this responsibility would rest on his shoulders. He had the money to distract himself as he wished as compensation, which had worked very well . . . until now. Now he wanted something more. And he had no way of getting it.

The performances at Celeste weren't enough, despite hearing from Craig that she had some particularly amazing things to pull out of the magic *Papillon* hat in the coming months.

He looked over at the large picture he'd had put in his office; one of the best pictures of her, in his opinion. She was perfectly illuminated by the lights in the skin-tight cobalt-blue costume that she'd performed in, the magnificent colours in the cascade of curls bright against the dark background. Taken almost exactly side on, it showed her at full stretch, arms out, hands tilted back like the tips of wings on a bird, face as composed as ever behind her mask.

He looked at the other wall, smiling as he saw the satellite picture of her standing on top of the car just after she'd thrown her hat. Two sides of a coin: the professional, controlled artiste and the reckless daredevil. He could not decide which he liked best.

He thought of the Manhattan skyscrapers outside his window. If she were there would she dare to jump off one? She was so alive, so full of passion and joy. But was she happy? He knew he wasn't. Knew that position and power had not provided one single moment of blissful freedom or joy. Being unmarried and childless, despite it being a conscious decision once more after recent events, felt like a long rest of his life.

Why did he want her? She was a mystery, it was true. And unobtainable – always the ultimate frustration. But it was more than that. He'd found out from Mac that the comms system his men used had been hacked into and the first time they'd tried to reactivate it, the whole system had frozen and Michael Jackson's 'Leave Me Alone' had played loud and clear in all their ears. It had to be a message from her, and she'd obviously instructed the guys who'd hacked into it to play that particular tune.

He had tried to run a trace back, but had got nowhere. Whatever security they had set up was infuriatingly superior. He'd immediately got his tech teams working on something better and more powerful, had had the whole system ripped out and reinstalled with the upgrade – which was costly – but he suspected they were already ten steps ahead.

Donny must still be feeling rather smug about it all, keeping Daryl completely in the dark. Must be proud that she'd managed to grab the earpiece and sabotage his own comms unit and, no doubt, share the information with his team. Which perhaps explained why he'd been subjected to a week of harassment whenever he'd gone anywhere in the car, as unmarked vehicles with very aggressive drivers had done their best to make his journeys difficult, and at times dangerous. Luckily, he had Geoffrey for such eventualities. He had driven in far worse situations and across much worse terrain, and was trained at the very highest level. Like Mac, he had seen combat for a number of years before using his talents in a different service than that of the state.

But he was sure Donny didn't know about his orchestrated attacks on the *Papillon*; if he did he wouldn't have hesitated to take a more proactive stance, surely? She was the main attraction and money-spinner at Celeste, after all. He had to admit, though, that the radio silence on this matter was rather worrying.

There was one other issue, however, that flummoxed him. Why would Donny be so protective of a mere performer – albeit a magnificent one – and subject Harvey to such appalling treatment, twice? The second time at the very hands of this girl who had stated quite succinctly, and with great authority, that their 'score was settled'. What gave her that authority? Or indeed who?

His thoughts then turned to Donny's girl, the redhead he had never seen, and another complete enigma. But in this respect, there was one thing he was fairly certain he was right about: 'Kitten' was, in fact, this girl – the 'secretary' he had spoken to on the phone. His mind went back to the conversation he'd overheard the night he'd offered Donny his helicopter; the night of the mysterious chase through the city that had sent Donny and his boys into a frenzy as they'd watched it on Donny's handheld; the night he'd heard him use the word 'Kitten' . . . but why would anyone be chasing a kid? And why had she been out anyway? She hadn't been at the show with him – he'd searched everywhere for a redhead who might resemble her, and be as beautiful as Donny claimed she was – so surely she'd been at home?

And on that subject, he still couldn't fathom why Donny waited – if he still was, and he was pretty sure he was – until she was of legal age and really was as beautiful as he claimed. How could he resist taking her to bed? She had to be sixteen by now, right? Sixteen was the legal age in most countries, and the majority of teenagers didn't make it to eighteen anyway, by their own choice.

And speaking of waiting, waiting was all he had when it came to the *Papillon*. And he didn't really know what he was waiting for either. A miracle? Yeah, like he believed in those. He couldn't do anything else. He'd had a team try to find out where she was from, who she was. Where she went to when she was in LA. But her identity had been black-carded – no name, no face, no address – which he knew wasn't personal but for her protection. But still . . . a connection with a mob boss wasn't necessarily the end of the world; in fact, if that should come to light, it would greatly add to her allure, surely? The media machine would love that. She looked so pure, so fresh, and so young, so to discover that she was connected with one of America's most ruthless . . . well, she could make millions from just a single interview. But how to find her? Somebody must know where she went when she got on the plane and left Vegas . . .

And then it hit him. And for a moment he could have laughed loudly. But then he felt like an utter dimwit as the fog of his stressed-out, over-worked brain began to clear. Why was a young girl performing in Vegas leaving on a plane after every show? Why was she black-carded – which was either because of government or mob protection – so that she was untraceable? *He'd seen Donny laughing with Franny Laperta at Celeste.* Why hadn't he figured it out earlier? LA was just a short hop from Vegas, and Capello was friends with Laperta. The *Papillon* was under Laperta's protection . . . Donny's 'girl' had been sent away . . .

Daryl almost slapped his forehead: *La Papillon de la Magie Noire was Donny's girl!*

Where and why else would Donny send her other than a city run by a man who would watch over her as carefully as he did? How could he have been so stupid? All the pieces were there: the *high-diving* competition; the computer whiz-kid he spoke about (the snatched and hacked into earpiece!); Donny's attendance at the shows; his treatment of Harvey, and her authority in telling Harvey their score was settled. She *knew* who was watching her back; *he* now knew who was watching her back! *Donny-Fucking-Capello.* And he'd been too busy, too self-absorbed, to join the dots!

He pressed the intercom. He had to get to LA!

"Mac."

"Yes, Mr Blackmoor?"

"Get a plane organised for tomorrow night, 7pm. I'm going to go to LA for a few days, soak up some sun."

There was a pause. He expected no less. It was an unusual request.

"Certainly, sir. Are there any . . . others coming?"

Daryl knew Mac was referring to his Cherries. But he did not want them in LA. What happened in LA would be private.

"No."

"Very good, sir."

Disconnect.

Another button.

"Marlene."

"Mr Blackmoor, sir?"

"Cancel everything from Wednesday to Saturday and rearrange. I'm going to LA for a few days. Send anything urgent to me now; anything else will have to wait."

A moment of stunned silence.

"Yes, sir."

Daryl Blackmoor was going 'butterfly' catching. Only he didn't have a net. And he definitely didn't think it would fit in a jar.

Donny would kill him. Personally. But that didn't put him off. Not for a second.

MAC HAD BEEN less than pleased by Daryl's decision to take himself off in a new BMW convertible. Without a chauffeur. Or a bodyguard. It had been a long and bitter argument that had got Mac rubbed very much up the wrong way, but there was only going to be one winner. Which was why Daryl was now cruising LA, the wind in his hair, shades on, feeling strangely free. He'd even ditched the suit for white chinos and a blue linen shirt, and not shaved for a couple of days either. He'd chosen the car because it was low-key enough so no one would pay him a blind bit of notice, but beast enough so that it was fun to drive – and would get him out of a situation if needed. But the novelty of having nothing specific to do, or nowhere pressing to go, served to highlight the lack of friends to visit, or a significant other in the passenger seat. And like a slam to the head, the loneliness returned. *Perhaps I should have brought Harvey.* But with another slam to the head he realised what a dumb idea that was. What was wrong with him? He'd be instantly condemned by association if she clapped eyes on Harvey!

He let out a long sigh of frustration and tapped the onboard screen for some music. *Where would she go? What did she do during the day? How do you find one girl in a whole city?* And LA was not just any city – it was a sprawling mass of humanity dozens of miles across. *Why have I even come? This is hopeless.*

He pulled up at a junction, the hot sun on his face irritating him with its brightness, and leaned an elbow on the side of the door, vaguely aware of another convertible pulling up next to him with two 'babes' in bikini tops and cowboy hats. They threw him some smiles over their large, dark shades but he didn't respond. Neither was a patch on her. Didn't even a strike a match.

He looked at the dash at the song: Razorlight, 'Wire to Wire', and started listening to the lyrics: '*What is love but a strangest of feelings? A sin you swallow for the rest of your life, you've been looking for someone to believe in, for someone to love you, until your eyes run dry.*' How apt. '*She lives by disillusion's glow . . .*' Yep.

Something caught his eye. A flash of gold. He pulled his shades down. A girl running. Blonde hair – he'd worked out that the 'redhead' part of 'I'm Donny's redhead secretary' had been a ruse – along with the large, dark shades and a trilby. But she was moving too fast for him see her, along the pavement behind a row of cars. Was it? . . . The lights changed and he pulled away, level with her, close enough that he could have shouted if he'd been able to speak. He spied black dots in her ears and knew she had wireless earphones in. She'd stop at the crossing waiting for the next lights to change, wouldn't she?

Doubt washed over him. It couldn't be her.

He had no choice but to stop at the lights, looked again, willing her to stop. He had to be sure. But she didn't stop. Carried on running. And it was then that he saw what he'd watched on screen a hundred times over: the fluidity, the poetry of her movements. His throat closed. His heart stopped. And then she dived into the road, not breaking her stride, ignoring the hoot of a car horn, and he froze, watching in horror. It had to be her, didn't it? Only she would be so bold! Where was she going? How on earth would he be able to follow her?

He cursed the lights as he started to lose sight of her, slammed the stick in gear as they changed and roared across the junction. *Where was she*?

He cruised along the road, looking down the side streets, swerving late around a bend when he saw the slim figure in denim shorts and a short white t-shirt sprinting across the street in the glare of the sunshine. He could feel his heart racing – at least it was beating now. He could barely look away from her. He turned the onboard camera in her direction. He had to record her.

There was nothing unusual about the display of athleticism that followed, as for the sheer hell of it she spun a few turns around a lamppost and into a side street. There were no people in sight. And no cars. He came off the gas. Didn't want to alert her, despite her having earphones in, to the roar of the BMW's engine. This didn't feel like LA at all. At least not the LA he knew. This was like stepping over into a different world. But where she went, he would follow. Without question.

She slowed slightly and turned into a car park, and he forced himself to drive on, trying not to look in her direction. Unless he was very much mistaken, and he rarely was in such things, she had arrived at a very dubious-looking strip club. It was a dive, a real dump. No doubt with similarly dubious and shabby clientele. He would go once around the block and park up. *What the hell was she doing here?*

MYSTY WAS THINKING exactly the same thing. When she had turned her iPod off and stowed her earpieces in the back pocket of her shorts, she looked at the building in disgust, putting her hands on her hips. Her dance buddy Angelique didn't really work here, did she? She glanced up at the hot-pink neon sign that glowed, grotesque and tacky, in the bright sunshine, some bits of it no longer working – which seemed appropriate. She wished she'd bought Lazarus.

She didn't know she was being watched by a pair of very keen eyes from behind shades as dark as her own from the edge of the car park. Eyes which saw the bunched eyebrows of a displeased scowl, the hands on the hips, the curl of her lips momentarily in distaste. He heard her sigh loudly as she walked towards the door, her body language expressing her reluctance. What the hell was going on? Why was she going in there if she didn't want to? *There was no way in hell Donny would approve of this*!

Resolutely she pushed through the door and disappeared.

Daryl followed her, wondering what on earth he was doing hovering outside this rank establishment. No one knew where he was. He must be mad. At the same time, he knew he'd have followed her into much worse places if put to it. He gritted his teeth and went through the doors, and the smell hit him: dank, musty air laced with old alcohol, cigarette smoke and sweat. Those were the smells he could identify. The rest, he really didn't want to think about.

A central stage, lit by meagre lights and raised up to about four feet, was unmissable; just as unmissable as the curvaceous gyrating woman, naked but for the predictable thong, heels and nipple tassels. He couldn't see her face, but he didn't think it would change his opinion. He was only interested in one thing: finding the girl. But that wasn't hard as she stood out like a white swan in a scrapyard. He wondered if this was a place where she met someone, covertly, but it didn't look like it. Still, he kept his distance and observed.

The drinkers who looked him over seemed disinterested and their sullen eyes returned to the stage, where the woman moved badly to uninspiring music played on a poor-quality sound system. What should he do? Order a beer and try to look inconspicuous? He retreated to the back of the room, leaning his elbow on it a second after his brain said don't. It was sticky and he shuddered, tried not to think about germs and STDs. A bottle of beer was banged down on the counter unceremoniously, without a glass; not that he wanted one considering the hygiene of the place. He kept his repulsion concealed behind a mask of bored indifference and enjoyed the novelty of paying for something with real dollars. Probably the first time in years he had done so.

"Are you Mr Kelly?"

He watched, waiting to see what she did. Even over the appalling music he could hear her voice. He'd never forgotten her voice. Now, it was firm, yet pleasant.

"For you I can be anyone you like."

She had addressed an overweight cowboy lookalike, belly bulging over dirty jeans which were too old, and too tight. He had big gold rings on fingers. Sovereigns. And an ugly worn face from too much cheap booze and roll-up cigarettes. The tobacco-stained sideburns and a moustache were so out of fashion he wondered if they'd ever been in, and a greasy, lank grey ponytail hung down his back.

"That's really nice, but I'm only interested in a Mr Kelly," she replied calmly.

"Well, I am him. And what can I do for you, sweet-cheeks?"

"My friend Angelique, she works here. Her boyfriend decided to *decorate* her face again, and busted her arm, so she can't work today. I said I'd fill her dance slot."

"Really? Well, that sure ain't a problem with me. I'd be happy to make it permanent for you if you're any good. Just head out back and choose a costume, some songs, and start doing your thing. I can't wait to see what you got under that cute little t-shirt."

Mr Kelly leaned back, flicked some of the ash from the end of his cigarette and nudged the guy next to him, a big ugly brute like his boss, his face also showing hungry appreciation of her body.

"Well, that's going be a bit of problem, you see, because she said it was dancing. I'm a *dancer*. Not a *stripper*."

"Well, that sure is a real shame . . . you too high and mighty to strip? It's honest work, darlin', any of my girls'll tell you that."

"I'm sure it is, but I'm not stripping."

"You don't get up there, Angel doesn't need to bother coming back." He pointed his roll-up at her, aggressively, trying to intimidate, and Daryl saw the muscles tighten in her jaw. She didn't like his attitude; Daryl didn't blame her. What was she was going to do about it? It was going to be interesting, he knew that much. He'd never been so captivated, and yet so utterly out of his depth. This was not how he imagined meeting her, but then he was the one trespassing . . . of sorts.

"That's a shame, but I'd say it's a good thing. She deserves better than the scum she has as a boyfriend, and the scum she clearly has as a boss. No one in their right mind would work in a place like this for a man like you."

A couple of the guys looked over at the verbal brawl, and the woman on the stage glanced over too; but they were obviously used to such behaviour and returned to their drinking and ogling, the bad music still rattling out of the shoddy speakers. But Daryl almost choked on his beer. What was she doing? He didn't doubt the result of her insults would be explosive.

"Did you really say what I think you said?"

"Yes. Every single word of it."

There was a long pause. Should he leave? Would it be cowardly? How had he got himself into this?

"Clint. Take this little bitch and get her in a costume. Bones, you help her too."

As she was marched away, Daryl slunk onto the cleanest chair he could find at the back of the room. To rescue her would certainly be one way to get into her good books, but he'd never been in a bar fight in his life for God's sake! He didn't fight people. Not in real life. In boardrooms, yes. With media and lawyers, yes. But not like this! And although he had done some martial arts training, it was more for fitness and control. The best he could do was go and get a couple of cash cards out of the car – if it was still there – and bribe them.

His turmoil was brought to a swift end when he heard a crash and a sharp cry of pain, and a few seconds later, she was frog-marched back to Mr Kelly, her t-shirt off, revealing the sports top underneath. She looked positively mutinous with her shades gone, even in the dim light, and one of the guys was holding his nose, blood dripping down his chin. He resisted the urge to grin. But he felt edgy. Unsure. Why was she so calm? What if this got out of control?

As he had feared, things took a sharp turn for the worst as Kelly banged down his glass on the bar and stood up, clearly resentful of this interruption to his day.

"You really are making this very difficult for yourself. Put her over a table. I'm going teach this little cunt a bit of respect." Even as she swore in protest, hands pulled her back and threw her forwards over a table. "Turn her over, I want to see her scream. $20 for anyone else who wants a ride after I'm finished." Kelly's smile was pure evil, his eyes feasting on her breasts, the expanse of soft pure skin, and a few lecherous chuckles were heard as the clientele's attention was drawn to the unfolding scene.

Daryl felt nausea grip his belly, and he let go of his beer bottle. He couldn't watch this. What was she doing? Was she playing with them? What about her ability to punch?! He thought about Harvey and his guy with the bruised solar plexus.

Kelly reached for his belt, undid it and yanked it from the loops, and it was all she needed. Her first kick caught him on the chin and made him stumble backwards, whilst she punched the other guy straight in the face causing his head to snap back before he crashed to the floor. Instantly she turned and blocked the blow from the other goon, punched him in the face, then the throat, and kicked him hard in the groin. Vaulting over the table on one hand, she landed in front of Kelly, who had recovered a little but was looking horrified. The woman still danced. But the other guys were torn now between her gyrating crotch and the fight. Kelly's brawls weren't anything new, but she was, and this was too interesting to ignore.

"You know, I really don't like it when people threaten me." She tilted her head to one side as she spoke, and stood back, jumped, rotated in the air once, and kicked his chest, sending him flying into the bar, where his limbs flailed at the impact and he slumped, trousers falling round his thighs revealing dirty grey underwear.

Daryl was in her line of sight, mesmerised by her; yet she was oblivious to him, her focus on the revolting Kelly. What should he do? He had nowhere to go. Had to stay rooted to his chair. Was she done yet?

No, not done at all apparently, as she purposefully strode over, hauled Kelly up by the scruff of his neck and dragged him face-first along the bar, before hurling him into another table, luckily an empty one. Finally there was a moment of stillness, and Daryl dared let out a breath.

No one moved. Or spoke. At some point the music had stopped. The woman on the stage was no longer dancing, and the girl behind the bar had retreated to the back wall, pressed up against the almost-empty shelves.

Time to leave.

But eight men stood up, each as slack-faced and dishevelled as the other; but the undercurrent of hostility was unmistakable: there was some sense of loyalty, even in dives like this.

Daryl placed his hands against the edge of the table, ready to shove it at someone – or else push himself up and what? go to her aid? – and watched as she flicked her hair back, rolled her shoulders, and then went forward to meet the first punch with a cup-block around his fist with enough force it jarred the man's arm shoulder from its socket. A second later he hit the floor following the punch to the side of his head. Another of the guys tried to smash a bar stool down on her and missed, because she moved like nothing Daryl had ever seen before. Another was thrown over the top of the bar, to crash into the shelves; a third was launched over her back after they tried grabbing her by the throat . . . and he could only stare as she swiftly despatched with the rest.

Finally, however, there was silence, and displaced dust floated in the musty air as if trying to make a break for freedom. In the centre of the debris of overturned tables and broken chairs, she stood, perfectly unharmed, breathing hard. Daryl realised his hands were still braced on the edge of the table. He would have helped her . . . except she hadn't needed him.

Those who had wanted to teach her some kind of lesson stayed low, or crawled a short distance away to nurse whatever felt broken or bruised. She, however, turned to the bar, grabbed a beer from the fridge, brushed off the top of a stool and hopped onto it.

She levered the top off on the edge of the bar, wiped the bottle and took a swig – and then grimaced in immediate disgust. She then lobbed the offending bottle over her shoulder, uncaring of the smash that followed.

"Jesus Christ. Does no one else care that the beer is warm?"

Daryl felt his jaw go slack in wonderment at her insolence, her gall.

Her focus shifted back to Kelly, and she prowled back over to where he had dragged himself onto a surviving chair, and sat down opposite on another.

"Now, Mr Kelly," she said with all the poise of a cute girl scout persuading someone to let her sell lemonade outside their house. "I don't like you, and I don't like your bar. I know how you treat your girls. I know what happens upstairs too. I know about all of it, so here's the thing: Angelique isn't ever coming back, for starters, and some of my friends aren't very impressed with your other side-lines. Like dealing. You've offended a helluva lotta people without seeming to notice. But they've noticed you. So I suggest after I walk out of here, you think very carefully about the choices you make from now on."

The look on Kelly's face told her he hadn't liked one word of her short oration. He might be ugly, crude, out-dated and immoral, but he wasn't stupid. He could add it up.

Getting no reply, she stood, as if her work there was done, eyed Kelly speculatively for a second and turned away, striding for the door, snatching up a chair leg as she went.

Just as she got to the door, a colossal but vacant-looking man walked in – and from the look of him, he wasn't as gifted in the brains department as he was in the sheer physical size department.

"Grab her!"

The shout was instantaneous, and she suddenly found herself, feet off the ground, face to face with the huge guy.

Oh hell! Daryl realised this was the moment he was going to have to step in and pay for having sat in the shadows for so long. No one gets to sit on the edge of a black hole of chaos without eventually getting sucked in! Hardening his mind to what he might have to do, he was unprepared yet again for what she did next.

She kissed the man.

A second later she swung the chair leg at his head and he dropped her. And then she was gone.

Daryl stood up casually, carefully, wanting to remain unnoticed; but no one paid him any attention – all eyes were on the damage or the injuries incurred. Heading through the door into the backstage area, he saw women in costumes or robes and they looked at him with frightened, overly-made-up eyes. He put his hands up in a gesture of peace, quietly asking if there was a fire exit he could use. They pointed, and as he crept away he felt their fear – not because of the fighting, but something else . . . Did Kelly threaten to rape them all if they refused to strip, or did he pimp them out? Was that what the girl had been referring to when she spoke about his 'side-lines'? And what happened upstairs?

On his way out he spied something on the floor: a small white t-shirt. He picked it up, realising it was hers. He had never picked up a single item of clothing in his whole life. It was so small, such a simple thing to do, and yet it felt so precious.

He exited quickly through the even more run-down back entrance and ran to his car, relieved to see it was still there, realised he was shaking. Was this real life? How people lived? Where was she now? He jumped in, firing up the ignition using the car's ID software on his LifeTime, and started the engine, quickly scanning the road for her. He saw her running along the street ahead, far in the distance, amazed at how far she'd got already, and pressed down the accelerator, caution now tossed away like an empty chocolate wrapper.

He pulled up level with her. This was not how he'd wanted it to be. But she looked round at him, face expressionless, eyes safe behind the shades. He couldn't breathe. *Oh God, help me now. How could you be so beautiful?* She didn't look away. Appeared to be searching his face. What was she looking for? What should he say?

"You need a ride?"

"No. Thank you."

How is she so composed! Her face is unreadable!

"Are you sure?"

They both heard the squeal of tyres and she looked around as his eyes went to the rear-view mirror. A dusty old SUV was accelerating towards them at breakneck pace: clearly her warning hadn't been enough. She looked at the BMW, the smartly-dressed well-spoken driver. There were seconds left to make a decision.

Daryl felt he had to say something. Prove he wasn't going to hurt her. "I have your t-shirt . . . you left it . . ."

She catapulted over the door and onto the passenger seat, landing one foot and one knee down, arms braced. Relief flooded his brain like nothing he'd ever felt before, and he sent the powerful BMW flying down the road. Suddenly a gunshot reported and something pinged off the car. Then again. He flinched; she didn't. Daryl realised he wasn't even wearing a seat belt, tried to reach for it, steering one-handed, the end of the street looming. *Mac would kill me with his bare hands!*

"Have you got a gun?"

What the . . .? This was not how he'd imagined their first conversation!

"A what?"

"*A gun*!" she repeated with a hint of impatience.

"You're going to shoot them?"

"Just the tyres," she said, as if it were obvious, as if it were normal.

"Glove compartment. Code 2759."

She reached over and pressed the numbers into the security pad, pulled out the weapon and shut the panel with her foot as if she did it all the time – and all with the same ease with which she checked the weapon for rounds, before turning to face their enemy who were yelling and gesticulating wildly.

"There are only two bullets," was her only comment, as if remarking on the leather seats.

"How many do you want?"

"Two's plenty. Only, what else have you been shooting?" she replied coolly, snapping the clip in and bringing the gun up, using her raised knee and aiming it over the back of the car at the SUV just as another shot was fired. Daryl flinched involuntarily, again, and she then fired twice, a perfect double-tap, and in the rear-view mirror he saw the SUV jerk suddenly as first one then the other front tyre blew out. It had been going too fast to stop safely, and the momentum threw it over in spectacular style, whereupon it rolled before grinding to a halt upside down in a churning cloud of dust.

He looked at the road, then at her. She was putting the gun away. Then she sat back down and pulled on her t-shirt.

"So . . ." she said slowly, eyes on him – and for the first time in God knew how long, Daryl Augustus Bartholomew Blackmoor actually felt self-conscious; he wasn't looking his best; why hadn't he shaved? – ". . . this your ride?"

Again, not the question he was expecting, and he slowed a little as they had no other pursuers and had entered a more residential area. He did not want to get stopped by the traffic cops.

"Yes."

"Are you sure?"

"Why wouldn't it be?"

"Why would you risk it getting shot at if it was yours? Either you're so rich you don't mind a few holes or you stole it."

Stole it? And God, a few bullet holes feel like a price worth paying to finally get to meet you!

"You think I stole it!" He wanted to smile. He could trash it a hundred thousand times over and not care less.

"I'm suspicious. I also don't want to get pulled over by cops looking for a stolen vehicle."

"I assure you, it's my car."

Still, she didn't look away, and he didn't like the feeling of being judged, weighed up, of someone questioning his word. No one did that. At least not when they knew who he was.

"Fine. It's your car. So, what are you?"

"*What* am I?"

"Yes. What are you? How many guys do you think drive a car like this and hang around streets like that? Are you a drug dealer?"

"A *drug* dealer?" This was unbelievable!

"Yeah. They drive these kinds of cars."

"Really?"

"Yeah, really."

"How would you know that?"

"You really aren't from LA, are you?"

She seemed amused by his ignorance and he forced himself to keep quiet. Lecturing her on who he was, was definitely not an option. It also wasn't the time to point out that with her clipped English accent, she didn't sound like she was from LA either.

"No."

"Because if you were, you'd know drug dealers drive BMWs; the mob drive white limos or Bentleys; and the gangster boys drive SUVs." Her tone was dry, as if irritated by having to explain such things. "So, what are you, if you're not a drug dealer?"

"I'm a photographer. I'm visiting LA." *Where had that come from?*

"Right."

She didn't sound impressed. Or interested. The one female on the planet he wanted to be interested in him and he was failing miserably! He could have thumped the steering wheel.

"You alright now?" he tried, hoping to steer the conversation to her, not him.

"Yeah, I'm peachy. Thanks for asking." No one else he had met in his entire life had ever used the word 'peachy', and he almost laughed out loud.

She leaned her head forward to re-tie the shoelace on her sneakers. She was close to him, and a length of her hair brushed his arm as she flicked it back. A jolt of electricity went up his arm to his spine. Jesus Christ, he was on edge.

"You want to go get a drink or something?" He cursed himself for his lack of subtlety, cringing to hear the words out loud. How long had it been since he'd had to ask a woman that? He'd *never* asked a woman that!

She laughed, a burst of hilarity that surprised him and confirmed his own lack of confidence.

"*Why?*" She looked at him, a huge smile of genuine amusement on her face. How he wished she'd take off the damn shades so he could bask in the real beauty of her.

"I figure you owe me. I got you out of there, didn't I?"

She lost her smile in a second. "I owe *you*? After you sat there with your beer and did nothing while a fifteen-year-old girl was about to get gang-raped because she wouldn't take her clothes off? I certainly do not owe you." She turned her head away in disgust. "And, for the record, I didn't need a ride with you; I deal with shit like that all the time. I only got in because you had my t-shirt. It's one of my favourites." She knew that wasn't strictly true; but hey, she could bullshit with the best of them.

Daryl felt crushed. Yet felt a long-dormant conscience shake itself to life. Her bluntness was like a slap, but he saw her point of view with complete clarity. He had just sat there, despite intending to step in. If not for her own ability and courage, bad things would have happened, he knew that.

"What were you hoping for, a go yourself after they'd finished with me?" The question was another verbal slap, and he felt his hands tighten on the wheel.

"No."

She didn't seem to care about his answer, didn't even look at him.

"You're fifteen?" *Act dumb, Daryl, don't give anything away.*

"Yes. And no, I know I don't look it," she replied tightly. "I've had men trying it on with me since I was barely in double-figures. And I've been attacked by plenty of guys who should know better. What is it with you guys? Is that all we're good for? So, anyway, that's why I've got pretty good at defending myself."

She sounded genuinely sad, and looked away at the pleasant gardens of the wealthy in the leafy suburb they were heading through, back towards the centre of LA.

Daryl felt a sense of shame wash over him, even as the hot LA sunshine baked the earth and his hands held onto the steering wheel like everything was normal. It was a most uncomfortable revelation, like he'd had some unexpected party prank pulled on him. He also felt disgust for all the thoughts he'd had about her without knowing her at all; at men for their uncontrollable lust for women; at Harvey for what he did to her; and for the horrors she had experienced because of the merciless world that held more perils than havens. Especially for someone so beautiful. *Now I understand why Donny won't touch her.*

"You're a little better than good," he replied quietly, trying to defuse the issue. "You're actually pretty impressive." She half smiled; he saw her in the wing mirror. "Do you have family here?" *Still play dumb, Daryl.*

"Did you see someone else out there fighting for me?" She gave a short laugh; she hadn't said it derisively. "I don't think you're a photographer."

"No?"

"No. But never mind. It's not like it matters."

He was disappointed she didn't make more effort to find out the truth; but relieved that she didn't. She didn't seem to be offended with his white lie. But was it really that obvious? He was very good at being believable. He glanced at her. The way she was sitting in the seat, leaning on the door, told him she wasn't entirely comfortable being in the car with him.

"You look like some rich boy," she then said. "Where did you go? Harvard? You look like the Harvard type."

She looked away again, as if that took him down in her estimation.

He couldn't believe that he, Daryl Blackmoor, was being criticised and found wanting by this impudent, incredible fifteen-year-old with such casual aplomb.

"Yes. As it happens. How do you know what a Harvard type is anyway?"

"I went there." She paused as if deciding what whether it was safe to reveal more. "I visited because I was offered an open scholarship. You all look the same. Or maybe it's just that none of you are different." He almost stalled the car. *An open scholarship? That was . . . almost unheard of.* The gravity of that statement eclipsed the insult that had followed.

"You didn't take it?"

"No. I wouldn't ever fit in." Her face clouded as she remembered, and he had to agree. She would stand out a mile. "Plus, I couldn't afford to go. Not even for a week."

"Surely someone would have sponsored you to go if you're that smart?" Daryl could think of fifty people – one person, in particular, so why hadn't he? – who would have done; he would have done, and offered her a job after graduation without hesitation. But he had to continue to pretend he knew nothing about her.

"Someone would have, but I couldn't accept. I don't like debt. To anyone, for anything."

Daryl couldn't help but wonder, apart from her obvious pride, why she would reject Donny's support.

"It's funny," she then said. "I spent so many years wanting to go there and when it came to it . . . it wasn't right. My mother and grandmother went to Cambridge, in England, and they loved it. I always thought it would make them proud of me to know I went to Harvard, even though they're . . ." She paused, realising she was voicing thoughts that had never before been shared, and that she was straying into territory she very much kept locked away. "Well . . . it's strange when you realise the dream you had was the wrong dream. It's hard to give it up, as much as you know it's the right decision."

Daryl was staring dead ahead, rather taken aback by the admission, driving now unaware of any particular destination. These were wise words from a fifteen-year-old. Her voice was much softer than it had been before, and he realised just how much it meant to her. Had meant. To want something so badly and have to give it up because of a lack of money; an achievement extinguished that would have been a tribute to her dead family. Never had he expected anything so poignant from this bonfire of attitude.

He didn't realise how long the silence had become as he pondered her thoughts, and startled when she suddenly said, "What? Amazed the alley cat you picked up has a brain too?"

He looked round at her sharply. *Alley cat? What?*

"No. Just thinking. And there's nothing alley cat about you, kitten, and I think you know that."

Shit! He realised he'd just used the name for her that Donny did! He froze. Would it trigger an alarm in her head? She was way too smart to miss it, or overlook it. He shot her a sideways glance, but she simply said, "Are you going to drop me off somewhere, because if you just keep going you will end up driving into the sea?"

"Where do you want me to drop you?"

He didn't want her to go just yet. He didn't want to stop and watch her walk away. He wanted her to stay just where she was, in his car, next to him.

"Anywhere is fine."

"Home?"

"No, just anywhere."

"You want to go to the police station?"

"Are you joking? Why the hell would I do that?"

"To report those guys back there."

"Hell, I wouldn't trust the cops to dot their i's or cross their t's. No, there's another type of justice in LA, and it don't come dressed in uniform." Her disgust was obvious, and he knew exactly who she meant. And he liked the way she'd dropped into bad grammar because the fancy had taken her. "There's a likelihood that place will be a pile of ashes by the time dawn rolls around anyway." Her face was serious but calm. She had no fear of them, the mob bosses.

"Sounds like you've got some pretty impressive friends."

"One big happy family."

She smiled at the craziness of it, of the people she knew, trusted, and often helped. She glanced at her watch; he saw her do so.

"Is that a *watch?*"

"Yep, an old-fashioned digital watch. And yes, I know it's older than I am."

"Don't you have a LifeTime?" he asked in disbelief. He didn't know anyone who hadn't.

"Nope." She seemed perfectly happy with her negative answer. And her outdated watch.

"What kind of dancing do you do?" He silently cursed as he saw traffic ahead. He was afraid she'd just get out. And then cursed again. He hoped she realised he'd heard her mention dancing back at the strip club, and hadn't almost dumped himself in it. Again. Why was he so nervous?

"Every type and any type. Depends on the music."

She looked away; he inwardly sighed with relief.

"So, what's your name?" he ventured. What did he have to lose by asking?

"My name doesn't matter. Shortly, I will get out of your car, and you will carry on with your life and I with mine. All very simple."

"I'll keep driving until you give me your name." He smiled at his attempt at an ultimatum and looked around, hoping to have softened her with the tease.

"If you knew who was sitting in your car, you'd know that wasn't much of a threat."

For a split second, she looked over her shades at him, and he tried to see the colour of her eyes . . . but there was too much shadow. Her reproof was absolute, but loaded with such mischief that he would never forget it. In that brief, unforeseen moment, he felt like he'd seen a glimpse of the woman she would be. And, somehow, he knew time would only make her stronger.

He started to slow for the queue of traffic at the junction. He really didn't want to. Knew this was it. But she stayed still.

"Jesus Christ! Are you bleeding?" she suddenly said, looking at his shirt. "And is that blood on the wing mirror?"

Daryl scanned his arm and then the mirror, alarmed, and looked back at her. "Where? I can't see . . ."

He was looking at an empty seat.

She'd bailed.

Damn it!

He'd had been played. *Well and truly played.*

Infuriated, he slammed the car into gear and swung off into a side street. She would have got out of the car at some point, but he didn't want it to be like this! He tried to curb his anger, his utter frustration. He'd seen her, hadn't he? She'd sat in his car, conversed with him, for Christ's sake. It was more than he'd dared to dream, finding her in this city, but . . .

He considered turning around and trying to find her again, but he needed to go back to his house. He'd been out for hours. No doubt Mac would be having kittens. But he tried to console himself with the fact that his trip had been a success, of sorts.

LATER ON THAT evening, Daryl set out to a particularly well-recommended restaurant, thoroughly enjoying the novelty of driving himself again – much to Mac's absolute horror once more. His step was as light as his mood, his mind somewhat more at ease than it had been for some time. He'd spent a number of hours processing the pictures from the car, picking out his favourite shots and book-marking them to be made into pictures for his walls. He couldn't help but feel a small thrill of success, as much as he wished she hadn't bailed on him. He now had a very real sensation of her. A smile. Her hair brushing against his arm. But there was something else: he respected her. Even admired her. And he appreciated it was a novel feeling for a man for whom women were merely playthings.

The balmy night air was comforting and he'd kept the roof down, had changed into dark blue trousers and a white shirt, and still hadn't shaved. It was rare for him to be in LA. He'd visited maybe a few dozen times, and for specific reasons like business or awards ceremonies, and then he was gone. He'd never really explored the city, and he was enjoying himself immensely. Had never felt more alive. Was it that he'd had a girl, *the girl*, leap into his car? That they'd been shot at? That he'd seen . . . life?

He smiled quietly to himself, thinking of the lecture Mac would give him if he knew. He smiled even more when he imagined Mac finding out what *she* could do. *That would be quite something.*

Across from him to the right he heard a sudden roar of noise, and five motorbikes pulled up at the lights. He thought instantly of her. Segments of conversations with Donny and the images he'd tried to conjure up in his mind flooded back. Could it possibly? . . . He swivelled the camera and his head. And saw the blonde hair. Saw the tight black leathers, the black helmet and visor. Saw her shake her head at the rider next to her. And then the lights changed and she roared away, her friends in hot pursuit. *He couldn't believe his luck! Stuff dinner!*

He annoyed a good number of people by changing lanes and then putting his foot down, listening for the sound of the bike engines above the sound of his own, scanning the road ahead and the side streets. He drove round and round. Where would they go? He was on the verge of frustration when he spotted another group of bikers. They were all parking up at the far end of a poorly-lit street, and he also looked for a place to park. He watched them for a few minutes, saw the bags they were carrying, the animated conversations. Were they having a street party?

He called Mac and asked him to cancel his reservation, and disconnected as soon as his faithful bodyguard started asking for his location. He had far more interesting things to see than a menu. He then got out of the car, realising that he had no idea what he was doing, or if this was even a good idea, but just the chance she was here was enough. Worse case? He would call Mac and get rescued.

TRYING TO APPEAR more relaxed than he felt, he arrived at a basketball court – and spotted her immediately. She was surrounded by a host of people of all ages and ethnicities in the centre of the court. There was some kind of ritual handshake going on, and hugs. Thankfully a large crowd was gathering around the edges, providing him with the camouflage to remain unnoticed, and he was able to have a good look around.

What was happening? He saw a stage had been erected, and five chairs were placed on a second tier at the back. And a sound system had been set up with speakers all around the courts. To the left of him was a table with a selection of drinks and big troughs of ice holding bottles of beer. It was like going back ten years to his college days and going to some mad party . . . except that there was a much greater sense of freedom here. It was more relaxed. Less organised.

And then a short, trim, bouncy black guy with the cheekiest smile he'd ever seen appeared on the stage and cried, "Welcome, welcome!" He had a top hat in one hand, and a silver-topped cane in the other. "It's good to see you all looking so lively tonight!" There was a cheer. "As you all know, tonight is the last dance-off. So, all those already knocked out – thank you for coming and lending your support and helping to drink the beer!" Loud laughter. "Of course, next week everyone is back in and the new draw will be made. Tonight, however . . ." – he paused dramatically and looked around, smiling, seeing the eager faces – "we have only six teams left and *one prize*. Only one team will take the title, and I'm curious to see if our current holders are going to make it an eighth win?" His eyes came to rest on one person somewhere deep in the crowd, and a good number of people followed his gaze and there was some playful shoving. "I do have it on good authority that if they do win, their lead choreographer is going to be tied hand and foot for *at least* three weeks." There was a chorus of laughter from everyone.

"I'd like to see anyone try!"

Daryl grinned. He knew that voice.

"So! You all know the way it works . . ."

He went on to explain the rules, emphasising fairness and that heckling or trying to otherwise distract the dancers was prohibited, and Daryl could feel the anticipation. He then called up Team Red with a final cry of "Let's get this party started!"

Five judges – he assumed – took their places on the chairs, with old-fashioned clipboards and pens, and he felt a nudge to his arm.

"Hey, dude, you wanna beer?"

He turned to the pierced and tattooed guy to his side.

"Yeah, yeah sure. That would be great." He had some cash in his pocket and reached for it.

"No charge, dude."

This was a revelation! He was passed a beer, and the guy moved on with his ice bucket checking everyone had one. *Free beer? How did that work?* He took a welcome swig. It was cold, and slid nicely down his throat.

Considering the collection of interesting haircuts, piercings, tattoos and dreadlocks, he didn't feel at all threatened. These weren't girls and guys out for a fight or trouble, they just wanted to dance, or watch the dancing. They weren't rich; not all of them were pretty; they were just united by their love of whatever was about to unfold. It felt so refreshing to be around people so passionate about something that it made them so happy. And the atmosphere was great. Far better than the low-toned, defensive, watchful ambience he usually endured at his formal work-dinners, or vain social gatherings where people seemed to spend more time showing off than enjoying themselves.

He looked up from his silent contemplations. *What team was she in?* He had no way of knowing, and couldn't ask anyone because he didn't know her name. He would just have to watch and look for that flash of golden hair.

He knew immediately she wasn't in Team Red. It was good for amateurs, and he'd seen much worse. And Coolio's 'Gangster's Paradise' was a song he liked. Other teams followed, but by the time the last team walked onto the stage, he decided he must have missed her, and he was grossly disappointed . . . but then a cheer rose. *Was that her?* He saw the hair – *it was her*!

Suddenly, he was paying attention again. The music started: Eminem's 'My Name Is'. How on earth was she going to dance to that? She wasn't a gangster, or a rapper! But she proved him completely wrong. With her cap pulled down, baggy jeans and a white t-shirt with a loose check shirt over the top she was clearly the leader. It was not just hypnotising to watch, but actually kind of funny seeing her capture the quirky moves and rude sense of humour of the rapper himself. Even down to the clutching of the groin that was done with unashamed commitment. And . . . *it all worked.*

He thought it was great, and then she just blew them all away. Completely in time with the music, and while the others did a set routine of interwoven moves, she launched into one of her somersault routines, and then a breakdancing sequence that had everyone roaring with approval. And then the music stopped, all of them in their final poses.

He didn't consciously decide to clap but he did, and was astonished to then hear himself cheering with the rest. His heart was pounding. Needless to say, her team, Team Indigo, went through, and he sensed something else: pride?

He was not going anywhere, and was handed another beer as the second round began. But he was only interested in one team, and there they were, there she was. Franz Ferdinand's 'No You Girls' thumped through the sound system, and partnered by a tall, black dancer, as toned as himself and undeniably handsome, he felt distinctly uncomfortable as to the lyrics '*flick your cigarette and kiss me / meet me where your eye won't flick me*' she went to her partner's arms, the other dancers spiralling around them. Their heads got so close Daryl felt his fingers bunch, the movement of their bodies forceful, almost like a tango. It was intense. Would they kiss? Why was he feeling . . .

But it was clear for her that there was nothing there except for the dancing, there was no kiss, just the fluidity of her body that he had witnessed so many times before. Still Daryl wished it was him dancing with her – not that he could dance. But just to feel those hands on him, feel the energy of her body as she moved in perfect timing and harmony with him.

Again, the cheering was loud. And long.

It was the last round, and he could feel the tension in the air heighten. There were now only two teams left: Green and Indigo. The audience had swelled so much that the people at the front sat down around the dance area so the people behind could see, and he saw a dark-haired girl from one of the previous acts – he vaguely remembered her – and his golden girl on the platform with the master of ceremonies. He was swirling his cane, and it looked like they were tossing a coin as to who was going to go first.

The other girl won the toss and chose to go first, and he enjoyed the long-legged stroll of Girl Indigo back to her team, not looking displeased in the least. To his amazement, one of them handed her a beer and she took a long swig, then leaned back against one of the other male dancers. There was such easy familiarity between them all, the people all close, touching but without sexuality. They were like one big family. And he marvelled at the organisation of the thing; the solidarity of it; the connectiveness of it. He had been wrong to think it was unorganised.

Team Green had chosen "Umbrella" by Rhianna, and the dancing was good. Well-timed, full of movement and all put together beautifully, expressing the right emotions for the song. Daryl felt mildly impressed, and saw the team were happy with themselves too, as if surprised they'd pulled it off as well as they had. He looked round to look at Team Indigo, and saw them cheering with everyone else.

Then Indigo were called up, and Daryl watched as she pulled off her t-shirt and tossed it over her shoulder, leaving her in a bikini top with ties that wound round her body. He could see the well-proportioned curves, the muscles that she knew how to use better than anyone he'd ever seen.

'Right Round' by Flo Rida started, and if he'd thought she was brilliant before, now he simply didn't have a word for it. '*You spin my head right round right round when you go down down . . .*' The beauty of her moves, fast-slow, fast-slow, was beyond anything he'd seen her do – even at Celeste – and the final chorus he would never forget, as she became lost in her interpretation, and the audience fell into complete silence. Only the music was heard, until the final bars, and she was still.

When the cheering erupted he felt the collective appreciation of hundreds of people, saw the dark-haired girl offer her hand, congratulating what had been a flawless, unbeatable performance. The girls exchanged a few words, and then with an arm round each other's waists, walked to the edge of the stage, where they were handed a beer. They then toasted each other, and took a swallow. The lack of conceit and the camaraderie was astonishing, and once more he felt something move in his soul.

Who was this beer-drinking, ass-kicking, dance miracle of a fifteen-year-old? This was not what he'd expected to find in LA. But as much as he was surprised, at the same time he *wasn't*. It suited her personality, every little bit of her incredible, beautiful personality.

"Pretty amazing, isn't she?" the guy next to him said, and Daryl emerged from his reverie.

"And then some," he agreed without hesitation. "I've never seen anything like it," he added, hoping the guy might open up and share some more information with him – like her name.

"I doubt you would anywhere, she's got so much talent it's unreal." They shared a smile and looked over to the stage. Team Indigo was being formally announced as the winners. Again. "Are you new? I've not seen you before." It wasn't an accusation, it was just a question. "Guilty as charged." Daryl didn't want to lie or make up stories; but it was time to get the conversation back to on her. "Does she always win?"

"Yup." A swig of beer. "She sort of came up with the whole thing. There were some small groups of dancers, but there was fighting about space or music, and rivalry, and then she had this big showdown one night with Leisha – the girl with dark hair – and hell, I won't forget that night."

"They fought?"

"Naaah. They had a dance-off. Mysty won, of course, but instead of doing what everyone thought she'd do and throw it in Leisha's face, she offered her hand, said well done, and asked if she'd dance again. And now everyone gets on. Everyone has their chance to use the space. We do this every week . . . best night of the week."

And just like that he had her name; but dare he push it and ask for a surname?

"New people join every week . . ." the guy continued, but Daryl was somewhat distracted at finally discovering her name and barely heard him, "so it's best to ask if they have space for a new member, or if you want to start your own team."

Daryl realised the guy was trying to be helpful, thinking he'd want to dance himself, or set up another team. Him dance? Ballroom dancing yes; explosive modern dancing, *no*!

"Is this it or is there more?" Daryl quickly asked, not sure how long he dared stay, thinking that he perhaps ought to make a discreet exit.

"The competition's over till next week, and a new draw will take place for the music, but now we just kick back, have a beer, and dance to whatever tunes come on."

Daryl was intending to make his excuses and head off when the guy next to him changed everything, like twisting a steering wheel, sending a car off the road to career down a most unexpected route. "Woohoooo! Mysty, you go girl!" he called out.

It was a loud, enthusiastic shout and she looked over, perhaps recognising the voice. She raised a hand and waved, and then did a double-take. Her attention fixed on Daryl with an intensity that disintegrated the distance between them.

Oh shit.

Daryl was glad no one heard him swallow.

His beer-drinking friend wandered off as someone approached and greeted him, leaving Daryl standing alone by the wire mesh at the edge of the court . . . with a very angry-looking girl walking straight towards him.

"What the *fuck* are you doing here?"

"I'm not doing any harm."

"That doesn't really answer the question, does it? Are you following me?"

"Maybe I just came to say goodbye after you disappeared from my car earlier." His answer somehow surprised her and her brow snapped together. He imagined her eyes were bright with emotion. Bright behind those goddammed shades.

"You're *not* a photographer."

"So what?"

"So it makes you a liar as well as a scumbag who goes to dirty horrible strip clubs!"

Wow, Daryl, you're getting both barrels. He almost smiled. So rarely had he been called anything, let alone a scumbag. He noticed people looking over.

"I'm not a native; I didn't know it was such a dive."

"Jesus Christ, a *blind man* would have been able to tell you it was a shithole. Didn't you *look* at the place before you walked in there? And why did you stay if it was so bad? To watch the '*entertainment*'?" She shook her head, impatient, finding his answers inadequate and not liking the way he so calmly shrugged everything off. He was such a loser. "I do hope you've been entertained once more?" She tilted her head and crossed her arms, challenging him.

"Beyond expectation."

The answer didn't please her; in fact, he guessed it was one of those answers she didn't care for much.

"So, are you going to dance? Or do you just stand and drink beer and watch other people?"

He tried to ignore the stabs of guilt and inadequacy. When had he ever felt either?

"I can't dance half so well as anyone here."

The admission interested her clearly, as her eyebrows moved up, but the lower part of her face didn't express any emotion.

"It's not about how well you can dance; it's about how it makes you *feel*." He was just pondering that statement, when she added, "So, if you won't dance, you should drive away in that pretty little car of yours and leave us alone. Leave *me* alone. This isn't a spectator sport."

And with that she turned and marched away, calling "Moses!" The master of ceremonies looked up instantly at her commanding shout. "Get 'Low' on for me. Let's *really* get the party started."

There was a loud chorus of approval, and Daryl wondered what was going to happen next as everyone seemed to move at once, turning to face the stage once more. The music started, and she prowled into the space where previously so many had competed for the crown that she had won.

Daryl had seen many things in his life, seen many very alluring female dances, but nothing came close to the next four minutes. She stopped in the centre of the floor and then she moved with the '*apple bottom jeans*' in the song. Such was her recognised superiority that most of the people stood back to watch; but some of her female teammates came forward to join her in the sexy gyrations, everyone singing '*the whole club was looking at her*' with hands up in the air, moving their bodies in time but not encroaching on the dance space taken up by their champion.

Three guys joined her, however, entwining their bodies, rubbing against each other as she tilted her head back against their shoulder or chest and bent her knees, the ripple of bodies together carrying them up and down. Daryl felt both jealous and captivated, until she put a hand out and pushed them away so she could step back into her own space, bringing the song to a rhythmic, pulsating, gyrating climax.

It was only when the song finished that Daryl realised he was rock hard. But he doubted he was the only one. He'd heard that song before, somehow, somewhere, but he never thought he see it danced to like that!

Nobody moved until she did. Ruffling one of the kneeling male dancer's hair, she stepped away and disappeared into the crowd even as everyone cheered in approbation. *Jesus Christ.* For the first time in his life Daryl Blackmoor wished he could dance. *Really* dance. Not just take women for an elegant waltz or impersonal foxtrot about a ballroom or on the dancefloor of a high-class club. He wanted to lose himself in the music, give his whole body over to it, nothing held back, like she had.

He took another sip of his beer. One more song and then he would go. But then he had a thought. He walked around the edge of the crowd to Moses, still in his top hat and cane, looking through some lists on a clipboard.

"Hi."

"Hey, new boy, you having a good time?"

Clearly Moses knew everyone, and the whites of his eyes were stark against the deep-brown irises and the dark mahogany of his skin, his mouth in a wide smile of perfect teeth. He was someone Daryl imagined it was very hard to dislike, but for all his familiarity, it was a little odd being spoken to like some twelve-year-old kid turning up for their first football practice. It wasn't appropriate in the least, considering who he was, but Moses didn't know that.

"Yeah, it's really impressive. Did you organise all this?" Flattery always helped.

"Well, I do at the moment 'coz I can no longer dance. It doesn't take too much. It's all about the moves and the music, you know?" He glanced back down at the list.

"I was wondering if you'd be able to arrange a little bit of further excitement?"

He was instantly suspicious, and the smile faded a little.

"Dude if you're with some gang or something we don't have anything to do with that. No drugs, no gang shit, no *nothing*."

"No, nothing like that." Daryl saw the slight relaxation on the guarded face. "I'm just amazed at the quality of the dancing, really. I'm visiting with friends in LA, and I ain't seen nothing like this before." The smile returned at the praise, and Daryl felt rather shocked at his use of slang – she really was getting to him. "And I was wondering if you'd maybe call a dance-off between your two leading ladies? Apparently, that's how this all came about?" He slipped six hundred dollars into the pocket of

Moses' jeans, and the guy didn't need to look to know it was money that had been offered. "I'm only here for another half-hour and I'm leaving LA tomorrow. Nothing more to it than that."

Daryl knew he'd got the approach right, and the mention of his leaving meant there would be no repeat. It was a one-time thing. Nothing to be concerned about.

"Well, I guess there's no harm in that. Both girls love to dance. But you know there'll only be one winner, right? I mean, Mysty could out-dance *anyone*."

"I know."

"Fine. I'll see what I can do. You better get yourself a ring-side seat."

Daryl nodded his thanks and backed away, stopping off at the beer table and grabbing another, pushing a couple more $100 notes in the donations jar for the 'Beer Fund' as it was so succinctly put. He liked that. And so did many others it would appear, as the jar was pretty full. Incredible really. Were things really run like this, by voluntary contributions?

He sipped his new ice-cold beer, promising it would be his last considering he was driving and watched. He knew he was getting looks from some of the guys – no doubt not pleased about his being there after she'd perhaps told them how they'd met – and heard Moses shout for Leisha and Mysty.

They listened to what Moses had to say, and he saw them put their arms around each other again. It seemed they were friends as well as dance rivals, and the respect between the two of them was admirable. He'd witnessed lots of people with far less talent who behaved very badly, shoving it in people's faces and getting aggressive with the competition. Not her though.

"Everyone!" Moses stood up on the stage. "We have something a little extra tonight!" A cheer of excitement. "Leisha and Mysty have agreed to one final round to tonight's competition. We're going to have a one-on-one dance-off!" An even bigger cheer. "So, everyone, grab a piece of paper and a pen – which you'll find down here – and put a song in the hat." He pointed to his top hat. "The only rule is, it that has to be from the noughties and have been a number one either in the US or the UK.

The winner will be whoever gets the loudest cheer after the two dances have been done. Ladies, while we leave them to nominate your tunes, shall we toss for who goes first?"

Ten minutes later, with the girls sitting on the edge of the stage, Moses took his hat and shook it around a bit.

"Going first is Leisha with . . ." He pulled out a screwed-up piece of paper. "Cascada with 'Evacuate the Dancefloor'!" A big cheer. And Leisha didn't look too unhappy. Moses held up his hands for silence again. "Going second is Mysty with . . ." Another piece of paper. "Lady Gaga and 'Poker Face'!"

Daryl almost laughed at her reaction. She hit her forehead with a hand and fell back onto the stage, making Leisha giggle. She might hide behind her shades, but she wasn't in the least bit affected! Leisha then jumped up and Mysty sat up, and leant back on her hands to watch her friend.

It was a tall order to get allocated a piece of music and have to dance to it with no rehearsal, so what Leisha managed was pretty impressive, although it got a bit disjointed and didn't run with the music half as well as the pre-prepared pieces she'd done. While Daryl didn't think it was great, it wasn't terrible, and it was a hundred times better than anything he could have done, so he joined in with the enthusiastic applause.

His attention now, however, was on Girl Indigo, his stomach a knot of anticipation. Not a Gaga fan, he knew the music, knew Poker Face had been huge – and a source of irony, of sorts, in his world.

"Mysty?" Moses looked at her and she stood, a little reluctantly.

"Can I use your hat and cane, Moses?"

He smiled and handed them over.

And everyone went quiet, waiting for the magic to start.

To everyone's surprise she didn't strike a pose, but got down on the floor, dead centre, and curled into a ball, chest on her knees, arms out stretched, the cane lying under her finger tips. The music then started, the familiar notes playing out in the warm night air.

What followed what such a piece of cheeky, sassy, daring dance incorporating the provocative lyrics that he didn't quite know how to react. '*I want to roll with him, a hard pair we will be / a little gamble and it's fun when you're with me*' and his eyebrows rose with surprise at her saucy use of the cane. '*Russian roulette is not the same without a gun,*' and it was raised like a rifle . . . pointing straight . . . at him. '*And if it's love if it's not rough it isn't fun,*' with legs apart, hands together and raised up as if in handcuffs. And his erection was beyond his control as she arched her back to '*I'll get him hard*', running her fingers along the cane and peeping out from the hat . . .

The rest of the song was a blur. And then the silence again after the last beats, before everybody erupted.

How could she just do that? Just walk onto a stage and execute a perfectly choreographed show?

Moses beckoned the two girls over, and Mysty took off the top hat and put it on Moses' head, and handed him the cane.

"Girls, this is your cut. You were as sensational as ever!" He held out $200 to each of them and they both looked at the money, then at each other, not understanding.

"Where did the money come from, Moses?" she asked.

The smile faltered on Moses' face when he heard the suspicion in her question. She made no move to take it, and neither did Leisha.

"Some dude, I don't know . . . tall, white shirt, shades. A new boy, visiting LA. He asked for a dance-off and gave me $600 – that's pretty generous."

"We don't dance for money here, Moses! You know that! It's not about that!" Mysty cried, and the audience froze. Daryl froze. She ran a hand through her hair, clearly desperately upset. "Do you know who that guy is? He's the pervert I found in that shithole strip club today, where they decided that because I wasn't going to strip, they would pin me to a table and . . . he did *nothing*! I was only there to defend my friend! Now he turns up here? *And you accept his money*?" Moses looked at the notes, seriously regretting his decision. "You take it all back to him, right now."

Moses put the two lots of notes together, added it to his cut – and headed straight for Daryl. *This isn't what was meant to happen. She was never meant to know! What have I done?* His heart sank. And began to shrivel as everyone's attention now turned to him. The bad guy.

"Dude. Your money. We can't accept it, I'm afraid. I shouldn't have taken it, and I wouldn't have if I'd known . . . I-I think you should leave. Find someplace else to enjoy LA."

Daryl didn't take the money, so Moses reached forward and put it in his shirt pocket, and then turned and walked away. Daryl was given no time to react, however, because immediately behind Moses was Mysty, and she placed herself right in front of him, two feet away. She did not speak. She didn't need to. Her body exuded hostility. A couple of the guys stepped forward, silently indicating that if she needed help they were there, but she waved them away. *I'm OK, I can handle this.* They saw the look and gave her some space, walked back over to the beer table. But they were not happy. Nobody – not least this stuck-up rich boy – upset one of their own. Somebody needed to be taught a little lesson.

"You won." He ended the silence, his voice quiet. He slid his hands into his pockets.

"You're a real pain in the arse, you know that? Why couldn't you just leave? Didn't you get enough entertainment earlier?"

"Do you know how rare a talent like yours is?" he offered, but it sounded weak, pathetic.

"That's my business, not yours. I'm not a performing monkey. And I don't hide in the shadows watching like a complete coward, not even brave enough to dance!" She reached out and pushed him in the shoulder, and it was enough to make him fight to hold his balance.

Daryl paused, taken aback by being confronted with both a rubbishing of his perspective of artists – not that she knew about that, of course – and being found wanting for not daring to join in. He looked down at where she'd touched him, outraged yet hungry for more, feeling a surge of sensation. He felt a muscle twitch in his jaw, trying to wade through the emotions just to keep up. No one had ever called him a coward, and he really didn't like it, and it goaded him enough to reply with anger: "You made Moses give me the money back. *What's wrong with you*? Was that not enough?" He took a nonchalant swig of his beer.

"I don't come here to get paid to dance."

"How about a private show? Name any figure you like. Maybe you could then buy yourself a watch that isn't older than you are?" He took hold of her wrist and tapped the screen of her precious watch with his forefinger. He knew as soon as he'd said the words they would be a red rag to a bull, and he wished he could retract them . . . but he had another reason for wanting the contact that sent a shot of adrenaline into his bloodstream.

"I won't ever sell myself, and certainly not to a man like you! I wouldn't touch your money if I was starving!"

"You're half-drunk and you can still out-dance everyone! And you wonder why I wanted to see you dance again?"

"I am not half-drunk. I was drinking alcohol-free. I ride a motorbike, for God's sake." She took another step towards him. She was so close he could feel the full heat of her rage. And her body. "You . . ." – she looked him up and down in disgust – "are a predator. You only care about what you want and getting it when you want it. You just move through the world taking what you want, thinking you can buy anything. I've known plenty of people like you, and you know what? *I did not like them, and I do not like you.* So, do yourself a favour – fuck off or you'll need to use your immense wealth on some surgery, *Mr Photographer*. You don't belong here, and you never will."

Daryl was stunned into silence. She'd pegged him. He *was* a predator. His only care was what he wanted, when he wanted it; but no one, absolutely no one, had ever refused his advances or his money. She was right. He didn't fit in. So why, for the first time in his life, had he felt so alive? And why, in God's name, did he suddenly want a cigarette?

"This isn't the end, you know," he said quietly, finally finding his voice, and tapping a guy on the shoulder he asked for a cigarette. The guy shrugged and offered one, and a light.

For some reason that seemed to utterly throw her. "Are you stupid or something? Why the hell are you smoking?"

"You're telling me to fuck off and you care if I smoke?"

"Telling you to fuck off is different from watching you poison yourself!"

"Why?

"Why? Are you stupid or something?"

There was no answer to that. He took a drag, feeling the familiar rush from his college days, before his father and the family doctor had weighed in on the issue. If there was ever a night for breaking rules, it was this one.

Outraged at how unaffected he seemed to be by their argument, she whipped out a hand and took the cigarette and popped it in his beer bottle. He didn't attempt to protest.

"I think you'll find the gate is behind you, so before some of these guys rearrange you a bit – even though they know I'm more than capable of doing it myself – I suggest you really do leave now. Oh, and don't come back to LA. Not ever."

"This isn't the end you know," he told her departing back.

She didn't turn, just gave him two fingers over her shoulder. Succinct.

"Cody!" she yelled, and a guy at the beer stand responded, launching a bottle of beer into the air. She jumped, and mid-flight caught the bottle as it arched through the air, flicked the lid off and took a swig as she landed.

Man. Daryl imagined taking her to one of his parties. She'd probably end up emptying the punchbowl over someone's head and then jumping off the balcony to escape all his arrogant, fawning friends. And him, of course.

He watched her enter the embrace of her friends and he sighed. It was time to go. He strolled over to the beer table, shoved the $600 into the donations pot, dumped his ruined beer in the bin, and walked away, slipping the earpiece into his ear as he stepped outside the gate. He headed over to his car, now able to hear whatever she said thanks to the bug he'd stuck on her watch face when he'd grabbed her wrist. He knew it wouldn't stay there for long, but hopefully long enough to be interesting. It had been wild hope that had made him slip the miniscule transparent bug into his pocket as he'd left the house, just in case . . . He was getting used to expecting the unexpected.

"You OK, Mysty?" Manson asked – one of the guys who'd approached her earlier to see if she needed help.

"I will be as soon as that jerk drives off."

Walking through the dappled shadows to his car he smiled: pain in the arse, jerk – he was so loved.

"Yeah, well, he might not find that so easy."

"Manson, what have you done?"

Daryl didn't need Manson to answer. As he got close to his car he could smell it: as well as various words being scrawled on the outside of his car in what looked like lipstick, gasoline had been poured into the inside of the car.

"We just . . . gave him a little extra gas for the ride home. Thought it might put him off trying to pick anyone else up."

"Guys! You didn't have to do that! He was *leaving*!"

He could hear the frustration in her voice. And it surprised him that there was no satisfaction in her tone to suggest she was pleased that his car's interior had been trashed. But then she didn't seem vicious or underhand. She'd thrown her insults and done her fighting, up front and to his face, which he respected her for, despite wishing he'd earned her favour, not her insults.

After placing the half-smoked cigarette safely on the wall behind him, he reached in and removed the memory card from his onboard camera. He then opened the glove compartment to retrieve the back-up card which saved footage automatically to one of his cloud databases – when he designed things, he didn't take chances. He slipped them into his pocket, pressed the red button on his LT.

Reaching for the cigarette he took a long, sweet drag. And tossed it into the open car.

He felt the heat of the flames on his back as they shot into the air, unhampered by a roof, and strolled away, heading up the road, embracing his last few moments of freedom. Mac would be there in less than a minute. An explosion then split the night air, but he didn't look round. He calculated he was far enough away, and there wasn't much fuel in the tank anyway.

He was surprised by her silence. Was she watching? Finally speechless?

A black Bentley pulled up in front of him and Mac, who was looking most displeased, opened the door. Daryl just smiled. He glanced out of the blacked-out window as the car pulled away and saw her. She was silhouetted, standing in the gateway of the baseball court. There were two guys either side of her and none of them moved. Daryl sat back, pulled off his shades and listened:

"That was a really dumb thing to do. The cops will see that and we'll get no end of hassle. How are we going to put it out? Manson, see if there's a fire extinguisher anywhere."

How had this evening gone so wrong? Who was that guy? And how come he turned up in that shithole of a strip club, and here? And then after toasting his new BMW, got into chauffeur-driven Bentley that appeared quite by magic? Was he mob? Was he trying to mess with her to get to Donny? She put her earpiece in.

"Fabio."

"Kitten! Did you win?"

"Erm, yeah, I did. Look, can you run a plate for me, I'm probably being paranoid, but nothing about today has been normal."

Smart girl, Daryl thought, knowing what she was about to do would get her nowhere.

"Sure, fire away."

"LAH7492NY. The format is in itself suspicious. Can you get a name? Or even a company?"

There was a short pause as Fabio typed the plate into his computer. "Nope. Nothing. It's like it doesn't exist. You sure that's right?"

"Quite sure. There has to be something out there. I wonder . . ."

"Where is the car? You want me to put a black mark on it?"

"Not much point. It's currently burning itself into a charred crisp."

"Wow, you have had an exciting day."

"You could say. I have some new signature-tracing software. I'll let you know if I get anything." By which she meant she'd hack into a couple of databases and have a look; but Fabio didn't know that and wondered what software she was talking about that he hadn't heard of. Daryl frowned too. What she did know that he didn't?

"You go home and get some rest now, OK? You know you're not as good as his Highness at staying up all night."

"Never will be either! Is he OK?"

Daryl heard the concern in her voice for Donny. It rankled.

"Yeah, he's OK. Except you're not here."

"I have a seriously busy day tomorrow, but I'll call him in the afternoon."

What on earth was she so busy with? Daryl wondered.

"Sure thing, kiddo. Ride safe."

"Always do, Fabio. Ciao."

DARYL GOT OUT of the car just as he heard:

"Hey, Mysty, you heading off?" – a male voice.

"Yep."

"Us too."

"We'll walk with you."

Daryl quickly made his way to his office and pulled up the satellite feed over that area and homed in on her. She was walking to her bike, pulling her jacket on, two others with her.

"I have five hours of hell tomorrow from 7am till 12, mitigated only by the fact I have the best evening ahead of me."

He smiled at the use of the 'mitigated' – what fifteen-year-old used words like that?

She swung a leg over the bike and fired it up. Pulled on her helmet. The guys did the same. And with a nod she pulled away, slowly, smoothly, the guys riding with her – at a pace that surprised him – and he tracked their progress with the satellite. The roads were quiet, and they rode three-abreast down the centre of the street, not bothering to stick to the lanes.

"You going to be at the Bowl on Saturday night?"

"Must I really answer that for you?"

The Bowl?

The guys just laughed and then one of them nodded towards a couple of traffic cops at the side of the road.

"Shit, we'd best get back in lane!" he said.

But instead of pulling them over, to Daryl's utter amazement, they just raised their hands in greeting. One of them pulled off his helmet.

"Hey, Mysty! When we going to get our new picture?"

"Next week! I promise!" she called back, clearly not surprised by the question.

"What the? *Who are you*?" he then said as they rode past.

She didn't answer that, just said, "Well, I guess I'll be seeing you two in all the usual places sometime soon."

Daryl wasn't expecting the burst of speed, but heard the roar of the 899 as she disappeared from the satellite's view. He tried to switch to a different camera but he was too slow – and she was too fast. He lost her visually. And then he lost her completely: the bug had obviously come unstuck with the rapid acceleration.

For a moment, he sat completely still in the silence, his head in his hands. And then a slow smile spread across his face.

It hadn't been the most conventional of beginnings, but it was most certainly *a* beginning . . .